More praise for
The Glorious Cause

"Engaging, accessible, and surprisingly suspenseful, *The Glorious Cause* will leave you eager to learn more about the American Revolution and the fascinating people who fought it. . . . A good reminder of how close that most glorious of causes, American independence, came to meeting an ignominious defeat."
—*Book Street USA*

"The accessible narrative moves with great fluidity. The battle scenes are graphically—even excitingly—written, but Shaara does not neglect the equally important diplomatic side of events as the new nation sought crucial European allies in its struggle for independence. . . . Shaara understands the history of the time, and he's clearly a good writer."
—*Booklist*

"Rich, exciting, and compelling, *The Glorious Cause* will inform and entertain. . . . The dialog rings true, and the history is accurate."
—*Library Journal*

By Jeff Shaara
Published by Ballantine Books

THE
GLORIOUS
CAUSE

A Novel of the American Revolution

JEFF SHAARA

BALLANTINE BOOKS · NEW YORK

A Ballantine Book
Published by The Random House Ballantine Publishing Group
Copyright © 2002 by Jeffrey M. Shaara

Portraits:
George Washington by James Peale, ca 1787–90, after Charles Wilson Peale (courtesy of Independence National Historic Park); Portrait of Benjamin Franklin by Joseph Sifrede Duplessis, 1783 (collections of the New York Public Library, Astor, Lenox and Tilden Foundations); Nathanael Greene by Charles Wilson Peale, ca 1783 (courtesy of Independence National Historic Park); Charles Cornwallis, 1st Marquess Cornwallis by Thomas Gainsborough (courtesy of the National Portrait Gallery, London)

Ballantine and the Ballantine colophon are registered trademarks of Random House, Inc.

www.ballantinebooks.com

ISBN 0-345-42758-0

Maps by Mapping Specialists

Manufactured in the United States of America

First Hardcover Edition: November 2002
First Mass Market Edition: June 2003

OPM   10   9   8   7   6   5   4   3   2   1

Dedicated to my great-grandparents
Giuseppe and Anna Sciarra
who left Italy one hundred years ago,
and brought their dreams to America.
The legacy of our founding fathers
takes many forms.

TO THE READER

THIS IS THE SECOND OF A TWO-VOLUME SERIES THAT TELLS THE story of the American Revolution from the points of view of several key participants. This story follows a time line that begins in August 1776, shortly after the signing of the Declaration of Independence, and follows the progress of the war itself to its conclusion. However, this is not what anyone would describe as a history textbook.

By definition, this is a novel. The story is told by the characters themselves, from their perspective, through their actions, dialogue, and thoughts. However, the events, and each character's contributions to those events, are as historically accurate as I could present them. Through research that includes memoirs, written accounts, diaries, and collections of letters and documents, I have attempted to reach into the minds of each character, to show you their world as they saw it.

This story is told primarily from the points of view of George Washington, Nathanael Greene, Benjamin Franklin, and Charles Cornwallis. Throughout, there are numerous other characters, including names that are familiar (I hope) to every schoolchild: the Marquis de Lafayette, Nathan Hale, Benedict Arnold, "Mad Anthony" Wayne, John Paul Jones, "Light-Horse Harry" Lee.

While I never knowingly alter any direct quote, or change the wording of any written document, the spoken language of the time presents a challenge to the modern ear. Though speech is certainly less formal than what was written (as is true today), there is, to our ears, a stilted and sometimes poetic quality to their language. While I am careful to remain true to the era, the dialogue must still be understandable to the modern reader. I have thus attempted to tread a fine line between the old and the new, avoiding at all costs any anachronistic words or phrases. I have also purposely avoided the use of foreign accents. The English characters in this story certainly spoke with "veddy" proper British accents. Those French and German characters who spoke English at all, naturally spoke with accents appropriate to their native tongues. For me to write this dialogue with every inflection ("Ya, I yam comink, Cheneral Vashington . . .") would have been a needless interruption of the flow of the story and a distraction to the reader. I am aware of the accents. I am asking you to be as well. For this, I hope I am forgiven.

As you move through the events of this extraordinary time, you may be surprised by the primitive nature of the war. There were no railroads, no telegraphs, no West Point training. The weapons were smoothbore cannon and flintlocks, to which words like *accuracy* and *reliability* simply don't apply. The most useful weapon was the bayonet. And for much of the war, the Americans didn't have them. It often surprises people how few soldiers actually fought in the most critical battles. Very often, three thousand men was considered an "army." (By contrast, in 1863, the two armies at Gettysburg totaled close to two hundred thousand troops.)

The American Revolution was in many ways our first civil war, and eventually became the first true world war. But regardless of the scope and the numbers, it was a war fought by individuals, whose sacrifice and dedication secured the existence of this nation. It is regrettably easy for us to take for granted the freedoms we live under without considering who paid the price to secure them. That is only one reason among many that these extraordinary people *must* be remembered. That is, after all, the purpose of this story.

—JEFF SHAARA
JUNE 2002

INTRODUCTION

AT THE END OF THE FRENCH AND INDIAN WAR IN 1763, THE VICtorious British government is nearly bankrupt from the costs of the war. Beginning in 1765 with the Stamp Act, the young King George III begins to enact a series of taxes, feeling that the American colonists who have benefited from the protection of the British army should show their appreciation by paying the cost. As these taxes are enacted by the British Parliament, the response in America is not what the king expects. For nearly a century, the American colonies have been allowed to manage most of their own affairs, and each has its own colonial legislature. The king's policies begin to intrude upon the fragile autonomy of the colonies, and the protests grow.

Hiding from the harsh eye of British law, a secretive group of men organize to protest the policies of King George. They call themselves the Sons of Liberty. They are led by Samuel Adams, a man with a talent for propaganda, who recognizes that the true power in the colonies lies in the hands of the people. The only means of tapping that power is by appealing to emotion. In 1770, what begins as the mean-spirited taunting of a British sentry grows into a violent mob, which escalates further into a panicked response from British troops, who kill five civilians. As tragic as the event is, the event itself is not as significant as how it is used. The Sons of Liberty label the tragedy the Boston Massacre, and for the first time, newspapers become an effective tool of protest. With relentless energy, and a considerable skill at manipulation of facts, Adams raises the awareness of the people of Boston to what he describes as outright oppression by the British. The protests continue, escalate, and in 1773, in a hard slap at British authority, three shiploads of British tea are tossed into Boston Harbor.

Throughout this entire process, King George and his government are utterly baffled by the outcries against what they still believe are reasonable demands. Though they occasionally bend to the protests, the king will never concede the last word, and he views the upstart colonists with increasing hostility.

Throughout the British empire, no citizens of any colony are granted the full rights of Englishmen, something the British government blithely takes for granted. The Americans see differently, and in 1775, each colonial assembly chooses men to represent them at the First Continental Congress, an attempt to unite the thirteen colonies into one voice. Meeting in Philadelphia, the congress is a strange mix of cultures and special interests, each of the colonies separated by boundaries far more cultural than geographical. For the first time, Americans begin to understand their true diversity, and the challenge of creating a united voice is nearly impossible to overcome. Despite their differences a spirit of cooperation brings them together the following year, when the Second Continental Congress convenes.

The Continental Congress is an assemblage of the finest minds in the colonies, and as the men come to know each other, the single voice finally begins to form. King George and his government refuse all attempts at reconciliation, regard the congress as a criminal body, and, by doing so, further strengthen congress' unity. King George and his ministers have unknowingly made a disastrous blunder.

Though the congress continues to press for a peaceful resolution to the controversies, the British government turns a deaf ear to any correspondence the congress will offer. The king's hostility and impatience grows, and he inflames the protests by sweeping away many of the limited freedoms the colonists already enjoy. To quiet what he believes are assaults on his absolute authority, he sends his army to Boston, to occupy the city. Under General Thomas Gage, the British begin to demonstrate their power, confiscating arms and supplies used by local militia and declaring the Sons of Liberty criminals. In April 1775, Gage sends the army across the Massachusetts countryside on a mission to capture colonial munitions and, if possible, to capture Sam Adams. The outrage from the local citizenry results in a surprising show of militia, which results in the battles of Lexington and Concord. Concord is a British disaster, and Gage's men retreat back to Boston, pursued by angry citizens who exact a horrifying toll on the British troops. Emboldened by their success, the militia continues to organize, and they fortify a position on the Charlestown peninsula, overlooking Boston itself. With his position in the city now threatened, Gage orders the British army to sweep the colonial rabble off the peninsula. Twenty-five hundred British regulars march against the militia, and in what becomes known as the Battle of Breed's (or Bunker) Hill, the British succeed in capturing the ground, but lose an astonishing forty percent of their men. For the first time, the British army realizes that it may be facing far more than a band of farmers who will run merely at the sight of a line of redcoats. Requiring a scapegoat for the embarrassment of Breed's Hill, King George replaces Thomas Gage with General William Howe, and strengthens the armed presence in Boston. But the militia continues to gather and organize, and the British are quickly sealed into the city.

The Continental Congress is slow to adopt any measures that will further inflame an already dangerous situation, but through the efforts of Sam Adams and his cousin John, and the sympathy toward the New Englanders from the influential representatives from Virginia, notably Patrick Henry and Richard Henry Lee, the congress agrees to appoint a commander in chief to go to Boston and assume command of what has become a blend of militia from several colonies. Since their primary concern is the selection of a man with experience, their choice is Colonel George Washington, of the Virginia Militia. Washington accepts with extreme reluctance and goes to Boston to present his commission to men who have no use for such an outsider. Washington exhibits astounding patience, and a skill at choosing subordinates, and gradually, the ragged militia units begin to take shape as an army.

In an astounding stroke of tactical skill, in one single night, Washington occupies Dorchester Heights, south of Boston, and General Howe wakes to find his entire position within range of colonial cannon. Rather than attack Washington's army, Howe abandons Boston.

In Philadelphia, the Continental Congress has continued lengthy and rancorous debate, many men of great influence still clinging to the notion that America must remain part of Britain and remain loyal to the king. Facing a nearly hopeless deadlock, the congress is stunned to learn that King George has declared the colonies to be in a state of rebellion, that any hope of reconciliation or compromise has been swept away by the hand of the monarch, who will accept nothing but the complete capitulation of his subjects. The move sways the congress to begin, for the first time, talk of independence.

While the congress debates, the American people have begun to read a pamphlet, written by an unknown expatriate Englishman named Thomas Paine. "Common Sense" finds its way to every street corner and public square, and the logic and clarity of Paine's arguments against the rule of monarchy sway American public opinion far more effectively than anything the congress has done. Realizing that the citizenry is far more willing to pursue a course of independence than they are, more voices in the congress call for a formal declaration. A committee is appointed, and a document is prepared, written primarily by a young Virginia lawyer, Thomas Jefferson. After more debate, the document is formally adopted. On July 4, 1776, the Declaration of Independence is given final approval, and copies are sent to every corner of the thirteen colonies.

Though the British army has sailed away from Boston Harbor, Washington will not celebrate his victory and moves his army rapidly to the one logical place the British might yet appear, New York City. He fortifies the city as much as possible, but it is nearly an indefensible position. When the British fleet arrives, Washington understands that the Declaration of Independence will have no meaning if he cannot win what is now an inevitable war.

GEORGE WASHINGTON

Born 1732, in Westmoreland County, Virginia, grows up with a love of the land around him, develops considerable skills as both a farmer and surveyor. When he is twenty years old he inherits the estate of Mount Vernon upon the death of his brother, Lawrence.

Joining the Virginia Militia soon after, Washington receives the traditional officer's commission due a prominent landowner. Without any military training, Washington commands a column of militia assigned to confront a settlement of French trappers who, according to the British royal governor, are trespassing on British soil. Washington marches his men into a confrontation, and when the French do not obey his demands to leave the area, he fires on them. The incident sparks enormous outrage in both England and France, and marks the beginning of the French and Indian War.

Though chastised for his unwise and costly show of force, Washington is allowed to retain his commission as lieutenant colonel, and in 1755, is assigned to accompany British general Edward Braddock on a campaign to confront the French, who have secured a strong outpost at the head of the Ohio River. Braddock's expedition is ambushed by a well-hidden force of French troops and their Indian allies, and the result is the first great British disaster on American soil. Braddock and most of his officers are killed, and only through the efforts of George Washington do any of the British force survive capture. Washington's heroism erases the stain of his earlier blunder, and he is promoted to full colonel of militia.

He yearns for a commission in the regular British army, but when he is repeatedly denied, he retires from the service, frustrated by the arrogant British prejudice toward colonial officers. He returns to Mount Vernon and attempts to settle into the peaceful life of a gentleman farmer.

In 1759, he marries a widow, Martha Dandridge Custis, whose wealth far exceeds his own. The marriage thus produces a couple who rank among the wealthiest in Virginia. Together, they charm Virginia society with their grace and quiet affection, and though Martha has two children of her own, Washington hopes to rear his own offspring. But their marriage produces no children.

By his status alone he is expected to participate in Virginia politics, and eventually is chosen to attend the Continental Congress. Though he has been ignored and insulted by the British, he harbors no particular hostility toward King George. As the British abuse turns from matters of policy to matters of violent confrontation, Washington leans closer to the voices favoring independence. Never one to speak out, he is nevertheless a strong presence in the congress, and by his experience is a natural choice to lead the new army.

His success in holding the army together in Boston stems from his quiet and stoic demonstration of authority, though he will occasionally display a fierce temper. He is a large man by any standards, and his size alone gives him a martial presence that commands attention, if not outright respect. Though still

seen by many of the New Englanders as an outsider, he demonstrates considerable talent for choosing capable senior officers,
notably Charles Lee, Israel Putnam, and Nathanael Greene. He
does much to weed out the incompetent and local political big-
wigs from important positions of command. He understands more
than anyone in the army that they must become professionals if
they are to confront the British.

He is not present in Philadelphia to sign the Declaration of
Independence, but he embraces the principle with absolute dedication. On July 9, 1776, he orders the document read to his assembled troops in New York. The response is a riot of patriotic
emotions, from his army and from the citizenry of the city. It is
the inspiration he must have if he is to lead this band of untrained
amateurs against the finest army in the world.

NATHANAEL GREENE

Born 1742, in Warwick, Rhode Island, into a founding family
of that colony. His father is a successful businessman, owner of
an ironworks, and a Quaker minister of limited tolerance, who
despises books and any source of education for his children beyond the teachings of his religion. It is not a doctrine Greene can
follow, and in 1773, after outspoken protest against the strict
tenets he is expected to observe, Greene is dismissed from the
Quaker community.

Greene manages his father's business until 1771, when the senior dies. Leaving the ironworks to the care of his brothers,
Greene moves to Coventry, Rhode Island, develops friendships
with men who are active politically, and begins to understand the
seriousness of the issues swirling around the colony. Though
Greene serves in the Rhode Island Assembly, he is rarely outspoken and shows no inclination toward a career in politics. In 1774,
he marries Catharine "Kitty" Littlefield, who is twelve years his
junior.

He is an avid reader, and makes great efforts to secure books
of all types. Books, he writes, "inspire the mind to action and direct the passions." As events around Boston grow more incendiary, Greene follows many of those from Rhode Island who accept
the responsibility of lending assistance to their neighboring
colony. He and his friends establish the "Kentish Guards," but

Greene is afflicted with a slight deformity, a permanently stiff leg, and his friends consider that a disqualification from any sort of command. Embarrassed, he serves as a private.

He travels to Boston and witnesses the first great influx of British soldiers, but his mission is more personal than business. He has been told of a noted bookseller, and so, because of his voracious appetite for new reading material, he makes the acquaintance of the man who shares his literary passion. The bookseller is Henry Knox.

Greene returns to Rhode Island, where he receives news of the bloodshed at Lexington and Concord. He is one of two men chosen by the Committee of Safety to organize their colony's contribution to the rapidly growing continental forces forming around Boston. Authorized by the colonial assembly, the newly organized body is called the "Army of Observation." Greene is surprised to be elected brigadier general, attributes the selection to prominent members of the assembly who are longtime friends of his well-known family. He accepts reluctantly, knowing full well he has no qualifications for command. By the end of May 1775, he is marching to Boston.

His Rhode Islanders do not participate in the action at Breed's Hill, yet the troops make a favorable impression by their discipline and willingness to train. When Washington arrives to assume command, Greene writes him a letter of welcome and is invited to meet the new commander at Washington's headquarters. The commanding general has already endured the slights and insults from those who refuse to acknowledge his authority, but Greene has no pretensions about his own rank, and welcomes the guiding hand of an experienced soldier. Greene's cordiality is a pleasant surprise to Washington, and a friendship is born. Upon Washington's recommendation, Greene receives a commission as one of the first brigadiers in the Continental army. At thirty-three, he is also the youngest.

Though Rhode Island is threatened severely by British raids, Greene insists his men remain at their posts near Boston. *"We must expect to make partial sacrifices for the public good. I love the colony of Rhode Island . . . but I am not so attached as to be willing to injure the common cause."*

Greene becomes more visible at headquarters as a man who both understands and proposes sound strategy, and when the British evacuate Boston, Washington grants him command of the city. When news of the Declaration reaches Greene, he is one of the first to suggest to Washington that a war can only be won if the colonies are aligned with a foreign power, notably France.

With the threat shifting toward New York, Greene marches out of Boston in April 1776. When he arrives at his new post, he is promoted to major general and assumes command of the troops on Long Island. He observes the British ships sailing into New York Harbor, but is taken ill and can only observe from the misery of a sickbed as Washington confronts the growing threat of full-scale war.

BENJAMIN FRANKLIN

Born 1706, in Boston, to a modest working-class family. As a teen he demonstrates a flair for the printing trade, apprentices to his brother in a family business. He runs away to Philadelphia, pursues the trade with anyone who will employ him and, within a few years, rises from the most menial of positions to control of his own business.

In 1730, he marries Deborah Read, who provides him with two children, only one of whom, Sally, will survive to adulthood. He also has an illegitimate son, William, whom he neither hides nor excuses.

As a young adult, he discovers a talent for the written word and proceeds to become the most famed social commentator and satirist of his day. Through his numerous articles, and the publication of his magazine, *Poor Richard's Almanack,* Franklin becomes famous and quite wealthy.

He is recognized as Philadelphia's most illustrious citizen and founds a lengthy list of community organizations aimed at both mind and body, as well as the public safety. He founds the colony's first fire department, library, and an academy that will become the University of Pennsylvania.

Not content merely to write, he expands his interests into science and involves himself in some of the most radical experiments of his day, involving electricity and magnetism, fluid mechanics and meteorology, among many other fields.

He serves the British crown as postmaster general of the colonies and travels frequently to England. In the mid-1760s, he makes a journey that will take him away from Philadelphia for more than ten years, during which time his wife dies.

As his stature increases, he travels throughout Europe, entertains and impresses the monarchies and intellectual elite of several nations. He is the most famous American in England and serves as the legislative representative to the royal government from four different colonies, which quickly draws him into the escalating controversies. His love of England blinds him to the seriousness of colonial protest, but as protest escalates into violence, he witnesses firsthand the blithe dismissal of all things American and the base corruption behind much of British policy. Finally understanding that colonists are in fact second-class citizens, Franklin begins to work to ease tensions. But instead he experiences what he feels is a fatal arrogance on the part of the British. When he is targeted personally, his love affair with England comes to an end, and in early 1775, he returns to Philadelphia.

His son William has become the royal governor of New Jersey and remains fiercely loyal to the king. It is a stance Franklin cannot tolerate, and the two men permanently sever their relationship.

As a delegate to the Second Continental Congress, Franklin does not engage in the debates, but serves as a quiet sage, and ultimately has considerable influence in bringing about the approval of the Declaration of Independence. Along with John Adams, Franklin assists Thomas Jefferson in the document's creation.

He serves on a committee that opens the first contact with Britain's traditional enemy, France, seeking to form an alliance that can provide the colonies with the means of defending themselves, as well as opening up fresh lines of trade and commerce closed by the British. The diplomatic efforts are discreet and dangerous. Once King George declares the colonies to be in rebellion, any nation that makes contact with the American congress is trespassing into British affairs and risks a war of its own. But the French see an opportunity to gain power through an alliance with America at the expense of her hated rival, and the congress is granted permission to send representatives to Paris to begin negotiations for credit and a possible military alliance. The first to go is Silas Deane, and Franklin follows in late 1776. Though he well understands that France is risking war with England, Franklin is more concerned with the survival of his own nation.

CHARLES CORNWALLIS

Born 1738, in London, England, to an aristocratic family, which affords him the opportunity to attend Eton College. He is a rugged and physically athletic young man but suffers an eye injury that gives him a permanent "droop" to his eyelid, which some confuse with sleepy disinterest. At seventeen, he joins the army, receives a commission as ensign, attends the famed military academy at Turin, Italy. Called into active service, he is engaged in several significant actions during the Seven Years War with France.

He sails to England in 1760, is elected to Parliament, and receives a promotion to lieutenant colonel. He returns again to the war on the European mainland, continues to demonstrate a skill in the field, and by the end of the war, he once again takes his place in Parliament.

His father carries the title as first earl Cornwallis, and upon his death in 1762, Charles inherits the title, as second earl. In 1768, he marries Jemima Tullekin Jones, the daughter of a professional soldier. She is a tall, beautiful woman of quiet grace, and he is madly in love. They have two children.

He continues his service in the army, and though he is not particularly supportive of the king's policies in America, he is nevertheless a loyal officer. In 1770, he is given the prestigious title of constable of the Tower of London, a post he will maintain for most of his life, though he is rarely there. Promoted to major general in 1775, he sails to America a year later, to rendezvous with Henry Clinton off the coast of Charleston, South Carolina. The attempted invasion of that coast is thwarted by the unexpectedly brilliant defenses constructed by William Moultrie, and the British invasion fleet suffers considerable losses. The battle is a severe embarrassment to the British navy and to Henry Clinton, and prevents the British from gaining a foothold in the southern colonies for another four years. Cornwallis has his first taste of the rivalry and bickering between army and navy, and he suffers his first experience as a subordinate to Henry Clinton.

Withdrawing northward, the British fleet, along with Cornwallis' infantry, sets sail for Staten Island, where they will join Commanding General William Howe. His mission is as it has always been, to confront and defeat the enemies of his king. As he sails into New York Harbor, he sees an enormous fleet already in place, feels a sharp sense of pride from the impressive show of strength. The British are, after all, the most powerful empire on earth.

Cornwallis understands the task that awaits them: the elimination of a rebellion against their king by the destruction of their so-called army. He knows little of this man George Washington, knows little about the rebel army itself. When he greets William Howe, he hears the confidence, the boastful talk that this absurd uprising will be put down quickly, that they might all return home by Christmas. By nature a subdued man, Cornwallis does not partake of the boisterous toasting to their certain glorious success. Though Howe seems oblivious, Cornwallis knows that somewhere beyond the show of British might, there are men with muskets who are fighting for a cause.

PART ONE

Actuated by the Most Glorious Cause that mankind ever fought in, I am determined to defend this post to the very last extremity.
> COL. ROBERT MAGAW, responding to the British demand for surrender of Fort Washington, New York, November 15, 1776

GEORGE WASHINGTON

1. THE FISHERMAN

He had sat out the raw misery of the storm through most of the night, keeping his boat tight against the shore. She was pulled up on soft ground between two large rocks, his private mooring, a hiding place he had known since he was a boy. The boat would be safe there, from weather or the occasional vandal, but this time the storm was different, the rain driven by a howling wind that might push the waves hard beneath the boat, damaging her against the rocks. His wife would not worry, would keep the fireplace lit, would not protest even though he would stay out all night. She had heard him speak of it too often, his love of the water, the pursuit of the fish that seemed to call to him in a way few wives understand. This time she did not expect him to return home for at least two days, and so as he huddled under a ledge of rock, soaked by the amazing violence of the storm, he did not worry for her, thought only of tomorrow, the new dawn, hoping that the storm would be gone.

He would rarely fish in the darkness, but the late summer had been hot, breathless days that kept the fish silent, sent them away to some invisible place every fisherman seeks. He had thought of drifting with the tide along the edge of Gravesend Bay, without even his small sail, just easing along the first deep water offshore, hoping to tempt something from below into an ill-timed assault on his handmade hooks. But as the sun went down, the breeze had not calmed, and he had stared wide-eyed at a terrifying burst of lightning, warning him from the distance, a great show from the lower tip of New York, moving toward him from the distant shores of New Jersey. The storm had blown hard across the harbor, and he barely made it to his private wharf before the hard rain slapped his face and soaked his clothes. He had used his long push pole to slide the boat between the rocks,

jumping out and then moving quickly under the ledges that
faced away from the water. There was nowhere else to go, no
thought of a fire, no blessed coffee, nothing but the hard crack of
thunder. He had tried to lift himself up, keep his breeches off the
ground, the dirt beneath him turning to mud as the flow of rain-
water found him, small rivers in the soil. But the rock ledge was
low and tight, and he could not escape, had settled into the misery, simply to wait it out until the dawn.

Before first light, the rain had stopped, and the quiet had
awakened him. He groaned his way into the open air, his joints
crying in stiffness, the air chilling him through the wetness of his
shirt. But then he could see the first glow in the east, and he listened for the sound, the winds gone, only a soft breeze flowing
through the trees behind him. He had always believed that after a
strong rain, the fish would move, emerging from their own shelter, hungry, looking for whatever he might offer them. It was a
lesson taught him by his father, who had fished this same water,
who knew Gravesend Bay better than anyone in the villages, the
way a farmer knows his land, every rock, every hole. He had begun to go out with his father when he was barely old enough to
hold the stout fishing pole, had cheered with pure joy when the
old man had wrestled with the fury of some unknown creature,
and shared the pride of his father's success, the fish flopping and
writhing in the bottom of the boat, the old man's quiet joy. His
father was gone now, but the lessons remained. He looked at the
boat, his father's boat, cared for by the hand of the son, thought,
It's time to go fishing.

There was a great deal of water in the boat, and he scooped
out as much as he could, then turned it on its side, a great splash
on muddy ground, the last bit of water spilling away. He was in a
hurry now, did not look at the glow on the horizon, knew that the
dawn would give way to another hot day, and he slid the boat
quickly off the shore, one last push as he waded out beside it,
then jumped, lifting himself into the stern. He pushed with the
long pole, the boat cutting through the low ripples on the water,
and he measured the shallowness, knew that in another hundred
yards it would drop off. He examined his fishing pole, felt the familiar excitement, knew that in the early morning, he might find
a big one, a striped bass perhaps, or hook into a big blue, a fight
that could pull his boat for a half mile into the great bay. If the
breeze was right, he could drift along the slope of the drop-off,

where the flounder might strike, the amazingly ugly fish that his wife would not touch until he cut away the ugliness.

The push pole suddenly went deep, the bottom falling away, and he set it down along the rail of the boat, tested the wind, thought of raising the small sail. He reached for the hard wad of bait in his pocket, ignored the smell, picked up the fishing pole . . . then froze, stared hard to the south, across the narrows, saw a reflection, caught by the first sunlight. It was a ship, fat and heavy, in full sail, coming straight toward him. Beyond, he could see two more, smaller frigates, more sails, and he stared at the bows of each ship, cutting through the water, thought, They will turn soon. They must be going out to sea.

He had often thought of sailors, the crews who manned the great ships, what kind of life could be had living only on the water. The harbor had filled with them only weeks before, more ships than he thought there were in the world, a vast navy, all the might of legend come to life. They were still there, a forest of bare masts and rigging, wrapping along the shoreline and wharves of Staten Island, extending out into the harbor. They had stayed at anchor for the most part, the navy knowing—as did the villagers—that on Governor's Island there were cannon, a curious battery placed by the rebels to keep Lord Howe's ships from sailing close to New York. The villagers had mostly laughed at the idea, that these men who had come down from Boston would dare to threaten His Majesty's navy, would have the arrogance to believe they could keep the mighty ships in their anchorage. But there had been no conflict, no real activity on either side. The hot talk in the taverns had grown quiet, the inaction breeding boredom in those who never really knew what would happen anyway. He was among them, excited when the navy arrived, the amazing sight of so many troops making camp on Staten Island, a vast sea of tents. But then nothing had happened, and many had gone back to their routine. And so, he had once again returned to Gravesend Bay to pursue the fish.

His father had told him about the British navy, the mightiest armada in the world, the vast power of the king that kept all his enemies at bay. But his father had no fire for politics, and the son knew only the talk, words like *Whig* and *Tory*, and issues that excited some, but, to many more like him, seemed very far away. He had heard the arguments, the complaints and protests, the threats and hot talk that meant very little to him. He had thought it strange that so many people could make such protest against their king, especially in the face of all those ships, the vast army, the enormous guns. And yet the voices had grown louder, the protests erupting into great public gatherings. He had been in New York when this man Washington had come. He had seen what those people called an army, heard some of the speeches, more new words, talk of a congress and independence. He thought it odd that the people wanted to be rid of their king, the one man responsible for their security, for protecting them from what he supposed to be all manner of enemies: Indians, the French, even pirates, who could sail close to these very shores, attacking the helpless, stealing anything they pleased. He had never actually seen a pirate, of course, or a Frenchman. There were Indians occasionally, in New York, or so he had heard. He admired these ships, this great mass of power, had felt as so many had felt out there on Long Island, that there could be no danger, no enemy who could harm the colonials as long as the great ships were there to protect them. But the rebels had cannon too. All it meant to him was that he should probably not fish around Governor's Island.

He had not fished around Staten Island either. It was unfamiliar water, too long a trip for his small boat to risk. If the wind turned against him, or a storm blew up, he would be helpless, have to make for land in a place where rumors sprouted. There had been talk from men who had been to Staten Island, who had seen the foreigners. He didn't know why they would be with the king's army, but the men at the tavern swore they had seen them. They were called Hessians, and some said they were savages, frightening men, strange uniforms and stranger faces. He had laughed at the descriptions, knew some of the men could spin a good yarn, but still . . . why would the king bring these men to New York?

He watched the three ships, his hands moving automatically to rig up his fishing pole. He had often seen smaller ships moving past Gravesend Bay, some near the shallows where he fished. There were sails only when they were heading for the open water, or, as he had seen lately, when they came in, the end of some long journey he could only imagine. The sailors had often called out to him, men up in the rigging, on the rails. He had always waved politely, wondered if they envied him, captain and crew of his own boat. But then someone had shot at him, a puff of smoke from a lookout, the strange *zip* of the musket ball passing overhead, a small punch in the water behind his boat. He had not understood that, thought it a ridiculous, frightening mistake, but the lesson was learned. Now, when the navy ships moved past he made ready, turned his boat toward the shore, an instinct inside him to move to safety, to keep his fat rocks in sight.

He thought now of doing the same, the three ships still bearing toward him. It was odd, something wrong. He did not move, still watched them, thought, They should be turning about before now, the deeper water is behind them. If they keep on this course, they will run aground. He had never seen such a mass of power so close. The larger ship was now barely two hundred yards away, then he heard shouts, the ship beginning to veer slowly to one side. The sails began to drop, the rigging alive with men, sounds of canvas flapping, the rattle of chain. He could see the anchor suddenly dropping, a hard splash as it thrust downward. He set the fishing pole down, his heart racing cold in his chest, his hands feeling for the paddle, no time to put up the sail. In short moments, the rigging of the great ship was bare, the tall masts naked against the glow from the east. He began to move the paddle in the water, pulling his boat backward, unable to take his eyes away from the flank of the ship, the rows of cannon staring straight toward him, toward the land behind him. The other ships moved in behind, slow maneuvering, more sails disappearing, and he kept paddling, his boat barely pushing into the tide, the breeze against his back. He glanced behind him, saw his rocks, the sanctuary, the agonizing distance, moved the paddle faster, chopping at the water. He expected to hear the musket ball again, but they seemed not to notice him, or better, they were ignoring him. The sandy bottom was visible beneath his boat now, and he grabbed quickly for the push pole, stood, balanced precariously, the boat rocking under his feet.

He strained against the push pole, the boat lurching under him, but then he stopped. Beyond the smaller ships there was something new, motion again, but different, no sails, no great masts. He stepped up on his seat, tried to see more detail, could tell the boats were flat, the motion coming from rows of oars. He saw more of them, and slowly they reached the warships, but did not stop, kept moving, still coming toward him. He was frozen for a long moment, his mind absorbing through his confusion. The flatboats kept coming, a vast swarm, the motion of the oars bringing them closer. He began to see reflections, a mass of color, red and white and silver. And now he understood. The boats were filled with soldiers.

HE HAD REACHED THE ROCKS, PULLED THE BOAT BETWEEN THEM, slid it hard onto the shore with sweating hands. The soldiers had ignored him, and he thought of leaving, running the long trail back to his house, telling his wife. He climbed up on the taller rock, could see a great fleet of small flat barges. They had begun to reach the shore, sliding to a stop a hundred yards away from his perch, one after another, shouts, the men suddenly emerging, each boat emptying. He felt a strange thrill, saw the uniforms clearly now, the red and white of the British soldiers, the colors that inspired an empire. He was truly excited, the fear gone, made a small laugh, thought, No, there is no danger. I should go out, salute them, welcome them to Long Island. He saw different uniforms, brighter red, gold trim, officers. If I can find the commander, bring him to my house . . .

He tried to imagine his wife's face. He laughed again, saw now that the empty boats were moving offshore, sliding between those that still held their passengers. He tried to count, three dozen, No . . . my God. The flotilla stretched all the way past the warships still, an endless sea of flat motion. He could hear sounds now, over the quick shouts of men, the rhythm of drums, and a strange screeching noise. The sounds began to come together, the music of bagpipes, and the boat released its cargo, a different red, men in tartan, and he stared, thought, By God . . . they're wearin' . . . *skirts*. He pictured his wife, knew she wouldn't believe him, thought of running again, bringing her back here, to see this amazing sight. He wanted to stand up high on the rock, pulled his knees up, but something held him down, frozen. There was a ripple of sound behind him, from the sandy hills, a line of thin woods. The soldiers seemed not to hear, no change in their voices, their activity. But he turned, looked back, saw bits of smoke in the trees. *Musket fire.* He couldn't see who was shooting, thought, My God, what foolishness. Who dares to fire at the king's troops? He huddled down against the rock, peered out toward the soldiers again, saw men in line, moving off the narrow beach, an officer leading them up the rise toward the trees. The musket fire slowed, just the single pop, then another. Then the woods were quiet, the British troops moving up closer. He felt an odd twist in his stomach, thought, Was that a battle? Was it over? He was amazed, thought, You do not shoot at soldiers. He tried to think who it might have been, had heard something about rebels who had come across the East River, to build some kind of fort near Brooklyn. Is that who was in the woods? He was anxious to move away now, to go home, to tell his wife this strange story. He looked out toward the boats again, could suddenly hear music, different, brass and drums. One of the boats reached the shore closer to him, and the colors were not red. The sunlight reflected off a mass of metal, men with gold helmets. The uniforms were blue, and the men began to move onto the shore with crisp steps, forming a neat rectangle. He stared, saw they nearly all wore their hair tied in a long queue, a braid protruding from the helmets, each man with a moustache. There were officers here too, and when their men moved off the shore, the officers turned, looked toward him, one man motioning with his arm, pointing. He felt the cold in his chest again, began to back down the rock. But he could not leave just yet, had to see, peeked up over the edge, saw six of the blue uniforms moving down the beach in his direction. Now the welcome was erased from his mind. He could hear their voices now, words that he didn't understand. This must be . . . could they be . . . *Hessians*?

He dropped down from the rocks, fought the urge to run, glanced at his boat. No, I cannot just leave her here. They might take her. He felt his hands shaking, the strange voices moving closer, just beyond the far side of the big rocks. He took a deep breath, fixed a smile on his face, moved around the boat, saw them now, saw for the first time the long muskets, the hard sharp steel, the bayonets moving down, pointing at him. There was one in a different uniform, the man holding a sword, who motioned toward him, unsmiling, said, "A spy, yes?"

He shook his head, tried to laugh.

"Oh, no, sir. Just fishing." He pointed toward the boat, his hand shaking. "See? Just fishing, sir."

The officer glanced at the boat, said something to the soldiers beside him, and the men moved quickly, the bayonets suddenly coming forward, the sharp flash of steel, the work of men who

know their business. The officer gave a short command, and the
soldiers backed away, stood again in a tight line. The officer
glanced down at the man who lay fallen into his boat, nodded,
made a brief smile.

"A spy. Yes."

---

2. CORNWALLIS

LONG ISLAND, NEW YORK, AUGUST 22, 1776

HE HAD BEEN WITH THE FIRST WAVE, BRINGING HIS OWN MEN
ashore in a great show of martial elegance. The uniforms were
spotless, the men well practiced in their drill, and as the regiments moved in line up the rise away from the water, not a man
among them had any doubt that if the rebels dared to stand in
front of them, the memories of Breed's Hill and Concord would
be wiped away in one bloody charge.

They had made camp near the small village of Flatbush, and
when the tents were in line, and the equipment organized, he had
gone back to the water's edge to observe as the rest of the massive force came ashore. It was a marvelous armada, nearly
ninety flatboats, a vast spread of force punctuated by the power
of the big warships, standing guard, great birds of prey watching over their flocks, keeping their men safe for the landing.
No force of rebels could have held them back. In fact, there
had been no opposition at all, except for a brief scattering of
musket fire.

Already the local civilians had come to the camp, all with details of what lay ahead, of the rebel position, the strength. Most of
the citizens in this area were staunchly loyal to the king, and it was
obvious they were relieved finally to be under direct protection of
the army. Nearly every farmer who came into camp fashioned
himself to be some kind of spy, eager to lend some assistance to
the army's intelligence. Cornwallis had heard that the musket
fire had come from some militia from Pennsylvania, and whether

or not the information was reliable, he had to wonder, were there no New Yorkers to defend their own soil? There would be meaning to that, something not to be ignored. General Howe had given little regard to the intelligence from the citizens, relying instead on the reports from his brother, Admiral Richard Howe. The admiral would stay with his ships, keeping a sharp watch for rebel movement from any quarter that might pose some threat to the landing. Cornwallis understood that of course General Howe would give much more credence to the reports from his brother. But Cornwallis listened to every civilian, sorted through hyperbole and careless boasting, focused on the small bits of real information, any hint of the weakness that could be of good use to this marvelous army.

They had landed nearly twenty thousand men, and combined with the great mass of naval power, it was the largest expedition the British military had ever assembled. They were not all English, of course, several thousand Hessian soldiers landing beside their new, or as some said, temporary allies. But Cornwallis had observed them coming ashore, could tell immediately that the Hessian discipline was absolute. Like the British, their uniforms were perfect, the weapons held in perfect symmetry. Even the faces of the men seemed identical, strange, as though a massive force of brothers. The uniforms were mostly blue, but then had come the *jagers*, in their green coats, the handpicked riflemen, recruited from the forests for their hunting skills. That would be something new here, men who fought as the rebels fought, relying on the keen eye and the well-placed shot, rather than the mass of power in the bayonet charge. It had excited him, the thought of the rebels discovering that not all their enemies observed the rules of war. Cornwallis still felt some uneasiness with that, not the disgust that rolled through headquarters, the outrage of Howe infecting the other officers. There was complaining already, how dare those rebels confront us by *not* confronting us? Cornwallis had read enough of Breed's Hill to know that it was a hollow protest, that if the rebels stayed put, it did not necessarily mean an easy fight. Howe would not talk of Breed's Hill, and there was no mention of it in headquarters, no criticizing in quiet conversation. Not one senior officer there would have assaulted the rebels any differently than Howe had done, except perhaps Clinton.

Cornwallis had never spoken to Henry Clinton about such things, it was simply not good form. Clinton would never speak openly, of course, but his silence betrayed a simmering disrespect for Howe. That sort of dissension was not tolerated, certainly not by a commander like William Howe, who carried a fragile pride. But Cornwallis had come to know Clinton well, suffering through the ridiculous disaster in South Carolina. Clinton had been stubborn, relying on bad intelligence and bad tactics, and it was Cornwallis' first taste of a war against the rebels. He had experienced the same outrage about their methods, the rebels who stayed put behind great fat logs, not understanding that when the British came to fight, the most proper response was to oblige. But the rebels had been perfectly satisfied to wreak havoc on the naval vessels, while the torturous heat and damnable insects wreaked havoc on the British troops. At least in New York, the countryside seemed well suited for a fight: rolling hills, hard ground, a place where cavalry could fight beside the bayonets. The coast of South Carolina was more swamp than land, the air thick with blight. Clinton had finally admitted defeat, that Charleston could not be taken without great loss, and both men had known Howe would understand that. Howe would never expect his subordinates to endure another Breed's Hill.

It was said with optimism that the Howe brothers made an effective partnership, the officers speaking quietly of how one man's weakness was bolstered by the other's strength. Admiral Howe was more matter-of-fact about strategy, had actually spoken out in support of some means of avoiding war, something the king and his ministers would never endorse publicly. But Richard Howe held a stronger political position in England, had quiet support from many who stood in opposition to the king's policies. Even before Cornwallis had arrived in America, he understood that the admiral had more powerful friends than did his brother, that some in England, and perhaps right here at headquarters, still cast some blame on the general for the loss of Boston and the carnage they had endured at Breed's Hill. Cornwallis had no affection for William Howe, had known him only from their days serving together in Parliament. It was not Cornwallis' job to place blame or find fault with anyone. William Howe had full command of the army. It would be Cornwallis' duty to follow his orders.

AUGUST 26, 1776

They gathered at the home of a grateful Tory named DeNuys, a nervous little man who bowed and scraped before General Howe, gushing with unbridled relief that the great British army had been delivered by God, a force of angels to hold the great hordes of rabble away from his modest home.

The last of the foreign soldiers had been landed the day before, brought ashore by their commander, General de Heister. The old Hessian was barely mobile, and Cornwallis guessed him to be nearly seventy, a military man who had charged through wars on European soil before many of the British command were born. There was an arrogance to the old man, but it was not an obstacle, and de Heister knew his place at the table, the professional soldier's instinct of when to speak, when to offer an opinion. Like Cornwallis, de Heister understood that this was Howe's command. And like Cornwallis, de Heister felt that once the army had completed its landing on Long Island, it was time to go to work.

There had been a brisk skirmish near Cornwallis' camp, a unit of Hessian grenadiers actually surprised by a sudden burst of fire from a column of rebels. The fight had little consequence, and the Hessians, under their commander Karl von Donop, had pushed the rebels back into the woods with little effort. But the outburst had prodded Cornwallis to prod Howe. It was time to move.

It had been a long meal, a generous offering by the DeNuys family, as well as masses of food brought in from local farms, more Tories welcoming the army into their territory. Howe had been nearly giddy, thanking them in the name of the king, inspired by the eruption of support that flowed through the camps. Cornwallis had enjoyed the meal as they all had, but it was past now, and his impatience had begun to grow. Finally, after too many toasts of good wine, even Howe could not avoid the purpose of this meeting, to talk of what they must do next.

The scouts had made their reports, local men who could draw the maps, lay out the routes for the army to follow. Cornwallis had waited as long as he could, observed the protocol, could not begin any discussion of the business of the war without some cue from Howe. But the time had come, and he retrieved a map from beneath the table, spread it out. He studied the lines, made an effort to pay polite attention to the conversation around the long table, servants darting quickly behind them, tea and wine still flowing. Across from him, de Heister watched through tired eyes, and Cornwallis caught the look, thought, He will wait. He wants me to begin.

At the head of the table Howe was writing a note, handed it to an aide, said something in a low giggling voice, and Cornwallis looked down, pretended not to notice. It was an annoying practice, and Cornwallis could say nothing about it. It was not his place to judge. It was common knowledge that the commanding general would carry on with his mistress, love letters and silly notes, passed through the headquarters as though by schoolchildren. Cornwallis didn't believe himself prudish, but the presence of the women, bright flowery ornaments for the arms of the officers, made him uncomfortable. It was a parade of foppish finery, the gathering of trophies that some of the men seemed to require. He knew that his view was distinctly in the minority, that his devotion to his wife, though she was three thousand miles away, made him the exception. But it was the commanding general who set the standard, who seemed to be the most affected. Howe had made a conquest of one of his own officers' wives, rewarding the unfortunate subordinate with a promotion and soft duty in return for erasing the man's honor at having his wife become General Howe's bauble. Cornwallis would never comment, of course, and tried to avoid even a furtive glance, something that would be interpreted as disapproval. It was not his place. And, despite the distraction, sooner or later the commanding general would have to focus on the matter at hand.

He glanced again at Howe, who now seemed receptive to the men at the table. Howe noticed the map, and Cornwallis said, "General, with your permission, I have examined the terrain. This map confirms what I have seen." He waited, could not launch into a full-scale talk on strategy unless Howe gave him the opening. Clinton was beside him, began to nod, his own show of relief that the talk was turning away from the merely social. Howe took the cue, said, "Please continue, General. I enjoy a good plan."

"From the reports we have received from Lord Admiral Howe, and from the civilian sources, the rebel position is here." He pointed to the map. "They have placed themselves with their backs against the East River, and have moved advance forces

into positions that extend their front line . . . here. There are four
approaches to that position. Four roads we can use. The rebels
are in a defensive position in force on three of them. From all reports, they have not fortified at all . . . up here. It is the most
northerly route."

Clinton leaned close to him, looked at the map, said, "Yes, I
can confirm these positions." Clinton looked at Howe.

"Sir, I would suggest a general assault along the rebel front,
combined with a turning movement along the northern road."
Howe did not look at Clinton, and Cornwallis absorbed that,
knew their relationship had been more than strained, certainly
before Cornwallis had arrived, possibly even before Boston. It
was simply a case of two men who held tight to their own ideas
of strategy, not helped at all by Clinton's sensitivity about the
failure at Charleston. Howe was looking at Cornwallis now.

"General, do you agree with the position we now hold? Are
you satisfied with the placement of our strength?"

It was an odd question, even inappropriate. I am outranked by
three men here. This should not be my plan at all.

"Sir, General de Heister has great strength in the enemy's center." He didn't know what else to say, looked at the old Hessian,
who leaned forward, said in a quiet voice, "We are prepared."

Howe, who had always seemed uncomfortable around de
Heister, smiled politely at the old man, and said, "Yes, well, by
all means. It is perhaps time to end this matter. Do you all concur
then, that the rebels seem ready to receive a fight?"

Clinton stared at Cornwallis' map, said, "They have already
demonstrated their willingness to fight. The only reason they are
not fighting us right now is they know our strength. Mr. Washington cannot engage us in a general assault. I would imagine he
is wondering why we have not yet engaged him."

It was an indiscreet remark, and Cornwallis was surprised to
see a smile break through the ruggedness of de Heister's face.
He looked at Howe, expected to see anger at Clinton's impudence, but Howe had turned away, was speaking to an aide, reading something written on a piece of pink linen. The aide moved
away, and Howe turned toward them, said, "General Cornwallis,
if you believe it is a good plan, then perhaps you should pursue
it. I might even . . . join you on the march. It should be good
sport."

*   *   *

THEY WERE LED BY THREE SCOUTS, LOCAL MEN, CHOSEN FOR THEIR familiarity with the roads. Two of them had moved out ahead, leading a patrol of troops, a probing party, who would be the first to find any rebel position. The army had moved northeast, behind the dense ridge of woods and thickets known as the Heights of Guian, which hid the rebel lines. It was late, and very dark, and Cornwallis rode slowly on a road where all the landmarks, the familiar trails, were erased by the night. Behind him, nearly ten thousand men marched in sweaty silence. Clinton was beside him, and they both knew that Howe was nearby, that no decision could be made without his approval. Their guide stopped, waiting for them to ride up close, said in a whisper, "Jamaica, sir. We turn left here. Old Jamaica Road."

The man seemed nervous, glancing into the darkness, and Clinton said, "Are you certain?"

"Oh, yes, quite, sir. I'm wondering where they might be waiting."

Cornwallis understood, the man was referring to the rebels.

"I wouldn't concern yourself, young man. There are plenty of muskets between us and them. We'll find them soon enough." He looked toward Clinton, would wait for the next move, and Clinton turned to the staff behind them, motioned to an aide, and said, "Have one man locate General Howe, inform him we have reached the intersection. One man will remain here, guide the column to the left. Continue silence at all cost."

There was a sudden roll of thunder, from beyond the ridge. Both men turned, the sounds coming more behind them than down the Jamaica Road. Cornwallis pointed into the dark, said quietly, "Southeast. The rebel position. That would be . . . General de Heister."

The sweat in his shirt gave him a sudden chill, and he gripped the reins of the horse, thought, *Finally*. He listened in silence, the thunder now distinct, artillery, scattered bursts of musket fire. There was no rhythm to it, thick lines of men seeking each other in the dark. He knew de Heister was pushing forward, measuring the resistance the rebels would offer. He tried to hear some difference in the sounds, picking out the rebel cannon from their own, but the distance was too great, the percussion muffled by the lay of the land. Clinton said in a low voice, "I had wondered if the Hessians would fight in the dark. Superstitious lot, you know."

There was a pause in the sounds, then another burst, uneven. Cornwallis nodded to himself, thought, A good sign. If they were merely firing at shadows, the sounds would be steady, officers losing control of their men, volleys fired at nothing. If a man is affected by fear, he will shoot at anything and nothing, and he will not search for a real target. There was another pause, scattered pops, more silence. He fought to see in the dark, strained to hear. But there was a lull, no sounds at all.

Cornwallis said, "It is not a general engagement yet. General de Heister would have them advancing. Use the darkness. It is the rebels who will fire at shadows."

He thought of the Hessians now, had wondered about what kind of soldiers they were from the first time he had seen them. They seemed almost inhuman, but not in the way that inspired fear in the civilians. They fought as one man, a singular purpose, the ideal soldier, rigid obedience to the commands of the officers. Even the British command had been amazed at their appearance, many of the officers never having seen a Hessian before. And, they had learned quickly that not all of them were in fact Hessian. The troops came from several small kingdoms and duchies: Hesse-Cassel and Hesse-Hanau, who were accurately referred to as Hessians. But there were regiments from Brunswick and Waldeck, Anspach and Anhalt-Zerbst, all those lands controlled by men who would appreciate the generosity of King George, who would be paid a fee for every soldier they could muster or impress into service for the British cause. All during the landing at Gravesend Bay, he had seen the Hessians standing at attention in their boats, in a rigid, if somewhat unsteady formation. They had maintained that stance the entire way across the harbor, and he had smiled at that, some sort of show for their British counterparts, the absolute discipline, the first gesture from their commanders that this hired army would earn the king's gold.

In the colonies, the British had already planted rumors of their barbarism, confident that the ignorance of the rebels could expand those rumors into raw terror if the men in strange uniforms and polished helmets actually faced them on the battlefield. Cornwallis knew the foreigners were as well trained as any British unit, but there was a difference, the discipline coming from something beyond loyalty to a king or pride in their flag. They were recruited by force, often kidnapped by aggressive sergeants, held in line by the threats of the pure brutality that awaited them if they strayed. The training was inhumane at best, and orders were obeyed out of fear. He would never question a man like de Heister, but from their very demeanor, Cornwallis could sense that the Hessian soldiers had no pride in themselves, seemed to march in the mindless cadence of soldiers who had lost their humanity. *And if those men have a disregard for life, have been taught to have no respect for themselves as men, how will they regard their enemy? There could be a brutality in those men that we might not be comfortable with. Yes, certainly, it makes them a frightening army. But what kind of ally?*

He smiled, could not help thinking that, yes, rumors work in many ways. It had been his idea, to make discreet mention to de Heister, to plant an image solidly in the old commander that the rebels either scalped or ate the dead of their wounded enemies. It was a bizarre tale, and de Heister had listened to it with a somber nod, would betray nothing of his own skepticism at such a ridiculous ploy from his British ally. But Cornwallis knew, de Heister didn't have to believe it. He had soldiers who *would*. He knew Clinton was right: The Hessians could be a superstitious lot. Brutal or not, inhumane or not, this war might be won by the most efficient killers.

It was well after midnight, and the silence continued. Cornwallis moved into the intersection, Clinton followed, and both men stared into darkness toward the east, toward the narrow gap in the brush where the Jamaica Road would lead them. The advance patrol had instructions to report back to the main column by midnight, would certainly have found the rebel line by then, or at least have some good idea of the rebel position. Cornwallis could feel Clinton's impatience, and Clinton turned now, said to an aide, "Bring me a dozen men. I want them to move out on this road until they find what I expect them to find. It seems our first attempt . . . our advance patrol has become lost in the dark."

Cornwallis rode forward, knew several of the men who had disappeared down the road. Some were from his own regiment, the thirty-third, and those men would not be lost. He listened hard, heard a brief rumble from the southeast, more scattered firing. The new patrol began to gather behind Clinton, the quiet shuffle of boots, and now the darkness was shattered by a voice, a sharp call, horses' hoofbeats. The shock made him jump in the saddle, and he could see a lantern coming toward them from the west, the road alive with light, the faces of men. Clinton moved quickly past him, shouted, "Extinguish that light! What is the meaning of this! Whose troops are you?"

The light went low, but not out, and one man rode forward, said, "Sir! We have them, sir!"

Clinton seemed to sputter. "Who? You have who?"

Cornwallis eased his horse forward, could see smiles, recognized the young faces, said, "Please report, Captain."

The man seemed to calm. "We captured the rebels, sir. The road is clear."

Cornwallis moved past the young captain, Clinton close behind him. He could see the rest of the patrol now, the British uniforms, and then others, no uniform at all, sullen faces, staring at him. Clinton seemed confused. The sharp voice now gone, he said, "Where are they? How many rebels?"

"They're right here, sir. Five of them. That's all there were."

CLINTON AND CORNWALLIS MOVED THEIR COLUMN WESTWARD down the Jamaica Road, and the young captain was correct. The rebels had not fortified the northernmost avenue into their position. Only five militia officers had been sent that way to keep an eye on what their commander had assumed to be nothing at all. For the rest of the night, the British marched half their army through the gap in the dense woods, moving silently on a route that brought them behind the main lines of the rebels. By nine o'clock in the morning, the rebel position was trapped between the two great arms of Howe's army.

3. WASHINGTON

THE SOUNDS OF THE FIGHT ROLLED TOWARD HIM IN ONE GREAT chattering roar. He had expected it on the right, where his flank lay close to the East River, close to the British camps, and Howe had not disappointed him. Washington had put his best troops there, the veterans in an army that had very few veterans. The British had begun moving against his right flank the night before, slow and probing, and it was not unexpected. He knew both sides would do some feeling out, the land somewhat precarious, swampy, patches of thick woods, framed by the salt marshes and swift current of Gowanus Creek. That part of the field was commanded by William Alexander of New Jersey, a man known to the army as Lord Stirling. It was a semilegitimate title his family had brought from Scotland, which was recognized in few places outside his own circle. But the affectation caused Washington no difficulties, the title in no way a barrier to Stirling's dedication to American independence. Washington believed Stirling to be a solidly competent, if somewhat fiery field commander, and he knew that Stirling had nearly as much field experience as he did, was in fact a few years older. In an army where any experience at all had value, Washington felt that Stirling's somewhat violent temperament suited command of the most likely place in the field for a good hot fight.

In the center had been John Sullivan, a veteran from the siege of Boston, one of Washington's first trusted subordinates. He had placed Sullivan in command of those troops positioned in the field outside of the fortified position at Brooklyn Heights.

By rank, Charles Lee was his second in command, but Lee was still in Charleston. Though there was no doubt the American forces there had accomplished a stunning victory, Washington was beginning to hear reports that Lee had been a very small part of the whole affair, that he remained in South Carolina only to bask in the glow of the victory. It was the kind of talk Washington could not tolerate now. He had more pressing problems right in front of him.

With Lee in the Carolinas, Israel Putnam was the second in command in New York, and Washington had placed him in the works at Brooklyn Heights, the command center of the entire position on Long Island. Putnam was one of the heroes of the extraordinary fight on the Charlestown peninsula above Boston, what they all knew now as Breed's Hill. It had been the worst day of the war for the British, a victory that cost General Thomas Gage his command. Though there were quiet disagreements over what role Putnam had actually played, he had been in overall command of the field, and most reports said that Putnam had been responsible for keeping the militia withdrawal organized and preventing the British from inflicting the same casualties they had absorbed.

Despite Putnam's self-confidence, and his reputation in Massachusetts, Washington would have preferred to place Nathanael Greene in overall command on Long Island, while Washington himself would stay in New York and maintain command of the half of the army that still fortified the city. But Greene had fallen ill, a serious fever, was tended to by nervous doctors across the East River. With the British pushing forward into what could be the most serious confrontation of the war, Washington was without the one man who inspired his confidence. Dividing the Long Island command between Sullivan and Putnam was the only alternative.

The British had the troop strength to attack both Manhattan and Long Island, and even after Howe's armada had landed at Gravesend Bay, Washington could not be sure if it was meant as a feint, to mislead him on the true direction of the British attack. But Washington could not abandon the city just to meet the British on Long Island, and so he divided his army, an anguished decision to weaken an already outnumbered force in the face of such a powerful enemy. Washington believed he had no choice. The British simply had too many options.

When the first sounds of battle had finally broken out, Washington had come across the river himself, his doubts erased. The British had made no move toward Manhattan, and the outpost on Governor's Island had sent no word of any warships coming their way. Very soon after daylight, the attack had spread across the entire front, a British force pushing into Stirling and then a strong wave of Hessians moving against Sullivan. To the inexperienced troops who faced this well-disciplined army, the shock had been devastating. All along Sullivan's line, entire units simply melted away, some without firing a shot. The men who stood their ground discovered they could not reload quickly enough to hold away the terrifying sight of so many bayonets coming toward them, and when the fight became face-to-face, it was the steel, not the musketball, that did the horrible work. Stirling's men tried to hold their ground, but were soon pushed into the swamps, many trapped there, overtaken by the rapid advance of the well-disciplined attack. As both fronts pushed hard against Washington's lines, the men began to turn toward their one sanctuary, the safety of the fortified works on Brooklyn Heights. But there would be no organized retreat. Before Sullivan could even begin his own withdrawal, there had come a rush of messages from the far left, from the one place none of the commanders had expected. The British had appeared in a vast wave on the Jamaica Road, already behind Sullivan's left flank, were now closing in around him. The entire position outside of Brooklyn Heights was now close to being surrounded.

Washington stood high on a rampart of the works, could see gaps in the drifting smoke, the sharp breeze blowing from the north. He could see men moving toward him, toward the safety of the works, but it was not any kind of orderly retreat. It was chaos. As they reached the fortifications they began to climb up and through the obstacles, the cut trees and earthen walls, the rocks and crevices. He stared numbly at their wounds, the ripped shirts, men with no shoes, blank and dazed expressions, or worse, wide-eyed panic. Some moved slowly, in a haze of shock, others ran, scrambling to safety, and then running again, within the works, men who had lost themselves to their fear. The sounds came as well, screams, some of the wounded calling out, the ones who had used the last bit of their strength to reach the Heights, only to collapse, no strength to climb the sharp rocks. He began to shout to the men who lined the ramparts, pointing to the fallen, "Go! Bring them up!"

A few men had already climbed over, were helping the others, but many more just stared, absorbed by the horror. He wanted to shout again, but the officers took up the call, began to prod their

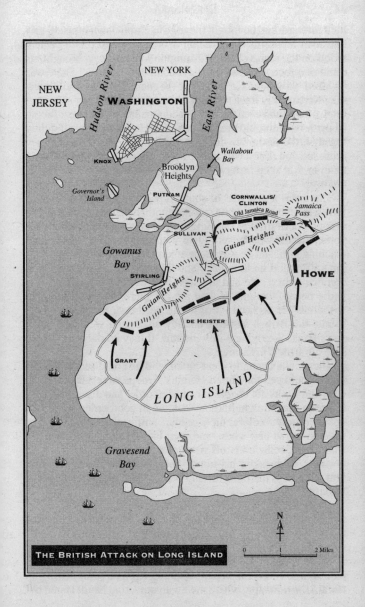

THE BRITISH ATTACK ON LONG ISLAND

men forward, and he fought the urge to climb down himself, saw one man trying to stand, using a broken musket as a crutch, blood on the man's chest. Washington looked away, brought his mind into focus. No, we must maintain our . . . what? There was no word. Courage? He looked at the men along the wall, knew they were mostly fresh recruits. None of them had ever seen anything of war, and even the officers commanding them were facing a horror no one could prepare them for. He pulled himself tightly together, the discipline directed inward. No, stay up here. They must see you. They will look to you. He shouted again, "Bring them in. But keep firm on the wall! Muskets at the ready. This is not over!"

There was a new roar of sound now, from straight in front of him, a fresh burst of white smoke, another chattering volley. The ground out in front of the Heights was an open plain, woods beyond, and the woods were alive with motion. The sounds kept reaching him, and he was more anxious now, the discipline slipping a bit, and he thought, I should ride out . . . see who is in command there. He had not seen Sullivan or Stirling since the battle began, thought, If they are out there, they will know to withdraw. He focused more to the northeast, heard very little sound, the British surprise already advancing well into Sullivan's flank. Surely he will withdraw. It may be the only way to save his army. *This* army.

The smoke began to clear again, and he could see across the plain, could see the Guian Heights. Troops were visible to the east, and it was not chaos, but signs of order and discipline, men in formation, straight lines, advancing in good order. But it was not the uneven colors, the irregular uniforms of his men. The lines were red and white, and then to the south, formations of sharp blue, reflections off rows of bayonets. He stared with a growing coldness in his mind. The lines were moving toward him, all across the field, driving before them scattered pieces of his army.

He looked back into the works, could see Putnam now, working to pull the shaken troops together, the men who had escaped wounds, whose panic had been brought under control. Gradually a line formed, men from various regiments gathering into a line of battle. Putnam was shouting something, officers repeating the calls, but few of the men paid attention to them, some staring up toward the ramparts, where men with quivering hands stared out at the same stunning sight that faced Washington. Some were looking toward him, and he saw it in their faces. This is the moment, the one instant that will decide their fate. If they run, abandon these works . . .

He would not look to the rear, give them any hint of what he was thinking. But he knew what was there. It was no accident the works were built with the rear against the East River. The design had been Stirling's, the man with a talent for engineering, for making the best use of the lay of the land. The river was a barrier to protect them. And he understood now, it was a barrier as well to their escape. Should they try to run, should the rout be complete, these men would have nowhere to go. He tried to wipe the thought from his mind, shouted again, "Hold firm! We are secure here!"

It was feeble, but he didn't know what else to say. The men on the rampart seemed to move with a pulse, each man fighting in his own heart the urge to run away. He knew that all it might take would be that one awful sight, one man with a horrible wound, one man who suddenly leaped from the ramparts, scrambled back toward the river, infecting them all. He looked for Putnam again, saw him still forming men into line, and Putnam looked at him, the older man's face a silent question.

"General Putnam, have these men remain ready! But there will be no advance. No one will move forward!"

Putnam nodded, understood what Washington was doing, that it was not only sound tactics in the face of an overwhelming force of the enemy, but those orders would calm the men. They would not be asked to do it again. Not this day.

He turned to his aide now, saw Tench Tilghman watching him, waiting for orders. The small thin man was holding the spyglass, and Washington motioned. Tilghman climbed a short ladder and handed him the glass. Washington took a breath, focused out on the closest line of troops he could see, a short line of blue coats. But it was not the sharp blue of the Hessians. These troops were facing the other way. There was a sudden burst of smoke, a volley, and out past them, a British line seemed to collapse, scattering into pieces. Washington said aloud, "Who is that? What . . . unit is that?"

He didn't expect an answer, but Tilghman said, "Marylanders, sir! Colonel Smallwood!"

Washington could hear the excitement in Tilghman's voice, still stared through the glass, could see more of his scattered men rallying to the Maryland line, bits of uniforms distinct now. His hands gripped the glass, yes! He is correct! The Maryland regiment. And . . . Delaware. Hazlet's men.

The British came together again, another advance against the Maryland line, and to one side of them, Washington could see men emerging from a thicket of trees, most of them running, more of the retreat, moving past their own solid line, the men who held their ground. He thought of the horse, I must go there. They are making a stand. It could rally the men! The field was bathed in smoke again, a fresh wave of volleys from the left, pushing more of Sullivan's men across the open ground, making their escape to the safety of the works. He watched the Maryland line still, could tell they were retreating in order, giving ground slowly, allowing the scattered troops to escape past them. But in front of them, he could see a growing force of British, and on one side, emerging from the same woods, a sharp reflection from more bayonets, a wave of blue, different, more Hessians. Men were climbing into the works all around him, and one man was suddenly at his feet, down below, shouted up to him, "Sir!"

The man could barely speak, his words bursting out in short breaths. Washington looked at him, and the man saluted shakily, said, "Sir! Colonel Smallwood requests reinforcements, sir! He asks . . . in the most urgent terms!"

Washington stared at the man, saw clear hard eyes, the man waiting for his answer. Washington looked again through the glass, and the man's impatience gave way.

"Sir! Colonel Smallwood . . ." Washington held up one hand, stopped the man, could see the Maryland line moving back toward him, a faster retreat now, but still good order. He felt relief, thought, No, Smallwood is saving his men. There can be no rallying now. This fight is done.

Smallwood was pulling his troops toward the safety of the Heights, a swarm of color pursuing them from three sides, a wave of gray smoke rolling over them, some of the Marylanders going down. Washington looked at Smallwood's man now, said, "It will not be necessary for you to return to Colonel Smallwood. There can be no reinforcements. The colonel understands that. He is in retreat."

The man tried to say something, a protest forming on his face. Washington forced himself to ignore him, stared again through the spyglass, the smoke blurring the view, the fight closing in all across the open ground. The sounds rolled in his direction, vast patches of smoke swirling around him. His men still came, the wounded still struggling, men helping each other, screams and shouts and panic. He stepped away from the rampart, looked for Putnam, thought, We must make ready. This is a good place for a fight. He shouted again, "Man the ramparts! Keep to your arms!"

Men still scrambled past him, some stumbling, and he could see the high rocky ground within the fortifications filled with what was left of Sullivan's command, every open space, some men sprawled out, some sitting, more of the wide-eyed shock. And, now for the first time, he saw that many of them were empty-handed, had left their muskets behind. Much of what remained of this army was nearly unarmed.

THE FIRING HAD STOPPED, AND ALL OUT IN FRONT OF BROOKLYN Heights, the British had brought their army into neat formation, stood in line now, officers straightening the formations, as though organizing a parade. They stood just beyond musket range, and whether through discipline or pure terror, Washington's men did not respond to this astounding target, no wild potshots at the great mass of power spread across the plain in front of them. He could hear music, a discordant rattling of drumbeats, a mix of rhythms, small groups of musicians and drummers, rallying their well-trained regiments. Behind the formation men on horseback were gathering, and Washington stared through the glass, tried to see them clearly, studied the grand uniforms. He could see one larger group, senior commanders, men with girth, heavy in the saddle, aides flittering about them. He didn't know the faces, thought, Howe, perhaps. Certainly he would be here, to see for himself what his army has accomplished. Their great . . . triumph. He was engulfed by the same shock that still spread through his army, that they had faced the might of King George, and had been swept from the field. And worse, it was not merely the confrontation, the power, but the tactics as well, the flanking move that had caught them all by surprise. His mind was too numb to think of blame, whether Sullivan or Putnam should have known better, whether someone should have protected against all the possible routes the enemy could have used. The

blame would be Washington's, after all, and there were far
greater concerns than which officer might not have performed.
He knew enough of the fight to know that many of Stirling's men
had made a valiant stand, Smallwood certainly, the Delaware
line, Atlee of Pennsylvania, Clark of Connecticut. But in the end,
the numbers against them were too strong, and so many of the
heroes would remain nameless, cut down by the bayonets or lost
in the swamps, a great many of them captured, including Stirling
himself.

He thought of Greene, but his mind was drifting, and he
thought, Would it have mattered? If Greene had been here,
would this army have stood up better, the deployment more
suited to the attack they faced? There was no reason to think so.
After all, it was not just the failure of the commanders that
caused the collapse. The men themselves could not face an
enemy this strong and stand firm.

The great mass of color in front of him began to blur, and he
backed away from the wall, fought to get control. Behind him
there was a swarm of sounds, faint screams and cries, the
wounded being tended to as best as they could be. Many were
quiet, those whose wounds were inside their own minds, staring
quietly at nothing, knowing that on this day they had shown very
little of what makes a soldier. But there were signs of an army as
well, officers still working their men into line, sorting through
the mingling crowd, separating companies and regiments. All
along the wall, the men who still had their muskets were climbing up, adding to the numbers, standing shoulder to shoulder,
many with the strength still to face what lay across the open
ground. In the rocks, Washington could see men climbing into
safe places, aiming, practicing the good shot, others slipping between, lining the gorges and small hills. He scanned along the
edge of the fortifications, thought, Of course, this is how it will
be after all. This is where the strength is in this army. We don't
have the numbers to face the enemy on open ground. But here, in
these rocks, on this hill, we are very strong indeed. He looked
out toward the British lines, saw no motion, the vast army just
standing, facing Brooklyn Heights like some strange enraptured
audience. He felt suddenly impatient, there was no reason to
wait any longer. He raised the glass again, focused on the largest
group of officers, thought of Howe. All right, you have waited

long enough. Perhaps too long. You have allowed us to make ready, the panic has passed, the chaos is now settling into a hard strong defense. Is that what you wanted? Is it more seemly for a British general to make war on a *prepared* enemy? Well, sir, we are prepared now. There were voices now, bits of sounds all along the British lines, orders calling out, a new burst of drumbeats. The rows of color began to ripple, like a great long ribbon flickering in the soft breeze. His heart pounded, and along the rampart his men began to shout, making ready, muskets coming to rest on the wall, facing the enemy. He could hear his officers, sharp orders, no firing, *wait,* and he nodded, thought, Yes, they would know. Some of these men were at Breed's Hill. They would know what will happen if they are patient. Let them come close, a truly wonderful target, fire as one great force. With this ground, Howe cannot make a rapid charge, there can be no great bayonet assault, and so, we will have time to reload, fire again. There was motion still, the drums moving the colored line in a rhythm, but there was something odd, the lines were narrowing, the formations growing deeper. He raised the glass again, stared at the first row of troops, expected to see the bayonets, saw instead the bright uniforms . . . from *behind*. Beside him, one man let out a cheer, and there was a silent pause, and then more men began to pick it up, the sounds echoing all down the ramparts, the men reacting to the sight, seeming to understand the mystery. Washington was still puzzled, still expected to see the great mass changing into line again, moving to a flank assault perhaps, slipping off to one side. But the columns grew longer, deeper, and he could see it plainly now. The mystery was solved. The movements were precise, the formations exact. But the British were not advancing. They were marching away.

AUGUST 29, 1776

He had brought more of his men across the East River, strengthening the forces in Brooklyn Heights, preparing the army for the assault that must still come. Through a long night he had watched the darkness, anticipating some move, a surprise attack. It was not the British style, of course, and he understood tradition, but the Hessians were still out there, and he knew that they might not have the same respect for a gentlemen's assault, especially the green-clad *jagers*, who were as comfortable in the dark as any of Washington's sharp-shooting woodsmen.

For two nights they had heard the sounds of the British camp, a vast sea of flickering fires, extending back into the woods. He had sent small scouting parties out, probing carefully toward the British flanks. There had been nothing significant to report, the vast bulk of the enemy staying put in their camps, only scattered eruptions of musket fire, British pickets shooting blindly at the indiscreet noises. But when each dawn had come, he could see that the British had been busy indeed, had made good use of the shovel, long snaking lines of entrenchments all along in front of his fortifications. If Howe had not been in a hurry to move against his fortifications, it did not mean the British were content to just sit and watch Brooklyn Heights. As the entrenchments grew longer and more complex, he had seen horses adding to the activity, drawing cannon, their crews setting the big guns behind great mounds of dirt, safe from his own artillery. It was clear now that Howe was not merely planning an assault. He was planning a siege.

By midmorning, a grim darkness had rolled over them from the west, and the rains came. It was not the quick violence of the thunderstorm, but a slow steady drizzle that grew harder as the day passed. By afternoon, the rains had soaked the ground and the men, and settled around them like a thick dark shroud.

AS THE DREARINESS OF THE AFTERNOON HAD PASSED, HE HAD RID-den among the troops, the horse slipping its way through the wet ravines and earthworks, the staff grumbling behind him. There were no cheers for the commanding general, the men huddled glumly in groups, some perched under ledges of rock, makeshift tents of blankets draped over muskets. The British had stayed put, again, and Washington knew instinctively that as the miserable day wore on, there would be no assault, Howe's men in no better position to fight the weather than they were Washington's fortified Heights. As he turned the horse back toward his headquarters, he sent aides out in search of the senior officers. He had not yet had a general council of the commanders, but he needed one now. It was not because of the men, or any move by the British. All along the fortified lines, he had told the men to check the pans on their muskets, and to those who had them, to check the condition of their cartridge boxes. Some of the men knew before he even told them. Their powder was soaking wet. And worse, no one had taken charge of the supplies. Boxes and cloth sacks of gunpowder were simply sitting in the rain. Throughout most of the Heights, there was almost no usable ammunition.

They gathered in a makeshift headquarters, an open-sided tent staked up behind a steep bank of rock. It was now one of the few dry places anyone could find. Most of the officers were as soaked as he was, and the moods were mixed. He still hoped to see more of the familiar faces, knew that all through the past two nights, men had continued to straggle in, finding their way in the darkness past the British. But as he looked at the faces, his last hopes were brought down. He looked at Putnam now, said, "We have heard nothing further? No word?"

Putnam shook his head, said nothing. Washington took a breath, said, "We do not have definite reports, and thus there is no way to make certain of the facts. But by all accounts, General Sullivan has not been seen. Those who saw him in the field are confident that he survived the action. It is a forlorn hope that he is alive and well, and, as the best alternative, is in the hands of the British as a prisoner."

He looked at the others, knew that Putnam was the only available senior commander, most of the others men of lesser rank, and certainly, lesser experience. One man seemed to surge forward, said, "Sir, if you will allow . . ."

"Everyone may speak, General Heath. This is a council of war. What have you to say?"

William Heath was a Massachusetts man, had served under Putnam in Boston, and if Heath had not distinguished himself for any particular action, the two men were at least accustomed to working together. He seemed full of protest, unsure how to begin, finally said, "Sir, I am at a loss to explain the actions of some of our most . . . *able* commanders."

There was sarcasm in the word, and Washington did not want to hear this, but Heath continued. "I have been made aware, sir, that certain regiments behaved with scandalous disregard for the safety of this army. I am told that the Marylanders carelessly burned a bridge that could have afforded a path of safe withdrawal . . ."

"General Heath, I did not call this council to pass censure on anyone. There is time enough for that later. I would point out to you that I myself observed Colonel Smallwood's regiment in heroic action, and I have since learned that those men performed with as much heroism on this ground as any unit in this army." There was a hand raised now, and Washington was surprised to see William Smallwood himself, the man's face emerging from a dripping dark coat.

"My apologies, Colonel. I intended no embarrassment. I did not realize you were here."

"General, I thank you for your approval. I cannot respond to General Heath's claim, but I can assure the commanding general that when I arrived on the field, Major Gist and the men of my command had already acquitted themselves under extreme hardship."

Washington could hear something in the man's voice, a sober calmness, the man about Washington's age, another veteran of the French and Indian War. Smallwood had been in New York on court-martial duty when the British attack began, his unit commanded first by Mordecai Gist. But Smallwood had come across the river quickly, would not allow his men to make the good fight without their commander. Washington had sought out the details as much as he could, knew that the Marylanders had been among those men who had held away an attack that could have destroyed Stirling's entire force. He knew nothing of the event Heath had referred to, some bridge being burned, knew the reports would be detailed later. He dreaded the aftermath of any battle, had been through this before, small men striking out with rumor and their pens at those who had done the work with musket and sword. It was the nature of war, and the nature of men who brought more ambition into battle than ability. And right now, Washington didn't want to hear any of it.

It was unusual that a colonel be at a council of war, but Smallwood had been called to this council because he was a veteran, and his immediate superior, Stirling, was absent. And it was apparent to the entire army that Smallwood's command was not only reliable, but might be some of the best troops Washington had.

"Gentlemen, I would prefer that each of us focus on the future, and not what has already occurred. Our losses have been heavy. And, I fear this weather has put us in a grave situation."

Putnam sniffed, said, "With all respects, General, my view is that the British have the disadvantage. We control the fortified ground, while they must come at us from the open. We control the hill, they must climb. If our powder is wet, so is theirs." Putnam stopped, and Washington watched the old man's face, saw the man's pride tempered a bit by a new thought, something unspoken.

"General Putnam, your comparisons to the glorious fight you commanded on Breed's Hill are noted. I have no doubt that you are correct in one regard. The British are taking their time, and will likely wait for a break in the weather. If they dry their powder, we will dry ours, and I am certain that in a duel of musket fire, their loss would be desperate. But as you know, General Putnam, the enemy has something we do not. They are proficient in the use of the bayonet. That is a superiority we cannot underestimate. As you know, this army does not possess . . . the bayonet."

He saw several faces go down, and Putnam nodded silently. It had become a fact that no one could overlook. Throughout the great fight they had just endured, the most effective tool of both the British and the Hessians was the bayonet. To the farmers and militia of Washington's army, many of whom fought with their own weapons, it was a piece of equipment that was completely foreign. As each of the commanders had learned, asking a man to fire his musket and then reload while enduring a bayonet charge made only for a brief battle. The men simply turned and ran away. Washington would not say it now, didn't have to. He could see that each man had already run the image through his mind, as Putnam had done. If the British come up that hill, we will cut them down, perhaps more than once. But this is not Breed's Hill. The enemy has brought nearly fifteen thousand men to our front. When they attack, they will continue to come, and no force will stay on that wall for long. Putnam said, "Is it assumed that General Howe intends to attack us?"

Washington glanced at the others, said, "He has his enemy right in front of him. I do not believe his king would find favor with General Howe sailing his army back to Staten Island."

Putnam seemed amused, a slight smile.

"I believe that General Howe is perhaps a friend to us. Or, he is no general after all."

There were small laughs, but Washington did not take up the lightness in their mood.

"I called this council because I consider it important to hear your views on possible strategy. There is no debate that we are in a dangerous situation here. We are faced with an enemy more than double our strength, and we have already demonstrated that we are not capable of pushing him away. General Howe must certainly grasp his advantage. Does anyone else have suggestion of strategy to offer?"

He searched the faces now, and no one spoke, the smiles gone. He said to Putnam, "Colonel Glover is not here?"

Putnam shook his head.

"He would be on the river, sir. Managing the boats. We're keeping a sharp eye down the river, in case the enemy attempts a run upstream."

Washington looked for Tilghman, saw him standing back just under the edge of the dripping canvas.

"Major, send for Colonel Glover. I would like him here."

They waited patiently, long minutes of quiet talk, and Washington saw Glover now, bringing his temper with him as he splashed through the mud. Washington could not help a smile, the short round man wiping a shower of water from his red hair. He was another man of Washington's age, and his temper had already become legendary, not for empty noise and bluster, but precision, the man's wrath aimed toward improving the efficiency of his men. John Glover, another Massachusetts man, commanded a regiment recruited from the tough fishermen around Marblehead, up the coast from Boston. It was Glover who had brought Washington across the river, the man making special mention of the direction of the wind, something Washington had not thought to value. Washington looked up now, the sharp breeze buffeting the canvas, and the others followed his look, most not realizing what he was seeing. It was still gusty from the north and west, and Washington understood the significance if the others did not.

When the works on Brooklyn Heights were designed, Putnam and Stirling had suggested that the mouth of the river be blocked by the sinking of old hulks and unusable ships, and the navigable channel below Brooklyn Heights was now crossed by a man-made brush line of masts and rigging, the topmost skeletons of the wrecked vessels. The senior commanders had thought the army secure in its Brooklyn position, that the barricade would prevent the British gunboats from sailing upriver and cutting half of Washington's army off from New York.

The water still dripped from Glover's face, and he looked at Washington now, said, "You sent for me, sir? Fine day for a war."

Washington motioned upward. "The wind is still holding. You expect that to change?"

Glover glanced at the others, who kept silent, knowing that Washington had a purpose in bringing this man to the council.

"Pardon me, sir. Would you be asking me to predict the weather now?" Glover's frankness had a way of disarming Washington, and he fought through the smile, brought himself to the seriousness of the matter.

"In a fashion, yes, Colonel. Do you anticipate the enemy ships will be held at bay for a while longer?"

Glover took the question seriously as well, said, "This storm is passing, lightening up already." He motioned to the west, across the river. "Sunset soon. You should see it through the clouds. By midnight, it'll be clear. Very clear. Full moon tonight." He paused, glanced at Putnam. "Can't say much for the wind one way or t'other."

Putnam had boasted loudly that no British ship of any consequence could sail through the barricade without ripping out its own hull. Washington knew he would have something to say, and Putnam obliged him.

"General Washington, if you mean to be concerned about the British navy, you know my feelings on that. We have made the necessary precautions to keep them out of the river. There is no danger here."

Glover tilted his head at Putnam, seemed to squint, and Washington knew Glover would make his point, would explain what Washington already believed to be true.

"You may speak freely here, Colonel Glover."

"Well, sir, I understand that your generals and such have a poor opinion of the British sailor. With all respects, sir, can't say I agree." He paused, looked hard at Washington, said, "All those sunken wrecks are a fine thing. But I've spent my life slippin' and cuttin' my way through rocks and whatnot, and if I know something about those lobster-backs out there, they been doin' a fair amount of the same. A good helmsman can get his boat past just about anything, especially in protected water like this here river. And, beggin' your pardon, sir, but if I was Mister Admiral *Lord* Howe, and I saw those little masts pokin' up at me out there, I'd simply take a flock of my smallest ketches, put one good heavy gun on each stern, raising the bow up high, and when the slack tide come, I'd pick my way right past that barricade. Then I'd commence to bustin' up the place. *This* place."

Putnam laughed now, said, "Colonel, I admire your, um, charming descriptions. But if Lord Howe agreed with your observations, then why hasn't he done exactly that? With all respect to your . . . seafaring skills, I have yet to see one ship sail within range of this position."

Washington pointed his finger to the rustle of the canvas above them.

"It's the wind, General. Colonel Glover, am I correct that since this action began, the wind has come from the north?"

Glover was all seriousness now, said, "General Washington, in my opinion, sir, we are able to stand safely here and have this little soirée for one reason only. The mouth of this river opens to the south. We have been blessed with a gale from the north that has prevented the British from entering the river. Forgive me, General Putnam, but I believe it is that wind, and that wind only, that has kept the British navy from sending a fleet right up our backsides. Sir."

The rain was slackening, and Washington could see a glimpse of the sunset, breaking through the clouds in the west.

"Gentlemen, if any of those warships make their way upriver . . ." He paused, saw the faces all watching him. There were no arguments, and his mind had formed the plan, the only opportunity his army might have to fight another day.

"Colonel Glover, can your boats be made ready in short order?"

"Certainly, sir."

"Then make ready. We are withdrawing from this position."

HE LEFT A SMALL FORCE ALONG THE RAMPARTS, GUARDING AGAINST a sudden move by the British. All through the night, Glover's Marblehead Regiment ferried the troops away and across the river, to the safety of Manhattan. Most of his army never knew his orders, had been told that they were being replaced by fresh troops, the only way Washington knew of preventing a panic, a mad noisy scramble to the boats. As the men marched to the water's edge, they were warned against sound, no mistake that might give the British some hint of what was happening. It was not perfect, and Washington could not keep the operation immune to human error. One section of the works was left completely unguarded for over an hour while the men marched away in the wrong order. But the error was corrected, and through the long night, few sounds came from the British camps. By midnight, the clouds had cleared away, and the wind was nearly calm, no longer a barrier to Lord Howe's navy. But the British ships would not move at night, would still have to negotiate the obstructions in the river, and so Glover's troop-laden boats crossed and recrossed the river unmolested.

Washington stayed on his horse, kept close to the shoreline, silently watching his men file out of the works. Most of the men never saw him, and if they did, it was only in silhouette, the big man on the great horse caught in the sudden flood of moonlight. To the army, the reflection on the river was a blessing, an aide to Glover's sailors, making easy navigation of the crossing to Manhattan, but to Washington, the full moon meant visibility to the British lookouts, and the constant danger that their move would be discovered.

Just before dawn, his fears were realized, a British patrol slipping forward, reaching the edge of the river without causing the usual alarm, their sergeant staring in wide-eyed amazement at the surge of activity in the river. The alarm went out, and Howe scrambled to bring his men to the scene, but then, as if on command, a thick bank of fog drifted over the river, covering the withdrawal. The British still came forward, made their way into the works of Brooklyn Heights without firing a shot, and some advanced all the way to the river's edge, caught a last glimpse of the big man stepping off, the rebel commander the last man to board the last boat. Washington's army had escaped.

4. CORNWALLIS

HE WAS WEARY OF THE REPORTS, MANIC BURSTS OF WORDS FROM the men who had first reached the river. He had finally ridden up himself, moving first through the farms, surprised by the destruction of the houses, shattered glass, broken doors, contents spread across the muddy roads. He understood now, the rumors floating through headquarters were accurate, reports of savage brutality by the Hessians. He didn't want to hear of it, but what he saw around him made it obvious. If there was no enemy in range, de Heister's men turned the frightening efficiency of their fight on whoever might lie in their path, soldier or civilian, rebel or Tory.

He reached the edge of a stand of trees, Brooklyn Heights now in front of him. He rode out across the open ground where the bodies still lay, the putrid smell rising with the dampness of the soggy ground, drifting past him as he guided the horse. Some of the corpses were British, and he could not avoid the horror of that, the good men who had fallen too close to the American position to be buried. He glanced back at his aide, the young Captain Hurst, but no words were necessary, the man already knowing the order.

"I'll see to it, sir. We'll have burial parties out here immediately."

Cornwallis made a quick nod, appreciated the young man's concern, something few of the senior officers ever cared to show.

He took the horse up through a narrow trail in the rocks, rode up straight into the place where Washington's ragged army had made its stand. The ground was a chewed-up pit of mud and debris, ripped clothes, and scraps of bandages. The horse stepped over a broken musket protruding from a deep puddle of brown water, and he could not escape the symbolism of that, the shattered arms of a shattered army, an army that should not have es-

caped. He clenched his fists around the smooth leather of the
reins, spurred the horse farther, closer to the high ground that
overlooked the river.

He could see it now, the shoreline of Manhattan, broken only
by the silhouettes of the great ships, Lord Howe's men-o-war
moving into position, some sailing upriver toward Hell Gate. Of
course, *now* we are in place. The thought stuck in his mind like a
sour piece of fruit. *Now* we can start our wonderful blockade, a
perfect trap around Brooklyn Heights for an enemy who is no
longer here.

No one was exactly certain what would happen next, and
General Howe had not revealed any details of a new strategy.
Cornwallis moved the horse along the shoreline, thought, There
could very well be no strategy at all. After all, we have gone to so
very much trouble to make a truly fine camp here. The army is
rested, the casualty figures somewhat complete, and clearly in
our favor. By anyone's measure, this was an absolute triumph.
The rebels lost a quarter of their strength, possibly more. We
have so many prisoners we don't know where to house them.
And the dead . . . we don't know yet. So many of them are still out
there. We may never know how many we killed. Those swamps,
the creeks and thickets will hide bodies for years.

He saw a group of officers farther upriver, moved the horse
that way, the aides behind him in single file. He could see Clinton now, surrounded by his staff, Clinton's expression a reflection of his own sullen mood. Cornwallis saluted, and both staffs
moved away, protocol, the two senior commanders left alone.
There was a long moment, and finally Clinton said, "We made a
grand show, General. To those farmers and shopkeepers it must
have been an awe-inspiring sight, a perfect display of the king's
might. It is unfortunate that our commanding general didn't
know what to do with it."

It was another of Clinton's indiscretions, something he would
never say publicly. Clinton looked at him now, and Cornwallis
could see no concern on the man's face, thought, I suppose . . .
he trusts me.

"I had thought there might have been a better plan." It was as
far as Cornwallis would go with a superior. Clinton ignored his
caution, stared out toward the river, said, "There was no better
plan. There was a legacy to be adhered to, to be feared: the
legacy of Breed's Hill. I wish you had been there, General. Bos-

ton: another grand show, all the pageantry and bluster, marching up that hill to victory. Never mind that it was a disaster. The field was ours. Never mind that we left nearly half our troops on the ground. We were victorious. But it was a mistake that General Howe will not make again." He looked at Cornwallis now, black despair in his eyes. "I advised against that assault, you know. There was the perfect opportunity to go around, cut the rebel retreat from behind. It was almost too simple a plan. But of course, there would not have been such . . . *pageantry*."

Cornwallis knew little of the strategy of that awful day over a year ago, had read only what the ministry had put in the official dispatches. But of course, Clinton was always a strategist, had all the experience in Europe. He would always have his own plan, would dissent freely from his commander, even unwisely. It was easy now to say he might have been right about Breed's Hill. But this was a different fight. The rebels who poured into the fortifications here were *already* defeated, infected with panic. What kind of stand could they have made? For Howe to be ignorant of that was to be ignorant of the power of his own army. But worse, to know the enemy's weakness and not act upon it . . . well, there will be as much hindsight here as there was at Breed's Hill. He stayed silent, and Clinton pointed out across the river, said, "They cannot hold New York. The island is simply too big, and there are not enough of them. It is ours for the taking. Just like this place, right behind us."

Cornwallis had considered that, said, "What they have left of an army could well be dispersed already. They may have no more fight left. This war may be over. But if we must continue to fight, the army is rested, prepared. Has General Howe given you some indication of when we might proceed?" He kept the sarcasm out of his voice, and Clinton surprised him now, laughed.

"Proceed? You mean, make another grand assault against a weak and pitiful enemy? No, General, I have received no orders to prepare for a landing on Manhattan. Will there be one? Most certainly. Whether or not the army is rested and prepared is hardly the issue. When the enemy was in chaos, falling back into these fortifications in a complete rout, we were *prepared* then. If we had followed them with the same dispatch with which we had begun the attack, this war would certainly be over now. General Washington would be sharing tea with General Howe, his surrendered sword a souvenir, the object of pride to this command."

Cornwallis glanced at the staff officers, knew Clinton's voice was carrying. Clinton caught the look, lowered his voice, said, "General, I do not wish to make you uncomfortable. But I have confidence in your abilities, and I believe you agree with my assessment. It is not necessary for you to state that. Surely you feel as I do, that we have lost an astounding opportunity to crush this rebellion, or at the very least, to crush its army."

Cornwallis sorted his words, was still not entirely comfortable. "I believe, sir, that without an army, there is no rebellion."

Clinton let the meaningless words drift by, said, "Did you hear the reports of mass drownings? Some say that during their escape, the rebels lost dozens of boats capsized, men overboard, wholesale loss of life. Right out there, hundreds perhaps. Rather sad, don't you think?"

Cornwallis wasn't sure what Clinton meant, and Clinton went on, "Of course, I assume that hundreds of drowned rebels would have made something of a mess of the shore, or at the very least, would have been a grisly observation for Lord Howe's lookouts. That's the sadness, General. It was all fabrication. This army is forced to *create* tales of enemy disaster, because we are impotent to effect that disaster ourselves. It was right in our grasp. Now, we must begin again, march to the boats and cross another waterway, and see what kind of enemy awaits us over there."

Cornwallis was absorbed by Clinton's deep gloom, a mood darker than even his own. He looked back toward the Heights behind them, crowded with red uniforms, men sorting through the debris the rebels had left behind. He saw one man with a bayonet, poking at a pile of muddy rags, more men doing the same, all along the waterfront, their white leggings soiled by the filth of the trash. He thought of Howe, the official report that would go to London. It was a victory, we have the ground, the enemy fled before us in panic, leaving behind . . . their garbage. If there is still a war, if the rebel army escaped to fight us yet again, at least General Howe can be proud. By God, it was a grand show.

SEPTEMBER 8, 1776

They had gathered on Admiral Howe's flagship, the *Eagle*, a grand man-o-war that carried all the luxury appropriate to his command. The dinner had been enormous, an assortment of all the delicacies to be had around New York, many of the Tories still pouring out their good tidings and their generosity to the British command. The plates were gone now, the claret flowing freely, and Cornwallis had begun to feel a lift in his dark mood for the first time.

The rebels had abandoned Governor's Island, and some had thought it was another unfortunate escape, that the navy should have made more of an effort to capture the position. But the effect was positive, no more of the annoying potshots at the ships if they drifted too close, and if Lord Howe had been too hesitant to seize the small island, no one spoke of it. The only rebel artillery positions were in Manhattan, most on the southern tip, and the navy had been free to spread out through much of New York Harbor. The calmer waters of the protected bays were full of activity as well, the navy bringing the fleet of flatboats into formation, preparation for the army to make its move to Manhattan. Despite Clinton's not-so-subtle fury, General Howe continued to operate on a schedule of his own, perfectly satisfied to proceed on some deliberate timetable only he understood. But the sight of the flatboats brought back the excitement, and Cornwallis could not help but feel that no matter if General Howe's movement was slower than he would have liked, at least, now, there was movement.

The admiral sat at the end of the table, framed by an extraordinary chair, tall spires bathed in gold. The talk had begun to quiet, and with a subtle tilt of his head, the order was given, the servants quickly gone from the dining room.

Lord Howe looked at his brother, who sat on his right, a formal, familiar ceremony between them, a mutual permission for the discussion to begin. The admiral said, "Some of you have shown the courtesy to converse with our prisoner, Mr. John Sullivan. I am pleased to report that the rebel general is actually something of a gentleman, with some understanding of his rebellion's unfortunate predicament. Once it was explained to him that we desired only to end this war, he was enthusiastic about communicating that to his congress. Thus, he has been paroled, carrying with him to Philadelphia a document expressing our inclination to negotiate for the end of this war."

There were nods, low murmurs of approval, and Cornwallis

kept his eye on the admiral, could see a glow of self-satisfaction. Lord Howe continued, "As you know, the ministry has given to General Howe and myself the power to grant amnesty to anyone who wishes to receive it, assuming of course that those persons agree to end hostility to the king. To be frank, no one in this command believed that their congress would take heed of this suggestion. However, we feel that the events of the past two weeks have had an impact. Not only have we utterly defeated Mr. Washington's little army, but his evacuation of Long Island has indicated in the strongest light that he has no intention of putting himself at risk again." He raised his wineglass. "I offer a salute to my brother, General Howe, for his extraordinary success in persuading the rebels to take to their boats."

Pleasantries passed around the table, and Cornwallis tried to feel the spirit, thought, Of course, it has to be the rationale. We are, in fact, *happy* that Washington's army escaped. Lord Howe waited for the toast to conclude, made the appropriate nod to his brother, said, "It is highly likely that the rebel congress will see their situation differently now. Prospects for peace have never been greater. Mr. Sullivan has conveyed this message to his congress, along with means of discussing terms of a general peace. I have agreed to meet with anyone whom their congress wishes to send. They have wisely consented to this, and I am most pleased to inform you that a meeting on this subject will take place in a few days."

Cornwallis knew of the ministry's authorization, granting Lord Howe the power to deal directly with congress as a peace commissioner. What that actually meant, no one was sure, except Lord Howe himself. Cornwallis had no idea how the Continental Congress would respond to such an offer. But as the men around the table made their toasts of congratulation, Cornwallis tried to see past the words. Had Washington been bypassed, considered by Lord Howe to be irrelevant? Cornwallis knew now he had been wrong about Washington's army simply dissolving away. They were digging in, creating fortifications along the East River, all the way up to the mouth of the Harlem River. And the artillery was still in place on the southern tip of the island, guarding the access to the Hudson River. Whatever army Washington has left, he is certainly prepared to make another fight. Their retreat from Brooklyn Heights might have been a defeat, but it was not enough to end a war. Obviously Washington knows that, and just as surely, their congress will agree.

He raised his glass automatically, did not hear the words, General Howe returning the favor to his brother, offering meaningless praise for the admiral's diplomatic triumph. Cornwallis avoided the faces, thought, They might actually believe that this peace commission will find a way to end this war.

As he had sailed westward from England, he had nurtured a fantasy that his duty on this side of the Atlantic would be brief, that he might return home after one decisive battle, enjoying complete optimism that no band of rebels could stand up against the might of the king's forces. The embarrassment at Charleston had sent the dream far back in his mind, and now, he felt the gloom returning, the dream erased altogether. He thought of the flatboats, waiting in the harbor. So now they will sit idly by, will not be loaded until Lord Howe has his diplomatic meeting. And in New York, the rebels will continue to build their works and fortify their position, while once again, we delay.

5. FRANKLIN

SEPTEMBER 11, 1776

THEY HAD SPENT THE NIGHT IN BRUNSWICK, RISING EARLY TO COMplete the final part of the journey from Philadelphia. The confirmation had come from Howe's staff that a boat would be waiting for them when they reached Amboy.

Franklin had stayed in the carriage the entire way, could never have stood the journey on horseback, and even the relative softness of the chaise had jarred him into a general discomfort for most of the trip. For the entire journey he had ridden beside Edward Rutledge, the aristocratic young man from South Carolina. Rutledge was a small, thin man, with a high, tinny voice who had built his reputation in the congress as a leader of those men who would prefer to err on the side of caution. Rutledge had been an advocate of delaying the signing of a Declaration of Independence, but was pragmatic enough to understand that once the sentiment toward independence became unstoppable, the conservatives could delay no longer. Rutledge had finally changed his stance, had led South Carolina to sign the document after all. Though the man's self-interest for South Carolina placed him naturally at odds with many of the New Englanders, he had built a particular dislike for John Adams. The feeling was mutual. Now, Adams was the third member of their committee, and throughout the journey, Adams rode a horse beside the carriage. Franklin had wondered if there would be some kind of open conflict between the two men, Adams particularly prone to falling into a heated debate about those subjects on which he disagreed. But Adams was pragmatic as well, kept his distance from Rutledge throughout the trip. If they were to meet with Lord Howe, they must present a united front.

Franklin had watched Adams on the horse, the New Englander clearly as uncomfortable as Franklin was. Adams was a fair horseman, but his girth made riding awkward, the uneven stretches of roadway causing Adams the same agony that Franklin endured. Rutledge had occasionally offered polite conversation, and Franklin obliged him. Though he didn't care for Rutledge's politics, he didn't quite share Adams' strong dislike of the man, so they passed much of the time in idle pleasantries.

Franklin could hear the unmistakable sound of seagulls, thought, The water, we're getting closer. He looked out to see them, felt a sharp breath of salt air, chilling him. The morning had been surprisingly cool, and he pulled his coat a bit tighter, thought, At least there is no rain. If the weather turned for the worse, the meeting would have to be delayed. Though the crossing to Staten Island was a short one, Lord Howe had warned them that his small flatboat would not do well in inclement weather.

He sat back in the seat again, felt himself rolling over another steep drop in the road, the creaking of the carriage now etched in his mind. Rutledge made some sound of discomfort beside him, and Franklin glanced at the man, thought, You are young enough to be my grandson. I will hear no sound of ailments out of *you*. He caught himself, knew his own mood was suffering, looked back toward Adams, who rode close behind the carriage. Adams nodded toward him, pointed, said simply, "The shore."

Franklin looked that way, could see a wide salt marsh, saw grass moving in a slow wave with the chilly breeze. They were close to the small town of Amboy, houses appearing up along the road, the masts of small fishing boats in a cluster. Rutledge had seen them as well, said, "Well, finally. I won't mind leaving this uncomfortable box, I assure you."

Franklin didn't respond, thought, It couldn't have been any more uncomfortable than Adams' horse. He had wanted to suggest that Rutledge ride, giving Adams some respite, but the subject had not come up, and Franklin had realized that Rutledge was watching Adams as well, a silent glare of satisfaction on the man's birdlike face. Well, of course. Like children, vying to sit beside the father. Franklin scolded himself, Well, no it might not have anything to do with the pleasure of *my* company. There was one more place in the carriage, and Rutledge claimed it. Though John Adams may best him in every debate, though he may be the great orator and the man of influence, out here, Edward Rutledge gets the more comfortable seat. Franklin let out a breath, and the thought stayed with him. *Children.* Despite all the importance, the gravity of the issues we face, so many of those men in congress behave the same way. It could be the ruin of us all.

The carriage reached a small wharf, and Adams was already off the horse, working the pains out of his back. Rutledge was quickly down, reached back to assist Franklin, and the old man did not object. His foot reached the hard ground, the usual pain in his legs spreading up, and Franklin steadied himself against the carriage, waved Rutledge away, said, "Thank you, young man. I am sufficiently balanced."

Along the wharf, a group of militia had gathered, and Franklin waved to them, managed a smile, could tell by the points and stares he had been recognized, something he was accustomed to. The men drew up in an uneven line, and those with muskets tried to make a good show, some kind of military posture. Franklin tried to keep the smile in place, but the stiffness in his knees was slow to let go. He moved with uneven steps toward the ragged formation, and one man stepped toward them, a huge swarthy man with a thick beard. Franklin stopped, could feel Rutledge and Adams beside him, the man communicating pure menace, blocking their path to the wharf. The man saluted them, a great fat hand planted on the grime of his forehead.

"We are honored, gentlemen. Welcome to Amboy. I am Captain Dirth Foresdale, New Jersey Militia, in command of your guard. You are safe here."

The voice was deep and growling, and left no room for argument. Franklin smiled again, felt relief, thought, Well it's preferable you are with us rather than against us. Adams stepped forward, said, "Thank you, Captain. Have you received any word of our escort?"

Foresdale sniffed, his hands on his hips, emphasizing the profound expanse of his waist.

"Well, yes, sir, their boat is just below. They been here for a while now." He leaned closer, and Franklin caught the sudden smell of rum and fish. Foresdale lowered his voice, said, "Them lobster-backs stayed right there, kept to their boat. Smart. We'd have put up with none of their nonsense here, sir. My men are primed for a fight."

Adams seemed to vibrate beside him, and Franklin knew that Adams was holding tight to his words, that any incident with the British here would jeopardize the entire purpose of this conference. Franklin put a hand on Adams' arm, a silent message, Be calm, it's all right. Franklin kept his voice low, said, "Good work, sir. But we'll handle them from here. They won't dare attempt any intrigues in our presence."

Foresdale seemed skeptical, looked back toward the water, and Franklin could see the British for the first time, a small crew, and one officer, peering up toward them, the man's face wearing a cautious smile.

Franklin moved past the huge man, tried to avoid the billowing waves of unfortunate odor. Behind him, Adams followed, said, "Thank you again, Captain. We are in your debt."

Rutledge followed silently, and the three men moved toward the British officer, the man stepping up off the flatboat, his caution giving way to formal cordiality. He snapped his heels together, made a short bow, said, "Gentlemen, Admiral Lord Howe offers his respects. This craft is to carry you across to Staten Island. Lord Howe awaits you at the Billopp House, a short distance from the water's edge. You will be escorted there once you land. I am to remain here."

Franklin was studying the perfection of the man's uniform, the rich red, the gold trim, had not fully absorbed the man's words, and Adams said, "Why would you remain here?"

The officer glanced up past them, slight dread betrayed on the man's face, and Franklin knew he was considering the ragged men who answered to Captain Foresdale. The officer brought himself into composure, said, "Permit me, sir, but you are Mr. Adams, yes?"

"Yes, that is correct."

Rutledge said, "I am Edward Rutledge, sir. South Carolina. Representing the Continental Congress."

Franklin smiled, said simply, "Franklin."

The officer was still more interested in the line of militia, said, "For lack of any better description, gentlemen, I am to be your hostage. It is my duty to remain on this shore until your mission is complete, and you return safely here."

Franklin understood now, said, "An extraordinary courtesy, sir, but an unnecessary one. I don't believe any of us considers himself to be at risk of being kidnapped by Lord Howe."

Rutledge laughed, said, "A preposterous offer, sir. The honor of Lord Howe is well known. We do not come here with any fear of betrayal. Nonsense."

Franklin could see relief on the officer's face, thought, Well certainly, this wasn't his choice. Being held by Foresdale's men would likely be a more horrible duty than the man has ever endured. Franklin said, "You should certainly accompany us, sir. At the very least, it will demonstrate to Lord Howe that we have faith in his word, and his flag of truce."

Adams moved toward the flatboat, the handful of sailors coming to life. He looked back toward Franklin, shrugged his shoulders.

"I suppose I agree. After all, one British officer would hardly be an adequate trade for three congressmen. The least he could have done is sent his brother."

THE CONGRESS HAD DEBATED THE WISDOM OF SENDING ANY COMmittee to meet with Lord Howe, strong arguments made on both sides. When General Sullivan had arrived in Philadelphia to make his plea, he seemed not to understand that most of congress considered him utterly taken in by Howe's assurances of his power to make any kind of real peace offering. Franklin had

come away from the meetings and discussions with a new respect for Sullivan's gullibility. It was especially demoralizing,
since, of course, Sullivan was one of Washington's most senior
commanders. But the general had returned to captivity on Staten
Island, fulfilling the terms of his temporary parole, full of the
satisfaction that his service had possibly shortened the war.

In congress, there was a simple dilemma. If congress ignored
Lord Howe's offer of a meeting, they could be accused of casual
disregard for the plight of their own army. The Tory element in
the colonies could have made great cry, labeling the congress a
mass of bloodthirsty rebels who passed up a clear opportunity
for peace. That extreme view was no less ridiculous than the
other, which was to send a committee that could be seen as weak
and submissive, a defeated congress begging for mercy for their
defeated army.

The meeting would be awkward for one other reason: Lord
Howe requested that he not be required to accept the men of the
committee as members of congress, since congress was not recognized by the king to be a legal body of a legal government. The
men could only be received as individuals. Congress of course
would not accept this, and the committee appointed was officially representing congress, whether the British saw it that way
or not.

FRANKLIN WAS SURPRISED TO SEE LORD HOWE WAITING FOR THEM,
standing with a cluster of British staff officers at formal attention as the boat slid alongside a narrow dock. Behind Howe, two
lines of blue-coated Hessian soldiers lined a walkway that led up
to a modest house. Franklin was helped from the boat, paused a
moment to struggle with the stiffness again, disguised it by
straightening his coat and appearing to wait for Adams and Rutledge to join him on the dock. He moved forward then, could see
Howe smiling at him, the formality loosening. Howe came forward, held out a hand, said, "My dear Dr. Franklin! How good to
see you again! It has been far too long!"

Franklin took the admiral's hand, felt the grip slightly cold
and boneless.

"How kind of your lordship to recall our meeting."

"My sister sends her warmest affections, Doctor. She misses
her games of chess with you."

Franklin bristled at the ridiculous attempt at familiarity, thought, It is highly unlikely his sister knows of this meeting. It has only been confirmed for four days.

"Yes, well, your lordship must understand, at present there are other priorities." Howe put on a look of concern, said, "And, I must apologize. My brother, General Howe, offers his regrets. I had hoped the general would attend this meeting, but I'm sure you understand, army business and whatnot."

He heard the familiar grunt from Adams, and Franklin spoke quickly, cutting off any possibility of an indiscreet response.

"We appreciate that the general must attend to his duties. As your lordship is probably aware, General Howe is involved in a war."

The admiral seemed to absorb that for a moment, then looked closely at Franklin, laughed, said, "Ah, yes, very good, Doctor! Indeed!"

Howe was looking past him now, the obvious pleasantries complete, and Franklin thought, Well, it wasn't that funny. He motioned toward Adams, said, "Your lordship, may I present Mr. John Adams, of Massachusetts. And, Mr. Edward Rutledge, of South Carolina."

There were more pleasantries, Rutledge putting on the best social graces, Adams doing his best not to betray his discomfort. Lord Howe led them up the walkway. On either side, the Hessians held their rigid stance, a salute to the honored guests. Franklin tried to avoid the comparison to Foresdale's militia, focused instead on the flow of mindless chatter that came from Howe.

He had come to know Lord Howe in London, where the British ministry recognized that Franklin was the most influential, and certainly the most famous, colonist in their midst. It was believed in London that Lord Howe favored some reconciliation with America. He was considered to be a peripheral member of that group who did not share the king's enthusiasm for an all-out war. It was the admiral himself who had attempted to recruit Franklin in assisting the official opposition as a more outspoken and thus influential spokesman for the colonial cause. But Franklin understood that he could easily be made a sacrificial lamb. If the king's opposition in Parliament fell further out of favor, Franklin would be the obvious scapegoat. If they were successful, and the king backed down, all the credit would go to men like

Lord Howe. Franklin had left London profoundly disappointed that the opposition to the king was, in the end, toothless. The only effective way for him to serve the colonies was to serve congress directly, and so, he had gone home to Philadelphia.

Though Franklin shared congress' general feeling that this meeting would serve little constructive purpose, and Adams was downright negative in his sentiment, he felt that at least they should hear the latest version of what the supposed friends of America might have to say.

As they moved into the house, Franklin caught a new smell, nearly overwhelming, the odor of the army, musty rooms where soldiers had stayed. He thought of the Hessians: Well, certainly this may be their post. It made him feel uneasy, too intimate with such a strange enemy. He had expected something a bit more formal, a bit more grandeur befitting Lord Howe's position. But convenience had taken precedence over show. The Billopp House was close to the water, and would make their journey that much shorter.

They were escorted into the dining room, and Franklin was not surprised to see a lunch already laid out, platters of meat and bread, several bottles of wine. Howe was, after all, the good host. They were seated, and Franklin realized that through all of the man's continuous chatter, Howe might actually be nervous. He took comfort in the thought, glanced at both Adams and Rutledge, both men silent. The room was quickly cleared of staff and servants, and with a sudden rush, the main door was closed, and the four men were alone except for Howe's secretary, who sat discreetly in the corner, prepared to record what was said. But there were no minutes to be taken yet. Howe had continued to talk, reminiscing to Franklin of London, of times that used to be, of days that Franklin knew would never be again.

THE LUNCH WAS CONCLUDED, AND HOWE SPOKE AT LENGTH, AND nothing he said was a surprise. They listened patiently, even Adams holding in his responses until the appropriate time. Franklin appreciated that Howe had not seemed to lose his general affection toward the American people, believing that the war was a truly awful consequence of stubbornness on both sides. Howe stopped short of mentioning the king, of course, but beyond the platitudes, Franklin could see that Howe was framing his words in the vague language of the diplomat.

The lunch was stirring in his stomach, and Franklin avoided the wine, focused instead on Howe's words.

"You understand, of course, that this was never intended to be a meeting of British authority for the purpose of entertaining the American colonies as independent states." Howe paused, and Franklin suddenly realized it was the most substantive thing Howe had said. "I cannot acknowledge your congress as having any authority to address the king. I had hoped that, as gentlemen all, we could ultimately devise some outline to put an end to the calamities of war. I fear you have come here expecting more than I can readily offer."

No one spoke, and Howe seemed distressed, said, "His Majesty's most earnest desire is to make his American subjects happy, to offer whatever reform will address their grievances. Surely, every American colonist understands that the king was only concerned with obtaining aid from his colonies, a means of assisting the royal treasury in providing protection to the colonies' very interests."

Franklin leaned forward, said, "My lord, we cannot muse about those issues which we know to have long passed beneath the bridge."

Howe seemed subdued, said, "I concede to you that money is not the significant issue here. The colonies can produce more solid advantage to Great Britain by her commerce, her strength, and her men."

Franklin laughed, and Howe seemed surprised. Franklin said, "Quite, my lord. We have a pretty considerable number of men. In time, your government may come to realize that in a way none of us here is likely to discuss."

Howe nodded slowly, said, "It is desirable to put a stop to the destruction that will ruin England as sure as it will ruin America. Is there no way of withdrawing this claim of independence? Can we not find the means of opening a door to a full discussion of the matter?"

It was a question for all of them, and Franklin glanced at the others, said, "Your lordship is aware of the authority by which we attend this meeting. That authority speaks for itself. It is not likely, or desirable that we speak of reversing that. You have sent out troops, you have destroyed our towns. You plan even now the further destruction of our nation. That is the true voice of your king. Forgive me, your lordship, but his actions speak far louder than your lordship's words."

Adams had said almost nothing, stood now, and Franklin leaned back in his chair, was relieved someone else would speak. Adams moved slowly around the table, said, "Sir, congress has declared the independence of the American colonies. That declaration is not swept away because the king does not recognize it, or because his representative here finds it inconvenient to speak of it. It hardly matters to the congress if you dismiss us from legitimacy. The voice of the congress, the very energy that created the congress, comes not from a few like ourselves, but has risen from the voices and the energy of the American people. There is *nothing* you can do, no army, no amount of destruction can silence that voice."

Adams sat down, and Franklin could hear his breathing, the anger still in him. He shared Adams' spirit, had hoped that the man would state his case with that kind of fire. Rutledge rose uneasily, and Franklin knew that Rutledge would be conciliatory, the voice of moderation.

"Your lordship, I too share Mr. Adams' resolve, and can assure you that my home, South Carolina, will not waver from the cause of independence." Franklin was surprised, looked at Rutledge, who searched for words. "Your lordship, I had hoped to convince you that there is great benefit to England if she maintains a positive relationship with America. We can surely form an alliance that benefits us all. The farmers and merchants of my state would welcome trade with England . . ."

Franklin sat back, listened while Rutledge went on, words of friendship, the hopes of diplomacy. He could not fault the young man, realized that the committee was actually a fortunate mix, conciliatory and yet determined in a way the British had always failed to understand. Rutledge was through now, sat down, and Howe seemed weary, said, "I admit that I do not possess the authority, nor do I expect ever to have the authority to consider you representatives of a state independent of the crown of Great Britain. I am sorry that you gentlemen have come this far to so little purpose. If the colonies do not relinquish their claim to independence, I cannot speak further." Howe stood then, moved to a window, said, "If America will fall, I would feel the loss as for a brother."

Franklin glanced at Adams, said, "My lord, we will use our utmost endeavors to save your lordship that mortification."

Howe turned, a weak smile, and Franklin was surprised, thought, Well, he is not without humor. Howe lowered his head for a moment, said, "I suppose you will endeavor as well to give the king some employment in Europe."

Franklin did not respond, knew that any mention of foreign alliance was inappropriate, certainly the carefully guarded discussions with France. But of course, the consequences of such an alliance are well known to a man like Lord Howe. It could mean another war.

The meeting seemed to have reached a conclusion. Howe looked toward his secretary, said, "That will do, Mr. Strachey."

The man stood, bowed, left the room, and Howe kept the door open. Franklin led the men out, the staff jumping to attention, but there were no more pleasantries, and they did not hesitate, moved out through the front door of the house. The Hessians were still outside, and Franklin was surprised by that, thought, They were made to stand here the entire time. He glanced at the sun, settling low in the west. It's been . . . three hours at least. That requires discipline. He could not help seeing the image in his mind of the grotesque Captain Foresdale. Yes, well, what we lack in discipline, perhaps we make up for in sheer brutishness.

They were escorted to the boat, and quickly they were under way. Adams sat beside him, his face frozen in a sullen frown, and he said, "This certainly confirms that General Sullivan is prone to exaggeration. I do not believe Admiral Howe had any power to do anything at all, other than sending Sullivan to attempt to seduce us into renouncing our independence."

Franklin glanced back at the sailors, saw no one who seemed to care what they were saying, and he said in a low voice, "I am not surprised, Mr. Adams. The king is not about to let the reins slip from his hand. Anything proposed today would have had to go to London for approval. This was, to be sure, a waste of our time."

Adams made the grunt, said, "I do not wish to offend you, Doctor. I know that Lord Howe is your friend. I must admit that I was not terribly impressed with the man. Perhaps it is what we are taught to believe, that British gentlemen are somehow superior. I admit to being embarrassed at having those expectations.

He is simply a public official in a position where his competence stands trial with every act he performs. If he operates his navy with the same efficiency he operates his peace conferences, I do not fear so much for our chances."

Franklin stared toward the New Jersey shoreline, felt a wave of depression, his exhaustion now complete. No, there was no peace to be had at this conference, no reason to hope that anything had changed. Lord Howe claims not to want a war, and yet, there is nothing in all his talk about how to avert one. Mr. Adams is correct: This was a waste of time.

He looked at the British officer now, the would-be hostage, the man acknowledging him with a polite smile. Our enemy. Well, we made at least one mistake today. We should have left him with Mr. Foresdale, made him a prisoner of war. At least this day would have accomplished *something*.

6. CORNWALLIS

SEPTEMBER 15, 1776

HE HAD BEEN AWAKE NEARLY ALL NIGHT, ORGANIZING HIS MEN, making preparations for boarding the flatboats. By two o'clock in the morning, the boats were being loaded, the soldiers lining up tightly with little of the usual grumbling. Every soldier knew that when the boats embarked, the enemy was right across the East River, waiting for them, and though only the senior commanders knew exactly where they would land, to the troops it hardly mattered. They had already swept their enemy away from one field. Now, they would do it again.

The hours passed, the boats were full, and Cornwallis watched as the rest of the plan moved into precise action. Out in the river, five of Lord Howe's warships had moved into a single line, were now positioned close to the Manhattan shoreline. As the ships made their way upstream, there had been only a scattering of artillery fire from the rebel positions, and the message was clear.

Washington's cannon were simply not there in force, and the naval observers were certain that the only concentration of artillery around the city was still nestled into the rebel battery at the southern tip of the island. But even that threat was not enough to prevent Lord Howe from moving additional men-o-war up the Hudson River, on the west side of Manhattan Island. While Cornwallis waited to begin the short trip across the East River, he knew that the navy's big guns were already in position to cut off any rebel retreat into New Jersey. The immense size of the island might provide a number of defensive options for Washington, but it also put him at a disadvantage. There was simply no way the rebels could protect every place the British could anchor their warships, and no way to guard every possible location the British army could put ashore.

The flatboats moved out at six, Clinton leading the first wave, while Cornwallis followed close behind. The army was divided into three parts, and de Heister had requested that General Howe place Colonel Karl von Donop in command of the third segment of the invasion. Howe had not objected, would likely have allowed de Heister any latitude the old Hessian wanted. After Long Island, there was no doubt that the Hessians were a fierce and reliable ally.

The first light of the dawn provided the grand show: The flatboats again were in motion, oars breaking through the glassy calm of the river. As at Gravesend Bay three weeks before, the armada contained nearly ninety boats, fifty men in each, all making their way toward the landing point. As the light grew, so did the magnificence of the show. In the vast spreading formation, the uniforms of the British and Hessian troops covered the black water in great patches of color. Cornwallis could feel the pure energy, his impatience and anguish at the delays wiped away by the spectacular sight.

Down to the south, a rumble of cannon rolled toward them, and the men in the boats turned in one motion, questioning, wondering whose guns they were. Cornwallis paid no attention, knew that the navy had begun shelling the rebel battery in the city. No one expected Washington to be fooled by Lord Howe's cannon, that the rebels would believe the landing was coming right at their greatest strength. There was no hiding this great sea of flatboats. Cornwallis knew it was simply good tactics, a diversion to keep the rebel artillery occupied, holding them in one place.

His own boat pulled farther from the shore of Long Island, closer to the line of great ships that would give them protection. Around him, the voices grew, the sense of awe infecting the men, and the flatboat was soon passing close behind one of the navy frigates, the *Rose*, anchored broadside to the shore. The men in his boat were waving, some calling out, a breach of discipline, but Cornwallis said nothing, could see the sailors above them responding, could hear their cheers. Yes, they know. We are already a victorious army, and no power on this continent can stand up to us.

On the far shore, Cornwallis could see a long row of turned-up earth, motion behind, men gathering along the shore, rebels emerging from the safety of their earthworks to stare at the great force moving toward them. He smiled at that. Of course, those men have never seen anything to compare to this. As they will soon learn, it is the hand, no, the *fist* of God and King George, coming right down upon them.

The men at the oars pulled his boat steadily past the big ship, and he turned to see the great open maws of the gun ports. The troops were watching as well, and the flatboat was now past the frigate, between the big ship and the shoreline. Cornwallis gave his own silent command to the ships, All right, you may begin firing. But the big guns did not respond. Around him, the cheers and salutes grew quiet, and he could feel the changing mood of his men. One man shouted, "You may commence to firing!"

There was nervous laughter at the man's mock command, and Cornwallis stared still at the guns, thought, We cannot go much farther. He turned toward the shoreline, saw the mass of flatboats in front of him, Clinton's oarsmen now holding their boats in place, jamming up the smooth flow of the crossing. There was a drummer now, a signal to the sailors in each flatboat, and abruptly his own oarsmen began to pull the opposite way, their officer giving the command to hold the boat in a stationary position, fighting the slow current in the river. Cornwallis knew the naval officer had the boat under control, and there was nothing for him to do except wait with the rest of the landing force for the ships to begin their artillery barrage. He looked again at the frigate, felt like cursing, held to his own discipline. Can you not see us? We cannot go closer until . . .

From the rows of open ports, there was one sudden burst of smoke, a thunderous roar that ripped the air above him. The sky was alive with streaks of red and orange, and as quickly as the sound rocked him, the shoreline erupted in blasts of fire. The men in the flatboat were pushed low to the deck, the shock of the sudden cascade of sound. The volleys from each ship erupted without pause, the sharp blasts from huge guns punching the air in his lungs. He could hear smaller sounds now, dull pops from the swivel guns, the miniature cannon high in the rigging of each ship. All he could see of the river was a swirl of gray smoke, and the smell drifted over him, burning sulfur, the smoke blocking out the sunrise behind him. The roar of noise continued still, but the men in his boat began to recover from the shock, began pointing at the shore, the cheers resuming, and he saw it as well. The row of piled dirt was ragged and uneven, and the men who manned the earthwork were now out of sight, bathed in smoke and fire. The flatboat sat motionless in the water, and Cornwallis looked along the river, the other boats still waiting as his was, while above them, the great ships continued to pour their fire toward the rebel works. As the smoke masked what was happening onshore, the men seemed to settle down lower in the boat, the wonder of the bombardment already becoming routine. He knew it would be like this for a while, that the big guns would continue their work, that nothing else could happen until somewhere, someone gave the order to cease fire.

IT LASTED FOR AN HOUR, AND WHEN THE SOUNDS FINALLY STOPPED, the echoes in his ears gave way to the sounds of a new drumbeat, and quickly the flatboats resumed their motion toward the shore. He felt a thick layer of ash on his face, could see it on the men, the white in their uniforms tinged with the grime of the burnt powder. He tried to find the excitement again, focused on the shoreline, the smoking piles of dirt along the water's edge, what remained of the rebel works. But he was nagged by the one glaring inefficiency, the bad timing, the big ships waiting too long to begin the barrage. Someone did not communicate, someone missed the order. You don't wait until your own troops are in front of you to begin an artillery assault. He put the annoyance away, focused on the job in front of him. Along the shore, the first of Clinton's boats had landed, the mass of color spreading out on open ground. They moved quickly, columns shifting into line, marching out toward the right. He waited for the sounds of musket fire, the resistance, watched as more of Clinton's men and now von Donop's Hessians continued to roll ashore, the only sounds the shouts of the officers, the final slap of the oars in shallow water.

With a final hard pull by the oarsmen, his boat slid into soft sand, the men quickly climbing up and out, splashing their way forward, responding to an officer already onshore. The man saluted Cornwallis, who stepped out as well, his boots sinking into the churned-up mud. His troops were already moving away, and he followed them, the footing solid for a short way, then muddy again. He crossed over a shallow ditch, could smell sulfur again, the ground ripped by the artillery barrage. He saw one body, and it was a shock, not for the blood, or the man's shredded clothing. It was *one* body. The ditch had been the rebel entrenchment. And there were no signs of a fight, no wounded, none of the scattered chaos that litters the ground of every battle. He could hear a chatter of musket fire now, well out in front, on the far side of the meadow, and lines of his men moved that way, led by the captains, the sergeants holding them tightly in formation. The meadow was a swarm of activity, units moving into one long line, others, the flanks, marching out to both sides. He looked again at the shallow ditch, the mud, wisps of smoke still clinging to the wet ground. It was a good show indeed. And when they had their fill of it, the rebels simply . . . vanished.

FORTY-FIVE HUNDRED MEN HAD COME ASHORE AT A WIDE COVE known as Kip's Bay. It was chosen from a number of possible landing sites, the shoreline protected from wind, a favorable tide, the ground flat and open, a meadow with no obstruction other than what the rebels would provide. Inland, the meadow ended at woods, and beyond the woods the primary roadway, the Post Road, ran north and south along the east side of the island. The city of New York was to the south, and the landing had avoided a confrontation with any force the rebels might have positioned there. No one knew the exact strength the rebels had placed at Kip's Bay, but with some good fortune, Howe might have chosen a piece of ground that was lightly defended. When the army came ashore, the only opposition came from scattered clusters of musket fire, small groups of men who had backed into the woods, and many more who had simply run away. But

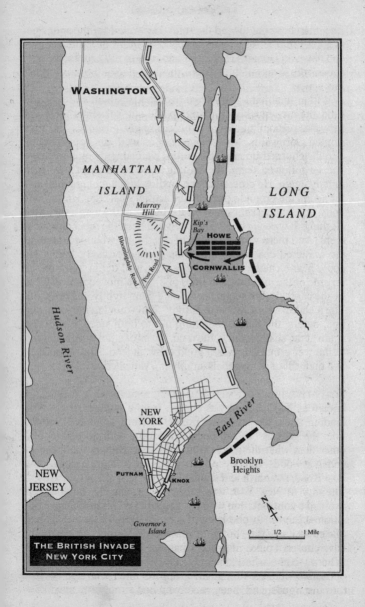

THE BRITISH INVADE
NEW YORK CITY

the Hessian, von Donop, had sent his *jagers* quickly forward, the green-coated marksmen, men whose method of fighting was familiar to the rebels. The *jagers* moved from rock to tree, each man precise at finding his target with a rifled musket, the skill of a marksman. If any of the rebels made a strong stand, the *jagers* would fall back to the lines of the men behind them, the massed body of Hessian troops who relied more on the bayonet. And, as had happened on Long Island, the combination was impossible for even veteran rebels to combat. In less than an hour, the first wave of Howe's invasion of Manhattan had swept away any resistance in front of them. As Cornwallis' men moved in formation across the meadow, there was the eerie sense of a simple parade-ground drill. Not only was there no organized opposition, but nearly every rebel in the area of Kip's Bay was in full flight.

HOWE HAD COME ASHORE AT THE REAR OF THE FIRST WAVE, HAD surveyed the scene of the landing with a puffed-up glow of accomplishment. Cornwallis and Clinton had met him, had made their reports, and Cornwallis had asked every officer he could find to confirm the most astounding report of all. No one could actually locate a single British or Hessian soldier who had been wounded. As Cornwallis gave Howe the report, even he didn't believe it. But Howe had nodded with a confident smile. Of course there were no casualties. It had been a good plan.

Cornwallis watched as Howe strutted along the shoreline, thought, I suppose this is customary. Give him his moment. No one can argue that this result was not worth many days of delay. Howe stared at the river for a long moment, and Cornwallis imagined him conversing with his brother, thought, They do seem to work well together.

Howe pointed out toward the river now, said aloud, "The remainder of the army is en route. We should have them all ashore here by this evening." He focused on the commanders now, said, "I take some pleasure in this, gentlemen. There is nothing as satisfying as a victory. By nightfall, we shall be in full strength, and shall march upon the enemy once again. This was, dare I say, a splendid operation. Splendid. London will only be pleased."

Couriers were gathering, more reports emerging from what little fighting there had been, mostly all in the woods. Cornwallis saw a senior officer approaching, a staff close behind, and the man seemed agitated, bursting with words. Cornwallis knew the man, John Vaughan, moving with a pronounced limp from a leg wound he had received on Long Island.

"Sir! Excuse me, General Howe!" Vaughan acknowledged Clinton and Cornwallis with a crisp nod, and said to Howe, "General, Colonel von Donop has taken his troops southward toward the city. I was not aware you had given this order, sir. My command has secured the heights around the Murray mansion, as ordered, and was awaiting further instruction, when we learned that the left flank was exposed by Colonel von Donop's march."

Vaughan seemed to run out of breath. Howe glanced at Clinton, said, "I gave no specific order to extend our position. However, Colonel von Donop enjoys the full confidence of General de Heister, and I am certain he saw a particular opportunity. It is probably a wise strategy to establish a strong front near the city, to prevent the rebels from assaulting us from that quarter." He looked at Clinton. "Don't you agree, General?"

"If the commanding general deems it proper to allow the Hessians to proceed with their own plan, then I have no objection." There was no emotion in Clinton's voice, and Howe seemed to ignore him. Vaughan found his energy again, said, "Sir, we have made every attempt to engage the rebels, without success. I deeply regret, sir, we have been unable to catch up to them."

All eyes were on Vaughan now, and there were small laughs, Vaughan himself still not getting the joke.

Clinton was not smiling, said, "General Vaughan, it is probably best you call your men back into a stable position. It is clear the rebels have offered you the field. I suggest you accept it."

Vaughan still seemed frustrated. Howe thought for a moment, said, "General Vaughan, you said we are in possession of the Murray mansion. Are the inhabitants present?"

Vaughan seemed deflated now. "Well, um, yes, sir. I spoke to Mrs. Murray myself. There was concern within the household about their safety, but I gave assurances no harm would come to them."

Howe smiled, put his hands together.

"Yes, excellent. We should go there. I am well acquainted with the Murrays. Fine hosts, staunch loyalists. We should offer them some comfort. No doubt, they have been subjected to considerable abuse by the rebels."

Howe moved to his horse, climbed up, said to Clinton, "You are invited, certainly, and General Cornwallis as well. Do make haste. For a wonderful day such as this, some refreshment is in order, and seeing that it is near the noon hour, perhaps in their gratefulness they will provide a hearty meal."

Howe was moving away, and Cornwallis looked at Vaughan, saw a look of distress spreading on the man's face.

"General Vaughan, I'm certain you are invited as well. General Howe did not mean to exclude you."

"Thank you, sir." Vaughan looked at Clinton now, said, "Sir, I believe we have considerable work yet in front of us. We observed a large number of rebels retreating to the north, and I would suspect that General Washington is gathering the greater part of his army in that quarter, along our right flank."

Clinton was still watching Howe's departure, the last of his staff now disappearing into the woods. Other officers had begun to gather, and Cornwallis could see men still emerging from the timberline, pulling into formation. Cornwallis said aloud, "Do we have any reports from the direction of the city? I have heard little from that direction since we made our first landing. Do we know if their main battery is still manned?"

Clinton said, "I've heard nothing, and I don't imagine the navy could drive a large force of rebels from those works. It's a strong position, and they have a great many guns there. It is unlikely they will give up that position without a sharp fight."

Cornwallis felt a stirring in his stomach, said, "Then, sir, should we not advance to the west, and do what we can to create some kind of barrier, especially on the main roads leading north? I have no doubt that General Vaughan is correct, and Washington will withdraw his forces to the only safe place they can gather, which is northward. Any rebel forces in the city can be easily cut off."

Clinton stared grimly to the west, past the meadow where more of their troops continued to gather, more strength coming into their formations. In the river behind them, the flatboats were beginning to land again, returning with the first units of the main body of the army. Clinton still said nothing, and Cornwallis could see the familiar glare on his face. No one spoke, waiting for the senior commander, and finally Clinton said, "We have been instructed to await the arrival of the remainder of the army.

We will not move from this vicinity until General Howe issues that order. The commanding general will not give that order until he feels we have the force to adequately crush the rebels, no matter in what direction they may be." He looked at Cornwallis.

"General, do you understand?"

Cornwallis was surprised at the question.

"Certainly, sir." He could see that Clinton wasn't satisfied with his answer, and Clinton said, "Do you understand that we have been ordered to maintain our present position for the rest of this day? We are not to advance *across* Manhattan, we are not to make any move to cut off the rebels in the city, no matter how disadvantaged they may be. The commanding general will not make any further advances until he has what he feels is a force adequate to the task, until the . . . *risk* has been eliminated."

Cornwallis understood now, Clinton was right. Howe was stopping again, would rest on the laurels of this one great victory, as though it was enough for one day. The report would be sent quickly to London, and the ministry would erupt with praise. For that reason alone, Howe would not take any kind of risk, not with the vast strength of the army still to be assembled on the shore. If it is a mistake, well, we do not know that yet. They are defeated certainly. But, again, we have allowed them to escape. The word dug into his mind, *escape*. How many times will we allow them to escape destruction? Surely General Howe understands that the war will continue as long as the rebels can make a fight, *somewhere*.

Clinton began to move away, his staff holding his horse for him. Cornwallis watched him climb up, and Clinton looked at him, said, "Best hurry, General. The war can wait. General Howe requires a hearty meal."

7. WASHINGTON

SEPTEMBER 15, 1776

THE SOUNDS OF CANNON FIRE HAD BROUGHT HIM SOUTHWARD, HIS staff fighting to keep up with the pace of his horse. As he reached the Post Road, he could see smoke rising from the river, but not enough to cloud the tall masts of the British warships. When their bombardment had stopped, he could see them clearly, and the dull thunder was replaced by scattered bursts of musket fire. As he moved past other units of militia, the men who guarded the landings from the Harlem River southward, the order had been given for the men to move toward the sounds of the fight. Along the northern stretches of the East River shoreline, what earthworks had been dug were quickly abandoned. They all knew now: The fight had been at Kip's Bay. From the west as well, near the Bloomingdale Road, men were advancing in support, some already reaching the crossroad where he stopped the horse.

The sounds of the battle had grown strangely quiet, and there was a new sound, voices, shouts, men now flowing up the Post Road toward him, others appearing out of patches of woods, across open fields. There were no British soldiers, just his own men, and they ran toward him with blind panic, stumbling into the road just below him, closer still. Though some were calling out, short gasps of warnings, curses, he could see many others were deathly silent, the faces staring straight ahead, purposeful, their fear driving them toward some imagined sanctuary, some place of safety they might never find. He could hear orders, hard commands from officers, trying to turn their men around, but then the officers were running as well, few stopping to form any kind of line. Washington was stunned by the sight, for a long moment just stared, felt a rising sickness. But then they began to move past him, some stumbling into the road right beside him, and now he called out to the staff gathered behind him, "Stop them! Hold them back!" He turned the horse sideways, and the aides did the same, blocking the road. He drew his sword, raised it high, began to shout as they forced their way past, "Stop! Hold here! Do not run! There is no danger!"

The wave of men parted around him, oblivious to any order, the shouts from the staff ignored as well. One man came straight toward him, launched himself into the horse's flank, Washington holding hard to the reins, the man staring through him, unseeing, blinded by his own terror. Washington raised his sword, the man still scrambling to push his way past, and Washington brought the flat of the sword down on the man's back, but the man slipped by and was quickly gone. There were more now, some still keeping to the road, but others had simply spread out into the fields around them, slowed only by their own exhaustion.

He heard new shouts, could see down the crossroad to the west, a column of his troops, saw General Mifflin, the Pennsylvanian. Mifflin was already ordering his men into the road in front of Washington, screening the commander from the tide of panic. Washington pointed with the sword toward a long low stone fence, said, "General, move your men into line. Take the wall!" Farther to the west, the stone framed a field of tall corn, and he rode that way, guiding more of Mifflin's men, said, "Take the cornfield! It will provide cover! Make ready!"

Mifflin was pulling his horse along with the flow of his men, putting them in place, and Washington felt a burst of relief, Finally, a fighting man, troops who can face the enemy. Thank God. More of his men were arriving now, the militia who had been up to the north, along the river, guarding the landing places that Howe had ignored. Washington guided them into place as well, the men lining up along fences that spread out to the east, some crouching low against rocks, muskets at the ready.

There were still refugees coming toward them, men staggering into the road, more of the panic. He could see there would be no fight in those men, and he shouted, "Let them pass!"

He pulled the horse beside the road, waved his sword, some of the men now walking, their energy gone. He saw faces looking at him, recognition, some of the men stopping to stare at him through the sweat and dirt on their faces.

"Take your position with these men! There is no enemy! You are not being pursued!"

His staff took up the same call, and some of the men seemed to understand, others collapsed to the ground, having run as far as their terror could take them. A few still had muskets, but only a few, and he saw more of them awakening to the moment, aware now of the growing strength of their own army. Slowly, they began to move to the fence lines, joining the fresh troops, the courage returning.

Mifflin's men were fully in place, and behind him, still other units were advancing, more strength. Washington directed them back behind the first troops, a second line of muskets. The officers had control now, and he moved his horse out into the Post Road, stared to the south, expecting to see the familiar columns of red and white, Howe's massed forces pushing their way north. The horse moved under him, and Washington held hard to the reins, Yes, I know. Right here! We will meet them right here. And we are prepared.

He could see a small hill, about a quarter mile away, the Post Road running up and over, then disappearing beyond. He knew that past the small hill, the road dropped off toward another much larger hill, crowned by the Murray estate, and then just below, Kip's Bay. He had not expected Howe to come ashore there, had thought they might land farther north, closer to the mouth of the Harlem River, farther from Washington's strength in the city. He knew the area around Kip's Bay was commanded by William Douglas, with a brigade of fresh Connecticut troops, green recruits who had not been with the army more than a few days. But south of the bay were more Connecticut troops, under James Wadsworth, experienced men, and Wadsworth would know to reinforce Douglas. He had no idea if the men who had retreated with such panic were Douglas' men, or Wadsworth's, or both. But for now, it made no difference.

From behind him, men continued to come forward, reinforcing his stand, and he sat high in the saddle, could hear some men calling out to him, would not acknowledge that, thought, This is not a moment for hat waving and celebration. Show me how you can fight. That is all I ask.

He continued to stare down the Post Road, could hear nothing but the men around him, but then something faint, a muffled rhythm. The men began to hear it as well, and the voices grew quiet. On the hill, he saw a flicker of red, saw a man, a single soldier suddenly crest the hill. The man stopped, seemed to wave, and now more men appeared, filling the road, some spreading out to each side. The muffled sound was now sharp, distinct, the careful rhythm of a lone drummer. The British came forward slowly, and Washington felt his heartbeat rising, expected to see a great mass of troops, but the British moved toward them down off the hill, and behind them, the hilltop was bare, the road empty. The British still moved forward, but the drum had stopped, the soldiers halting now, extending into a single line. Washington could see now, no officers, no one on a horse, thought, It's merely a scouting party, perhaps, sixty, seventy men. They will not come much closer, unless they have strength behind them. I must hold these men back, they might be tempted to charge them, an easy capture. We must see what they do first.

His thoughts were jarred by a sudden cascade of voices, men on either side of him. He expected to see them bursting forward, shouted, "No! Hold here . . ."

But they were not advancing. Instead, men were pulling away from their cover, the stone wall emptying, as they suddenly rushed out of the cornfield. It had begun with a few, but the infection spread, and all around him, men dropped their muskets, a sudden eruption of panic as his men, Mifflin's men, the others, abandoned their position. He stared in horror, felt a burn in his chest, his voice choked away, the infection now complete, hundreds of men filled the Post Road, scampering away across the fields. He tried to shout, made just a noise, no words, saw Mifflin riding back through his men, trying to turn them, and the anger rose inside of him, Damn them! Why do they run? His staff was close by, watching him, waiting for some instruction, and Washington felt the anger growing into a hot mindless rage. He spurred the horse, rode through the panicked men, slapping at them with his sword, his voice now harsh, raw. "Stop! You are cowards! Damn you!"

He saw a young officer, the man pushing past his own men, knocking one man to the ground, the officer scrambling over a fence, stumbling, tearing at his own canteen, throwing it aside. Others were doing the same, dropping whatever was in their hands, cartridge boxes, powder horns, littering the ground with the tools of his army. Washington tore the hat from his head, gripped it hard in his fist, still watched the young officer, the man now running away from him in full stride. Washington's hand was shaking, his hat bunched into a shapeless mass, and he threw it hard to the ground, shouted again, "*Damn* you!"

But there was no one to hear him now, just his staff, gathering slowly behind him, no one able to hold the troops from their manic retreat. He turned, looked again toward the British troops, saw them advancing again, the same small line, the drummer keeping the rhythm of their march. He slumped in the saddle, watched them come, the uniforms distinct, the sharp colors, the bayonets a bright silver reflection in the afternoon sun. They were nearly within musket range now, and still they kept their discipline, came forward at a steady march. He felt a strange sense of wonder, it was after all just one small unit, no real strength at all. Indeed, just a scouting party. He could see the sergeant leading them, close enough to see the features of the man's face, confident, watching him as a hawk watches his prey, moving closer. There is no need for them to fire a volley. No, they will just capture us. We are unprotected. He felt the horse suddenly jerk to one side, saw Tilghman close beside him, pulling on the bridle, the young man looking at him with a terror of his own.

"Sir! We must go!"

The horse was moving now, and Washington felt the reins that were still in his hand, could see the staff in motion, the sounds of the horses. Tilghman said again, *"Sir!"*

His mind snapped alive, and he spurred the flanks of the horse, and it responded, the familiar gallop. The staff was all around him, riding as he rode, moving up the Post Road, following the trail of debris left by his army.

HE HAD CAUGHT UP TO MANY OF THE RETREATING SOLDIERS, HAD accepted their uselessness to make a stand. The staff had gathered as many officers as could be found and began to guide the troops toward the one place they could find safety. The northern part of Manhattan Island was rocky, with a wide stretch of high ground known as Harlem Heights. There, while Howe had spent two weeks planning his invasion of Manhattan, Washington had placed his headquarters, and the greatest strength of his army, a naturally fortified position, tall cliffs and massive boulders that spread from the Hudson River on the west to the Harlem River on the east.

Washington rode westward now, reached another crossroad that intersected the Bloomingdale Road, the main north–south road on the western part of the island. He crested a hill, could see the Hudson River in front of him, a line of British warships sitting at anchor, part of Howe's grip on the island. He stopped the horse, the staff, other officers now gathering, more of his army finding their way to the safer roadway. Their movement was northward, and he made no attempt to stop them, knew that they would first have to gather on the rocky Heights if they were to have spirit for another fight.

The road was churned into dust, men moving past without seeing him, and he did not look at them, did not want to know whose men they were, whether or not they were Mifflin's men or had been a part of the collapse at Kip's Bay. There was the sound of a horse, then another, and Washington heard his name, the staff motioning. A horse emerged through the choking clouds, and Washington could see it was Israel Putnam. The short round man was holding tight to the reins of a horse whose hide was soaked with hot foam.

"General Washington! Thank God, sir! Thank God! I feared the worst!"

Washington waited for Putnam to collect himself, the exhausted horse lowering its head, Putnam wiping caked dirt from his face.

Putnam commanded the battery far to the south, and Washington knew how far he had come.

"General Putnam, I am pleased to see you are safe."

Putnam huffed, seemed not to notice the black mood in Washington's voice.

"Sir, I am not safe at all!" The words poured out of Putnam in a torrent. "We are in a deadly strait! My division is still occupying the battery. I must urge you, sir, to consider our immediate withdrawal! As best as we can determine, the entire British army is east of this position. If they advance across to the Bloomingdale Road, my men are cut off. The navy ships have been dueling with our guns down there, and I have no doubt they will attempt some sort of landing after dark. Colonel Knox is putting up a gallant fight, sir, but we are no match for an assault from land *and* sea! Sir, we must withdraw!"

Washington turned to the east, thought, No sound, no drums,

no advance. Nothing. He looked at Putnam, said, "Since you rode this far, I am assuming the Bloomingdale Road is still open all the way southward."

"Yes, sir! For now, that is! We cannot delay!"

"No, you cannot. Can you make the ride yourself, General?"

Putnam seemed insulted at the question, said, "I am here to protect my men, sir! I will make any ride necessary!"

Washington looked at the other horseman, a much younger man, the face familiar, Aaron Burr, a contentious man who had served briefly with Washington's staff.

"Major Burr, you are familiar with this road. If the enemy attempts to block it, can you guide General Putnam's troops on alternate routes?"

The young man seemed calm, unaffected by Putnam's excitement.

"Sir, I know every back road, all the trails. I can guarantee you we'll make good our escape."

Washington was already familiar with the young man's arrogance, tried to ignore the boast, said to Putnam, "Return to your command, General. Have Colonel Knox salvage what he can, but do not jeopardize your men by attempting to remove the cannon."

He saw the look of despair on Putnam's face, and Putnam said, "Sir, we have sixty-seven guns there. That's nearly half our artillery."

"You have four thousand men, General. Their safety is my first concern. If you do not succeed, this army has lost far more than cannon. Do not delay, General."

Putnam saluted, turned his horse, and the young Burr led the way. Washington looked to the west, the sun moving lower in the sky. He pulled the horse around, moved out into the road, the staff behind. He stopped suddenly, strained to hear, the only sound the movement of scattered men, all heading north. He thought of the scouting party, the small detachment of British troops who had so frightened his men. Scouting parties will be out in all directions. All it will take is one who moves west, who dares to go as far as the Bloomingdale Road. If they locate Putnam's column, Howe can throw a great force into their flank in short order. Putnam has four thousand men. Howe could bring twice that many. He thought of Henry Knox, the young rotund man, the bookseller who had become the best artilleryman in his

army. We need your guns, young man. But more, we need *you*.
He glanced back down the road to the south, the road open and
silent. He thought of Howe, the man's tactics: Why does he delay? Why does he not finish the job he had begun this morning?
He knows I will not abandon Putnam's men, he knows they will
retreat. That could be his plan, after all. Strike us when we are on
the march. He pushed the image from his mind, had seen enough
of retreat and panic for one day. He moved the horse again,
stared ahead to the high ground to the north, where the mass of
his army was digging in.

AS HE MOVED NORTHWARD, HE CONTINUED TO PASS THE GATHERING
troops, more of his army, seeking the safety of Harlem Heights.
He met officers as well, new orders going out, men sent back
to the southeast. As the Post Road cut more diagonally across
the island, it ran through a natural defile of rocks known as
McGown's Pass, where he was certain a small body of men
could hold back a much larger British advance. It was the last
piece of good ground his men could use to keep the British away
before they came to the flat plain in front of Harlem Heights. He
didn't know if it would work, but he gave the job to the Marylander, Smallwood, one of the few men whose troops he knew
would make a stand.

As the darkness spread, it began to rain. The shovels still
worked through the deepening mud, but the wounded and the
panic-stricken found whatever shelter they could, the sounds of
the rain muting the cries of their misery. Washington tried to ignore the rain, sat on his horse on a protruding point of rocks,
stared to the south. He had seen nothing of the British, and so, he
knew that Smallwood was doing his job, that the British had been
slowed down enough to halt for the night below McGown's Pass.

Putnam's division had made their escape, exhausted men who
had survived the incredible journey up the long route of the
Bloomingdale Road, a forced march led by the furious tenacity
of their commander. Though Knox had left behind many of his
guns, and the men had given up far more of their supplies than
the army could afford to lose, four thousand troops had slipped
past an enemy three times their number and were now safely in
Harlem Heights.

With Howe's occupation of New York, Washington had one
other concern, could not keep it from his mind. Nathanael Greene

was in a sickbed in the city, would surely have been captured, had von Donop's Hessians not been so interested in plunder. As the bleak night wore on, General Greene had made his escape as well, had ridden safely to the Heights, his arrival an astonishing, joyful surprise.

Washington was still out on the point of rocks, the horse quiet beneath him, could still hear the sound of shovels, the army doing its work to make the high ground safer still. The word of Greene's return had come from his staff, and he had sent them away, did not respond to their curiosity, why he did not join the welcome. He was enormously relieved that Greene had returned, perhaps too much so, felt a strange release of emotion at the news, but he kept it to himself, would not allow the staff to see him that way. There had been enough emotion today, this shameful, awful day. He was embarrassed still by his show of anger at his troops, and though no one else seemed to fault him, though no indiscreet comments came to him, he knew it had been a serious mistake to lose control of his demeanor. He felt the opposite about Greene, not rage, but pure joyful relief. The staff and the other senior officers already knew how much he valued Greene. When Greene had fallen ill, there was talk among the doctors that he might not survive, and Washington had been surprised at his emotions, a fear and sadness he was ashamed to admit. We are all soldiers, and General Greene is as likely as any of us to be killed. But I do need him. Beyond the politics, all the jealousies that infest this army, there is an honesty in the man, something I truly need.

As it grew late, the rain had begun to slacken, the first stars appearing, clouds drifting apart. It was only then that he had sent for Greene, knew the man might still be fragile from the illness. He would not ask him to endure the weather any more than he already had. He stared still toward the open plain in front of the Heights, as he had done at Brooklyn, wondered if the British would form the same way, a vast thick line. Behind him, he could hear the dull plod of a horse's hooves.

"Not such a pleasant day, I understand."

The voice was Greene's, and Washington did not look at him.

"It was not a pleasant day."

"Your Mr. Tilghman asked me if I would inform you that Colonel Smallwood has brought his men in."

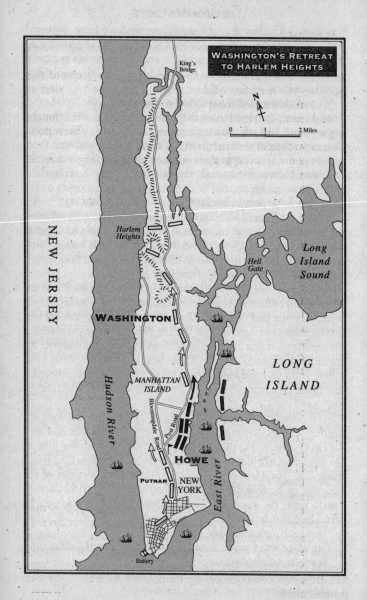

WASHINGTON'S RETREAT
TO HARLEM HEIGHTS

N

0   1   2 Miles

King's
Bridge

NEW JERSEY

Harlem
Heights

Hell
Gate

Long
Island
Sound

WASHINGTON

LONG
ISLAND

Hudson River

MANHATTAN
ISLAND

Bloomingdale Road

Post Road

HOWE

PUTNAM   NEW
          YORK

East River

Battery

Washington nodded, said, "Very good. Fine officer."

Greene moved his horse close up beside him, seemed to lower his voice.

"From what I've heard, yes. If anything is to come of this fight, we will need fine officers. We will need good soldiers as well. Could have used some today, so I'm told."

Washington had tried to erase the image from his mind, fought it now, could still see the men running away, leaving their positions in the face of a mere handful of the enemy.

"I do not wish to experience another day like today. I shouted out to them, shamelessly, even cursed them."

"Did they not deserve it?"

He stared into the darkness, more stars now appearing.

"I have wondered, Mr. Greene, is this the army with which I am to defend America? Can we do no better than to scamper away? We have done nothing but give up every patch of ground we have been required to defend. Now, we have lost New York. I had thought we could make a fight of it."

Greene said, "If we are to rely on militia, men pulled away from the tenderness of their homes, given muskets, instructed to stand up to an experienced army . . . what kind of fight do we expect of them? These are men who will flee from their own shadows. Howe was determined to have New York. He intends to make winter quarters there, so I'm told. The Tories in the city were gleefully vocal on the subject. British flags are already appearing in every shopwindow." He paused for a moment. "It is still possible we can burn the place. Without the city to make himself comfortable, Howe will have to keep moving, or build his camps, which could leave him at some disadvantage. It may be the best opportunity for us to strike at him."

Washington shook his head, said, "No. Congress instructed me to hold the city at all hazards." The words seemed to stick in his throat, and Washington knew what was coming.

"It seems you did not comply."

Washington saw no humor, said, "No, but it was the very reason we attempted to make our stand there. I would never have allowed General Putnam to remain in the city, to place his division in such peril if the congress had not wished it. To have simply handed New York to General Howe without a fight would have had disastrous consequences for the country. As it is . . . the loss is incalculable."

Greene sniffed.

"Congress. Is congress to fight this war? What do they know of battle? They expect one glorious fight, army facing army, like some childhood game. What strategy do they impart to you? Here's your authority to make war. But, do it without harming anything of value, such as New York."

Washington knew that Greene would speak his mind, would sometimes give in to the frustrations.

"Mr. Greene, the congress has expressed their confidence that we should not destroy New York because we will yet possess it again. Optimism is to be admired."

"Yes, sir, I love a good optimist. New York is a fine city to be sure. But it's just a city. It's not an army, and it cannot do anything to win a war. Right now, it is a collection of houses and buildings that will serve to give shelter to the enemy. There is only one good course remaining. Burn it. If we come to possess it again, then we can rebuild it."

Washington was feeling his own exhaustion, did not want to debate.

"Mr. Greene, if congress was to learn that we had destroyed New York of our own choice, the outcry would end this war, and not in the way we intend. If the people believe that the result of this war is the destruction of our most valued cities, then the sentiment for that war will disappear. I am aware that General Howe will make himself perfectly comfortable there, and I would do anything in my power to see that isn't so. But I must still answer to congress, and the congress will have none of it. We cannot burn New York." He paused, lowered his voice. "No matter how tempting the prospect."

He could see Greene turning in the saddle, heard a small grunt.

"Are you all right, General?"

Greene rubbed his stomach, said, "It comes and goes. I could use some sleep."

Behind them, the men still worked in the darkness, and Washington could hear low cursing and a quick profane response from the man's sergeant. Greene said, "They're going to be worn-out in the morning."

Washington turned the horse, could see nothing but the faint reflection from the shovels.

"Not all of them. And we must make ready. We cannot depend on General Howe to delay any further. This army requires some advantage, something to give these men confidence. We had none of that today. This is an excellent place to make a stand. General Howe has shown very little inclination toward speed. He takes his victories one at a time, savors them, possibly even celebrates them. But his generals are in their camp right now, making their plan for tomorrow. They know we are here. They know they must bring the fight to us, and thus far we have given them no reason to hesitate. I believe he has made mistakes, that we have been blessed by his delays. But if General Howe dares to push his army up these rocks, it could be a far greater mistake than just sitting still."

8. NATHAN HALE

HE CARRIED HIS DIPLOMA UNDER HIS COAT, THE ONLY OFFICIAL identification he could come up with. He had only been asked to show it once, to a hostile British colonel, suspicious of this plainly dressed man who traveled the country roads of Long Island at night, claiming to be a schoolmaster. The colonel had scanned the document with mild disgust, a low disrespectful comment about Yale College, as though any colonial school was far inferior to the most lowly grammar school in England. Hale had kept his hat in his hand, painfully polite, and the colonel could find no reason to hold this odd man in this dismal place. The colonel had more important work to do after all, patrolling the country roads for rebel raiding parties who were making off with cattle and grain. The colonel had not even taken the time to inspect the cloth bag Hale carried, heavy with books, texts in Latin, the classics. The British had simply resumed their march, patrolling the darkness for their enemy, while the schoolmaster was allowed to continue his journey. Hale had caught the officer's final insult, some curse about teaching anyone to read in this godless land, and Hale had said nothing, had resumed his long walk, the sweat in his clothes betraying more than the humid warmth of the evening.

His route had brought him across the waterway from the north, a careful, discreet crossing, avoiding the British naval patrols. He had planned to stay on Long Island, to visit the homes of the loyal citizens there, those who stayed close to the British camps. Teachers were rare now, so many having escaped the growing terror of the war, their schools shut down, some serving as hospitals for the wounded, classrooms now crowded with flat hard beds, bloody sheets, doctors overwhelmed by the new horror of their job. But when he had reached the homes along the north side of the island, presenting his credentials to curious and often nervous farmers, he began to hear unexpected news. The British were gone, had crossed the East River, a swift and efficient invasion of New York. The farmers were delighted to tell the story, all their confidence confirmed, the might of King George's army sweeping away the rebels, bringing an end to this ridiculous war.

His roundabout journey from Harlem Heights had taken days, and he had not been able to contact anyone in Washington's army, had received no official messages from anyone. Though the British actively patrolled the roads, it did not take him long to realize that the bulk of their army was simply gone. With soft footsteps through silent patches of woods, he had found the camp, amazed to have been standing alone in what were now empty fields of debris. The effect on him had been unexpected and strange, a sense of panic that he might have missed it all, that he had wasted too much time reaching his destination. If the camps were empty, then he had come to the wrong place. His job, after all, was to find out where the British were going next, but now, there was nothing for him to learn, and ultimately, this dangerous mission had become a waste of time. He had become more panicked by that than by the confrontation with the British colonel.

He had no choice but to continue the journey, and he found passage to the city with a sympathetic, though somewhat surprised, merchant, who made regular crossings from Brooklyn to

Governor's Island, then to the city itself. Once the rebel cannon had fallen silent, the man had resumed his regular trade run, had found himself ferrying more passengers out of the city, part of a vast exodus of refugees who would escape the British occupation. But Hale had convinced the man, there were still children in New York, and certainly their parents would want them occupied with more than the chaotic horror of an army occupation. They would still need teachers.

HIS HOME WAS IN CONNECTICUT, AND HE JOINED THE ARMY AFTER an anguished debate with himself, wondering if a soldier could contribute more to the country's cause than a man who gave education to the children. As the talk of war burst into the reality of Lexington and Concord, it was the British occupation of Boston that settled his argument. He had volunteered alongside many of his friends, made the march to Cambridge to join Washington's army, had sat in earthworks for long weeks staring at the red-coated soldiers who stared back at him. When the British evacuated Boston, Hale had moved with the army to New York, had camped with the Nineteenth Connecticut Regiment near the city. He was quickly made an officer, promoted almost immediately to captain, an acknowledgment of his education and intellect, the young man who had gone to Yale College when he was only fourteen. He didn't know much about being an officer, but the men who marched with him showed respect, a new experience for a man who had previously commanded only restless children.

There was respect from above as well, and he was offered the opportunity to join Colonel Thomas Knowlton's Rangers, formed from the Connecticut regiments, a handpicked squad that would serve directly under Washington. They would be an official scouting unit, gathering information and intelligence beyond the normal chain of command. The opportunity excited him, since his duties thus far had been mostly mundane. He had never yet faced the enemy in combat. His unit had remained encamped in New York, while the great battle took place on Long Island. Though many in the nineteenth were relieved to be safely on Manhattan Island, Hale had wondered if he would ever know that experience, what those men had gone through, the men who stood and faced the enemy, the men who were now *soldiers*.

Once the Rangers had been organized, Colonel Knowlton himself had gathered the entire group together, had walked among them speaking of a specific mission. It was a mission for just one man, and there would be no uniform, no musket. Knowlton did not use the word, but the message was plain: General Washington needed a *spy*, someone to move through the British camps, someone who could provide information on when and where the British would move next. No one had volunteered, and Knowlton acknowledged that the job was unseemly, unfit for a real soldier. There was no respect to be found by being a spy. And, of course, a soldier caught out of uniform, behind the lines of the enemy, would simply be hanged.

Throughout the night that followed, he had thought again of all he had missed so far, knew that Knowlton himself had fought at Breed's Hill, many of the men around him already taking their muskets into the line of fire, the campfires alive with tales of fights Hale could only imagine. No one spoke again of the new unpopular mission, but Hale could not escape the feeling that it was an opportunity, some way he could be useful. He had finally gone to Knowlton, had told him he would volunteer for the mission. Knowlton had accepted Hale's offer with few words, and Hale understood that the colonel himself was unsure of the honor in this sort of job. But the two men had gone straight to Washington's headquarters, and Hale had stood silently as Washington explained all he needed the young man to do. But that mission was on Long Island, and Washington could not have known that in a few days, everything would change. So now, Nathan Hale the schoolmaster was in New York.

SEPTEMBER 20, 1776

He had come to the city for the first time in late spring, when the army had arrived from Boston, the Nineteenth pitching their camp near the East River. The duty had been mundane and tedious, but then had come the curious order, and the entire army had marched and assembled on the great open Green. It had been over two months ago, on July 9, and it was one of the few times he had actually seen the commander in chief. Washington had ordered the troops to form a hollow square, the first time the men had seen their own strength assembled in one piece of open ground. Even the citizens had come, gathering around the Green in awe of the sight, so many men with muskets, the odd mix of uniforms, the sounds of the drums. But then, the drums had stopped, and Washington himself had called them to attention. He would always remember the voice of that officer who read them the document, the words of the Declaration of Independence. In the formation around him, no one had spoken, each man absorbing the words, the entire army understanding that something momentous had occurred. The congress in Philadelphia, that body of men that most knew little about, had somehow united all of the colonies into one voice, and now, that voice had officially broken their allegiance to King George.

As he walked through the Green now, that extraordinary day was nowhere in evidence. British troops spread out around campfires, much of the greenery was ripped up, pits dug for latrines, trees cut, piles of logs stacked. He caught the rank smell, moved quickly past, made his way westward. He moved into a side street, narrow, thick damp air, more smells, could hear voices in the houses, a woman crying, shouts of men. The woman was in obvious distress, and he thought of stopping, knocking on the door, but the accents were unmistakably English, the crude manner of the common soldier. He was in no position to be gallant.

He kept moving, wasn't sure where he was going, saw more side streets, narrow again, twisting. There was no sunlight here, the street thick with mud, and he heard a strange animal sound, quick motion in front of him. He could see a group of pigs bursting out of a deep wallow, scampering away from him. He shuddered at his own fright, a low nervous laugh, heard shouts in front of him. The darkness opened into sunlight ahead, and he could hear the pigs squealing, a harsh, sickening sound. He moved closer to the light, saw a group of British soldiers running, chasing the pigs, a sword, the awful game. He backed into the darkness again, moved through the thick mud, another side street. He stayed close to the sides of the houses, listened, more voices, women. He tried to hear the words, talk of food, a baby crying. He was surprised anyone with children was still there, that despite his own charade, he had believed that anyone with a family would be long gone from the city. He kept moving, the dark street ending, more sunlight. He looked down at the filth clinging to his shoes, knew he would take the smell with him. He stepped into open air again, looked across a wide street, felt a light breeze cleaning his lungs. Now there was a hand on his back, a hard push, and he stumbled into the street, his knees hitting hard on the cobblestones. He turned, saw a group of soldiers, laughing, one man pointing at him.

"Out of the way, clerk."

The men moved past, more laughter, and he held the anger, lowered his head, said quietly, "Yes, sir. As you wish, sir."

The soldiers were gone, and he sat on the rough stones, rubbed his knees. He did not take well to the role of the helpless weakling, had always been athletic, more fit for sports than any of his friends. But he could make no show, no protest of any kind. The last thing he needed was attention, especially from soldiers.

If there were citizens still in New York, they had to be either loyal to the king or so destitute they had no means of leaving. Both were dangerous to him, and he knew he could speak to no one, ask no specific questions. The Tories would take him straight to the provost's office, and the street people would see a reward, would find a way to draw him into some betrayal for which they would pocket a few shillings. If he was to observe the strength of the British positions around the city, the location of specific units, he would have to do it alone. Eavesdropping at windows had given him nothing. No, it would be the officers, the men with real information, and they were safely housed in the large estates, their debauchery brought to *them*, unlike the common soldiers.

He had walked for most of the day, his legs aching now, the strain of slogging quietly through muddy alleys. The frustration was growing, and he had already thought of giving it up, making his way carefully out of the city, finding some way to reach Harlem Heights. But then he remembered the meeting with Washington, the commander in chief asking him to do what so many would not. Even if the men of Knowlton's Rangers were uncertain of the honor in being a spy, Washington had made it clear. The mission was not only important, it was crucial. Now, with the British in the city, it might be all the more so. No matter the frustration, he had to accomplish *something*.

He moved to an open square, saw more soldiers, strange blue uniforms, polished brass helmets. It was a squad of Hessians marching in formation, muskets on shoulders, and on both sides of the street, civilians were staring silently, tight grim faces. The Hessians moved past, and the onlookers began to move again, slowly resuming their own business, and he thought, Even the Tories are frightened. It is one thing to receive General Howe with graciousness, to give lavish parties in his honor. It is quite another to try to live with these strange and foreign soldiers marching in your streets, who have shown no concern for your politics or your loyalties. If you are not in uniform, you could very well be their enemy, and they do not hesitate to act on that. He heard a burst of shouting from a house behind him, a woman's short scream. He turned, saw glass shattering, a book flying out the window, landing in the street in a heap of scattered paper. He stared at it, instinctive anger at the assault on the one thing he loved, wondered what the book was, thought of picking it up. There were more shouts, male now, and the woman screamed again. In the wide square, another group of soldiers appeared, British this time, but they made no move toward the house. Hale caught their glances that way, saw smiles, reacting to the screams of the woman only as some shared experience. He felt an icy chill, moved quickly away from the house, felt the violation of the woman in some place deep in his mind, the awful shame that there was nothing he could do. He rounded a corner, saw more soldiers, fought hard to keep his anger quiet. But these were different, powdered wigs, much gold on their uniform. The anger eased, and he focused on the opportunity, saw four men, dressed with the sharp scarlet coats of officers, *senior* officers. He fought the urge to duck away into the alley, was too far in the open, could only move past them, make no obvious motion. He kept his face down, nodded silently as they passed him, slowed his walk, listened to their conversation.

"The old place is quite handsome, I'm told. We shall move there tomorrow."

Hale turned, leaned against a wood wall, seemed to scrape the mud from his shoes, tried to hear more. They were walking slowly away from him, and he began to follow, kept his distance.

"Well, the general shall certainly approve. With the batteries now in place, there will be no call for movement. The firewood is accumulating nicely. And, to a warm hearth are drawn those who provide their own warmth. Certainly, we can make use of the local . . . ah . . . *flowers*."

The man laughed, joined by the others. Hale stayed back, could not risk them noticing him. He backed into an alley, ignored the crushing smells, thought, *Winter quarters.* Of course, this is no secret, it was always said that the British wanted to be in New York for the winter, plenty of housing, even for the soldiers. And, plenty of entertainment. Flowers indeed. He could not escape the sound of the woman's screams, closed his eyes for a moment. *Damn them!*

The daylight was fading, and he backed farther into the alley, thought, You've been on the street for too long, seen too many people. Someone will notice you. Best stay hidden for a while.

He felt his way around a corner, the smells of garbage and filth unavoidable. He felt the wetness in his shoes, stood in a place that never saw sunlight, thought, You should remember this alley. A good sanctuary. He looked up, saw a window, caught the flicker of a candle, and a head suddenly appeared, a sharp gaze down the alley toward the street. Hale stood motionless, and the man never looked down at him, withdrew back inside. Hale heard voices now, low talk, strained to hear.

"Aye, he's bringing it all tonight. Have ye got the lamp oil? There's already one barrel under the floor here . . ."

The accents were thick, Irish perhaps. The talk moved away from the window, just low murmurs now, and he felt a new excitement. These weren't soldiers, this was something else, talk of conspiracy. He felt a sudden stab of hopefulness. There may yet be people here who don't favor the British at all. He tried to recall the man's words . . . lamp oil . . . a barrel. Why would they want so much lamp oil? To sell? But the British wouldn't pay, they'd simply take it. He focused through the darkness, the daylight completely gone, moved farther back into the hidden corner, put his hand out, felt his way. The wall was rough, rotten planks, and his hand touched something that moved. There was a sudden clatter of falling wood, and he pulled back, his heart jumping. He reached down, wrapped his fingers around a long stick, could see a bulge at the top, felt it was crowned with straw. He picked it up, could tell that it was nearly as tall as he was, the straw gathered as on a broom. Odd, no place to be sweeping anything back here. His eyes were adjusting more to the darkness, the candle from the window a faint glow. There were more brooms farther back in the corner, the same shape, the straw pointing up, out of the mud. He moved his hand through the broomsticks, counted, eight, nine, a dozen. He still held the one in his hand, turned, looked out around the corner toward the street, quiet now. Why would someone store brooms . . . he looked up, the voices still there, the windowpane over his head brighter with the light of an oil lamp. *Lamp oil*. He held the broom away from him, stared at the straw. It's not a broom. It's a *torch*.

THE FIRST FIRES BEGAN AFTER MIDNIGHT, TORCHES TOSSED THROUGH broken windows of homes abandoned by their owners. The men had emerged from the house like a swarm of bees, and Hale had watched from across the street, stayed back in a dark corner as the men retrieved their torches. As they spread out through the narrow streets, he had followed one man, saw the torch suddenly ignite from a candle in the man's hand. The man thrust the torch into an open window, igniting the curtain, a sudden eruption of flame that quickly took hold of the dry wooden walls. Then the man moved on quickly, and Hale followed, the man turning into a narrow alley. As the fire spread higher, Hale grabbed a piece of wood, ripped it from the side of the house, wanted to light it with the rising flames, but he was in the open, too visible in the hard glow of firelight. He followed to where the man had disappeared, moved into the alley, then out to another street, could see men gathering around a fat barrel. More torches were handed out, each one dipped into the barrel, then ignited by a thick candle. Each man was quickly on his way, the torches coming alive in the darkness. Hale moved toward the man who stayed by the barrel, saw the face in the flickering candlelight, hard, old, and the man stared at him for a long moment, said, "I don't know you."

Hale held out the piece of ragged wood, said, "Does it matter? I am a patriot, sir, just as you."

The man took the wood from Hale's hand, dipped it in the oil, ignited it, said, "Get out of here!"

Hale ran now, was in a wide street, could see flickers of flame spreading out through the alleys. There were shouts now, and he moved quickly, saw a narrow lane, turned that way, the glow from his own torch casting a bright light between two houses. He stopped, looked both ways, houses on either side, thought, Which one . . . what should I do . . . and there was a voice above him. "What . . . who are you? I'll kill you!"

He saw a glimpse of the man's head, the voice unmistakably British. The house seemed to come alive with sounds, men scrambling, more curses. Hale looked up at the window, gauged the distance, put one hand on the bottom of the board, and with one quick motion, launched it up through the window.

THE CITY WAS ENGULFED IN FIRE, AND HE WATCHED THE EXTRAORDINARY scene from a low hill, tried to catch his breath, his whole body shaking with the exhaustion and the pure thrill of the long night's work. By now, the fires had spread to nearly a fourth of the city, and he could see entire houses collapsing into themselves, larger buildings, warehouses, even some of the grand homes now engulfed by the man-made hell.

It had not been long before the soldiers had swarmed the streets, and he had escaped by the strength of his legs, had run right through the grip of the troops sent to stop the chaos. There had been virtually no water, and when the soldiers could not extinguish the dozens of fires, they turned their energy instead to revenge. Troops began to round up anyone they could find in the street, and Hale had seen one screaming man simply thrown into a burning house, the rage of the soldiers building into their own inferno no officer could control.

He had been able to set a dozen or more of his own fires, and from the time that had passed, he knew the troops had not been mobilized with any kind of efficiency. As the fires had spread, there had been no general alarm, the soldiers only called out by word of mouth. In every church steeple, the bells were long gone, melted down by Washington's army for the critical supply of musket balls.

It was nearly dawn, and still he watched, could tell that many of the fires had begun to die away. The wind had shifted, and he cursed that one piece of bad fortune. He had thought the entire city would burn, but now he could see that many of the steeples and taller buildings were still intact, the flames all centered in only one part of the city. But it was a massive area of destruction, and no matter what happened, the British had lost a large part of their comfortable winter quarters. And more, even General Howe would know that right there in the city, in dark alleys and crumbling shacks, there were rebels who could still bring their war straight into the heart of his own headquarters.

Hale turned to the east, the sunlight just beginning to break over Long Island, dim gray light in the empty road. He began to move down from the hill, stared northward toward Harlem Heights, still several miles in front of him, and every route blocked by the British. Before the fires, he had made some notes, maps, descriptions of those British fortifications he could see up close. The location of Howe's headquarters was no secret in the city, and the position of the British cannon was simple to diagram, as was the largest gathering of troop barracks and tents. But with the spread of the fire, all of that seemed insignificant. But he still had his orders, thought, It is not up to me to decide what is important. General Washington will expect a report.

He felt his pocket, still had the diploma, his one piece of documentation, but he had no confidence now, his masquerade as a schoolmaster would mean nothing, not after the great fire. The British would round up every man who they could not label as a known Tory.

He thought of just hiding out, but he didn't know the land, and any farmer who saw him would likely report him. There would be no friends out here, not this close to the British camps. And, on the river, the British patrol ships would stop and inspect every boat, probably stop the waterway traffic altogether.

He still walked northward, felt the chill of the early morning, could smell smoke on his clothes. Well, they'll know where I've been. But still, I'm only a schoolmaster. He could see men now beside the road, moved closer to them, the road blocked, guards milling around a small stone building. He saw a crude wood sign, The Cedar's Tavern, could see that the men were standing, watching him. Now they stepped into the road, and one man said, "Hold there, sir. What is your business here?"

Hale scanned the uniforms, tried to appear dazed, unsteady, said, "I'm a schoolmaster. My home has been burned. I have nowhere to go."

The soldiers moved closer to him, one man now behind him.

"Yes, quite a shame. The army will do what it can for the citizens. You should go back to the city. There's nothing for you out here."

Another man emerged from the tavern, and Hale could see the uniform of an officer. The man smelled of an odd perfume, leaned close to Hale, said, "Look at me, sir."

Hale lifted his head, looked at the officer, saw a grim unsmiling glare. The man kept his stare deep into Hale's eyes, said, "Remove his shoes."

Hale felt his heart turn over in his chest, and there was a bayonet now, pointed at his gut. He sat down in the road, pulled his shoes off, thick mud caked on his hands.

The officer pointed, and one man picked up a shoe, peered inside, turned it over, impaled it sideways on the bayonet. The sole split, and Hale closed his eyes as a folded piece of paper fell to the ground. He lowered his head, heard the officer say, "Hand me that."

There was a quiet moment, and Hale sat with his eyes closed, knew the man was reading his report, his diagrams and sketches. The officer said, "Gentlemen, remember this. Always check the shoes. This is how spies carry their information. Pick him up."

Hale felt hands under his arms, stood now, and the officer said, "Take him to General Robertson. This will certainly provide him some amusement."

THEY HELD HIM IN A GREENHOUSE BESIDE AN EXTRAORDINARY home known as the Beekman mansion. It was General Howe's headquarters.

He sat barefoot on the hard ground, surrounded by the smells of the fire. He knew they had been talking about him behind the glass door, could see several officers come and go, many looking in on him, more than just curiosity. He tried to be polite, managed a faint smile, but the smiles were not returned. They had taken his diploma from his coat, his one official document, and it was the one piece of hope, that he was, after all, just a schoolmaster. There was no evidence at all to connect him to the army.

The door opened again, and two guards came in, bayonets pointed down at him, and behind them, an older man in a powdered wig. He had already been introduced to General Robertson.

"Stand up, Mr. Hale. If that is your name. Actually, we're about to determine that fact."

Robertson motioned for him to follow, and Hale obeyed, moved between the guards into a small room, saw another man, younger, much shorter, the face familiar, but the British uniform a surprise. Robertson said, "Young man, this is Samuel Hale, General Howe's deputy commissioner of prisoners. But, I don't need to introduce him to you, I'm sure." Robertson said to the other man, "Well?"

Hale avoided the eyes of the shorter man, who moved close to him now, reached up, pulled at Hale's collar.

"Yes, sir. The birthmark, same as I remember. This is my cousin, Nathan Hale. That is, *Captain* Nathan Hale, of the Nineteenth Connecticut Regiment, of the Continental Army."

Hale felt his breath drain from him, could still not look at his cousin's face. Robertson said, "Thank you, Commissioner. You may return to your post."

Robertson looked closely at Hale now, said, "Well, now. Your diploma is genuine. Most impressive."

Robertson moved away, motioned to the guards, said, "Bring him."

Hale felt a hand on his back, had no strength, his legs moving with slow unsteady motion. He climbed some stairs, did not look ahead, did not care where he was being led. A door opened, and he was surprised by the sudden aroma of food. His stomach began to ache, and Robertson said to the guards, "Hold him here."

Robertson was gone, and Hale tried to see the food, thought, Perhaps they will feed me. But the door opened, again, and Robertson was back, and another man, round, thick-faced, but no uniform, the man dressed in a robe, gold slippers beneath a long nightgown. The man was clearly annoyed, said, "This is him? Not much to look at. I had rather expected someone with a bit more . . . flair."

The man shuffled around behind him, then said, "So, tell me, young Mr. Hale. Did Mr. Washington send you here with instructions to burn this city?"

Hale said nothing, and Robertson said, "Mr. Hale, you will respond to General Howe."

Hale was stunned, looked at the heavy man, stared at Howe's disheveled dress. Howe scowled at him, said, "Rudeness is typical of rebels. I do not please you in my current state of attire? Well, I would add, Mr. Hale, that you do not please me by interrupting my morning repose. Have you no response to my question?"

Hale forced himself to stare straight ahead, said, "No, sir. You have all the information you require. My identity is known to you."

Howe moved away toward the door, said, "Yes, indeed. That it is." He pulled the door open, stopped, looked back toward Robertson now, said, "Hang him."

SEPTEMBER 22, 1776

He sat in the tent of John Montresor, a pleasant, somewhat formal man. Montresor was the chief engineering officer for the British army in America, but only carried the rank of captain, something that had made Hale curious. There was little conversation between the men, but Hale appreciated the man's graciousness, the engineer's tent situated by chance close to the ground where the executions were said to be held. Hale had been escorted on foot to the place, his feet still bare, a sweltering hot day. He was surprised when Montresor had given the order for the guards to bring Hale into the tent.

Hale had asked for some paper, and was surprised that Montresor accommodated him, providing a pen as well. The engineer had watched him as Hale wrote two letters, and Hale could not help noticing the sadness in the man's face. Hale didn't know how to react to that, there was no reason to beg anyone for mercy.

Montresor was watching him still as Hale completed the last letter, to his brother. Hale put the pen down, sat back in the chair, stared at the papers on the small table Montresor had allowed him to use. He had no way of knowing if the British would actually send the letters, if such a courtesy would be granted a spy. But he was encouraged by Montresor's manner, the man showing none of the arrogant hostility of the other officers.

"You attended Yale College, I am told."

"Yes."

"Fine school. Unusual to meet someone in your, um, profession who understands books."

Montresor seemed uncomfortable, and Hale said, "I don't have a profession anymore, sir. I was a schoolmaster. Now, I am, I suppose, simply a prisoner."

Montresor looked down a moment, said, "You are familiar, I assume, with Homer?"

"Certainly."

"I wonder about your own odyssey, this mission of yours. I

sense something of dignity in your bearing. Yet the job requires a man to practice deceit at every turn. Is this what your cause requires of you, that you sacrifice moral principles to achieve your ends?"

"Captain, this is a war. What is moral about any duty we perform, whose outcome is the destruction of another?"

"But, Mr. Hale, you must certainly agree that in war, a well-accomplished mission is regarded with honor and celebration, even by your enemy. Yet in this business of yours, capture means death. That very penalty suggests that a spy is regarded with disdain on either side. To a man of honor, especially a soldier . . . well, I am at a loss, Mr. Hale. As soldiers, our place is on the field."

"I'm sorry, Captain. But my place is where my nation requires my service. I had a mission to fulfill."

"Is that important now, Mr. Hale? Clearly you did not succeed. I wonder what would have happened if you had. Do you believe you would have won the war for General Washington? Was it so important that you accomplish this mission?"

"Those are two different questions, sir. I doubt my actions would win any war. And, yes, it was important that I do this. I joined General Washington's army because I wanted to be . . . useful."

"Then you are a tragic figure, Mr. Hale. You will die for no good purpose." He paused, and Hale could see a sadness in the man's eyes. "Schoolmaster. There is honor in that, Mr. Hale. If not for this war, you would have had a good life, no doubt. You are an educated man, in a profession where books do not matter. How terribly sad. I regret that you should come to this end. You should not be remembered as a failure."

Hale thought a moment. "How I am remembered will likely be decided by your army, sir. If you have the conscience to bury me in a forgotten grave and give my passing no mention, then, Captain, I will have failed indeed. But only because General Washington will not know that I performed my duty."

Hale heard a voice outside, and Montresor stood, moved to the opening in the tent, said something, looked back toward Hale. Hale did not need to be told. He stood, moved to the opening of the tent.

Outside, the man who had led him across the open ground was

waiting impatiently. Hale had come to know the man as Cunningham, the provost marshal, the man whose duties included the disposition of condemned prisoners. He was a big, grotesque man, spoke in a rough voice, a crude accent Hale could not place. The man's uniform was merely a huge black ill-fitting coat, his arms extending below the sleeves. He grabbed Hale by the shirt, pulled him forward, spun him around, and Montresor said, "That is hardly necessary, Marshal. He will not resist you."

Cunningham ignored him, and Hale's hands were clamped together behind his back. He felt Cunningham's hard grip, wrapping something around his wrists, the man's rum-soaked breath engulfing him. He spun Hale around, faced him, and Hale saw the man's hideous smile. Cunningham said, "There you go, now, rebel. All snug."

Hale glanced at Montresor, who was looking away, the sadness obvious on the man's face. Hale said, "I would request a clergyman, sir."

Montresor looked at Cunningham, a short questioning nod, but Hale could see that Montresor had no authority. Cunningham made a small grunt, said, "Pray to the devil, rebel."

The guards were there now, and Cunningham grabbed Hale's collar, pulled him roughly away from the tent, Hale stumbling as the big man dragged him. He tried to work his legs, noticed a wagon parked beside an old stout apple tree. Beside the wagon was a shallow hole, fresh earth, and a wooden coffin.

He had no air in his lungs, felt his legs give way again, but Cunningham held him up, the guards close behind him. Suddenly he was pulled up into the wagon, the hard wood rocking beneath him. He found his balance, straightened his legs, could see out now, an artillery park, rows of cannon, more wagons. There were a few soldiers gathering, and a small group of civilians. Now he saw children, running out across the open ground, some sort of game, the children oblivious to him, to what this all meant. He said again, "A clergyman . . ." but the rope was over his head now, Cunningham tightening it roughly on his throat, the words choked away. He tried to say a prayer, could not be angry at Cunningham, the man doing his job. There is no evil in that. Hale looked at the faces watching him, most of them expressionless, some turning away, and he saw Montresor, the only emotion he could see, the sadness etched hard in the engineer's face. He wanted to talk to the man again, wished there had been more time, something intriguing, an educated, civilized man, serving in the uncivilized hell of war. But it is what we must do, it is the time we live in. He remembered the meeting with Washington, and Colonel Knowlton, the importance, the seriousness, the commander in chief speaking to him with such quiet respect. He had kept that moment with him, Washington's concern, the weight of all of this on the man's shoulders, all of the war, all that this could mean. I *have* been a small part of it. I hope that somehow he will know that. I hope he will understand. I may have failed my mission, but I was some small part. I was . . . *useful*.

He tried to turn his head, but the rope rubbed him hard. He could only see Montresor, wondered why the man still watched him, realized, perhaps he has to. There is something in the man that will keep him here, some need for penance perhaps, that will make him see this. Thank you, sir.

Behind him, Cunningham said something, and Hale felt the wagon lurch slightly, the floorboards tilting beneath him. The rope was suddenly looser, and he took a long breath, looked again at Montresor, summoned the energy, the voice, said, "I only regret . . . that I have but one life . . . to lose for my country."

ON HARLEM HEIGHTS, THERE WAS LITTLE ACTIVITY, THE SOLDIERS at their posts, lookouts scanning the horizon across the plain below them. They had seen the flag of truce, the small parade of British horsemen, and Washington had sent Putnam to receive it. The officer who led the party was an engineer, John Montresor, a name vaguely familiar to Washington. Montresor had brought a letter from General Howe, a protest about some brutality from the rebel soldiers. But there was more meaning to the note, and the last paragraph, written as nearly an afterthought, had made it clear that Howe was telling him something more significant, a boasting of sorts. It was just a brief mention that a spy had been hanged, a man with a diploma in his pocket from Yale College.

Washington revealed nothing to his staff, folded the note away, moved out on the point of rocks, could see far to the south, where clouds of black smoke still rose over New York, where fires still burned in the wreckage of a quarter of the city. He glanced behind him, wasn't sure if Putnam was still there, looked again toward the south, said quietly, "It seems that Providence, or some good honest fellow, has done more for us than we could do for ourselves."

9. CORNWALLIS

HOWE HAD FINALLY ORDERED A LINE OF TROOPS TO PUSH ACROSS Manhattan Island, a tight seal to keep the rebels pinned on Harlem Heights. There had been one minor engagement near the rebel position, a place near the Hudson River called the Hollow Way. It was not part of Howe's instructions, but the response to a rebel patrol sent down into the plain beneath the Heights to determine where the British main lines might be positioned. The patrol was successful, and found themselves confronting the British Forty-second Highlanders, one of the most historic units in King George's army. The Highlanders were also known as the Black Watch, and brought into battle a reputation for brutal efficiency. Dressed in the kilts and tartan of their ancestors, and driven forward by a rolling cascade of bagpipe music, the Highlanders responded to the sudden encounter with the rebels by making an advance of their own, and the rebels, who were outnumbered, wisely withdrew. But Washington made use of the aggressiveness of the British. In quick response, he sent out another, larger force, Knowlton's Rangers and a company of Virginia riflemen. The intent was to flank and possibly surround the British, who had remained out in front, separated from Howe's main force. Despite a brief and brisk action, there was little positive result for either side, and when the Highlanders were reinforced by a company of Hessian reserves, the rebels retreated to their fortifications at Harlem Heights. The official report that reached Howe's headquarters indicated that among the casualties, two rebel officers had been killed, one of them the man who had founded the elite squad of Rangers, Colonel Thomas Knowlton.

OCTOBER 11, 1776

To the British, the skirmish with the Highlanders had seemed to remove any inclination the rebels had to leave the safety of their defenses, and beyond the occasional raid of some farmhouse, Cornwallis had heard nothing of any rebel movement at all.

He rode now through McGown's Pass, the tall rocks and narrow trails now the geographical center of the British line. The staff followed in single file, and Cornwallis tried to ignore their nervousness, men not accustomed to riding close to the front lines, some of them searching the rough ground to the north for the chance encounter with a rebel marksman.

He had been to a farmhouse, a low flat building bordered by an apple orchard, that served now as one of the many reconnaissance posts. The house had been owned by a man known to be sympathetic to the rebel cause, and the heavy front door had been branded with a crude letter *"R."* It was the custom now for the loyalist civilians to brand their traitorous neighbors. Once the British had completed their occupation of New York, the loyalists had been positively gleeful about identifying those citizens whose sympathies might lie with the rebels. Scattered through those sections of the city unaffected by the fire, many houses and storefronts were marked by the insignia. To the army, especially the Hessians, the carved letter was an open invitation to plunder. Most rebel sympathizers were long gone from the island, and the army occupied nearly every home that still supported a roof. But to the north of the city, in the open farm country, Cornwallis knew it was simply good fortune that some of these abandoned houses now provided the British lookouts with a view toward Harlem Heights.

What the British command did not anticipate was that the visible outposts would attract rebel deserters, and they came down from the Heights nearly every night. That morning Cornwallis had interviewed yet another group, dirty men with filthy clothing. Though he had occasionally seen some semblance of uniforms on distant rebel units, most of these men wore nothing to show they ever had been soldiers. The interviews were usually performed by a company commander, a job appropriate for an officer of lower rank. But Cornwallis enjoyed it, had come to appreciate the differences between the mind of the British soldier, and the rebels who opposed them. Besides the entertainment it gave him, he understood that his presence might actually result in an even greater willingness for the deserter to talk, most of them now desperately eager to please. He knew better than to believe all their expressions of newfound loyalty to the king, especially those who professed an immediate need to join the British army. Washington certainly would try to infiltrate the British lines, and Cornwallis considered it a challenging game to identify those deserters who were more likely just spies. It was not difficult for him to distinguish those rebels who brought a genuine desperation, hunger, sickness, and Cornwallis knew they would have no inhibitions about talking to their new benefactors. He knew it was the best chance for some piece of good intelligence, something significant that the deserters might not even recognize in their own rambling tales. The soldiers had been instructed to welcome the deserters as friends, to see to their needs, which usually meant only a simple meal, or a warm blanket. This morning's lot had been typical: talk of despair, how vast numbers of Washington's forces were simply giving up and going home, some militia units in open defiance, officers marching their men right out of camp, across the King's Bridge northward, insisting the war was over, that any opposition to the British army had been proven futile.

The group this morning had been typical in another way as well, something he had seen with growing frequency. There was no guilt in the men, no sense that they were betraying anything. The stories had become less sensational and more matter-of-fact. These men were through being soldiers, had endured just enough of the horror and the deprivations of war to believe that whatever the cause, the politics, the dispute with the king, the cause was not as important as their own discomfort. Cornwallis had not been surprised. He did not know what Washington's camp was like, of course, and the deserters would bring their own very biased version, but surely the message was clear. We are still the empire. We are Britain, we are centuries of history, and we are the mightiest army in the world. And you are part of a band of rebels who would presume to drive the empire away. With what? They cannot even feed you properly, arm you properly, put you into proper clothing. No, before too much longer, Mr. Washington may find he has no one left in his camp at all.

He moved the horse down a narrow gorge, saw scraps of clothing, a shattered musket, signs of the brief fight in McGown's
Pass that had once held Howe's men back. On that day, they escaped us a second time. And, now, once again, Mr. Washington
sits in his defenses and wonders why we do not complete the job.

He moved past the fresh earthworks, men suddenly appearing
from behind barricades of wood and rock, snapping to attention
when he passed. He did not look at them, knew their hopeful expressions by heart, good troops waiting impatiently for another
opportunity, and no one sure just when General Howe would
give it to them.

The sharp skirmish at the Hollow Way had resulted in ninety
casualties to the British, and Cornwallis had considered that a
prelude of what was surely to come. He had examined the
ground in front of the Heights, already preparing his own men
for the sequel, finding some way to draw a greater number of
Washington's men into another fight. A direct assault on the
Heights would have been foolish, perhaps, certainly costly. But
the rebels had shown little ability to stand up to any general engagement, whether or not they were behind fortifications. But
Cornwallis' preparations were suddenly stopped. Back at headquarters, Howe had responded to the results of the Hollow Way
skirmish very differently, and his orders had stunned Cornwallis, as they stunned nearly every officer in the army. Instead of
preparing for any kind of general assault, the British would build
a heavy line of fortifications all across Manhattan Island. They
would prepare a defensive line against a much smaller force that
had shown no intention of leaving their hill.

Cornwallis had naturally gone to Clinton, had heard the man's
rage yet again. Both men knew that Howe might never erase the
image of Breed's Hill as he formed his strategies. Every assault
against a rebel hilltop would provoke the memories of a victory
dearly bought and a lengthy casualty list that would stick hard in
the throats of London.

The soldiers along the line accepted their new orders with the
same resignation they had shown at Brooklyn. If they could not
attack their enemy, they would instead make good use of the
shovel and the axe. The work had gone quickly, the men driven
by the incentive that the order might still come at any time, to
form and be ready, to march and advance beyond their own new

defenses. But days became weeks, and no order had come. Cornwallis had gone to headquarters more than once, had become practiced at holding in his impatience. More often now he found Howe to be simply unavailable, his staff whispering indiscreet comments about the effects of the general's mistress. For more than three weeks, Howe had seemed content to keep his army in place, while Washington's vastly outnumbered army dressed its wounds.

Cornwallis rode clear of the fortifications, and the road leveled out, the rocks giving way to a flat hillside. Up ahead he could see a group of officers gathered at a narrow crossroad. They saw him and began to move their horses into line, official respect. He scanned the faces, several younger men, and the senior man, Alexander Leslie, the brigadier who had commanded the skirmish below Harlem Heights.

Leslie was slightly younger than Cornwallis, had served the army in nearly every major action of the war, was by anyone's estimate a capable and disciplined officer. Like Cornwallis, he was a sober man, not taken with the vices often available around the headquarters of most senior commanders. Cornwallis had tried to be less formal with Leslie, saw something in the man that could lead to friendship, but Leslie often seemed unapproachable, inflexible, adhering to protocol with the stiffness of a man whose uniform is too tight.

Cornwallis rode close, the line of men holding their horses in a rigid salute. He looked at Leslie, said, "Is there a problem here, General?"

Leslie seemed perplexed by the question, and responded, "By no means, sir. We were discussing the disposition of the artillery. As you know, sir, General Lord Percy will remain in command of this position, and once we are on the flatboats . . ."

"Flatboats?" The word jabbed at Cornwallis like a sword. "What flatboats?" His voice had cracked with the surprise, and Leslie seemed suddenly embarrassed for him, looked away for a moment, the other officers taking the cue, looking away as well. Cornwallis took a long breath, thought, Decorum, man. They need not know your every thought.

"General Leslie, allow me to repeat my question. Have you been ordered to make a crossing . . . somewhere?"

Leslie seemed uncertain how to respond, cleared his throat,

said, "The order came this morning, sir. General Howe . . . oh, dear me. Were you not informed? This is highly . . . it is not seemly for a junior officer to convey orders to his senior. I'm not at all certain what I should do . . ."

"Good God, General, just tell me where you're going. I've been out on the line all morning, questioning deserters. What orders?"

Cornwallis' explanation seemed to soothe the man, and Leslie said, "Oh, quite, sir. Yes, that would explain . . . Orders, sir, to board the flatboats in the East River. Lord Percy is to remain in command here, while the army makes the journey to the Throg's Neck. The orders are from General Howe, of course, sir." Leslie's discomfort seemed to return, and Cornwallis held up a hand, said, "All right, General. Don't trouble yourself further. I will go to headquarters immediately. Thank you for the information. You did nothing untoward. I am quite certain that as we speak, one of General Howe's couriers has been sent to find me out in this wilderness. As long as I remain near the advance lines, he will likely confine his search to whatever tavern he may find, until he can deliver his dispatch in safety."

He moved the horse, the staff coming alive behind him, then turned to Leslie again, ignored the grateful relief on the man's face.

"If you don't mind my asking, General, what the devil is a *throg's neck?*"

IT IS TIME, GENTLEMEN! WE HAVE THE REBELS EXACTLY WHERE WE wish them to be, and our only job now is to round them up! Rather like draining the water from a container of live fish. There lies Mr. Washington, ingloriously flopping about!"

There was laughter now, and Howe basked in the attention, a quick glance to the servants and staff. They began to laugh as well, as ordered. It was a grand party, the headquarters crowded with the brightest lights of loyalist New York. The banquet table was spread with every manner of treat that could be procured, the servants slipping in and out discreetly removing the rapidly emptying platters, bottles of wine flowing into a sea of glasses.

Howe moved around the table, and Cornwallis backed up a step, allowed him to pass, caught the smell of perfume, not all of it belonging to Howe. In one corner stood the plump blond woman who had been Howe's greatest priority in New York, and Cornwallis was used to her now, even the jokes about Mrs. Loring becoming stale. It was obvious to Cornwallis, if not to the entire senior command, that Howe was going to enjoy his dalliance no matter what anyone said, and no matter what military matters might arise. The war would not end without General Howe, and the commanders now understood, it would be General Howe who would decide *when*.

Howe took Mrs. Loring's hand, made a great show of kissing her white glove, and Cornwallis could not help thinking of her husband. What kind of man . . . he wiped the question away. He already knew the answer. Loring must certainly have sought some position requiring some level of prestige and no real work. Howe had promoted the man to be his commissioner of prisoners, a rather uncomplicated job that produced a reasonable salary. In his gratitude, all Loring had to do was ignore the behavior and the whereabouts of his wife. Howe returned to the table, poked among the sliced meats, and Cornwallis thought, A happy man. Well, of course. He has an accommodating woman, a jolly audience. And finally he has a plan.

Howe allowed the noisy commotion in the room to grow quiet, and the audience seemed to understand he was ready to speak again. He waited a last silent moment, dramatic effect, said, "Once we have burst upon the rear of the rebel position, it will be as wrapping them up in a bright red ribbon. It is quite likely that we shall not have to fire a shot!" Howe looked at Cornwallis, a knowing glance, said, "According to everything we are hearing from the deserters, there aren't but a handful of muskets left on that infernal hill anyway!"

Cornwallis was surprised, nodded to Howe, acknowledged the reference, a brief show of appreciation. Until that moment, he had no idea if his reports had actually been read at headquarters. Interviews with deserters could hardly compete with the festive social scene. Howe seemed to grow serious now, said, "Good citizens, as my fellow officers will attest, in the army, we have an instinct about these things. Frankly, this command was reluctant to inflict unnecessary losses on its own gallant soldiers. There had to be a strategy that would cause the rebels to submit, without the tragedy of so much loss of life. On *either* side, I might add."

Cornwallis let the words flow by him, knew he was caught in Howe's web, that Howe would use the festivity as a stage. Of course, he·will make a good show of kind sympathy to the rebels, their wives and children. We will fight and win a war and no one must suffer. He glanced around the room, saw several of the grand society ladies hanging attentively on Howe's every word. He looked for Clinton, was surprised to see that the man was gone, had slipped out of the room. Not wise, General. He looked toward Howe again, a glass of wine raised, yet another toast, the wine disappearing. Well, no matter. Tonight is not about strategy anyway, it is about good wine and accommodating women. Regrettably, General Howe, neither of those is sufficient cause for me to lose sleep.

He began to slip past some of the other officers, no one noticing, thought of Clinton again. He will have some particular view of this plan, certainly. And, before too much longer, we will all know if, this time, General Howe can outwit Mr. Washington.

OCTOBER 12, 1776

He had studied the maps, now knew exactly where Throg's Neck was, and why it was valuable to the army. The flatboats would carry most of the men northward, up the East River, then navigate through the treacherous swirling waters of Hell Gate, moving east into Long Island Sound. Throg's Neck was a spit of land that jutted southward into the Sound, and the maps showed it to be a convenient landing place for the troops. Once ashore, the march would begin northward, with the intention of cutting Washington's army off from their supply lines to New England. Once Washington realized that Howe's army was not only facing him on Harlem Heights, but was encircling him from behind, there would simply be no escape. Howe's plan might indeed work.

THE HELL GATE PASSAGE WAS APTLY NAMED, A TREACHEROUS, swirling confluence of channels, and as the flatboats bobbed and twisted their way through, one was ripped to timbers, sweeping terrified soldiers toward the rocky shoreline. Several had drowned, but most were rescued, only to board another boat to make the journey again. It was nearly miraculous that there had

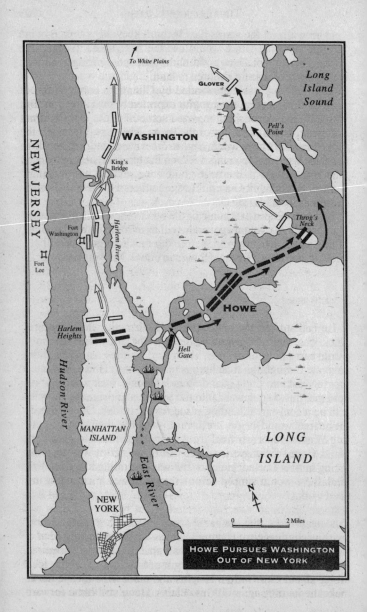

To White Plains

GLOVER

Long Island Sound

WASHINGTON

Pell's Point

King's Bridge

NEW JERSEY

Fort Washington

Harlem River

Throg's Neck

Fort Lee

HOWE

Harlem Heights

Hell Gate

MANHATTAN ISLAND

Hudson River

LONG ISLAND

East River

NEW YORK

N

0   1   2 Miles

HOWE PURSUES WASHINGTON
OUT OF NEW YORK

not been more loss, a testament to the skill of the sailors. By nine in the morning, nearly five thousand troops had reached the calmer waters off Throg's Neck, the flatboats holding at anchor, awaiting the order for the men to land.

The landing was commanded by Clinton, a combination of British and Hessian troops who expected little opposition. But the advance skirmishers reported something the maps had not shown. Throg's Neck was actually an island, and to reach the mainland, the troops would have to cross a wooden bridge, which passed over a watery marsh. When the skirmishers approached the bridge, they came under rebel musket fire, the mainland crawling with marksmen, a thick line of dirt and rocks thrown together as fortification. The bridge itself was of almost no use. The rebels had removed the planking. When Clinton received news of the setback, he ordered the entire column to halt. It was, after all, Howe's plan. Howe would have to decide what to do next.

The maps showed another landing area, farther to the northeast, called Pell's Point. But before the army could make their way to the flatboats, it began to rain, a hard, wind-driven storm that brought everything to a halt. The weather did not improve for the rest of the day, and Howe knew that he could not have so many troops unprotected against the elements. So he ordered them into shelter. Tents were landed, and Throg's Neck became a British camp.

To the dismay of Clinton and Cornwallis, Howe would not move the army by water as long as Long Island Sound was churned by the storms and blustery winds. For six days the British remained in their tents, waiting for the order to move to Pell's Point.

When the weather finally cleared to Howe's satisfaction, the army began the short journey, reinforced now by most of the units on Manhattan. Howe landed twenty thousand men on Pell's Point. As they advanced inland, they were not impeded by any marsh, but by the regiment of John Glover, the Marblehead fisherman. The land was farm country, cut by stone fences and hedgerows, and Glover backed away from the British advance with perfect precision, keeping Howe's army from any kind of orderly march. The delay was all that Washington required. Howe had given Washington the gift of time, and the entire rebel force abandoned Harlem Heights and made their escape northward to the hills around White Plains. Howe still came forward,

and confronted as much of Washington's force as he could find,
but Washington stayed away from a general engagement, withdrew from field to hill, and finally placed his army on another
stretch of high ground that only Howe seemed to fear. Instead of
pressing what might be a costly attack, Howe ordered his aston-
ished officers to turn the army around and march back to the flatboats. Cornwallis held tight to his frustration, and obeyed
Howe's orders. He recognized that there might be one bright spot
in Howe's amazing and puzzling strategy. There was still one
body of rebel troops on Manhattan Island, one strong outpost
protected by the high cliffs west of Harlem Heights, overlooking
the Hudson River. Above rugged, nearly impassable terrain, the
rebels had constructed a fortress, called Fort Washington. It was
the only place on the island that rebel forces still occupied, and it
was a significant position that Howe could not ignore. If the British were to retreat from White Plains, there would be no shame.
Howe could justify the move by planning the immediate capture
of the rebel stronghold. But Cornwallis understood, no matter
how much Howe tried to build enthusiasm for the new plan,
Washington had escaped again.

10. GREENE

NOVEMBER 6, 1776

AN ENORMOUS LUXURY HAD COME TO WASHINGTON'S ARMY IN THE
form of prisoners of war, captured in the various engagements
from Brooklyn to White Plains. As the numbers of these prisoners increased, so too had their rank. As Howe returned his troops
to their posts around New York, negotiations had begun, and
customary to the rules of war, officers had been exchanged. The
luxury resulted in the return to Washington's army of the two senior commanders captured on Long Island, Generals Sullivan
and Stirling. At nearly the same time, word had come to head-

quarters of another blessing, a piece of news whose effect was an immediate boost to the morale of the army. From his triumph in South Carolina, General Charles Lee had made the journey northward, and once again, was in place beside Washington as his second in command.

From the first organization of the army around Boston, Lee was seen as the one shining professional in an army of amateurs. Though Washington's appointment as commander in chief had seemed entirely appropriate, given his experience and his prominence in the key colony of Virginia, many were quietly relieved that congress had shown its true wisdom by appointing Lee as Washington's immediate subordinate. But to Greene, all the noise about Lee's prowess seemed to come more from Lee's opinion of himself than anything he had accomplished in the field. To many in the army, Lee's prestige was greatly increased by the victory at Charleston. But from most of what Greene had heard from the troops who had been there, Lee's great triumph belonged much more to the men who served under him.

Lee was by birth an Englishman, had served in the British army, reaching the rank of lieutenant colonel. When the French and Indian War concluded, so too did the need for a great many British officers, and Lee lost his command. Always one to seek adventure, Lee found it by traveling to Poland and so impressed the Polish king that he was promoted to major general in the Polish army. After his return to England, Lee's outspoken criticism of King George made life somewhat dangerous for him, and he followed up his words with actions, sailing to America. Though sentiment still favored Washington as the commander, many in the army and in the congress believed that Charles Lee was the finest military mind in the American cause. Now, Lee was back where so many claimed he could be put to the best use.

With Howe bringing his army back into New York, Washington could only guess where the British would move next. As long as Washington kept his troops out of harm's way and focused on a strong defense, Howe would not likely seek any direct assault. But the British could not be expected to sit quietly for long, and so Washington divided his army into four parts, each charged with the protection of a vital route out of New York. Lee would remain around White Plains with the largest force, nearly seven thousand men, guarding against any land assault toward New

England. General William Heath would command three thousand men at the Hudson River Highlands, an easily defended position about thirty miles above Manhattan, in the event the British navy attempted a strong push upriver. Washington himself would bring two thousand men southward into New Jersey, guarding against the rumored invasion of that state, which would provide Howe an open road to Philadelphia. The last position was the one already manned by the troops still in Manhattan, the seemingly impregnable fortress of Fort Washington. Immediately across the Hudson, on the New Jersey side, the army had constructed another fort, which Washington ordered to be named Fort Lee, in honor of the return of the general. The two forts faced each other across the wide river, were manned by nearly four thousand troops, and were both under the command of Nathanael Greene.

GREENE REMAINED MOSTLY ON THE WEST SIDE OF THE RIVER, would travel across to Fort Washington for meetings with the senior officers there. The only activity around the fort was the further construction of redoubts and earthworks along the high cliffs and rocky highlands of northern Manhattan Island, in a widening arc around the fort itself. The work was in the hands of Fort Washington's senior officer, Colonel Robert Magaw, a crusty Pennsylvanian, who brought a homespun sense of discipline to his command. Magaw had come from the rugged wilderness near Carlisle, but his background was not military at all. His crudeness masked his formal education, and he was what many referred to as a country lawyer.

The work around Fort Washington was an attempt to make a strong position much stronger, the cliffs, deep ravines, and swampy bottomlands providing a formidable barrier to any assault. Greene had observed some of the work himself, dirt piled on rock, stout branches sharpened and wedged into tight crevasses, the work performed by men whose energy was boosted by their confidence in the strength of their position.

It was midday, and he was returning to Fort Lee, full of the same confidence he had seen in Magaw and his men. As the small boat slid across the slow current, he could see British warships far to the south, anchored in line out from the city itself, an unnecessary wall of strength against the foolishness of any move Washington's men might make down the Hudson.

The boat moved in slow lurches, the oarsmen practiced, efficient, and Greene stared at the distant row of tall masts, thought of Howe, the great assembly of British power. Would he dare to attack us here? He had imagined the awful scene, British soldiers trapped in the rocks, a staggering loss, certainly, entire lines of British troops wiped away by the withering musket fire from above, American marksmen enjoying a picnic of target practice against any force trying to reach them. He knew that many of the other commanders believed that Howe could not allow the Americans to maintain such a strong position on Manhattan, and Greene could not dismiss that, but more, he had begun to wish it so. An American victory could be a catastrophe for the British.

The small boat reached the shore, and he stepped out, looked up toward the rocks of Fort Lee, began the slow awkward climb. The crippling stiffness in his leg was an embarrassment, though almost no one noticed it anymore. He had already experienced the prejudice, that a soldier must be sound in body, and he had expected teasing about his limp from the first day he drilled with his Rhode Island regiment. The ridicule had come less from the men around him than from his own mind, that voice that even now pushed him up the hill. No one on his staff would ever ask to assist him, whether he was stepping up through sharp rocks or climbing into the saddle of his horse. He did not have to tell them to stay back, the grim determination on his face all the instruction they would need.

He reached the top of the hill, held himself still for a long moment, recovering from the climb, his chest rolling with hard breaths. He looked away, disguising the exertion, would not have his aides or worse, his troops see him in any discomfort. He scanned the face of the cliff, could see all along the edge of the sharp drop-off, where cannon had been placed in low places in the rocks, their crews milling around them, the boring routine. The lookouts slouched in their towers above him, and the only sounds were low voices, quiet conversations, and, back in the wooden huts, the work of the cooks, the rattle of tin plates already piling up for the evening meal.

He moved out to the edge of the largest rock face, his particular perch, stared across to Fort Washington. There was routine over there as well, but not the same boredom. The men would still be working in shifts, shovels and axes trading hands, hard veterans growing harder by their good work.

The troops under his command were a mix, mostly from the mid-Atlantic states, Maryland and Delaware men, along with Magaw's Pennsylvanians, and Virginia riflemen. The New England men had mostly gone north with Lee, protecting the roads into their own states. Washington had been logical about how the army had been divided, and Greene could find no fault with the overall strategy. The one fault he did find was the burst of good cheer that had welcomed the return of Charles Lee.

He had never taken to the man, knew he was the exception, and so, he had kept quiet at the meetings. So many of Washington's commanders were quick to point to the man's vast experience, showed Lee a respect bordering on worship that had always annoyed Greene like the sting of a bee trapped inside his shirt. He pictured the man now, slovenly in dress, Lee's thin skeletal face punctuated by a long hooklike nose. Greene himself was no fanatic about personal cleanliness, and no one in the camps expected a soldier, even a senior officer, to bathe more than once a week. But Greene had endured Lee's personal aroma in more than one meeting, a cloud of odor that only a dog could ignore. Lee was surrounded always by his dogs, bragged of their prowess on the hunt, though Greene never knew anyone who had seen Lee hunting anything. To Greene, the dogs were yapping mongrels whose loyalty to their master was nearly equaled by the loyalty of the troops under him. Greene had often quizzed himself about his own dislike of the man, thought, I really have nothing against dogs. And it is not the man's personal habits, the hygiene. No one wins a war based on his habits of toiletry. It is much more about his demeanor, his indiscretion, the man's willingness to harp about his superiors, always behind their backs. He finds fault with every command, every commander. He boasts still of his criticisms of King George, and Thomas Gage, and even General Howe. So, what does he say now about General Washington? Or the congress? He certainly has little use for civilian authority, or for anyone beneath his rank, whether it be I, or Sullivan, or anyone else. The man enjoys his own glow, a firefly flittering in front of a mirror. Greene sat now, rested his stiff leg on a short ledge of rock. But it is not for me to say, after all. General Washington needs experienced commanders, and there is no one who inspires this army more than Charles Lee. He glanced up-river. I am just happy that he is up *there*.

Above him, a lookout called out, and he saw the man pointing to the south, down the river. Greene stood, leaned out, could see a ship, now three, sails full of wind, moving north. The lookout waved his hat, a short cheer, "Yeee! They're comin' again!"

Greene watched the artillerymen scrambling into position, the big guns prepared, bags of powder carried forward from the storage cellars deep in the rocks.

The ships were moving in single file, and now his spyglass was there, the good work of an aide, and Greene held it up, studied for a moment, said aloud, "One frigate. The other two are not warships. Transports, perhaps."

Around him, men were gathering along the edge of the drop-off, filling in the spaces between the cannon. He looked out across the river, could see the line of brush in the channel, the tangle of masts and broken timbers that barricaded the river. Well, he thought, we'll see if this time we have done it correctly.

As he had done off the shore of Brooklyn Heights, Israel Putnam had worked out a plan to block the passage of the British ships by clogging the navigable part of the Hudson River with sunken wrecks. Various excuses had been made for the failure in the East River, and Putnam had done the work with a renewed sense of purpose. But already the British had passed through the barrier twice, and each time, Putnam had raged at his men to re-inforce and improve the barrier, added more wrecks, then cut trees, floated out and lashed to the tops of the masts. Putnam was gone now, sent by Washington to command the outposts around Philadelphia. His former duties on the Hudson now fell to Greene, and Greene appreciated Putnam's intentions, the crucial necessity of stopping the British ships from sailing upriver. If the British could move freely in the Hudson, they could sail as far as the Highlands with impunity, threatening any colonial interests along the way, from farms and supply lines to the valuable crossings that Washington would need to maintain contact with the scattered parts of his army.

The three ships were in full sail, coming closer, and he glanced back at the artillerymen, saw the officers watching him, waiting for his command to fire. The cannon could easily reach all the way to the far shore, and in Fort Washington, he knew that

Magaw's gunners would be waiting as well. If the ships were slowed down by Putnam's barrier, they could be seriously damaged by the colonial guns. If the barrier took hold of the ships and tangled them in place, the cannon would blow them apart.

No longer needing the spyglass, he leaned out on a tall spire of rock, easily able to see the open gun ports of the frigate, thought, Probably a thirty-two-gunner. The other two ships were slightly smaller, and the strategy opened up in his mind. Of course, the two transports . . . this is a test. They would not risk three warships, the loss would be too great. The transports are probably lightly manned, the crews prepared to abandon ship if necessary. Well, then, we'll see if General Putnam knows his engineering.

The frigate was within a hundred yards of the first barriers, and he could see the sails sagging slightly, the ship slowing. It was the first sign he would need. He turned, pointed to the cannon closest to him, a massive thirty-two-pounder, and the gun roared to life, a sharp blast of smoke and flame that blew out past the rocks. All down through the cliff side, the rest of the guns answered, and he flattened his hands over his ears, stared out through the smoke. Across the river, he could see sharp flashes, more smoke, the guns in Fort Washington responding, and now in the river, the water around the ships erupted in tall plumes. The soldiers along the rocks began cheering, the fight distinctly one way, and he felt their spirit, raised his fist in the air. But the mood passed, and he thought, This is too simple, too foolish. Why do they attempt this? The cannon nearest him fired again, and he caught the officer's attention, made a sign with his hands, stop, cease fire. Let's see what we've done. The guns gradually fell silent, and quickly the smoke began to clear, the same breeze that filled the British sails. The frigate had turned slightly toward him, the transports close behind. The frigate had not fired at all, and he thought, All right, there is no need for a broadside, so you will make yourself a smaller target. The ship abruptly began to tack the other way, swinging back to broadside, then turning the other direction, its bow angled toward the far shore. Now the transports began following the same course, a careful, winding route. Across the river, Magaw's guns were still firing, holes appearing in the sails, one shot cracking a mast on the frigate. But still the ships moved upriver, sliding through the barrier. The frigate was past the last of the entanglements, had cleared the obstructions, the sails filling again. It swung about defiantly broadside, resuming its course upriver. Greene turned again to the artillery officer, who was waiting for his signal. The guns came to life again, the smoke once more blocking his view of the river. He could see Putnam in his mind, the fat old man who was so very sure of himself. There was one piece of the plan that Putnam had thought so very clever: a secret route through the barricade, mapped out only for the commanders, to allow any colonial ship to negotiate safely through the barrier. Well, General Putnam, your secret is out. Somehow, by the treachery of some deserter, some spy, somehow they know. And if they can make their way safely by day, it won't take them long to do it by night. And then, we are in serious trouble.

NOVEMBER 12, 1776

If we cannot prevent vessels passing up, and the enemy are possessed of the surrounding country, what valuable purpose can it answer to attempt to hold a post from which the expected benefit cannot be had? I am therefore inclined to think that it will not be prudent to hazard the men and stores at Mount Washington, but as you are on the spot, leave it up to you to give such orders as to evacuating Mount Washington as you judge best.

Greene was grateful for the tone of Washington's orders, appreciated that Washington would not make firm decisions without knowing the situation. He had put the paper away in his small desk with a sense of pride because he knew the order meant one other thing as well. The commanding general trusted him.

The comfortable feelings had drained away quickly, and Greene knew that staying in Fort Lee put him too far away from what could become an immediate problem. He had returned to Fort Washington, met with Magaw, who continued to be confident, insisting that no British force could carry those heights, that only a protracted and costly siege could loosen their hold on that wonderful ground. Greene could not tell Magaw to withdraw, not in the face of the man's absolute certainty. But that order was Greene's to give, and he sat alone in the small house that was his office, wrestling with both sides of the question. If he stayed put, and took Magaw at his word, a British attack could cost Howe a decisive battle. If Magaw was wrong, and Fort Washington was captured, the loss to the army in men and equipment would be devastating. He could not escape Washington's order, the words deep in his mind: *as you judge best.*

It was late in the day, and he could smell food, the fires already lit. His headquarters was just inland from the works of Fort Lee, and on the roads to the west, guard posts had been set up, the perimeter manned by a skirmish line to protect against a surprise assault from behind. There had not yet been any disturbance out that way, but he heard shouts now, a surprising jolt to his thoughts. He pulled himself upright, retrieved his sword, moved slowly to the door. He heard horses, hoofbeats slowing, and the voices were close now, his aides. He opened the door, was suddenly face-to-face with a tall, dust-covered man in a blue coat. Greene could not help a smile, saw it returned, said, "My word. A surprise. General Washington, welcome to Fort Lee."

Riding quickly, Washington had come with only a small guard, his part of the army making camp around his new headquarters at Hackensack, nearly six miles away. The man's face was drawn, the dust of a long day's march covering every part of him, and Greene's aides had quickly brought a comfortable chair, one man stoking the fire in the small stone fireplace of Greene's cabin. Washington sat heavily, had barely spoken, and Greene could feel the man's exhaustion, heard the deep steady breathing. There was coffee now, and Washington accepted it gratefully, held the steaming cup in his hands, continued to stare at the fire. Greene waved the staff away, the door closing, the two men now alone, the dark room lit only by the fire. Washington set the cup down beside him, and Greene could see more than the man's weariness, the sharp blue eyes dulled by sadness. Washington said, "I expected a better reception, General."

Greene sat upright, glanced around the room, a moment of slight panic.

"I'm sorry, sir, what is wrong?"

Washington saw the look, shook his head. "No, not here. Forgive me, Mr. Greene. I had thought . . . when I began the march toward Hackensack, I was given cause for optimism. The New Jersey officials I met along the way were most insistent that their state would rise to this occasion. I was given reason to expect a gathering of fresh militia, some five thousand strong. That's the reception I refer to."

"Five thousand New Jersey militia? Did they appear, sir?"

Washington looked at the fire again, said slowly, "Two hundred fourteen."

Greene didn't know how to respond, had seen no great outpouring of fresh troop strength himself since he had been at Fort Lee.

"I have heard of no such report, sir. I would certainly have advised you."

Washington held up his hand, said, "No, not your concern, Mr. Greene. I was overly optimistic. I expected this state to respond differently than the other twelve. But there is no good reason why. The congress has made many a call for enlistments in the army, for new regiments. The response continues to be . . . minimal. I should not be surprised that expecting five thousand local militia, only two hundred appear. And, of course, three-quarters of them have no muskets." He paused, looked at Greene again, the sadness reflected in the firelight. "All we are asking them to do . . . is defend their homes. Is there such sacrifice in that?"

Greene felt strangely helpless, an eager son, trying to cheer the father.

"Sir, we have close to four thousand in the outposts here. General, you know my lack of confidence in militia. With the ground we command, militia are not necessary."

Washington sat back in the chair, closed his eyes for a brief moment, then blinked hard, said, "So, you have decided not to withdraw?"

The arguments in Greene's mind flooded over him, and he sorted his words, said, "Sir, if we withdraw, the morale of the army will be damaged severely. We would ask them to abandon weeks of work, a defensive position that might well be . . . *perfect*. The high points to the north of the fort command the King's Bridge, the artillery easily controlling the crossing. The British cannot make use of that part of the island without great inconvenience. We overlook the main road southward for two miles, our guns control all the land from the Hudson to the Harlem River, and despite the ineffectiveness of the barricade, any ship passing upriver must come under severe fire." He thought a moment, found the word. "The place is indeed, sir, a *fortress*."

He expected the word to impress Washington, saw instead no change in expression, and Washington said, "If you were General Howe, and I described to you such a place as you have just done, what would be your response?"

Greene thought a moment, felt a cold hole opening in his mind. He knew the answer already, but he didn't want to say the words. Washington tilted his head now, still questioning, waiting for him to respond.

"If I was General Howe, I would say . . ." He paused. "We cannot allow the enemy to possess such a place. We must have that ground."

Washington said nothing, looked again at the fire. Greene studied him, thought, He wants to withdraw.

"Sir, if it is your decision that we abandon Fort Washington . . ."

Washington looked at him again, shook his head, said, "What I may wish is not as important as the wishes of congress. Mr. Greene, I believe we are in a perilous situation here. But the congress believes the peril lies more in the morale of the people, the willingness of this nation to support this war. If we continue to withdraw and retreat, giving ground at every confrontation, there is no doubt in congress that this war shall end itself. We might never have the resources to make another fight, might never face the enemy in battle. The nation might simply dissolve beneath us. The message from congress is that this ground not be abandoned except in the case of the most dire emergency. There was considerable unhappiness that New York fell to the British with such ease. Many in Philadelphia wonder if their city is to be next. What do I tell them, Mr. Greene?"

He could feel a sudden weight, a piece of the responsibility that Washington carried shifting to him.

"Sir, I would ask you to visit Fort Washington. I believe you will share my confidence. We should not withdraw."

Washington did not look at him, and Greene couldn't tell what the man was thinking. Washington began to shake his head, said, "Not tonight. I will return to Hackensack, see to the camps of my men. They must be prepared to move at a moment's notice should General Howe show a sudden urge to march to Philadelphia. Once the troops are in good order, I will return. General Howe has been extremely gracious about biding his time. Perhaps he will do so again."

NOVEMBER 16, 1776

The British had done as Greene feared, had sent flatboats up past the barricades by night, landing troops north of the King's Bridge. Those troops were now protected by British frigates, anchored both north and south of the two forts. All along the high cliffs of the Hudson, and across the northern tip of Manhattan, Greene's scouts reported considerable movement from every direction, more flatboats in the Harlem River, massed columns on the march from the south, moving up from below Harlem Heights.

Washington had returned, along with Putnam, and Greene had his boat transport them across the Hudson at first light, avoiding the danger from the British frigates. They gathered now at the Morris House, a grand home abandoned by its British owner. The house stood beside the Post Road, on a bluff that overlooked the Harlem River, the house itself considered safely inside the colonial lines. Magaw had come down from Fort Washington, brought a mood that was nearly festive, but Greene knew that Washington was no longer buoyed by the confident talk. If the British were indeed moving against the colonial fortifications, Washington would see their strength for himself.

The house had been preserved with some care, surprising, considering that its owner was a British officer. The commanders actually had chairs, the furniture mostly intact, but the staffs quickly discovered the house would provide no breakfast. The pantry was quite empty.

Greene acknowledged Magaw with a solid handshake, more respectful than the typical formality. Washington waited patiently for the cordiality to pass, said, "I have been informed, Colonel Magaw, that the British have demanded the surrender of your post."

The mood was immediately somber, and Magaw's smile was gone now. He said, "Yes, sir. Yesterday, a British officer under a flag of truce delivered a letter from General Howe. It stated plainly that if we did not lay down our arms, my men would be put to the sword." He paused, and Washington seemed to wait. Greene asked, "Your response, Colonel?"

"Why, sir, as you know, I informed General Howe that I would defend this post to the last extremity." Greene could see the expression on Magaw's face, disbelief that he could have offered any other response.

Washington nodded slowly, said, "Your strength then, Colonel?"

Magaw glanced at Greene, said, "With the reinforcements sent over by General Greene, sir, we have near three thousand."

Greene caught a quick look from Washington, knew the word would stick in the commander's mind, *reinforcements*. If they were not to withdraw, Greene knew he had to strengthen Magaw's force, increase even more the commitment to hold the ground. Otherwise, there was simply too much ground to defend. Washington said slowly, "I have been hearing assurances, Colonel, that you control the strongest fortifications we have yet defended. You have stated to General Greene that you believe you can hold Fort Washington and these hills until the end of the year. Am I correct?"

"I believe so, sir." Greene was surprised to see uncertainty on Magaw's face, the confidence suddenly fading. Magaw looked down for a moment, then at Greene, and said, "However, I must report with considerable regret, sir. My adjutant, Mr. Demont . . . seems to have . . . deserted."

There was a hard silence, and Washington leaned forward and said, "Your adjutant?"

"Yes, sir." Magaw was nervous now, seemed to avoid looking at Greene, who felt a growing chill.

Greene could not hold it back, the words flowing toward Magaw with black anger. "Are you telling us, Colonel, that the man who assisted you in preparations for this defense, the man who knows well the entire arrangement of these fortifications, that this man is now in the service of the British?"

Magaw seemed resigned to the obvious, said, "Well, sir, we don't know that for certain. But he did cross through the lines. We would have to assume that General Howe would appreciate his knowledge."

Greene felt his mind clouding, all the good design, all the work, possibly swept away by one man's betrayal. Washington sat back in his chair, said nothing, the room now under a pall of silence. Greene was watching him, wanted to say something, to bring back the confidence. It was still a strong position. Demont's betrayal would not change that.

The silence was broken by a roar of sound, and the door was thrust open, staff officers appearing. "Sir! The British!"

The men were all up and outside in a quick step, and Greene could see up a long rise, a line of troops, the sudden echo of bagpipe music. In the distance there were more sounds, the rolling thunder of artillery. To the south, where Magaw's men held strong earthworks, a battle began to rise toward them, smoke and musket fire. Greene looked for Magaw, who was already moving away, and Magaw shouted toward Washington, "Sir! I shall return to the fort!"

Musket balls began to punch the ground around them, popping the side of the house, and Greene could see the Highlanders moving down the hill, not toward them but farther down, toward a line of men emerging from below. Greene could see them now, Baxter's men, Pennsylvanians, a tight line, volleys going in both directions, the ground blanketed by smoke. The Morris House was empty now, and men were pulling Washington away. Greene pointed the way, guard troops waving them on, leading the officers to a trail, which cut through the hills toward the Hudson. Greene knew his boat was waiting for them, moved up close to Washington, the sounds of the fight behind them. No one spoke, Putnam huffing his way, the other men flanking Washington, protecting him. Out in front of him, Greene could hear more big guns, the sounds blending with the fight erupting on all sides. It was the British frigates, massed broadsides fired toward Magaw's fortifications.

They reached the Hudson, and the commanders stepped quickly into the boat. Greene waited until the others were in place, looked toward the north, to the highest ground where Magaw would be. The battle was now engulfing the entire position of Magaw's men, nearly two miles of lines engaged. Greene thought of the reinforcements, Yes, thank God. But is it enough?

The boat began to move, the oarsmen calling out to him, and he stepped through soft mud, climbed in. Down the river, the British frigate was shrouded in smoke, her guns firing in a continuous wave, sharp streaks in the air, the thunder rippling the surface of water. He sat now, Washington beside him, and the boat slid away from the shore, the oarsmen working frantically. They moved out into the open water, and the scene unfolded as they moved farther away, great columns of smoke to the north, beyond the fort, a sudden burst of firing, troops meeting their enemy on a new front, the battle rolling across some new piece of ground. Washington said, "We can do no more for Colonel Magaw just now."

Greene looked up toward the fort now, the British shells bursting above, streaks of fire showering beyond the hills.

"Yes, sir. God help him."

THEY WATCHED THE FIGHT FROM THE WALLS OF FORT LEE, COULD hear the waves of sound growing tighter, the battle a compacting circle. They could see very little detail, and Greene stood beside Washington as both men used the spyglass, long moments of quiet, while around them, Greene's men sat close to their guns, staring across the river in desperate silence.

It was afternoon, and to the south the smoke had cleared away. The fight had moved north, and Greene knew that the Morris House was far behind the British advance, that Baxter's Pennsylvanians had either withdrawn toward the fort, or were gone. As the fight drew closer to the fort itself, Greene could imagine the scene, the fort filling up with retreating men, scrambling up through the rocks, jamming their way into the tight space. The reinforcements would cause their own tragedy, a horrible piece of the puzzle he had not considered. There would be too many men to fit inside.

He still looked through the spyglass, bits of motion, colors, uniforms, men climbing rocks, bursts of smoke. His eyes were swollen with fatigue, and he lowered the glass, and Washington did the same, moved away from him, sat down on the rocks. Washington held the spyglass low in one hand, said, "Dark soon. If Colonel Magaw can hold out, we can send boats over, remove the men as best we can."

There was no confidence in Washington's words, and Greene motioned to an aide, said, "Prepare an order. Instruct Colonel Magaw to keep to his guns until dark."

The man was writing furiously, and now from the lookout above them, a sharp call, "Sir!"

Washington had stood, and Greene saw the lookout pointing out to the river, saw the small boat now, oars pulling it quickly across. The progress was agonizingly slow, and Greene could do nothing but wait, saw the boat slide into shore below them, the dispatch passed to an aide, the man climbing the hill with long hard strides. Washington had watched the scene without speaking,

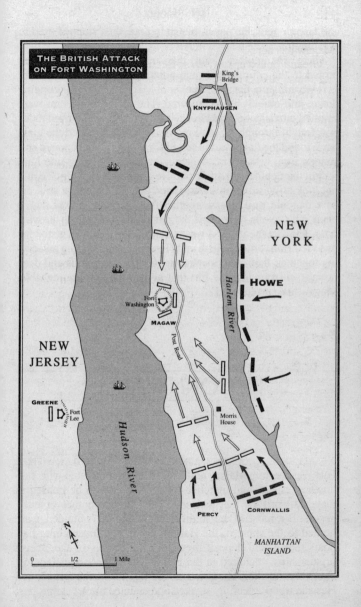

THE BRITISH ATTACK
ON FORT WASHINGTON

King's
Bridge

KNYPHAUSEN

NEW
YORK

Fort
Washington

MAGAW

Harlem River

HOWE

NEW
JERSEY

Post Road

GREENE

Fort
Lee

Morris
House

Hudson River

N

PERCY

CORNWALLIS

MANHATTAN
ISLAND

0   1/2   1 Mile

and Greene took the paper, began to read, then stopped, said to Washington, "The boats will not be necessary, sir."

There was another shout, then many more, and both men turned to the commotion, men pointing across the river. Over Fort Washington, the small flicker of Magaw's flag was dropping down, and quickly it disappeared. The men around him were stunned into silence, and Greene raised his spyglass, tried to focus, fought through the shaking in his hands, gripped the glass hard, found the flagpole. He stared for a long moment, heard soft sounds from beside him, Washington's grief digging into him, fought the tightness in his throat. He gripped the spyglass, could not look at Washington's tears, tried to hold the image still, the bare flagpole, and he saw another flicker, rising, a new flag, a blank white cloth. Now came the sounds, drifting across the wide river, and Greene knew it was cheering, the pure exhausted joy of a victorious army, British and Hessian troops singing and crying together, their voices echoing over the sharp hills and deep ravines, surrounding the fort that he had thought impregnable. Magaw had surrendered.

11. CORNWALLIS

NEARLY THREE THOUSAND PRISONERS WERE MARCHED AWAY FROM Fort Washington. Magaw and his officers were treated with customary respect, and marched toward the city, to be housed in makeshift prisons that had once been private homes or businesses. But most of the soldiers, including the wounded, were herded to the shore of the Harlem River, and loaded onto flatboats that would deposit them into the bowels of the British prison ships, anchored in the East River at Wallabout Bay. All along the fortified lines, and in the fort itself, the British and Hessian troops gleefully stacked and counted the rebel muskets, cleaned and repaired the rebel cannon, and hauled to their own camps the enormous stores of canvas, blankets, and food the rebels had surrendered.

NOVEMBER 20, 1776

He led the crossing of the Hudson River before dawn, flat-boats ferrying nearly six thousand troops to a landing place called Lower Closter, chosen for them by a local Tory farmer. They had been rowed upriver, reaching the far shore about six miles north of Fort Lee, and as he stepped ashore in gray mist, all he could see was the stark sheer wall of a cliff, looming tall above the riverbank. But the guide knew the land, and led him through a patch of dense brush that suddenly opened to a trail, narrow and tight, and nearly straight up the cliff.

Cornwallis was still not comfortable with the farmer's claims, eyed the perilous climb with skepticism, and behind him, he could hear short groans from the men, who began to see for themselves the job in front of them.

The farmer seemed not to appreciate Cornwallis' doubts, hissed at him with a sharp whisper, "This would be the only way up, General. You can follow me, or you can go back to your boats and find your own way."

Cornwallis ignored the man's impudence, thought, No, we are not returning to the boats. We are here, and we will climb. He fought the urge to give the man a warning, that any treachery would be rewarded with a Hessian bayonet. But he was in no mood for bluster or posturing. If this was the only way, then it was time to go. He glanced behind him, saw the Hessian officer who commanded the *jagers*, the troops that would lead the way, said, "Captain Ewald, you may follow Mr. Aldington." He glanced up, the daylight now showing the way, the trail a few feet wide at best, the steep ground covered with sharp rocks, an uneven road, no place for horses. Ewald moved quickly, and the Hessians began to file past, the farmer leading them up the hill. Cornwallis moved back toward the river, the flatboats still pulling ashore, more men stepping out into formation, waiting their turn to make the climb. He saw a cannon rolling up and out of one boat, the wheels set carefully on long wooden planks. The sailors held tight to the ropes, the big gun now ashore, and Cornwallis saw the blue coat of the artillery officer, said, "Major Landry, have your men retrieve those ropes. The horses must remain here until the men have reached the summit. The climb is too severe for the horses to draw the cannon. They must be pulled up by hand." Landry looked at the big gun, another one still in the boat, pulled by the sailors, and around the boat, the men were looking upward, eyeing the climb. Cornwallis knew what he was asking, said aloud, "No man will be compelled. I would ask the seamen first. You men are handy with the rope, but no order will be given. I ask instead for volunteers." He paused. "This is an important business today." It was an unusual request in an army where the men simply did what they were ordered to do. But Cornwallis would not abuse his men, knew that some were more suited for the work than others. If this day went as planned, they would need their strength.

Men glanced at each other, some still looking at the tall cliff, and some began to step forward, falling into line, Major Landry beside them, and Landry said, "General, these men are prepared for the work at hand."

Cornwallis smiled, said aloud, "Your king thanks you, gentlemen." He turned, looked up at the cliff, moved back through the brush, could see the last of the *jagers* disappearing up the trail. Hessian regulars were falling into line beside him, and he held up his hand, their officer giving the command to halt, to make way for the general. Cornwallis stepped up on a tall rock, took a long, deep breath, and began to climb.

IT WAS HIS FIRST TASTE OF INDEPENDENT COMMAND SINCE HE HAD come across the Atlantic, and for the first time, he knew that if there was delay or confusion, it would be no one's fault but his own. He had not pressed for the assignment, would not politic against anyone to secure a command. Howe had given him the mission with little fanfare, no eager congratulations on the good work Cornwallis had already accomplished. He had given up on trying to predict Howe's motives, his experience in the short months of this campaign teaching him that the general's mind worked in ways Cornwallis had never been trained to understand. But the mission was an honor nonetheless, and Cornwallis had even written Jemima, sharing his pride, knew that the daughter of a good honest soldier would understand that same pride in her husband. She knew how much his service meant to him, that his need for recognition had very little to do with the empty prestige that might come from praise from the ministry. His ambition was to win the war and return to his family. If General Howe believed that placing Cornwallis in command of a major assault would accomplish just that, it was all Cornwallis could ask for, and it had nothing to do with vanity.

This type of mission would normally have been Clinton's job, but Clinton was with the navy, on his way to Newport, Rhode Island, to capture the deepwater port, and if possible, the city of Providence. The strategy had much more to do with the simmering personality clash between Howe and Clinton than any sudden need to take control of Narragansett Bay. Clinton had been less and less discreet about his displeasure at Howe's delays, and the withdrawal from White Plains had caused an outburst that even Cornwallis could not ignore. He had endured Clinton's mutinous tirades long enough, and finally, exhausted by Clinton's disruptive complaints, he went to Howe himself, revealed Clinton's latest insubordination. Feeling betrayed by Cornwallis, Clinton spouted more anger around headquarters as to how he had been conspired against. He felt his authority had been usurped by Cornwallis' ambition to replace him, as though Cornwallis was driven by the same selfish pride as he himself. Clinton could never understand that Cornwallis had no wish to be suddenly closer to Howe's command, to have Howe looking so carefully over his shoulder. But with Clinton's departure, at least the army could operate without one of its senior commanders angrily disputing every order he received.

THE FARMER'S WORD WAS GOOD AFTER ALL, AND THE CLIMB HAD not been as difficult as he imagined. Soon the entire force was marching up the trail in good order. Once on top of the cliff, they formed again by column, marching without pause through the farm country that would lead them to Fort Lee.

His horse had been brought up, and he rode beside the Hessians, knew that out in front, Captain Ewald had the *jagers* spread all through the woods, an effective wave of skirmishers. Ewald knew to take captive anyone they found, an effort to keep word of their march from reaching Fort Lee. There were scattered farmhouses, and Cornwallis looked carefully at each one they passed for some sign that the *jagers* had gone beyond the job, the Hessian tendency toward mindless destruction, the brutalizing of any civilian. But the houses were undamaged, and there were no cries for help, no blood in the doorways. This was not a day for reprisal or plunder. The enemy was not here, but up ahead, and if the plan worked, the rebels in Fort Lee would be completely surprised by an overwhelming assault from the one place they would not expect: the one road that led inland, the only road the rebels could use for an escape route.

He saw three *jagers* moving back toward him, escorting a scowling civilian, and Cornwallis did not stop the horse, moved past the man, who cursed at him as he went by. Cornwallis smiled, ignored the man, thought, There will be much cursing by the end of this day. Just be grateful, sir, that you are not a soldier. Those Hessians might not be so gentle.

It was a reminder of something he hoped never to see again, and the smile faded. As Fort Washington fell, the Hessians were the closest to the main rebel position, had made their advance from the ground on the northernmost part of Manhattan, the most difficult terrain imaginable. They had pushed through swamps, climbed up over rocky cliffs, all the while enduring waves of musket fire and well-placed artillery from the rebel defense. The cost had been enormous, and most of Howe's casualties that day had in fact been among the Hessians. When they reached the walls of Fort Washington, and Magaw had surrendered, the exhaustion and brutality of the day gave way to revenge, and the Hessians would not recognize the white flag. The rebel prisoners were unarmed and helpless, and the Hessians had attacked them with the bayonet. It was a slaughter that had alarmed their own officers and horrified the British. Angry demands from red-coated officers had finally pushed the Hessian commanders into action, and the chaos had been brought to an end. The British had been outraged, the Hessians' officers mildly apologetic for the loss of control. Cornwallis had seen the aftermath, the rebel bodies stacked in bloody heaps, Hessian soldiers still shouting their curses at terrified prisoners.

He glanced to the side now, the rows of helmeted troops staring ahead, a mindless force, marching toward their duty. He thought of de Heister, the old Hessian general merely shrugging his shoulders when told what his men had done, his only comment, *"War turns man into beast."*

Well, perhaps. But it was a horror that would last, far beyond the emotion of that battle, of watching your own men die beside you. The British soldiers would look at their allies differently now. The Hessian soldier was simply not the same, was not taught respect for life. He looked again at the faces beside him, thought, If they fight out of fear of punishment, and not loyalty, then they still have a camaraderie that is no less powerful than our own. Even if you care nothing for generals or kings, you will come to care about the man beside you, the soldier who has shared every horror you have. And when *he* is killed, you will seek revenge. He looked ahead, another small house, more *jagers* emerging with another civilian in tow. This one was not cursing, seemed gripped by a raw terror, whimpering softly. Cornwallis looked at the man's tears, realized now, yes, the absolute fear. These people may hate us, might spit and curse at the British soldier. But they are terrified of the Hessians. The image of the slaughter at Fort Washington was still in his mind, and he felt the disgust, but something else as well. The rebels have forsaken the dignity of the civilized soldier, to fight a war befitting the savage. What the Hessians did to their prisoners is no different. If the rebels insist on waging an uncivilized war, we clearly have troops who will oblige them. Is that, after all, a bad thing?

He heard a sudden burst of musket fire, a brief chatter, could see troops in the trees ahead, Ewald's men coming together, rushing forward. There were more muskets now, but only a few, far to the front, and he turned, motioned to an aide, said, "Find Captain Ewald. I must know what they are confronting."

The man rode past him quickly, disappeared into the trees, and Cornwallis saw the face of a Hessian officer, looking at him, waiting some instruction.

"No, keep your men in column. We must not delay."

The officer nodded, and Cornwallis spurred the horse gently, moved up along the column, could hear more muskets far ahead, scattered, the trees clearing in front of him. He could see *jagers* still in motion, more of Ewald's men focusing on the direction of the firing, and now he saw a low thin cloud, just past the trees, thought, Smoke. But no, too wide, too much. It's not smoke. It's dust. It's an army on the march.

He saw his aide now, riding hard toward him, and the man

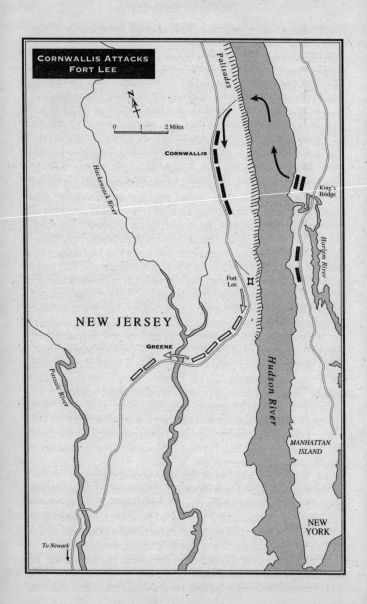

reined up, said, "General, Captain Ewald has located the rebel position! They are spread out to the west, on a road ahead. They are marching in quick order, sir. They know we are in pursuit! It has to be the garrison from Fort Lee, sir. Captain Ewald requests the army advance in strength. The enemy is not putting up a fight. The captain says he believes he can cut off their retreat!"

The man was out of breath, and Cornwallis said nothing. He reached into the pocket of his coat, retrieved the map, unfolded it. The road out of Fort Lee led southwestward, to a bridge on the Hackensack River. It was the only direction the rebels could retreat, and there was only one bridge that would allow them to escape across the river. If Ewald could move quickly enough, get to the bridge . . .

He folded the map, returned it to his coat, felt another piece of paper in his pocket, his fingers holding it for a moment. It was his orders from General Howe. He left it in his pocket, knew already what it said.

"You will advance on Fort Lee, and secure its capture."

There was no room for discretion, the orders distinct and definite, and what was not written on the paper had been made clear at his last meeting with Howe. The capture of Fort Lee was the highest priority.

The aide was staring at him, had said all he could, and Cornwallis looked up the road, more scattered musket fire, thought, No, we are not in pursuit of the enemy. We are in pursuit of a *place*.

"You will return to Captain Ewald and order him to break contact with the rebels. I do not wish him to suffer casualties. The life of one *jager* is worth more than ten of the enemy. He will follow his original instructions and advance his men only to Fort Lee."

THEY WERE CLOSE TO THE RIVER, AND THE HESSIANS HAD SPREAD into a line of battle, the response to more musket fire. But there was no force in their way, the fire coming only from scattered groups of rebels, who were quickly captured. They were stragglers from the main force, the sick and lame, or others, who for some reason of their own had stayed behind, had not marched with the rest of their army. Cornwallis ignored them, knew they were acting without orders. He focused instead on the fort itself, saw the Hessians moving past a group of small houses and huts, saw tents now, the smoke from a fire. The Hessians were quickly inside the fort, and he waited for the sounds of a fight, but there was only silence, and he knew what they had found. Nothing.

He reached the fort, his staff moving past him, but he knew there was no danger, ignored protocol, rode in with them. The Hessian officers had their men under control, the soldiers searching through rows of tents, opening wooden doors to tin huts, storerooms. There was a burst of wild laughter, and he looked out toward the river, saw a man sitting astride the barrel of a cannon, waving his hat, then falling forward, sliding to the ground. A soldier rushed toward the man, then stopped, his bayonet fixed on the man's back, but the man was still laughing, rolled over now, looked at the Hessian with wide eyes, then laughed again. The soldiers began to gather around the man, their sergeant reaching down, hauling the man to his feet. The man made a ragged salute, said, "Would you gentlemen care for a wee dram?"

The sergeant looked up at Cornwallis, who said, "Yes, quite drunk. He is harmless."

He climbed down from the horse, the fort now filling up with more soldiers, British as well. Cornwallis began to walk past a row of campfires, saw pots of boiling liquid, caught the smell of soup, roasted meat. The common area of the fort was crowded with piles of canvas, many of the tents struck but not packed. The soldiers were moving in and out of the shelters, opening all the doors to the storerooms and cellars, but the men were not looting, no one ripping through any abandoned debris. He could see that it was not debris at all. It was supplies, whole and useful, everything an army would have in their own fort, even their dinner.

The men were beginning to celebrate, the shock of what they had discovered turning into a party. He saw more rebels pulled by their shirts into the open, drunk as well, and he understood now. Of course, more stragglers, whose loyalty to their rum keg exceeded their loyalty to Mr. Washington.

He kept moving forward, closer to the sharp cliff that fell away to the river. In the rocks were the cannon, the big guns that had tormented the British ships. His men were examining them, and he could see that none had been spiked, none damaged. He thought of Howe, the order that would not let him pursue the rebels. Well, sir, you will be pleased. We have captured not only the fort, but every piece of equipment, every tent, every dinner plate, every gun. The rebels have simply left it all behind.

CORNWALLIS STAYED TRUE TO HOWE'S ORDERS, AND ONLY WHEN the fort and all its supplies had been secured did his troops begin the march in pursuit of the rebel garrison. They had crossed the Hackensack River in a blinding storm of sleet and rain, made worse by the destruction of the single bridge, repairs to which took several days. Cornwallis knew that Greene's men had joined up with Washington's, had stayed in one place for the several days that Cornwallis had been delayed. The rain-soaked roads could not disguise the misery of Washington's army, supplies and stragglers dropped all along the way, an army that could not keep itself together. Along every mile, Cornwallis' men scooped up prisoners, and he heard more tales of despair than he had ever heard from the deserters at Harlem Heights. Every farmhouse was filled with exhausted, barely clothed men, and when Cornwallis reached Brunswick, he knew that just across the Raritan River, Washington's army was melting away.

He paced the horse along the river, could see that the weather was turning foul again, a thick black sky moving toward him from the west. The chill cut through his uniform, and he reached for the heavy coat, an aide quickly beside him, pulling it over his shoulders. Upriver, he could see a group of rebels, a dozen perhaps, and he rode that way, ignored the faint objections from the staff, thought, It hardly matters, gentlemen. They have no muskets. He halted the horse, and the rebels began to wave, and he didn't know if they were taunting or surrendering. He looked at the sky over their heads. Another night like the last few, and the rebels will likely beg for mercy. Mr. Washington cannot want a fight, not under these conditions. Surely he is outnumbered by two or three to one. And everything we have seen tells us that those men have very little fight in them. He looked down the river again, where the engineers were repairing the bridge. Gentlemen, I implore you. Do make haste.

The army was back in whatever cover they could find, mostly in patches of woods, and he had relaxed the usual discipline, allowing the men to gather branches and moss, any kind of protection against the weather. When the march out of Fort Lee had clearly become a pursuit, he had ordered the army to leave their tents behind, the men already encumbered by the weight of their

packs and muskets. Once the weather changed for the worse, he
had regretted the order. But their means of making a dry camp
was well behind them now, and they would need their rest. They
had endured the same march as Washington, and the toll was
etched on their faces. Even as they gathered up the rebel stragglers, his own men were dropping in place, staggering through
muddy roads in blind fatigue. There is some blessing in this delay after all. And still, right there, across this river, Washington's
army is waiting.

The wind howled past him, and he turned the horse, cursed
the winter, knew it would only get worse in the weeks ahead. He
shivered, pulled again at the coat, and his staff was up close to
him now, knew without him saying anything that he had enough
of this for today. He began to move the horse, saw another rider
coming from the east, the man led by a *jager*. He recognized the
man with dread, one of Howe's aides.

The man was shivering, retrieved a packet from his saddle,
said, "General Cornwallis, I am pleased to find you, sir." Cornwallis said nothing, was in no mood for pleasant chat. "General
Howe offers his congratulations on the extraordinary progress of
your march, and advises you that the general himself will be
joining you here at Brunswick."

The dread had now turned ice-cold, and Cornwallis said,
"Here? General Howe is coming here?"

"Oh, quite, sir. The general has ordered you to remain at post
here until he arrives. He is quite eager to accompany you on the
chase, sir."

"When might the general arrive?"

"Oh, um, any day now, sir."

Cornwallis could see a bland pleasantness on the man's face,
oblivious to the significance of his message. Cornwallis moved
the horse again, felt another blast of wind, left the man sitting
alone, moved toward a long row of small houses. So, we shall
sit tight and wait for General Howe. And he will arrive *any
day now*.

DECEMBER 7, 1776

It took Howe nearly a week to fight the elements and his own
habit of making a comfortable camp at every stop along the way.

When he had finally reached Brunswick, Cornwallis' engineers had finished their work, and the army was ready to cross the Raritan. But Washington's army was no longer anywhere to be seen.

With Howe now commanding the column, the pursuit began again. Every day brought more rebel prisoners, and once the weather dried out, and the roads hardened, Cornwallis had seen for himself the dark streaks and stains on the road, the blood from the bare feet of Washington's men.

Cornwallis could make no excuses, could not avoid riding alongside his superior, that sort of decorum so very important to Howe. Around them, the army had made good time, Howe not holding them back, beyond the luxury of allowing the men to sleep until well after daylight. It was frustrating to Cornwallis, an annoying lapse of efficiency, but he would not make any objection to Howe, knew the morale of his men had to be kept high. They were moving farther and farther inland, away from the security of their supply base, and away from any significant help should they suddenly find themselves in a fight.

They reached the outskirts of Princeton, and Cornwallis could see the *jagers* swarming through the college, helmeted soldiers appearing in the windows of the large building, Nassau Hall. There had been no trouble, no snipers, nothing at all to cause alarm. The college was nearly empty, ghostlike. Cornwallis knew that the college president, John Witherspoon, was an outspoken rebel, would respond to the British advance by closing the college, sending the young men scurrying through the countryside, ridiculous threats of grave consequences should they stay in the town.

Most of the townspeople had left as well, but in the streets he could see the curious emerging. There were more stragglers, of course, those who would collapse into the small comforts of the town. Already his advance patrols were rounding them up.

The *jagers* were out in front again, and the reports kept coming to him in a steady stream. Washington's army could not be far ahead. The sound of axes was echoing through the woods, the rebels cutting trees, dropping them across the road just in front of the army's progress, a feeble attempt to hold Howe back.

They rode past a small tavern, and Cornwallis saw a British flag in the window, thought, How long has that been there? Likely not while Mr. Washington was in the area. I wonder if that fellow is a true loyalist, or just someone with an instinct for the pragmatic.

Howe had issued a proclamation, calling for loyal subjects to the king to step forward, a reassuring statement that those citizens out here, who had been so far from the protection of British forces, were now safe, and could state their loyalty without fear. In return, they would receive a certificate signed by Howe, guaranteeing them protection from any harassment from the British troops. The response had been encouraging, though not overwhelming, but reports had already begun to come into camp from irate Tories, protesting that their farms, and occasionally their daughters, were being abused by the Hessians, who showed no understanding at all of Howe's reassuring words. But Howe continued to believe it was a major step in bringing the countryside back into the fold. Cornwallis understood now: To Howe, this was the most important part of the entire mission.

As they moved farther into the town, more of the citizens came out into the road. He glanced at Howe, saw a silent pride on the man's soft face. He could see that Howe shared none of his own frustration, seemed unconcerned that Washington was staying just far enough in front of them to avoid a fight. Howe was waving now, and Cornwallis saw a group of women emerging from a small house, flowers in their hands. An old man appeared, bent and gray, held a British flag, and Cornwallis had the sudden sense of being in a parade. It brought back memories of Europe, the celebration of war, as though some kind of grand spectacle justified any of the horror.

Howe was reacting to the attention with a broad smile, and Cornwallis focused ahead, listened for the sounds of the army, any sign that the *jagers* had actually caught up to Washington's main body. Howe was waving again, responding to a small group of cheering boys, said, "Marvelous. It's like coming home. This truly is England, all of it. Every house, every farm, every town."

Cornwallis didn't know if Howe expected him to respond, thought, Of course, in the end, it's not about armies, or this chase of a beaten enemy. Howe was enjoying the countryside, appraising it in ways Cornwallis had never understood until now. It was the European way, conquer your enemy by conquering his land, measure your victory by acreage. We are occupying their property, their towns are falling under our command. This is not about catching Washington, or defeating his army. Howe's proclamation to the loyalists was all about pacification, reassuring the people that we will protect them from the rabble, reassuring them that their king has returned to take control. There is logic to it, I suppose. The rebels claim their power comes from the people, that it is the people who give legitimacy to their congress. Take that away, and there is no revolution at all.

Up ahead, he heard more muskets, could hear a musket ball whistle by overhead. Howe was waving still, a flirtation with a young girl, and Cornwallis thought, He didn't hear it. He didn't hear any of it.

DECEMBER 8, 1776

There had been musket fire for most of the day, scattered and brief, and very few stragglers had appeared. He knew that Trenton was very close, the *jagers* pushing and probing forward, testing the resistance that Washington might have placed in their path. There had not been any kind of real engagement, mostly marksmen, rebels who hid themselves close to the wrecks of small bridges, more of the annoying obstacles to slow the column. The *jagers* would pursue, a brief fruitless chase, but the rebels knew the land. Each time the game was played out, the main column would be forced to halt, and after a time, Cornwallis would begin the cumbersome task of putting the army in motion again.

Howe had stayed behind, rising very late, had been gracious enough to allow Cornwallis and the army to begin the march without him. It was a blessed relief, and Cornwallis had the troops up and on the road quickly. Cornwallis had put a spark of energy in his orders, knowing that Washington had increased the space between them slightly. If he could inspire the men to a day or two of hard marching, they might still catch the main rebel column. But the army was encumbered by the weight of its packs and the fatigue in its legs, and the rebels were close to the one place that might finally offer them another escape, this time into Pennsylvania. Beyond Trenton was the Delaware River, and a wide river could mean opportunity for either side. If Washington's troops could be caught on the near shore of the river, unable to find a means across, their despair and panic would surely result in a rapid surrender, and Howe would have a glorious victory. But if the rebels crossed the river . . .

He would not focus on that, knew that Pennsylvania would allow Washington to move in many directions, his meager force vanishing into the vast farmlands. It is winter, after all, and there can be no long marches in winter. The weather had continued to change, from chilly and dry to the icy misery of blinding storms. He tried to imagine the scene in the rebel camp, each day closer to bloody disaster or some kind of salvation. Washington knows his situation, of course. The man is no fool. He has a dwindling army of shopkeepers and farmers, and he cannot stand up to us at all, not now, not after so much of his strength has simply fallen away. He needs the river, and he needs us to dawdle and delay. Cornwallis turned in the saddle, looked back down the moving column, did not see Howe. He felt relief, looked again to the front, saw a church steeple above a thicket of trees, then more buildings, small houses, shops. They had reached Trenton.

THE TROOPS RACED AHEAD OF HIM, AND HE WAVED THEM FORWARD with the sword, but there were few sounds, scattered pops, the sudden burst from one cannon. But it was not a fight, there were no lines of rebels waiting for them, the cannon his own, a futile shot across the river.

He reined in the horse, looked across from a high bluff, could see rebels in motion, pulling boats up the far bank. The shoreline was a solid mass of boats, all shapes and sizes, some crude and unfinished, fishing vessels and simple rafts. But the boats were empty, their human cargo already gone. His men were firing across the river, at the last of Washington's rear guard, but there was little return fire. He ignored the pleas from his staff to back away, knew there was no danger. No, it could not have been more perfect. We gave them exactly what they required, exactly the amount of time they would need to safely cross the river. General Howe will have his critics again, his enemies in London claiming he delayed with purpose, leniency to the rebels. They will not know how it is to be out here, marching this army through eighty miles of bad roads and dismal weather.

He felt himself sagging in the saddle, drained by the long days of this ridiculous pursuit, this absurd chase through land that meant nothing to anyone but General Howe. The last of the rebels were moving off, disappearing into the trees, while around him, his men continued to form solid lines along the edge of the river. Officers were beginning to gather, and he heard the curses of the sergeants, could hear Hessian troops shouting something across the river, their own curses. There was no shooting, the targets far away, the enemy beyond even his own imagination. The word rolled through his brain, *Pennsylvania,* his mind a fog of weariness and anger. He felt paralyzed, could not even see the river, stared at nothing, swallowed up by the great wide hole in his mind, the abyss, where that man and that ridiculous army had disappeared, had escaped again.

DECEMBER 14, 1776

They had stayed in Trenton for several days, the army settling into their camps in a dull haze of frustration. He had sent scouts out along the river, and the reports had not surprised him at all. There were no boats to be found, none, of any shape or kind. Washington had been very thorough. For many miles in both directions, the rebels had pulled every craft that could float to the west side of the Delaware River.

He was pacing the shoreline, staring at muddy water, had made this his routine now, walking out every day, while Howe kept to his lavish and comfortable headquarters. But Cornwallis did not dwell on the mud and the stark skeletons of trees, the dreariness of winter in New Jersey. His mind was on Jemima, imagining the sight of her waiting on the wharf, standing alone, as though he was the only passenger on the ship, just husband and wife, coming together after the torment of the months of separation. He thought of his walk down the plank, maintaining his decorum, teasing her, seeming to search the wharf for someone else, all the while watching her, until finally she scolded him, Charles! Pay attention! It was their private argument, and there was no hostility to it, just the tease, when his mind would drift away to some other place, or the writing of some letter that was not for her. Charles! What of me? And he would pretend to go on with his work, wait for her to move closer, trying to distract him, and he would suddenly drop the pen, push the papers away, wrap his arms around her thin frame, bathe himself in her perfume.

Even when the children came, they had their privacy, and neither of them would allow parenthood to prevent their playfulness. He thought of her laughter, like soft music, her beautiful voice, those eyes, that beautiful face.

The image faded, his thoughts jolted by the sounds of the horse, the sight of his aide. He knew that Howe expected him for lunch, a tradition now, and Cornwallis felt a dull sickness in his stomach, could not think of food. His aide dismounted, said nothing, the message known to both of them already. Cornwallis could see the man's anguish, said, "Yes, yes, Colonel, do not be so troubled. I'm coming. I do not wish to keep General Howe waiting." The man seemed relieved, and Cornwallis moved past him, climbed on the horse, slapped the reins. The streets were crowded with Hessians, formations of sharp blue, polished helmets in long straight rows. They stepped aside with precision, their officer stiffly at attention as he passed, and he nodded to the man, habit now.

As he approached Howe's headquarters, he could not avoid looking out toward a wide field, out behind a row of houses. He had seen it first from the window of Howe's headquarters, something Howe himself had not noticed. Cornwallis had pointed it out, and Howe had dismissed his suggestion with a brief shrug of his thick shoulders, and so Cornwallis would not mention it again. But each time he rode by the field, he stared out at this place, the sawmill, row upon row of cut timbers, a vast field of the raw materials they could have used to build boats.

He rode up slowly to Howe's headquarters, stepped down heavily off the horse, adjusted his coat over the discomfort in his stomach. There was music coming from inside, some kind of odd Hessian horn, the irregular beats of a large drum. A guard held the door open for him, and he stepped inside, was jolted by the smell, something hard and pungent. The table was piled with large platters of fat tubes, some gray, some red, some seemingly no color at all. The men saw him now, calls of good cheer, some in broken English, and he stepped forward, put on his best effort at a smile.

Howe was at the head of the table, said aloud, "Welcome, General! We have a surprise today! Colonel Rall has insisted that his camp prepare our lunch. It seems that we are in a part of the colonies where some of his people have settled."

Rall stood now, an older, frail man, with a stiff, unsmiling formality, and Cornwallis said, "Well, Colonel, thank you for your kindness."

Rall looked to the side, an aide whispering to him, and Cornwallis thought, Of course, the good colonel speaks no English at all. He was familiar with Rall's aide, a friendly young lieutenant named Piel. Piel motioned to a chair, said, "General, if you please. We have procured some of the finest luxuries of our own country from the farms around Trenton. It has given our soldiers much joy. Please."

Piel was still pointing to the chair, and Cornwallis sat, the smell numbing him. He stared at the massive platters, could not help the thought: It appears to be one very large intestine. He still had the smile, felt his jaw stiffening, saw Howe now stabbing at a fat sausage, the juice spraying the table. Cornwallis scanned the rest of the table, saw no vegetables, nothing to delay the inevitable, and he reached out with a fork, carefully stabbed a sausage of his own. The Hessians had waited for him, and now there was a surge of forks, men heaping the plump links on their plates.

He could see Howe thoroughly enjoying himself, and Howe said, "Excellent, when you acquire the taste. Enjoy, General."

Cornwallis poked and prodded, knew he was being watched, cut a small sliver off the end, brought it to his mouth. Howe said, "General, we have been discussing the winter quarters. I believe it is best to have the Hessians remain here. We will establish outposts back through New Jersey, generally on the same route of our march, Princeton, Brunswick, and so forth."

Cornwallis did not taste the meat in his mouth, stared at Howe, who frowned, said, "Is there a problem, General? Dinner not to your liking?"

He swallowed the meat, said, "No, sir, the meal is fine. Winter quarters? Are we not to pursue the enemy?"

Howe laughed, said, "Pursue whom? Where? Really now, General. In winter, one makes winter quarters. You are well aware there is no purpose served by attempting any march through winter conditions. The conditions here are far too severe for us to take the field. We currently occupy a string of towns that will provide us adequate shelter and a friendly environment. It would be foolish to move farther into unfamiliar terrain. I have decided to place Colonel Rall in command here, with Colonel von Donop down the river in Bordentown. General Grant will assume command at Brunswick, and you . . ." Howe paused, seemed to inflate, a knowing smile. "You, General, may make plans for a visit home. I believe that sort of thing is in order. You may accompany me to New York, and make preparations for a crossing."

Cornwallis was stunned that Howe would have taken such notice of his sentiments.

"General Howe, I am grateful. I assure you, sir, I would return as rapidly as possible."

"Of course, General. I consider the journey to be one of refreshment. I would request that you return after a stay of no more than a month, in time for us to resume this campaign at the appropriate time. I have already issued a dispatch to be sent to the ministry, advising Lord Germain that I do not feel there is the smallest prospect for finishing this matter before spring."

THE BRITISH TROOPS WERE MARCHING EASTWARD, ON THE SAME muddy road that had brought them to the edge of Pennsylvania. Cornwallis stayed a while longer in the town, fought the urge to push himself quickly back to New York. He was already planning the time he would have with Jemima, but the army had no such luxury, and he would not parade his own privilege of a journey to England in front of the men who would keep to their posts in this dismal place. His duty was still in Trenton, seeing to the disposition of the defenses there, and he had already met with Rall, to offer the Hessian some last-minute instructions, ensure the man's preparations for the security of his position. The shore of the Delaware River was, after all, the farthest post in a line that stretched all the way to New York. But Rall had been arrogant, even dismissive, seemed to be insulted that Cornwallis would question his judgment. It was a discussion that could do no one any good, and Cornwallis knew when to step away. Howe was right after all. Winter in this part of the colonies was a miserable affair, and nothing would be decided until spring. In the meantime, he could enjoy an all-too-brief visit with his family.

He climbed the horse, moved out past his staff, knew they would fall in line behind him. He followed the column out to the main road, the horse bouncing him unevenly, felt the rumble in his stomach, the Hessian delicacy not settling comfortably. Most of his men were well out on the road, the town occupied only by

Hessians. He pushed the horse past another formation of blue coats, saw the familiar rigid salute from an officer, the carefully drilled show of respect. They are not all as stubborn and arrogant as Colonel Rall, he thought. But no one can question his qualifications as a soldier. He has fought all over Europe. He can certainly handle himself in Trenton.

12. WASHINGTON

THEY HAD KEPT TO THE ROADS WITH AS MUCH ENERGY AS ANYONE could expect, often without the opportunity to prepare the most simple of meals. In the open roads between the towns they would often eat what was available only in the greatest haste, no time for campfires, the men subsisting mostly on raw flour. What had not been left behind in Fort Lee had been burned along the march, tents, blankets, anything to lighten the load, and to prevent the stores from falling into the hands of the British. Through each town they marched, the citizens who were still there had come forward, curiosity turning to horror, and finally, to pity for this amazing sight, barefoot men with rags for clothes, marching two by two, relentless in their retreat.

All along the journey, Washington had sent letters northward to Charles Lee, whose unopposed forces nearly doubled what Washington had on the march. The letters were polite, suggestive, imploring Lee to send what he felt he could spare, any strength he felt comfortable parting with. Lee had responded with a disturbing lack of concern, vague pronouncements to Washington that Lee felt his army should continue to remain whole, that his own position was the more important. Around Washington, the senior commanders were beginning to bristle toward Lee, astounded at the man's arrogant assumption of an independent command. Washington responded by making his letters more direct, finally ordering Lee to march southward to add his forces to Washington's, but again, Lee made excuses. To men like Greene and Stirling, Lee was insubordinate at best, and treasonous at worst. But Washington held down any such talk, kept his own anger inside, continued to order Lee to march. He would not yet believe that this man who was so loved by the army, who was thought to be the consummate professional soldier, would blatantly disobey Washington's orders. When Lee finally agreed to bring part of his forces to join Washington, he moved with deliberate slowness, the message clear again. Certainly Lee knew that once he was alongside Washington, he would no longer command his own situation, could not play his particular game of war free from Washington's interference.

Horatio Gates had been ordered to send reinforcements from the outposts he commanded north of Albany, the force that had been deployed to protect against a British advance from Canada. Gates had delayed as well, but did not have Charles Lee's backbone for flagrant disobedience. Washington learned that Gates had sent nearly fifteen hundred troops on the march toward Trenton. There was still no word from Lee on how many men he would bring, but Washington had kept his optimism, believed that by the time Lee reached Trenton, the army would be strong enough to make some kind of effective resistance against Howe. But both columns of reinforcements were still many miles away when Washington marched into Trenton. Once his army had crossed the Delaware River into Pennsylvania, not only were Lee's forces of no help, they were in a perilously isolated position of their own. Until the reinforcements arrived, Washington's army had dwindled to fewer than three thousand men, and the escape over the river was not cause for a celebration to anyone. The lookouts had kept a sharp watch on Howe's army as it gathered across the river, but there was no sign that Howe intended to come across. Washington made no great show of his wise strategy, the removal of all boats from the New Jersey shore, though around him, the entire army believed that it was the only thing keeping Howe on the far side of the river.

DECEMBER 15, 1776

He rode the horse through a stand of tall trees, the limbs stark and bare. He looked across to the church steeples, the streets of

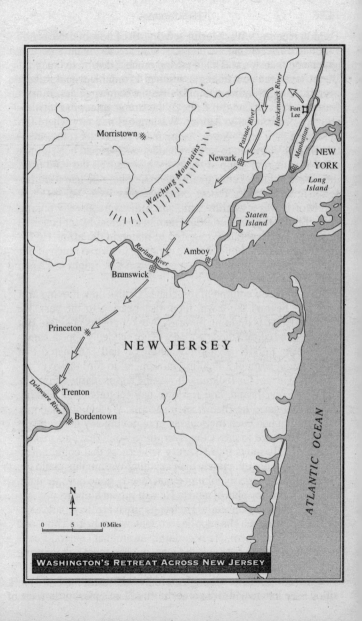

WASHINGTON'S RETREAT ACROSS NEW JERSEY

Trenton teeming with colorful activity, all of it from the army of William Howe. He felt no danger, could see no visible sign that anyone on that side was even paying much attention to the river. He retrieved the new field glasses, a gift from his friend Robert Morris, so much more compact than the long spyglass. Morris was a member of congress, one of the strong voices in Philadelphia who continued to support Washington in a city where the defeats of their army were causing many to wonder if the selection of this Virginian to be commander in chief had been a mistake. Washington gripped the ivory glasses, felt the gold trim, the lenses a much better quality than anything he had used before. He had wondered how expensive they were, but he knew that Morris was a wealthy man, and some were already talking about him as the most qualified man in congress to engineer the financing so desperately required to maintain the army. He focused the glasses, thought, If we continue to lose so much of our strength, money might not be a concern. There might not be an army left to feed.

He could see a column of red-coated British now, moving up a long rise beyond the town, then disappearing to the east. He thought, Howe is dividing his army, weakening his position. But we cannot be certain those troops will not suddenly appear somewhere else, upriver perhaps. Washington had considered that Howe might attempt a flanking movement, to ford the river beyond the view of his lookouts. It was the lesson learned from the fight on Long Island, and if Howe had forgotten the flanking tactics that gave the British such success, Washington had not. Washington had been meticulous in removing any boats, and if the British were to cross the river, they would have to make a march of fifty miles into a wintry wilderness that could defeat them much more effectively than anything Washington could do. He studied the British column again, nearly gone now, thought, No, this is not any plan of attack. He will spread his army east, reinforce Princeton certainly. He has no great artillery park here, no massed wagons. His supplies are somewhere behind him, and he must protect them. He is certainly aware that General Lee is marching down on his flank and rear, and he cannot risk ignoring us in that quarter.

It was as optimistic a thought as he could form about Lee's position. The letters had still come, more of Lee's insubordination, couched in the phrases of a man who is growing more and more bold with his own importance. Lee had now proposed that he keep himself completely free of Washington, suggesting that only an incompetent commander must remain close to his superior's oversight. The letter had done little to endear Lee to the generals around Washington's camp, and even his admirers were beginning to ask how much more of this kind of arrogance Washington would tolerate. But rather than pull Lee in by the collar, Washington had no choice but to submit. Lee's position and the army around him were too important for Washington to give in to a dispute about rank and protocol. Lee insisted he should remain near Morristown and maintain a threat to Howe's outposts. Lee had been matter-of-fact in his belief that Howe was intending to march all the way to Philadelphia, winter or not. Washington had read Lee's rambling analysis with a quaking anger, but he would still not reveal that to anyone else, no matter what the sentiment in headquarters was toward Lee. He knew that Lee was wrong, could see it now for himself. Howe was not massing an army along the river. He was already drawing back.

As the British column disappeared to the east, he focused on the town, saw more troops in formation, Hessians, filling an open green, a sharp reflection of sunlight from their brass helmets. Behind them, rows of dark low buildings were shrouded in the smoke from their chimneys, and Washington lowered the glasses now, thought, No, they are not going anywhere. They are in winter quarters.

Riders were coming up behind him, and he turned the horse, his escort of guards moving aside. He saw Tilghman, was surprised to see Greene, riding beside him. Greene had been spending most of his time with his own division, constant drilling. It was some sort of penance for the disaster of Fort Washington, and Washington could not interfere, knew that the responsibility was shared by both of them. But Washington would answer to the congress. Greene was answering to himself. There had been no reproaches, no need for Washington to make mention of the awful mistake, the poor decision to try to hold the forts. Greene would learn from the tragedy, and nothing like it would ever happen again.

The two men moved through the trees toward him, unsmiling,

no calls of greeting, and Washington waited for them to draw close, said, "Official business, gentlemen?"

Tilghman glanced at Greene, said, "A packet of letters has arrived, sir, addressed to Colonel Reed. The colonel is in Philadelphia, and I thought, sir, in light of events, there might be some importance in reviewing their contents."

Washington still didn't know why Greene was there, said, "You suggesting I read Mr. Reed's private mail, Major?"

"I'm not at all certain it is private, sir. It could certainly be something official. The packet is from the headquarters of General Lee."

Washington was unsure why this was important, but clearly Tilghman was agitated, and Washington held out his hand, said, "Yes, well, you may be correct, Major. Let's have a look."

Joseph Reed was Washington's staff secretary, a Philadelphia lawyer. Washington made use of the man's considerable talent for writing by having Reed draft orders and compose many of the letters Washington had to issue as part of the routine business of command. Reed was a definite contrast to Tilghman, the two men roughly the same age, but the redheaded Tilghman was more plainspoken, with an unrivaled passion for the cause of independence. Unlike the more professional Reed, who saw the staff work as employment, Tilghman had volunteered, was unpaid, and carried no rank as authorized by congress. The title of "major" was Washington's own salute to the young man, whose discretion and loyalty to Washington were absolute.

Washington examined the letters, saw one with Lee's own handwriting, something with which he was quite familiar by now. He hesitated, thought, Well, yes, this one could certainly be official business. He opened it slowly, began to read, stopped, looked at Greene, who sat expressionless. Washington read further,

> . . . *lament with you that fatal indecision of mind which in war is a much greater disqualification than stupidity or even want of personal courage . . . eternal defeat and miscarriage must attend the man . . . cursed with indecision.*

It felt like a fist, a sharp punch in his stomach, and he lowered the letter, a silent moment, and Greene said, "More of the usual, sir? More recommendations on how we should better serve Lee's strategy?"

Greene had become Lee's most vocal critic, and Washington would not have allowed such a comment in headquarters. But out here, Greene was only stating what Washington was feeling himself. He did not respond to Greene's sarcasm, said, "It seems that Mr. Reed has been in correspondence with General Lee . . . on the subject of my unsuitability to command this army." He paused, felt a cold fog in his chest, said, "This is not for the camp, gentlemen. I have revealed too much already."

Tilghman was wide-eyed.

"Oh, certainly not, sir."

Washington looked at Greene.

"General? Am I understood?"

Greene stared at the paper in Washington's hand, said, "There is a great deal of this kind of talk going around, sir. Not here, but in Philadelphia, certainly."

"I am aware, General, that there are those in congress who have their own designs on my command. It is a cross every commander bears. I had hoped that among my own staff . . ." He saw the image of Reed in his mind, a man he considered a friend. "I had hoped there would be loyalty."

Greene did not hold back, said angrily, "No commander should bear scheming and duplicity. This is near treasonous, sir. Colonel Reed is conspiring with General Lee . . ."

"No, Mr. Greene. Colonel Reed has apparently expressed some misgivings to General Lee, and General Lee has responded with his own view. There is no act of treason here. Merely opinions. I regret they should come from my own staff."

"And, sir, where is Colonel Reed now? He is in Philadelphia, speaking those words to members of congress. No doubt had he received this letter first, he would have related Lee's message as well."

Washington was weary of the subject, said, "We will discuss this no further. These men have a right to feel discouraged. This army has done very little to inspire anyone to our cause. I admit, I am distressed by Colonel Reed's willingness to communicate his feelings directly to General Lee. But we know, gentlemen, that their views are not isolated ones. Look around you, Mr. Greene. Entire companies have abandoned this army. Enlistments are expiring daily, and you might as well attempt to stop the wind as to prevent them from going home. Many of the reinforcements we received from General Gates arrived in camp only to depart again. I was distressed to learn that General Gates has failed to secure their reenlistment before he sent them to this command. Many more terms expire at the end of the year. If I cannot find some means of persuading these men to remain with this army, by January, we will have in this camp fewer than fifteen hundred men." He paused, could see Greene absorbing the words, the numbers. "So there is disaffection? Discouragement? A lack of faith in my abilities? That can be no surprise, gentlemen. I had so hoped to persuade General Lee to join his men to this camp. He inspires the congress and the army in ways I do not. We must not be so concerned with allegiances and loyalties, and who conspires against whom. We must do everything in our power to hold this army together. If we do not, then I believe . . . the game is nearly up."

He felt his hands shaking, gripped the letter still. He was embarrassed, regretted the outburst. He folded the letter slowly, steadied himself, returned it to its envelope, said, "Major, you will see that this is forwarded to Colonel Reed, accompanied by my apology for having opened it. It is after all, his personal correspondence. There will be no judgment. We will say no more about this."

Tilghman took the letter, seemed nervous, said, "Sir, I do not understand Colonel Reed. But I hope you do not believe there is disloyalty on your staff. I assure you, sir." The man was near tears, and Washington wanted to put that aside, erase the moment.

"Mr. Tilghman, I do not require your reassurances. No cause that was ever worthy was without its turmoil, its trials, its hopelessness. We are not defeated yet."

There were more horsemen, some of his guard leading a courier through the trees, and Tilghman reacted quickly, turned his horse, rode past the guard to intercept the man. The courier pointed up toward Washington and was clearly agitated, his arms in motion, then calmed, the message delivered. Washington could see Tilghman's reaction to the message, the young man lowering his head, his face in his hands. Washington looked away for a moment, stared across the river, and Greene said, "No doubt, word of some new piece of good fortune."

Tilghman was moving again, rode up close, and Washington saw tears, and Tilghman said, "Sir, there is news. General Lee . . . has been captured by the British."

* * *

IT HAD BEEN NEARLY TOO EASY, LEE CARELESSLY SPENDING THE night at a private home well outside the protection of his own camp, a patrol of British cavalry stumbling on the place, bagging the extraordinary quarry with almost no resistance. Washington could only be certain that General Howe would take very good care of a man whose ambition might be of more use to the British than to Washington.

The troops who had marched with Lee began to arrive in camp, commanded by John Sullivan. Though the enlistments continued to expire, Washington knew that for a short while at least, he could keep a force of several thousand men in the field. But he could not prevent the desertions, and those who remained were suffering the misery of a camp without adequate food and shelter, enduring the increasing bitterness of winter with rags for clothes.

The false rumors of Howe's certain advance on Philadelphia had thrown the city into panic, and no one had reacted with more panic than the congress. Nearly the entire body had gone, were attempting to establish a quorum in Baltimore, some means of maintaining the semblance of a government.

Since the earliest days of the war, most of congress had favored supplying the army with militia, troops who answered first to their own state. It was a means of controlling the army, many believing that a professional, permanent military would result in abuses to the very freedoms they were fighting for. But when the panic engulfed them, many in the congress had put aside their earlier misgivings. Men like John Adams and Robert Morris understood that reality often has a way of pushing aside idealism. As they made plans to abandon Philadelphia, the congress voted Washington absolute power to direct all matters relating to the army and the war. Though congress expressed its approval of Washington as the one man who could be trusted with such unlimited authority, he had been granted, in effect, the power of a military dictator.

DECEMBER 22, 1776

The panic in Philadelphia produced another surprise. Israel Putnam encouraged militia to come out, and faced with the

sudden threat to the safety of their homes, over twelve hundred
men had enlisted for a six-week term. When they actually appeared, Washington had met them with stunned delight. They
were not trained soldiers, of course, and Washington had come
to share Greene's skepticism whether any force of militia could
make a strong stand in combat. But the fresh troops were a godsend to the morale of the army, a sign that all was not lost, that
the rest of the country was not ignoring the plight of its soldiers.

The congress had decreed one more bit of support for his
army, but the reception from the troops was a mix of amusement
and disgust. With a grand show of patriotic reverence, congress
had decreed that the country, and presumably the army, observe
a "day of fasting," thought to be a necessary show of humility in
such a time of peril. Washington ignored the rude comments
from his men, knew as well as anyone that such a gesture meant
very little to the troops who had to struggle to find any decent
meal.

With a force of six thousand men, Washington knew he had
the best opportunity he might ever see again to make some sharp
blow to the enemy across the river. In barely a week's time, two-
thirds of his strength would see their enlistments expire. Everywhere he rode, all through the camps, the men were looking to
him, the commanders, Greene and Stirling, Sullivan and Knox.
Every man knew that if Washington was to quiet his critics, put a
stop to all the conspiracies to remove him from command, something positive would have to happen. They were simply running
out of time.

THE MAN HAD BEEN ARRESTED BY A PATROL OF LOCAL MILITIA, A
loudmouthed Tory, known throughout this part of New Jersey as
a trader in cattle and other goods, a provider of supplies to the
British. His name was Honeyman, and he made no secret of his
fierce loyalty to King George, had engaged in more than one fistfight in the taverns around Trenton, daring to shout into the face
of any rebel sympathizer, quick to curse their misplaced loyalty
to the cause of independence.

He put up a good fight, kicking and cracking his whip at the
militiamen who managed to finally drag him from his carriage,
subduing him only with a heavy rope. All the way to the camp he
cursed them, and when they had heard enough, they plugged his

mouth with a rag, yet still he fought, his rage coming through in grunts and high-pitched moans.

When he reached the camp, he was surrounded by guards, the gag still in his mouth, and the troops began to gather, making good fun of this violent misfit. The local men all knew him by reputation and told his story, and the response from the others was predictable. Some men lined up to kick at him, gave him back curses of their own. But none of the physical abuse silenced the fiery loyalty of Honeyman's dedication to his king. The sport played itself out, and when the turmoil had subsided, the guards brought him to Washington, the staff assuming that this man might be useful after all, might be inclined to reveal some bit of information. The guards themselves were skeptical that the man could be of any use for anything but a hanging, and when Washington ordered them away, there was surprise and deep concern that this crazed Tory would be allowed so close to the commander, that Washington would tolerate the presence of this violent man in his office. Even the staff was surprised when suddenly, the door to the office was closed by Washington himself.

ARE YOU ALL RIGHT, MR. HONEYMAN?"

The ropes were gone now, and Honeyman flexed his jaw, laughed, said, "They could have used a *clean* handkerchief. But, just a spot of rum would wash away the taste."

Washington brought out a glass, and Honeyman drank it in one quick gulp, and with a raspy breath said, "Better. Much better. Perhaps one more, sir. Helps the memory, you know."

Washington knew the routine, poured another, and Honeyman put it away as well. Honeyman saw a chair now, dropped down, tested the soreness in his side, said, "At least one of your young fellows has boots still. I'll be feeling that kick for a day or two." He laughed, and Washington sat patiently, and now the complaining was past, and Honeyman said, "Last things first, General. Have you considered the manner of my escape?"

"We'll lock you in the guardhouse. There are loose boards in one corner. Wait for the distraction, the guard will change about midnight."

Honeyman rubbed his chin, said, "They'll get off a shot or two. Worrisome bunch. They shoot better than the British."

"They had better."

It was not a joke, and Honeyman, all business now, said, "The cattle business is doing very well in these parts, General. Sold a nice fat herd to Colonel Rall just yesterday. He has twelve hundred mouths to feed, you know. Hessians all. And, of course, there's Colonel von Donop, a few miles below, Bordentown, about the same number. From the barrels of good spirits I seen stacked up in Trenton, them fellows are looking to a nice party come Christmas Day. A very nice party. It's particular to them folks, you know. Hessians, whatnot. They do like their Christmas."

Washington sat back in the chair, listened to every detail of Honeyman's report, felt his heart beating faster in his chest. Honeyman kept talking, details of the British garrison in Princeton, the location of the rural outposts along the road, while Washington listened silently, his breathing in a quick steady rhythm, the plan forming in his mind. It was more than troop numbers and placement of guns. The key was the certainty that bored soldiers in winter quarters would be allowed their one celebration, their one pause from the routine of marching and formations in the bone-chilling cold. The morning after their celebration, there would be the fog of sleep, the aftermath of the holiday that would leave most of Rall's men in no condition to fight anyone. Christmas indeed.

13. WASHINGTON

DECEMBER 25, 1776

HE HAD BEEN NEAR THE BANK OF THE RIVER SINCE FIRST DARK, had felt the wind rising, the temperature dropping as each hour ticked by. The troops had been kept at drill, practicing formations for most of the afternoon. Though the men didn't understand the sudden flurry of activity, their officers had been ordered to keep them close at hand, no lapses in discipline, no opportunity for a potential deserter to find himself alone. As the day grew sharply colder, the drilling had kept the men in motion and so they were not stiffened and uncomfortable. By nightfall, the entire army had a sense that something would happen, very soon, and that it was important.

He sat on a wooden box, an old beehive, wrote orders out carefully, handed each one to waiting couriers, looking hard into the eyes of each man. There could be no idleness, no distraction in these riders. Each commander must know what was expected of him, of the men in his command.

Along the Delaware, the army had prepared for three separate crossings. Horatio Gates was the farthest south, would lead the fresh militia across the river near Bordentown, an attack against von Donop's forces, which was to be more of a diversion than a general action. If successful, von Donop would be cut off from Trenton, would have no role to play in what might occur there.

Opposite Trenton, Washington had ordered General James Ewing to ferry eight hundred militia to the creek along the southern edge of the town, to bottle up any retreat by Rall's Hessians in that direction.

Washington himself would lead the main body of the army, twenty-four hundred experienced men, the divisions of Greene and Sullivan. Their crossing would come nine miles north of the town, a place known as McKonkey's Ferry. Once across the river, the march would be south, along two parallel roads, Sullivan close to the river, Greene farther inland. If the plan was to work at all, the two columns would have to reach Trenton at about the same time, the combined strength the only way Washington could hope to bring an effective attack.

It was a complicated plan at best, a three-pronged assault that depended on the reliability of each commander. And it was not to be. Late in the afternoon, as Washington marched his men north to McKonkey's, he had been stunned to receive a note from Gates, who had decided to leave his camp and make a sudden trip to Philadelphia. There were rumors swirling around Gates, that with Lee captured, Gates was politicking to his friends in congress, revealing his own ambition by making the most of the failures of Washington's leadership. Washington had not wanted to believe it possible, Gates having come to the army in the first place because of his friendship to Washington. But there was no time now for dealing with whatever intrigue Gates had in mind.

Washington had immediately ordered Gates' men to be led by his subordinate, General John Cadwalader.

As darkness had come, and the weather turned more severe, there arrived more bad news from down the river. Washington was shocked to learn that both Cadwalader and Ewing had abandoned any hope of crossing the river. Washington had read the words with stoic silence, two of his three prongs defeated before the assault could even begin. If Washington halted his own march and ended the mission altogether, their unique opportunity would be lost. The ambitious plan was reduced to one faint hope. He still had the most experienced men in the army under his command, and the march upriver had gone smoothly. At McKonkey's, the boats were waiting.

THEY LINED THE BANK IN A SOLID ROW, AND AROUND EACH BOAT men were working, some testing the long stout push poles, some tending to the boats themselves. Washington finished the last of his orders, saw John Glover coming toward him, the man's face hard and unsmiling, the scowl of a man going about his work. Glover saluted him, and Washington could see sweat on the man's brow, defiance of the sharp cold.

"Colonel, are we ready?"

He tried to hide the impatience, had no reason to scold Glover for anything, and the stocky man stared at him, said, "These boats . . . damnedest thing I ever seen. We loaded one of 'em up with Colonel Knox's cannon, and she just sat up tall, like she was still empty. I don't know how this fellow Durham figured how to build these things, but I doubt anyone can sink one."

Washington could see through the darkness, low lanternlight, the long fat boats rocking slightly, the crews still making their preparations.

"They use them for hauling iron ore down the river, so I'm told, Colonel. They have a shallow draft." He tried to sound knowledgeable, Glover listening with tolerance, and he felt foolish now explaining anything about boats to Glover. There was a sudden blast of wind, and Glover turned northward, said, "Aye, sir. Shallow draft. That they do. I have to tell you, General, there's a brute of a storm kicking up." Washington followed Glover's gaze, stared into the biting blackness, the wind watering his eyes. He knew to trust the man's instinct about the weather, and Glover said, "It'll be snowing before long. The ice is already coming up in the river. These boats will be frozen in place pretty quick." He looked at Washington. "We best be moving pretty soon, General. The Durham boats are heavy enough to take a pounding, but the ice and the wind's gonna play hell with the crossing. It's blowin' straight down the river."

Washington saw formations of men lit by lamplight, the troops massing just beyond the riverbank. He looked at Glover again, the man focused on his men at the boats. He saw Henry Knox, the artilleryman supervising the cannon, rolling more of them close to the water's edge. Knox saw him as well, made a brief wave, then turned again to his gun crews. He shouted something, and his men moved quickly, the cannon suddenly lurching forward, the men hoisting and heaving on the ropes. There would be eighteen cannon carried across, and every one was precious. It was all the artillery Colonel Knox had left.

One by one the big guns rolled into the Durham boats, their crews alongside, and Glover was shouting, pointing, his own men boarding each boat, securing the big guns. Glover looked at him, and Washington could see impatience, the man with no interest in a conversation, not now. Washington said, "Return to your boats, Colonel."

Glover smiled for the first time, said, "God bless us, sir. I'll see you on the other side."

As he moved away, the storm Glover predicted began to swirl around him, the wind buffeting Washington with a howling fury. It was more ice than snow, and he felt the sting in his face and eyes. He held up his hand, a shield, letting him see the specks of light from the lanterns bouncing with the movement of the men who carried them, barely visible now, faint reflections through the blinding sleet.

He stepped away from the river, climbed the narrow bank, and farther up he saw Greene, stepping down to the water's edge. All through the darkness, the commanders moved out in front of their men, and along the river, Glover's fishermen were standing beside each boat, their work complete, each of them aware that the moment was close. He could feel their energy, could see Greene looking at him, knew they were waiting for his order. Close beside him, Tilghman had brought a drummer, a very young, very thin man, a ragged coat over bare legs. The man was shivering, stared at Washington with wide eyes, Washington turned toward the river, could not look at the drummer, knew so

many of them had so little. He pushed the thought away, pointed
to the drum, the young man responding, the sounds of the storm
suddenly cut by a steady roll of the drum, then several sharp
beats, and another roll. Out in the darkness, more drummers
knew to pick up the rhythm. As the sounds echoed over the army,
the men began to come forward, stepping in line to the long fat
boats. He could see Greene, close to the water, guiding his men,
seating them tightly into each boat, Glover's men standing high
on each rail, the men holding tight to the push poles. Some of the
soldiers had sticks of their own, to ward off the ice in the river,
the stark white shapes that floated past them, some already
thumping and ramming the boats. He tried to see in both directions, but farther away, the darkness and the storm blanketed his
men, the flickers of light the only sign that his army was moving
at all.

After a few minutes there was a shout from Glover, and Washington saw the fishermen gathering at the stern of each boat.
Glover held his arm in the air for a brief moment, his own signal,
and Washington saw it come down, and just as quickly, the boats
began to move, sliding away from the shore. Washington did not
feel the wind now, ignored the flecks of ice biting his face. He
held his hands at his side, clenched his fists, felt a sharp tightness
in his throat. If God has any mercy for our cause . . . let these
men have their one good day.

THE FIRST WAVE OF BOATS HAD GONE ACROSS AND RETURNED
empty, and it was his time. He stepped into the boat, moved to
the front, sat himself in the center of the bow, waited for the boat
to fill behind him. He looked at the rail, thick and heavy, could
see a large piece of ice float by, close enough to touch. Behind
him, Tilghman was in place, and the boat was rocking slightly as
the last of the troops stepped in.

He tried to keep his hands covered, the bite of the wind cutting
through his gloves, and he pulled his coat around his shoulders
tightly. Tilghman leaned close to him, said, "Sir! The flag is
boarded!"

Washington turned, saw a man holding tightly to the pole, the
ragged cloth wrapped securely. The last man was seated now,
and at the stern, Glover's men were waiting for the order. He
waved his arm, and the boat slid forward, the bow settling slightly
into the water. Two men were standing up beside him, pushed

their long poles downward, began to walk back to the stern, then quickly were up again. The boat slid past more ice, was suddenly rocked by a collision, more ice now sliding along the sides of the boat. He focused into the darkness ahead, his fists still a tight clench, could see a dull shape, the bluffs of the shoreline in front of him. The boat kept moving, more ice punching the sides, and he saw a flicker of light, one lantern, on the far shore. The snow was blowing harder, and he shielded his eyes, saw more lanterns, more light, the shapes of men, shadows moving. The boat suddenly stopped, rocked slightly to one side, and men were splashing toward him, one lantern held high. He stood up, steadied himself, one hand on the rail, saw a hand, ignored it, stepped down into the water. The sudden wetness shocked him, the boots soaked through quickly, and he stepped through a thin layer of ice, made his way quickly to the bank. His horse had been ferried across already, and waited for him up on the bluff. He climbed up, tried to ignore the sharp cold in his boots, saw more lanterns, the men spreading forward in column on the road. He looked back toward the river, could see the whiteness, the ice that was growing thicker still. He could see nothing of the shore they had left, the wind blowing the snow in a low moan, but he knew there was nothing to see. His army was *here*, had made it across without accident, without a single man lost.

He rode up to the front of the column, Tilghman close behind, saw Greene now, the only lantern still lit. Washington glanced at Tilghman, said, "The time, Major?"

"It is nearly four o'clock, sir."

Washington grimaced, said nothing, thought, The crossing should have been completed by midnight. But we could not know how bad the weather would become. And I will find no fault with Glover's fishermen. But we will not reach Trenton until daylight. He looked at Greene now, saw Sullivan moving up beside him, said, "Nine miles, gentlemen. With dispatch. Absolute silence. No stragglers. You may commence the march."

DECEMBER 26, 1776

The army divided at an intersection five miles north of Trenton, and Washington waited only a minute while Sullivan's columns moved out on the river road. Knox's cannon were divided equally, nine to each column, and Greene's men did not halt, kept moving on the inland road that would take them into Trenton from the north. Out in front, a company of Virginians led the way, men whose instructions were explicit. There could be no sound, no alarm given to whatever Hessian outposts might lie in their path.

He rode beside Greene in total darkness. The storm was as fierce as it had been all night, and the road was paved in a slippery sheet of ice. He strained to hear any sound, some sign that the Virginians had come up against some opposition, some trouble, yet one more piece of bad news. But the road was empty, and the storm carried them forward in blessed silence, the wind ripping the trees, skeletal patches of woods giving way to rolling snow-covered fields.

His hands were aching, and he realized he had not eased his grip on the reins for a very long time. He flexed his fingers, thought, We must be very close. It has been too long. He would not ask the time, knew the daylight would come over them no matter how fast they moved now, that the plan was already set in motion, that God had his hand on anything that would happen now. He saw a thin row of trees lining the road, bending with the wind, leaning forward toward Trenton, pointing the way. The branches were framed by a light gray sky, and his stomach jumped, the first glow of the dawn. He would not look that way, stared ahead instead, tried to see nothing at all, only the darkness, only that which would hide his army. He felt his own breathing, the sharp cold in his chest coming out in a visible fog with each short breath. He could see the road now as well, stretching out in front of him, the first time he had been able to see the tracks in the ice, the footsteps of the men leading the way. He wanted to say a prayer, thought of those men, the Virginians, the coincidence, men from his own state leading them into whatever lay ahead. What will they see, who will be waiting for them, what kind of preparation will Rall make? Was there a party after all? We have our spies, does Rall have his? They could be waiting for us, just over the next rise, the next patch of woods. Howe might have ordered him to keep ready, cancel any sort of celebration. There can be no Christmas, not in war.

He fought to control the voices in his mind, the doubts streaking through him. He focused on the Virginians moving ahead, and beyond he could see a house, small, barely a shack. There was a flurry of sounds, the wind muting a sudden chatter of muskets. Beside him, Greene gave a quick shout, and a company of troops began to run forward, a slow jog, cracking through the muddy ice. Washington spurred the horse, knew it had to be the first Hessian guard post, their first confrontation, the voices in his mind silent now. He kept moving forward, had to see, heard Greene moving beside him, the troops leading them forward at a quick trot.

He saw the Hessians in the road now, a dozen or more, forming a line, their muskets erupting in one volley. But the Virginians were on them, and the Hessians began to run, darting out of the road, trying to form another line, behind a stone fence, another volley. Washington pushed forward with Greene's men, the confrontation one-sided, too many Virginians, the Hessians withdrawing again. He watched them with amazement, no panic in those men, retreating in good order, stopping to load and fire, astounding discipline. But his men were too many and pushing too hard, and the Hessians could not hold them, gave way, disappeared over the crest of a hill. His men ran beyond the crest as well, and he followed, reached the top, could see the ground falling away in a long slope. There were more houses, and down the long hill was the town itself, spread out in a beautiful panorama, dark buildings coated with snow, the white streets swept clean by the storm. He stopped the horse, and around him, the main column began to spread out in line, and there was movement in the town, the houses beginning to empty, the streets coming alive. He heard a new sound, muffled, deep and thunderous, then again, a hard thump. He stood high in the stirrups, waited for the sounds again, low thunder, and suddenly there was a bright flash down below in the town, a smashing cascade of fire. He looked out toward the direction of the river, nothing to see, the snow clouding the sky. Greene was close to him now, unable to hide his own excitement.

"I believe, sir, that would be General Sullivan!"

Washington could hear the cannon rumbling in a steady rhythm, and around him, more of Knox's guns were rolling into place. He moved the horse off to one side, saw two cannon lining up side by side, the wheels nearly touching. With quick precision, the gunners were scrambling around them, and suddenly they both fired, one great roar, smoke and fire blowing through the snow, a storm of their own. Out in the field beside him, Greene had his men in line, muskets ready, those who had bayonets leading the way. Greene looked at him, had his sword in the air, and Knox's cannon fired again, the sound filling him, and there were no words, nothing he needed to say. He raised his arm, looked hard at Greene, and pointed down the hill toward the town. With a sharp cry, growing into a long high cheer, the troops began to charge into Trenton.

THE ROUT WAS COMPLETE, THE HESSIANS COMPLETELY STUNNED BY the surprise assault. Those who managed to man their guns, or form some kind of line of resistance were quickly swept away by Knox's cannon. Many were not panicked by the sudden assault and kept their retreat with the order of disciplined soldiers. But retreat they did, some southward, across the Assunpink Creek, the one place where they would have been surrounded had Ewing brought his militia across the river. Many more pulled out to the east, the road toward Princeton, small bodies of troops quickly surrounded by the swarming advance of Washington's men. As they filled the town, the two armies fought hand to hand, house to house, but the surprise was too complete, and the Hessians could not hold their ground.

He stayed on the hill, watched it all through the field glasses, thought of moving closer, but the height was the best vantage point to see everything. The smoke was held low by the storm, and he noticed the wind, still blowing against his back, wondered if it had helped his men, any Hessian resistance facing right into the storm. Couriers were moving all around him, and he finally heard from Sullivan, an aide bringing him word of a rapid sweep along the river, Knox's guns blowing quickly past any resistance.

He searched through the field glasses to find the one place that should have been the headquarters, could make out a row of cannon that had not been fired, one flag that rose high on a staff. He saw a brief fight outside, his own men pushing past, thought, If Rall was there, he cannot be any longer. Knox's cannon were suddenly quiet. He looked that way, saw Knox himself moving toward him, a beaming smile on the man's face, and Knox said, "I have ordered the guns to cease, sir. There seem to be no present

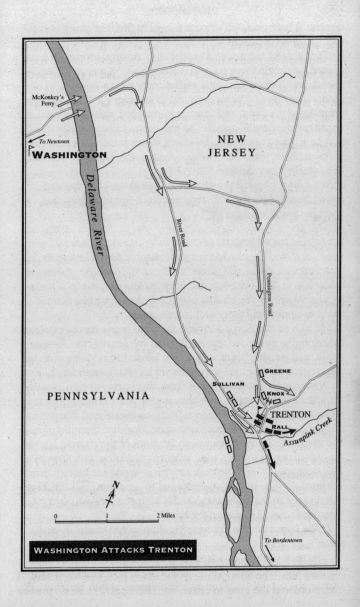

McKonkey's
Ferry

To Newtown

WASHINGTON

**NEW
JERSEY**

Delaware River

River Road

Pennington Road

PENNSYLVANIA

SULLIVAN

GREENE

KNOX

TRENTON

RALL

Assunpink Creek

N

0   1   2 Miles

To Bordentown

WASHINGTON ATTACKS TRENTON

targets." There was still scattered musket fire, but mostly south-ward, beyond the town.

"We should advance, Colonel, the danger seems to have passed. Maintain these guns in this position." Knox started to respond, and behind him, one of the cannoneers shouted, "Their colors are down! They've struck their colors!" The man was pointing to the town, and Washington turned, raised the glasses, could see the bare flagstaff. The gun crews were joyously shouting, hats going up, a raucous cheer. Knox joined his men, gave his own cheer, and after a long joyous moment, Knox said, "Has to be Rall's headquarters!"

Washington raised the glasses, stared at the bare flagstaff, allowed himself to feel the celebration, a broad smile, said, "It must be. Yes. So it must be."

A LONG LINE OF HESSIAN SOLDIERS WAS HERDED DOWN THE WIDE street, and Washington moved aside, waited for them to pass. He watched as a squad of Greene's men completed the search of a small house. The windows had been broken out, the door kicked in, and when the search was complete, their sergeant pointed to the next house, and the search began again.

He moved the horse forward, watched many more prisoners emerging from a side street, flanked by guards, the Hessians silent and sullen, heads down. He moved past them, saw the church, the place where they had told him Rall was being held.

Washington climbed down from the horse, moved into the darkness of the church, saw the narrow pews draped in bloody white cloth, the wounded Hessians lying end to end. There were soft cries now, moans from one man, bloodier than the others, the man's life flowing away onto the floor of the church. He saw an older man in a sharp blue uniform, standing with several of Greene's troops, and the man saw him, wiped his bloody hands on his coat. The troops straightened to attention, and Washington nodded to the man, wondered if he spoke English, said, "Are you the doctor? Do you understand?"

"Yes, I am a doctor. I believe you have come to see my patient, here."

The man backed up a step, and Washington could see a man on the floor, a thick blanket folded under him. Washington leaned closer, the face old, sunken eyes looking up at him, another officer kneeling beside him. The wounded man said something, his voice faint, and the officer stood now, said, "I am Lieutenant Piel, sir. May I assume you are General Washington?" Washington nodded slowly, still looked to the older man, and Piel said, "This is Colonel Johann Gottlieb Rall, sir, in command of the Trenton cantonment. He is . . . *we* are your prisoners, sir."

Rall's face was a pale gray, empty eyes staring past him, barely conscious. Piel spoke to him, and Rall seemed to focus, responded to Piel, who said, "General, Colonel Rall asks no favors for himself. He wishes only that you offer some kindness to his men."

Washington removed his hat, could see death on the man's face, said, "Tell the colonel that his men will not be abused."

Piel conveyed the message, and Washington backed away, moved to the open door. He stepped outside, took a breath of clean air, rid himself of the smell of the church. The doctor had followed him, said, "He will not survive this day, General."

Washington wasn't sure how to respond, said, "We regret the loss of so many."

The doctor reached into his pocket, pulled out a folded piece of paper, handed it to Washington.

"I thought perhaps you should see this, General. I found it in Colonel Rall's pocket when he was brought here. The note is written in English, thus it is not likely Colonel Rall knew what it said. He is a somewhat stubborn man, did not appreciate the need for an interpreter. Lieutenant Piel is much abused, I'm afraid. I do not know if this is proper, General, but this note mentions you."

Washington took the paper, saw bloodstains, read the words,

> . . . *a considerable force of rebels is on the roads north of Trenton* . . .

He handed the paper back to the man, said, "It is not improper of you, Doctor. You are no doubt correct. It is apparent he did not read it."

Washington climbed the horse, the doctor disappearing back into the church. The horse carried him into the streets again, and everywhere he looked, his soldiers were in motion, hauling wagons of supplies, men carrying armloads of muskets. He saw

Knox again, the man bouncing heavily on horseback, directing the flow of six brass cannon, hitched now to the horses that would carry them away. Knox saw him, waved to him with joyous informality, moved away with his new guns.

He saw Greene coming toward him, more officers, the horses at a gallop. As they reined up Greene said, "Sir! We have the first reports. The provost has estimated around a thousand prisoners, sir. Perhaps a hundred dead."

This was the part that Washington dreaded, but saw none of that on Greene's face.

"General Greene, what were our losses?"

Greene laughed, an odd response, and beside him, another man said, "Colonel Knox had some difficulty, two of his officers received light wounds. Two other men are unaccounted for, lost possibly on the march last night." The man stopped, and Washington waited for more, said, "What else?"

Greene was still smiling, said, "Nothing else, sir. There were no other casualties."

Washington felt a strange numbness, disbelief.

"Thank God for that."

Greene's smile faded, and he looked at Washington with concern.

"Are you all right, sir? This was a perfect victory, General. Your strategy was without flaw."

He heard men cheering now, saw a regimental flag held high, the men who captured it parading it through the streets. When they saw the officers, hats went up, the flag held out, and behind them, more men, a second flag, one man holding it aloft on the point of a bayonet. Greene raised his hat, and the men returned the salute. More troops were gathering, and there was music, and Washington saw a drummer, the young man who had given the signal on the bank of the river, the young man's legs covered now, ill-fitting stockings from the trunk of some Hessian soldier. It was a small symbol, one man's comfort, the spoils of this extraordinary victory. Through all the joy around him, the music and the cheering, he felt a strange sense of amazement. He thought of Rall, that one curious piece of paper that could have changed everything. The man will die never understanding that he has been defeated by his own arrogance. It is the arrogance of them all, of William Howe and King George, all those who so blithely dismiss this army. Yet we have a purpose, and if we are allowed the opportunity, we will *defeat* you.

All through the town, the army went about its work, but the celebrations were few, the officers and their men seeming to know as much as Washington did. If the war was to be won, this day was only one victory. There had to be many more.

The flags were packed away now, the music muted, and Washington rode back up the long hill, could see Knox's two guns still in position. He stopped the horse, pulled it slowly around, looked out over the town, realized for the first time the snow had stopped. He rode slowly into the open field, held up his hand, kept the staff away. He wanted a moment by himself, would not have them close by just now. He was feeling the fatigue of the long night, his hold on the emotions breaking down, the command slipping, giving way to his tears. He looked out across the town, could see his army at work, knew there would have to be a new plan, immediate and definite, securing this victory, that the captured supplies and prisoners would have to be taken back across the river, the army made ready to make the best advantage of this day. But he could not think of that now, needed just this one long quiet moment. He sat back in the saddle, and the tears stopped, and for the first time in this awful war, he began to feel the joy. We have won the day. This was a *victory*. It is a glorious day for our country.

14. WASHINGTON

DECEMBER 30, 1776

HE HAD BEEN BACK ACROSS THE DELAWARE TWICE, SEEING TO THE transfer of the captured supplies and the disposition of the enormous number of Hessian prisoners. John Glover's Marblehead fishermen had manned the boats once more, had crossed and recrossed the icy river, carrying load upon load of equipment, tents and muskets, and the Hessians themselves. By now the prisoners had reached Philadelphia, had been paraded into the city to an audience who would be awed by their martial appearance, the sharp uniforms an astounding contrast to the ragged clothing of the men who guarded them.

Washington had come back into Trenton, had surveyed the town with an eye to its defense, but the town itself was not as important as the protection of his army. Scouting and raiding parties were sent into the countryside, their first priority to keep an eye on the British position, the strength of the garrison at Princeton, and beyond. He knew that Howe would not let him just settle into Trenton and bide his time for the rest of the winter. The loss in both men and prestige was a sharp and bloody wound that Howe could never just ignore. There would certainly be a response. The question Washington had to answer was when, and how strong.

Below the town, the Assunpink Creek provided a barrier, and so he moved his men into position behind the creek, with their backs to the Delaware River. On the road that led northeast toward Princeton, he sent Colonel Edward Hand, with his regiment of Pennsylvania marksmen. Hand would resist whatever force came down the road from Trenton, buying Washington's men the precious time to construct a solid line of defense.

Down the river at Bordentown, Cadwalader's militia had finally crossed, only to find that the Hessians there had wisely withdrawn. Washington had no need for a separate force miles to the south, and Cadwalader was ordered to bring his men to Trenton. There would be a bit of delay, since the militia had taken readily to the job of pursuing the Hessian retreat. It was the kind of fighting the unskilled soldiers could perform with raucous enthusiasm. Their enemy was running away from them.

If the British responded as Washington believed they must, there would have to be a new plan. To just sit and wait at Trenton was unlikely to bring any kind of success. But there could be no strategy until he knew what he was facing. From the beginning of the New York campaign, his strategy had formed itself around the needs of the moment, dealing with the new crisis at hand. Well before the British would reach his defenses, Washington had a crisis of a different sort. Many of those men who had already served, who had become veterans, were now preparing to leave, their enlistments expired. Washington had recently received a newly published pamphlet, authored by Thomas Paine, which expressed exactly the sentiment that Washington had to communicate to his troops. *The Crisis* was a call for the country to offer up its men as soldiers, an earnest and passionate plea for sacrifice as the only means of saving the country. Washington had read the paper and envied Paine's eloquence, had little confidence in his own. But he would make the effort, speak to the men, and offer his own plea for his army to remain together. Though he might still raise an army for a spring campaign, the new recruits would have none of the backbone of these soldiers, and whatever advantage had been gained against the British would be lost. The victory at Trenton would mean nothing at all.

THE SOLDIERS LINED UP ALONG THE BANKS OF THE RIVER, SUMmoned by the drums of their regiments. Washington waited for the entire line to settle into place, looked at each man, rugged faces, little trace of a uniform, some with arms wrapped in shredded blankets, rags tied around their feet. He was surprised to see the quiet respect, no grumbling, no one protesting why they would have to hear a speech from the commanding general. When the drums grew quiet, he rode out in front of them, sat high on the white horse, gathered his energy.

"You here today are soldiers. At long last we have cause to celebrate. You have given your nation a victory. But it is not the final battle, and your nation is desperate that you remain here to ensure that our triumph does not simply fade away." He gazed along the front line, tried to feel their mood, but the faces were mostly expressionless, simply watching him, waiting for more. His words seemed flat, his nervousness was growing, his frustration at the clumsiness, the unskilled oratory.

"We are anticipating reinforcements. You have heard the rumors, and I believe them to be true, that several hundred men are on the march here from Philadelphia. Some of you feel that it is *their* turn. Your place in the line of fire should be held by someone else, someone who has not yet done his part. I hope you will reconsider. If the raw recruit stands beside another raw recruit, it is not an army. But if he stands beside *you*, if he stands beside a soldier, then he will fight like a soldier. We cannot train so many fresh recruits for the duty that lies so close in front of us. I need you to show them what they must do. I beseech you to remain, to reenlist." There was still no response from the men, and he began to feel a blossoming depression. His words were not reaching them.

He had begged congress to send him funds, enough to provide a bounty to each man who reenlisted. But he had heard nothing thus far, knew that with their scamper to Baltimore, most of the congress was more interested in preserving their own necks than in providing for his army. And now the men in front of him were showing no enthusiasm for his words, and his frustration was growing. If a bounty was required, if that was what would inspire them, he would pay it himself.

"Any man who remains, who shall sign up for six more weeks, will be paid a bounty of ten dollars." It was pure desperation, and he saw men glancing at each other. No one seemed convinced. "I would ask you now, any man who chooses to reenlist, please step forward."

He moved the horse away, turned, watched them. There were low murmurs along the lines, but no one moved. He gave them a long moment, but still the formation was motionless. He lowered his head, let out one long breath, and blinked hard, felt himself engulfed by utter sadness. He moved the horse closer again, would not be embarrassed by his own emotions. If these men were to leave, his own pride would matter very little.

"Allow me . . . one last thought. In the campaign just passed, you and I have become an army. If that has no meaning to you, then I would ask you to imagine what is happening . . . out there. If you could see across this land, if you could see the enemy who faces us, who gathers his strength for the next fight, you would know that today he is looking at us with a different eye. Many of you had little faith you could stand up to the might of the British soldier. Now, those soldiers are confused and uncertain, have learned that your muskets, your cannon are as deadly as theirs. Many of you have feared the Hessians. Now, they fear *you*. You men have done everything that I have asked you to do. You have marched and fought and retreated and defended your ground. There are those outside this army who say that by retreating we have been disgraced. I do not agree. We are a small army, facing an enormous foe. We must seek opportunity, we must fight this war to our advantage. We have given way when there was no other option. But we are not vanquished. And today, we stand here as victors, on ground where the *enemy* gave way." There were nods now, and he felt a stab of energy, the words flowing finally.

"No army rises to greatness by the starch and finery of its uniform, no victory relies on the decorations that drape the chest of its commander. The victory you won on this ground was won by every man in this line. You won this fight for your wives, your homes, for your country. Everything you hold dear has been made more secure by your patriotism and your heroism. I know of your fatigue, I know of the hardships you have endured. But without you, I do not believe this nation can survive. If you will consent to serve for even one month longer, you will preserve the cause of liberty. I believe it is this army alone that can decide our destiny."

He ran out of words, overwhelmed again by the sadness, the frustration, moved the horse away again, stared down, his eyes clouded by despair. He waited for a long moment, resigned to the difficult job ahead, the new recruits, the men who might be coming from Philadelphia. The silence was broken by a voice, a low mumble, the man clearing his throat now. Washington looked up, saw one man making his way forward, slipping through the lines of men in front of him. Washington saw a ragged beard, the man's shirt a filthy rag, saw the man's bare feet now, the skin dark and red, hardened by the marching through the muddy snow. The man was out in front of the first line now, and Washington could see he was older, the beard flecked with gray. He looked up at Washington with a crooked frown, seemed to appraise him, said, "I don't believe you ever lied to us, General. I'll not go home while my country needs me."

The man stood alone for a moment, and now the lines were wavering, small sounds, and another man stepped forward, stood beside the older man.

"I'll not leave you, sir. Truth is, I got no place else to go."

One by one the men came forward, and as their number grew, the cheers came, the men saluting their commander as they saluted their own resolve. He sat upright in the saddle now. There were no words, just a wide smile, the space in front of him filled now with a sea of rugged faces, hands in the air, their enthusiasm flowing out, inspired by the words of their commander.

The cheering began to slow, the men now falling out of formation, the drums beating again, the staff taking charge of the business of the army, the men lining up to sign the papers. He heard hoofbeats, turned to see some of his guards escorting a carriage, a single passenger, trailed by a small group of armed militia. The man was waving to him now, calling out, "General! Sir!"

The carriage halted on the narrow road, and Washington nudged the horse that way, saw the man raise two fat canvas bags.

"General! I am here on the most urgent business, sir! I was instructed to bring this to you with the utmost haste!"

Washington was puzzled.

"Do I know you, sir? What is this?"

"I am under the instruction of Mr. Morris, sir. Robert Morris. He has instructed me to release this only to you." The man looked at the guards, seemed uncertain, lowered his voice, said, "It is . . . money, sir. Fifty thousand dollars in currency and silver. He said you had considerable need, sir."

Washington felt a raw shock, stared at the heavy bags, thought now of his friend Morris, the one congressman who had not abandoned Philadelphia, who had gone about his desperate work to raise the funds Washington would need to pay his army.

NEARLY TWELVE HUNDRED OF HIS VETERANS HAD REENLISTED FOR a six-week term, and every man among them had received his ten-dollar bounty. But there were others who would not stay, and Washington could find no fault with those who were weak with sickness, who had suffered the extreme hardships that weeks of poor clothing and bad food had caused. But there were others, and he sat across from one man now, could see embarrassment on the man's face, the short, heavy New Englander staring down at the floor, his hat in his hand. Washington had not expected the man to come to headquarters with such a dismal message, but it was clear the decision had been made.

"Colonel Glover, is there no convincing you to delay?"

Glover shook his head.

"General, I'd be lying to you if I said I wasn't looking forward to gettin' back home, sir. You have to understand, it's not patriotism alone that holds my boys here. It's a love of the boats, the water. If I have to make excuses for that, then I will. We done our part, to be sure, but there's a good many others in this country who haven't done a stinkin' damn thing for this army. Every man in the Marblehead regiment knows of someone up home who've been stayin' put and makin' their fortunes on the sea. And you know, sir, I'm not talkin' about fishing. Most of those scoundrels are raiding any boat they can find, could care less whether it's the king's goods or our own. But you know you can trust my boys, sir. No one will be keepin' anything for himself. We'll be helpin' the cause just as much, just in other ways."

"Colonel, you're talking about privateering. Raiding enemy shipping. It's piracy, you know."

Glover sat back, and Washington saw a smile.

"Now, General, we both knows that it's them pirates that's been givin' considerable assistance to this war. You can't deny it, sir. The only ones who are chokin' on that word is the British. I hear that the congress is mighty appreciative. Between the captured guns, the supplies, and the boats themselves, well, my boys feel like they're missin' out on all the fun, beggin' your pardon, sir. If this country wants to build a navy, or have any say in who runs the waterways around here, it needs men like us. After all, sir, it's the one thing we're good at."

Washington felt a small hole open inside of him, said, "You have been of great value to this army, Colonel."

"Aye, sir, and we will yet be! But I'm figurin' you won't be needin' the services of a good boatsman around here for a while, and there's good work to be done up north."

Washington could make no good argument, knew that Glover's men had more right than anyone in the army to claim they had done their duty. Glover thought for a moment.

"Not all of us is leaving, sir. Some got no family, and for reasons unexplained, they've taken to these mud swamps. So, if you're needin' somebody to row you across some godless bog hole, there's some of 'em still be of service."

It was small consolation to Washington, and Glover seemed to understand that. Washington saw the man's face reflecting his own sadness. Glover stood, said, "Sir, with your permission, we'll be headin' out."

Washington stood as well.

"May God go with you and your men, Colonel. Your country is grateful to you."

"Thank you, sir."

Glover did not wait, would not drag out the moment, was out the door. Washington stood alone for a long moment, thought of the retreat from Long Island, the crossing of the Delaware. *If he never returns, there will be no shame. He has saved this army more than once. He may yet do it again.*

---

15. CORNWALLIS

JANUARY 2, 1777

THE REACTION IN HOWE'S HEADQUARTERS TO RALL'S DISASTER WAS loud and frantic, and Cornwallis' journey to England was abruptly canceled. Again he assumed command of the army in New Jersey, crossed the Hudson, and made the journey from Amboy to Princeton in one long grueling day, a ride of over fifty miles. Cornwallis had left the headquarters escaping a firestorm of words from Howe, the man's so carefully orchestrated schedule now a complete shambles. There would be no winter quarters for the army, not yet, the civilized tradition interrupted by the astounding spectacle of this barbaric band of rebels, who would so insult the rules of war by a surprise attack on a celebration of Christmas. De Heister had been the brunt of much of Howe's tirade, and Cornwallis knew that the old Hessian would bear the shame for the whole debacle, that Colonel Rall had been his choice for the defense of Trenton. De Heister's own account of the defeat was already on its way across the Atlantic, and as Cornwallis had ridden away from Howe's headquarters, he didn't know if he would ever see de Heister again. By the time Cornwallis returned to New York, the old man might be gone, recalled by a Hessian king who had no patience for defeat.

The reports had come to Howe's headquarters one after another, every commander offering his own excuses, scrambling to paint the best picture of his role in the catastrophe at Trenton. Yet no one could put to paper the exact rebel strength or where they had placed their army.

Von Donop had responded to Rall's collapse by withdrawing his men from Bordentown, knowing that with Trenton in the hands of the rebels, no other position along the Delaware River was likely to be safe. And worse, the Hessian colonel came to realize that the rebels were pursuing him not from Trenton, but from Bordentown itself, a new wave of troops who had crossed the river after Rall's defeat. Von Donop made his way across unfamiliar farm roads, through icy streams, a frantic and miserable march to reach the safety of the British defenses at Princeton. Despite the discipline of his veterans, the utter defeat of their comrades infected the Hessian regiment with a simmering panic, and when bands of rebels began to harass their flanks, filling each night with the terror of sniper fire, the withdrawal boiled over into a chaotic retreat. To von Donop's men, it seemed that every farmer had a musket, every family was seeking bloody revenge for Hessian plunder. Von Donop's stragglers joined the few Hessians who had escaped Trenton, and as they scattered throughout the countryside, many of them simply deserted, helped by Cadwalader's militia and local farmers to cross the Delaware and find their way toward Philadelphia. As much as von Donop intended to reach Princeton, to rejoin the British in a counterattack, many of his soldiers had other ideas, were in no mood for another surprise assault.

Those British units that could be mobilized in short order were now on the move westward. From Amboy to Brunswick to Princeton, the scene was frantic determination. The reinforcements marched with unaccustomed speed, inspired by the commander who quickly overtook them. Cornwallis had ridden past the columns of fresh British regiments refusing to believe that the defeat in Trenton was anything more than the sloppy arrogance of Colonel Rall, a soldier who built no defense because he had no fear of his enemy. It had been so very common in this army, a philosophy that came from Howe himself. So many of the commanders had accepted it as absolute. No rebel can stand up to a proper soldier. Since the fight at Brooklyn, there was constant congratulation at headquarters, victory after victory, driving the rabble away with the pomp and pageantry the empire expected. But there are lessons in victory as well as defeat, and

Cornwallis believed that too many of the senior officers had learned nothing about their enemy. Even Howe's lesson from Breed's Hill seemed to be forgotten. As Cornwallis pushed the horse across the New Jersey farmlands, he was already seeing Washington in a different way. *He* is a man who learns. Yes, he understands that his men cannot stand up in a general engagement. Washington knows his own limitations, his army's weaknesses. He is a soldier after all, and he will elude us because he *must* elude us. He can only succeed if we allow him to, if we are vulnerable, if we make a *mistake*. And Colonel Rall provided him one.

The headquarters at Princeton was under the command of Cornwallis' friend Alexander Leslie, but the overall commander of the lengthy line of New Jersey posts was General James Grant. Grant was an accomplished veteran of English wars dating back over thirty years, and brought to his command a thorough disregard for the rebels, and especially for the leadership of George Washington. Grant had once made the boisterous claim to a session of Parliament that with an army of five thousand men, he could conquer all of America himself. It was a speech designed to please the newspapers, but there were no rebel marksmen in the halls of Parliament. Cornwallis would not embarrass Grant, was not riding to the front to find fault. Grant was still an exceptional field commander, and though his boastful disdain for the rebels had become a sad irony, Cornwallis knew there was an opportunity still, that if Washington was to hold on to his victory in Trenton, he might attempt to hold Trenton itself. Despite Rall's defeat, one thing had not changed. If there was a major confrontation, the rebels were still no match for the British army. Though Howe might believe fighting in winter to be uncivilized, there might yet be an opportunity to end this war.

He rode into Princeton wondering how Grant would respond to his arrival, knew that the older man would certainly not expect him so soon. Nothing had ever been done in this army with speed, but delays now could give Washington a dangerous power. The longer the British took to respond, the greater the chance that public opinion would swing toward the rebel cause. The result could be a sudden influx of militia to Washington's army, an enormous increase in morale. Whether or not that would matter on the battlefield, it would certainly matter to congress, and to Parliament.

He rode past the college again, saw a few lanterns, guard posts placed at the intersections. He led a company of dragoons, and the guards welcomed the horsemen with raised arms and cheers, few realizing that Cornwallis himself was among them. They turned down a side street, moved toward headquarters, and Cornwallis began to dread seeing Grant, thought, He should not have been in command of such an important position, especially with its most vulnerable outpost manned by Hessians. It was a problem for most of the British commanders, the awkward relationship between British and Hessian officers that might now be worse than ever. But the chain of command should always prevail, and Cornwallis knew that if you made a decent effort at diplomacy, you could give an order to anyone in the Hessian command. Tradition or not, pride or not, the Hessians were subordinate to their British counterparts. Even Grant would understand that the Hessians had been humbled now. One of their senior officers had lost his life in their worst defeat of the war.

It was very late, and he climbed down from the horse with a stiffening pain in every joint in his body. Just outside the town, he had overtaken a column of Highlanders, and he could hear their bagpipes. He stretched his back, thought, They've marched as far as I have ridden, and there will be no complaining from their lot. There shall not be a word out of me either.

The dragoons had dispersed, one of Grant's staff guiding them to a camp. Cornwallis' staff had been strung out on the road, the last pair of aides now arriving. He showed patience, waited for them to dismount their exhausted horses. He scanned their faces, saw the twists and frowns, younger men all.

"Rest your bones, gentlemen. This journey is not yet over. We will be moving out in the morning. I suggest you find something to eat."

He could hear small moans, had no patience for complaining, stepped gingerly toward the headquarters, sharp pains in both hips. The doorway was alive with firelight, and he thought of food, but there were no smells, the evening meal long past. He straightened himself, waited for the stoic guards to open the door. The bagpipes behind him were drowned out by music of a different kind now, from inside the headquarters. He could hear a violin and bad singing, and not all of it from men. He stepped inside, was surprised at the festive mood, men around a table, several bottles emptied, a group of brightly dressed women gathered around a pair of musicians. The music stopped, and the voices grew quiet, and he brushed at the dust on his disheveled uniform, was in no mood for pleasantries. He saw Grant, the older man sitting tall in a chair, looking at him with a strained smile. Grant suddenly rose, said, "Ah, General Cornwallis, welcome. Forgive me, sir, but you appear to be in need of a rather stiff beverage."

Cornwallis felt his weariness giving way to annoyance.

"No, General Grant, I do not require any *beverage*." The word came out of him with a spitting hiss. "I did not expect to find a party. It is certainly not in *my* honor. Whose honor might it be? A memorial for Colonel Rall perhaps? General de Heister? Or perhaps you would have us salute the man who brought so many of us back out here? Would that be *General* Washington?" There was complete silence, and he saw Grant's expression change, regretted his outburst, No, there is no need to shame the man.

Grant motioned to the women.

"Ladies, you will excuse us. The musicians may leave."

There were disappointed protests from the women, but they obeyed, and the dresses swirled past Cornwallis, a cloud of perfume engulfing him. Grant waited for the room to clear.

"General, if you feel it is appropriate, then I offer my apologies. This may seem to be a party, only because there has been a considerable brightening of spirit in this camp. Over the past two days, the arrival of the reinforcements has brought a new vigor to these proceedings. Not a man here fails to see that there will be a considerable and inevitable turnabout, a glorious reversal in the affairs of this past week."

It was the speech of a man accustomed to giving speeches. Cornwallis looked around the room, familiar faces all, Leslie giving him a small self-conscious nod. He moved to a chair, sat slowly, a stab of pain in his back, blinked hard, fought the dust in his eyes, said, "I have had an exceptionally tiresome day. It would not be prudent of any one of you to ask my particular view toward the affairs of this past week."

He could see Grant deflate now, and the man seemed to slump as he sat. Cornwallis thought, No, do not worry, General, I did not come here to censure you. "Do we know the disposition and strength of the rebel forces? Where exactly is Mr. Washington?"

No one spoke, and he could see faces turning toward Grant. Cornwallis wiped at his face with dirty gloves, said, "Do you have a report for me, General Grant?"

"I can only relate to you what our scouts have determined, sir. The rebels have occupied Trenton and seem content to remain there. They have made forays toward our position, capturing a miniscule amount of supplies, wagons and whatnot, but of no consequence. I do not know, precisely, where Mr. Washington may be found."

Cornwallis heard the familiar tone in Grant's voice, the arrogant dismissal of Washington, thought, Hardly the time, General. He felt a cavernous hole in his stomach, the exhaustion of the day blossoming into an overwhelming desire for a simple plate of bread and meat.

"I require some rest, gentlemen, thus I will be brief. Tomorrow morning, this army will advance in column toward Trenton. We will confront whatever defensive position the rebels have constructed. If Mr. Washington chooses to remain on this side of the river, his army will be annihilated. Good evening, gentlemen."

Cornwallis stood slowly, and around the room, the others stood as well. He turned toward the door, was suddenly frozen in place by Grant's booming voice.

"Quite so, sir! Let us sweep up this rabble once and for all! They are certainly no match for us! I shall enjoy seeing Mr. Washington wearing a rope!"

Cornwallis looked at Grant's purposeful grin, fought the words in his mind, wanted to wipe away the man's arrogance, thought, That rabble has just given us a thorough thrashing, and you have already forgotten? He sorted out his words, said, "Let us not dwell on what *should* be, General. Let us use the means we have at hand, and make it so. Whether or not Mr. Washington is a match for this army is still to be determined. I intend to find out."

THE MARCH BEGAN EARLY, AND IMMEDIATELY THEY WERE CONfronted by musket fire from carefully hidden defenses. Across every creek bed the ground had been littered with cut trees, and in every narrow pass the woods held marksmen. As the army inched its way closer to Trenton, the resistance became more organized, stronger, rebel earthworks concealing well-placed cannon, entire companies of riflemen chasing the British skirmishers back to their main column. Over each hill, past each patch of woods, the constant pressure from the rebels had to be met, and Cornwallis was forced to spread the army into a line of battle. Each time they would push forward with bayonets ready, only to find the rebels vanishing in front of them. The regiments would assemble again into the column of march, only to hear another burst of musket fire. By the time they reached Trenton, it was after dark. The ten-mile march had taken over ten hours.

THE DRAGOONS HAD SPREAD OUT THROUGH THE STREETS OF TRENton, harassed only by the occasional sniper. His staff was nervous, but Cornwallis pushed ahead, saw to the placing of the army, the wider streets giving them room to make camp. He would not be as careless as Rall, would not scatter his cannon in useless display, but kept the guns together, their crews ready to move on short notice, anywhere they were needed.

There had been a brisk fight along Assunpink Creek, and the main body of the army was still facing the enemy on the far side, separated by a short span of icy water. With artillery on both sides covering one bridge it was a standoff for the moment, neither side wanting to venture into a difficult fight in the dark.

He eased his horse down narrow streets, the staff carrying no lantern, no target for a marksman. He could not see the condition of the houses, and it didn't matter after all. It was a town already trampled by two armies, and surely the rebels had abused what the Hessians did not destroy.

There was a sharp whine, and down a side street the smashing of wood and glass. Yes, of course you will drop your iron, just enough to keep us on edge, to lose us some sleep. He knew the name, Knox, the rotund bookseller from Boston. How is it you know your artillery? But then, your entire army is made up of men like you. A gun in one hand, and a military manual in the other. How in God's name could the Hessians have allowed you such an advantage?

Couriers were riding past him, reporting the troop placements to his staff, the men speaking in low whispers. He could make out a line of soldiers forming close to the creek, and he nudged

the side of his horse, rode that way. Past a double line of crouching soldiers he could see the ground fall away to black water, and farther down, he could see the bridge that had been such an object of contention. He knew the soldiers were waiting for orders, that if he decided to engage the rebels again, they would surge ahead, right down into the water. He stopped the horse, heard low voices, the officers', saw another line of men adding to the strength. Across the creek, the skyline was lit by a long row of rebel campfires, the reflection on the faces of the British troops who stared at them. He felt himself shiver, thought, A crossing here will be difficult even in daylight. They fought to a stalemate today. In the dark, nothing good can be accomplished, and these men already know that. Those who have just arrived are too exhausted even to try.

He stared at the distant campfires, could hear the sound of shovels, axes, the rebels strengthening their defense. Yes, Mr. Washington, you know that as well. But *behind* you is a wide river, and unless you have all your boats, you aren't going anywhere at all. He turned the horse, surprising his aides, said, "I wish to see General Grant. I must learn what the scouts have to say."

THE WINDOWS WERE COVERED IN BLACK CLOTH, HIDING THE HEADquarters from the continuing annoyance of the rebel cannon. Grant was laying out a map, and Cornwallis moved around the small table, pointed to the creek, said, "Is there any one place more suited for a crossing? The bridge will be the focus of their artillery. How shallow is the water along this stretch, here?"

Grant looked to an aide, who stepped forward, said, "General, according to the men who fought there today, there are depths to a man's chest along most of the creek. Some more shallow areas, of course, but we do not have the exact locations."

There was a knock at the door, it opened slightly, and one of Grant's aides held a black cloth up to shield the lantern. A voice from outside said, "Excuse me, sirs. Scout's arrived."

Grant motioned, and quickly the man was inside, the door closing behind him. Cornwallis was studying the map, saw the scout's face, unfamiliar, was surprised to see the gray hair of a veteran. The scout was wide-eyed, seemed surprised by the presence of Cornwallis, said, "Sirs! Forgive the interruption. I have just returned from the river just north of town. We have scouted up that direction for a good bit. We ran into a bit of a flurry, rather like stumbling over a bee's nest. No casualties though, sir. Even their squirrel hunters can't shoot in the dark. But sir, the rebels have got their boats under pretty strong guard."

Cornwallis absorbed the word.

"*Boats?* You found the rebels' boats?"

The man's confidence seemed to wilt under Cornwallis' stare, said, "Um . . . yes, sir. Quite. Just above the town."

Cornwallis was skeptical.

"Do you mean that the rebels are separated from their boats? What of the river south of town?"

The scout showed no hesitation.

"No, sir. I was down the river myself when the artillery fire stopped. We were trying to find some route to get in behind the rebel position, slipped our way right out to the river proper. There are no boats there. They're all upriver, sir."

Cornwallis felt a surge of enthusiasm, looked at Grant, said, "General, can you tell me how the rebels might escape across the river, if *we* are between their men and their boats?"

Grant understood, was smiling now, said, "No, sir. I cannot."

Behind him, another man spoke. "General, it is our best chance! We can take it to them right now!"

There were murmurs of agreement, and Cornwallis looked around the room, saw that the comment had come from his quartermaster.

"Thank you for your suggestion, Mr. Erskine." Grant was looking at him with the same hopefulness, and Cornwallis rubbed his hands together, said, "Gentlemen, they cannot reach their boats tonight. There is no need for haste. Crossing the Assunpink Creek will be a deadly affair in the dark, and there is no point in distressing the troops so severely. This army needs its rest. We will be fresh in the morning."

He was feeling the spirit now, the first time in a long while, the sense that finally something good would happen. They were a long way from New York, from General Howe, from the politics and foppery of the city. Out here it was army against army, strength against strength, and when the sun came up, they would have their confrontation. It was all he had hoped for, and it was coming to pass from an unexpected surprise. This time it was

Washington who had made the mistake. He looked at the map, ran his finger around the rebel position, the campfires, tried to imagine the desperation of those men as they dug their earthworks, the utter terror of what they would face in the morning. He smiled, thought of Washington. You have backed yourself into a dangerous and desperate position, and now you will pay the price. He looked around the room, could see the optimism, their excitement building with his.

"Gentlemen, we have him. We finally have him. Tomorrow morning, we shall bag the fox."

16. WASHINGTON

JANUARY 3, 1777

JOSEPH REED HAD PUT HIS EMBARRASSMENT ASIDE AND AGREED TO return to headquarters, and Washington would make no comment about the man's indiscretions with Charles Lee. Reed's response to Washington's generosity was to take responsibility for leading a scouting party in the direction of Princeton. Reed had a home in Trenton, knew the land and the roadways, and if the army was to find the means of escaping Cornwallis' certain attack, Reed was certain he could find it.

The council of war had been a quiet affair, no one obsessed with his own glory, every senior commander aware that the army was facing a serious dilemma. They could not remain behind Assunpink Creek in the face of the strength Cornwallis brought against them. Despite the good work of the men with the shovels, if the British succeeded in crossing the creek, the boats could not be brought down quickly enough to make an escape. If Cornwallis pressed them hard against the river, Washington's men would have nowhere to go.

The Assunpink Creek wound its way farther inland and gradually grew more shallow, cutting through woods and farmlands where the maps were incomplete. But Reed had made his own

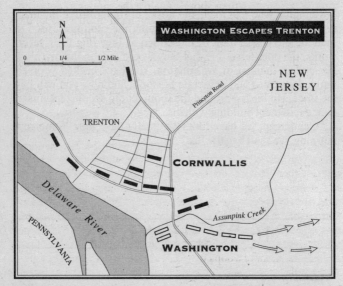

sketch, the route to a narrow trail that paralleled the Post Road to
Princeton. The scouting party had picked their way back from
Princeton without confronting a single British soldier. If Cornwallis was even aware of the trail, no one in the British camp had
taken care to patrol it. Reed estimated the British had only three
regiments still in Princeton, around twelve hundred men, and
beyond, their enormous supply depot at Brunswick was barely
defended. If the army could push another night march, the surprise might overwhelm both positions and put Cornwallis in a
serious hole.

For several days, the weather had been mild, a thaw that mud-
died the roads, but this night, when darkness came the winter
returned, and temperatures plunged again. When the ground began to harden, Washington knew that the men and the cannon
would have a much easier march. A little after midnight, the
army slipped away from the fortifications behind Assunpink
Creek and began to follow Reed's trail. The wheels of the cannon
had been wrapped in cloth, and every man knew that before the
hard cold dawn, they would need absolute quiet.

Behind Assunpink Creek, Washington had ordered four hundred men to continue their noisy work all night long, stoking the

campfires, clanging their shovels against the stumps of cut trees, all a very good show of an army digging itself in. Just before the first light, they too would follow the trail away from their hard work, their mission accomplished. If the plan was successful, Cornwallis would still bombard the earthworks, would still send his men swarming through the chilly waters of the Assunpink. On the crest of the long rise, Washington's campfires would still be smoldering, but the trenches would be empty.

HE RODE IN THE STILL DARKNESS, TRYING TO REMEMBER HIS WORDS that had inspired the men to stay with the army, but his memory was a fog, the only vivid picture in his mind the single veteran who led them forward. Around him, the soldiers marched as they had marched down to Trenton, each man holding himself in the road by keeping close to the man in front of him. But the soldiers were exhausted beyond anything they had experienced before, and at each pause in the march, men would simply collapse where they stood, others falling asleep while still on their feet. Behind them, more troops would be marching still, and the collision would jar them all into sudden alarm. The sudden surprises were not all harmless. Far back in the column the silence had been shattered by a sudden wave of shouting, and Washington had ridden back to find that Cadwalader's militia had suddenly panicked, a bizarre rumor spreading through the men that they were suddenly surrounded by the Hessians they had once pursued. The outburst had slowed the march, but the panic was mostly contained, only a few men disappearing into the night, chased by a nightmare that might pursue them all the way to Philadelphia.

As the army drew closer to Princeton, Washington could not keep the daylight away, and as at Trenton, the march took longer than he had planned. The last two miles would find the army bathed in stark rising sunlight, a brisk cold windless day. But there had been no sign at all of British soldiers, no patrol, no scouts. As the men continued their slow shuffle along the narrow trail, hidden from the vast rolling fields, he was feeling the mix of excitement and relief, convinced that Cornwallis still had no idea where these troops had gone.

THEY MOVED THROUGH THICK TREES THAT RAN ALONGSIDE A NARrow deep creek called Stony Brook. The creek ran straight up to the Post Road, where it flowed beneath a wooden bridge, a key barricade to slowing down any march by the British. He could see another road, turning away to the right, leading out into an open field, then dropping down into a long ravine. Washington stopped the horse, and Reed pointed.

"The back road. That will lead us south of the town."

There was pride in Reed's voice, and Washington nodded silently, thought, Every piece of information he has given me has been accurate. Sullivan's division was already following Reed's map, the column marching toward the ravine, and behind Sullivan came one of Greene's brigades, commanded by Hugh Mercer. Mercer was actually a doctor, another of the old veterans, a crusty Scotsman Washington had known since the French and Indian War.

It was no accident that Mercer was now beside him, that he had been given the most important assignment of the mission. Mercer was to lead a force of three hundred fifty men straight up the Stony Brook, and destroy the bridge over the Post Road. Once the bridge was gone, it would be a simple matter for marksmen to seriously delay any British crossing, whether it be a retreat by the troops in Princeton or the sudden appearance of Cornwallis, who would certainly move quickly once Washington's escape was revealed.

Washington pointed along the wooded trail, and Mercer smiled at him, unusual for the stern Scotsman.

"General, we'll see you on t'other side a'hell."

Mercer saluted him, and his men were quickly in motion. Washington watched him until his column had moved beyond the intersection, thought of the wilderness in Virginia, the disaster of General Braddock. It had been twenty years now, and he could still recall marching with Mercer alongside British troops who even then despised anything American. Godspeed, General Mercer. We may all have our sweet memories of this day.

More troops in the long column were moving past him, turning onto the back road. He spurred the horse, rode quickly alongside them, broke out past the trees, felt the warmth of the sunlight. To the left, a wide grassy field rose up away from him, obscuring his view of the Post Road. He turned out into the field, the horse stepping through a thin layer of glistening frost. He climbed the long slope, could see the hill cresting around a pair of farmhouses. Behind him, he saw Sullivan's men, the head of the column farther east, a ripple of motion as the men moved through the ravine. They did not have to be prodded now, there was no falling out for sleep. They all knew how close they were to the British, that they had yet to be discovered, that so far, everything had happened according to plan.

Above him on the hill, he saw a rider, an officer, coming down from the crest. The man rode past a line of skirmishers, and Washington motioned to Tilghman, who moved up the hill. The officer met Tilghman on the slope, and Washington could see the man pointing back up the hill. Washington spurred his horse, moved closer. Tilghman said, "Sir, Major Wilkinson reports a column of British troops up on the Post Road. They were on the march west, but have turned, and are in line moving this way."

"How many?"

Wilkinson shook his head, said, "Could only see one regiment at most, sir. They had already crossed the bridge. General Mercer's men were coming out of the trees, moving out this way."

Washington digested the image, thought, Mercer has seen the British, must know he can no longer destroy the bridge. He could see nothing, the hillside still blocking any view of the main road. So the British are on the march, but where? Only one regiment? It came together in his mind now. These British are marching *west*, toward Trenton. It was the first time he knew for certain that Cornwallis had been fooled. If Cornwallis was still expecting a sharp fight along the Assunpink Creek, he would certainly order the Princeton garrison to send reserve strength to Trenton. These troops had no doubt begun their march at first light. From that vantage point, they could certainly have spotted Mercer. It is simply bad fortune. If we had only been here earlier . . .

There was musket fire now, up toward the bridge, where Mercer's men would certainly be. He rode that way, glanced behind him down the hill, the last of the main column below him. He focused again on the sounds, one solid volley, scattered shots. He said to Tilghman, "Go to the main column. Divert the three units of the rear guard this way, have them advance in haste. I will see what we are facing. General Sullivan and the remainder of the column must keep moving toward Princeton."

Tilghman was gone quickly, and Washington was surrounded by his skirmishers, the men pulling closer to his horse, protecting their commander. He listened again, another sharp volley, but it was not as many muskets. He knew Mercer would make the good fight, but he had to see. He reached the crest of the hill, could hear the shouts of men blending in with the scattered firing. There was a thick grove of trees, an orchard, a dense cloud of smoke rising above. To his right was the highest point along the crest, framed by the two farmhouses. He watched the fight in the orchard, then looked anxiously behind him, some sign of the advance of his men from the road. Finally they came, a solid line, and he saw Edward Hand's Pennsylvanians, followed by a line of Virginia riflemen. As they moved past him, they were running, every man seeing the fight. Washington focused again on the orchard, but the firing had stopped, just shouts, and Mercer's men emerged from the orchard, some stumbling, wounded, others in a fast run.

He could see bits of color now, the British moving through the orchard, some pursuing Mercer's retreat. Up on the rise, more British suddenly appeared, spreading into line, moving toward Hand's men. The two regiments moved toward each other, no firing, Hand's men allowing Mercer's refugees to stream past. He began to shout at the retreating men, "Stop! Hold here! Fall in with these men!" Other officers were assembling, some quieting the panic, and the veterans responded, many of Mercer's men gathering in their own fear, falling in behind Hand's line. The British were still advancing, and Washington took off his hat, saw the last of Mercer's retreating men, some scattered behind Hand's line, some wandering, dazed, some moving forward again, absorbed by the advance of Hand's men. He saw one small group still running back, stumbling, exhausted men, and they were close to him now, the faces looking at him, the men slowing, fighting for breath, and he shouted at them, "Come with us! They are but a handful! We shall have them!"

He waved the hat, spurred the horse, and the men responded, found their way into the line of the Pennsylvanians, and he cheered them, knew they would not falter now. Nearly all of Mercer's men were advancing again into the brief fight they had just lost, their panic erased by the strength of the men beside them. The British were less than fifty yards away, the gap between the two armies closing rapidly, and he spurred the horse, bolted forward, was out in front of Hand's men, stopped the horse between the two lines. The British were barely thirty yards from him, halted their line, and he waved the hat again, looked back at his men, shouted, "Halt!"

The soldiers were facing each other, a long silent moment, Washington between them still, and he raised the hat, shouted, "Fire!"

A smoky blast erupted around him from both sides, the musket fire engulfing him in a roar of sounds. The horse jumped, and he held tight to the reins, stared hard toward the British, could hear the cries and groans, most of the British line a heap of fallen bodies. The men who were not hit were pulling back, the British officers waving their swords, the retreat orderly, but then, the order was gone. They began to run, scrambling back along the side of the hill in a rolling wave of red. His men were around him, wildly cheering, the men looking at him with awestruck relief. Tilghman was there, grabbing the reins, shouting, screaming something, a prayer, some kind of curse, crying relief. Washington could not hear the young man's words, his ears still ringing from the cascade of musket fire, the voices of his men. But he focused on the British, disappearing out toward the Post Road, leaving so many of their own in the field around him.

SULLIVAN'S MEN HAD MET THEIR OWN RESISTANCE CLOSER TO THE town, had driven more of the British garrison away in a glorious rout. The British were in full retreat, some escaping west on the road to Trenton. Others were in full flight, disappearing into the countryside. Both wings of Washington's assault closed in on the town itself. As he reached the open grounds of the college, there was a new scattering of musket fire, piercing the air around him, his men rushing forward on the roads, officers up front pointing the way. He could see flashes now, bursts of firing from the windows of Nassau Hall. Around the large building, his men were beginning to return fire, but they were in the open, British troops smashing out windows, firing from the protection of the brick walls. Cannon were rolling past him, and he looked for Knox, but the guns were manned by another officer, a very young man he had come to know at Harlem Heights. Washington remembered the first meeting, Knox pointing him out, giving the commander notice to watch this young man, some instinct Knox had, that Alexander Hamilton would perform an exceptional service to this army. Washington moved closer, would not interfere as

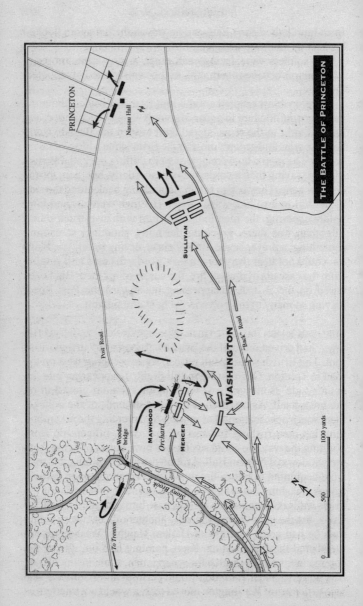

THE BATTLE OF PRINCETON

PRINCETON

Nassau Hall

SULLIVAN

Post Road

WASHINGTON

"Back" Road

MAWHOOD

Orchard

MERCER

Stony Brook

Wooden bridge

To Trenton

N

0   500   1000 yards

the guns were unhitched and swung around, and now Hamilton looked toward him, seemed to wait for instructions. Well, yes. I would not have anyone destroying this college without orders. Washington was beside the guns now, said, "Captain Hamilton, the enemy is causing us some inconvenience. Are you carrying solid shot? Can you provide them some discouragement?"

Hamilton was all seriousness, gave a crisp order, his crew loading the brass six-pounders, and he put his hand on the wheel of one gun now, said, "General, upon your order, sir."

The musket fire was still coming from Nassau Hall, and Washington heard one ball whiz closely overhead, could see a British soldier in a first-floor window, the man staring at him with recognition, and Washington thought, No need to give him another opportunity.

"Captain, you may fire."

The two guns jumped to life, the blasts of smoke rising quickly, and Washington could see shattered brick, a ragged hole in the wall just around the corner where his British assailant had been. Now there was a shout, and a dozen men surged forward, began to push through the doors of the Hall. The windows were vacant now, the British position in obvious turmoil, and suddenly, from the same window where the marksman had missed his opportunity, a white cloth appeared. More white began to emerge from the windows of the upper floors, and more of Washington's men pushed inside. Quickly the British were herded out, a dozen, then more, their number growing. From around the college officers were gathering troops, sending them quickly to surround the British, who continued to flow out of Nassau Hall. Washington backed away, saw Hamilton pulling the guns back, making room in the open yard. Finally the men who emerged through the doorway were his own, and Washington scanned the British, silent, sullen faces, nearly two hundred men, half a regiment of prisoners.

His troops were gathering still, some only staring, others laughing, calling out to the British, who did not respond, the captured men seeming to press together, closing ranks against this new kind of assault. Washington thought, How odd that they would fear us. Are we so unknown to them?

He saw one man burst out of the doorway of the Hall, the man running toward the cannon now, gripping a bottle of some dark liquid, and the man shouted toward Hamilton, "Captain, you're a fine shot, sir! You blowed a hole right through a painting of King George!"

From the upper floors of Nassau Hall, more of his men were cheering, calling out, some displaying bits of uniforms, British hats, swords. There was no longer any battle, the mood of the army changing abruptly to a celebration. All through the surrounding houses and shops, men were emerging with British prisoners, supply officers mostly, noncombatants. Others carried all manner of British uniforms, packs, supplies of every kind. One man was pulling a small wagon by himself, and Washington could see the cargo, a stack of white cloth, fresh tents, blankets. He would not stop them, knew that out on the Post Road Mercer's men were holding tight, a careful eye toward Trenton, artillery pieces now doing the job of destroying the bridge over Stony Brook. He knew Cornwallis would surely be coming, but for the moment, there was no danger. The men had desperate needs, and the blankets and clothing of the British would replace many of the rags his men carried. He was actually enjoying the spectacle, the pure joy of his army, another extraordinary day, another gift to the nation, another victory.

Men began to emerge from Nassau Hall again, and there was something new, a man holding a loaf of bread, and another a bottle, the man shouting, "There's a fine feast here! We done interrupted their lunch!"

Men began to flood into the hall, and Washington knew he could not keep them from a meal, would not try. The officers were filling in the gaps around the British prisoners, were now herding them away in the road, and Washington felt his own hunger, could smell what the troops had discovered, some kind of soldier's mess in Nassau Hall, a delicious odor of something still cooking. He climbed down from the horse, and Tilghman was beside him, the young man stepping in front of him, blocking the way. Washington stopped, said, "It seems the British have obliged us with a meal. If we are fortunate, there will be enough for all. However, if we do not make haste, the men may consume every scrap before we can find something for ourselves."

Tilghman did not reflect Washington's good spirits, seemed not to hear him, said, "Sir, I have to say . . . you put a mighty fright in us today. We all thought . . . well, sir, we all thought you had put yourself in harm's way. We were greatly relieved that you survived."

He was surprised by Tilghman's emotions, looked at the rest of the staff, some men nodding, echoing what Tilghman had said. He tried to recall the moment, the horse carrying him out in front of the men.

"Gentlemen, a commander must lead his men."

Tilghman began to protest, and Washington held up a hand.

"I am grateful for your concern. In the heat of battle, we do not always think of our own safety. And, as you can see, on this day, I was blessed by the hand of the Almighty. Indeed, on this day . . . we were all blessed."

HE RODE BACK ACROSS THE WIDE HILLSIDE, THE GROUND STILL LIT-tered with heaps of red. Some of the wounded had been moved, but there were many more still to be tended, and he moved past them holding the thought away from his mind. On the crest of the hill, the two farmhouses were now hospitals, and before he could put his army into motion again, before he could begin any kind of new march, he had to visit the men who would stay behind. And one of them was Hugh Mercer.

He stepped into the house, could hear the sounds of the dying, sharp screams and low groans. Every room was lined with men, and their clothing showed a mix from both armies. He saw women, kneeling, wrapping bloody limbs, and he moved past them without speaking, thought, The farmer, perhaps, his family. Their peaceful home was suddenly the center of a battlefield, and yet they remain here to help. We are blessed with such people as these.

He glanced into a small room, saw a man in a British uniform, the insignia of a doctor, bent over, tending to a man in a blue coat. Washington looked over the doctor's shoulder, saw the wounded man's face, and his heart turned cold. It was Mercer.

The doctor looked up at him, no recognition, and Washington said, "Sir, if you please, I would speak to my officer."

The doctor said nothing, moved quickly to another man, and Washington knelt, relieved to see Mercer's clear eyes, said, "General, it is nothing serious, I pray."

Mercer smiled slightly.

"Can't say for sure, sir. Told that chap I'm a doctor myself, he didn't believe me, wouldn't tell me anything. I do know one thing, sir. I'm about as full of holes as a man can be and still be in one piece."

Washington could see bloody rips in Mercer's coat, spots of blood on the man's legs.

"They thought I was you, sir."

Washington was puzzled, said, "The British?"

Mercer nodded. "Thought they had captured the commander in chief. They were mighty rude about it too, as though General Washington would have been so unwise as to walk himself right into the line of fire. I took it as an insult, sir. On your behalf, of course. No excuse for myself."

Washington could not help thinking of the scolding from Tilghman, and Mercer took a long deep breath, gripped Washington by the arm, raised his head slightly, said, "We hurt 'em, General. Dropped a good many. We got off three good volleys, but I give the redcoats their due, they kept coming. They shot my horse, didn't have much choice but to lead the men on foot. But we couldn't stand up to the bayonets. I ordered them to fall back, and then . . . well, I wasn't about to let a redcoat insult you, sir."

Mercer laid his head down, another long breath, and Washington felt the man's grip loosen on his arm.

"You did your part, General. We won the day."

The man's eyes were closed now, and Washington felt himself shake, put a quivering hand on a bloody stain on the man's chest, could still feel movement, soft slow breaths, thought, *Thank God.* He looked for the British doctor, but the man was out of the room, and Washington stood, stared down at the old Scotsman, blood on every part of his clothes. He backed away slowly, the smell of the room filling him, the doctor moving past him again, carrying a wad of white linen, going about his work with calm precision. Washington stood in the doorway for a moment, looked again at Mercer.

"God bless you, General. We won the day."

AFTER THE FOOD HAD BEEN CONSUMED, AND THE ARMY HAD GATH-ered as much of the British supplies as they could carry, he assembled the officers to survey the condition of his troops. The British supply depot at Brunswick was another hard day's march, and Cornwallis would be pursuing them from behind, but no matter how much speed the British commander could make, Washington's men had the head start. He was still not sure of the British troop strength at Brunswick, the reports from the scouts inconsistent. Some believed it was unprotected, and Washington wondered if those reports were more wishful thinking than good scouting. But others believed that Howe had continued to send reinforcements from Amboy, and any move on Brunswick might involve another sharp fight. The spirit of the army might be willing, but every officer understood that to push the men on yet another forced march, to the probability of yet another fight would exceed what his men could endure. With Cornwallis in pursuit, any hesitation on the march, any need to stop the army even for a brief rest could result in a sudden disastrous attack from behind.

The road to Brunswick divided at Kingston, the army arriving at dark as a storm of fresh snow began to cover the trees. When the army reached the intersection, their commander agonized still over his decision, the dangerous temptation to continue marching the men toward Brunswick. Most of the men were still in rags, again leaving a trail of bloody footprints, and no matter the stores that might wait for them in Brunswick, they were still a brutally exhausted army. Few of the men knew what the intersection meant, and when Washington gave the order to march on the left fork, few knew that they were heading northward, to a place called Morristown. There they could make camp safely, would be protected, surrounded by great fat hills. Cornwallis would not follow them, would listen instead to the orders from General Howe, the British commander who would finally be allowed his winter quarters. If Washington's men didn't know the roads, didn't realize that they would finally have some rest, every man understood that in the past ten days, the tall man on the large white horse had led them through the battles that had inspired their nation, shocked their enemy, and changed the war.

PART TWO

BENJAMIN FRANKLIN

17. FRANKLIN

HE HAD ARRIVED ON THE COAST OF FRANCE IN EARLY DECEMBER, after a tormenting voyage that had aggravated every ailment he suffered. In the past, crossing the Atlantic had always been an adventure, a time for experiment, long hours testing the currents, the water temperature, all the fun of exploration. But his age was betraying him, and though he turned his efforts again to the science of the ocean, the aches and pains sapped him of any enthusiasm. By the time the ship moved close to the French coast, he was ready to feel dry land under his swollen feet. But there was one more torment. The winds kept the ship away from its intended port of call, and in frustration he disembarked at the wretched coastal town of Auray, welcomed by no one.

He was accompanied by his two grandsons. Temple was now seventeen, the boy displaying an interest in politics that would not be considered unusual, given his father's notoriety as one of King George's most loyal governors. Franklin had been careful not to influence Temple by speaking ill of the boy's father, even though Temple was more aware than anyone that the break between his father and grandfather was permanent and absolute. Franklin had convinced himself that the boy's eagerness to accompany him abroad, possibly as his secretary, was a victory of sorts, if not for America, then for the old man himself.

Benny was seven, his daughter Sally's son, and politics was nowhere in the younger boy's mind. The journey was the adventure of a lifetime, the youngster traveling with his grandfather to worlds that barely existed in a seven-year-old's imagination.

The difficulties of the sea voyage extended onto land. Since they had not disembarked at a major seaport, finding comfortable passage inland was a challenge. Eventually, they reached Paris, after a nerve-fraying ride through desolate forests said to be overrun with ruthless bandits. For Benny, it was yet another adventure. For Franklin, it was the final tormenting chapter in a journey that had been far too difficult a distraction for the work he had come to do.

When they finally reached Paris, he moved them into the comforts of the Hotel d'Hambourg. Franklin was relieved to find that Temple could manage mostly for himself, the young man adapting immediately to the social settings, basking in the attention his famous grandfather attracted. The young man was already catching the eye of a number of flirtatious daughters of society.

But Franklin was uneasy about caring for Benny. He was, after all, only a child, and would still require considerable schooling. Franklin had once believed that his influence, his wise counsel would be all the boy would ever need, but it was an old man's vanity, and he learned that quickly on the long voyage across the Atlantic. Sally had warned him of her son's boisterous curiosity, and Benny had engulfed his grandfather in endless questions about ships and oceans and France. Even if Franklin had wanted to provide so much enlightenment, his ailments dampened his enthusiasm for the sudden foray into being a parent.

FRANKLIN HAD BEEN INVOLVED IN THE NEGOTIATIONS WITH FRANCE for over a year, but only in the most discreet and secretive way. To any foreign government America was still officially a part of the British empire, and no one in the French government would risk a confrontation with their eternal enemy by openly meddling in King George's internal affairs. But the finances of making war had created a disaster for the American cause far worse than any rout on a battlefield. Congress was operating in bankruptcy, and no amount of debate or meetings in committees could solve the problem of supplying Washington's army. The troops themselves might be accustomed to late pay, but many did not yet know what Franklin knew, that the congress had exhausted every means of feeding and clothing them, not to mention the purchase of guns and ammunition, horses and wagons.

From the earliest days of the congress, Franklin had supported the attempt at a foreign alliance, that in order to achieve independence, there might first have to be some kind of dependence on a foreign power who saw the loss to England as a gain for themselves. The most logical choice was France, the one country whose conflicts with England had produced centuries of warfare. But France was not eager to renew a war she had lost thirteen years earlier.

With Franklin's prodding, France had offered a gesture of friendship by accepting an unofficial visitor from congress, whose duties would be harmless enough, a man who would only provide information of events in America. That man was Silas Deane, a Connecticut congressman with a particular talent for finance. Despite the public face of the French court, Deane's real mission was to pursue any form of assistance France would be willing to provide, presumably in the form of military hardware. But France could not do business directly with America without risking war with Britain. Thus, Deane's mission had involved him in convoluted deal-making, the French nervously offering minimal assistance through nefarious business channels. The result had been a slow trickle of munitions from French manufacturers which could reach America only after sailing through the French West Indies, where the goods could be transferred to American ships.

Once the Declaration of Independence had been signed, the French government could feel more comfortable speaking directly to official representatives of the American congress, though a war with Britain was still the likely outcome. As the desperation in supplying Washington's army increased, congress responded by naming three commissioners to openly negotiate for French involvement. Deane would remain in Paris as one of them. Franklin was an obvious choice, with his experience in Paris, and his familiarity with the French court. The third commissioner was to have been Thomas Jefferson, and Franklin had been enthusiastic to be working again with the young Virginian. He had enormous respect for Jefferson's mind, and for his humility. The negotiations with the French would be ticklish certainly, and Jefferson would never be one to make some grand show in Paris, placing his own ambitions ahead of the job at hand. But as Jefferson was preparing to sail for France, his wife had fallen ill, and the young man had chosen to remain in Virginia. The congress replaced him with a man who contrasted completely with Jefferson's quiet subtlety, another Virginian. His name was Arthur Lee.

Lee was the brother of one of the stalwart champions of the Declaration of Independence, Richard Henry Lee. But Arthur

Lee possessed none of his brother's gift for diplomacy or passion
for any cause other than his own. Franklin had known him from
their time in London, Lee serving as the colonial representative
from Virginia, as Franklin had done for four other colonies. Lee
fancied himself a shrewd manipulator of public policy, and
while in London he grew close to those members of Parliament
who openly opposed the policies of King George. Once the king
declared the colonies to be in open rebellion, there was no official purpose to Lee staying in London. To his few friends in
Philadelphia, it was an appropriate next step for Lee to join
Deane's efforts in France. But the news that Arthur Lee would be
arriving in Paris seriously dampened Franklin's enthusiasm. He
had no confidence that Lee would bring anything to the negotiations beyond loud impatience. Even worse, Franklin was certain
that Arthur Lee despised him.

When Lee reached Paris, he initiated an immediate conflict
with Silas Deane, and a small flood of letters from Lee was already sailing to Philadelphia. Deane's offense had been to carry
on business negotiations without Lee's involvement. It was the
worst kind of wound to a man like Arthur Lee. He was accusing
Deane of ignoring him.

Deane was deeply immersed in a complicated arrangement for
French loans that had to be funneled secretly through a private
company. Franklin trusted Deane, and by the time he had reached
Paris, he understood that Deane's negotiations were nearly complete, and the transfer of funds to congress was already in progress.
He welcomed Deane's talents in the areas of high finance, and
Deane returned the favor by suggesting that Franklin serve as the
spokesman for the commission, an obvious choice, since Franklin
was quite simply the most famous American in the world. Once
again, Arthur Lee's prickly sensitivity was bruised.

With his grandsons firmly in the care of motherly hands,
Franklin began to focus on his mission. They did not have long
to wait, the first official welcome coming to Franklin's hotel, an
invitation for their first meeting at the French Foreign Ministry.

JANUARY 9, 1777

The man's name was Charles Gravier, and he carried the title
of the Count of Vergennes, had held the position as the Minister

of Foreign Affairs to King Louis XVI since the young king's ascension to the throne barely two years earlier. Vergennes was an immensely intelligent and charming man, and had become an immediate favorite of both Louis and the young king's Austrian wife, Marie Antoinette. Louis had inherited a court divided in its support for the American cause, but Vergennes had been firmly on the side of the Americans from the beginning. His opposition had come mainly from the stubbornness of the conservative finance minister, Baron Turgot. But Turgot was soon replaced, the young king showing no patience for disagreements in his court. Though Vergennes brought the support of his king to the negotiating table, Franklin believed that there must still be some discomfort for a well-entrenched monarch like Louis. The only news from America was a dismal report of loss and retreat by the American army. It would certainly be inappropriate to ask the French for a commitment of troops or a fleet of ships. Louis would be cautious, hesitant to risk a war with England by granting full support to a rebel army that had yet to prove it could stand up against the might of the British.

Franklin was concerned as well that the issue at the very core of their negotiations was independence for a people who were struggling to throw off the yoke of their own monarch. Whatever value Vergennes placed on American independence, George III and Louis XVI were of the same mold. England and France were traditional enemies, and Louis might delight in King George's crisis, but if the Americans were successful, the passion for independence might spread, and every monarch in Europe might suddenly find himself immersed in a revolution of his own. It was a delicate political reality, and Franklin knew that Vergennes would have to tread carefully. There was indeed a game to be played.

VERGENNES HAD NOT YET ARRIVED, AND THE AMERICANS HAD BEEN led to what the servant described as a parlor. The room was enormous, ornate powder blue walls trimmed with delicate designs in gold leaf, and in the center of each wall hung an enormous mirror. There was a fireplace on one wall, dwarfed by an enormous portrait of King Louis, his image carved into a disc of white marble nearly three feet wide.

Franklin was familiar with the grand halls of royalty, had been entertained in some of Europe's most imposing mansions, but as he studied the ornate gilded carvings that framed one of the enormous mirrors, he could not help but be impressed. The French do have a way, he thought. Dwarf the man by engulfing him in splendor. It is a statement, I suppose, a lesson for the *little* people, the very notion of a monarch who so towers above us all. He backed away from the mirror, felt his sore feet cushioned by a soft Persian rug that spread across the width of the room.

To one side, Deane was studying a part of the oak floor not covered by the rug, an intricate design of diamonds and detailed parquet. He put his hand down, feeling the wood, said to Franklin, "Marvelous, I must say. Not merely a floor, but a work of art!"

Deane's secretary, Edward Bancroft, stood close by, seemed amused by Deane's sense of wonder.

Franklin had thought it appropriate for at least one secretary to be present, that anything said in these meetings must surely be recorded. Bancroft was the obvious choice, a Massachusetts man who had worked with several of the colonial representatives in London. Franklin had known him for years, a pleasant and sociable man, and he had been pleased to hear that Deane had secured Bancroft's services. Franklin was still determined to groom his grandson Temple as his own secretary, but the position was too new to the seventeen-year-old to bring him to such an important meeting. Bancroft could certainly fill the role for all three of them.

Arthur Lee had moved to the far end of the room, as detached from the others as he could be and still be in the same space. Lee was staring at a mirror, and Franklin caught the man looking at him in the reflection.

"Rather lovely place, wouldn't you say, Mr. Lee?"

He put as much pleasantness in the words as he could, some means of breaking through the shroud of gloom that enveloped Lee. Lee did not turn, said, "Lovely, yes."

There was nothing pleasant in Lee's words. Deane glanced at Franklin, a brief shake of his head, and Franklin said quietly, "We must strive for appearances, Mr. Deane. I have done this sort of thing before. United front is most important."

Lee turned now, said, "Yes, Dr. Franklin, you have done all of this before. Mr. Deane, we must be certain to watch and learn."

There was hard sarcasm in Lee's voice, and Franklin felt frustration, didn't know what else to say. He turned again to the mirror, could see Lee's back in the reflection, the man doing everything he could to create a gulf between them. Lee was somewhat younger than Deane, both men in their late thirties. Deane's face was adorned with a pleasant openness, a soft roundness given easily to a smile. It was a sharp contrast to Lee's stern glare, a tight aristocratic handsomeness that made him seem much older than Deane.

Franklin saw Deane again studying the intricate woodwork of the floor, busying himself with a mindless distraction. Franklin thought, We cannot demonstrate this sort of conflict to the French. Mr. Lee must surely know that.

Franklin had always known Lee to be a man who placed great value on his own abilities, but he thought, Does he truly believe this job is for him alone? Clearly I cannot counsel him. He assumes anything I say to be a show of vanity, as though we must go about these negotiations by my instruction only. If he is excluded from anything here, it is by his own doing.

He realized that they had been waiting for several minutes, felt a nervous twinge, thought, Is that their plan? Are we to be kept waiting as a show of our unimportance? It was a familiar annoying experience from his days in London. British officials delighted in making a disdainful show when confronted by any issue concerning the colonies. Surely, it cannot be like that here. They would not have invited us here just to humiliate us. I only hope we make a suitable impression. He glanced at himself in the grand mirror, thought, Well, old man, if you intended to make *this* impression, there could not be a more perfect setting than a house too beautiful to live in.

He was wearing a fur cap, a simple brown covering that did not hide the uncoiffed hair that straggled down to his shoulders. It was the most modest attire he could fashion together, a simple brown coat over a stark white shirt, none of the ruffles and lace and adornments the French elite considered a requirement for high fashion. If the French had not yet formed their own image of what an American was, Franklin invented one, and offered it to all of France with no embarrassment. There would be none of the fineries, none of the personal trappings of luxury, and certainly, nothing that would make him appear to have once been *English*.

He wore his spectacles always, kept them low on his nose, peered up over them to the tall ceiling. He marveled at the chandelier right above him, the one understated piece of décor in the room, a ring of tall candles emerging from a small explosion of glass beads, glittering like a mountain of diamonds. He moved to one side, thought, No doubt a capable craftsman fastened it securely. But anyone can have a bad day. No point in placing myself under anything whose sudden collapse could dice me into small bits.

He saw Deane and Bancroft moving toward a long table perched squarely in the center of the room. It was surrounded by ornate chairs, and Deane stood behind one, looked at Franklin, said, "Doctor, would you care to sit?"

Franklin shook his head.

"Not appropriate, Mr. Deane. We must endure the wait."

Bancroft leaned close to Deane, said, "Protocol requires us to stand until our host has arrived."

He appreciated Deane's gesture as much as he appreciated Bancroft's knowledge of decorum. He flexed his feet into the rug, bent his knee slightly, and a sharp pain ran all the way up his back. He looked at himself in the mirror again, frowned at the expanse of his waist, thought, Too many lavish dinners, too much standing about. I must return to my routine, the long walks. Perhaps this stiffness will be relieved.

There was a flurry of noise, and the tall glass doors swung open, servants stepping in quickly, standing to one side. More men appeared, with pads of paper, all of them falling into what seemed to be a reception line. Now another man appeared, said in a loud voice, *"Le Comte de Vergennes."*

The man seemed to be speaking to a roomful of people, and his voice drew the four men closer to the door. Franklin steadied himself behind one of the chairs, saw Vergennes appear in a rush, the man trying to gather himself. Vergennes looked at Franklin with utter horror.

"Oh, my word, Dr. Franklin! Forgive me! I was detained at the royal court. The queen insisted." Vergennes seemed to catch himself, suddenly aware of the indiscreet comment, and the ears of his staff. He looked at the other three men, produced a smile, said, "On behalf of His Majesty, King Louis, welcome to Paris."

He turned, said something in French, and two of his assistants seated themselves behind him, on either side of a small table that held their inkstands, each with a pad of paper perched firmly on one knee. The rest of the entourage was quickly gone, the double doors coming closed with a soft click. They had gathered close to the table, and Vergennes said, "Gentlemen, I sincerely apologize. You should not have been made to wait. Were you offered some refreshment?" He looked at Franklin now, said, "Please do not take offense, Doctor. This was an accident, nothing to be interpreted otherwise. You are as welcome here as anyone can be. Please, do sit down."

Franklin was surprised, thought, Apparently he reads my thoughts. This might make things interesting.

"Please, Your Excellency, an apology is unnecessary. It is of no concern. We were enjoying your décor."

Vergennes sat, the others followed, and Vergennes said, "Your kindness does not erase our rudeness, sir."

Franklin felt himself settle into soft luxury, the strain in his legs letting go. Vergennes was still watching him, said, "Has your stay in Paris been to your liking, Doctor? Is there anything I can do to make you, any of you, more comfortable?"

The others did not speak, and Franklin fought the urge to make a poorly timed joke about sending a French army to invade England. He turned slightly in the chair, still easing the pains.

"I for one am quite satisfactory, Your Excellency. An old man's bones have no sense of humor."

Vergennes smiled again.

"Then we have already established one thing in common, Doctor."

Vergennes was older than he expected, and Franklin saw sharp dark eyes focused on him through thick drooping lids, the look of a man who was always tired. Franklin looked toward the others, saw Deane nod to him, a signal that he expected Franklin to do the talking. Lee was simply staring down, and Franklin said, "If I may be allowed, Your Excellency. A formal introduction is in order. We come here as official representatives of the Congress of the United States of America, and are fully empowered by that body to propose and negotiate a treaty of commerce between France and the United States."

Vergennes waited until the formal speech was complete, smiled again, said, "What would you propose of us, Doctor?"

"Your Excellency, we are waging a war for our survival. We could ask any willing government for an alliance that would sweep away our disadvantage in battle, but this we do not do." Vergennes was all seriousness now, waited for Franklin to continue. "The financial credit of the United States is of paramount importance. We request assistance in the purchase of those goods which may assist us in fighting this war. As Your Excellency is certainly aware, Mr. Deane has been successful in his meetings with French business interests. In addition, the French government has shown a generous spirit by allowing American ships to anchor in French ports. We would ask that Your Excellency continue this generosity. Further, we would hope that Your Excellency might find the means of sending those ships back home laden with supplies."

Vergennes waited for more, but Franklin was through, thought, That is sufficient for a first meeting. We must not overdo it. He sat back in the chair, looked at the others, could see a look of satisfaction on Deane's face, the man who had already done so much to secure private funds. Deane's job would be much simpler if France would desist from the intrigue and openly offer supplies and credit to the Americans. Lee looked up at Franklin now, seemed to wait for more as well. Franklin tilted his head, a gesture of politeness, said, "Do you have anything to add, Mr. Lee?" Lee pondered the question, and Franklin gripped the edge of the table, silently begged Lee not to say a word.

"Thank you, Doctor. Not at this time."

Franklin let out a long breath. Thank you, sir. We cannot ask them for too much. This is not yet the time.

Vergennes was looking at him with a question on his face, and Franklin waited, knew the man was assembling the proper words, the skill of the diplomat.

"Doctor, please be assured I mean this as no offense. America is a vast land, and your resources have yet to be developed. I am confident that when your craftsmen and your farmers fully explore the potential of your country, you will be a valuable partner to any nation. But that is the future. The present offers a difficult portrait. In your current crisis, the one resource you can call upon is your strength of numbers. I would imagine your government could field an army many times the force required for your defense. There is curiosity here, Doctor. Why must America look beyond her own borders?"

It was a question Franklin had expected.

"Your Excellency, we take no offense. Your Excellency asks a simple question which has difficult answers. We represent a congress who must work within the authority granted to it by the states. There is no means for us to compel anyone to take up arms. There is a general feeling in the congress, and throughout America that the assembly of a professional army is a threat to the very freedoms we are fighting to secure."

Vergennes pondered the statement.

"You cannot achieve your independence if you do not have the spirit to fight for it."

"Your Excellency, no nation on this earth has accomplished what America is attempting to do. Where do we go for instruction, for guidance? Is there any nation prepared to offer us a model to follow, who can provide wise counsel for our congress, so that we may know how to build a nation? It may be that the only way for America to survive is to impress its citizens by force, to compel men to take up arms against their will. But such a success would cost us the very principles for which we fight. Is this a contradiction? Perhaps. The congress is not a professional government. It is composed of men such as those before you here." He paused, thought a moment. "When the British were persuaded to evacuate Boston, the congress voted in celebration to grant General Washington a gold medal. To the General's credit, he will not wear it. He beseeches us instead to put our gold to better use, to pay for clothes and food for his soldiers. I am embarrassed to admit to Your Excellency that we do not possess the means to do that. It is not simply a lack of spirit. It is a lack of experience, and a lack of resources. We are a nation of amateurs, fighting a war against an empire of professionals. If America survives, it will have to survive on the backs of the inexperienced. And, I must be candid, sir. We require assistance."

THE RESPONSE CAME IN LESS THAN TWO WEEKS, AND HE STARED at the gold seal on the document in tearful disbelief. He read the words over again, thought, There must be conditions, some restriction, some clause here . . . but there was nothing beyond the simple and extraordinary decree. The French government had granted the American congress two million francs to assist them in their war effort, with a guarantee of two million more for each year the war went on.

He lowered the document, looked now at the courier, a young man sent by Vergennes to deliver the document.

"I suppose, sir, this is official."

The man spoke only broken English, smiled now, said something that Franklin's swirling mind would not grasp. Franklin looked again at the thick gold seal of King Louis.

"Well, yes. Of course this is official."

The young man seemed ready to leave, and Franklin looked at him again.

"Young sir, please express my profound . . . our most esteemed . . ." He stopped, thought, Good God man, how does one respond to this?

"Please tell Count Vergennes that America thanks him."

The young man seemed to be satisfied, was quickly away. Franklin closed the door, moved across the room to the window, could see the young man emerging from the hotel entrance, climbing now into a grand carriage. He backed away from the window, sat slowly in his soft chair. There was silence now, and he held the paper up, thought, This could change so much. And there's no one here to show it to.

He tried to relax the spasms in his stomach, the utter thrill of the success. This will cause trouble at the French court, that's for certain. The English will howl like wild dogs, and no one will be surprised if a war is declared either here or in London. But he would not think of that now, held the paper against his chest. He would have to write his own letter to the congress, a footnote to this document, send the papers on the fastest ship available. He thought of Vergennes. What did he say to the king? Was it a difficult job convincing Louis to open up his treasury? And what must we still do in return?

His mission was far from accomplished, but in his hand was the first success, the unmistakable message that America had found an ally. The door to the French court was slowly swinging open.

18. FRANKLIN

THE SMALL SHIP REACHED THE DOCKS AT LE HAVRE WITH A MESsage that tore across the French countryside like a bolt of lightning. George Washington had bloodied the British at Trenton and Princeton, a pair of stunning defeats to Howe's army that brought cheers and celebration to the halls of King Louis. Franklin received the news as he had received the gift from Vergennes, staring through damp eyes at the glorious words on a simple piece of paper. He did not yet know what this would do for his negotiations. Certainly the gloom would be lifted, and no matter what news might follow, for a while at least, the French would know that the Americans could do more than make broad and grandiose pronouncements about independence. They could fight for it as well.

Vergennes had summoned Franklin as soon as the news had reached the French court, and within minutes of the invitation, Franklin was dressed and had summoned his carriage. As he stepped out of the hotel, a small crowd was waiting, and he heard his name, surprising calls of congratulation, as though this one old man had accomplished such a feat three thousand miles away. He was accustomed to being recognized, but this was different, and he was amazed that word of Washington's victories had spread so quickly beyond the official halls of government. The carriage was not yet there, and he stood alone, while the crowd grew, more of the passersby clamoring for a look at this celebrated American. As their joy flooded over him, he began to relax, would board the carriage in due time, would enjoy the moment, the extraordinary show of affection from a people he was still trying to know.

He had begun a healthy routine again, would brave the chilly days for long walks through the wide streets. There was always attention, the old round man moving slowly past the shops and small cafés dressed still in the style that seemed to amuse the socialites. He would always wear his trademark plain fur hat and dull brown coat, and always the tiny glasses perched on his nose. By appearance alone his fame had spread, far beyond the drawing rooms of the elite. As he made his daily walks, people stopped him on the street, if only to speak to him, and his responses were polite, if somewhat inaccurate. He had tried to master the French language, had become fluent enough to understand most of what was spoken to him, but his failing was in the details, and his poor grammar and clumsy pronunciation only added to his charm. To the poor and working classes, his lack of concern for pomp and grandeur was making him a hero, and within a few weeks, his image had begun to appear in stone and wax and paper, adorning the modest walls and hearths of simple homes all over Paris. In clothing shops, merchants began to stock more goods of the color brown, described now as the Franklin Hue. Hat shops began to sell the Franklin Hat, his simple fur now reproduced as an object of popular fashion.

His image was not all accident. His purpose from the beginning was to show that America was not so obsessed with finery as with the substance of its own crisis. He had hoped that his appearance would at the very least draw attention to his purpose for being there, a humble man from a humble nation. It could only help his cause, and it had seemed to work. To those in and around the royal court, he continued to be a charming and curious oddity, sought after for his graciousness and his vast collection of stories. But the sudden outpouring of affection from the people was a surprise, both to Franklin and to the elite. There had been some of this in London, but the response there had not been so positive, his image more a symbol of the annoying rebellion. But the French workers had made him an icon, the consummate American, a symbol of a dynamic people who would throw off their chains. There was something in their response that reached him beyond his grateful vanity, a gnawing sense that beneath their affection was another voice, aimed perhaps at their own government, a growl of discontentment that his appearance had brought to the surface. But he could not focus on that, the old man's limited strength keeping his mind on the job he still had to do. The celebration of Franklin by the French people had naturally added to the jealousy and resentment of Arthur Lee.

The three commissioners had agreed that an effort should be made to seek aid from King Charles of Spain, and Lee had leapt at the opportunity to leave Paris. Spain and France were allied in a somewhat weak coalition against England, the rivalry for control of the oceans that had produced centuries of warfare. Spain did not possess France's wealth, but there was motivation in Madrid for Charles to join with Louis should war actually erupt on this side of the Atlantic. England controlled Gibraltar, the impregnable fortress that guarded the entrance to the Mediterranean Sea. That the English should occupy what was in effect part of the Spanish mainland was an embarrassment to Spanish pride. If any war was to be fought against England, King Charles had one eye firmly focused on claiming Gibraltar.

While Lee was making the journey to Madrid, Deane had once again resumed his complicated negotiations for the discreet shipments of supplies. He was frequently away from Paris, though neither Deane nor Franklin considered his absence a problem. Today, it just meant that Franklin would respond to Vergennes' invitation by himself.

THE RECEPTION FROM VERGENNES WAS AS ENTHUSIASTIC AS THE man's official position would allow, and Franklin could sense the joyous mood in every one of the French servants and secretaries. The scene had begun as before, Franklin escorted to the powder blue room, but there was no waiting now, Vergennes arriving seconds after Franklin was left alone. Franklin still didn't know why Vergennes had called him, would not allow his optimism to run wild, knew that all of the old issues were still in place. Washington's victories had certainly eased some of the pessimism of the French court, but the war in America had not yet ended. Louis would understand that with the coming of spring, the British would resolve to reverse their embarrassments in New Jersey. Even if the French were now to offer direct military assistance to the Continental Congress, it would not make a direct impact in America for many months. Washington's army and the American cause might yet be swept away.

THEY SAT AGAIN AT THE GRAND TABLE, FRANKLIN ADJUSTING HIM-self to the comfort of the soft chair. Behind Vergennes, the two familiar secretaries flanked the small table, inkstands full, preparing to record what was said.

"Doctor, I have received confirmation from the navy that four American ships, bearing military supplies, have been at anchor in Le Havre. As a result of the most stern protests from the English, I have not allowed these ships to sail. If I did, it would be a clear violation of our treaty with England and could lead to a declaration of war. However, only this morning I received the dreadful news that the carelessness of the port guards has allowed these ships to escape to the open sea. Where they will reappear is a source of extreme speculation. However, I leave such speculation to the English."

Franklin could not hide his smile, examined Vergennes' expression for any break in the man's formal seriousness.

"Thank you, Your Excellency. For, um, not speculating."

"There is no reason to thank me, Doctor. Those ships will be the objects of a widespread search by British warships. There is no guarantee any of them will reach their intended port. Wherever that might be."

Franklin tried to mimic Vergennes' seriousness.

"Your Excellency is quite correct. I wish only for the safety of their crews . . . and cargo."

He was adapting easily to the rules of the game. The English had grudgingly accepted the French gifts of money to America, King George no more eager than the French to declare another war. But openly supplying the Americans with French weaponry was an escalation the British could not ignore. American ships that docked in French ports were free to take on whatever cargo their captains could arrange. But the only way they could carry that cargo anywhere beyond French waters was by eluding the official orders to stay put. This meant nothing more than setting sail after dark, when the French harbormasters, under discreet instruction from Vergennes, simply turned the other way.

"Doctor, are you familiar with Viscount David Stormont?"

Franklin knew the name, the British ambassador to France.

"I have not made his acquaintance, Your Excellency."

"It's not likely you will. He was here this morning, as expected, with his shrill protest of the escape of your supply ships. He made a rather hasty exit, not wishing to inflict upon himself the poison of actually meeting the *rebel* Dr. Franklin."

Franklin smiled, but Vergennes was not amused by his own humor.

"Lord Stormont is a man filled with regrettable excitement. His job is to issue protest, and he is a man quite expert of performing his job. It has become a tedious routine, which even Mr. Stormont knows will bear no good results."

Franklin sensed a gravity to Vergennes' voice, a deeper meaning beyond his words. Franklin did not understand, tried to lighten the moment.

"I regret I should be such a fly in Lord Stormont's ointment, Your Excellency."

Vergennes seemed not to hear him.

"I must reveal something to you, Doctor, for which I hope you will not take offense. By my instruction, the police have been watching over you. I thought it a prudent precaution. Paris is not a dangerous city, Doctor, but you are a famous man, and vulnerable to a variety of evils. Should any harm come to you, it would be a severe embarrassment to King Louis. I am not ashamed to admit that it would cause me considerable distress as well."

The news itself did not surprise him. That Vergennes would reveal it with such a somber tone did.

"I am not offended, Your Excellency. I admit to being somewhat cavalier in my habits. It is of comfort that your security officers have one eye on my well-being."

Vergennes was still somber, said, "Doctor, we are not the only ones watching you. My invitation to you today was not public information, and yet Lord Stormont knew you were coming. This morning, by his careless complaint, he has revealed what we have long suspected to be true."

Franklin was puzzled by Vergennes' dark mood, said, "Your Excellency, I have long believed that the best remedy when surrounded by spies is to behave in a manner which, if made public, will cause no one to blush. If I believed that the valet in my hotel was a spy, which he probably is, I would be more concerned with the quality of his service than anything he could learn from me."

Vergennes did not react as Franklin expected, folded his hands together on the table, stared down for a moment, said, "I am not so concerned that the English should have spies in Paris. It is a fact of life in Paris, as it is in London. My concern, Doctor, is that Lord Stormont is a man of ruthless purpose, and I believe he is a danger to you. Officially he is here to protest anything that might be offensive to his king. Unofficially he is the primary employer of English agents in Paris. What he revealed today is that they know as much about your whereabouts and your activities as I do. If the relationship between France and America should continue to improve, Lord Stormont might consider that an extreme offense he cannot ignore. Today, he made a dramatic show, spitting venom in my office. Tomorrow, that venom might take a different, more silent form. Doctor, I do not wish to frighten you. But I earnestly suggest you take care to avoid dark streets."

MARCH 1777

Outside the Hotel d'Hambourg, the crowds had continued to gather, hoping to catch some glimpse of the famous American. The scheduled visitors came as well, men with their own nefarious proposals for assisting the American cause. Some wore uniforms, offered their service to the American army with extravagant claims of heroism, a pedigree of leadership that the great General Washington would surely find useful. Franklin had exhausted himself with politeness, receiving anyone who claimed to need his attention, but the demands became insufferable, his peaceful routine obliterated. But worse, through all the inconvenience to his time and energy he was tormented by Vergennes' warnings. Franklin was not so concerned about the danger to himself. The congress would certainly find among its number many men who would be capable of playing the diplomatic game. But each day, he would watch his grandsons depart the safety of the hotel to go about their routines, Temple running Franklin's essential errands, Benny attending school. Such worries began to assault his sleep, any noise from the street jolting him awake. Within a few days, the dilemma turned to decision. They could not stay in Paris. To the dismay of his admirers in the street, and the neighbors who called him their friend, Franklin and his grandsons boarded a carriage, trailed by another that held the effects of his growing office. The journey was not far, down winding roads, up a wide pleasant hill a short way beyond the city, a small village called Passy.

The owner of the Hotel Valentinois had made himself known as an admirer of both the American cause and Franklin himself.

Franklin was furnished a suite of rooms that opened onto a large garden, and despite his protest, the owner would accept no payment of rent.

They settled with ease into the very different atmosphere of the pleasant village. Benny was immediately enrolled in a boarding school nearby, which would keep the boy occupied six days a week. Temple had seemed unsure if the new residence would take him too far from the Parisian girls. The ballrooms were always open to the grandson of the great man, but even the impatience of a seventeen-year-old was not tested by the short ride to the city.

Franklin's new routine was enhanced by the luxurious grounds of the hotel, and he walked often past the bare patches of black dirt, already raked clean by a host of gardeners, who eyed the calendar for the start of the season, the first warm days that would allow for the first seeding.

He set up his office with a new energy, had invited Deane to do the same, enough space provided so that both men could have their privacy but still share the convenience of close communication.

Packages were coming to him from America, the routes safe enough for American ships to reach French ports without difficulty. He knew the English were still protesting, but the packages he was receiving were harmless, came mostly from Philadelphia, wrapped by the hand of his daughter Sally.

He sifted through the careful wrappings, mostly clothing for his grandsons, his daughter certain that Franklin would never understand what a small boy required. He would never protest, could not tell her that the ladies of the village had taken both boys into their care with the same charmed enthusiasm as the women in the city. Anything Benny required, whether pencils for school or stockings to match the fashion of the village were amply provided.

He searched the bottom of the crate, ran his hands through the packing cloth, felt a lump, retrieved a small wooden box. It was not from Sally, the writing formal, his name printed in simple black letters. He slid open the top, saw two small bottles of liquid, one dark, the other nearly clear, saw a note curled around them. He held up one of the bottles, thought, Ink, certainly. Not likely that American ink is so much superior to what I can find here. He unfolded the note now, read slowly, the letter from John Jay, the congressman from New York.

My Dear Doctor,

    I am most trusting that you will find good use for the enclosed. It is the invention of my brother, James. A like shipment has been sent to Mr. Deane as well. If you find its use to be of benefit, a larger supply can be secured for you. I regret that the formula is contained in the mind of my brother alone.

There was another small piece of paper with instructions, and Franklin thought, So, one bottle is for writing, another for reading. How very strange.

He pulled a pen and paper out of the drawer of his desk, wiped the tip of the pen clean with his handkerchief. Now he opened the darker bottle, dipped, wrote his name on the paper. He sat back, waited for the ink to dry, and suddenly, his name began to fade, then vanish altogether, the paper now blank. He laughed, said aloud, "Well, a fine trick. However, writing with water will accomplish the same feat."

He opened the second bottle, glanced at the instruction, wet his handkerchief from the bottle, wiped it over the blank paper. Instantly, his name reappeared. He let out a laugh, looked at the paper closely, thought, Well, now, this can very well ensure that our dispatches can be moved about without Mr. Stormont or anyone else knowing our intent. All credit to James Jay. He has invented invisible ink.

AS THE SPRING WARMED THE AIR, FRANKLIN STAYED CLOSE TO HIS office, responding to the letters from congress, passing along the continuing flow of requests to Vergennes and the French court. Despite the willingness of Vergennes to meet with him, despite the success of the carefully planned arrangements with Deane's contacts, there was still no formal alliance with the French. Franklin understood that French support would remain limited, that neither France nor England was eager to begin a new war. All Franklin could do was press on, still confident that Vergennes would continue to speak to his king about assistance to America. But both men knew that Louis would remain cautious, and Franklin had to concede that with the new spring would come a new British strategy, and a new campaign. So much would depend on the news that came from America.

19. CORNWALLIS

WHILE HOWE AND MOST OF THE SENIOR COMMANDERS HAD SPENT their winter quarters nestled into the social comforts of New York, Cornwallis had been with his troops still stationed between Brunswick and Amboy. The weather had been unusually mild, the late winter mostly chilly and damp, and the tedious boredom so common to winter quarters was made worse by intermittent warm spells, which thawed the frozen ground to a muddy swamp. A warm winter breeds disease, and entire squads were brought down by sickness. As the supply sergeants attempted to feed the troops from the farms in the area, they came under constant attack from small bands of militia, who would strike hard, then melt away into the brush. What should have been minor foraging missions became large-scale troop movements, entire companies of redcoats required to protect every small wagon of confiscated supplies. By the end of January, Cornwallis had learned that foraging the countryside of New Jersey had become a waste of time. The Tory farmers were long gone, fearing reprisals from local militia, and any barn that might hold precious grain or horses was just as likely to contain a company of rebel marksmen.

The only alternative supply line came from New York, from the occupied farmlands of Long Island and Staten Island. But the naval crews suffered as much as the infantry, boats unloading in Amboy peppered by deadly musket fire from grassy fields along the water. Any boat attempting to move up the Raritan was subject to cannon fire from guns hidden by Washington in strategic positions along the northern banks of the river.

As bad as conditions were for the men, it was worse for the horses. Without fresh forage, many simply died, and those who survived were so weakened they were useless as mounts for the dragoons.

As the sun finally warmed the ground, the sickness began to ease, and every man in Cornwallis' army welcomed the blessed spring. Cornwallis knew the mood of his men. As the stifling wooden huts were replaced by white canvas tents, every soldier turned his thoughts toward the north, where Washington still held his army. The British probed and scouted the ground toward Morristown as far as Washington's skirmishers would allow, brief sharp fights that bruised both sides. But Cornwallis already knew that Washington had found an ideal place to defend, and the army could only launch their assaults on small rebel outposts, or attempt quick strikes at supply stations, where Washington might be storing munitions. The only way to bring Washington out of the hills and into a general engagement was by giving him a target too tempting to resist. Time and again, Cornwallis would advance his men out in column from Brunswick, a feint to the west, as though his eight thousand men were suddenly on the march to Trenton. But Washington had stayed put, no ruse of vulnerability by Cornwallis had worked. As long as Cornwallis was not reinforced from New York, it was simply a standoff. Washington would not attack, and Cornwallis could not dislodge him from Morristown. Until Howe made a decision about where and when the campaign would resume, the British soldiers in New Jersey would continue to endure Washington's sniping at their flanks, and the rebels' annoying disruptions in their supply lines.

As spring rolled toward summer, Howe had given his army no plan, had instead conducted a tediously slow debate over strategy with his superior in London, Lord George Germain. While Howe waited for official approval of some new plan of action, much of the British command idled away the months in the comforts of their mistresses and the fine dining rooms of the city. To Cornwallis, it was another frustrating exercise in futility. He could only bide his time, nursing his army back to health, remaining close to his headquarters in Brunswick angrily waiting for Howe to make up his mind.

JUNE 5, 1777

Cornwallis had avoided the dinners, the formal occasions so sought after by the officers in New York. He always had the good excuse for staying away from the city, some new assault by the rebels requiring his attention, his own mission to capture some particular goal, spies constantly bringing him word of Washington's shifting movements. But the invitation this time was not social, and Cornwallis could not hide his own expectations that, finally, something more specific was being discussed at headquarters, something that might put his army into motion.

He arrived at the headquarters at midday, and as he rode through the streets of New York, he saw formations of men at drill, supply wagons gathered into great squares, artillery parks alive with gun crews, fresh maintenance on cannon that had sat idle since December. There was energy to the movements that could only mean Howe was making some preparation for a march.

The house itself was a bustle of activity, Howe's staff welcoming him as they rushed past, each with some dispatch in urgent need of delivery. It had been months since Cornwallis felt his own enthusiasm rising, the anticipation returning, that wonderful surge of strength that spreads through the army when the new campaign grows close. He moved into the grand parlor, the familiar meeting room where Howe had summoned the senior officers. The men had gathered loosely around the wide table, and Cornwallis moved into the room to salutes and handshakes. He nodded to Leslie, knew his subordinate would already be there, the young man having crossed the Hudson that morning. The Hessian von Donop stood beside a tall window, made a slight bow toward him, and Cornwallis saw the old Hessian, Wilhelm Knyphausen seated beside him. Von Donop bent low, spoke to the old man, who looked up at Cornwallis with a solemn stare, and Cornwallis thought, It must be official. Knyphausen has replaced de Heister. One old soldier carries the shame of Trenton back to his country, replaced by another. Cornwallis said, "General Knyphausen, I hope you are well."

Knyphausen glanced up at von Donop, who translated Cornwallis' greeting, and the old man raised his hand slightly, said something in a low voice. Von Donop said, "Thank you, General."

It was all that Knyphausen ever said, and Cornwallis had wondered if it was the language alone, many of the Hessians speaking enough English to participate if they chose to. But more often the Hessians seemed content to sit quietly in the meetings while their British counterparts worked out their strategy. It is courtesy, I suppose. It is, after all, our war. He moved closer to the table, could feel the enthusiasm he shared with the other officers, scanned the room, saw one man moving a chair close to the table, no uniform. Cornwallis felt a bolt of shock. It was Charles Lee.

Howe was not yet there, and as Lee pulled himself up to the table, the others grew mostly quiet, watching Lee, as though each man was reluctant to speak in the presence of the prisoner, who had once been a part of their army.

Lee gave him a polite smile, and Cornwallis said, "Mr. Lee. Are you now a *guest* of this command?"

It was a poor joke, but Lee seemed inflated by the words.

"Oh, quite so, General. I must ask, however, do you have some objection of referring to me by my title? I am a lieutenant general, you know."

He could see Lee was serious, and Cornwallis glanced at the others, all silent now.

"Not in this army, sir. As I recall, your title here was . . . lieutenant colonel. Or perhaps, *deserter*?"

Lee seemed stabbed by the word, looked away, said, "If my king had only given me my due, I assure you, sir, I would be in this army today."

Cornwallis regretted the insult, could feel the awkwardness of the moment, the others shifting nervously, and he was already weary of the confrontation.

"Mr. Lee, I am not concerned with any of your deeds or the injustices which may have befallen you. Clearly you are here because General Howe has invited you."

"Quite right, General!" Howe burst into the room with a flurry, pointed to Lee, said, "The good general has been most helpful in seeking an end to this unfortunate rebellion. It would not be prudent of me to reveal to you, Mr. Lee, the exact strategy we are to employ; however, your king may yet find it in his heart to forgive your most recent transgressions."

Lee puffed up again, looked at Cornwallis, said, "I respect your views, sir. But I assure you, my only purpose here is to bring this regrettable war to an end. I have no doubt that this army will prevail, but as you may agree, any victory must be accomplished by a considerable loss of life. Is that not to be avoided?"

Lee's sudden smile gave Cornwallis an uncomfortable chill, and he thought, Is this to be the purpose of the meeting? After all this time, we will now operate by the strategy of a traitor? Howe seemed to sense his discomfort, said, "Mr. Lee, perhaps it is best if you are returned to the *Centurion*. I wish to discuss, um, current events with my commanders. You understand, of course."

Lee was sulking now, and Cornwallis watched him, felt rising disgust, thought, A poor actor. He changes his mood with each passing word. Everything in the man is for his own benefit, changing with the moment. Howe motioned past him, and Cornwallis turned, saw two guards at the door. Lee stood slowly, and Cornwallis was surprised that the man was much smaller than he remembered, his thin frame bent in a crooked slouch. Lee moved past, avoided looking at him now, stopped at the door, said to Howe, "My respects, sir. I wish you good fortune in the campaign ahead."

Howe bowed slightly, said cheerily, "Thank you, Mr. Lee!"

The guards escorted Lee away, and Howe's mood abruptly changed. He waited a moment, stared out through the doorway, said in a low voice, "I am out of patience with the man's ingratiating pleasantness."

Cornwallis was relieved by Howe's words, said, "Sir, am I to understand that Mr. Lee has offered this command a strategy for ending the war?"

Howe sat now.

"Quite so, General. The wind blows in our favor again, and Mr. Lee is the weather vane. He believes we should invade Maryland and Delaware, and thus divide the colonies. He feels the war will end itself on that account. He considers Mr. Washington to be quite the imbecile, is rather insistent that his congress should be put in chains, since they did not place him in command. Mr. Lee claims that the war would have already been over, and that he would have been our savior, delivering the peace by delivering the colonies back to their king. Quite a bit of bombast in the man."

There were small laughs from around the room, but Cornwallis did not see the humor.

"The man is a traitor to both sides. Since we have him, perhaps it is our duty to hang him first."

Howe held up his hand, said, "I appreciate your passion, General, but the matter has gone beyond our control. Lord Germain had requested we ship Mr. Lee to London for trial, and he is presently being quartered in my brother's care aboard the *Centurion*. However, we have received a letter from the rebels which has given us reason to delay any action regarding Mr. Lee. I must give credit to Mr. Washington for understanding the rules of war. It seems that he has close at hand five Hessian officers of high rank. He states that our treatment of Mr. Lee shall influence his treatment of the Hessians. It is an appropriate demand. Mr. Lee shall remain in shipboard in New York until such time as he might be exchanged."

Cornwallis smiled now.

"I should imagine that prospect concerns Mr. Lee. If we don't hang him, Mr. Washington might. However, five Hessian officers is too great a price for the rebels to part with on his account."

Howe shrugged. "Perhaps. It is not our concern at the moment." The matter had passed, and Howe looked around the room, motioned to an aide, and a map was unrolled on the table. Cornwallis leaned close, saw the line of the Hudson River northward, Albany, and farther up, Lake Champlain. Howe said, "Lord Germain has given his approval to General Burgoyne's plan."

Cornwallis was confused, had heard brief rumors about Burgoyne and some new strategy, but had no idea Burgoyne was anywhere close to the colonies.

"Sir, excuse me, but . . . General Burgoyne?"

Howe's face showed a curl of annoyance, said, "Yes, General. Gentleman Johnny has been busy. You may have thought he has been in London, more concerned with his writing than his military career. But it seems he is instead scripting a role for himself in this war. With all respects to Lord Germain, General Burgoyne has charmed his way into the hearts of the ministry. He is presently preparing to move a force of seven thousand British and Hessian troops southward from Canada, through Lake Champlain, overland to the Hudson River and down to Albany. With this accomplished, New York will be under the crown's control, and New England will be severed from the remaining colonies. Gentleman Johnny will thus have crushed the rebellion."

There was no enthusiasm in Howe's words, and Cornwallis could see frowns now, some of the men around him uncomfortable with Howe's sarcasm. Cornwallis scanned the map, absorbed the plan.

To one side a voice, Charles Grey's, said, "Sir, with all respects, this plan has, as you say, been sanctioned by Lord Germain. But it has also received the approval of His Majesty. I do not believe I am alone in this room when I say I have utmost respect for the abilities of General Burgoyne. This plan is sound, and could very well bring the rebels to capitulation." There were nods, murmurs of approval, and Cornwallis stared at the map as he sorted out the words, more comments supporting Burgoyne. He was surprised at the dissension, more surprised that Howe was letting them have their say.

John Burgoyne had served with Howe and Clinton in Boston, as subordinates to Thomas Gage. But while Howe and Clinton had pressed forward their plans for defeating the budding rebellion, Burgoyne had spent much of his time engaged in his passion for writing plays, while at the same time, he sent a continuous stream of complaints to London, decrying the efficiency and abilities of his fellow generals. He was the oldest of the group, and to many, including William Howe, he had an inflated notion of his abilities. After the debacle at Breed's Hill, Burgoyne went to Canada, helping Governor Guy Carleton defend against rebel invasions of the valuable colony. But the Canadian winters held no appeal, and Burgoyne had returned to England.

Cornwallis had little contact with the man, knew him much more by reputation, knew that the nickname "Gentleman Johnny" had come from the man's own troops, a reflection on Burgoyne's empathy to the conditions of his men, something Cornwallis was known for as well. Though Cornwallis believed that Burgoyne was content to sail home to a prestigious retirement, he could see now that the man had spent his time in England carefully nursing his ambition, and had certainly succeeded in finding the willing ear of the king. And among Howe's command, Burgoyne clearly had his allies.

Cornwallis was surprised at Howe's tolerance of the dissent, but the protests were mild, respectful, and when the officers had run through their words, Howe said, "Your concerns are noted, gentlemen. I have no wish to impugn the reputation of General Burgoyne."

Cornwallis saw frowns, thought, That's exactly what you intended. He looked at the map again, tried to fathom the plan, but he couldn't assemble it in his mind.

"Sir, forgive me. I am trying to understand. General Burgoyne must sail the length of Lake Champlain. He must thus attack Fort Ticonderoga, must then move his wagons and artillery across this terrain, here. That is a great deal of countryside."

"Yes, General. You are stating the obvious."

Cornwallis ignored the comment, continued, "Do we have the means . . . how is he to navigate the country?"

Howe jumped at the question, said, "He is to be guided by a thousand Indians! Marvelous! And to add to his movements, it is believed that the loyalists in the area will flock to his march as well, providing their own assistance. Can you imagine that, General? His Majesty's good citizens marching side by side with the savages who torment them."

Grey stood now, and Cornwallis saw anger on the man's face, and Grey said, "Sir! I must protest! Do you deny that this plan could end this war?"

Howe glared at Grey.

"And what of us, General Grey? What of the soldiers in this army, who have given so much to the king's service? We have suffered the agonies of war, vanquished our enemy, as we have been bloodied by him. I have repeatedly offered my own strategies to Lord Germain, and now I receive word of this ridiculous plan of action. Will General Burgoyne succeed? Possibly. Will it bring this war to a conclusion? I have my doubts. I have insisted to Lord Germain for months now that this rebellion will be crushed by the year's end and that we can accomplish that from right here!" His words choked away, and Cornwallis saw red-faced anger, understood now. Of course, if Burgoyne ends the war, he reaps the rewards. That's what this is about, after all. Howe had his composure again, and Cornwallis said, "Sir, if the purpose of this plan is to capture Albany, why cannot we pursue that goal from this direction? If General Burgoyne was to bring his forces to New York, is not a campaign in force up the Hudson River a more effective means of reaching that place? His army could join with the troops already here. The rebels could not possibly hold back such strength."

Howe looked at him for a moment, and Cornwallis saw weariness. Howe said, "You are not a student of history, General. The route through New York has always come from Canada. The route southward through Lake Champlain has been consecrated by history. Lord Germain and His Majesty both appreciate that, General. We must adhere to tradition."

Grey said, "General Cornwallis, the strategy is to blaze a chasm through the colony of New York that will divide the rebel effort. From what I have seen of General Burgoyne's strategy, Albany is merely the junction. His army to ours. Certainly there will be a combining of forces."

The enthusiasm that had filled him was gone, and Cornwallis looked at Howe, said, "We are to join him in Albany? Move our forces north?"

Howe said, "General Burgoyne anticipates that we will effect a junction with his army once he has captured Albany. I have no doubt that once we know him to have arrived there, we can move a portion of our strength upriver. We should have sufficient time to complete *my own plans*."

The words were spoken with slow gravity, Howe watching them all for reaction.

"General Burgoyne is not the only man who has secured the approval of Lord Germain. I did not intend this meeting to focus entirely on Gentleman Johnny's war. I am preparing orders for each of you. This army will soon commence to march across New Jersey, with two purposes. First, I intend to draw the rebel army out of their base in Morristown in order to destroy them once and for all. General Cornwallis, you have made this attempt and failed. It is not for any lack of skill on your part. You simply did not have the resources at hand to offer Mr. Washington a sizable enough prize. I propose to march eighteen thousand men toward the Delaware River, with a train of supplies and boats, sufficient to allow us to cross unmolested. If we are fortunate, however, we *will be* molested. Mr. Washington cannot just sit in his hilltops and watch us go by. He must come down and offer us a fight. What he may not expect is how large a fight that will be." Howe paused, clearly enjoying the moment.

Cornwallis said, "Forgive me, sir, but if he chooses not to confront us . . ."

"General, if he does not confront us, then he will enable us to pursue the second goal of this plan. He may sit on his hills all the while and enjoy the spectacle of this army crossing into Pennsylvania and capturing Philadelphia!"

The word flowed through the room, each man digesting it, and the response was muted, not what Howe was expecting.

"Gentlemen, do you not see? It lies there as a great ripe plum, guarded by the most fragile of militia! The rebel capital! It is the one positive advantage we can gain from General Burgoyne's mission. The rebels must stay focused northward. Mr. Washington may perhaps divide his army and send reinforcements to their people around Albany. We can perhaps make a feint, move ships upriver toward the Highlands, drawing their attention in that direction. But any move the rebels make will come to naught! Once we are in Philadelphia, the heart of this rebellion will be crushed. How can these rebels wage war if their capital is conquered?"

CORNWALLIS HAD FINALLY SEEN THE LETTER FROM BURGOYNE, THE plan spelled out in enormous detail. There was no confusion as to either the line of march or the ultimate goal. Burgoyne insisted that with Howe's strength added to his own, their combined armies could devastate any rebel opposition and subdue all of New England in short order. There was one confusing gap in the plan, and Cornwallis was still not certain how the two armies were to join, whether Burgoyne expected Howe to advance farther northward than Albany, or whether Howe was to remain in New York and wait for Burgoyne to summon him up the Hudson. In either case, Howe did not seem concerned, his own orders from Germain granting him the discretion to march on Philadelphia in the manner he chose. Howe had settled the disagreements with his subordinates, reassuring Grey and the others that once the rebel capital had been secured, they could return to New York in plenty of time to join forces with Burgoyne.

If both armies were successful, Cornwallis believed the combined loss could crush the rebel spirit out of every colony, and he began to spread Howe's enthusiasm to his men. Finally, after so many months of waiting, the army would resume their march.

They embarked from the wharves at Amboy on June 12, began to march inland over the same roads that had carried Howe's army to Trenton six months before. As Cornwallis led his men along the southern banks of the Raritan, he tried to share their high spirits. It was, after all, the soldiers' opportunity for revenge, to sweep away the disasters of winter. But his gloom was returning, and he scolded himself, his enthusiasm dampened by the cold image in his mind, another great column of men and equipment, three hundred miles to the north, beginning their march as well. The grand strategy required cooperation and timing between two separate armies who were too distant from each other to communicate, and Cornwallis knew that no matter how sound the mission, how complete the plan, each army was led by a commander whose eyes were firmly focused on his own place in history.

Howe ordered him to maneuver as far west as Hillsborough, Cornwallis leading one wing of the army while Knyphausen's Hessians moved on a more southerly route toward Princeton. But there was no rebel army to face them. Washington had advanced his army out of his camp at Morristown, but only as far as Middlebrook, settling the rebels into another series of stout hills, this time within ten miles of Brunswick. As Howe marched his army toward Princeton, Washington would not take the bait, and abruptly, Cornwallis received orders to turn back, to gather the entire army at Brunswick. Howe was determined to bring Washington off his hills, and the next march was north, toward Metuchen, an attempt to outflank the rebels. But again Washington stayed in his defenses, and Howe's frustration spread through the entire army. But Cornwallis knew that no matter how much his men wanted a fight, Howe would not order them to attack a position they could never carry. After eighteen days of marching and countermarching, Cornwallis realized that Howe had made a huge mistake. Howe's plan was to continue on to Philadelphia, but Cornwallis knew they could not just march past Middlebrook as though the rebels weren't there. Washington's army would be coiled for a strike at the rear of Howe's army, could seriously torment the flanks and rear guard all the way to the Delaware River. If Howe attempted to move into Pennsylvania, Washington could strike him during the crossing of the river, the very tactic Cornwallis had failed to accomplish in December. As Cornwallis watched Howe's plan unravel, he knew that Howe was still focused on Philadelphia, the strategy fixed in his mind, stubborn and inflexible. If they could not assault the rebel capital by land, Howe would find another way.

On June 30, the army was ordered to march again, this time back to Amboy, to board the boats that would carry them to Staten Island. Once again Cornwallis shared the mood of his

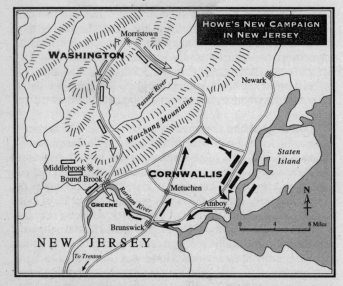

men, the utter disbelief that nearly three weeks of maneuvers and marching had gained them a few sharp skirmishes and nothing else. As Cornwallis stepped away from the wharf at Amboy, he fought the despair, the frustration mixed with a growing sense of alarm. Precious time had been lost, the time they would need to capture Philadelphia and return to assist Burgoyne, the time they would need to bring this war to a conclusion before another winter brought Howe and his grand strategies to yet another standstill.

20. GREENE

FOR WEEKS HE HAD MAINTAINED HIS POSITION ON THE HILLS NORTH of the Raritan, watching the great one-sided chess game play out below him, the British throwing up earthworks around Brunswick, then marching west, then back again. Washington had finally ordered him down to pursue Howe's rear guard, and when the British had turned and marched back to Brunswick, Greene had followed. He had maneuvered his troops with great care, knew that if the British realized he had come down from the safety of the hills, they might suddenly turn back on him, his men perhaps caught in the open, no time to build their own defenses. But when Howe had abandoned his march toward Princeton, it had been no ruse, no bait to draw Greene too close. It was as though the British were more focused on their own display, a strategy that made little sense to Washington.

Greene would not be careless, kept close enough to the British to monitor their movements, but not so close that a sudden burst of British mobility might catch his division in a fight he didn't want. But there was nothing about the British that suggested mobility, either in their movements or the planning of their commander. Greene could only wonder at the mind of William Howe, that once the man put some plan to paper, the strategy required no further thought, simply did not allow for the possibility of change.

When the British had gathered back into their defenses at Brunswick, Washington had ordered Greene once more to pull back to the safety of the hills, in case Howe ordered a sudden thrust toward Princeton. But when the British took to the road again, they went north, leaving Greene to worry if Washington had fortified the passes into the hills with sufficient strength. But

Stirling was there, a strong force dug into good ground, and the British thrust at Washington's eastern flank had dissolved as quickly as it began. This time, when Howe withdrew his men back into Brunswick, they did not stop to occupy their own carefully built defenses. As Greene eased down from the heights again, the redcoats were already marching east, this time toward Amboy. Greene had pursued them, small skirmishes, quick jabs at the British rear, but the British were in full retreat, had boarded their boats at the wharves and, just as quickly, sailed away. When Greene reached Amboy, not a shot had been fired. As Greene's men spread along the waterfront, Howe's baffled troops were once again pitching their tents on Staten Island.

Greene had stood with his troops, astounded that the British would expend so much energy, and waste so much time only to see their commander change his mind. Then the amazement of Greene's men changed to celebration. It was not so much a victory as it was satisfaction, the British march across New Jersey ending where it had begun so many months before.

As he glassed the British ships now anchored close to Staten Island, Greene thought of Washington, who had accepted the blame for the defeats in New York, who shouldered the despair of the entire nation that they could not bring to the field enough strength to hold the British away. Greene would never forget that one awful day, the catastrophe at Fort Washington. The commanding general had placed no blame, but Greene knew what others had said, knew there was grumbling in congress. Nothing was ever said in headquarters, and Greene knew now that Washington was not a man to cast blame away from himself, would not allow any criticism of his commanders to be voiced in the camps.

Throughout the desperate retreat across New Jersey, Greene had realized that the men who kept to the march were held by a loyalty to Washington that had nothing to do with strategy. Greene did not know how to explain it, knew it was something in the men's hearts. He wondered if Washington himself was aware of the affection and loyalty of the men in this army. That loyalty had been tested, and might be again, but for now, they had their reward. As he stood on the shores of Amboy, he knew that for the first time in many months, not a single British soldier had his foot in New Jersey.

*　　*　　*

THE LONG ENCAMPMENT AT MORRISTOWN HAD REVITALIZED THE army. Their stunning accomplishments on the battlefield had inspired new confidence that brought in an amazing abundance of food from the farms. They were strengthened as well by the arrival of French merchant ships, bearing the fruits of the careful negotiations in Paris. Besides the much-needed supplies of cloth and gunpowder, the army was receiving troop strength as well, a sudden inflow of new volunteers to the regiments. Greene had shared Washington's despair at the loss of so many of the veterans whose enlistments had expired, but Greene could not find fault with those men who wished to return to their homes. With the British firmly in their winter camps, the desperation had tempered, and the deluge of new recruits swelled the army to nearly eleven thousand men, many persuaded to sign eighteen-month enlistments. Though Greene had little faith in new recruits, and no faith at all in local militia, he hoped that the commanders would have the luxury of time, perhaps two months of drill and training to bring the army back to its feet. As the long weeks passed, Greene had grown nervous, knew that the recruits were still too raw, still finding their way into the soldier's life. Washington had cautioned them to expect a new British campaign by April, but they had been granted yet another luxury, this time by their enemy. Amazingly, the British camps had remained quiet until June.

With the army safely protected by the hill country around them, many of the commanders could enjoy the refreshing company of their wives. Martha Washington had arrived in March, and the monotony of headquarters had changed into a whirlwind of gaiety. He had seen the immediate change in Washington himself, and it made his own loneliness that much more difficult. Greene had spent many long nights deeply worried about his wife, Kitty. Her pregnancy had been difficult, made more so by the sudden chaotic presence of the British troops who had swarmed into Rhode Island under Clinton. But the baby had come in March, and though Kitty was as ill afterward as she had been during the pregnancy, her letters began to come more often, softening his worry. He had been surprised that anyone around the headquarters would share his concern, would distract themselves with his troubles during the pleasant mood of the winter camp. He was more surprised that the wife of his commander would do so much to comfort his fears, that she would help him write the soothing letters to his ailing wife, would share and celebrate his grateful relief when the baby girl was born safely. It was only fitting that the infant would be named Martha Washington Greene.

When Howe began his chaotic march through New Jersey, Washington ordered the social fineries to end. By mid-June, the wives, Martha included, were on their way home.

THERE WAS A NOTICEABLE QUIET, THE MOOD AROUND THE TABLE considerably subdued. Greene sat to Washington's right, studied the formal document, ignoring the dense brick of corn bread on his plate. He finished reading, his appetite crushed by a hard twist of anger. Sullivan sat across from him, said, "Do you agree?"

Greene tossed the paper toward the center of the table.

"Of course I agree. What manner of fools do we obey? Are they so consumed by their vanity . . . ?" He stopped, glanced at Washington, who was eating, seeming to ignore the anger. Knox sat at the far end of the table, leaned forward on his heavy arms, his round face a portrait of gloomy resignation.

"Has anyone actually heard of this fellow? Du Coudray?"

Greene pushed his plate away.

"Of course not. He's another in the parade, another feathered peacock, bringing his French superiority to the congress in yet another grand display! And they bow and coo and adorn him with all manner of compliments. And, the finest compliment of all, Mr. du Coudray, since you have come all the way from France, please accept this gift of our army. It is *yours*."

Sullivan sat back, his anger more subdued.

"Not the army, actually. Just the artillery."

The word seemed to punch at Knox, the heavy man sinking lower in his chair. Greene grabbed for the document again, fought the urge to crush it in his hands, said, "You are too generous, John. By their gracious and trembling hands, the congress has dated his rank of major general so far back as to predate our own commissions. He outranks us. He has never even seen a continental soldier, and yet, because of his sublime French manner, and his skill at flattering the congress, he now will supersede our commands."

He tossed the paper down again, looked at Washington, saw the man mashing the dry corn bread into a plate of dark gravy. Washington filled a fork, raised it toward his mouth, the contents now spilling off onto the plate. Washington huffed, began the process again.

"The food has grown worse since the wives have left."

Greene knew Washington was ignoring their hot protests, felt his anger draining away slowly.

"Sir, do you not share our outrage at the congress? This fellow . . ." He looked at the paper again. "This fellow Philippe-Charles . . . du Coudray brings here some letter of recommendation from Silas Deane, and suddenly, the congress decides he is in command of everything in this army!"

Washington prodded the corn bread again.

"Mr. Greene, if I reacted with anger to each foolishness that emerges from the congress, I would be in a constant state of agitation. *That* would be of very little benefit to this army. Do I share your outrage? Certainly. But we are all under the authority of the congress. This very country can maintain its existence only by the will of the congress."

Greene stared at him, felt an explosion brewing, fought it, could not raise his voice to Washington.

"Sir!"

It was both a question and a complaint. Washington put his fork down, looked around the table.

"I do not know if Mr. du Coudray will become an asset to this army, but there is one inescapable fact. He is French. He brings with him not only a letter from Mr. Deane but the high regard of the French court. We are not in a position to insult or disregard French officers who have come to our shores to be of service. The congress has not met the needs of this army, despite my every plea. If they find pleasure in anointing foreign officers according to the splendor of their uniforms, we must accept that. Insulting congressmen will not secure shoes for our men. Allowing them to feel a constructive part of our efforts might."

Knox stared at Washington with drooping sadness.

"Sir, does this mean I am no longer in command of the artillery?"

Washington took another bite, seemed to force a swallow.

"General Knox, you will command the artillery in this army until I order otherwise."

Greene was feeling confused now.

"But, sir, you said we must obey the congress. This order says that this du Coudray fellow now outranks every one of us but you."

Washington seemed to stifle a smile.

"Mr. Greene, I never said we must *obey* every whim of the congress. Since they delight in issuing paper, perhaps you gentlemen should issue some paper of your own. If three of my most experienced commanders threatened to resign, congress would respond with some outrage of their own. How dare you, and so forth. They might even request that I deal with your insolence by removing you myself."

Greene felt a headache brewing.

"Sir, this is madness. With all this army has accomplished, must we be subject to this absurd meddling?"

Washington was all seriousness now.

"Mr. Greene, it is the nature of the world. What else can we do? There is fear enough in Philadelphia that this army will vanquish the British, and then vanquish the congress itself. They grant me the power to raise an army, and so fear that power that they do nothing to provide for the very army they seek. The meddling is constant because the fear is constant. They fear the dangers of military power, while they know that without this army, they would hang from British gallows. They meddle because they must. I accept that meddling because *I* must. I despair that this army will face destruction from the congress long before we face it from the British. Despite their rhetoric and their fears, every one of them knows this army is the only salvation. Despite their meddling, they must ultimately seek my approval." He paused, and Greene saw the familiar sadness, the weight of so much settling on the man's broad shoulders. "As for Mr. du Coudray, I have given thought to his position. Since he feels suited to an artillery command, I will recommend that congress grant him a title, something with grandeur that will satisfy the man's ambition, such as inspector general of ordnance and military manufactories. You see, Mr. Greene? Often, it is no more than a game."

Greene looked across at Sullivan, who was beginning to smile, saw Knox now rising a bit, his dark mood lifting. Greene was still angry, knew that Washington was trying to put the best face on a dismal portrait. He backed his chair away from the table, stood.

"With all respects, sir, if it is a game, it is a desperate game."

JULY 10, 1777

Washington had repositioned the army, organizing the new recruits into their respective units and placing those units where they would be the most useful. The headquarters was still at Morristown, though Washington had stayed on the move, nervously inspecting the defenses up the Hudson toward Peekskill. Stirling's division had been sent upriver, reinforcing Israel Putnam, who now commanded the defense of the Highlands. Greene remained near Brunswick, and all along the Jersey shore, lookouts kept a sharp watch for movement by the British ships. For several days, that movement had been continuous and confusing. Clusters of frigates would suddenly file up the Hudson, raising the alarm up toward the Highlands. But quickly the ships would reverse course and return to the harbor. Another small fleet would then raise sails and disappear eastward past Gravesend Bay. Soon, those ships would return as well, only to sail southward past Staten Island. Washington's spies began to reach him with conflicting reports of British intentions. Some claimed that Howe was forming an armada to invade somewhere to the south, the Delaware River perhaps, some insisting that the British were planning another direct assault on the Jersey shore. Since every armada had eventually returned to its anchorage in the harbor, Washington realized that Howe was either maddeningly indecisive about his own intentions or was simply playing a game with him. Washington cautioned Greene and the others to stay vigilant, that despite all the apparent nonsense of the navy's movements, eventually Howe's true intentions would be revealed.

Greene carried his breakfast with him, a hard biscuit stuffed with a small piece of dried meat. He worked the stiff leg in a careful rhythm, climbing the tall hill as he had done for days, his aide following with the field glasses. It was already hot, the air smothering him in dampness, his shirt cold with sweat. He reached the one tall rock, leaned against it for a moment, his breathing slower, tried to ignore the pain in his stiff leg. He grabbed a tuft of brush above him, pulled himself up through a crag on the rock, his good leg now holding him. He lifted himself to the top of the lookout, could finally see the harbor clearly, and the mouth of the Hudson. There was a reflection, motion, one small frigate coming down out of the river, a patrol perhaps, Howe's futile effort at keeping the river free of the nighttime traffic. The aide was beside him now, handed him the glasses, and Greene scanned across to the city, patches of black still evident.

"They have not yet cleaned up the remnants of the fire, Mr. Hovey. They will not make the effort until they believe it is truly their city."

The man beside him stood at silent attention, something Greene was used to now, the young lieutenant always formal, few words. He knew Hovey was always watching him closely, there to help if Greene stumbled, if the leg suddenly gave way. He appreciated the young man's attentiveness, appreciated more that Hovey would never speak of it.

Greene lowered the glasses, thought of the Tories, so many loyalists from the countryside scampering into New York for sanctuary. It is so much like Boston, stuffed full like herring in a barrel with British sympathizers who have nowhere else to go. Is there not something to be learned from that? If this was still *their* country, why would the Tories have such a need to flee? If we are but a rabble, the dregs of your empire, why have you not subdued us?

There was a voice behind him, from below the rock, "Sir! General Washington approaches."

He moved to the edge of the rock, saw Washington dismount his horse, the big man now climbing the slope of the hill, trailed by the ever-present Tilghman. There was another aide as well, and Greene was pleased to see the young Hamilton, the artillery captain so impressing Washington that the commander had named him to his staff. It was more than just a reward for good service. Despite Joseph Reed's valuable assistance at Princeton, Reed could not avoid the stain of his betrayal, the indiscreet correspondences with Charles Lee. Washington had accepted Reed's resignation, and the young lawyer was gone, had returned to his home in Philadelphia. His replacement had to be a man of letters, someone who could turn the proper phrase. That man was Alexander Hamilton.

Washington moved up close to the tall rock now, said, "I am not a young man, Mr. Greene. May I have a word with you without scaling these heights?"

Greene stepped down to the crag in the rock.

"Certainly, sir. Allow me a moment."

Hovey was quickly in front, moved down the rock before him. Greene slid down, guiding the stiff leg through the gap in the rock, and he landed with both feet on the solid ground, hid the pain, pulled himself upright. He saluted Washington.

"There has been little change, sir. The ships are spread out in several areas of the harbor. If General Howe has some plan, he is not revealing it today."

Washington was frowning, staring away, and Greene knew not to interrupt his thoughts. Washington glanced around him, seemed to appraise the staffs, the company of riflemen spread out down below, the skirmish line who kept their muskets toward the river.

"General Greene, will you accompany me?"

Washington moved back down the hill toward the horses, and Greene followed, could feel the man's mood, thought, Something is wrong. He glanced back toward the harbor, No, the enemy has shown us nothing. Something of congress, perhaps? Another French peacock? The exercise was familiar, trying to cut through Washington's deliberate routine. It was not a sport he enjoyed, a product of his impatience, but he knew that Washington was assembling his words, and Greene would just have to wait. They moved past the horses, stepped down into tall grass, away from the morning sun, the air cooler. Washington stopped, looked around them, and Greene thought, The men. He's looking for those who might hear too much. Washington seemed satisfied they were alone, said in a low voice, "Mr. Greene, this is not a day I hoped I would ever see. I received a dispatch this morning from General St. Clair. He has abandoned Fort Ticonderoga. Burgoyne has taken possession of the fort."

The word punched through him like a spear.

"Abandoned?"

Washington nodded slowly.

"I have not yet received a full report, but I have faith in Arthur St. Clair, and I have no reason to believe he would not perform his duty." He paused, and Greene digested the word still in his mind. Washington said, "I had hoped the fort would be a major obstacle to the plans of General Burgoyne. Its loss is unaccountable, a most unfortunate event. Now we must make preparations. General Howe may already know of his victory. He will certainly take advantage, make every effort to combine a considerable force with Burgoyne's army. I do not see how we can entirely prevent that."

"Can St. Clair still fight? Is there anything to slow Burgoyne's advance? Perhaps Burgoyne will do for us what Howe has always done. He may decide to stop at Ticonderoga and celebrate his victory. It could give us time to move troops to that front."

Greene was running the names through his mind, the numbers, the strength they could muster toward Albany. Washington was staring down, said, "I do not know where Mr. St. Clair has gone, or his men. He only had a force of three thousand around the fort, and many of those were new recruits. Still, I believed that was adequate. The fort was a strong position. But now, whatever force St. Clair can still employ is barely a skirmish line should Burgoyne continue his march. We will send support immediately. General Gates is in active command there."

Greene sniffed, the sound more audible than he had intended.

"Mr. Greene, we cannot afford to debate the merits of anyone's command. The congress has deemed it proper that Horatio Gates lead that department. There is no time for argument."

Greene looked down.

"Of course not, sir."

It was more of the meddling, but this time a product of Gates' own efforts, the man taking every opportunity to campaign directly to the congress for what Gates insisted was his proper place, an independent command, out from the direct control of Washington. The congress had agreed, few in Philadelphia showing any grasp of the legacy of Charles Lee, those commanders who believed their own cause outshone that of the army. But Washington had moved beyond Greene's indiscretion.

"I wish you to send the Eleventh Virginia, Morgan's riflemen, to accompany two regiments being detached from General Putnam's command at Peekskill."

"Sir, my entire division can be prepared in short order. They are ready for a fight. I will march them with all speed, sir."

Washington held up a hand.

"No, Mr. Greene. What I require is that you remain close at hand. General Howe is still in New York. Until he makes his intentions known to us, we cannot commit any large force. I have summoned General Arnold from Philadelphia. He has already demonstrated considerable skill in that theater. I am hoping he will agree to organize what resistance can be assembled north of Albany."

The name brought more thoughts of the congress to Greene's mind, a bungling of promotions that had nearly cost the army one of its most able field commanders.

Benedict Arnold had distinguished himself from the earliest days of the war, stood side by side with Ethan Allen the day Ticonderoga was first taken from the British, an astounding accomplishment that provided the Continental Army nearly all of its artillery pieces. Arnold had continued his good work, defending Ticonderoga against a major British assault the year before. But when the congress granted promotions to a new group of major generals, they were hesitant to commission too many men from any one state. Some in the congress believed that Connecticut had already provided a disproportionate share of senior commanders, and thus Arnold, the Connecticut native, was passed over in favor of men from other states. Congress never seemed to consider ability to be as important as appeasing the tender feelings of various state assemblies. Washington had been given no say in the matter, but he recognized the ridiculous injustice and campaigned angrily on Arnold's behalf. Finally, Arnold had received his promotion. Despite the insult from congress, Arnold continued to exert himself with considerable skill in the field. For the past several weeks, he had been in command of the militia that guarded Philadelphia.

Greene knew that if Washington required a capable commander to take the field against Burgoyne's advance, there were few in the army who could take charge of a dangerous situation with as much skill as Benedict Arnold.

Washington began to walk slowly back up the hill, said, "Are you certain the ships are still at anchor?"

Greene followed, knew Washington would see for himself, and he waited until they reached the crest of the hill, pointed, said, "One group of frigates, a dozen, perhaps, near the mouth of the river. Several more, and at least six ships of the line out in the middle of the harbor. There's another group of smaller gunboats and a good many transports still at Staten Island. They do not appear to be making ready."

Washington had raised his field glasses, lowered them again, said, "General Howe is a mystery. He may not yet know of their capture of Ticonderoga, but still . . . I would be moving my strength upriver. I would not wait."

"General, he has done a great deal of waiting." Greene smiled, but Washington was grim, focused, and Greene said, "Perhaps, sir, he knows we are expecting him, that we are reinforcing the Highlands."

Washington made a small grunt, said, "Mr. Greene, when have we ever prevented them from gaining a river? A year ago I heard nothing but confidence about our strong defense of New York. You were a witness to our arrogance there. We have no engineers in this army. We build our fortifications by consulting outdated textbooks, written by the very enemy we are trying to hold away. General Putnam is confident he can keep the British from passing his works at the Highlands." Washington paused, raised the glasses again.

Greene said, "With respects to General Putnam, sir, we have not prevented the British from passing anywhere. The Highlands may be no different."

Washington looked at him, his expression softer, a small nod.

"It is essential for an effective commander to learn from mistakes, whether his own, or the mistakes of others. Thank you, Mr. Greene."

Washington looked away again, and Greene sorted through the small puzzle, realized now that Washington had tested him. The stain of Fort Washington had been with him for a while, but he saw past that, could see that Washington was telling him to learn from the error. He suddenly felt very good, wanted to say something to return the favor, somehow lift the burden he could feel in the man beside him.

"Sir, the loss of Ticonderoga could be a minor affair. Burgoyne is still a long distance from here. Even if Howe combines forces with him they cannot secure the entire length of the river. We can surely find the means to sever their hold."

Washington said nothing for a long moment, stared at the harbor, then looked around, again careful of those who might hear.

"Mr. Greene, there are many people in this country who be-

lieve that by the size of this land alone, we cannot be defeated. It
is natural to assume that no army on earth can subdue a nation as
large as this one. But our victory will not be won because we
control the most land. It is won by the defeat of the enemy's
army. We suffer the inefficiency of congress, but congress re-
flects the will of the people, and the people are our only means of
maintaining this army. The loss of Ticonderoga is not so important to this army as it is to the people. If they lose faith in us, they
will not support us. What we accomplished at Trenton transformed their mood, and you witnessed the result. New recruits,
ample rations. But when faith is justified, it becomes expectation. I have endured a flood of letters from congress, questioning
why we were so idle at Morristown. I am scolded, advised in the
strongest terms to strike out again, produce more victories, as
though it is simply a matter of will. The congress is aware that
the optimism of the people can change easily into hopelessness,
that the support for this army is as fragile as a flicker of candlelight. It may only take one great defeat, one powerful blow by the
British to extinguish it."

"Sir, clearly then, General Howe does not grasp that. He has
had opportunity to deliver such a blow, and has failed to do so."

"Yes, Mr. Greene, there is the mystery. I have heard rumors of
grumbling in the British high command, that the Howe brothers
may be our friends after all, that all their enthusiasm for peace is
reflected by their poor strategy."

"That would be . . . treason, of the highest sort."

"Quite so, Mr. Greene, which is why I don't believe it. General Howe is experienced in the European ways, that defeating
your opponent is best accomplished, not by defeating his army,
but by capturing his capital."

Washington looked again at the harbor, slowly raised his hand
in front of his chest, made a fist, his voice now loud, excited.

"That's the answer, Mr. Greene! That is why those ships are
still at anchor. No matter how sound the strategy, how important
it may be to Burgoyne, Howe doesn't *want* to go north. He wants
to go south. He has his eye on Philadelphia, after all."

THE SHIPS IN THE HARBOR HAD CONTINUED THEIR STRANGE GAME,
and Greene continued to observe them, the obvious trickery, sails
going north, then south, as though Howe expected Washington

to uproot his army to follow every feint. Then a letter had come to headquarters, captured in the hand of a spy. The man claimed to be traveling to Burgoyne, overland, when everyone in camp knew that the British dispatches were moving far quicker by water. The spy had stumbled down a road clearly controlled by Washington's guards, claimed to have been lost, and the letter he carried in his pocket was written in a code so simple, the sergeant who carried him to headquarters had already broken it. Washington read the letter with disguised amusement, made a loud pronouncement to the spy that the captured dispatch was an invaluable piece of intelligence. The supposed spy had been released, and the guard posts were discreetly ordered to allow the man to make his way to whatever boat would carry him back to General Howe. He would certainly report his mission a success, that Washington had captured the details of Howe's explicit plan. The document was a detailed letter to Burgoyne, stating that Howe's army would board their ships and sail north, supporting Burgoyne's march by first invading Boston, the very harbor that Howe himself had once abandoned. With the spy long gone, Washington had called his commanders together, and there had been no debate. When Greene returned to his men, the British ships were raising sails, were already heading out to sea. Howe's absurd charade only convinced Washington what they had already suspected. The British were on their way to Philadelphia.

21. WASHINGTON

JULY 31, 1777

THE ARMY HAD HALTED AT THE RIVER CROSSINGS ABOVE TRENTON, waiting for his order to advance into Pennsylvania. As confident as Washington was that Philadelphia was Howe's target, he could not escape his nagging discomfort of marching so much of his strength away from the Hudson River.

The British were masters of the sail, and the spies in New York estimated that Howe's fleet numbered well over two hundred ships, from the large men-o-war, down to the small gunboats. Movement on that scale was difficult at best, and any inclement weather could cause chaos for so many ships moving in unison along the same route. The fleet would surely take the shortest path, minimizing their vulnerability, and the one direct artery that led to Philadelphia was the Delaware River.

Washington had constructed small outposts along the river on the southern New Jersey shore, fortified positions that were unlikely to keep the British away, but could at least give Washington the information he was so anxious to receive. Once Howe's fleet was spotted, Washington could feel much more secure about marching his army into Pennsylvania.

For over a week nothing had been heard, and he rode through the streets of Trenton exercising his nervousness, waiting for any word of the location of Howe's massive force. Much of the damage in town had been repaired, few signs remaining of the battles, or from the occupation by the British and Hessian troops. Most of the citizens were back to their daily routine, and when the homes were empty, or the storefronts shuttered, it was presumed that the owners were Tories, many of whom had escaped the wrath of their neighbors by fleeing to New York.

His troops were kept outside of town, no need to risk any kind of confrontation with the citizens. But the activity in the streets showed no sign that these people were at war with anybody. He rode past merchants who mostly ignored him, took the horse down along the Assunpink, crossed the bridge his men had fought so hard to control. He prodded the horse up the ridge, could still see patches of blackened ash, where his men had built their great campfires, disguising his march toward Princeton. He did not stop, had already moved beyond the memory, could not focus on a victory now long past. The details in his mind were on what lay ahead, the anguish at Howe's disappearance, the message the next courier might bring. He knew there was only one certainty for his army. Along the Delaware River, they were completely removed from Howe's strategy, caught in between the possibilities. There might be clumsiness in the movements of the naval armada, but there was also strength. There were British troops still in New York, but Washington knew that Howe had been reinforced by London, could have nearly twenty thousand troops on those ships, a great fist of power that could suddenly appear anywhere, could be landed ashore and marched inland long before Washington could maneuver to meet them. If he was wrong about Howe's intent, Washington could not chance a march closer to Philadelphia. If Howe's massive force suddenly appeared again in New York Harbor, not only the Hudson River Valley, but most of New Jersey could be captured, wrapped up under British control without much of a fight.

He eased the horse down toward the wide river, could see the boats were already in place, manned by the Marbleheaders, the fishermen who had not gone home. It was his one advantage, a smaller army crossing a river with its own craft. If Washington had to move his men quickly, the river would not delay his march, and if Howe surprised him, made a sudden push toward a confrontation, the river was a perfect defensive line.

He turned the horse, the hooves sloshing through the soft muddy ground, the men on the riverbank standing aside, some raising hats, low cheers, salutes. He could see that many were still barefoot, and it was not because of the mud. The cargo from the French ships had included shoes as well as an abundance of cloth, and the seamstresses around Morristown had made an extraordinary effort at producing new shirts and pants for the men. But nothing could be done with the shoes. For most of the men in his army, the shoes did not fit. The jokes had come, the men turning their irritation into humor, a variety of explanations why French feet were apparently so much smaller than those of the Americans. But if his troops had put their best face on the situation, to Washington it was yet another frustration, knowing that another long march had to be made by men whose bare feet could cripple the army. Worse, the autumn months would give way quickly to a new winter. Without adequate shoes, the men could not march at all.

He continued to ride along the riverbank, studied the boats, looked across the river, saw a few more scattered on the far bank. He moved past a larger Durham boat, saw one man standing out in the bow, holding a long fishing pole. The man suddenly tugged at something, the pole curving down to the water. The man let out a shout, his solitary battle suddenly churning the water around him. Washington stopped the horse, the staff holding back be-

hind him, and he watched the combat, the man struggling to hold
the pole out of the water. There was a large splash, and the man
tumbled back into the boat, the pole in two pieces. Washington
realized now the fisherman had attracted an audience, and the
men around him began to laugh, some applauding. The fisherman struggled to his feet, frowning as he rubbed a bruised elbow, was suddenly aware of Washington.

"Oh, sir! Cursed thing got away! Busted my pole!"

Washington could not help a smile, a welcome break in his
mood.

"What kind of fish was it, soldier?"

The troops around Washington were quiet now, sharing the
fisherman's surprise at the question. The man still nursed the
pain in his elbow, said, "It weren't no Tory fish, I can tell you
that, sir. They just float right on up and beg you to take 'em in.
No fun a'tall. Had to be an American fish. Nothin' else put up
that kind of scrap."

The men around him began to cheer, and Washington still
smiled, knew it was all for his benefit, an overdone show.

"Thank you, soldier. Best leave the American fish alone. These
rivers need plenty of scouts."

He nudged the horse, began to move again, the troops returning to their work. He tried to recall the last time he had gone fishing, stepping through the mud and rocks of the Potomac, the
details long forgotten. He was not a good fisherman, was more
in love with his land than the water it touched, had envied those
who were so skilled.

His smile began to fade, and he turned away from the river,
glanced back at the staff, Tilghman suddenly up beside him.

"Sir? May I be of service?"

The young man was always serious, and Washington said,
"You a fisherman, Mr. Tilghman?"

The young man absorbed the surprising question.

"Uh, somewhat, sir. Much younger. Been a long time, sir."

"I should like to know how to do that. I am told that the Potomac is quite full of fish, all varieties. Can you teach me?"

He saw a puzzled look on Tilghman's face, and the young man
said, "I would be honored to accompany you, sir."

Washington looked ahead, thought of Howe, and his brother, a
man who must certainly be at home on any water.

"All that time at sea. Do you suppose Admiral Howe takes the time to fish?"

There was a silent pause, Tilghman weighing his words.

"I don't know, sir. May I get you something, sir? Are you feeling all right?"

The horse carried him up to the crest above the riverbank, and the image was firmly in his mind now, the Potomac, the sweeping view from the porch of Mount Vernon, orange sunsets painting the forests below the river.

"Sir?"

The soft daydream was pushed away by Tilghman's voice, and the view of Trenton, the town spread out before him. He could see formations of troops, the officers following his orders to keep the men busy.

"No, thank you, Mr. Tilghman. We will speak of this at a later time. Be sure that the regimental commanders are instructed again. They will post provost guards on the roads. There will be no mischief in the town, the men must do nothing to anger the citizens. I do not know how long we must remain here."

There was a horseman now, unarmed, no uniform, the man led by a squad of troops. Washington felt his heart jump, the troops now depositing the man close to him.

"Your Excellency, greetings, sir!"

It was a title Washington despised, and he frowned, but said nothing. He had tried to keep his staff from referring to him with such a regal salute, but there was one place where the word graced every document he received: *Congress*. The man was oblivious, said, "General Washington, I am here at the request of Congressman Morris. A courier has come to Philadelphia from your fortress on the Delaware cape. The congress is in quite a state, Your Excellency! Your presence is urgently required! The British fleet has been sighted!"

He felt his heart pounding, a flood of relief. Finally! It was no deception, no trickery after all. Howe has revealed his plan. He spun the horse, studied the faces of his aides.

"You will carry immediate word to the commanders. We will commence to cross the river with all speed, and march southward toward Philadelphia." He looked at Tilghman now.

"Send a message to General Sullivan. Instruct him to prepare his division to march at the first word. He is to remain near the

Hudson until I am absolutely certain of General Howe's intentions. But he should be prepared to join us with all haste."

He spurred the horse, moved toward his own camp, heard Tilghman issuing the specific instructions to each of his couriers. The word was already spreading to the men, and he rode past fresh shouts, salutes, but his mind was out in front of his army, detailing the plan for the next day, and beyond. The British would certainly sail as far upriver as their ships could navigate. The courier's word struck him now: *fortress*. No, gentlemen, we have no such thing. But if we can march this army with dispatch, we can at least meet the enemy on ground of our own choosing. The congress will certainly make plans to leave the city, and that courier was correct. I must go there immediately, and advise them, do what I can to reassure them that this army is prepared. It appears the wait is over.

AUGUST 1, 1777

As Washington made his way quickly to Philadelphia, the journey was being made from a different direction as well by a young man finding his way northward from the coast of the Carolinas. The man had come from France, his ship slipping through the porous blockade the British had thrown up around the American ports. His long ride would carry him first past dismal swamps and patches of flat farm country, worked by families who spoke less of war than of survival. As he pushed northward into Virginia, the land became more forgiving, and the people seemed to change as well, many more offering their encouragement to this young visitor. He received greetings and salutes of hope and encouragement that his mission was worthy, that somewhere to the north, a very good man was leading the American army in a desperate fight, a necessary fight. The young Frenchman was welcomed even more by the small towns along the rugged coast and waterways of Maryland, from people who had given so many of their own men to the fight, who believed still in the value of their cause, and who spoke as well of this man Washington, who bore the weight of their cause. When the young man reached Philadelphia, he found a city of loud voices, meeting rooms and taverns boiling with opinions, men freely offering their great pronouncements, solutions both wise and ridiculous, hot debates not of the value of the war itself, but of the quality of the men who commanded the fight. It was here that he heard the first angry attacks on Washington from those who championed other names unfamiliar to the young man, Gates and Lee and Arnold. It was unlike anything the young man had ever heard. The French army from which he had come would never be so outspoken against the authority of their king. America was a different land after all, and a land in the midst of a revolution with a spirit and substance that had appealed to him from his first readings of the words of Sam Adams and Tom Paine. He was not a soldier of fortune, had come from a family of some means in his own country. He was not a mere adventurer, though he would not avoid adventure. He did not come with the pretense of experience, though experience was his goal. Above all, he did not come to America to lord his supposed wisdom over Washington, the one man whose wisdom would determine so much.

During his time in Philadelphia, the young Frenchman had attended meetings and hearings in the congress, was flattered to be received as an honored guest, granted the opportunity to speak, to offer his services. He had hoped to ride northward, to find the camps of Washington's army, but then came word from his hosts that Washington would soon be in the city, a pleasant surprise. He was flattered to receive an invitation to a dinner, and the promise of an introduction to Washington. Though he held a title in the French court, though he had dined in the very presence of his king, the opportunity actually to address the commanding general threw him into knots of nervousness. His lack of experience, his very youth was betraying him. He was, after all, not yet twenty years old.

The young man could not keep the nervousness away, dressed for the dinner with clumsy fingers fumbling with the fineries of French silk and lace. Throughout the long journey, he had worked on his English, and he continued to practice, stood in front of a narrow mirror rehearsing his introduction, a formal sweeping bow, then again, with no bow at all. The nervousness grew worse, and he tried to calm himself by speaking to the mirror, imagining the introduction to the great Washington, very soon now, and he made the bow again, one last time, said, "With your pleasure, General, I am Marie-Joseph-Paul-Yves-Roch-Gilbert du Motier, the Marquis de Lafayette."

* * *

WASHINGTON HAD TRIED TO BE DISCREET, RODE THROUGH THE CITY streets with no fanfare, but the word of his visit had preceded him, and by the time he reached the City Tavern, there was already a crowd.

He was not sure who would attend the dinner beyond his friend Robert Morris, and of course, a variety of congressmen. He had received word of a foreign guest, and the news had smothered whatever enthusiasm he felt for this social occasion. He had learned to dread any meeting with yet another in the unending line of foreign dignitaries, men who flowed over with self-importance, with their boisterous demands for authority. He thought of Greene's word, *peacock,* so aptly describing the spectacle of the grand uniforms, filled by so many men of loud ambition and no ability. His dread had only increased when he learned that this particular guest was hardly a man at all, but a boy who brought a man's title, and who no doubt had expectations of receiving a man's respect. Still, the young man was French, was said to have some close acquaintance with King Louis. The French had continued to plague Washington's headquarters with their insistence on assuming immediate command, none more so than the ever-vocal du Coudray, who had assaulted both congress and Washington himself with his demands for a senior command in the next confrontation with the British.

As Washington climbed down from the horse, he acknowledged the polite cheers of the small crowd, thought of Greene, relieved that his subordinate was not accompanying him. No, Mr. Greene, this would not be your sort of affair. This might be an evening of careful diplomacy. Your impatience would not do. Our cause is not aided by insulting the very people whose assistance we require so desperately. If this young marquis is truly close to King Louis, we should, at the very least, be polite to him.

THE DINNER HAD BEEN A MIX OF BOISTEROUS GOOD CHEER AND subdued advice, and Washington had endured it all with a graciousness that had drained his energy. The wine was flowing freely now, and the conversation was steering away from talk of the war, the one subject that had kept the evening entirely sober. Washington had given up any thoughts of using the evening to

campaign for the urgent needs of his army. The few members of
congress were concerned mostly with their short time left in the
city. It was not quite panic, but it was clear that every one of the
dinner guests had his eye on the door, each one planning his
journey southward. There was talk of assembling the congress
at York, Pennsylvania, far enough from the potential danger, yet
close enough to Washington so the lines of communication would
not likely be cut. Throughout all the talk, Washington could not
bring himself to further destroy their good cheer by reminding
them that if his army was not supplied, the British could conquer
much more than Philadelphia.

As the evening had grown late, the pleasantries and good
manners were replaced by more serious talk of the danger to the
city, more advice on military defenses from men who had never
seen their enemy. Washington would not offer any details of his
plans for the defense of Philadelphia, knew that even among
friends, strategy was a risky thing to divulge. He endured instead
the advice, allowing the men to point their fingers at him, the
wine loosening their inhibitions, and their tongues.

He had nearly forgotten the young Frenchman. Lafayette sat
against the far wall, had spent most of the long evening smiling
politely. He was a small man, thin, not especially handsome,
with red, nearly blond hair that had already receded above a tall
forehead. Washington was surprised that he had been so quiet,
did not seem to carry the air of the self-important. There had
been toasts to the French alliance, to Lafayette himself, but the
young man never placed himself at the center of attention. It was
a relief to Washington, that the evening might not be a spectacle
of vanity after all.

The voices were droning on around him, and he could not focus, was feeling the strain of his day in the saddle. He shifted
himself slightly in the chair, blinked hard through tired eyes,
looked across at the young Frenchman now, saw fatigue, thought,
Yes, young man, ambition is a strenuous cause. You've no doubt
been hard at it. Throughout the evening, Washington had noticed
Lafayette watching him, the young man especially attentive when
Washington spoke. He could see the young man fidgeting now,
strangely nervous, and Washington thought, Well, I cannot avoid
the issue much longer. At least he does not seem to be as bold as
Mr. du Coudray. He waited for a lull in the conversation.

"Tell me, Mr. Lafayette, what are your intentions here?"

Washington regretted his bluntness, tried to smile, take the rude edge away from his words. Lafayette looked at him with wide eyes, the room now silent. The Frenchman stood.

"General Washington, I have here a document." He fumbled in his pocket, produced a folded piece of gray paper, opened it, and Washington could see the young man's hands shaking. "Sir, since I am still learning the complications of your language, it is possible that I can answer best by reading to you the commission your congress has so generously bestowed." Lafayette read now,

Whereas the Marquis de Lafayette, in consequence of his ardent zeal for the cause of liberty in which the United States are engaged, has left his family and friends, and crossed the ocean at his own expense to offer his services to the said states without wishing to accept of any pension or pay whatever and as he earnestly desires to engage in our cause, Congress have resolved, that his services be accepted, and that, in consideration of his patriotism, his family and illustrious relations, he shall hold the rank and commission of major general in the army of the United States.

Washington felt the familiar stab in his stomach, could hear Greene's voice in his mind, the explosion of sarcasm. *Major general?* Well, he is after all, only nineteen. A lieutenant general should be at least twenty. Lafayette was looking at him with gentle hopefulness, and Washington realized that the young man was not demanding anything.

"Mr. Lafayette, while I certainly respect the wisdom of our congress, I must ask you again. What are your intentions? Do you expect me to provide you with your own command, something appropriate to your . . . rank?"

He dreaded the answer, waited, the room completely silent now, all eyes on Lafayette. Washington could see the young man's expression change, the nervousness replaced by confidence.

"General, I have every wish to command a division in your army. But I do not yet have the experience. I was most insistent on one point to the congress, and asked them to make special mention in this document. Since I am not yet of much value to your cause, I do not wish to be paid. I requested the rank they assigned to me, because I believe I can be of service in that rank. But I remain a volunteer, sir. I have come here to learn, not to teach."

Lafayette sat down, and the faces turned to Washington. The young man was still looking at him, and Washington again saw the confidence, the eyes of a man who seemed above all to be honest with himself. Washington had never thought himself wise in reading a man, in knowing a man's character by the look in his eye. But he had seen that look before, in Henry Knox, Nathanael Greene, the men who had become his most trusted commanders. He had seen it as well in the most loyal and reliable member of his staff. Washington had to convince a reluctant congress to promote Tench Tilghman to lieutenant colonel, but Tilghman would still not take pay for his job. If Lafayette was truly a volunteer, it was a welcome comparison. Lafayette seemed to be waiting for his response.

"Mr. Lafayette, this army will survive on the backs of its volunteers. I should like you to begin your service by joining my staff."

AUGUST 22, 1777

Washington was stunned to learn that Howe's navy had disappeared off the Delaware capes, the great mass of ships abruptly raising their sails and vanishing beyond the horizon as quickly as they had appeared. The reports from the outposts offered no answers, and for several days he had felt a rising alarm, the familiar despair, wondering if Howe had indeed fooled him, that even now the British navy was sailing again through New York Harbor, already launching a massive push up the Hudson River that Washington was too weak and too distant to stop.

Though there was no hint where the ships had sailed, Washington began to receive a different report from the scouts along the south Jersey coast, that several British vessels had attempted to pass his artillery positions, coming under a brisk fire from guns whose effectiveness was doubtful. But when Howe's ships confronted the obstructions Putnam had placed in the river, they made no attempt to slip through. Unlike that dismal day on the

Hudson, when Nathanael Greene could only watch Howe's ships mock the barricades, this time, the British had turned back, did not attempt to pass. It was a surprise, and Washington had to believe that, finally, Putnam had devised a means to block a river that might actually have worked. But that success had come with a disadvantage. If Howe could not sail up the Delaware, he had certainly altered his plan. It was a question that burned in Washington's mind. What was Howe's *new* plan?

The army made camp north of Philadelphia in a small village called Germantown. Washington found himself with no strategy of his own, no way to know if anything he did would be the correct move. As the days passed, there was still no information, no word from any quarter to explain where Howe had sailed.

The rumors began to fly, word of a panic in Boston, a great fleet appearing on the horizon that was actually no more than a bank of fog. The debate swirled through the camps, some of the men believing that Howe had gone farther south, would attack Charleston. Through it all, Washington kept his focus on two fronts. The sheer size of the fleet meant that Howe could not simply play a game, was still vulnerable to the wind and seas, would have to point his armada in one direction. It was a massive operation, and with the enormous number of troops on board, there had to be a mission far more serious than just another feint. If the British navy was at home on the water, their army, especially the Hessians, certainly was not. Washington had to believe that no commander would inflict such senseless discomfort on so many good soldiers for long.

Washington stayed close to his tents, passed the time by studying his maps, holding himself awake in dull candlelight until the lines on paper blurred into sleep. His officers had stopped offering their own theories, exhausted as well by the pure guesswork, strategy that meant nothing until Howe gave them the answer.

It was very late, and sleep had not come. He stood in the warm air outside his tent, listened to the sounds of the night, the low chatter of insects, felt the sweat in his clothes. There was no breeze, and he strained to hear the sound, the familiar rhythm of hoofbeats that would break the silence, the blessed courier who would bring him word. Spread out beyond the town, the army was mostly asleep, and he was as tired as any of his men, but there was no rest tonight, a dull pain from a hard knot in the back of his neck that would not give him peace. He could see a soft glow in a nearby tent, knew it was Tilghman, the young man probably watching him even now, keeping out of sight until Washington gave some sign, some hint that he required his aide. Washington stared at the light, saw flickers of motion, the night creatures drawn to the glow. His mind was drifting, and he fought it, tried to keep himself in the moment. How much longer can we remain here? He had asked himself the question every night, and his officers were asking as well, some believing still that Howe would appear at Charleston before anywhere else. If that is true, we will not know for many days yet, and there will be little we can do about it. Seven hundred miles on foot would destroy this army.

He pushed the thought away. No, Howe will still come to Philadelphia, or he will go back to New York. If Philadelphia cannot be assaulted by way of the Delaware River, the alternative is the Chesapeake Bay. If he returns to New York, it is possible he has received explicit orders from London, to unite his army with Burgoyne. He shook his head, sorted through the fog of thoughts. That is the one great mystery, more perplexing than where they have taken their ships. How can he simply abandon Burgoyne? It would have been logical to wait in New York for Burgoyne to march southward, some plan perhaps to push up the Hudson at the appropriate time. But for Howe simply to sail away, put such a great distance between their forces . . . how can London have approved such a strategy?

He turned his head to the side, pulled at the knot in his neck, tried to relieve the dull ache in his head. He turned into the tent, a faint glow of light, the one candle nearly burned down, a small flame barely surviving above a small pool of wax. He stared at the light, thought, It must be New York after all. Perhaps that is best. We cannot hope to confront them down here in a general engagement. There is little cause to sacrifice this army merely for the protection of Philadelphia. The congress would never understand that of course. If we can make a wise confrontation, we will do so, but ultimately the city has no value beyond the symbolic. If Howe occupies the city, he must fortify it, and that will be so much more difficult than defending the island of New York. Surely he knows that the congress will simply move to another location. It is one luxury we have, a government that is mobile. Nothing like that in Europe, certainly. And, there is still Burgoyne. He fought the blur in his mind. New York. He will go to New York, and we must return as well. We will march tomorrow. But . . . would Sullivan not have sent word?

He shook his head, moved to the bed, sat down. The exhaustion was complete now, his head pounding, and he reached out toward the candle, pinched the flame between his fingers. He expected darkness, was surprised that he could still see, the walls of the tent a dull gray. He wiped his hands on his face. So, another day has begun. He took a deep breath, stood up slowly, thought of Tilghman. I hope you are more wise than I am, Colonel. Perhaps you had some sleep. He stepped out into the dawn, still no breeze, a low mist hugging the ground. He could see campfires now, brought to new life by the men who rose early, the night sounds replaced by an army slowly coming awake. He saw Tilghman emerging from his tent, others as well, Hamilton, and now the different uniform, the young Lafayette. They began to move toward him, and he tried to summon the energy, fought to keep his eyes open, tried to think of the instructions, what might happen today. We should go to New York. We have waited long enough.

Tilghman was motionless, staring out, and Washington stretched his arms, thought of coffee, realized now that the others were staring away as well, at the road to the south. Now he heard the sound, the hoofbeats, then more, and he could see soldiers, the guards, emerging from the gray light. The horses were pulled to a stop, and one man dismounted, came toward him quickly, a civilian. The man held up a paper, said, "Your Excellency! I bring you a message from Philadelphia, from John Hancock, sir!"

Tilghman had the paper now, handed it to Washington, who broke the wax seal, held the paper out, fought the dim light, tried to focus on the words. He read for a moment, felt a low fire rising inside of him, his mind clearing, the orders forming, the instructions for the new day. He looked at Tilghman.

"Colonel, prepare the men to move. We will march south, through Philadelphia. According to Mr. Hancock, the British fleet has been sighted well up the Chesapeake Bay. It seems that General Howe is coming ashore after all."

The staff was gathering close, and Washington began to give instructions to each man, Hamilton writing it all down on paper. They began to move away, and he turned, stepped into the tent, stood for a long moment, thought of Howe. Your men will be anxious to leave their ships, to march on dry land again. And if we are blessed, we will find good ground, we will stand firmly in your way, and give you a fight that will send you home. And perhaps I will have the opportunity to ask you myself. Why did you abandon General Burgoyne?

22. CORNWALLIS

AUGUST 25, 1777

HE STEPPED ONTO DRY LAND FOR THE FIRST TIME IN MORE THAN SIX weeks. Behind him, the men filed out of the flatboat in a wave of grateful relief, their sickness and misery already drifting away with the breezes that swept out across Chesapeake Bay. The shoreline was swarming with troops, and there was very little order, the officers allowing their men to drift away from the beach, every man thanking God and General Howe for finally putting them ashore. Within the first few minutes of their landing, whole companies had surged inland, a desperate exodus away from the water, as though the water itself was the plague that had so infected them.

They had made the landing at a place called the Head of Elk, the northernmost tip of the Chesapeake. Cornwallis had studied the charts and maps of the area, knew that the army would make their base on a piece of land that was still sixty miles from their goal. Philadelphia was no closer now than it was to Brunswick, the same camps where his army had spent so many months of useless waiting. A march southward across New Jersey might have taken two weeks, a confrontation with the rebels already decided a month or more ago. Now, they would begin a campaign across an unknown piece of ground, a countryside he had never seen, seeking an enemy who might appear around any curve, on any ridge.

Cornwallis watched the fleet of flatboats continuing to gather along the narrow beach, those still full weaving their way through the chaos of the empty boats, the sailors losing their discipline, shouts and curses, some striking out with their oars and push poles. A ship with sickness is a curse to anyone who sails her, and tempers were hot, impatience with the mass of traffic along the shore. The sailors had suffered the company of the soldiers who had come to hate every part of the voyage, and every part of the ships that brought them. As each boat released another swarm of exhausted faces, Cornwallis shared the feeling with them, that the useless torment, the absurd torture of this fine army was finally past.

HOWE HAD ALLOWED THREE DAYS OF REST FOR THE GRATEFUL SOLdiers, who regained their stamina in relative quiet along the banks of the Chesapeake. The supply officers had been busy, organizing the Head of Elk into a massive depot for provisions, unloading the extraordinary amount of equipment from the huge armada of transports. As the camps were erected, there had been sightings of rebel troops, but no combat. Cornwallis had seen the reports from the scouting parties. They were hardly troops at all, small companies of local militia, led by no one who seemed willing to risk an encounter. It was far different from the camps in New Jersey, where his men were harassed and tormented by riflemen with deadly aim.

Despite the peacefulness of the camps at Head of Elk, Cornwallis was as eager to move as his men. His division would lead the advance, seven thousand men who finally seemed fit for a new campaign. They marched away from Head of Elk on August 28, led by Tory guides, the only men among them who had any idea what might lie ahead.

From the first day out of New York Harbor, the weather had been insufferably hot, and the ships had become steaming ovens, their decks too small to accommodate the sheer numbers of men who suffered beneath them. Once dry land was beneath their feet, the morale of the troops had soared, but there was little relief from the heat, and the enthusiasm for the march had quickly drained away. They moved northeast, past wide swamps and patches of scrub forest, the air dense and wet, swarming with insects. After several days, Howe had granted them the privilege of marching at night, but the darkness did not cool the air, and there was no breeze to carry away the invisible pests. As the men grew accustomed to starlight, the march seemed to pick up momentum. There had even been music again, drummers setting the cadence, fifes and bugles and bagpipes carrying the men forward. But then, the rains came.

SEPTEMBER 8, 1777

Cornwallis pulled his coat tighter around him. It was not a chill, but the soaking wetness of his uniform. The wind was flailing the trees above him, the darkness complete. Despite the effort of his staff, no lantern was surviving the gale. He had given up trying to see anything, no need to look ahead, nothing in front of him but soldiers, each man keeping to the road by following the tracks of the man in front of him. Still he would make the attempt, the rain pelting his face, driving hard into his eyes. He leaned forward in the saddle, lowered his head, tried to blink the water away, but he knew immediately that it was a mistake, a gust of wind driving a stream of warm water under his collar, down his back. He sat upright again, twisted slightly in the saddle. The slow rocking of the horse was scraping him from below, the soaking wetness turning his undergarments into harsh rags. He tried to find a comfortable position, settle into the rhythm of the horse's gait, but the animal seemed as miserable as he was, picked its way through the mud with uneasy steps.

The horse was new to him, one of the few that had survived the journey. It had dismayed him to see the horses coming ashore, emaciated animals disembarking from their own small fleet of flatboats. He had seen the staggering animals led by their handlers, sad men whose duty gave way to pity, leading the horses to patches of green, any kind of grass the animals would try to eat. After a short time, Cornwallis could not watch them, had turned away from the pitiful sight of exposed ribs, hollow stomachs. The length of time the ships spent at sea had surprised the supply officers, and as the journey lengthened, it became clear that the ships could not carry enough forage for the horses to survive. In just a few weeks they began to die. He had no special love for horses, had always enjoyed a capable mount, but the long sea journey had opened up a new horror in him, the spectacle of the helpless animal who endures its own starvation without complaint. Once it began, it was constant. Each day the animal transport ships met the dawn by sliding carcasses over the side, the animals who had not survived the night. When Howe ordered the armada out of the Delaware River, it was obvious that the fleet had many long days still to sail, and the request came from the supply officers, permission to cast off the weaker animals, those whose survival was in doubt. They would simply be pushed overboard, the most humane way for the horse transports to preserve the supply of grain and fresh water for those animals that still had strength. Cornwallis had objected at first, horrified at the waste and the cruelty. Even Howe had reacted to that, and Cornwallis could not avoid the feeling that Howe might have more sympathy for the horses than for the suffering of his men. But the supply officers made their case, and Howe had given the order with one condition: The crews of the transports would carry out the grim duty after dark. Even now, in the roaring misery of the rain, Cornwallis could hear that awful sound, the heavy splashes that would echo across the black water. He thought of the one small consolation, the only kind of peace he could find through those dreadful nights. At least, as they drown, they don't cry out.

He could hear the wind again, knew there were thick trees around him, another deep patch of woods. He heard the familiar whine, the mosquitoes darting around his face. He wiped at the air, a useless gesture, the movement opening up a new part of his uniform to a small flood of water. The mosquitoes swarmed over them from the woods, the patches of low ground, swampy, the birthplace of so much human misery. These narrow roads were the only way through, and he knew that out in front, the skirmish line was probably massed into the road itself, that no officer would order his men into these swamps at night. It hardly matters, he thought. The rebels are nowhere to be seen. They are in their homes, with their wives. Dry clothes.

There was a sudden burst of light above him, a hard slam of thunder. The lightning reflected off the men in the road, and he jumped as they did, jarred awake by the startling sight. The horse seemed to stagger, and he held the reins hard, pulled the animal to halt. The horse grew calm again, and he nudged it with his boots, the animal resuming the uneven gait. A fresh gust of rain blew into his face, clouding his eyes yet again, and he blinked hard, thought, Even the ships were not this bad. Well, perhaps.

He felt a sharp sting on his ear now, slapped it away, could not help a small quiet laugh. A soldier's life. Torture by design. He thought of the stories from his childhood, the stern lesson from a frightening schoolmaster. We shall be punished for our sins. And, so, here we are, in all our biblical absurdity. We have suffered the plague of locusts, and the flood of Noah. What is left? Shall Mr. Washington part the colony of Pennsylvania, and swallow us up? Perhaps that will be the fate of General Burgoyne, guilty as he is of the sin of ambition. How dare this man usurp the glory rightfully due to General Howe?

The horse stumbled, and he pitched forward, caught himself on the horse's mane. Behind him came a voice, one of his aides, "Sir! You all right?"

"Quite so, Major."

The humor was gone now, and he pulled himself upright, thought, So they are watching you after all. Not everyone sleeps in the saddle. I suppose, if *this* army is going to match the successes of our rivals, we should stay perfectly awake. Gentleman Johnny must have no advantage.

They had received news of Burgoyne's capture of Ticonderoga with a mix of congratulation and dismay. Howe had sent his formal letter of salute of course, a job well done. But Cornwallis knew that Burgoyne's victory had given a new urgency to Howe's own plans, that if the insurrection in the colonies was to be defeated, it must still be decided on Howe's terms, and not by the actions of this playwright who had so boldly thrust himself into Howe's war. But then the mood around headquarters had changed, Howe himself spreading a strange jubilation, and Cornwallis realized that Burgoyne's success meant that Howe could proceed with his own march toward Philadelphia, not be so concerned about returning to New York after all. Clearly, in the Champlain Valley, Burgoyne had matters in hand.

Before Howe had set sail, the army had received reinforcements, and Cornwallis knew that his division marched in the lead of an army of nearly eighteen thousand men. No one could be sure of

the exact rebel strength, but Washington's seasoned veterans
could not number more than three or four thousand. Tory spies
had assured Howe that any larger force the rebels brought to a
confrontation would be composed of fresh troops and worthless
militia.

SEPTEMBER 9, 1777

The rain had stopped with the sunrise, and Howe had ordered
a halt to the march. The men flowed out into rolling fields, and
Cornwallis was relieved to see that the landscape was changing,
more of the rolling farmlands than the miserable swamps. The
farms were not as groomed as they had been in New Jersey,
fewer stout fences, few of the stone walls that had given the rebel
marksmen such effective cover. Out in front, the lead units had
spread out into a line of defense, the usual precaution against the
sudden appearance of rebel riflemen. But there had been no
sounds of firing, no resistance at all. For several days the scouts
had spread out through the countryside without detection, and
most had already brought their reports. The main force of rebels
had marched through Philadelphia and advanced down near
Wilmington. It was clear that Washington intended to bar the approach to Philadelphia, had moved the rebel army southward as
Howe had moved north. The Tories had brought estimates every
day of what they were facing, talk of as many as twelve thousand
rebel troops, a number Howe considered ridiculous. But Cornwallis knew that numbers might not be as important as ground,
and Washington would choose his ground with great care.

Cornwallis' uniform was still soaking wet, and he led his men
into a vast grassy field. He saw officers gathering, one moving
toward him with a bearing of stiff formality.

"Sir, we regret to report that the men have lost the use of much
of their powder. The storm has caused quite the inconvenience,
sir."

"Major, there is no apparent sign of the enemy. Do what you
can to dry the powder stores, and send word to General Howe
that most of our cartridges are likely ruined. We will feed the
men as adequately as we can. I have no doubt that General Howe
will resume this march with all haste."

The officers moved away, and he looked at the sky, a sea of small clouds moving eastward. The air was thick and hazy, and he felt a warm breeze, thought, At least no rain today. If the roads dry out, we will make good time.

There was a splashing of hoofbeats, and he saw Howe's flag emerging from down the road, let out a deep breath, no breakfast just yet. He stepped close to his horse, could see Howe himself. He glanced to his staff, saw them already climbing up into their saddles, thought, All right, so we will now learn what we are to do today. He pulled himself up into the saddle, felt the heavy wetness in his clothes. Howe was coming toward him, and he saw Charles Grey now as well, a long line of staff officers. Howe said, "Good morning, General. I regret we must make brief our rest. There is considerable news this morning."

There was no pleasantness in Howe's words, the man not even looking at him. Cornwallis had seen the look before, thought, Something has happened.

"Is the news to be shared with your command, sir?"

Howe focused on him now.

"Oh, quite, General. No need for secrets these days. The letter was brought from the fleet this morning. It seems that General Burgoyne has run into some difficulty. His jaunty parade through the wilderness was struck a somewhat unfavorable blow. Some place called Bennington, I believe. A large contingent of his Hessians was sent off on some foraging expedition, and was rather rudely handled by the rebels."

Howe seemed distracted, stared away, and Cornwallis felt uneasy, said, "Is that all, sir? What of General Burgoyne? How great a loss, sir?"

Howe seemed not to hear, and Cornwallis felt his impatience rising. Howe turned to an aide.

"The letter, Colonel, if you please."

The aide retrieved a folded paper from a bag, and Howe held it up, said to Cornwallis, "The fates are on the side of General Burgoyne, even if the Gods of War are not. This unfortunate incident has cost General Burgoyne a thousand good men, irreplaceable in his present situation. And, in an annoying display of coincidence, I have also received this letter, sent to me by Lord Germain, dated back in May. Damnably slow ships. Lord Germain feels it is imperative that this army cooperate with General Burgoyne as our *first* priority. While he assures me that he supports my designs on capturing Philadelphia, we have been instructed to complete this mission, then make every effort to return to New York, in time to lend assistance to General Burgoyne." Howe paused, stared away again, said, "I never considered Lord Germain to possess the talents of a seer. But clearly he had his doubts about General Burgoyne's plan from the beginning. It is a mystery, then, why he approved that plan." Howe looked at the paper without reading it. "It is almost as though this was never intended to reach me before we sailed."

Grey moved closer now, said, "General Howe, we cannot withdraw now. We have come too far . . ."

Howe exploded now, his voice punching the air, "Of course we do not withdraw! We are on this ground with purpose, and that purpose is to occupy the rebel capital! From everything we have heard, Mr. Washington is making ready to prevent that from happening. This is exactly what I had hoped, exactly the means I had laid out for winning this war!"

Cornwallis saw a frown on Grey's face, and understood that Grey was deferring to him, the only man who was senior enough to make an argument with Howe. Cornwallis said, "Sir, I agree that Philadelphia is still our goal. May I ask, sir, if Lord Germain's orders allow us the discretion of completing our mission?"

"Oh, we will complete our mission, General. Only then will we give serious consideration to General Burgoyne's situation. The general has placed himself in jeopardy at his own responsibility. *Assist him*. Lord Germain should have known better." Howe looked past Cornwallis, toward the field where the soldiers were drying their belts, tending to their equipment. "Prepare your men, General Cornwallis. We must resume the march."

Howe moved away now, and Grey lingered, moved close to Cornwallis, said nothing for a long moment. Cornwallis turned to his staff, said, "General Howe was clear in his orders. Inform the regimental commanders. Prepare the men to march."

The staff obeyed, moved quickly away, and Grey said in a low voice, "Lord Germain is not required to *know better*. We are to follow his orders."

Cornwallis shifted in his saddle, the dampness still scraping him.

"Lord Germain is not here, Charles. A great deal can happen in a few weeks. If General Howe can win this war, John Bur-

goyne will not require anyone's assistance. The contest will be
done, regardless of who Lord Germain wishes to place in favor."

"So, is that what this is about, after all? I had hoped this command could rise above such bickering. Must this be some sort of
tawdry race? All glory to the man most pleasing to Lord Germain? Is not the king best served by obedience to his orders?"

"I am not privileged to know what pleases my king, Charles. It
is not my place, or yours, to judge the actions or the motives of
General Howe. It is our place to obey him. And right now, it is
my duty to lead my troops into this road. You should do the
same."

Grey seemed depressed by his words, saluted him, said, "Yes,
sir. It will be done."

Grey moved away, followed by two aides who had stayed out
near the road. Cornwallis watched him for a long moment,
thought, He is too experienced to be so naïve. None of this is
new to this army. We all know of ambition and intrigue, glory
and pettiness. It is simply the way. It has always been the way. If
General Howe fails, he will pay the price, and we will follow
someone else. Whether there is glory or blame cannot matter.
What matters is those men who are waiting for us up ahead.

SEPTEMBER 10, 1777

The ground was rolling, open fields cut by shallow ravines,
farmland and forest, intersected by narrow creeks. The scouts
had led the skirmish lines toward a great mass of rebels, but they
had not been in place long, there was no sign of a strong defensive line. Howe had ridden to the front with him, the two men
scouting the land, seeking the strength of rebel positions. They
found themselves scouted in return, rebels appearing close,
across the banks of a narrow deep creek. They came within a
hundred yards of each other, both parties withdrawing quickly.
But Cornwallis had raised his field glasses, had caught a clear
glimpse of one man, the distinct uniform of a senior officer. But
his curiosity was replaced by Howe's excitement, the army so
close to the goal, so close to the confrontation, that finally Washington would give them a fight.

The army continued to maneuver, and along the narrow stream,

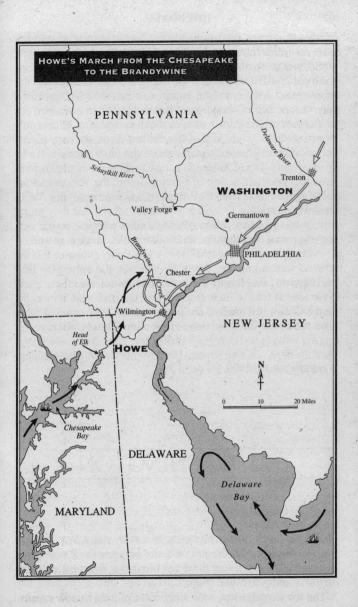

HOWE'S MARCH FROM THE CHESAPEAKE
TO THE BRANDYWINE

PENNSYLVANIA

Schuylkill River

Delaware River

Trenton

WASHINGTON

Valley Forge

Germantown

Brandywine Creek

PHILADELPHIA

Chester

Wilmington

NEW JERSEY

Head of Elk

HOWE

N

0   10   20 Miles

Chesapeake Bay

DELAWARE

Delaware Bay

MARYLAND

Washington responded, until finally, the two armies faced each other, skirmish line to skirmish line. Cornwallis studied the maps, sought out more of the local scouts, the men who could give him the location of the crossings, the valuable fords. The lines on the maps meant nothing to him except that the rebels had anchored their troops behind the stream. But as the Tories examined the maps, they added information to the drawings, and he was surprised when they told him of the shallow fords, so many places for an army to cross upstream, above the rebel position. As he worked and planned, he began to realize there was a weakness to the rebel position, a way of moving across the stream and assaulting the rebels from their flank. It was a surprise, that for all the advantages this ground provided the rebels, that they might have made a mistake, hasty reconnaissance perhaps, poor scouting of ground that might be unfamiliar to Washington as well.

As the plan came together, Howe was easily convinced. If the ground was unfamiliar, the tactic was not, the same plan they had used on Long Island. Then, the water was at the rebels' back. This time it was to their front. When the plan was firm in his mind, Cornwallis studied the maps one last time, studied more than the pencil lines. He noticed the names, crude letters marking the villages and crossings, Buffington, Kennett, Chadd's Ford. And the deep winding stream, Brandywine Creek, that Washington must have felt was his great ally.

23. WASHINGTON

SEPTEMBER 11, 1777

WITH THE FIRST LIGHT, THE CREEK HAD BEEN SHROUDED IN A LOW carpet of fog, but as the sun rose, the air grew thick and warm, the hum of insects filling the dense brush that hid much of Washington's army. He had placed his troops into a compact line along the Brandywine, with a regiment of light infantry spread just across the creek, the men who would seek out the first contact with Howe's advancing army. By midmorning, those men had scampered across the Brandywine in a hasty retreat, pursued by the enemy who was not British but Hessian. The blue-coated soldiers did not follow the Americans across the fords of the Brandywine, and it was clear that the Hessians had not intended to start a general engagement. Instead, they backed away along a high ridge west of the creek, just beyond the view of Washington's lookouts. As the enemy troops disappeared, the lookouts could see a line of black specks spreading along the crest of the hill, the Hessian field artillery moving into place. By the time the sun had cleared the treetops, the Hessians brought their cannon to life, punching the air above Washington's men with a barrage of ineffective fire. Knox had responded, and for most of an hour, both sides carried on the duel, lobbing shells blindly into enemy positions, troops and guns mostly hidden by dense thickets and patches of woods.

Washington had placed Greene in command of the ground that faced the Hessians, with Sullivan on the right, anchoring the flank upstream. The Brandywine was crossed by several shallow fords, and toward Sullivan's far flank, a crossing called Wistar's Ford stood out boldly on the maps. Washington's own map was drawn by Sullivan's scouts, and showed that the next crossing beyond Wistar was twelve miles upstream, a far longer march than the British would make with the Americans so close. Washington was hopeful that Howe's scouts would tell their commander that the American position was flawed, could easily be flanked from the Wistar crossing, or even from some of the fords closer in. If Howe read his maps, the strategy must be obvious to him, a plan that would recall the British flank attack on Long Island, Howe's first major success of the war.

As the Hessians continued their futile artillery barrage, their troops showed no sign of making ready for anything but sitting tight, and it was becoming clear to Washington that Howe had ordered the Hessians to provide a grand show, a demonstration in force. Washington had offered the bait. It was the first sign that Howe had taken it.

Directly in front of the Hessians, Greene's troops stood watch over two shallow fords on the creek, the crossings that the Hessians would certainly use if they launched an attack. On the

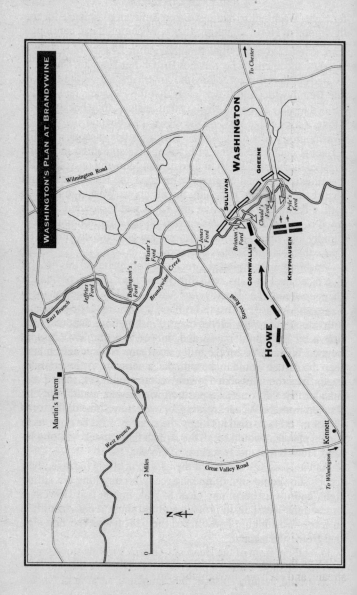

far right, Washington had instructed Sullivan to prepare for the likelihood of Howe's flanking attack. Washington had cautioned Sullivan to keep a sharp eye, to have scouting parties manning every crossroad, every ford where Howe's troops might suddenly appear. If Howe could be convinced that he was springing a cleverly conceived trap, then Washington could spring a trap of his own. With the Hessians staying put across the creek, Washington could only wait for his own scouting reports, some confirmation that Howe had indeed divided his army. A game was afoot, and a mystery as well, Howe's whereabouts still unknown, no sign from across the creek that the troops who faced him were anything but Hessians, no more than a third of Howe's strength.

The first reports had finally come into camp at midmorning, word from upstream that a British column was marching north, toward the upper fords. He had read the paper with sweating hands, nervous excitement at the first real evidence that Howe was following the very plan that Washington had hoped for. If the scouts would continue to do their job, Washington knew that they would find the British troops, most likely Cornwallis' men, exactly where he wanted him: on the march, vulnerable, spread out along the roads upstream. Sullivan had been ordered to make ready, prepare to drive his men across the fords and surprise the British before they could form any kind of defense. Sullivan's attack need only hold the British in place, while Washington sprung his own trap on the Hessians. Once Howe's march had been confirmed, Greene would lead a massive strike straight across the creek, a sudden roaring assault into and around the Hessians. Before Howe could react, Washington could rout the Hessians, and then, with Greene turning northward, the rest of Howe's army would be surrounded.

All Washington needed now was the reports from the scouts, some confirmation of just where Howe and the rest of his army had gone.

General,
A large body of the enemy, from every account five thousand, with sixteen or eighteen fieldpieces marched along this road just now. . . . I believe General Howe is with this party . . .

It was the third dispatch that Sullivan had forwarded downstream, and each one brought the same piece of news. Sullivan's scouts reported that Howe had indeed divided his army, was marching exactly as Washington wished him to. He handed the letter to Tilghman, moved to the doorway of the small house, his headquarters, could see Greene in the distance, standing on a small bluff, staring out through field glasses across the creek toward the Hessians. Above him, the air was ripped by cannon fire, the Hessians continuing their display, Knox and his guns continuing to respond. Washington motioned that way, said, "Have General Greene report to me here."

He expected Tilghman, heard instead the voice of Lafayette, who said, "I will retrieve him, sir."

The young man was quickly on his horse, and Washington watched him gallop hard over the stretch of uneven ground. He is perhaps trying too hard, he thought. I should speak to him about that. It is not necessary for a commander to learn first to be a courier.

In the distance he saw Lafayette rein up beside Greene, the message delivered, and Greene looked back toward the house, was quickly up on his horse, both men now riding hard toward the headquarters.

He knew that Greene had been skeptical of the value of this young Frenchman, like Washington himself, had suffered through the preening and boasting of too many foreign officers, none of whom had shown any talent for leading an army. Washington had not yet seen any of that in Lafayette, and he knew that Greene respected his commander's instinct. Greene's legendary impatience had been tempered, and he would not be dismissive of the young Frenchman until Lafayette proved himself one way or the other. But there had been no bluster from Lafayette, the young man true to his word that he expected no favor from Washington until he had earned the right. Though Greene had withheld his judgment, he was cautious with his friendship, as though he expected Lafayette still to burst into plumage, assume the character of yet another foreign peacock. Washington watched as the two men moved through the brush, thought, I do not believe he will disappoint us, Mr. Greene. This army is desperate for good commanders, for leadership on every level. If Mr. Lafayette can fill those shoes, we must allow him room to do so.

The sky was cut again by a streak of fire, the shell bursting in the brush in front of the house. Washington hunched his shoulders, a reflex, the cloud of smoke obscuring the two riders. His heart froze for a long moment, and then they appeared, emerging through the smoke, and he let out a long slow breath. Tilghman was suddenly in front of him.

"Sir, we must move to safer ground!"

"It was not marksmanship, Colonel, but fortune. I cannot remove myself from any place the enemy may strike. This place is as safe as any on this ground."

The two men reined up beside the house, and Washington moved forward, thought, There is no time for a formal meeting. Greene was still on his horse, and Washington said, "General, we have received another confirmation that the enemy is marching upstream." He saw the grim concentration on Greene's face, a slow nod, and Washington looked back at Tilghman, said, "Send word to General Knox. Have him cease his cannon fire."

"Sir!"

"General Greene, it is time. Have your division advance across the creek to their front and assault the Hessian position. Report to me on your progress. May Almighty God bless you with success."

Greene was upright in the saddle, and there was no smile, no outburst of bravado. Greene looked at him, his hands gripped hard around the leather reins, said, "It will be done, sir."

The man was gone quickly, and Washington looked to his staff, said, "Mr. Hamilton, take word to General Sullivan. He is to advance across the creek and seek a confrontation with the enemy in his quarter. Request in the strongest terms that General Sullivan keep me informed of events. Do you understand?"

Hamilton's face had the same look he had seen from Greene, and the young man said, "Right away, sir!"

Hamilton was already to his horse, and with one quick shout was gone.

Washington stepped back to the entrance of the small house, stared for a long while, could see movement in the brush along the creek, Greene's men rising from their cover, forming their lines. The first wave was already at the creek, officers leading them to the shallow fords. The Hessian guns continued to pound the air, but there was no aim, nothing to show they were even aware that the attack was coming toward them. Washington could hear the men in the creek now, shouts and splashes, saw field guns moving up behind them, the cannon that would give covering fire, or even better, might be put to use close to the enemy. We know where their guns are, and if we are quick, they will not be able to protect them. He looked for Knox, the round man astride the horse, but the movement along the creek held his attention, more of Greene's troops marching through the rocky stream. He thought of climbing the horse, moving closer, but he could do them no good now. No, I must remain here. There is too much at stake. They must be able to find me.

As Greene's men flowed across the creek, Washington felt his nervousness surging through him, knew that once across, they would have to gather, form again into good order. The Hessians are too far back to prevent that, and certainly their officers will hold them ready behind that hill, or, if they are scattered into smaller units, there will be a mad scramble to bring them into line. They cannot be expecting us to attack, and that may be all the advantage we require. The momentum is ours, and Mr. Greene will know to shift his lines to exploit their weakness.

There was nothing for him to see, no sounds of a fight yet, and he moved to the small office in the house, stood beside the desk, could not sit, still listened for the first sounds of Greene's assault.

"Sir!"

Tilghman was back, standing in the open doorway, breathing heavily, and Washington saw a paper in his hand.

"Sir, a message has just arrived from General Sullivan!"

Washington took the paper, thought, It is too soon for word of his assault. There has been no sound of a fight in that direction.

General,

Since I sent you the message by Major Moore, I have heard nothing of the enemy about the forks of the Brandywine, and am confident they are not in that quarter, so that the earlier information must be wrong.

There was a long silent moment, and Washington stared at Sullivan's note, names of fords, mention of roads that were unfamiliar, not on any map Washington had seen. He felt a cold sickness, a sudden dark panic, listened for a long moment, still no sounds from across the creek. He looked at Tilghman now, said, "We must pull them back. It could be a trap."

The words flowed from him in a soft voice, and he saw Tilghman's confusion.

"Go to General Greene immediately. Halt his advance. Tell him that General Sullivan has offered new information. He does not believe the British are in his quarter. It is quite possible that Howe is still right up there, close beside the Hessians. Have General Greene reverse his advance, and return his men to the near side of the creek."

Tilghman seemed stung by the words, and Washington pointed across the creek, said, "*Now,* Colonel!"

Tilghman was quickly away, and Washington stared at the paper still in his hand, thought of John Sullivan. How can you not be certain? Must I go up there myself? No one can hide the march of an army. Have you not examined the roads? We move this army on information, and when that information is contradictory, we can do nothing at all. He wanted Sullivan there now, wanted to ask him, how can you send me reports that claim one thing, then change your mind? What am I to think? How are we to *act*?

Lafayette was in the doorway, a look of silent concern, and Washington moved to his chair, sat numbly, and Lafayette said, "Should I ride to General Sullivan, sir? If he is mistaken . . ."

"He is already mistaken, Mr. Lafayette. Either General Howe is upstream, or he is not, and I have letters claiming both." All the excitement of the morning, all the optimism was drained from him, and he spread the papers on the small table in front of him, shook his head, heard a loud noise outside, a hard shout, and Lafayette was out quickly. The noise continued, coming into the house now, angry and profane, and Washington could not erase the daze in his mind, saw Lafayette again, who said, "Sir, there is a gentleman here, who claims to have information."

The man pushed into the small office now, and Washington stared up at a fierce hulk of a man, the dark skin of an Indian.

"I am no gentleman, sir! But I do have information! If you do not withdraw this army, you will be surrounded! The British are coming across the creek at Jeffries Ford this very minute!"

Washington felt himself pushed back in his chair, pressed by the man's thunderous voice. He could see others coming into the room, guards, men with bayonets, and the big man ignored the commotion behind him, said, "I will not speak to anyone but you, sir! You are in great peril!"

"Who *are* you, sir?"

The man backed away, seemed caught off guard by the question.

"I am Thomas Cheney. A farmer. I was riding along the creek up north a ways, and I ran straight into a flock of those lobster-backs!"

"Mr. Cheney, do you not think I would have been informed of this? General Sullivan . . ."

"Bah! Sullivan! I tried to tell him, and he ignores me, his men laughing, say I'm crazy-drunk. I am neither, sir!"

Tilghman was beside the man now.

"Are you aware, farmer, that spies are hanged? General, I am deeply sorry. I just returned . . . if I had been outside, he would not have been allowed to enter."

Cheney ignored Tilghman, said, "I am not a spy, I am not a Tory, and I am not lying!" Cheney glanced at Washington's papers, saw a map, said, "Look! See here!" He grabbed the map, ran his finger over the lines, said, "No, this is wrong! Up here, there is a ford. Jeffries! That's where they are coming across!"

Washington felt a growing anger, blending with his frustration.

"Sir, I cannot just take your word. We have scouts in that quarter. Mr. Tilghman, escort this gentleman outside. Mr. Cheney, we will hold you here. You must understand . . ."

"Oh, I understand, sir! I will go out there and sit under a big oak tree, and watch your army get swallowed up!"

The man turned, and Tilghman followed him out, the guards moving out as well. His head was swirling, and he looked at the map. Wrong? The map is wrong? Is that man lying? How do we know?

Lafayette was in the doorway, said quietly, "Sir, General Greene has returned."

"Yes, I'm certain he has."

There was the sound of boots now, and Greene burst into the room, his face a black flame.

"*Why,* sir? We were in position, there was no sign of opposition! Why did we halt?"

"Calm yourself, General. Mr. Sullivan reports that there is no sign of the enemy upstream. From the nature of his information, it is possible that General Howe made a feint in that direction to mislead us. You might have advanced your division into the entire British army. We have no choice but to hold our position, Mr. Greene. We must know where the British strength lies. We must find General Howe."

Greene stared at him with an open mouth, said nothing, and Washington added Greene's impatience to his own. There was a knock at the door, and Hamilton was there, seemed surprised to see Greene, said, "General Washington, General Sullivan awaits your next instruction. He assumed that in light of his new information, you would not want to risk having his division cross the creek."

Hamilton seemed unsure, seemed to wilt under Greene's hard scowl. Washington felt a wave of misery now, the perfect plan, the carefully arranged trap now replaced by a complete lack of initiative.

"Mr. Hamilton, I wish you to return to General Sullivan and instruct him to continue scouting the crossings above his position. We must locate General Howe."

Tilghman burst into the room, pointed behind him, said, "Sir! You must come!"

Tilghman was gone again, and Washington thought, What else must we endure? He pulled himself up from the chair, could hear shouts from outside, moved past Greene, who followed him outside.

The staff was all there, and all faces were turned to the north. He could hear it now, a steady roar of sound, not from the far side of the creek, but up above them, behind Sullivan's line. It rolled across the low hills and thick brush in a steady rumbling wave, a storm of muskets, punctuated by the deep thunder of cannon fire. All around him, the voices were silent, each man trying to grasp the obvious, that Sullivan was suddenly engulfed in a fight no one predicted, from a direction no one had expected. Greene moved out in front of him, stared as they all stared, said in a cold hiss, "It seems that General Howe has found *us*."

THE COLLAPSE OF SULLIVAN'S FLANK WAS COMPLETE, SOME UNITS fleeing in utter panic, but most holding themselves in good order, fighting as they retreated. As Howe's assault against Sullivan's position roared to life, the Hessians had responded as well, had launched their own assault across Brandywine Creek over the same fords that Greene had abandoned. Though pockets of resistance slowed the British advance, Washington knew he could not hold his position, and by nightfall, the ground along Brandywine Creek was fully in British hands. With Greene serving as a strong rear guard, Washington gathered those troops who could still fight and withdrew them to the town of Chester.

THE STRANGE FARMER WAS LONG GONE, AND WASHINGTON STOOD in the dark, thought of the man's name, Cheney, his profane fury at being ignored. Indeed, sir. You were correct in every detail.

Most of the army's equipment had been salvaged, and the camp was taking shape in the darkness around him. He watched as a group of men nursed a small fire, brush and sticks piled on, the flame growing, a soft glow spreading across the ground around him. As the fire engulfed the darkness, his eyes were captured by the light, and for a long moment, he felt lost in the flame. He had not allowed himself a moment's rest in nearly two days, and he stood alone in the soft glow, his mind drifting through a soft fog. In so many of these quiet moments, he saw the face of his older brother, saw it now, Lawrence, the good soldier, leading him on the wonderful expeditions through the rugged country around Mount Vernon. His brother was the scout, the experienced woodsman, but as Washington had grown older, his brother had grown curious about the surveyor's instruments that Washington would carry. As Washington taught himself more and more of the craft, Lawrence paid more attention, and the memory still brought a smile, the one day when they stopped on the trail, when the sixteen-year-old began to explain how to map the valley below them, details of the ground, turning the landmarks into mathematics, mapping his way through an unknown land. It was the first time he actually impressed his older brother, the first time he knew that Lawrence respected him. But the guiding hand fell away, Lawrence weakening, the horrible fits of coughing from the consumption that would kill him. Lawrence had died when Washington was only twenty, and Washington had often wondered that if his brother had survived, would he be in the commander's shoes now? The years had not dimmed his reverence for the man who had so impressed the boy, the man who still might have been Virginia's finest soldier. And today, he thought, I have brought shame to you yet again. But it is different than the defeats of a year ago. It was not for lack of courage, there was little of the pure raw panic of untested soldiers. On this day, we put up a good fight, there was no chaotic retreat. But it was a retreat nonetheless, the utter and complete failure of a very good plan. And if it is not the men, if this army

had indeed been ready for a fight, then the failure was nowhere
else but in their commander.

He had walked out in the open field to hear the words of his
men, as though they would not notice him, would pour out their
anger whether he was there or not. It would be his penance, to
overhear their protests, that if he heard a vocal gathering around
a campfire, he would invite them to face him, to pour out their
frustration. But there had been none of that, the men tending to
their business, the business of making camp, caring for the
wounded, the companies and regiments finding their own from
the scattered masses in the retreat.

He knew there would be noisy outrage about this day, if not in
his own camp then certainly from the congress, hasty calls for
blame, some falling on John Sullivan. He would not listen to any
of that, would do everything to deflect the responsibility from
anyone in his command. There can be only one man responsible
for this kind of failure. If the congress must pass judgment, they
will do so on me, not on these soldiers. He turned away from the
fire, could not escape the irony, the one talent in the boy that his
brother had felt such pride. Washington knew maps, could survey the land as well as anyone in Virginia. And on this day, the
defeat, the collapse had come for want of one good map.

Cheney had been right about that as well, that the maps Washington had were both inaccurate and incomplete. He knew the
name now, not just from the strange dark man, but from Sullivan's officers. Jeffries Ford was barely two miles above Sullivan's position, not twelve, and if Washington knew nothing of it,
Howe certainly did. By the time Sullivan realized he was out-
flanked, the British artillery was already firing into his lines.

The staff was putting his headquarters together, and Washington knew they were preparing some sort of supper, whatever could
be gathered together. He turned away from the fire, his eyes blinded
by the darkness, thickened by exhaustion. He blinked hard, wiped
his face with dirty hands, heard a voice behind him.

"May I intrude, sir?"

Washington looked for the face, his eyes still adjusting, but
the voice was familiar.

"You are not intruding, Mr. Lafayette. Is the supper prepared?"

"Very soon, sir. I thought I should see to your service. May I
get you something?"

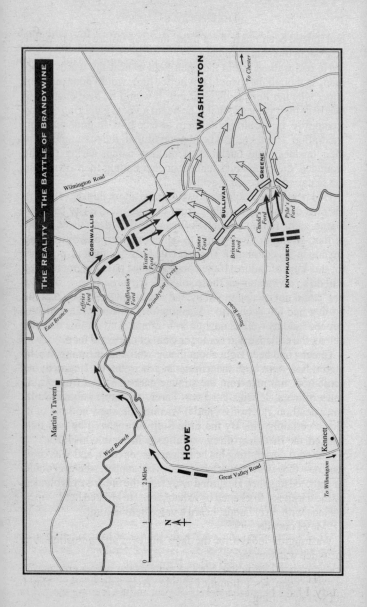

The young man's face was lit by the glow of fire, and Washington began to walk, saw Lafayette following him, the Frenchman moving with a pronounced limp. He stopped, said, "Are you injured, General?"

Lafayette put a hand on his leg, said, "A minor wound, sir. It is wrapped securely. It is proof that the British are poor marksmen. No one would purposely shoot a man performing such minor duties as myself."

It was pure modesty. Washington knew that Lafayette had ridden out through Sullivan's retreat, had rallied the men into defensive lines, had done as much as anyone on the field to keep the army in good order.

"I should like to examine that wound myself, Mr. Lafayette. We should not chance carelessness. This army cannot afford to lose the services of its most able officers."

He strained to see the bandage, could tell only that it was tied in a bundle above the young man's boot top. He realized Lafayette was staring at him, and the young man said, "You embarrass me with the compliment, sir."

Washington straightened, said, "The embarrassment is mine. No, that is too generous. The shame is mine. This army deserved more from its commander."

Lafayette did not respond, and he was grateful for the silence. He did not want this exchange of platitudes, meaningless conversation to soothe the wounds to his pride. He began to walk again, slowly, allowing for the young man's limp. Lafayette said, "May I inquire, sir, what you were doing? Were you speaking to the men?"

"No, I was . . . listening, actually. I thought perhaps it would be a good thing, that I should walk among the men and hear their words."

"If I may be allowed to ask, sir, what did you expect to hear?"

Washington looked down, thought a moment.

"Anger. Despair. After today, I wonder how many of them will be driven to desert. I hoped to dissuade them, convince them that this was not *their* defeat."

Lafayette stopped, and Washington saw him massaging his leg, and the young man said, "I have heard nothing like that."

"No, I can't say I did either. Surprising."

"I cannot agree, sir. This army knows defeat, and it knows victory. I have heard the stories of your militia leaving the field in great haste, never to be seen again. But that is not these men. The enemy won this day, but only this day. These men are still an army, they are still prepared to fight. There will be *another* day."

Washington waited for Lafayette to walk again, was close to his tent now, could see the staff at work, another campfire. Lafayette began to move away.

"With your permission, sir. I must tend to my bandage."

The young man disappeared into a tent, and Washington could see the man's shadow moving in the glow of candlelight. It would take a European officer to see war that way, he thought. They have been fighting the same enemies for centuries, and one more day of battle changes very little. If he is correct, then I have much to be thankful for. But there is still tomorrow, and we may awake to find ourselves closely pursued by the enemy. Surely they will not allow us to escape, while they celebrate their victory. If General Howe presses his advantage, how will we respond? And if these men will indeed make another stand, will their commander be up to the challenge?

He could smell something cooking, saw the staff gathering around a low crude table. There was laughter, surprising him, and he wanted to scold them, quiet them with some stern command. Is it not disrespect, after all? We have left men dead on the field today, and there must be respect. We must repay our debt.

He could not hold the anger, felt his eyes closing, forced them open. He backed away into the darkness, could not share their mood, thought, I am not yet ready to look past this day. Mr. Lafayette may be correct, and there will certainly be another opportunity for this army. But I have believed it would ultimately be decided by one sharp engagement, a single massive blow, that this war will be won or lost in one awful bloody day, on ground just like we lost today. Congress believes that, the entire nation seems to believe it. Our enemy has that capability, the power to accomplish that. But I am not certain that we do. And if we cannot strike such a blow, then we have but one other course. We must simply lengthen the war, test the resolve of our enemies by wearing them down. How much support will their Parliament give to an endless conflict? And the congress? He thought of Lafayette, the man's enthusiasm, his willingness to do whatever is required. We need a great many more like him, officers, certainly, but soldiers as well. That spirit may be this army's one salvation, since we are deficient in so many ways, so unlike those countries whose history is so shaped by war and professional armies. The British show no discomfort employing foreign soldiers to support their cause. It may be that our best hope of victory will come from a foreign shore as well. French ships filled with cloth and gunpowder are all well and good, but it may be that unless we are strengthened by the power and the spirit of their army, this war will simply drain this country dry.

HOWE RESUMED HIS PURSUIT OF WASHINGTON'S ARMY WITH THE same dedicated slowness that had marked his entire campaign. For two weeks the two tired armies parried in a tedious twisting dance through the Pennsylvania countryside, kept apart by Washington's careful maneuvering and the deep waters of the Schuylkill River. If Washington's army was indeed prepared for another hard fight, Howe seemed unwilling to expend the energy required to bring it to pass. Finally, with Washington unable to do anything to keep Howe from accomplishing his primary mission, on September 26, the British army made a joyful parade of marching unopposed into Philadelphia.

24. CORNWALLIS

PHILADELPHIA, OCTOBER 1777

HE HAD LED THE COLUMN THAT MARCHED INTO THE CITY, AND while the enthusiasm from the citizens was exactly as he had expected, he was surprised that the crowds who lined the streets were mostly women and children. But it was a grand show nonetheless, an outpouring of grateful relief, a city offering its salute, as though the king himself had brought liberation to their city, and with one swift blow had destroyed the rebellion. What followed had been expected as well, parties, dinners, offerings of lavish gifts, the social matrons and their daughters fluttering about these gallant heroes with a generosity that Cornwallis found embarrassing.

While Howe and many of the British officers seemed to bask in the glow of the giddy attention from their new hosts, Cornwallis had focused on housing his men, and it had not escaped him that so many of the fine homes that were available to the army had simply been abandoned by their owners.

He knew better than to mention the matter to Howe, that from the first campaigns into New Jersey, both Howe and the ministry in London had been cavalier in their expectations that so many colonists were still loyal to the crown. For so many months, throughout every campaign the British had launched onto the soil of New Jersey, and now Pennsylvania, Howe and Germain had always believed that a vast army of loyalists would emerge from their tormented hiding places and flock to the army, would provide much-needed troop strength that Howe required to crush Washington's rebels. Instead, the Tories had been strangely silent, and beyond the occasional show of a British flag, placed hastily in a shopwindow, or some farmer who might offer a wagonload of supplies, these same loyalists had shown very little inclination to actually fight for their cause. If Howe was dismayed by the indifference of the citizens, he hid it well, continued to issue the calls to arms, as though he still believed there were vast pockets of loyalist sympathy, that great throngs of men would still gather to take up the king's muskets as well as his flag. Lord Germain had accepted Howe's vision with certainty, had even used those expectations as the excuse to put off Howe's unending pleas for reinforcements, the troops who Cornwallis knew would be needed if the British were to make a quick end to the war. While some smaller units of fresh soldiers had arrived from England, they had proven to be more of an inconvenience than a blessing.

It was typical for recruits to create problems of discipline, but over the past few months, the poor quality of the new troops seemed to point to an even greater problem. Howe paid little heed to the new units, was too focused on his own strategies to make introductions to unfamiliar junior officers. But Cornwallis recognized quickly that the men who marched from the ships now were a different breed of soldier. The ministry was obviously scouring the prisons, and entire companies of men carried criminal records. Others seemed to have no history at all, their officers admitting that the recruitment drives had been such a failure, that men were being swept up into the service straight from their wretched homes in the filthy streets of the British cities. Despite all of Howe's optimism that an army might yet emerge from the colonial countryside, the message coming from England was that under the king's very nose, the war was becoming more and more unpopular.

It was still a mystery to him where so many of the men of Philadelphia had gone. Even if the Tories were unwilling to offer more than words to His Majesty's cause, Cornwallis could not fathom that so many capable men from the colonial capital would accept a role in the army of the rebellion. As he made his rounds through the camps of his men, visits to the officers under his command, he studied the abandoned homes, wondering if their leaving the city might have nothing to do with loyalty to one cause or another. Perhaps the men of Philadelphia were too accustomed to the soft and pleasant life of America's largest community to serve any cause at all. Perhaps they had simply disappeared into the countryside, and once the war had concluded, they would return to their homes and their families, prepared to serve whichever government awaited them. Regardless, the women who remained weren't revealing anything, beyond a not-so-subtle ability to charm the officers who were occupying their homes.

He knew many of his officers were taking full advantage of the hospitality, and he would not object to it as long as the army kept its overall discipline. There had not yet been any serious problems of looting, or abuse of the citizens, which surprised Cornwallis. All around the camps, notices had been posted, warnings of strictest discipline for those who would violate the civilians or their property. On the march from the Head of Elk, there had been the usual problems, houses burned, pantries and barns ransacked, debate in the ranks if the Hessians had been more responsible than some of the new British recruits. There was punishment, of course, and several soldiers had been hanged, dozens were flogged. But Cornwallis had long ago issued his own order to his division. There would always be hanging for the most serious offenders, but the use of the whip was stopped. He had long believed that flogging was simply a man's ticket to

misbehave, that any man could endure a bloody back if his crime
was to his liking. To some of the old veterans, scars from the
whip were a badge of honor, a sign of their virility, and he had
heard of men who goaded their comrades into some criminal act
just to test their mettle. He knew that you could not change a
man's character by punishing him, that if a man was inclined to
abuse or steal from a citizen, the whip was merely his cost. He
focused instead on the officers, inspiring his junior commanders
to exercise discipline over their men under the threat of censure
from the high command. The threat of demotion in rank or dismissal from the service was a severe embarrassment to a British
officer, and Cornwallis knew that threat would be more effective
than any damage that could come from a whip.

OCTOBER 4, 1777

While Cornwallis occupied Philadelphia, Howe had established his main headquarters at Germantown, five miles north of
the city. Washington's army was still close, and with Cornwallis
protecting the city from direct assault, Howe felt that dividing
his army, and placing a large force in a more rural area would allow them better mobility to respond to any sudden moves that
the rebels might make.

Cornwallis was relieved that the Hessians seemed content to
stay in their camps, had caused no problems in the city. Under
the command of Wilhelm Knyphausen, the Hessians seemed
more subdued, more accepting of order. Cornwallis had wondered if there was more to the man than he had seen of de Heister. Both were aged men, veterans of many wars and several
monarchs. With Knyphausen in command the change in the
Hessian camps was clear, and Cornwallis could not let that pass
without some attempt at understanding their commander.

Knyphausen still spoke no English, and at the councils, Howe
had lost patience with the translators, had begun to avoid speaking toward the old man at all, addressing his remarks directly to
von Donop, or whoever else might be by Knyphausen's side. It
was a serious show of disrespect, and Cornwallis had wondered
if Knyphausen was as unaware as he seemed, or in fact, if the old
man's dazed expression hid a greater understanding than anyone
realized.

He turned out of the main street and rode through the front entrance trailed by his surprised staff, stopped the horse on a wide platform of flat stones. He looked toward the front yard, the river, saw no one moving, and he knew he was hesitating, his eye following the splendor of the house, the ornate woodwork along the roof. He looked toward the back door, realized there were guards standing stiffly to each side, green-coated *jagers*, their helmets polished to a silver sheen, each man's hair braided in a tight black queue that reached nearly halfway down his back. He expected them to acknowledge him, but they stared ahead, ignoring him and his staff. He studied them for a moment, thought, I suppose it's a bit late to just turn around and leave. Surely they will tell someone.

Cornwallis climbed down from the horse, felt he was in some very foreign place, a place where a man in a British uniform was completely insignificant. He looked back at his aides.

"Perhaps we should have sent word. I should have considered that the Hessians might expect an appointment."

He stepped across the stone carriageway, and the door opened abruptly, a blue-coated officer emerging, stopping suddenly, saying something in German, some word of surprise. There was another man behind him, and Cornwallis heard more German, and the second man moved up, said, "General Cornwallis, welcome, sir. Please, our apologies. We were not aware you were coming. I am Captain Heisel."

Cornwallis was surprised at the man's skill with English, could see that Heisel was genuinely concerned.

"The apology is mine, Captain. I was performing my routine, and realized that I had not offered my respects to General Knyphausen. I can certainly return at a later time."

The man stiffened, said, "Certainly not, sir. General Knyphausen is in the library. I will inform him you are here. It will only be a moment, sir. Please come inside, your men as well."

Both officers stepped back inside, and Cornwallis climbed the short steps, moved past the two guards who were still facing out, their eyes following him closely. His staff followed him into the house, and he saw a small parlor to one side, said, "My men can remain here, if that is acceptable."

Heisel moved that way, stood beside the door, said, "Certainly, sir. Gentlemen, please be comfortable. I will arrange refreshment."

He looked at his aides, a silent order, *Stay here,* and there was no protest. They filed into the small room, and Cornwallis waited for Heisel, who moved quickly, said, "Please, General, if you will allow me . . ."

There was a long hall that led through the center of the house, and Cornwallis saw another man emerging from one side, recognized von Donop, who saw him, said, "Ah, General! A pleasant surprise!"

Von Donop came forward, smiling broadly, something Cornwallis had never seen. He managed a smile of his own, and von Donop was suddenly serious, said, "Is there a problem, General? Are we in some difficulty?"

"Oh, no, quite the opposite, Colonel. I would prefer that this be a social visit."

The smile returned, and von Donop said, "We are honored, General. General Knyphausen is right this way. He will be delighted to see you, sir!"

He followed von Donop into the hall, felt thick carpet under his boots, thought, I have never known General Knyphausen to be delighted about anything. At least they're making a good show. This should be interesting.

Von Donop motioned toward an open door, and Cornwallis saw the old man now, sitting in one corner, dwarfed by a wall of books. The room was musty, the familiar smell of old paper, and Cornwallis could not help but marvel at the amazing collection of books. Knyphausen stood up slowly, and Cornwallis saw that the old man was out of uniform, was suddenly embarrassed, realized he had never seen any Hessian officer without his full dress coat.

"Forgive me, General Knyphausen. I should have made an appointment." He was very self-conscious now, thought, I am, after all, the junior officer here. He looked at von Donop, expected the man to translate his apology, but the colonel held out one hand, said, "Please, sir. You are an honored guest. The general has remarked many times that he wished to make your better acquaintance."

Cornwallis looked at the old man, was surprised that Knyphausen was even aware of his name. Knyphausen was looking at him, pointed silently to a chair, and Cornwallis still felt awkward, said, "A wonderful library. Surprising. Few like it in the colonies, I'm sure." He moved to the chair, waited for Knyphausen to return to his seat, the old man moving slowly, settling back into his chair. Cornwallis sat as well, felt the soft leather under him, looked again at von Donop.

"If it is not too much of a bother, Colonel, your service at translation is much appreciated." Von Donop said something to Knyphausen, and the old man made a small laugh, a brief wave of his hand. Von Donop said, "Thank you, General. That won't be necessary. I hope to see you before you depart."

Cornwallis was surprised to see von Donop move to the door, and the man was gone, the door to the library pulled shut. Cornwallis felt the air in the room grow heavier, stared at the wall of books across from him, thought, Well, not quite what I had in mind. This might be a brief visit. Knyphausen pointed to a book, resting on a table beside him.

"Gibbon."

Cornwallis saw now, *The History of the Decline and Fall of the Roman Empire.*

"Ah, yes. A masterwork, sir. Certainly. I'm not aware if it is available in German. I should see about that, arrange a copy for you." Knyphausen was looking at the book, and Cornwallis was feeling the self-conscious frustration, the chasm of language between them, the silent moment unnerving him. Knyphausen said, "Thank you, General. It won't be necessary."

The man's words stunned him, distinct, laced with the thick syrup of a German accent.

"I was not aware, sir. Forgive me, I was always under the belief that you did not speak English."

The lines in the old man's face showed a soft smile.

"It is often more useful to spy on your friends than on your enemies."

Cornwallis absorbed the words, and Knyphausen said, "No, my apologies, General. I did not mean to use such a crude word. My English is poor. What I meant . . ."

"What you meant, sir, is that a man can learn a great deal about those around him if they don't know he is listening."

"Does that offend you, General? It might certainly offend General Howe."

Cornwallis thought a moment, Yes, it certainly might.

"Why, sir, have you revealed this to me?"

Knyphausen looked at him, seemed to study him for a long moment.

"Why did you come here, General? Surely you did not wish to speak of the weather. General Howe is gone to Germantown, so you cannot be here to discuss strategy."

"I felt the need to offer my appreciation, sir. Since I am in command of the garrison in the city, I am pleased that your command . . . um, I had hoped to express . . ." The words were choked away, and he stopped with a self-conscious lurch. Knyphausen held up a crooked hand, soothed him with another smile.

"My men . . . we are behaving ourselves, eh, General? You are welcome. Tell me, are you comfortable speaking about General Howe?" Cornwallis saw a sharp glint of steel in the old man's eye, no sign of the haze he had seen at the councils. Knyphausen seemed to sense the awkwardness of his question, said, "You may be assured, General, these doors are closed. It is simply that I have some concerns. I believe you share them."

"Forgive me, sir, I'm not certain I understand."

"That's what you are supposed to say. But I believe you understand very well." Knyphausen tapped the book beside him, said, "Gibbon. Englishman. Knows something of history. There is history right here, General, this city. We are history, you and me. And General Howe. There is a tragedy brewing here. For you. Not so much for me."

Cornwallis was hanging on the man's words, could feel the wisdom, not just from the man's years, but more, something unexpected.

"I'm sorry, sir. Why not for you?"

"I am a mercenary, General! Even now, Colonel von Donop is supervising the accounts, preparing the casualty lists from the battle along the Brandywine Creek. Once the lists are complete, they must be presented to your king. For every man in my command that was killed, King George must pay the archduke three times the normal price per soldier. General Washington and his rebel marksmen have done a fine job in bringing gold to my country's treasury." He laughed, shook his head. "You find it disturbing that a general is pleased with the death of his men? I admit, it is an arrangement that has its problems. For example, we may claim a man as killed, if he is only missing. This means, if one of my men deserts, the archduke is paid. You can imagine, General, that places me in a difficult situation. As a commander, I am supposed to punish deserters. But to please my monarch, I am to allow them, even *encourage* them, to run away." Knyphausen seemed to lose focus, and Cornwallis waited for more, thought, What has this to do with General Howe? The old man rubbed his face, wiped his eyes. "This is not how I was trained to fight a war." He looked at Cornwallis, the sharpness in his eye returning. "As your hireling, I am to obey every order and submit to the strategy of General Howe. It has sometimes been difficult."

Cornwallis said nothing, was not sure how far Knyphausen would go.

"How will you end this war, General Cornwallis?"

He thought a moment, said, "We must first defeat the rebel army."

Knyphausen seemed to jump at the words.

"Yes! So then, why do we sit in this pleasant city? Winter is still far away, and I feel as though I am in winter quarters."

Cornwallis felt the discomfort returning, said, "Sir, General Howe is aware of our mission. We will attack the rebels when the time is right."

"Please, do not take offense, General. I do not mention this to insult you, or General Howe. This is a conversation between two good soldiers, nothing more."

Cornwallis heard the compliment, said, "Thank you, sir. But, you must understand, I am not comfortable criticizing my superior officer. It is not appropriate, sir."

"All right then, I will speak, and you just listen. You have your honor to protect, your duty to perform. I have been through all of that. An old man learns that time is short. If I do not speak my mind while I am able . . . well, death provides ample time for silence. It cannot be helped." He laughed again, and Cornwallis could not help a smile. "You still have time to win this war, General. But your army has made two mistakes in this campaign. You have captured the rebel capital as a substitute for capturing its army. There is no value here. General Howe would disagree, and he may have convinced London of that. But even the rebels know that we have done nothing here to end this war." He paused, looked at Cornwallis with a hard stare. "I was surprised that you supported General Howe's decision to capture this city. You are certainly a good tactician. I had thought you were a better strategist."

"You said *two* mistakes, sir."

"All right, General, you do not have to justify your decisions to me. The second mistake. You have failed to assist General Burgoyne. General Clinton is in New York furious that he is unable to obey Lord Germain's order, to support your army up north. I too receive letters. Baron von Riedesel commands the Brunswick troops with General Burgoyne. He is a good man, a very good soldier. He has communicated his displeasure, and the displeasure of General Burgoyne that so little cooperation has been provided by General Howe. I was told, as were you, that General Howe would capture Philadelphia and return in time to assist General Burgoyne's campaign. And yet, here we sit, a very long way from New York, with a rebel army still opposing us. There is talk in your headquarters that General Howe has expressed his wish that General Burgoyne's mission fail. Is that accurate?"

Cornwallis felt the heat of embarrassment rolling up his face, looked down at the floor.

"No need to answer. I said I would talk. General Howe believes that he will have favor with your king if he succeeds, and Burgoyne is defeated. That is a serious error in judgment. General Howe is the commander in chief. On this continent, he is responsible for every victory, and every defeat."

Cornwallis slowly raised his head, saw Knyphausen looking at him, a strange sadness on the man's face. The old man tapped the book again.

"Remember Gibbon, General, the lessons of history. Your king rules an empire as did the Caesars. You and I, we serve, we share the same duty, to defeat the king's enemies. If we fail, *this* old man will return to Hesse-Cassel with stories for his grandchildren. What will you do?"

Cornwallis shared the man's sadness now, said, "I will continue to serve. Surely, an old soldier knows that."

"Yes, of course. But good soldiers should have good commanders. It does not always happen, of course. That's why men like Edward Gibbon have so much to write about."

There was a soft knock on the door, and von Donop appeared,

said, "General Cornwallis! Forgive me, sir. There is an urgent message from General Howe. His troops are engaging the rebels at Germantown."

HE LED THREE REGIMENTS, MEN WHO HAD HEARD THE SOUNDS OF the fight well before he did. They marched through the fog along the bank of the Schuylkill, and when the river made a sweeping turn to the left, he rode straight, the guides leading him toward the heart of Germantown, and the low roll of thunder. As they reached the first houses, the fog began to lift, and for the first time he could see the town itself, one main road leading away to the west. The sounds were drifting away on the far side, the battle slowing, scattered shots, the artillery silent. As he moved past the houses, there was a new sound, closer, the houses already filled with wounded, makeshift hospitals. It was a sound every soldier dreaded, and the men behind him seemed to quicken their step, the column pressing forward. He responded as well, spurred the horse, thought, The fight is moving well beyond the town. We are surely driving them back. He looked behind him, the officers waiting for his order, and he saw Leslie, said, "Prepare to advance. I will locate General Howe."

There were still low patches of fog, and he saw horses, flags, a cluster of color riding toward him. He stopped his horse, and Leslie moved up beside him, and he said in a low voice, "I seem to have found him."

The riders came slowly, a deliberate parade, Howe leading the pack. They were close now, and Howe raised his hand, punched the air with a fist.

"General Cornwallis! Perfect, marvelous day! The matter has been concluded! Dare I say, this was a fine victory for His Majesty's soldiers!"

Cornwallis saluted him, said, "General, three regiments at your service, sir."

"No need! Did you not hear me? The matter has been settled! The rebels have been swept completely away! I must say, that rabble did a sprightly job of stumbling about the place. The fog was quite a disadvantage for them. There was a moment when I thought we were in a serious scrape, that Washington had sprung quite the surprise. But, hah! In short order, we found our mettle and drove them right back into their forest!"

He had never heard Howe so animated, the man now turning to his aides.

"Make careful count of the rebel casualties. This will play well with Lord Germain!" He looked at Cornwallis again, said, "They dared to come right at us, and we stood tall! London will find no fault with this command on this day!" Howe looked past him, seemed to see the column of reinforcements for the first time.

"Too late, General! This one was mine! I'd say you should return your men to the city."

Howe moved away, his entourage keeping pace. Leslie was beside him now, and Cornwallis said, "It seems the commanding general did not require our services after all. Have the column rested, issue them some food. And then, Mr. Leslie, I suppose we should return to Philadelphia."

The order passed along the line behind him, the drummers taking up the call, and his men began to file out beyond the houses. He nudged the horse, moved forward, made his way past more of the houses, saw broken glass, one roof punched by an artillery shell. As he moved toward the far side of the small town, he could see troops dragging the bodies aside, lining up the dead, a long row of red uniforms. Beyond, he saw fences draped with color, blue and brown, more rebel bodies spread out in a small field. He rode forward, saw a patch of open ground to the left, one large stout house, the yard a vast carpet of bodies, nearly all rebels, several British soldiers picking through them. He saw an officer, moving slowly around the house, and Cornwallis stopped the horse. The man noticed him, stood upright, but no salute. Cornwallis could see he was very young, short red hair, saw a smear of blood on the man's face, and he said, "Well fought, Lieutenant."

The man seemed unsure, looked around at the rebel bodies, some moving slightly, badly wounded.

"It was very close, sir. There was good fortune here today. If not for the bloody fog, they might have run straight over us. I'm ashamed to say it, sir, but so many of my men wouldn't fight. They just ran away. It was a bloody awful surprise, sir."

The young man seemed dazed, and Cornwallis said, "Are you wounded, Lieutenant?"

The young man put a hand inside his coat, felt, probed.

"A small one, sir."

Cornwallis saw the man's bloody fingers now, said to Leslie, "Get him some assistance. Now."

The staff was down, moving toward the man, helping him toward a horse. Cornwallis moved past the large house, the road opening up beyond the town, larger farms, more rebel bodies spread along the fences, some in the road. He saw a blue coat, dirty white pants, the body of a rebel officer, the man lying face-down in thick grass. He looked at the man's uniform, gold braid on the collar, a short sword still in his hand, thought, He died moving forward, leading his men. He felt a strange anger, thought of Howe. Enjoy your bloody damned parade, General. But there was more to this day than your perfect little victory. We soundly defeated these rebels at Brandywine, and yet, here they are again. He looked out across the open ground, a hundred bodies, more, thought, This was no skirmish, no raiding party. It was a well-planned, large-scale attack. That lieutenant may be correct. Fortune, indeed. General Howe can tell London anything he damned well pleases. But these rebels are far from defeated.

25. WASHINGTON

OCTOBER 7, 1777

HE ASSEMBLED THE ARMY NEAR SHIPPACK CREEK, A MARCH OF twenty miles from the site of their chaotic fight at Germantown. Their casualties nearly equaled what they had lost at Brandy-wine, more than a thousand men killed, wounded, and captured, and in the space of three weeks, the two fights had cost Washington more than twenty percent of his army.

The British encampment at Germantown had been a wonderfully ripe target, the town itself approachable by several good roads. From all he had learned about the British position, Washington knew that if they made their march at night, two strong

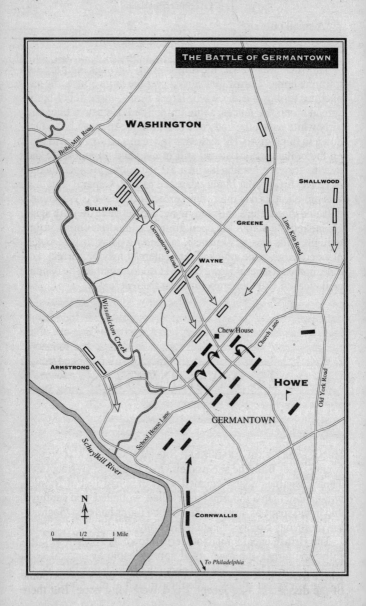

forces could converge on the enemy lines in a pinching assault that not even Howe's regulars could withstand.

He had advanced along the main road with Sullivan, while Greene led his division up to the north, would come into the town on the British flank. It was good strategy, driven by the fire of the men who saw the chance to avenge their defeat at Brandy-wine. The initial attack had driven the British back in total confusion, but then the confusion had swept over both armies, the entire field shrouded in dense fog. But the key to the strategy was coordination between the two prongs of the attack, the timing that both divisions would begin their assault at the same time. Greene's route had been longer than expected, his division led by a guide whose self-proclaimed skill had proven dreadfully over-stated. Though Sullivan's attack had panicked the British into a stampeding retreat, when Greene's men finally arrived, they stumbled right into Sullivan's flank. Blinded by the fog, and their own nervousness, both wings of Washington's assault began to fire into their own positions. When the British managed to re-form and make a stand, the confusion in Washington's lines became panic. Since Washington still believed they had achieved a complete victory, he was astounded to witness the sudden collapse of his entire attack, waves of his men returning out of the fog, pursued by little more than the sound of their own footsteps. Despite the utter vulnerability of Washington's panicked troops, Howe did not drive forward a pursuit. Once clear of the town, the retreat had slowed, and as had happened at Brandywine, Washington's army managed to salvage itself.

As the army gathered, Washington was surprised that the men who shouldered the muskets seemed to take it in stride, were even boastful of having carried an attack straight to the heart of the British headquarters. There was little evidence of shame in the camps, more the sense that it could have worked, that this time, success was very close, a fight that was turned more by bad fortune than any fault of their own.

But if the foot soldiers could shrug off the stain, Washington could not, and immediately he began to hear a new round of criticism. The defeat at Germantown gave new energy to those who were unraveling the frayed edges around his command, men whose frustrations were giving volume to their angry voices. Some of the dissenters, like Joseph Reed, were long gone. But there were others, men who Washington had believed were supportive of his efforts, surprised when they began to carry their disaffection to the congress. Some were valuable officers who had grown miserable under Washington's command, men like Benjamin Rush, the physician who had served as surgeon general, or Thomas Mifflin, the field commander who had become quartermaster general. There were open discussions now, suggestions of incompetence and indecision, complaints that Washington was too reliant and too respectful of unproven officers like Greene and the young Lafayette. Even Washington's staunch supporters had to wonder if the commanding general was so burdened by the hardships of pursuing the war that he had lost his ability to make sound decisions.

When the congress again fled Philadelphia, they carried fresh dispatches from up north, the first reports of the struggle Horatio Gates was waging against Burgoyne. It was one report in particular that gave Washington's critics fresh ammunition. Word came of a victory against the British, a place called Freeman's Farm, that had halted Burgoyne's campaign and possibly placed Burgoyne's army in some jeopardy. There could be no quick confirmation, but those who were speaking out against Washington took advantage, some already making a champion of Gates, the man some felt was the most likely to achieve some success in this war. With Charles Lee still in the hands of the British, many had begun to anoint Gates as the new savior, the one man certainly capable of finding the victory that had so eluded the helpless Washington.

AS HE HAD DONE AT CHESTER, WASHINGTON WAITED FOR THE DARK-
ness and walked among the campfires. His gloom was absolute, a dark chasm of private despair that he would not inflict upon the men at his headquarters. After the fight at Germantown, the army had extended their march to nearly forty-five miles in two days, a stunning display of energy from men who were still without shoes and much of anything to eat. For two days they had collapsed around Shippack Creek in heaps of exhaustion, recovering not just from that one extraordinary march, but from the weeks of marching and fighting, the constant pursuit and escape from Howe's army.

He moved along a thin line of trees, stepped into the open

where the campfires flickered in a ragged pattern across the fields. He heard the crack of a twig behind him, did not turn, knew it was the guards, keeping their discreet distance. He knew that Tilghman would not let him just wander off, would send at least a few of the handpicked Virginians to follow him. Thank you, Mr. Tilghman. With you in my camp, I have no need of a Guardian Angel. He could not blame the young aide, knew that where the lookouts were posted, a nervous sentry might see this large man slipping quietly through darkness and make a tragic mistake. No, Mr. Tilghman, I will not endanger myself.

He moved closer to the nearest fire, the light catching a row of dark bundles, realized it was men sleeping in the open. He moved away, would not disturb them, saw movement around another fire, a man standing up, another coming out of a small tent. He stayed back, heard their voices now, more men gathering close, and he could see something on the ground between them, playing cards, a game of some sort. He did not approve of gambling in the camps, had seen too many fights, had issued too many orders for punishment for such a destructive activity. But exercises in discipline seemed meaningless now. He could not deprive these men of anything they needed, not after his latest mistake, another battle whose failure cut a deep swath through any optimism he could muster. He thought of Greene, Sullivan, Knox, the men he must rely on, must hold to the same standards that the congress was placing on him. There seemed to be a new standard now as well, so much encouragement coming from Gates and his stand against Burgoyne. Washington knew Gates well, a former British officer who had settled in Virginia. He had a reputation as a disagreeable, combative man, which was only enhanced by his appearance. He was very short, somewhat round, peered at the world through amazingly thick spectacles, his face locked in a perpetual frown. He had come to the Continental Army at Washington's own request, was the first adjutant the congress had named, had been the first to serve Washington as Tilghman did now.

Though Washington had been far less critical then many around the headquarters, he had never thought Gates particularly capable of command. But he could not openly question the accuracy of the reports from Gates, knew that his critics would jump on his doubts as a show of jealousy, pettiness toward the one commander in this army who might actually be succeeding.

He was still staring out toward the fires, tried to sweep the image of Gates from his mind. You cannot dwell on that which you cannot change. This is what is important, this ground, this camp, so many good men. Is there faith still, that I can lead them into another fight? There is a burden enough in being outfought by your enemies. But this command is under a siege of a different sort, from congress, from the successes of Mr. Gates. If he prevails, what shame and dishonor will these men suffer if they are outdone in *every* instance? This is not Europe, these are not men compelled to serve, we are not such an army that we do not *feel* these things. Will they continue to obey this command if I do not give them something in return?

OCTOBER 18, 1777

The report came first to Putnam's command in the Hudson River Highlands, was sent by rider across New Jersey, ferried across the Delaware by the same crossing where nearly a year ago, Washington had had his finest hour. But no one spoke of Trenton anymore, few seemed to recall the triumph of Princeton. Old memories are replaced by fresh triumphs, and the army had a new cause for celebration, a new roster of heroes, a cheerful outburst for that other army, far to the north, and the man who led them. The place was in every conversation, its name repeated by every soldier, in letters home, reports to congress and the states, a place high up the Hudson River called Saratoga. Putnam's report said that Gates had not only defeated Burgoyne's army, but had captured the entire force and would negotiate its surrender.

Washington had ordered Knox to fire a thirteen-gun salute, and he issued his own congratulations to Gates' efforts, posted the words throughout the camp, *Let every face brighten, and every heart expand . . .*

The details in the report were plain enough, but Washington had yet to hear any word from Gates himself, and despite the jubilation that rolled through his camp, Washington could not simply accept as fact the report that came by way of Israel Putnam, a man who was himself relying on information that had merely been passed along by courier. He held tight to his skepticism, knew that there was already the speculation that with Burgoyne eliminated, Gates would march south and join his army to Washington's. The issue of who would assume overall command was already a hot topic in congress, and Washington knew that the rumors were drifting around his own headquarters as well, speculation that despite issues of rank, Gates would no longer serve as anyone's subordinate.

Whether or not Gates saw himself as the new savior of the cause, Washington was still his commanding officer, and still felt entitled to the man's report. After several days of complete silence, Washington lost all patience for waiting. At the end of October, he sent Alexander Hamilton on the long ride north, to visit Gates himself, the young man carrying Washington's order for Gates to send a large percentage of his strength southward. Whether or not Gates would come himself, or even obey the order were concerns Washington kept to himself.

NOVEMBER 4, 1777

The British had withdrawn their army entirely into Philadelphia, had fortified the city with a series of strong earthworks, Howe not risking any exposure to his army that might result in another surprise like Germantown. But the British had essentially cut themselves off from any reliable supply line, the ships at Head of Elk too far away to be of practical use. The danger to the British was their very hold on Philadelphia, that without the ships, the army simply could not be fed. The Delaware River was the most obvious artery for Howe, but a vast fleet of British supply ships was forced to wait far down the river. The Americans had constructed two significant forts on the New Jersey shore, Mercer and Mifflin, manned by enough artillery to keep any British shipping at bay. Both Howe and Washington recognized the critical importance of controlling the river, and for nearly a month, the British launched repeated assaults by land and sea, brutal and bloody attacks led by some of Howe's finest officers. On November 15, the last American position was overrun, and the British finally controlled the Delaware. Though another devastating defeat for the Americans, both sides understood that the cost had been enormous, not just for the troops, but for their commanders. One name emerged from the reports, familiar even to Washington. Howe had lost one of his most able commanders, and the Hessians one of their finest officers. Among the dead was Colonel Karl von Donop.

NOVEMBER 28, 1777

Washington knew that British troop strength had been weakened in the city, that the assault on the forts down the river had been led by Cornwallis himself. But Washington was weakened as well; Greene, accompanied by Lafayette, had led nearly three thousand men who were still on the New Jersey side of the river, the detachment Washington had hoped would rescue the beleaguered outposts. They had been too late to turn the fight, the forts already surrendered when Greene drew close. Now it would take several days for Greene to return, and Washington could only wonder if there was any way he could still drive the British out of Philadelphia.

He eased the horse along a wide crest, the hill overlooking the entire city. He was surprised they had seen no sign of a British outpost, no lookouts, no one patrolling the farms beyond the city itself. He stopped, raised his field glasses, thought, No, Howe is content to stay put. He is already thinking of his very pleasant winter quarters. He moved the glasses toward the river, could see a row of masts, the activity along the waterfront. The flags were evident as well, the perfect symbol for the British achievement, the flag of their king flying over the American capital. He had expected a great deal more outcry from the congress, knew that there would be ample amounts of anguish from a government that has lost its seat. But the congress was reestablished at York now, and though there was plenty of controversy, he had received very little of the shrill advice he expected, that Philadelphia should be retaken at all costs. No, this is not Europe after all, and even if General Howe does not understand that, we do. Philadelphia was a name on a map, and though most considered it the venue for the government, it had no real meaning as the capital city, nothing so historical that its loss was any kind of devastating blow to the army. In some ways, he thought, it serves us better. It is one quite visible place, just as New York. The enemy is *right there*, right where we can see them.

The wind was blowing, and he put the glasses away, pulled his coat tighter around him. Winter indeed. We may predict one thing about General Howe. There will be no campaign now, no great long march, no threat.

He had already scouted the most practical location for his own army to camp for the winter. They would avoid the towns, could not so abuse the citizens who were so completely abused already, some of the outlying communities extremely crowded with those who had escaped the city itself. He had considered moving farther west, the safer hamlets and hill country, but the British would certainly take advantage. With his army far away, Washington knew that Howe could make uncontested forays to the farm country near the city. It was a vastly fertile land, and what the British did not take they might very well destroy. It was essential that throughout the winter Washington keep his troops close enough to Philadelphia to watch over Howe's movements, to guard the many avenues the British could use to venture into the surrounding countryside. Since there was no suitable town, Washington had scouted the land for the most suitable location to build one, would have the men construct their own camp, making good use of the lumber from the dense woodlands in the area. If the location was secure, guarded by water, or sharp hills, Howe was unlikely to attempt any kind of surprise attack.

He turned the horse, the staff moving with him, felt the sharp chill again. I do not relish another winter, certainly not for these men, who have already endured so much. But the construction will provide activity, keep them engaged in healthy work, and if we are fortunate, a kind Providence will bless us with a gentle season. He moved the horse down along a narrow creek, through a stand of trees, already bare of leaves. The wind whistled above him, and he glanced out to the west, to the darkening sky. He was still unsure if the ground he had chosen was the best place, but it was only eighteen miles from the British lines, was wrapped by a deep bend in the Schuylkill River, a high prominence that would hold away any assault Howe might make.

Despite Howe's success in opening the Delaware River, and what Washington still believed were his own failures to win his confrontations with Howe's troops, the mood of the army was surprisingly buoyant. Some would wonder at our very survival, he thought, would marvel that this war has lasted yet another year. It may be our greatest opportunity, our most effective weapon, to prolong the fight. Did any one of us truly believe this would be a brief affair? Perhaps it is unfitting for a nation to be born simply by a wave of a hand, or even the acclamation of its people. If we are worthy of all we profess to fight for, then perhaps the Almighty is requiring us to demonstrate that. If that is my part in this, then I will do the best I can. If congress believes someone else should take command, I will accept that as well. In the end, it is the goal that will matter, not who carries the torch.

The horse found the road, and he waited for the men behind him to file into place. He paused a moment, looked at the faces, the ragged coats, said, "Gentlemen, we will march the men tomorrow. I wish us to occupy that good ground with haste. I do not believe General Howe will interfere, but we can leave nothing to fate. When we reach the camps, we will issue instructions on the order of march. We will prepare a sufficient number of maps. There will be no confusion. If we are blessed by a Divine hand, then we will be afforded a gentle winter, and that ground at Valley Forge will provide us a safe location."

He turned, spurred the horse, the wind still cutting into him. He blinked through the cold air, fought to see, realized it was starting to snow.

26. FRANKLIN

PARIS, NOVEMBER 1777

THE QUIET GARDENS OF PASSY HAD NOT GIVEN HIM THE ESCAPE HE had sought. If he had any thoughts that removing himself from the bustle of Paris meant a much more relaxed focus on his work, he knew now that his celebrity had come with an annoying price. For weeks on end, no matter his other appointments, no

matter the fullness of his calendar, he found himself fending off
the constant stream of visitors to his home, so many of whom
were seeking his approval, a letter of introduction or recommendation to the congress, some avenue for opportunity in America.

They came with appointments or without, men from all levels
of society, clerks and bankers, carpenters and dandies, offering
services that most had no ability to provide. Franklin had made a
game of predicting their particular story, would watch through
the window as they emerged from elegant carriages, or climbed
down from swaybacked horses. The sport was the only consolation to the assault on his intelligence, as though he was blind to
their ambitions and their motivations for leaving France. No
matter their performance, he created his own category of appli-
cant. Some were fleeing some personal difficulty, usually an escape from a creditor. Others had personal problems of a different
sort, usually involving one or more women, a mix of revenge or
jealousy. Then there were the soldiers, and Franklin categorized
them as either genuine or counterfeit. In either case, they poured
forth their requests, cloaked in a well-rehearsed passion for the
American cause. Franklin had come to dread the appearance of a
man in uniform. The more finery on the man's coat, the more
outrageous his expectations. More than one man insisted on sup-
planting Washington himself, as though no American could possibly measure himself in the company of a Frenchman with
obscure medals on his chest. Franklin was aware that Silas Deane
had succumbed to these presentations, had annoyed congress
with letters of introduction for some men who Franklin was convinced would never see any form of battlefield.

But not all the applicants for service had been pretenders, and
Franklin had heard of the young man, this Marquis de Lafayette,
a man whom King Louis considered so valuable to his own military that Lafayette could make the journey only by violating the
king's orders that he not go. The only way the young man could
avoid the king's decree, and the ship captains who would certainly obey it, was by purchasing a ship and hiring its crew with
his own funds. It could have been the fancy of just another
wealthy adventurer, but Franklin learned from his friends in the
French court that if this particular young man was provided the
opportunity, Washington himself might benefit from his service.

Lafayette had been the joyous exception, and Franklin had

come to accept that if he was to accomplish any work at all, the reports to congress, even his personal letters, he must first usher the waiting applicants through his sitting room.

He welcomed the presence of Deane, could always depend on the younger man's energy in hastening the process. For a long hour they had endured the angry spouting from a strange old man, and neither Franklin nor Deane had been able to grasp what the man was demanding, his French twisted by the man's age and some infirmity of his speech. The man's presentation was concluded by his exhaustion, and Deane had graciously escorted the man out to his carriage. Franklin waited for him in the parlor, and Deane returned, said, "Rather odd chap, that one. I heard something about horses, 'Lord High' horseman . . . or some such."

Franklin moved toward the sitting room, said, "You understood more than I did. I could only gather something about wanting to command all the horses. Perhaps he was asking to be named major general of livestock. He could oversee the lieutenant of chickens, organize the goat brigade." He settled into his chair, felt the giddy humor, the complete lack of patience for the process. He sighed, tested the soreness in his joints. "Just a pathetic old man, I suppose, whose good days are past. We should be more tolerant, Silas. But they do not make it easy."

Deane sat across the room from him, looked into a teacup, sniffed, "Cold. More coffee, Doctor? I'll retrieve it myself."

"No, thank you."

Deane was out of the chair already, disappeared toward the back of the house, and Franklin thought, He has learned a great deal. Not so impressed anymore by every man in a uniform. Not sure if that lesson has been learned by the congress, which must certainly give dismay to General Washington.

Deane returned, a steaming cup in his hand, and he stopped in the doorway, looked out through the front window.

"A carriage. I thought we had completed our punishment for today."

Franklin heard the beat of the horses, listened more to the pain in his bones and stayed in the chair.

"What have we this time?"

"Simple craft. No one of wealth, that's certain. Oh dear. He has a uniform."

Deane went to the door, and Franklin heard the voice, very foreign, and Deane seemed excited now, some recognition. Franklin waited, and Deane led the man into the sitting room, said, "Dr. Benjamin Franklin, I am pleased to introduce to you Baron Frederick William Augustus von Steuben. In my last meeting with Monsieur de Beaumarchais, the baron's name was mentioned prominently. I did not expect him to make the visit here. Monsieur Beaumarchais has suggested the baron may be of service to our cause."

Franklin stood slowly, studied the man who stood at stiff attention. Von Steuben was a tall, handsome man, a high forehead, and Franklin thought, He somewhat resembles General Washington. Same age, or close.

"Baron, it is my pleasure to welcome you to Passy."

Von Steuben seemed unsure, smiled slightly, a short, crisp bow, reached into his pocket, pulled out a letter. Deane handed it to Franklin, who studied the wax seal, the gold embossing of the French War Ministry. He opened the letter, read for a moment, said, "It seems you have made a considerable impression on Count Saint-Germain. You may be the first man to visit here who has actually impressed someone worthy." He read again, then looked at von Steuben, studied the man's unfamiliar uniform. "Yes, of course, Prussian. You served with Frederick the Great. Tell me, Baron, what may we offer you?"

Von Steuben looked at Deane, the uncertainty returning and Deane said, "He speaks no English, Doctor." Deane began to speak in French, and von Steuben's face seemed to lighten, the words finding their way. The Prussian made another bow toward Franklin, said in a ragged display of French, "I seek service, sir. I bring the respectful salute of King Frederick, for your cause. I have considerable training in the art and practice of war. I ask only for an opportunity."

Deane looked at Franklin, said, in French, "Doctor, Monsieur Beaumarchais has told me that the baron brings a considerable amount of skill. He is currently, um, my apologies, Baron. He is currently without position. He holds the rank of captain in the Prussian army."

Franklin sorted through Deane's words, saw a short nod from von Steuben. He thought a moment, said, "Baron, the French War Ministry feels you are qualified for service to any army in the world. I have no reason to doubt that. However, I see one problem." He sorted through his words. "The congress is deluged with men of high rank, vast claims of experience, most of them absurd. I fear that your rank of captain will not attract much attention." Franklin moved to his writing desk, sat, retrieved his pen from the inkstand. He looked at Deane, said in English, "Mr. Deane, I have a solution. If you agree that the baron is indeed one of the few capable men who has come through this parlor, then we should provide him with a letter of introduction that will cause him to be noticed. I propose we . . . elevate him somewhat." He began to write, glanced up at von Steuben, who was watching him with puzzled curiosity. Franklin returned to the paper, the pen scratching out the words. He finished, held up the paper, said, "There. Mr. Deane, I would ask you to translate this for the baron, so that he may know what he is carrying."

Deane read the paper, smiled now, said, "Only you would have the courage, Doctor."

Deane began slowly, read the words aloud to von Steuben in French, and Franklin saw the man's eyes grow wide, the Prussian now looking at Franklin with some apprehension.

Deane saw the look, interrupted his reading, said, "I'm not certain the baron is comfortable with this, Doctor."

"Nonsense. Never knew a military man to turn down a promotion."

Deane began again.

"The gentleman who accompanies this letter is the Baron von Steuben, who honors us from his position in the service of the king of Prussia, whom he attended in all his campaigns, being his aide-de-camp, quartermaster general, and lately achieved the rank of lieutenant general . . ."

DECEMBER 1777

He had taken Temple to the opera, a lavish production of a new work by Franz Joseph Haydn, *Il Mondo della Luna*. The young man had protested at first, but Franklin would hear none of it, had been dedicated to injecting his eldest grandson with a significant dose of culture. He knew Temple would have been much happier spending the evening with the young ladies of Passy, and throughout the carriage ride into Paris, the young man had sulked and growled his displeasure. But once inside the grand opera house, Temple's mood had brightened considerably. The vast audience that flowed through the portals of the hall were the cream of Parisian society, and as both the young man and his grandfather noted, there were more beautiful women in attendance at this one event than could be found in the entire village of Passy. Though he could not be certain that Temple had acquired any appreciation for the works of Haydn, the society women who took notice of this eminent Doctor Franklin, took special notice of his grandson, and the young man found himself fluttered over by a giggling flock of colorfully adorned young maidens. Temple would never protest an evening at the opera again.

They would remain in Paris for the night, Franklin having been granted an appointment with Vergennes the next day. He had made arrangements to stay at a comfortable hotel in the city, had been discreet about his planning, expected that if the news of his evening in Paris was announced, someone would certainly insist on making a fuss, some sort of reception. Temple would no doubt enjoy the attention, but Franklin's patience for social banter was fragile. Despite his love of the opera, after such a long evening, he was more interested in a good night's sleep.

They arrived at the hotel to find the wide entryway choked with traffic, carriages and their drivers maneuvering clumsily. His own carriage halted in the street, and Franklin peered out the side, his driver pointing. "Monsieur. My apologies. There is so much . . . busy."

"No matter, my good man. We will make the walk from here. If you would kindly retrieve our bags . . ."

The driver was quickly down, opened the door, and Franklin eased himself out, stepped down on the uneven cobblestones. He looked back at Temple, said, "You see? Someone in the hotel must have revealed our stay to every guest in the place. Now they have spread the word to every corner of the city. There is truly no escaping the crowd."

Temple was beside him, the young man holding discreetly to Franklin's arm, supporting him, steadying him as they stepped over the treacherous roadway. "I should have a word with the manager. Clearly he has no respect for my privacy."

"Yes, Grandfather."

The young man's tone was sarcastic, and Franklin could tell that Temple was skeptical. *Why else would such a crowd assemble? It seems he must see for himself. He is more like me than even he knows. Ah, well, if we must endure an adoring audience, at least I can use this to instruct him, some guidance on the proper way of showing humble appreciation to one's admirers.*

They wound their way through the carriages, reached the entryway, the door held open by two men adorned in the costumes of Roman guards. Franklin smiled as he passed them, thought, *Ah, the French. They do so seek the absurd in their fashion.*

The lobby was more quiet than he expected, and he led Temple to the reception desk, a young man writing furiously on a pad of paper.

"Excuse me, sir. We have arrived. Will you kindly direct my grandson and myself to our proper station?"

The clerk ignored him for a moment, continued to scribble, looked up now, showed a mild shock. "Oh! Dr. Franklin! Yes, your room is prepared, sir!"

Their baggage had been set beside him, and the clerk seemed to study the emptiness of the lobby, an annoyed frown.

"There is no one to assist. I am sorry, sir. The servants are all engaged with the reception in our grand hall. I shall have to assist you myself. If you will wait just one moment."

The clerk went back to his pad, was scowling, annoyed at having to suffer such an inconvenience, and Franklin said, "Shouldn't we attend the reception first? There is ample time for us to retire afterward."

The clerk seemed perplexed, said, "Are you attending, sir? I was not aware."

Franklin was perplexed himself, and Temple leaned forward, said in a low voice to the clerk, "May we know who the reception is for, sir?"

The clerk smiled now, a show of pride.

"We are honored tonight to receive a most famous Englishman, sir, Mr. Edward Gibbon." The clerk lowered his voice, said to Franklin, "You know, sir, I am told he writes books!"

Franklin looked at Temple, saw feigned disinterest. *Well, no, he is not so much like me after all.* He had the wisdom *not* to as-

sume that I am the center of every universe. The clerk was out
from behind his desk, hoisted their two small bags, said, "If you
will follow me, sir. Your room is this way."

"Doctor! Dr. Franklin!"

The woman's voice was familiar, and he saw the flutter of silk,
a bright yellow flower moving toward him.

"My word, Madame Brillon! How very . . . surprising to see
you."

She moved close, took his arm, and Franklin was suddenly
self-conscious, overwhelmed by a wave of her perfume, the stiff
tower of her hair soaring high above them both. Temple began to
back away slowly, and Franklin said, "Temple, you recall my
friend, Madame Anne-Louise Brillon. What, my dear madame,
has brought you away from Passy?"

"Really, Doctor, do I require an excuse? My husband is
scarcely aware if I am home or not." She laughed now, a girlish
giggle, and he felt her grip tighten.

"You exaggerate, madame," then thought, Well, no, she does
not. Her husband was an assistant to a government minister, con-
nected to the dreary operations of the king's treasury, a much
older man than the energetic woman who still held tightly to
Franklin's arm. Franklin had assumed her to be in her thirties,
and from their first meeting in Passy, she had placed a strong
grip on both his arm and his daydreams. He knew that Temple's
daydreams had run rampant as well, and more than once
Franklin had to insist to his grandson that Madame Brillon was
much more of a daughter to him than anything scandalous. If he
did have scandalous thoughts, he was not about to reveal them to
his grandson.

"Do come, Doctor! Mr. Gibbon is a most fascinating man! I
had thought him to be much older, but he is far closer to my own
age than . . . I mean, such insight into history . . ."

Franklin would not let her be embarrassed, interrupted, "Yes,
that explains the costumes at the door. Roman. A salute to his
work."

She gripped him hard again, said, "Oh, Doctor. You know how
much I am drawn to men of experience."

He glanced at Temple, felt a rising heat on his face, said, "I
should enjoy meeting Mr. Gibbon. However, it is not acceptable
for me to invite myself. There might be some Englishmen present who would find my company to be objectionable."

"Nonsense, Doctor!" She released him now, said to the clerk, "Excuse me, young sir, I would like to carry a note from Dr. Franklin to Mr. Gibbon."

The young man dropped the bags, an unceremonious thump beside Franklin, returned to his desk, tore through papers, scrambled to find something suitable, then produced a pen, said, "Madame, please proceed. I will write."

Franklin could see a blush on the clerk's face as well, thought, Yes, young man, she has that effect. She took Franklin's arm again, her softness melting him, and she dictated to the clerk, "Dr. Benjamin Franklin requests the honor and the pleasure of a meeting with Mr. Gibbon."

IT HAD BEEN NEARLY AN HOUR, AND TEMPLE HAD RETIRED TO THEIR room, the young man's endurance not what Franklin had hoped. He sat alone in the lobby, thought, Historians, even English ones, have some value, surely. I should instruct my grandson to show respect. One day he might regret his impatience.

Madame Brillon had returned angrily to the reception. Her patience had become exhausted as well, more insulted than Franklin himself for his being made to wait just to enjoy the company of the famous author. He was fighting the rising tide of sleep, the chair beneath him more comfortable with each tiring moment. He fumbled for his watch, but his tired eyes would not see the details, and the effort to retrieve his spectacles was simply too much work. He found himself thinking of Madame Brillon's anger, relieved that it had not been directed at him. She is most charming, he thought, a thoroughly delightful companion. His eyes were closed now, and he was breathing in the scent of her perfume, was suddenly jarred awake by a burst of sound. He pulled himself upright in the chair, could see her marching toward him from the long hall, a flurry of motion, and she was there now, the clerk following her, nervous, a paper in his hand.

"Really! I am offended, Doctor! How dare anyone suggest . . . oh, the arrogance!"

Franklin took the note from the clerk, read aloud, "It is with regret that though I hold much admiration and respect for the good doctor, I cannot place myself in conversation with a man so identified with the rebel cause. Though I would enjoy such a meeting, I must maintain the strictest loyalty to my king. Edward Gibbon."

Madame Brillon made an angry sound, said, "To think that I made this journey just to pay my respects to such a man! How utterly rude!"

Franklin stared at the paper, said, "My dear, I am a subscriber to the rhetorical skill that is best described as the *last word*. Young man, allow me a moment, then I would ask you to return to the reception, and convey my response." He wrote,

> *Mr. Gibbon. I have read your note with understanding. As much as I admire your previous work involving the fall of Rome, I should like to offer, that when you take up your pen to write the Decline and Fall of the British Empire, I shall gladly furnish you with the ample materials in my possession. Benjamin Franklin*

HE TOOK TEMPLE WITH HIM TO THE MEETING WITH VERGENNES, HAD already made good use of his grandson as his personal secretary. He knew that Arthur Lee suspected every servant, every employee around any of them as being a spy, while Deane seemed to ignore completely the same threat. Franklin found himself somewhat in the middle, but a secretary was a position too important to be filled carelessly. Temple had solved his dilemma. What the boy lacked in worldliness, he compensated for in loyalty and an inexhaustible desire to please.

Over the past few months, the meetings with the French court had produced little in the way of progress, and certainly nothing that should be kept from the ears of anyone's secretary. It was a growing frustration for Franklin, as it had been for the other commissioners as well. Lee's mission to Spain had been a complete failure, the Spanish king refusing even to meet with an American representative, even more hesitant than the French about provoking the anger of King George III. Lee had resumed his mission in another direction, traveling on to Berlin. He went at the invitation of the Prussian King Frederick, who had a legendary hatred for the English monarch. But Lee's efforts were futile there as well, Frederick reluctant to widen a war that so many in Europe believed was simply an English problem.

Franklin had done his best to hide his despair over the news from America. The defeat of Washington's army at Brandywine had erased any of the momentum from the victories in New Jersey. Franklin knew that around the French court, the friends of America were becoming more uncomfortable that their support for this rebellion might have unfortunate political consequences if their king suddenly turned his back on the whole affair.

They were to meet in the office of Conrad Alexandre Gerard, a subordinate of Vergennes, and one of the few French officials Franklin could speak to with complete frankness. Gerard did not share the stiff formality so common in the French court, seemed immune to the fear that his words might cause his king some indigestion. Despite Franklin's deepening relationship with Vergennes, even in friendship, Vergennes seemed to couch his conversations in careful subtleties, precise and polite, but always with one eye toward the fragile temper of King Louis.

Gerard's reception room was similar to that of Vergennes, more like the grand ballroom of some astonishing palace than any place devoted simply to business. When Franklin and Temple disembarked from their carriage, they were met by the customary secretary, the man gushing out his usual greetings, as though Franklin was the most influential visitor ever received at the palace. Franklin had heard it all before, assumed that the man's patronizing flood of compliments was well rehearsed, the same delivery to any visitor. The man was always accompanied by an escort of soldiers, emphasizing the point that though Franklin might be a celebrated guest, the king's security was still the priority.

It was Temple's first visit to Versailles, and Franklin had one eye focused on his grandson as their escort led them through the extraordinary halls. Franklin had become accustomed to the fineries, the walls, floors and ceiling bathed in luxurious detail, but he expected Temple to gawk in wide-eyed wonder, assumed the young man would be as captivated by the grandeur as his hosts expected him to be. Instead, Temple seemed to focus on the soldier in front of them, and Franklin could see now he was matching the man's steps, mimicking his march. The secretary was a tour guide as well, pointing out certain artifacts, explaining in thick English the history they passed. Franklin made a polite show of paying attention, annoyed that his grandson was not.

They reached the end of a long hall, and their escorts stood aside. The secretary motioned toward a grand entryway to the reception hall, and Franklin stepped in first, his eye caught by the rich scarlet draperies framing the enormous windows. The walls were a creamy white, bordered in gold, and much like Vergennes' office, enormous mirrors stood between the windows. The secretary left them alone, the doors closing softly, and Franklin could hold his impatience no longer, said in a hushed voice, "Temple! Can you not show some respect? Are you so accustomed to palaces that you cannot at least *pretend* to be impressed?"

Temple seemed stung by Franklin's scolding, looked around the room, said, "Yes, sir, I am impressed. I am impressed by how much money the French have spent decorating their halls. If America had this much gold in our treasury, the war would already be over. We would not need to come to this place to beg for our means."

Franklin was shocked, stared at him for a long moment.

"My apologies, Temple. You are quite correct. It is an appropriate reminder."

Temple was studying the room, and Franklin realized how much he cared for the young man, thought, A man indeed. Years ago Temple's father William had accepted with perfect ease the appointment by King George as royal governor of New Jersey. Franklin had never been comfortable with his son's attitude, as though by the appointment alone, William had earned the right to surround himself with such finery and baubles as these. Temple was William's illegitimate son, a source of scandal that often came to life during the early days of the Revolution. But Temple had seemed immune to the controversies surrounding his father, had been doted on by a stepmother who placed a desperate value on social position. For the first time, Franklin understood that his grandson had seen past the absurdity of the façade, had formed his own opinions of the dangerous trappings of title. He was suddenly proud of the young man, thought, He is so . . . American. And you, old man, so accustomed to all this grandeur, if you become a bit too impressed, remember the wisdom from this . . . *boy*.

The door opened behind him, and a parade of men entered.

"Ah, Doctor, welcome yet again! And this young man is your grandson, yes?"

Gerard was all smiles, and Temple responded with perfect politeness, said, "I am honored to be allowed to attend, sir."

Gerard smiled at Franklin, said, "His grandfather's grace! Excellent! Please, let us be seated!"

Franklin saw Vergennes then, made a short bow toward the older man, who had said nothing yet, unusual, allowing his subordinate to make the first introductions. Vergennes returned his bow with a forced smile, said, "A pleasure as always, Doctor."

He felt something uncomfortable in Vergennes' words, thought, He has something on his mind. Well, let's get to it. The chairs were pulled out, and Franklin waited for his hosts to sit, aware that Temple had done the same.

Gerard was still full of pleasantries, was speaking to Temple, the mundane questions about the young man's experiences in Paris. Franklin did not hear the words, focused on Vergennes, could see that the older man was avoiding his gaze. Franklin said, "Excuse me, Your Excellency, Monsieur Gerard, but certainly you are aware that I have requested this meeting to resume that most unpleasant of my official duties. I must request in the strongest terms you will allow, that your government acknowledge and accept the terms we have previously requested. My country has a desperate need for an alliance with a foreign power. By all that His Majesty King Louis has generously provided, my congress is convinced that a formal alliance with France is the most suitable and desirable partnership we could achieve."

Gerard glanced toward Vergennes, and Franklin was certain now, Yes, he has something to say, something official. Vergennes leaned forward, put his hands on the table, stared down at them for a moment, said, "Doctor, His Majesty continues to be concerned about the state of affairs in your country. You must certainly be aware that the loss of your capital city to the English is a blow to your cause not easily repaired. It would have been better had your army demonstrated some success against General Howe. His Majesty is concerned that your situation has worsened to such a level that the repayment of his generous loans to your cause may be in jeopardy."

The word bored a deep hole in his brain. *Loans.* So, Louis has changed his mind. The generous grants of assistance have become *loans*. There was a silent moment, and Gerard said, "Ah, but of course, Doctor, your General Washington made an admirable assault at . . . yes, at Germantown. Quite impressive! Following up a defeat with an attack!"

Vergennes allowed Gerard to have his say, stared at the table in front of him, said, "It would have been better, of course, if General Washington had *prevailed* at Germantown."

Franklin felt a cold sickness, a chill flowing down through his stiff legs. He had made an extraordinary effort to put the best appearances to the situation in Pennsylvania. It had been Gerard himself who had informed Franklin that Philadelphia had fallen, and Franklin had responded with a joke, that in fact, Howe had instead been captured by the city. There was a seriousness to the quip, Franklin desperate to communicate a different view to the French, that the fall of Philadelphia was not such a catastrophe after all. Howe's occupation and defense of the city would surely cost more in British troop strength than it would gain them. But Franklin was not a military man, could not be clear in the details, could not paint a positive portrait of a loss that even he felt in some awful place. His daughter was there, young Benny's family, and his aging sister Jane, and he had heard nothing from them since the reports of the horrible turn of events. But it was still his job to make a fight of a different sort, that if Washington had his struggles on the battlefield, Franklin must still wage a different war at Versailles. He looked at Vergennes, could see the man's discomfort. Yes, you know very well what you have said, the meaning of your new word. *Loan.*

Vergennes met his eyes for the first time, and Franklin saw regret, a hint of sadness. So, it may not have been your decision, you may not have agreed. But you had no choice, you have made it official. The king of France now believes an alliance is unwise. He took a deep breath. No anger, be careful. You must still do your job.

"Your Excellency, forgive me, but I detect a hesitation in Your Excellency's words, something I have not heard before. Surely, His Majesty King Louis is aware still that an alliance between France and America will benefit both. The alternative is a tragedy that will destroy not only my country, but my people. If no one will support our struggle, if there is no hope that America can survive as an independent nation, our only recourse is a treaty with England. Regardless of how ruinous such a treaty is to my country, it will certainly be of great distress to France. England reunited with America will be a force that no other nation may hope to rival." He sat back then, saw somber faces on both men. "It was not so long ago that France was compelled to yield to English might. King Louis might fear a return to those days. I assure His Majesty, as I assure anyone who hears my words. Unless America survives, France will always be at the mercy of English domination."

He was exhausted, had not come to this meeting expecting such a change in French attitude. The smile was gone from Gerard's face, who looked at Vergennes, then said, "Doctor, we are not so far removed from America that we do not feel its despair. But you are aware that if France enters a formal alliance with your country, it will commence a state of war between France and England. If America is defeated in battle, then King George will be free to use all of his resources against our valuable islands in the West Indies, and against France herself. His Majesty must weigh the risks. He must make wise alliances. King George has already done so. He has secured the service of the Hessians, the Anspachers, Waldeckians, Brunswickers, all who support England in her campaign. You see, Doctor, it is not merely a war against England that we risk."

Franklin was fighting the anger, a hard effort to hold in his words. How can you toss out such feeble excuses for backing away from the alliance? He looked at Vergennes, knew that Gerard was only filling the empty space in the conversation, that Vergennes would ultimately be the only voice that would have weight with the king.

"Your Excellency, so much has already been done, so much of a foundation already laid. I had thought we were so very close, that the formal alliance was itself more ceremony than meaning."

He knew he was oversimplifying, but he wanted Vergennes to say it, to make plain what the king's position was. The old man responded.

"Doctor, without a formal alliance, France is still removed from the conflict. His Majesty has provided no soldiers, no warships. A formal alliance is a line that once crossed, cannot be undone."

"Your Excellency, I hear the words, I appreciate the exercise in diplomacy." He held back the words, fought his own frustration, saw the grim stare from Vergennes. "Your Excellency, I do not wish to offend, but I am fighting for my nation's existence. Surely, Your Excellency would grant me the kindness to plead my position with honesty. France has an opportunity to lead the rest of Europe in an alliance against the greatest military power that none of you are able to defeat alone. You mention the Germanic lands, as though you fear monarchs whose only power is the gold they find by selling their citizens into military slavery. Such men are not to be feared, because they do not have the support of their own people. If I did not believe that, I would not be an American. Any despot who enriches himself at the expense of his people is not to be feared. He is to be reviled. Does Your Excellency require evidence of this? What of King Frederick of Prussia, who will not allow the Hessian troops to cross his soil, to use his ports? What of the Dutch, the Danes, what of Catherine of Russia? King George sought alliances with all of them, and was completely rebuffed. No one benefits from a powerful England. And if France does not assist us, if you turn away from this alliance, England may well maintain her power over my country. And, over yours."

He felt sweat in his clothes, realized his hands were shaking. His heart was pounding in his chest, and he tried to focus the fog in his eyes, said quietly, "Your Excellency, my country is in desperate straits."

His voice was shaking, and Temple put a hand on his shoulder now, said, "Grandfather . . . ?"

Franklin touched the young man's hand, nodded slowly, said quietly, "It's all right."

Vergennes was watching him intently, and Franklin saw concern on the man's face.

"I apologize for my impudence, Your Excellency."

Vergennes started to speak, stopped, seemed to weigh his words.

"Doctor, I do not fault you for your passion. If we have witnessed one remarkable result of your conflict, it is the passion of your people for your cause. Do not be concerned. There is no offense taken in this room. But, Doctor, these words will remain *in this room*. His Majesty is very clear. France will not start a war by allying herself with a cause that is already drowning in defeat. If your cause can be achieved, France will gladly become your ally. We will do more than offer you arms and gold. But no nation will respect your independence until you demonstrate that your independence can be achieved."

"Your Excellency is saying that France will assist us when we prove we no longer require your assistance."

He stood slowly, Temple reacting quickly, helping him up. He steadied himself against the table, saw a sad resignation on Vergennes' face.

"Doctor, I must serve my king."

The meeting was over, and Franklin felt Temple holding him, guiding him to the door. The escort was waiting for them outside, and Franklin began to find his strength again, his legs more steady. He tapped his grandson's arm, said quietly, "It's all right. I can walk."

They moved into the grand hall, and Franklin felt the lush carpet under his sore feet, was grateful for the one bit of luxury. The soldiers led them out slowly, the walk much longer than he remembered. They moved past the artwork, the porcelain and silk, and he ignored it all, focused on the floor in front of him, the slow march of the men who would lead him outside. His mind was already drifting toward Passy, to the gardens, the quiet, the solitude of his office. It is where a man goes to retire, he thought. Perhaps I will stay here, after all. I may not have the strength to go home, another difficult voyage. He thought of his sister now, fragile Jane, a woman of enormous sadness, relying so on her famous brother for survival. I hope you are safe, my dear. And Sally. At least my grandsons are with me, out of harm's way.

Then he could see the sunlight, blue sky, the soldiers standing aside. He searched for his carriage, tried to pick out the one from a long row of carriages, thought, So many visitors, all the business of government, all those who preen and fawn before their king.

Temple was out ahead of him, the young man saying something to a driver. Franklin blinked against the brightness of the sun, thought, His eyes are sharper than mine. Good to have him along. I should tell him that. He started to say something to the young man, realized that Temple was farther away, directing the carriage out of the line, and he thought, I suppose it can wait. I had so hoped this would be a good experience for him, that his grandfather could show off a bit, perhaps impress this boy with all my vast skills at diplomacy. Instead, he will recall that I groveled to them. Begged. I should be ashamed.

The carriage was close, and Temple was beside him again,

helping him as he climbed slowly up. Temple was in quickly, and Franklin felt the young man's hand tugging at his coat, sealing him against the cold. He wanted to apologize, try to ease Temple's disappointment, tried to put the words together, and Temple said, "I wish I could tell them . . . the congress, I mean. I wish I could tell them how you stood up to the French. The whole country should know."

DECEMBER 4, 1777

The ship came from Boston, had escaped the dangerous net the British navy had spread throughout the North Atlantic. Though the passengers were few, one man disembarked with serious purpose, and found the fastest means to reach Paris. His name was Jonathan Loring Austin, a Massachusetts attorney, schooled by the hand of John Adams. Austin made his way to Passy with one mission, to deliver the news to the American commissioners. The word had already reached every corner of the thirteen states, was still celebrated from barrooms and offices to the camps of soldiers. Burgoyne's entire army had been defeated, and over five thousand British and Hessian troops had surrendered at Saratoga.

Within hours, all of Paris had heard the news. Franklin waited at Passy with renewed patience, hoped that word of the astounding American victory would bring a change in the attitude of King Louis. He was not disappointed. Within two days, Gerard came to Passy carrying Vergennes' message of congratulations. Within a week, the foreign ministry was inviting the American envoys to present another proposal for an alliance, which Franklin sent by the hand of his grandson. In another week, Vergennes met Franklin, Deane, and Lee with the news that the government of France had sent envoys to King Charles of Spain. If Spain agreed to join France in declaring war on England, then both nations would form an official alliance with the United States of America. Franklin's cautious enthusiasm gave way to a new despair. King Louis, whose lust for high-stakes gambling was legendary, was hedging his bets. Though the cheering for the American victory still rolled through the streets of Paris, at Versailles, the French court would only risk a war if total victory was a safe bet.

27. WASHINGTON

FOR DAYS, THE RHYTHMIC SOUND OF AXES ROLLED OVER THE plateau, the forests below teeming with men who knew only one duty now. They had begun their winter camps by sleeping in the ragged canvas tents, but Washington knew that canvas would shield no one from winter. If the army was to subsist and survive in a winter quarter, they would have to build solid structures. The ground had been chosen with the vast stretches of woods in mind, and no one complained when the tools were handed out. Already the snow had covered the plateau where the cabins would be built, and already sick men were filling the nearby farmhouses, the health of the army decaying. Each day, fewer men were able to answer the call to duty, fewer men made the difficult trek down into the trees, fewer men had the strength to haul the stout logs up to the heights of the camp.

He had begged the congress to secure horses and wagons, and neither had appeared. Washington watched as the men formed their own teams, wrapping themselves in leather harnesses, straining with hard groans as they pulled the cut timbers up the hill. On the plateau itself, men with some training in carpentry guided the others, notching the logs, each cabin rising slowly as the timbers were set upon each other. Stiff red hands worked frozen mud and clay, filling the gaps in the logs, sealing out the cold. As the walls grew higher, the men worked from the inside out, seeking protection from the sharp wind. Washington had hoped they would find some ingenious method of building a roof, something more weatherproof than thatched sticks and muddy grass. But once the doors were built, slabs of split oak, a dozen men could finally huddle inside, protected against the hard freezing wind. The grassy, porous roofs would have to do.

Each cabin had a chimney to vent the choking smoke from a variety of crude hearths. The men who had some experience with brick making or masonry, or some skill with molding clay, could construct an efficient escape for the smoke from their blessed fires. Others relied on wooden chimneys and fireboxes caked thick with mud to make them fireproof.

Inside, the snow and grass beneath their feet was trampled down to wet bare dirt that would become the floor of each cabin. As the cabins filled with men, the wetness of the bare earthen floors rose up to swallow them in a soft cauldron of sickness. Though the fires in the crude hearths would eventually dry the ground, the cold still seeped in, and the troops scoured the countryside for straw, for any kind of ground cover. But the barns had been stripped clean of hay, the feed so desperately needed for livestock. What straw could be found was soon matted and worn, but it could not be replaced, and so even when soiled, it could not be discarded. Soon, mold and filth was all that remained, and many of the men found that their only protection against the earth beneath them was the clothing on their backs.

They were still soldiers, and the camp was still the vulnerable home of an army whose enemy was barely twenty miles away, and so the official duties would continue. Provosts and lookouts and pickets were still posted, guarding against a sudden assault by the enemy, or keeping watch on those who might attempt to desert. Washington could not stop the desertions, of course, knew that any man who feels a festering passion for going home will somehow find the means of escaping the army. They would leave mostly at night, some slipping away from the outposts, some from the cabins themselves. Many would not go far before the cold and snow and their own wretched weakness would drag them down, some freezing to death in the roadways, found by patrols the next day. Others would never be found, would stumble into gullies deep with soft snow, swallowed up by the frozen misery they were so desperate to escape.

Despite the loss of numbers, Washington had begun to detect some new form of camaraderie. Each cabin was its own small community, and when one man did not return from his night watch, the others would make good use of the small bit of vacant space while cursing the man's weakness. It was rarely infectious, a man's desperate escape regarded more as a tragedy. It was better to learn a man's character now, in the camp, than on the line when you might have desperate need for his musket. The men who kept to their duty understood that a deserter was less likely to find his way home than to suffer a lonely death. There was simply nowhere to go, no place close enough to offer sanctuary where a man could find any better protection against the weather than the cabins at Valley Forge.

Few had coats, and the shoes that were still serviceable could not stand up to the constant freezing and thawing that came with the daily routine. Most of the men had worn through their pants and shirts, many could only wrap themselves in what remained of blankets. In each cabin, the man whose lot it was to make the march to the frozen outpost would be dressed by the men around him, each man contributing some small bit of protection, anything that might help their comrade survive the watch.

Despite the hard winter, despite the blasts of wind that swirled the snow, in a few short weeks, what had once been a bare grassy plateau cut by a few ravines, was now a town. Washington's army had constructed more than a thousand wooden structures, great long rows of cabins spread out over a camp that was nearly two miles long.

WASHINGTON MADE A DAILY INSPECTION, RODE ALONG THE TRAM-pled snow-packed lanes, through great clouds of black smoke from the low chimneys. The men had built cabins for more than just their own quarters, and beyond the rows of barracks were other structures, a blacksmith shop, supply sheds. There were larger cabins as well, what had quickly become vastly overflowing hospitals.

More than a year ago he had ordered the army to construct a central hospital facility in the small Moravian town of Bethlehem, a means of bringing together as many doctors and other volunteers whose sole duty was the care of the sick and wounded. But Bethlehem was fifty miles from Valley Forge, and unless a man was suffering from smallpox, or some other ailment that might endanger the entire camp, it was impractical to risk such lengthy transport. The tragic alternative was the structures they had built at Valley Forge, and very soon the hospital cabins were places to be avoided, the source of nightmarish stories of fever and dysentery, of men dying in their own filth. But avoiding the hospitals did not always erase the horror, and the awful sounds would echo across the snowy fields, the screams of men who suffered the amputation of frostbitten or infected limbs.

The numbers of sick were still growing, nearly a third of his army was suffering some serious illness, and another third were huddled in their cabins with the ailments that stripped them of any ability to fight. The men who were excused from duty found that the shelters could cause problems of their own. Sealed up in their cabins, their eyes and lungs would suffer from the stifling dry heat of the wood fires, eyes and lungs burnt with smoke. But to escape the cabins meant exposure, hands and fingers split, feet swollen into lameness. As he heard and endured the suffering of his men, Washington was grateful that Howe was so fond of quiet winters, would make no attempt to interrupt the comfort of the British troops. Eleven thousand men had moved into Valley Forge, but Washington knew that on any given day, fewer than three thousand could have put up any kind of fight.

While so many of his men had worked on the cabins, others had been busy with the shovel, digging entrenchments and redoubts, earthworks along the roads that gave access to the camp. There were inner lines as well as outer, the crucial necessity of having some good defensive line to fall back to. More often, he would ride out along the outer lines, heavy earthworks facing south and east, the roads that led to Philadelphia. Out past the works, the ground fell away, a long hill easily protected by artillery. As he rode along the far left flank, he could see the Schuylkill, and the new bridge just built by his men. It was constructed for the purpose of foraging, the most convenient means of sending wagons out to the north and west. But Washington knew that it was something else as well. Despite the strength of the ground, the stout defenses, if Howe did launch an attack, he might very well overwhelm any meager force Washington could summon. The bridge would be the army's one avenue of escape.

The outposts and picket posts were few and scattered along the river itself, and served little purpose than to watch the far side, some sign of a British patrol perhaps. The plateau fell away to the river's edge in a steep drop along much of the northern flank, and he stayed up on the flat roadway, would not risk the horse's legs on a sharp slope of icy ground. The staff would be grateful; they were not the skilled rider that he was. He glanced behind him, saw Tilghman huddled in the saddle, his arms pulling tightly to his coat. Around his shoulders was draped a blanket, the man's face barely visible. Washington stopped the horse, waited for the aides to come up, said, "We're nearly done, gentlemen. I do not enjoy this duty any more than you, but as long as the men are suffering in our protection, we will pay our respects by observing them with the same decorum we would exhibit at headquarters."

Tilghman emerged from his covering, removed the blanket, had received his subtle message. Washington spurred the horse, moved out again, could see the final picket post in front of them, saw the men coming together, muskets upright. Beyond the post, the ground fell away to the west, and he could see a lone column of smoke, rising from the chimney of his headquarters. He rode close to the pickets, stopped, could see one of the men bareheaded, thought, Not wise, then he saw the man's feet, dark and red, and beneath them, the man's hat, crushed flat, the only protection the man had against the icy ground. The sight horrified him, and he said, "Have you no cover for your feet, soldier?"

The man began to speak, but the words were held back by a sudden wave of shivering. Beside him, a man said, "Have *you*, sir?"

There was no emotion in the man's voice, no expectation of a reply. Washington avoided the sight of the man's bare feet, scanned their muskets, saw no gloves, cracked and cut hands wrapped tightly around the dull wooden stocks of their weapons. He wanted to respond, we are trying, we are making every effort . . . but the words would not come, held away by the tightness in his throat. There could be no good answer after all, no anger toward the man, who only spoke what they all were feeling. He could not help but stare at the clothing, some of it barely there, one man's legs naked from the knee down to the rags that wrapped his feet. There were remnants of blankets around some of them, large holes revealing the torn strips of a shirt, patches of filthy color, scraps of cloth that were never meant for clothing. Each man was looking at him, hollow black eyes, and he fought for the words, some response, something to comfort them.

"Your country is proud of you. Your sacrifice will be rewarded, so help me God."

He moved the horse, was past them, heard no cheers, no grateful salutes to his concern. Is it a lie, after all? If our country is proud of what we do, why have they not provided? How can they allow their soldiers to suffer the nakedness, to go without the basic comforts, or worse, the basic necessities of survival. He could see the headquarters now, the house nestled down near the junction of the river and the Valley Creek. For a long while he had kept to his tent, would not move into the house until the cabins had been built, would not allow his men to suffer in their tents while their commander lived in comfort. The gesture had been appreciated by the troops, but down in York, the congress could only criticize, letters condemning him for putting his men into camp at all. He had read the protests with a hard grip on his temper, fat men in wool suits, tobacco and brandy, soft leather chairs, insisting that his army should attack, and attack again. It was the consequence of the success of Horatio Gates, the simpleminded assumptions that one man's victory can so easily be achieved on every front. If Washington's army failed to win, it was only because they failed to attack, the mindless strategy of men whose only knowledge of war is the inconvenience of hearing about it.

He eased the horse down the slippery roadway, saw a man emerging from the house, then another, Hamilton, pointing up toward him now. The first man was quickly up on his horse, and Washington thought, I will be there in a moment. What could be so urgent that you cannot wait?

The man rode unsteadily up toward him, the horse struggling in the deeper snow, and Washington did not stop, was feeling the chill himself that had so plagued Tilghman. He recognized the man now, Major Deere, the quartermaster department, one of Mifflin's people, rarely seen in the field. The man turned the horse, moved beside him, and Washington simply looked at him, said nothing.

"Sir! I have some unfortunate news!"

Washington said nothing, thought, Certainly. Why else be in such haste?

"The wagons have arrived with the latest victuals. There is a problem, however. It seems that in an effort to, um, lighten their load, the drivers drained the brine from the barrels of pork. I am sorry to report, sir, that the meat has . . . spoiled, sir."

Washington sagged in the saddle, said, "How much meat?"

"I regret . . . all of it, sir."

He closed his eyes, his head down, could not feel anger. His mind was a sea of fog, no words at all, just one vision, the bare feet of the shivering soldier. For all the shortages, food had not yet been a problem, the one item that the quartermaster had seemed to secure. At least the men had been fed, and if it was not always what they hoped for, no one had yet gone hungry. Washington rode the horse into the yard of the headquarters, an aide emerging to take the reins. He climbed down, his boots sinking into soft snow. He moved slowly toward the door of the house, climbed the short steps. He passed the flag, the dark blue square dotted by white stars, held up in a soft flutter by the light breeze. The door was open now, Hamilton standing to one side, waiting for him. The smoky warmth rolled toward him, and he moved into the hall, turned into his office, was surprised, pleased to see Lafayette, the young man rising out of his chair. He expected the usual smile from the Frenchman, but Lafayette looked at him with a somber frown.

"Yes, Mr. Lafayette, I just received the news. Countless barrels of pork, now useless. We shall have to find some other means . . ." He stopped, saw a look of confusion on the young man's face. "What is it, Mr. Lafayette?"

"Forgive me, sir, I did not know about the pork. That is most tragic, sir. I brought you . . . this. The message arrived a short time ago. It was not sealed, and I persuaded Mr. Hamilton that I should examine it in your absence. Forgive the indiscretion, sir."

Washington saw a paper in the young man's hand, reached out, the automatic response, held the paper in his hand for a long moment.

"Is this . . . bad news, Mr. Lafayette?"

"It is unfortunate, sir."

He unfolded the paper, was surprised to see the name of Patrick Henry. He tried to focus his eyes on the man's writing, saw it was merely an introduction, Henry forwarding some other letter to Washington's hand. He read for a moment, said, "It seems my friend Mr. Henry has been the recipient of another of these anonymous essays which are circulating around the congress. He has enclosed it . . . oh, well, I misspoke. This one is not so anonymous after all. There is no signature, but I recognize the handwriting. This is from the hand of my friend, Dr. Rush." He held the letter up, caught the light from the window, began to read, felt the words knotting up deep inside of him, a chill rising in his chest.

"Dr. Rush clearly believes that the cause of our country's woes can be placed firmly at my feet."

Lafayette said, "It is outrageous, sir! He does not even sign his name! What manner of cowardice is this?"

Washington continued to read, and he made a small sound, the words cutting into him,

> But is our case desperate? By no means. We have wisdom, virtue and strength enough to save us if they should be called into action. The northern army has shown us what Americans are capable of doing with a GENERAL at their head. The spirit of the southern army is no ways inferior to the spirit of the northern. A Gates, a Lee, or a Conway would in a few weeks render them an irresistible body of men . . .

He lowered the paper.

"Dr. Rush has joined that ever-growing cabal who champion those men who believe themselves more capable of commanding this army. This is disappointing, Mr. Lafayette. But not so much as to incite your anger."

"I must disagree, sir! Conway? This is surely a product of his indiscreet blathering to congress. The man has inspired nothing short of an insurrection against your command, and, of course, he has found a willing partner in the ambitions of General Gates!"

Thomas Conway was an Irishman who had come to the army from France, another in the long line of puffed-up martinets, generally despised by everyone at headquarters. But Conway had gone a step further than so many of those who simply displayed their medals. He had taken his campaign to congress with unceasing energy, had been open and aggressive about his own qualifications for command. Congress had tried to appease the man by granting him a major general's rank, with the position of "inspector general." As such, he would not answer to Washington, but directly to the congressional Board of War. It was an absurd arrangement, and could not disguise the growing dissatisfaction with Washington's power. When Conway had presented himself at headquarters, Washington had essentially ignored him, but Conway would not go away quietly. The man's words came back to him now, Conway's own letter, an astounding comment to Gates that had come to Washington's hand:

Heaven has been determined to save your country; or a weak general and bad counselors would have ruined it . . .

Washington folded Henry's letter, slipped it into his coat. "Thank you, Mr. Lafayette."

He moved to his chair, put a hand on the back of his tall desk, stood quietly for a moment. Lafayette said, "Sir, how will you respond to this? This is outrageous! These men are clearly advancing their efforts to undermine your command!"

Washington stared toward the window, his mind a soft blur, his thoughts as bleak as the white ground that spread out beyond the house.

"Dr. Rush has been my friend for . . . years. He put his signature to the Declaration of Independence, spent so many months in the congress working for our cause. I cannot just ignore his sentiment. It is one matter to dismiss the voice of a man like your Mr. Conway. I don't fear those who are blind with ambition. Their blindness will lead them to failure, to mistakes, to unwise alliances. But Benjamin Rush is not of that cloth. He resigned as surgeon general of this army because he could not tolerate the inefficiencies in that department. While we have desperate need of his service, I have to respect his decision. This . . . I'm not certain I can respect at all. At the very least, he could have had the courage to sign his name."

He turned, looked at Lafayette, saw Tilghman there, Hamilton behind him.

"What response is appropriate, gentlemen? I cannot prevent men in this army from believing in their own abilities, and I cannot prevent any man in this country from having his say. This may be my just reward. If my efforts do not meet those of the commanders who now find such favor with the country, then this intrigue against me is justified." He looked at the faces, saw the outrage that he was too tired to feel himself. Tilghman said, "If you do not respond, sir, allow us to speak in your place. Allow your men to send their own message to the congress, or to General Gates, or to whoever else will spout such insubordination! No one in this camp will follow anyone but you, sir!"

Lafayette said, "I am ashamed, sir, that I believed General Conway to be an adequate commander. It is an embarrassment to me that French officers continue to infect this army with their zeal for glory. It cannot be ignored, sir!"

Washington sat down, settled heavily into the chair.

"Your loyalty is noted. I will handle this matter in a way most appropriate. You are dismissed, gentlemen."

He knew they would continue to protest, could not hear it just then. The room emptied, and he sat alone for a moment, but there was no time for the luxury of daydreaming. He called out, "Mr. Lafayette, if you please."

Lafayette returned, and Washington said, "I have heard nothing of progress in our negotiations with your king. Do you have any information, have you received any word?"

"Sir, I would have informed you at the first moment. I regret, I have heard nothing as well."

Washington sat back in the chair, looked at the desk, the scattering of papers, said, "We are in a desperate time. I appreciate your outrage and your loyalty, Mr. Lafayette. But I cannot summon energy for such causes while this army endures." The anger rose up, unstoppable now, and he rolled his hand into a tight fist, pounded slowly, softly on the desk. The words came out in a low hard growl, *"I do not comprehend how the congress can hear our pleas and continue to ignore them so."* He paused, rubbed his hands together, held on to the anger, pushed it away. "This army is dying, Mr. Lafayette, a slow, quiet death. We are weaker daily, and even if we survive the winter, I do not believe the coming of spring will bring a miraculous cure. We cannot clothe the men, we cannot provide the means to protect them from the cold. And if that is not sufficient cause for despair, now there are difficulties with the food. We cannot always be faulted for sickness, but starvation is another matter. I cannot comprehend that the congress will not provide for the survival of this army, that these men, these very good men, will be allowed to suffer so."

"Surely not, sir."

Washington thought a moment, said, "We *need* your assistance, Mr. Lafayette. It is no longer about money or credit or ships filled with gunpowder. It is about soldiers, the power of *your* nation to turn this war against our enemy. I do not see how this army can be brought to the field in three or four months and face the might of General Howe again. Your king must understand the need, must certainly know that an alliance with America is desirable."

"I'm sorry, sir. There is little I can offer, except hope."

"Well then, Mr. Lafayette, let us pray for the abilities and the wisdom of Dr. Franklin."

28. FRANKLIN

DECEMBER 1777

THERE WAS A FLY IN THE OINTMENT, AND HIS NAME WAS KING Charles III. The Spanish monarch was the nephew of Louis XVI, and a man of fragile sensitivity about his place in the hierarchy of European politics. The question put to him by the French government, whether or not he would enter a war with the hated English, put Charles squarely on the spot. His response was more of a personal message to his uncle at Versailles. Charles understood that an alliance with France did not change his stature as the lesser power, that his uncle King Louis would likely reap the greater glory and the greater spoils of any victory over the English. Worse, the Spanish seemed to feel they had much more to lose if America gained her independence. Certainly the American people would continue to flex their muscles, would look toward Mexico, perhaps, or other Spanish territories that America would find desirable to add to her own lands. And Charles had little confidence that he could maintain control over the colonies of Central and South America, or his islands in the Caribbean against what might become the new fashion of the day, distant colonies rising against their oppressive monarchs. The arguments swirling around him in Madrid were too strong for him to take any risks beyond his own borders. It was a rare opportunity for Charles to have the last word with his uncle Louis. His response was no. The Spanish would not join any alliance with the Americans.

DECEMBER 31, 1777

Franklin received the word from Vergennes on the last day of the year, the final capstone to a miserable holiday.

He had left the other two envoys in his house, would not even discuss the matter, the words choked away by the heat of his anger. He had grabbed his coat, wrapped himself against the cold, moved out through the bleak and desolate gardens. He knew Temple was watching him from the window, the young man always concerned for him. Yes, I would be concerned as well. This old man cannot endure many more years like this one. Failure does not contribute to longevity.

Just before Christmas, the usual stiffness in his joints had erupted into an attack of gout, and the painful swelling in his feet and knees had threatened to keep him confined to a chair. He walked with a slow limp, tried to ignore the severe pain in his left foot, his severely swollen toe suffering the tightness of his shoes. But he would not stay indoors, could not face the pitiable Deane, who had reacted to the news by collapsing into tears. Lee was worse, suspicious still of anyone and any event that did not focus on him, and Franklin knew that in Lee's mind the collapse of the French alliance would produce a conspiracy, that somehow Lee would conjure up demons that would convince him even Franklin was profiting from Spain's refusal, some bribe perhaps, a bizarre exercise in fantasy from Lee's illogical mind. No, Mr. Lee, sometimes events just . . . happen. There need not be any greater reason, any despicable plot, any intent by some force of evil to point its rotten finger directly at *you*. We are dealing, after all, with monarchs, men who control their own fate only if they control the fate of everyone around them. It is a challenge to even the most enlightened, and despite their greed for artwork and the splendor of their palaces, there is little to suggest enlightenment in the minds of these despots.

He had reached the edge of the property, stopped at a low stone wall. He felt his shoulders slump, thought, It is not necessary to be so angry at Arthur Lee. He is no more to blame than I am. Well, perhaps I am to blame, after all. I relied on faith that Vergennes is dedicated to an alliance. Despite Mr. Lee's lack of trust, we agree on one thing. We had expectations of success, and we were handed failure.

He looked back at the main house, realized he had come too far. Now, you old fool, you must walk that far again. He flexed his foot, the pain shocking him, tearing up through his leg, and he nearly lost his balance. He eased himself to the wall, sat slowly, the cold in the stone rising through him. He took a deep breath, looked at his hands, deep red, numb from the cold. You truly are an old fool. There is supposed to be wisdom in age, and you stumble out into a winter morning with no more thought than an anxious house pet. He looked up, tried to focus on the skeletons of tree limbs around him, absorbed the silence, thought, Not a bird, not a single furry varmint. They're tucked away no doubt in some warm nest. Your intellect has sunk below the level of the dumb beasts. The silence was broken now, Temple rushing up the path toward him.

"Grandfather! Let me help you!"

The young man carried a blanket, wrapped Franklin, and he didn't protest.

"Come inside, Grandfather. It's too cold for a walk."

Franklin felt the young man's hands lifting him, and he tried to shift his weight, ease the pain in his foot. They began to move, Temple holding him tightly by the arm. He wanted to say something, but the sadness was overwhelming him. He was limping even more than before, and after a few steps, said, "We have failed, it seems. A fitting conclusion to our efforts, a long walk in the desert of winter."

Temple seemed not to hear him, said, "Grandfather, Mr. Deane is still waiting to speak to you. He is concerned about you."

"Hmm, yes, it is his nature. What of Lee?"

"Mr. Lee is gone, sir. He said he would seek some new solution to our difficulties."

"Wonderful. I shall await that with childlike glee."

They were close to the house now, and Franklin could see the door opening, Deane stepping out.

"Doctor, you should not venture out so."

"Yes, Mr. Deane, my grandson has imparted that lesson already."

They climbed the short steps, and Franklin could feel the heat from the house, saw the fire in the hearth, limped his way back toward his chair.

Deane sat across from him, his customary place, waited for Franklin to warm his hands, then said, "Doctor, we have another course."

Franklin flexed his fingers, rubbed at the redness.

"What do you suggest? We can always pack our bags and move this expedition to Moscow, spend our remaining days courting the favor of Empress Catherine."

Deane made a small grunt, looked at Temple, who stood behind Franklin's chair.

"Mr. Franklin, would you allow me a private moment with your grandfather?"

"Certainly, sir."

Temple was out of the room now, and Franklin was curious, saw a different expression on Deane's face, hard, angry.

"Doctor, I wish you to cease this course!" The words came out in a burst, and Franklin was surprised, said, "What course is that?"

"You are not the victim in this matter. Yet you behave as though the French have given affront to you alone. I would rather spend our energies in constructing a positive result for our nation, than . . . forgive me, Doctor . . . than in wallowing in our own personal despair."

He had never seen Deane angry before, felt himself swelling up with responses, but the force of Deane's temper kept him quiet.

"As you know, Doctor, I have been in discussion with Paul Wentworth. He has been in Paris for some time, representing the interests of the British ministry. He wishes to speak to you."

Franklin knew that Deane had been approached by British representatives, had kept far away from any of that. It was a risk to his relationship with Vergennes that Franklin would not take.

"Doctor, Mr. Wentworth claims that there is a movement afoot in the British cabinet to find the avenue toward a reconciliation with America. There is considerable regret that this war has gone beyond anyone's expectations. Without the French alliance, what choice do we have but to consider some agreement with England that might prevent further bloodshed?"

"Are you suggesting that we enter into a discussion of surrender terms?"

"No, Doctor. And neither is Mr. Wentworth. He has not gone so far as to state it plainly, but I believe there is great fear in London that our alliance with France is close at hand. He has communicated a desire to interrupt that by forging some agreeable treaty between England and America."

"How agreeable?"

Deane shook his head.

"He is vague about specific terms. Which is why you should meet with him. He is considered to be the most influential member of the British officials in Paris. I certainly understand your fear that the French would know of this."

Franklin thought a moment, said, "He is more than an influential official. Count Vergennes considers him to be the chief British spy in France. If I was to meet with him, it could cause a stir at Versailles."

"That might be unavoidable, Doctor."

Franklin sat upright, stared into the fire.

"It might be more than that, Silas. It might be most desirable. The French have every reason to hope for American independence, whether they risk their own necks or not. But if America seeks a renewed alliance with England, if we can secure some peace that sits well with both congress and King George . . ." He looked at Deane now, felt the energy returning, his mind awakening. He slapped the arm of his chair, said, "Silas, contact your friend Mr. Wentworth. I wish to meet with him. I am eager to hear his propositions."

"I can arrange some discreet location, Doctor. We can make every effort to prevent Count Vergennes from hearing of it."

"No, Silas. I wish the meeting to take place right here, in this house. As for Vergennes hearing about the meeting? I am depending on it."

JANUARY 6, 1778

Franklin was polite to the extreme, welcomed Wentworth into his parlor with a smile, could not help thinking of the seductive graciousness of the spider. He did not know Wentworth other than the casual passing in London, the man serving as the colonial representative to Rhode Island. Wentworth's only other connection to the colonies was by family, a cousin to John Wentworth, the last royal governor of that colony. But now, neither Wentworth nor his cousin had any official connection to America. Both their positions had been erased by the start of the war.

Wentworth carried himself with the stiffness of an English aristocrat, the attitude of a man who must force himself to endure the company of anyone of a lower station. Franklin enjoyed Wentworth's discomfort, made all the more entertaining by the man's purpose for being there. Wentworth's mission was, after all, to convince Franklin that there was a real hope that England and America could set aside their differences and ignore nearly three years of astounding violence.

Franklin had purposely allowed Wentworth to make his case, allowed the flood of patronizing words to fill the room, all the carefully rehearsed platitudes and expressions of mutual benefit. After nearly twenty minutes, he could feel that Wentworth was tiring, the man's voice, and his ingratiating smile fraying around the edges. Franklin waited for a pause in the man's presentation, said, "Your loyalty to your king is admirable, sir."

The comment seemed to puzzle Wentworth, had nothing to do with what he was saying.

"Doctor?"

"You are a most loyal English citizen. Your king would be proud."

"Thank you, I'm sure."

There was silence now, and Franklin knew he had changed the course of the man's entire presentation.

"Tell me, Mr. Wentworth, it must be a maddening experience for the ministry to deal with such rabble as we find in congress."

It was a casting of bait, and after a moment Wentworth said, "I admit to you, Doctor, that I share the curiosity of many in Parliament how such a body of men, who claim to represent their nation, can so readily reveal those affairs of state which should be kept private. There has not been a single example of a private correspondence between my government and yours that has not suddenly become a topic of display for your newspapers, or posted in every town square. How does any government expect to conduct its business by revealing every policy and every negotiation to its people?"

Franklin shrugged. "That's a question I cannot answer, sir. Some in your Parliament would claim that government can only be accomplished by men of breeding, that men of congress must be men of title. Certainly, most men who perform the duties that Mr. Deane, Mr. Lee, and myself have attempted here, would, in your government, be men of title."

Wentworth took the bait again.

"Absolutely, Doctor! I see we are of the same mind on this matter! What you are so delicately proposing, sir, is that you gentlemen could be disposed to accepting King George's terms if there was, ah, ample reward."

"Mr. Wentworth, I have proposed nothing of the sort."

Wentworth smiled now, said, "Ah! Yes! Well, very good, sir! Your message is received and shall be delivered."

"You are certainly mistaken, sir. But since you have mentioned the word, what are the terms, exactly, that your government is proposing?"

Wentworth seemed to be enjoying himself now, said, "Very good, indeed, sir. You are a master at diplomacy. Quite simply put, sir, it is a matter of fact that an alliance of England and America creates an empire that is unequaled in the world. There is mutual benefit in matters of defense and in matters of commerce. The marketplace alone that we each bring to our respective merchants and craftsmen is extraordinary! We share the common language, which, to be frank, Doctor, is a decided advantage for you, I'm sure!"

Franklin laughed at the man's joke, thought, If anyone was unclear if you were a spy or not, you have just provided the evidence. How else would a man of no acquaintance know of the inefficiency of my French?

"Doctor, I must assume that you represent the views of your congress, and carry considerable weight there."

"I would not say that, sir."

"Ah, of course. Nonetheless, Doctor, I will speak as though you do. The ministry is prepared to withdraw the demands placed upon the colonies by the various acts put into place since 1763. Since these acts were so odious to you, and seemed to produce such hostility to the crown, the king himself is willing to concede that they were enacted in error."

Franklin could not hold back, said, "Why did you not consider this to be an option *three years ago*?"

Wentworth seemed surprised by the question.

"I don't actually know, Doctor. Certainly could have saved us all a bit of trouble, yes?"

"A *bit*, yes. What of independence, sir? You have not mentioned the very heart of the matter."

"Ah, Doctor, because it is not the heart of the matter. It simply cannot be. What King George is proposing is to put aside every issue that produced this conflict in the first place, to admit the errors of his government. There will no longer be any *need* for independence. All our differences will be settled!"

"That might not be acceptable to the congress."

"Ah, yes, I see. Just as you three here, your congress is composed of men who have a sensitivity to their place in the empire. A trivial matter, Doctor. The king would surely grant as many titles as required. Your congress could create its own House of Lords, modeled on the very foundations of our own. How very perfect. Marvelous. The king should enjoy the notion."

Franklin was growing weary of the game, said, "I have made no such offer. I'm not certain that independence can be swept away with such a casual gesture."

"Doctor, there is nothing casual in the power of His Majesty's soldiers. I assure you, King George is willing to wage war on your soil for ten years to achieve his aims."

"Mr. Wentworth, the American people are willing to fight for fifty years to see that he does not." He had endured all he could of Wentworth's smugness, leaned forward in his chair, thought, It is time for the second act of this play. He conjured up the anger in his mind, let the words fill the cauldron, then slowly allowed it to spill out. He began with a low growl.

"How dare you, sir! You come into my home and insult me and my country with solicitous bribes? You suggest that under your control, we can become an empire to rule the world, and yet, I have seen Ireland, I have seen what your domination has produced! You do not cooperate, you do not create a marketplace. You take, you plunder, you strip the land of those goods which suit you. You return only misery and oppression!"

Wentworth was sitting back in the chair, shocked into silence by the outburst. Franklin felt the churning inside of his mind still, leaned toward Wentworth, said, "You dare to mention your king's soldiers! They have burned our towns, killed and tortured our citizens, laid siege to our fine cities! And, as if your own soldiers are not capable of inflicting sufficient horrors, your king

employs foreign barbarians to further his revenge on the innocent, those who only wish to live in freedom from the outrage of
your king's absurd policies, which change with the wind, to suit
whatever madness he may this day enjoy!"

"Doctor, your anger is most unseemly. I bid you, do not allow
your passions to undo our good work. I did not intend to offer
you fuel for your anger. If I have given you personal offense . . ."

"It is not personal, sir. It is *national*! It is the *outrage* of my
country pouring forth, the *disgust* at your notions of how we
must serve the whims of your monarch, and the corrupt policies
of your ministry! Your country is an ailing patient, sir, rife with
disease and infection. My country is young in spirit and body,
and seeks alliances with those whose sight is toward the future.
We have no interest in holding tightly to the sickness of the
past!"

He realized he was shouting, had worked himself into a frenzy
of raw anger. He stopped, felt his heart tearing through his chest,
his hands shaking. Wentworth was staring dumbly, his mouth
open, and Franklin sat back in the chair, let his breathing flow
out. He felt the control returning, sat silently for a moment, then
reached for his watch, thought, Nearly two hours. Sufficient
time, certainly, to impress any French observer. He looked at
Wentworth, who seemed completely lost. Franklin was calm, the
job complete. The polite smile returned, and he said, "Mr. Deane
should be arriving shortly. Since the hour is growing late, and
my cook here does admirable work, I would be delighted if you
would stay for supper."

JANUARY 7, 1778

Franklin could never be sure if Vergennes' spies had made
their report, but a message from the French Foreign Ministry
was too sudden to be coincidence. The word came less than one
day after Franklin's meeting with Wentworth, carried by the
hand of Gerard himself, signed by Vergennes. If the American envoys would agree to negotiate no further with anyone representing
the English government, the creation of the necessary paper would
begin immediately. Gerard was discreet, would say only that there
had been a change of heart in the French court. For reasons unex-

plained, King Louis XVI had been persuaded that France would make official its own alliance with the Americans.

29. WASHINGTON

VALLEY FORGE, PENNSYLVANIA, JANUARY 1778

THE MAN WAS HUGE, A SCOWLING HULK, RODE AT THE HEAD OF A long column of troops who were as ragged as their commander. They passed through the outposts to unexpected cheers, moved through the frozen earthworks as huddled soldiers rose to greet them. They pushed their way up the long snowy hill to the plateau, each man amazed at the sight of this strange new town, built by the hands of Washington's army. The cabins were waiting, the grim vacancies created by so many who were sick or simply gone. As they spread into their new homes, their fresh fires added new clouds of smoke to the vast sea of black air that drifted over Valley Forge. They did not complain of the choking misery of the cabins, the hard cold ground kept away by the thin layers of worn blankets. Instead, they were grateful for the shelter, the long miserable march from Saratoga now complete. It was a homecoming of sorts, this hearty regiment of Virginians, led by the crude and powerful man who inspired as much good humor in the army as the passion for a good fight. With word of the return of these lean and victorious riflemen, the stories began to flow, the pride of accomplishment, these men who had done so much to destroy Gentleman Johnny Burgoyne. As their revelry began, their leader continued on to headquarters. Daniel Morgan had returned to Washington's command.

THE RECEPTION HAD BEEN BOISTEROUS, A DINNER IN THE MESS cabin that was as lavish as any they could assemble. The senior officers had all come, and Washington could see that the towering Virginian had lost none of his flair for dramatics. He enjoyed the tales of Morgan's long march, knew some were more tall than others. Throughout the long evening, the huge man's antics gave the entire command a blessed distraction from the difficulties in the camp, and Washington knew tomorrow he would hear of the antics of Morgan's men, a certain distraction for the rest of the army as well. Nearly three years earlier, Morgan had been the first Virginian to march soldiers to Boston, his sharpshooting riflemen the first company of southern troops to join New England's effort against the British. They had been a rowdy and undisciplined lot, had tormented Washington with their drunken brawls. But their reputation for astounding marksmanship, and the hard line with which they faced the enemy excused their behavior. When Burgoyne's march toward Ticonderoga seemed a desperate crisis, congress had found comfort in sending Horatio Gates. Washington had felt more comfort in sending Daniel Morgan.

IT WAS VERY LATE, AND HE HAD SENT MOST OF HIS STAFF TO THEIR quarters. One by one, the senior officers had offered their compliments, some finding difficulty in the climb to their saddles, struggling through an alcoholic haze. With the party nearly over, he had invited Morgan to the main house. He waited for a final good-bye, Morgan shouting something crude out the door, horses moving away, and Washington moved out of the hall, into his office. Greene followed, and Morgan was quickly there, his laughter subdued now by the change in location. The light was soft, the fire low in the hearth, and Morgan seemed to understand that the house was quiet, that the time for festivities had passed.

Washington pointed to a stout wooden chair, and Morgan dropped down, leaned the chair back, a precarious perch, and Greene laughed, said, "I must say, Daniel, you do take a toll on the furniture."

Greene sat as well, and Morgan produced a bottle from his belt, held it up to the firelight, frowned at the emptiness, said, "Furniture is meant to be used, Nat. Like this brew. We've used a good bit of this tonight." He set the bottle on the small table beside him, said to Washington, "You have some men of great capacity in your command, George. Haven't known too many generals to survive for long with such an appetite for spirits. That quality is best reserved for the foot soldier."

Washington smiled at the informality, Morgan's trademark, the man's words slurred more by his lack of teeth than any injury from the alcohol.

"We do not often imbibe to this degree, Daniel. It is not . . . encouraged. However, this was a special occasion. With all you have heard this evening, I would add my own salute. Welcome back."

"Wouldn't be anywhere else, George. That fat little sparrow not to my taste as a commander."

Greene seemed to light up at the description, smiled broadly, said, "We do exercise some caution here, Daniel. We're too close to his friends in congress to offer such frank commentary on General Gates. He is, after all, the hero of Saratoga."

Morgan sniffed, frowned again, and Washington could see that Morgan did not find the comment amusing. Washington said, "I should like to hear your account of those days, Daniel. Most of congress, and from what I hear, much of the nation feels Mr. Gates is our best hope for victory."

Morgan stood up suddenly, the chair rattling behind him, tumbling to one side.

"Your damned congress knows as much about fighting . . . by God! The hero of Saratoga? Well, of course, it was simple to predict how his reputation would come bursting out of that place. He's down there in York right now, no doubt filling them with all his grand exploits. *Sparrow* was too kind, George. The man is a . . . vulture. Lives off the efforts of everyone else. Keeps himself out of danger, while his men do the work. That little turnip wouldn't know a line of battle if it trampled him under its boots!"

Morgan was stalking around the room now like some great cat, his thick arms moving as he spoke.

"Hero? The heroes of that fight were Benedict Arnold, and Enoch Poor, and old Ebenezer Learned. My riflemen played some smart role as well. I had to *seek out* General Gates to get my orders to advance. He was back in his headquarters having a card game with some British officer. He would rather have spent that day reminiscing with a prisoner than leading his men into battle. And, damned if he didn't come prancing out in the field just as we had the enemy in full rout! Then he began to spout all this talk . . . glorious victory! *His* glorious victory! There was some in my group had to hold tight to their muskets, or they mighta drawed a bead on that fat little partridge!"

His fury had exhausted him, and he moved back to the chair, set it upright with a sharp clatter, sat again.

"Hero of Saratoga! I'd plant my boot right where that hero does his best work!"

Washington was stunned, saw Greene staring openmouthed, a smile now spreading across Greene's face, and he said, "Well, now General Washington, what do you think about that? Am I mistaken, or was that a right smart bit of fresh breeze that blew through this place?"

Morgan sat with his arms crossed on his chest, still mumbling to himself. Washington didn't know how to respond, focused on Greene's obvious pleasure.

"It is not a habit we should encourage. However, I am grateful for your candor, Daniel. I was aware that Mr. Gates had a desire to elevate his station. I was not aware that he would be so clumsy about it. It is not for me to make light of this, nor to contradict his version of events at Saratoga. He was in command. He does have the privilege of claiming the victory. But you are correct. He is in York right now, assuming his new duties on the Board of War. I suppose we should be grateful that his new position has removed him from the battle."

"Board of War?" Morgan unfolded his arms, leaned forward, his hands on his knees. "What in blazes is that?"

Greene said, "You have been too far away, Daniel. Congress has decided that they had best administrate this war from behind. General Washington is still in command in the field. But the Board of War will determine what that command shall be."

Morgan sat back in the chair, seemed dazed.

"From behind? Then General Gates is in the right place."

Washington looked toward the door, saw movement, Tilghman peering in.

"Sir, can I get you anything?"

"Thank you, no, Colonel. We will be retiring soon. You may as well."

Morgan watched the man move away, said in a low voice, "Should we be concerned about spies, George? With all the talk about intrigue . . ."

"Mr. Tilghman is most loyal, I assure you. I have no fears about the men in this command. We have had our difficulties, certainly, some of those who have shown themselves to be more concerned with their place in history than in the good of this army."

Greene said, "The intrigue is not in this camp, Daniel. It's in York. There is considerable effort being made to sway the congress to replace the general with someone of a more heroic quality."

Morgan shook his head.

"You mean Gates. How far is York? Twenty miles? Twenty-five?"

Greene nodded.

"Maybe I should pay a visit to this Board of War. Kick in a door or two. I'll show them some heroics."

Washington looked at Morgan closely, thought, He cannot truly be serious.

"Daniel, there is no time for issuing threats to those who oppose this command. If you are correct about Mr. Gates, the truth will prevail, the man himself will determine his place in this war. We can only do what is required of us at the moment, and our situation in this camp is most difficult. I would hope you would confine your efforts to the welfare of your men. The Board of War is my concern, and they have not yet intruded into the business of this army. If we are fortunate, they will confine their lofty opinions to the meeting rooms in York."

HE STARED AT THE LETTER WITH A FEELING OF COLD SICKNESS.

"Mr. Tilghman?"

"Sir?"

"Summon Mr. Lafayette."

He sat back in the chair, stared at the window, could see the row of cabins across the open ground, the housing for his guards. The ground was cut by deep trails, winding through the hard mounds of snowdrifts, dirty snow flattened by the boots of his men. The mood of the camp had been brightened by several days of sunshine, an icy blue sky that caused snow blindness for many of the lookouts, the men whose reddened eyes still suffered from the smoke of their cabins. But the blue sky was gone now, swept away by a blanket of dull gray. He stared above the hill behind the guard cabins, thought, There will be snow again, certainly. He would not focus anymore on the letter still in his hand, the official dispatch from the Board of War, had read it too many times already. He heard sounds now, saw Lafayette in the doorway. The young man said, "You require my presence, sir?"

Washington pointed to a chair, and Lafayette sat quickly.

"You have received orders."

He handed Lafayette the paper, who read slowly then looked at Washington, questioning, the young man's usual smile replaced by uncertainty.

"What is this, sir? I am to go to . . ."

"Canada. The Board of War has been busy. They seem to believe that an attack against Governor Carleton's outposts will bring the Canadian people to our side. They are assuming that a Frenchman in command of the force would inspire the French Canadians to join your effort."

Lafayette scanned the paper again.

"Did you know of this, sir?"

"Read the last bit, the bottom of the page."

The Board will be happy on this, as well as every other occasion, to receive your opinion and advice.

"They did not consult me, and despite their graciousness, I am confident that my opinion would likely be ignored. I am pleased on one account, however. If this mission is to succeed, I know of no other officer who I would rather see in your stead."

Lafayette seemed unconvinced, said, "This states that General Conway is to be my second. Am I to be grateful for that?"

"There is more to that than you are reading, Mr. Lafayette. Mr. Conway has no doubt campaigned for this mission, for the purpose of keeping an eye on you. I caution you to expect some pressure from the Board themselves, and from Mr. Gates in particular. You would be a formidable ally to their efforts at removing me from command. They will test you, I am quite certain."

"This is madness, sir! A mission to Canada, while it is still winter? I am to . . . *journey to Albany, and assume command of the forces* waiting me there. What forces? How could this mission be arranged and communicated to such a distance without you knowing of it?"

Washington shrugged.

"These are questions that can only be answered when your mission has commenced. Take good care, Mr. Lafayette. If you are successful, then all of America will salute your conquest of Canada. If you are not . . . then you will return to me. Either way, this nation has the advantage."

FEBRUARY 12, 1778

The guards were becoming accustomed to visitors, carriages heavy with well-dressed men, mostly from congress. Many were responding to Washington's complaints with a skeptical eye, would visit Valley Forge to see for themselves why the commanding general had become so annoyingly insistent with his tirades against their presumed neglect. The guards barely noticed them now, a cursory glance, even the officers waving the visitors casually through the outpost. With the visitors past, the guards would make their crude jokes, inspired not by humor, but by bitterness. A congressman would expect a reception, a formal dinner at least, and by now even the foot soldiers knew that Washington was doing all he could to conserve the precious food around headquarters. He must surely dread these visits from the aristocratic prigs in York, who seemed to regard these outings as some winter holiday, a vacation at the expense of the army that protected them.

It had been a quiet afternoon, the men huddled around a shallow pit in the ground, their small fire protected from the wind by a fat bank of hard snow. Their replacements would soon arrive, and the men would not wait to eat, one man securing a small sack of flour. They watched hungrily as he prepared their meal, the raw flour mixed with melted snow, kneaded to a thick paste, flattened on a flat piece of iron. It was a highlight of their day, but it would not go uninterrupted, and they rose from their shelter to the sound of horses, a carriage, then a wagon, packed high with bundles and crates, rocking precariously on its grinding springs. The caravan was led by two horsemen, men with short sabers and pistols in their belts. One of the guards moved into the road, halting the strange procession, and an officer suddenly emerged from the carriage, said, "Who might be in command here?"

The guard looked toward the fire, and another man stepped up over the mound of snow, his hands black with ash, smeared with the paste of the flour.

"That would be myself, sir. Captain Roe. What is your pleasure, sir? A bit of dinner perhaps? We have firecake and water, and, if that's not to your liking, we have water and firecake."

There were small chuckles from the men, and the officer said nothing, allowed the men their moment of fun.

"Captain, I am Colonel Meade. These men are courtesy of General Smallwood's brigade, from his camp at Wilmington. On the authority of General Washington, you will allow us to pass."

Roe seemed unimpressed with the man's bluster, said, "I will, eh? Possible. You don't appear to be a spy. Are you?"

Meade was growing impatient.

"See here, Captain. We have important business."

"Everybody does, Colonel."

More of his men were emerging from the snowbank, curiosity giving way to annoyance, their meal delayed. Roe moved closer to the carriage, said, "Best take a look at what you got there. Any spies inside here?"

Roe leaned into the window of the carriage, then seemed to jump back, made a small surprised grunt, and now his men could see the face of a woman, peering out at them.

"Captain Roe, thank you for your courtesy. Colonel Meade, do be polite. These men are only performing their duty. Perhaps you should make an introduction."

Meade made a short bow toward the woman, said, "Captain, will you please allow us to pass? I assure you, there are no spies here. This is . . . the wife of General Washington."

SHE MOVED TO THE HOUSE ON MEADE'S ARM, HER COAT BRUSHING the snowbanks that lined the deep path. The sentries had been alerted, stood in line on both sides of the door, and as she reached the steps, Meade stepped aside, the guard opening the door with a crisp turn. She stepped inside the house, the unmistakable aroma of the kitchen, could see the hall now lined with men, all standing straight, their backs against the wall. She felt her hands shaking, was already nervous, would never insist on such a formal display. She recognized some of the faces, could not just allow them to stare blankly ahead, said, "Mr. Tilghman, how wonderful to see you again! And, Mr. Harrison. Mr. Hamilton. How nice." She stopped in front of another, very young, handsome.

"I'm afraid I do not know you, young man."

The officer responded with a whisper, "No, ma'am. Major John Laurens, ma'am."

"Mr. Laurens, I am pleased to make your acquaintance."

She moved past the last of the staff, small greetings, quiet introductions, could see now they had served as a reception line, leading her toward a parlor, to the right of the hall. She turned, could not help a small gasp, saw the tall man standing alone in the center of the room, waiting for her. She could hear the movement of soft footsteps in the hall behind her, the staff slipping away, and she said a silent thank-you for their discretion. He smiled now, and she tried to smile as well, fought the tears. For a long moment, they stood in silence, neither one moving, as though neither one knew what to do. She studied his face, saw the deep lines, the blue eyes soft with weariness, his cheeks thin, pale. His broad shoulders were rounded, seemed to sag, his whole form showing a sadness she could not bear to see. She could not hold back any longer, moved close to him, wrapped her small arms around him, felt his now enveloping her. They stood quietly, the only sound the crackle from the fire in the hearth behind him, and she felt the warmth on his back, her fingers moving slowly on the rough wool of his coat. He said in a soft voice, "Thank God you are here."

She would not let him go, not yet, hid her tears in his shirt, and he patted her lightly on the back.

"Let us go upstairs. My room . . . our room is there. We should have a moment of privacy."

She would not look at his face, was embarrassed at her emotions, held tightly to his arm as he led her to the stairway. The hall was empty now, the kitchen silent, no one in the house making a sound. He was in full uniform, and she could hear the sword on his belt tapping the wall as they climbed the narrow steps, the boards squeaking from the weight. He led her through another hall, another room much like the parlor, warmed by a crackling fire. He closed the door behind her, and she felt his hands on her shoulders, felt him turning her toward him, touching her hair, pulling her close. She wrapped him again, but this time he was not the general. The rough uniform could not disguise the man. He seemed to melt against her, and she felt a strange frailness in his arms, could hear the sadness in his breathing, soft cries now, every part of him finally able to let go of the exhaustion, his own emotion. She was no longer embarrassed at her own tears, held him tightly, would hold him, would feel his soft cries as long as he needed.

30. WASHINGTON

FEBRUARY 1778

HER DAY HAD BEGUN EARLY, A GENTLE KNOCK AT THEIR BEDROOM door, the soft apology as the man moved quickly in the darkness to light the fire in the small bedroom hearth. Washington was awake and up quickly, and she watched him in the glow of firelight as he fastened the buttons of his uniform and pulled on his boots. She sat up in the bed, and he responded by lighting a candle, said in a quiet voice, "I thought you would remain here. There is no need for you to rise so early."

"Nonsense, *Old Man*. A general's wife should set a good example."

It was the first time she had called him by her pet name in a long time, and he leaned closer to her, covered her hand with his, said, "Not around the staff, please. In their eyes, I am old enough as it is."

She was surprised by his good humor, watched as he stood up, pulled his heavy coat down from the hook on the wall.

"I will come for you a bit later. Perhaps we can ride out in the country. It is quite beautiful here."

"What must you do today, George?"

He absorbed the question, said slowly, "Many things. We are waging war with the quartermaster department. Mr. Mifflin resigned his post there because I would not sacrifice this army merely to save his home in Philadelphia. The congress has not found it necessary to replace him, thus, for some time now, there has been no one in charge. It is a vexing problem, and possibly the most important difficulty we face. So many of my urgent requests have been ignored that I am certain my dispatches are regarded as fuel for their fires. The troops have not received any meat in two weeks, and when I warned the commissary of the consequences, the possibility of mutiny in the ranks, their response was, 'Give them bread.' I am astounded at the lack of empathy for our suffering."

"Perhaps you should appoint your own officers to command that department."

"It is not so simple as that. I can suggest, but it is congress who must make the appointment. There are so few of them in attendance at York that nothing is accomplished, nothing but the posturing and complaining from the Board of War. If Mr. Mifflin had performed his duty as quartermaster general with the same zeal he places on his performance at the Board . . ." He paused, and she could hear his breathing. "I regret you must hear this."

"You may speak to me of anything, George. Is it not better to unburden yourself here, to me, than to risk offending someone else? I know your temper. You will endure in silence until the most unfortunate moment."

"That is troublesome, Martha. I was not aware . . ."

"Old Man, as long as I am your wife, I will help you any way I can. You are suffering so from the vanity and foolishness of those men. When you went to the first congress, it seemed very different. Your letters said nothing of meanness and backbiting."

He moved to a small table, poured water from a stout pitcher into a small cup. He drank, set the cup down, said, "So many of the good men have simply gone home. The congress is very different now. The men who made the first journey to Philadelphia, they were *statesmen*, they brought a spirit that no one expected, that no one had ever seen. The debates between John Adams and Mr. Dickinson . . . Martha, it was as if God himself was speaking to us, enlightening us to what man could accomplish. In the end, nearly every man in that hall believed we could change the course of history, that we could create a revolution that could affect all of mankind. It was extraordinary, and it was somewhat frightening. You know when they selected me for this command, I did not go to Boston with much faith in my abilities. I feared that those men had made a grievous error. Now, so many of them have returned to their homes, their own lives, as though the job of building this nation is complete. Many in the congress now are men of ambition and petty concerns, their minds consumed with simplistic notions of war and command. They plot and scheme behind my back. The idealism has been replaced by the mundane."

She slid out of the bed, moved across the small room toward the growing fire, stared into the flames.

"You can always come home. Mount Vernon could use your strong hands."

"How can I abandon my post? I am surprised you would even suggest . . . I should retire, in the midst of this crisis? What of this army, what of the men loyal to my command? I have a duty here . . ." His voice was rising, and she turned, was smiling at him.

"You see? It is still important to you, no matter what happens in congress."

His hand was hanging in midair, the unfinished gesture, and he dropped it to his side, shook his head. She moved toward him.

"You will do what is right, Old Man. You will not allow congress or Thomas Mifflin or even Horatio Gates to keep you from your duty." She turned toward the window, could see a gray light, pointed.

"You will do what *they* require of you. I know very little of congress, except that few of them have ever been soldiers. Despite all their intrigue and pettiness, they must respect that. This is, after all, a war. This country is not depending on the congress, they are depending on the army, they are looking to you. Those men in York are simply envious of that."

"But I have not given this country, or the congress, the one thing they know of war, the one thing they expect of their army. *Victories*."

"Do you have faith in these men?"

He looked toward the gray light of the window.

"If this army is fed and clothed, if they are led by good officers, they will defeat anyone on this earth."

"Then you know what you must do. You must see to their food and clothing. The officers . . . I don't believe they will disappoint. They are led by *you*."

GREENE RODE BESIDE HIM, AND THEY MOVED OUT AWAY FROM THE house, followed the roadway blackened by the wheels of the army. His breath was a white fog, the morning air biting his face, an icy dampness. He led Greene out through the open ground beyond the cabins of his guards, along the base of the low hill, past the stumps of cut trees, long gone for lumber and firewood. They moved past the blacksmith shed, could hear the sharp strike of steel on steel, the men whose work never stopped, the constant repairs to wagons and equipment. They continued up the rise, out on the crest, the artillery park on the left, Knox's guns arranged in neat rows, the brass barrels glistening under a thin layer of ice. He could see across much of the camp, the morning mist gray with the smoke from the cabins. He had not spoken since he climbed the horse, and Greene knew to wait, that Washington would begin the conversation in his own way. They moved down again, a shallow ravine, and to one side there was a gathering of men and wagons, and the carcasses of horses. Slowly they were hoisted up and piled on each wagon, to be hauled away by a pair of scrawny animals that were barely alive themselves. He had seen it before, but was still shocked, felt himself flinch, a spasm of sickness. He turned away, spurred the horse up the hill again, and Greene was beside him quickly, said, "I have made certain they haul the carcasses beyond the outposts. The ground is too frozen to bury anything. We have located a deep cut out to the west . . ."

"I am certain the duty is handled, Mr. Greene. It is most unpleasant."

"Yes, sir."

He rode slowly, began to think of Mount Vernon, the pride he felt when he walked through the stables, his affection for the tall stout horses.

"At home, the loss of a good horse filled me with great sadness. They always perform, no matter the duty, the weather, no matter their age. They are a blessed beast. God has given the horse a special place on this earth. I have often thought that God judges man on how we treat the horse. What better measure of character is there than how we respect the beast that takes on our burdens?"

"That we have made the horse a beast of burden might bring punishment enough." Greene made a low laugh, and Washington said, "You are not a man of the land, Mr. Greene. With all respects, you cannot understand."

Greene did not respond, and Washington said, "My apologies. I did not wish to offend you."

"None taken, sir. But you are not quite correct. An iron mill requires the labor of horses. My father relied greatly on his teams. I rode often when I was a boy. Even with the . . . problem in my leg."

They moved into a wide trail, the dirty snow banked high to one side. They were among the cabins now, and Washington saw a small open campfire, unusual, pulled the horse that way. There were four men, and they stood now, surprised, and Washington could see a metal pot hung above the fire, a rising column of steam.

"Gentlemen, do not let us disturb you. Are you cooking?"

They glanced at each other, and one man raised a spoon from the pot, poured the dark brown liquid into a small cup.

"Aye, sir. Soup, it is. One of the fellows here got a might lucky chasin' a rabbit. This here pot's done made us several days of good eatin'."

Greene moved the horse forward, closer to the fire, said, "Several days? How big was the rabbit?"

"Oh, the rabbit's been gone a while now, sir."

The man stirred the bubbling brew, and Washington could see something round and dark, the spoon knocking it with a metallic click.

"What is in the soup, soldier?"

The man moved the object around, said, "That'd be a rock, sir. We always hear tell that there's strength in rocks. We figured if we boil it a while, it might lend something to the soup."

Greene leaned out, looked down into the pot.

"That appears to be . . . leaves. Seems your soup is a bit . . . soiled."

The man spooned up the bits of brown.

"Oh, no, sir. Not only leaves, but pine needles as well. The best soup has to have . . . vegetables."

Washington pulled his horse back.

"General Greene, we should be on our way."

They left the men to their fire, and Washington moved back into the roadway, then crossed to the far side, climbing the horse over the bank of snow. They were moving toward the edge of the plateau, the ground falling away in a wide sweep. Below, the outer line of earthworks cut across the hillside, and Greene moved up beside him.

"Forgive me, sir. Where are we going?"

Washington had left the staff behind, ordering them to keep to their work at the headquarters. They were followed only by a handful of his guards, and he stopped the horse, turned.

"Captain Gibbs, have your men remain somewhat farther back. I wish to speak to General Greene in privacy."

The man obeyed, held the guards in place while Washington moved away. Greene followed, was close beside him again.

"Privacy? I am honored, sir."

"Don't be, Mr. Greene. I find that my temper is short these days. I do not wish to make an unfortunate demonstration for the men."

"Certainly, sir."

"Mr. Greene, we have men eating dirty water and calling it soup. How long will they tolerate these conditions? How long must I? Are we so helpless? Our raids on the British supply wagons have been ineffective. General Howe has purchased the loyalty of most of the farms around Philadelphia because he can offer payment in hard currency. We offer nothing but continental paper." He stopped, turned toward the guards, saw they were at a suitable distance.

"I have exhausted the congress with my pleas, so much so that they have now *suggested* that this army simply take what it wants from anyone who can assist us. We are to secure food by the point of the bayonet. Those farmers who have not yet found sympathy with the British will certainly do so now. What manner of solution is that? I am dismayed that your foraging expeditions have been so ineffective. We manage to gather a lengthy train of wagons, and they return to this camp nearly empty. What is the explanation?"

"Sir, the farms simply do not have the means to feed this army, whether we pay them with specie or threaten them with the bayonet."

"Then what would *you* suggest, Mr. Greene?"

"We require a quartermaster who will not be so hesitant to insult those who control so much of the goods we require."

"What do you mean?"

"Sir, it has been suggested in many quarters that a great deal of supply is sitting idly in warehouses along the coast. There is simply no means to compel anyone to transport it. Several states are claiming possession of the French goods that happen to arrive in their ports, taking the opportunity to better clothe their own militia, with no regard for the needs of the whole. The supplies that do find the means to reach us are mistreated, or stolen by the men whose job it is to transport them. I have seen barrels of flour spilled in great heaps beside the roadway, no doubt too much of a bother for some wagoneer who preferred his own hearth rather than the completion of his mission. We had wagons of meal and flour arrive here last week in broken barrels, soaked with rain, already molded beyond use."

"Mr. Greene, you are telling me nothing I do not already know. I asked you for a suggestion."

"A quartermaster. Someone who understands the needs of this army, and the means to satisfy those needs. Someone who is not so enamored by the drawing rooms of congress. Someone who will carry a whip into those halls to secure what we need. Someone with a *backbone*. Sir."

"Mr. Greene, I agree. I would like you to volunteer for the position. Congress will be so informed, and I will insist they make official the appointment in a rapid manner."

Greene looked at him with wide eyes.

"Me?"

"Since the position comes only with the rank of brigadier general, you may retain your rank on the line."

"Surely there is . . . is there no one else . . . *me,* sir?"

"There is no one more capable in this army. You will not sacrifice your command. When General Howe resumes his campaign, I will require the services of every capable officer. But I will also require a capable army, men who have the strength and the means to march and fight. That . . . will be your job."

Greene slumped in the saddle, stared down the long hill.

"General Washington, may I be allowed to volunteer my services as quartermaster general of this command?"

"We are grateful for your service, Mr. Greene."

THE CONGRESS RELUCTANTLY APPROVED WASHINGTON'S SELECtion, and within days, Greene had made a loud presence before the Board of War, had inserted himself into the comfortable parlors of the men who had been so free in their criticism and campaigns against Washington. The congress began to hear another side of Gates' story, Greene visited in York by Morgan and Stirling, men who told their own tales of Saratoga, who gave many in the congress a different view of Gates and his friend Conway.

Greene inserted himself as well into the soft complacency of the commissary offices, with a fiery impatience for the bumbling and bickering of the quartermaster staff. Though some took immediate offense at this intrusion into their private domain, others accepted Greene's authority, and Washington began to hear a new rumbling from York, that the rusted machinery that had caused so much suffering to his army might finally begin to move.

A LETTER HAD COME FROM LAFAYETTE, AND WASHINGTON READ THE report with a mix of anger and relief. The Board of War had made loud its boasts to the young Frenchman that three thousand troops would be waiting for his arrival in Albany, fully prepared for the march into Canada. They would be joined as well by an outpouring of militia from the area, the call going out to so many of those who had served Gates' command against Burgoyne. But Lafayette arrived in Albany to find that the troops numbered barely over a thousand and that no one had made any effort to bring out the militia units at all.

The army had never been able to mount a successful invasion of Canada, and despite his faith in Lafayette's zeal and ability, this mission had never inspired Washington's confidence. The mission was simply halted, and he was relieved that the young man would return to Valley Forge, to wait with the rest of the command for the new campaigns of spring.

Washington ordered Lafayette's letter copied and sent to the congress. Now, the Board of War would discover that their casual planning and boisterous predictions had collapsed around them, that men who shaped and viewed their strategy through the bottom of a wineglass could not manipulate his army for their own designs. It was a public embarrassment to the Board of War, and a hard blow to those who had championed Horatio Gates as their one true military leader.

At Valley Forge, Martha's presence added a softness to the headquarters that brought other wives to camp, Kitty Greene, Lucy Knox, and a subdued but refreshing social scene. There would not be the finery and ballroom antics of the British, but muted gatherings more fitting to the mood of the army, to the resources they could muster, and the gentle style of the one woman who brought it together.

The wagon that had followed Martha into camp had brought the small luxuries that would most readily survive the journey, cheese and nuts, hard breads and dried fruit. It was a welcome addition to the typical routine, and now, in the cold evenings, the headquarters was a softer place, a beacon of candlelight. The mood of the house spread to the army as well, and even the angry protests from men who had seen neither meat nor rum were muted by her presence.

By late February, there was a new routine, music and singing, even Washington aware that the army was changing, the horrors and sacrifice now a shared experience that united the men in their cause. There was no militia now, the army at Valley Forge did not suffer from the sudden loss of regiments, or the sudden arrival of raw, undisciplined troops. There were few expiring enlistments, the men more focused on enduring the rest of the winter with as little misery as the weather would offer and as much sustenance as the new quartermaster could provide.

They had visitors still, and Washington relied on Martha's natural cordiality with the civilians. With the foreign soldiers, Washington had accepted his role, had become practiced at diplomacy. The congress had been chastened, was not as likely to bestow vast authority on every European officer who demanded it. But the foreigners continued to come, some smarting from the lack of gratitude from the congress, some just seeking their opportunity for glory and adventure. As the papers were forwarded to Valley Forge, one man stood out, and Washington had taken special note, the man carrying a letter from Ben Franklin. He was a Prussian, unusual, and word came to Washington that the man had impressed the congress with the same humility they had seen in Lafayette. Like the young Frenchman, he came only as a volunteer, sought service by any means Washington himself would suggest. Washington found himself eager to meet this man who had both charmed and impressed his American hosts, this man who carried such lofty credentials, such a close relationship to Frederick the Great. The Prussian king was Europe's finest soldier, and now, Washington would receive into his army one of King Frederick's most celebrated aides, Baron Frederick von Steuben.

FEBRUARY 23, 1778

He waited just beyond the outposts on the road that came from York. His guards were in formation behind him, a wide arcing line, several of his staff just inside their ranks. Washington held the horse in the middle of the road, watched as a cluster of riders made their way up a long hill, the horses stepping high through a fresh layer of loose snow. He caught sight of a dog, a thin rail of an animal, bounding rapidly behind the horses.

They were close enough that he could see the details of their uniforms, and he thought, American, how odd. Well, perhaps not so odd after all. If they are to serve in this army, they should dress the part. How better to make a favorable impression, especially for a man who claims to serve as a volunteer. It was obvious which one was von Steuben, an older man, large in the saddle. There was something on the man's chest, bouncing as he rode, a large flat disc, a medal nearly the size of a bread plate. There was another medal as well, pinned in place, a massive star, and as the man rode closer, Washington could see bits of color, the star encrusted with jewels. The parade halted, only a few yards in front of him, and Washington looked at the older man, said, "General von Steuben, welcome to Valley Forge. Welcome to the army of the United States of America."

The man nodded, formal, did not smile, and another man rode forward, said, "General Washington, I am Peter Duponceau, aide and secretary to General von Steuben. I also serve as the general's interpreter. General von Steuben is somewhat deficient in his use of the English language. However, I assure you, this will not be a disadvantage. I am instructing him daily. The general is most joyful to make your acquaintance, sir."

Von Steuben made a brief, curt smile, said something in German, and Washington felt awkward, did not enjoy interpreters.

"I was not aware General von Steuben did not . . . um, well, no matter. Thank you, Mr. Duponceau. Your presence is most welcome."

There was a low voice behind him, and Hamilton said, "Sir, with your permission, does the general speak French?"

Washington looked at Duponceau, who said, "Most assuredly."

Hamilton rode forward, said, "Sir, if you will allow, I can assist as well."

"Very well. General von Steuben, this is Major Hamilton of my staff."

Hamilton made a slight bow, said something in French, and von Steuben responded with a brief word, another polite smile. Washington said, "We should retire to the camp. General, if your men will accompany us."

The parade began to move, von Steuben easing his horse up just behind Washington. It was more formality than Washington required, and he thought, Probably a European custom. I should tell him to ride beside me. He glanced back, saw Duponceau, and the man caught his look, moved quickly forward.

"Sir? May I be of service?"

The dog was now out in front of him, a prancing, delicate gait, then suddenly racing out into the trees, and von Steuben gave a quick shout, the dog quickly returning to the road. Washington could not help thinking of Charles Lee, the man's fixation on dogs, noisy hounds accompanying him everywhere. But von Steuben bore no other resemblance to Charles Lee, and Washington put the unfortunate comparison aside, realizing Duponceau was beside him still.

"May I inquire . . . the breed of dog?"

"It is an Italian greyhound, sir. A special favorite of the general."

"Greyhound. Very well. Uh, Mr. Duponceau, it is not necessary for the general to ride behind me. In this army, we prefer not to be so formal. Please ask if he would care to ride alongside."

Duponceau eased back, and in a short moment von Steuben moved up next to him, said something in French. Washington heard a short laugh, and behind him Hamilton said, "My apologies, sir. Forgive my outburst."

Washington looked at von Steuben, examined the man's martial bearing, riding stiffly upright in the saddle, the amazing medals displayed on the man's broad chest. The Prussian acknowledged the glance, a crisp nod, and Washington said, "Will someone kindly inform me what he said?"

Hamilton was close to him now, said, "He is honored, sir, to be riding beside the king of America."

31. VON STEUBEN

It was like nothing von Steuben had ever seen, drummers and musicians filling the cold air with discordant noise, the spectacle of what could have been so many vagabonds and high-waymen gathered into loose formations of order. But if the appearance of Washington's army was a shocking surprise, the shock was deepened by the number of troops. When the cabins had emptied, and the lines formed, he could make an estimate of the strength of this army, the force that would soon be called upon to resume their fight. He didn't know how many men were sick, or on leave, or how many had simply disappeared into the countryside. But in front of him now, shivering in respectful silence, stood no more than five thousand men.

He had been misinformed of the dress of the continental officer, and before he left France, he had adorned himself and his staff in coats that he soon learned bore an unfortunate resemblance to the scarlet facings of the British. He wisely accepted the stern advice from sympathetic militia officers, had secured a coat of blue, his staff doing the same. But a Continental uniform did not guarantee safe passage, nor a warm meal. Though they had received hospitality, they were also confronted by unexpected hostility, and the message had been made plain. This was a divided land, peopled by those whose loyalties lay clearly in two separate camps. It was his first surprise, that not every American believed in this Revolution, that from one farmhouse to the next might come a complete change in sympathy, some of these people still holding tightly to their allegiance to King George.

Von Steuben had left the Prussian army nearly fifteen years before, something the congress did not know, and something Franklin had neglected to mention in his letter. A man whose talents were distinctly military had endured difficult years as a civilian, and when von Steuben had recently sought another military position, King Frederick had advised him to travel to France. Every soldier knows that war creates opportunity, and despite the glowing portrait Ben Franklin had painted for the congress, von Steuben had gone to France merely in search of much-needed employment. Now, on the snowy plateau of Valley Forge, he had been received and celebrated as an honored guest.

As he studied the army he had come to serve, as he pored through the records Washington provided him, studied the structure and behavior of the Continental Army, his thoughts turned to those skills he had already mastered. Von Steuben understood more than any man in America the kind of discipline and training that was required to stand up against the might of the British.

Throughout that first inspection of the army, he had seen not only the tragedy of their dress, but the pride in their brotherhood. As he and Washington had ridden slowly through the formation, they had saluted him with raucous cheers. He knew that Washington had intended it to be a show for the Prussian. But von Steuben saw their faces, could see where the attention was focused, knew that their show of emotional enthusiasm was less for some Prussian soldier than for their commanding general. It was the intangible ingredient of every great army, the love of the troops for the leader they served. Despite his dismay at their appearance, he could feel that these men bore the hearts of soldiers, that strange and frightening force that drove men to march into the guns of their enemy. It was the first great challenge to building an effective army, and Washington had already put it behind them. To von Steuben, it was the first encouraging sign, the one piece of hope he could muster for the duty that still faced these men.

Organizing the departments, the accounting for supplies and munitions, the process of leave and enlistment, all had their priority. But papers and files and the staffing of offices could wait. Nothing was as important as the training of the men.

MARCH 1778

Von Steuben had assembled a hundred men, a select few chosen from each division, those whose sense of discipline had been made clear, either on the battlefield, or on the march. Most were junior officers, all were young, and von Steuben had marched them to a quiet patch of open ground, out away from the eyes of the rest of the camp.

They stood in a column of two, and he rode the horse down alongside them, tried not to notice the amazing lack of clothing. Behind him, the two American aides, Captains North and Walker, gave instructions, straightened the formation. He rode again to the front of the column, sat stiffly up on his horse, said to North, "Line of battle. With all haste."

The shout went out, and the men began to shift their ground, from the vertical to the horizontal, the men gathering in a ragged crowd, then spreading to the sides. Within a minute or more they were facing him in two wide rows, the men pulling themselves close beside each other, eliminating any gaps in the line. They were looking at him now with satisfied smiles, and he showed no change in his expression, said, "Return to column of march."

The men began to shift again, the lines collapsing into a stumbling mass, one man falling, knocking another man to the ground. The collisions were many, and the men down in the snow were laughing, one man launching a snowball at another. Gradually they shifted back into line, some of them laughing still, but coming to some kind of order.

"Gentlemen, if this was a battle, you would not be so concerned with repeating this move. You would all be dead, probably by the bayonet of the Hessians."

The laughter had stopped, and he motioned to his aides, said, "Captain North, Captain Walker, assume a position at the head of each line." He moved the horse around to the side, said, "You will follow the steps of the man in front of you. When he turns, he will pivot sharply. You will do the same. When he stops, you will stop. When he resumes his march, you will resume yours. Captains North and Walker will begin the shift. From column of march to line of battle. Now!"

The two aides made their turns, the men close behind, following. As more of the line made the turn, the crispness dissolved, the men at the rear still milling slowly past.

"No! Crisp! Pivot! By damned, we will do this again! No! Better I will show you!"

He climbed down from the horse, grabbed a musket from one of the men, glanced at the rusty bayonet, could see a coating of rust on the barrel as well.

"This is a disgrace! Before you complete these lessons, you will learn to care for your weapon. You will understand that a bayonet is not a tool for you to roast your supper!" He pulled the musket close to his chest. "Now, you will march . . . the order to halt! Now, the order to shift to column . . . so! Pivot . . . turn . . . *crisply*!"

He made the move again, swung the musket up to his chest, marched with a high stiff kick, prancing his way across the snowy field, a one-man army. He stopped now, stood stiffly, the musket straight down by his side.

"You are facing the enemy! You will wait for the order! The officer will give the order to load, thus!" He reached into his belt, pulled a nonexistent musket ball from an imaginary cartridge box, went through the motion of loading the musket.

"See? Now, the officer will order you to firing position!"

He dropped to one knee, raised the musket to his shoulder.

"Fire! *Powwww!* Now, the enemy is fleeing before you! The officer orders . . . charge bayonets!" He jogged forward now, the musket pointing straight out, made a high-pitched scream, "Aaaaaaaaaa!"

He stopped, slashed and cut the musket through the air, then suddenly stood at attention again, the musket by his side.

"The enemy is defeated! He has retired from the field! He could not stand up to your discipline!"

He realized he was exhausted, felt his breathing, sweat in his clothes, saw now embarrassment on the faces of his aides. Across the field, he heard the sound of cheering, saw that he had an audience, a thin line of men ringing the field. Now the cheering was close by, the men in his formation joining in, some bending over with laughter, men dropping to their knees. He looked down for a moment, thought, Yes, a comical sight, certainly. The only man on this field who knows what a soldier must do. He handed the musket to Walker, moved to the horse, North holding the reins. He climbed up, the laughter now growing quiet.

"This amuses you, gentlemen. Enjoy your moment of levity. But you will perform this drill a hundred times . . . a thousand times. When you leave this field, you will perform it in your dreams, you will march these steps in your mind while you eat, while you perform your toilet. When I release you from this field, you will return to your regiments, and you will perform this for your men, *you* will be the teacher. If you do not think of this as important, then you will not survive against your enemy. I assure you, General Howe's soldiers have performed this exact drill, they can perform it in the darkest night, in a driving rain, and they can perform it perfectly as they die from your musket fire." He paused, looked out over the faces, saw all eyes watching him. "Without drill, an army is nothing more than a mob. Without drill, a soldier is a musket with one ball. When that ball is discharged, there is nothing remaining. That is when you die by the bayonet. Have any of you ever participated in fisticuffs?"

There were low laughs, and several hands were raised.

"Yes, well, this very method of drill will assure your victory in a one-man war as well. Two men, shouting angrily at each other, then the blows come, a rapid uncontrolled flailing of arms and fists. Is that familiar?"

There were nods, small comments, mostly agreement.

"I would offer you an advantage. If you ever find yourself in the unfortunate circumstance of such combat, remember this drill. Why? When your opponent begins his wild assault, you take one step back, you wait for the moment, you might even endure his blows, the ridiculous meaningless pummeling, but you are skilled, you are disciplined, you will wait. You focus on your target, and you make one solid punch, you launch your disciplined assault right at his vulnerable point. With one sharp precise blow, you will defeat him. It is no different than facing a thousand men. It is the difference between a mob and an army. Discipline, patience, the carefully aimed maneuver, the perfectly placed blow. I assure you. General Howe knows this. King Frederick the Great knows this. Now . . . *you* know it. It is my duty to prevent you from forgetting it."

HE GAVE THE HUNDRED MEN THE TITLE OF *INSPECTORS*, AND WITHIN days, the continuous drill had shaped them into the teachers he required them to be. It was not always smooth, and he was not always as controlled with his temper as he hoped to be, but even his fury was endearing. More, the inspectors were impressed by von Steuben's willingness to embarrass himself, the prestigious officer who would soil his boots, shoulder a musket, kneel and crawl and march in their lines. As the first inspectors gained their skill, others began to line up, volunteering to become his next company of students, and thus, teachers themselves.

Though his focus remained tightly on the men close at hand, he could not avoid being distracted by the one blue-coated horseman who would appear occasionally among his audience. Washington did not come often, but come he did, and von Steuben would snap his men into line, the volume of his words just a bit louder, a discreet glance toward the big man on the white horse who would observe only awhile, then move away to other duties. After so many days von Steuben had come to understand that Washington was a man of few compliments, few outbursts of emotion. But if the words weren't spoken, von Steuben had seen it in the man's eyes, Washington's quiet approval. The men in the drill knew, and now, their commander did as well. The army was indeed changing its shape.

HE HAD MADE THE ACQUAINTANCE OF ALL OF WASHINGTON'S SEnior commanders, had felt the bonds between those for whom Washington seemed to have a special respect. Nathanael Greene came to headquarters many times, and those who dared to speak behind his back did so well out of the presence of Washington himself. Greene seemed to possess a Prussian's impatience, and von Steuben was surprised to learn that the man had no background as a soldier. There were jealousies toward the man, some minor complaining that Washington relied on the Rhode Islander to an extreme. The complaints were few though, and even the men who groused quietly that Greene had not actually accomplished much on the battlefield seemed to believe that if the crisis came, he would be the man to emerge.

Von Steuben was making regular visits to headquarters, a guest for dinner nearly three times per week. The makeshift dining room was always crowded, a mingling of senior officers, staff, cooks and maids, and the wonderful company of the women. He had taken immediately to Martha, the quiet smiling woman, always polite, always gracious, a kind word at every turn. But her soft graciousness could not hide a hard core of authority, and von Steuben knew that the headquarters was not managed by the instruction of the commanding general. It was run by his wife.

He took his time reaching the headquarters, knowing he was still somewhat early for dinner. He enjoyed walking through the camp, appreciated the cordiality of the troops, something rare in European armies. As he stepped carefully down the snowy hill, his mind was focused, his latest project, a means of shortening the Prussian Manual at Arms, a version that might be distributed on paper to every company of men. He stepped along the icy banks of a small creek, thought, It must be brief, concise, something that can be learned in days, not months. Yet it must contain the essential formations, commands. He stopped, looked across the muddy snow to the house, the tall plume of gray smoke rising above. He could feel the softness under his boots, the snow melting, the creek more muddy than frozen. He studied the open ground, thought, Yes, it will be spring soon. He looked down toward the river, beyond the house, could see speckled patches of white and pink spread through the thickets of brush, the first buds, trees with names he didn't know. He glanced down to the mud caking his boots, thought, That will be a problem. The roads will swallow an army, so no one will move for a while. But it will dry quickly. Already the warm air is coming. He looked down into the creek, the water moving in a narrow swift rush, driven by the thaw on the hill behind him.

He thought of the day's drill, the formations. In Europe, men train for months to be called recruits. Here, we must train in weeks to be called soldiers. What army in Europe would endure what these men have suffered? He heard it still, the cries that met every officer, every tour by any man on horseback, from Washington to the occasional civilian. They call out from their dismal beds, *no meat, no soldier*. They make their protest, and then . . . they go about their duty. In Europe, this army would have simply dissolved, great bloody riots. He looked at the house again. They would come here as a mob, would have destroyed this place, taken every scrap of clothing and food, stolen every boot, and if the officers could not escape, they would be hanged. But the Americans . . . simply endure. If this army prevails in this war, it may be by the very suffering they have endured here, by their very survival. It is as if they understand that their cause is more important than their suffering. The British will never understand that. Even King Frederick would not understand. In Prussia, Austria, France, you instruct a soldier what to do, and he does it. Here, you tell them and they ask . . . why? Give us a good reason. If the reason is adequate, the deed is accomplished. It is a curious people.

He saw guards emerging from the house, the young Captain Gibbs now stepping down, the men moving away from the house, toward the creek. Gibbs saw him, seemed surprised, said, "General von Steuben, may I help you, sir?"

He could hear the distinct Virginia accent in the man's voice, so different from the New England men.

"No, thank you, Captain. I'll be to dinner now."

"General Washington is in the dining cabin, sir. If there's anything at all we can do, please inquire."

The young man moved away, the guards falling into line behind him, a slow march toward their quarters. They hopped across the creek in turn, the mud splattering beneath them, and von Steuben watched them for a long moment, then made a wide step across the creek himself, moved to the door of the house.

THE DINNER WAS COMPLETE, BROUGHT TO A CLOSE BY A SONG, AN unfamiliar melody, words von Steuben didn't know. It had been Mrs. Washington's idea, a frequent conclusion to the meals now, something prayerful, solemn. He had tried to follow the words, could understand that it was a call for mercy, for sparing the lives of the young. He had stayed quiet, absorbing their mood, had focused on Washington, could see the man staring downward, his eyes closing, the words filled with obvious meaning. But when the song was finished, the mood passed, the officers and their wives rose from the table, solemnity giving way to smiles and cordiality. It was another of those odd American habits, finding a moment to reflect solely on the sadness, the horror of the world beyond these pleasant walls. As he stepped out into the chilly night, he thought, It is another difference, something that separates them from Europe. So often the foreign officers are men of high breeding and titled family, so far removed from the rabble of their army. They command vast armies of men they rarely see, and certainly never speak to, soldiers whose lives are reduced to sketches on paper, to lines of a map. The generals learn it from their monarchs, those who are barricaded in their own grand palaces, removed farther still from the people whose lives they hold in their hands. It is no wonder these men love their commander. It is an emotion that flows in both directions.

The party was dispersing, Washington's staff assisting the ladies to their waiting carriages. Washington was not there, and von Steuben thought, He is already into the main house. Duponceau had pointed it out to him his first few days in the camp, Washington's private entryway, the escape route from the social scene that might otherwise capture him in the dining area. It was a narrow door, cut into the side of the main house, that led directly to Washington's office. Von Steuben looked at the guard, ever-present, one of Gibbs' Virginians, a gruff-looking man who stood squarely in front of the door. Von Steuben smiled, thought, Not everything about this army is so casual.

He moved around the outside of the house, climbed the steps, moved inside, found himself alone in the hall. To one side he could hear the clatter of pewter dishes in the kitchen, small talk from the maids. He lingered in the hall for a moment, saw the glow of light from the far end of the hall, Washington's office, and now a voice behind him, "General, are you lost?"

He turned, was towering over the petite round woman, said, "Mrs. Washington . . . no, not lost. Waiting. A moment only."

"Are you waiting to see my husband? I am certain he is alone. Most everyone has retired. I was preparing to do the same."

"Oh, thank you, yes. I will see him. Only a moment."

She was smiling at him, the contagious softness that brought out a smile of his own.

"Are you not married, General? Your wife would certainly be welcome in this camp."

"Oh, no, there is no wife. Difficult for me . . . my duties."

"Forgive me, General. I do not mean to be impolite. I must say, your English is improving rather nicely."

"Thank you, *ma'am*." He exaggerated the word, the touch of Virginia, and she laughed, her hand covering her mouth.

"I am proud to say, ma'am, I have entirely read *Robinson Crusoe*."

"Marvelous, General. You should be proud. I shall be pleased to send for more books, if you would like. I believe everyone in this army would be honored by your efforts at our language. Many of the European officers have done very well with their

English. My husband tells me that General Lafayette is nearly flawless."

"Ah, yes. I do not meet General Lafayette yet, ma'am."

"I have not either, General. He is to return here soon, I believe. My husband has a great affection for the young man. I am looking forward to making his acquaintance. I have never known my husband to make such a fuss over one of his officers. He regards General Lafayette very much as he would his own son."

Von Steuben smiled again, had run out of words. He began to feel awkward, and she looked away, said, "Dear me, General, I truly must retire. I'm certain my husband will be pleased by your visit. I do not know any reason why you must continue to wait in the hall."

He made a deep bow, realized she had sensed the uncomfortable moment, had removed it with the skill of a perfect hostess.

"Mrs. Washington, it has been my pleasure to speak for you."

She laughed, her hand again on her mouth.

"Not quite correct, General. You're learning though. Good evening, sir."

She began to climb the stairs, and he waited for a moment, could hear her steps above him. He looked again down the hall, heard nothing from Washington's office. He eased closer, made a sharp rap on the wall, peeked around the edge of the door, said, "General? Permit me, sir?"

Washington was at the tall desk, sat back, said, "Mr. von Steuben, by all means. Please, come in. Sit there."

Von Steuben obeyed, kept his back straight, his hands at his sides. Washington said, "I did not see Mr. Duponceau this evening. Is he feeling all right?"

"Oh, quite, yes, sir. I excused him. I wished to . . . speak without him tonight."

"Very well. Excellent. I admire the young man. Difficult duty, being an interpreter. I cannot imagine seeing my words pass through another man. Something is surely lost." Washington seemed concerned, said, "If I am speaking too rapidly . . . please tell me."

"Oh, no, sir. Not at all. It is good for my lessons. I can understand . . . mostly." Von Steuben tried to relax, always felt tense around Washington, realized now it was the first time they had ever been alone.

"Did you wish to speak to me?"

"Oh, General, I apologize. I should not take your time."

"Speak to me, General."

"Sir, I observe your Captain Gibbs."

"Caleb Gibbs? Yes, I selected him myself, captain of the guard. I know his family well. Is there some problem?"

"Oh, no, sir. Well, yes. Problem is that your guard is . . . all from Virginia, correct?"

"Yes. I required loyalty, General. In the beginning of this campaign, there was discussion in this army about hostility between the states. I regret some of that still prevails. It was thought that a guard from New Hampshire or New Jersey might not be so . . . efficient as one from my home. Virginians would tend to be more protective of Virginians."

Von Steuben was frowning now.

"You don't agree, General?"

"I agree with the . . . principle. But I disagree that it is necessary today. In fact, sir, I am feeling it is wrong. It could be a problem."

Washington seemed surprised, said, "Please continue."

"Sir, you have soldiers here from all over America. From what I see, they all follow you as their commander. This entire army is example of loyalty for the world. It is amazement. I have a suggestion, sir. I believe it is better for this army if you return their loyalty."

"How do you mean?"

"They show you their loyalty. Show yours . . . to them. Your guard should be from each state. You select a few men from each state, you send message to all states. You respect *them*, you believe they will serve you as well as Virginians. Captain Gibbs, if he is a good officer, he can command more than just Virginians."

Washington stared at him for a long moment, seemed to ponder the thought. Von Steuben felt uneasy, the tenseness returning, and Washington began to nod slowly, pointed his finger at him, said, "An unprejudiced eye. I am not accustomed to that in this command. I believe you are correct. Very well, if I am to have personal guards from every state, you will select them for me."

Von Steuben was flattered.

"Yes, sir. I am happy to, sir."

He was already thinking of the men from his drill classes,

several who had stood out, who had shown a quick grasp of the lessons.

"I will begin tomorrow, sir. I should retire, now, sir. I have used your time too much."

Washington looked at his desk, held up a piece of paper.

"*This* is how my time is spent, General. I was writing another letter to congress. I write perhaps ten per week. It is the most tedious duty of this command. This particular letter . . . I am attempting to inspire some of those gentlemen down there to compel their home states to release new recruits to this army. The states continue to raise regiments, and are then determined to keep them within their borders as local defense forces. I have tried to communicate the obvious, that neither Delaware nor Connecticut nor New Hampshire is presently under siege."

Von Steuben could hear the weariness in his voice, said, "Forgive me, sir. I do not understand so much of this . . . congress. In Europe, that word has become exalted. All that we know from Philadelphia, your Declaration of Independence. Inspires great respect, your congress is such men of character. When I visited through York, I saw . . . please, I am apologizing, sir."

"Speak your mind, General. We are alone here."

"There were but few. I hoped to see great hall of men, debating issues. I saw instead . . . parties. Food and wine. I was invited to stay, very kind hospitality. But I could not see that anyone there was fighting a war."

Washington smiled, but von Steuben could see it was not good humor.

"Very astute observation, General. I cannot compel them to do anything they do not wish to do. And yet, my authority rests solely in their hands."

"But . . . the states. The congress has no authority to the states?"

"That's the most serious difficulty facing this army, General. Congress represents the American people, but it has no real authority. Congress can make requests of the state assemblies, but it cannot compel anything. My army is a continental army, composed of men from all thirteen states. This war is a war of independence for all thirteen states. But no state is obliged to offer support to the men who cross beyond their borders."

"Sir, you are saying that this army fights for a government that is not . . . real. It has no power. How do you fight a war?"

"This is a war about an ideal, General. The American people are united in a cause. If we lose this war, if I am captured, I will likely be hanged. Every one of my officers here faces the same fate. Even . . . you. But what the British, what King George does not understand is that what happens to this army is not important. The *cause* cannot be defeated. No king, no army can capture a man's mind, or the minds of an entire country. There is inspiration in that, General. In some ways, the American people have already won this war, because they have experienced what it is like to cast off an oppressive ruler. They have come to accept that they have rights, that no supreme power can command any of us to bow before him, except the Almighty God."

"But, sir, what if you *win* this war? You have no government?"

Washington looked down at his desk, thought a moment.

"General, in a hall in Philadelphia, I was a witness to an extraordinary gathering of genius. Those men helped create this war by creating the foundation on which we fight. If we triumph in battle, those men, or men just like them must undertake a new responsibility. We are saying to England, your system does not work here. We will build our own system, and we *will* make it work. Despite all that I have experienced with this new congress, General, I must believe that we *can* make it work. I must hold to the faith that driving the British from this land is not the conclusion of our efforts, but the beginning. None of us can say what will follow. But the American people have come too far simply to turn back, to return to the domination of a king who regards this nation as his own property, to abuse and exploit as he will. It is my job to fight, General. If we are victorious, the job of creating a government, of creating a nation . . . that will fall to someone else, a congress perhaps, some gathering of the same genius that has brought us this far. If that does not occur, if it is not within us to create something permanent here, to give meaning to *America* . . . then there is no reason for us to fight this war."

32. HOWE

THE PLAY WAS *HENRY IV, PART ONE,* AND HE HAD WHISKED HIS MIS-
tress through the hall in a flurry of color, her gown swirling
around them in a grand display that was meant only for her. He
knew she enjoyed the attention, seemed oblivious to the stares
and low comments. He paid little attention to the response from
the other officers, and even less to their disapproving wives.
Those voices were faint enough as it was, muted by the overwhelming number of officers whose arms were draped by mistresses of their own. Many were a product of the hospitality of
Philadelphia, some had come from England. By now, any mention of scandal was nearly rehearsed, simply a part of the show,
of each evening's entertainment. It had become the dreary routine, the long winter evenings punctuated by whatever form of
gala could be arranged. The effort came primarily from Major
John André, a man who seemed adapted to life in the center of a
social whirlwind. André had organized the theater company, was
usually its star actor, a man clearly at home in front of an adoring
audience, especially an audience of so many women. He was the
perfect man to lighten the dark mood of winter, to fill the calendar with every manner of ball and celebration, plays and perfor-
mances by anyone who might break the monotony of winter
quarters. The manic social scene had been a delight to Howe, for
a while. But the plays were becoming redundant, only so many
roles for André to master, only so many times Howe could sit
through yet another performance of Shakespeare. Tonight had
been a particular chore, and despite the delight of Mrs. Loring's
parade through the crowd, Howe had finally conceded, he had
absorbed as much of Philadelphia as he could. He was bored to
death.

The daylight hours were passed by the occasional drill, some meaningless march by some regiment through the streets, the unnecessary reminder of their presence to a civilian population who were increasingly hostile to the army in their midst. There was little of Philadelphia that reminded any of its citizens of what once was, not even to the most basic functions of government. The British had swept aside any municipal position, from police to street cleaning, all administration now a part of the army's duty. The city was, after all, a fortress, the home to a British force that numbered nineteen thousand men. There was no place in the daily routine for the concern of private citizens, while the army's needs were so great. The result was a city that was falling slowly into ruin. Howe avoided the unpleasantness of the filthy streets, kept himself behind closed doors of the mansion that was his headquarters. As the snow had melted, the smells had emerged, and he avoided the inquiries that came even from his own generals. From civilian and soldier came the protests for how the sanitary concerns could have been ignored, and what might be done now that the spring thaw was certain to ripen the sewers even more. The civilians were actually becoming organized in their protests, and he had deflected the outcry from some annoying committee by simply blaming the Hessians. He had sent an official complaint to General Knyphausen, pointing out the unfortunate habit of the Hessians to stable horses inside various homes, and worse, to deal with their sanitary problems by shoveling the manure straight into the basements. With the warmer weather, the consequence of that was driving even the Hessians to find different quarters, the houses they left behind utterly destroyed. When Howe first learned of this unusual form of abuse, he was amused by the Hessian efficiency. When his remedy had no effect, either on Knyphausen or the outrage of the citizens, he issued a new order, this one to the civilians. Anyone who sought to interrupt the business of the army by voicing loud protest was offered the opportunity to leave, a subtle suggestion that they should perhaps make arrangements to join Mr. Washington at *his* camp.

As the distractions of theater and Mrs. Loring had begun to grow stale, he had taken to the faro hall, a gambling den established to provide entertainment even to the lowest-ranking officers. It was yet another scandal, and he endured another round of complaints, some of the commanders speaking out on behalf of their subordinates. The card game was less entertainment than a place for young lieutenants and captains to be sheared with the precision of a barber, and throughout the winter, some of the least experienced officers had gambled themselves into bankruptcy, some even forced to resign their commissions. Howe's investigation of the game had been conducted by means of his regular participation. Whether or not the game was honest hardly mattered. General Howe seemed to win with astounding regularity. Any further complaints were simply ignored.

IS THERE STILL NO ATTACK TO BE MADE?"

The room was quiet, no one willing to respond, and he looked toward Charles Grey, said, "Well, General? Are we to sit here, captive in our own complacency?"

Grey was an older man, thoroughly capable, and Howe had always felt the man's subtle lack of respect.

"I have made my reports previously, General Howe. I have no reason to amend them."

"Ah, yes, indeed, General Grey. I am merely attempting to make more current that which I must communicate to Lord Germain. By your reports, then, I may advise the ministry that the rebels have continued to occupy an unassailable position at Valley Forge. Any attempt on our part to dislodge them would cost us far more than the benefits to be gained. Is that our consensus?"

He scanned the room, saw dull stares, some heads down, still no one speaking.

"Now, gentlemen, let us not give these meetings such a downward cast. Despite what may be transpiring in Parliament, or what excuses General Burgoyne may be presenting there on his own behalf, it is not *this* army who has suffered a defeat. It is not *this* army who has forced Lord Germain and Lord North to champion the cause of capitulation to the rebels. No, gentlemen, *this* army is holding well to its guns! Spring is drawing close! No matter what superior position Mr. Washington now commands, the rebel army is disintegrating before our very eyes! Once conditions permit, our new campaign will make short work of our foe, and of this war!"

He concluded the meeting, did not speak to anyone as they left the grand hall, the dining room of his headquarters. He stayed in his chair, waited for the last man to leave, Knyphausen, the old Hessian looking at him with undisguised sadness. His aides were there now, and he said, "Away! Close the door. Do not disturb me."

The cavernous room was silent, and he sat back in the chair, let the feigned enthusiasm slip away, thought, It was a grand show. But I am truly sick of it, of the advice, of the criticism, of the meaningful glances. What was that look from Knyphausen? Pity? Every one of them knows that this command is tottering on the precipice. He thought of his words, *new campaign*. He had already received instructions from Lord Germain, a shift in strategy. It was widely assumed that the French were close to some agreement with the rebels, and if a French fleet was to throw their weight to the war, it could be a disaster for British land forces. Already, a strong line of British warships was required to maintain the flow of supplies up the Delaware River, and if the French attempted to blockade the waterway, the results could prove disastrous, not just to Howe in Philadelphia, but to Clinton's forces in New York. From Newport to the Chesapeake there was simply not enough British shipping in American waters to protect itself, while also protecting the army. The ministry's answer was to shift the entire focus of the war, from a land-based operation to a naval war. He stared at the table in front of him, reached for the half-empty wineglass, thought, The might of the British, conducting a war of plunder and arson. That's all it will amount to, blockading and burning cities, from Charleston to Boston. No man who has ever been a soldier would agree to such conduct. What honor is there in a war waged from the safety of a ship, against an enemy who can evade you by moving himself a mile inland? What victory can be gained? Asinine!

He had heard of the debates in London, the king's opposition launching an all-out assault against the continuation of the war. The rumors that France would enter the war had rattled the complacency of Parliament, men who might suddenly find their seaside estates under fire from French warships. The opposition leaders had introduced a measure to satisfy all demands of the colonies, to reverse all those policies that had inspired the war in the first place, granting the colonies every demand they had sought except outright independence. Even now, he thought, they are putting the absurd policy into action, a new *peace commission*, preparing to sail over here to . . . what? To pretend this army doesn't even exist? To beg for mercy from that ridiculous congress? This is the cost, this is the price I must pay, the empire must pay for Burgoyne's folly! It is not bad enough that he hurls himself into a wilderness he knows nothing about, that he relies on savages to guide him. Now, while his entire command is held prisoner in Boston, he is allowed to return to London and regale the Parliament with all the justifications for his failure. Certainly he is laying blame squarely at my feet. It is his nature, his very character to cast fault in every direction. How am I to defend myself from so far away? Who will speak for me? My wife?

He had received a letter from his wife, Frances, that she had indeed petitioned the ministry to give him a fair hearing, not to toss away his career solely on the words of John Burgoyne. It was an embarrassment to him, made worse when he learned that his mother, Dowager Countess Howe, had joined in the campaign. We go to war, and it is our women who must do the fighting. Well, my dear, you are not so well informed. I have already sought my relief from this unfortunate predicament. If anyone is to speak on my behalf, it must surely be me. But first, I must be allowed to leave *this* infernal place.

The wave of sniping at his command had begun to reach him only a few weeks after he occupied Philadelphia. News of his victory at Germantown had been received in London with a far different eye than he expected. It was not seen as a victory at all, but another example of his own failure, the opinions voiced loudly in the Parliament that Howe had allowed the rebels to escape yet again. His critics had now become his enemies, their hostility so infecting the ministry that Germain had subtly stripped him of independence. It was not formal, nothing so humiliating. But Howe could feel Germain's intrusions, the increasing flow of dispatches, less of the counseling and more direct instruction. Germain had always given priority to Howe's own strategies, but that had changed. Now the orders were distinct and intrusive and left no room for discussion. With Burgoyne clawing at him as well, Howe had no choice. He could neither defend himself nor command as long as he was in America. The only alternative was to offer his resignation. His brother had done the same, a show of family unity. But Howe knew he was the target, not the admiral. All that remained was the word from Germain. Either the resignation would be accepted, and he could return to London to salvage some piece of his personal honor, or it would be refused.

Refusal meant that Germain would have to back away again, allow Howe to manage his own strategy, that King George had somehow come to Howe's defense. It is the only means I have left, he thought. The only way I can maintain this command is if the king himself supports me. He knew there was one point strongly in his favor. King George despised John Burgoyne.

The meetings with his commanders had become farcical, just like the one he had just concluded. No one would speak openly about anything that was not a safe subject, the old career men like Charles Grey and James Grant already secure enough in their retirement not to cause any ripples now. They all seemed to grow meeker with the absence of Cornwallis.

He could not deny the man's request to sail to England, the same request that a year ago was preempted by Washington's astounding success at Trenton. With Philadelphia secure, and the army firmly in winter quarters, Cornwallis had finally embarked in mid-December. Howe had heard nothing from his friends in London about any kind of intrigue or campaign by Cornwallis against him, thought, No, it is not his way. He has responsibilities of his own, and he is the one man in this command who truly misses his wife. He will enjoy his time there, as he well deserves to do. They will inquire of him though, Germain, North, perhaps even the king. They will seek his version of events, of my fitness for command. Surely he wants command of his own, would accept the promotion with enthusiasm. But it is not his way to conspire, certainly not with Burgoyne.

He finished the wine, set the glass aside, raised himself slowly out of the soft chair. He looked at another chair, the second one on his left. It was the position at the table where Cornwallis always sat, a strange tradition that Howe had never really noticed until recently. I rather miss the man, he thought. The others do as well. They sit around this room like so many stuffed pheasants, no one with an original idea. He will speak up, always has. He is not afraid of giving offense. It is not always the best sort of reputation to have. It has certainly damaged the regard this army has for Henry Clinton. Ah, but they are two different men. Clinton is a man driven by anger, a man who only wants to rule his roost, who will accept no counsel, no argument. It will likely serve him well. He is certainly next in line to *this* command. He moved to the tall windows, stared out at the empty street. He pictured

Clinton in his mind, marching into headquarters like some rabid demon, his first task to sweep away any sign of William Howe. If that day is to come, I will not relish it. If there has been one advantage to our theater of war, it has been that Henry Clinton is far away from me. We have accomplished so much here, so many good fights, so much conquest. We sit here proudly in the enemy's capital, their government vanquished, their army a rotting shambles. And yet, men like Clinton and Lord Germain, even my own generals, Knyphausen certainly, they believe we are losing this war. There is power in that kind of pessimism, the power to drain the fighting spirit from this army. How dare they, after all? I have earned my place at this table. And instead of recognition, I am criticized. This army stands poised, complete, strong, moving into a new spring, what will likely be the final spring of this war. I have never failed to drive the enemy before me, and yet my government despairs that we should fight them from ships.

He heard a small noise out beyond the wide doors, a low voice. The staff waits for me, hovering, as though I should not have a moment's idle time. Well, of course, we must prepare for this evening's gala event, whatever it might be. Wednesday? That would be a ball, dancing to the same dismal musicians, Mrs. Loring positively giddy while I suffer through another minuet.

APRIL 14, 1778

The bundle was small, with few of the usual attachments, no other letters from various ministers, from anyone at all but Lord Germain. The one order was specific and direct. Howe was to send two thousand troops by sea to attack the rebel ports in New England. He tossed the order aside, knew the ridiculous tactic was a simple show of authority. It was a far more complicated maneuver than Germain's stroke with a pen. Weakening his army in Philadelphia was a cataclysmic mistake, that Admiral Howe would argue the move was utterly impractical. But those were petty details, and he could not pretend to care, focused instead on the one other letter, this one more direct still, signed again by Lord George Germain.

. . . General William Howe is officially recalled, his duties concluded as commander-in-chief of British forces in North America . . .

The order was brief, and the final paragraph cut slowly into him like a cold steel sword. His successor had been notified, was already making preparations to sail for Philadelphia. Henry Clinton was now in command of the army.

---

33. WASHINGTON

MAY 3, 1778

HE HAD BEGUN TO HEAR RUMORS, VARIOUS CIVILIAN VISITORS bringing their own version of what might be happening in France. It was all annoyingly vague, and Washington had finally written to congress, requesting some official confirmation, some hint that the rumors might actually be true. But no reply had come, a strange silence from the men who were supposed to know so much about every current event, especially if it involved negotiations with the French government. He considered riding to York himself, to face the men who brought the rumors from France, or those who had the letters in hand. But a journey away from Valley Forge was not a wise idea, even for a day or two. While spies had reported little movement by the enemy, he could not risk a sudden assault from Philadelphia. And there were concerns closer to home. The spring warmth had turned the camp into a quagmire of mud, and with it came always the danger of disease. His priority had to be Valley Forge. What was occurring in France, and what they knew of it in congress, would simply have to wait.

He had ordered a general cleansing of the camp, the cabins emptied of all bedding, the accumulated decay opened up to the warm air. With the cabins clean, the focus turned to the men, and Washington was delighted by the sudden arrival of supplies of soap and vinegar. The men were lined up along the banks of the Schuylkill, and each man was instructed to bathe, allowing himself no more than ten minutes in the water. Washington had always believed, as did his doctors, that immersing a man's body in water for a lengthy soaking could inspire a variety of illnesses. But the caution expressed in his orders was hardly necessary. Despite the welcoming bath, every man who stepped gingerly into the river realized that winter was not so far behind them after all. Even this late in the season, the waters of the river were cascading down from melting ice far upstream. Any man who could actually endure a full ten-minute bath found his skin turning blue.

With the warming air came the pungent aroma of the filthy ground around the cabins. Squads of men were given shovels, the alleys and narrow roads scraped clean, the rancid dirt hauled away. With the melting of the snow, the grass had returned to the fields, and though it was not ideal feed for the horses, they were allowed to graze, as were the small herds of cattle that began to arrive on the hardening roads.

The wagons were arriving with a frequency that surprised everyone in the camp. With a new spirit, and the authority that Greene carried straight into the halls of congress, the supplies had begun to move, a slow trickle that was now widening into a steady flow. From the docks of New England, from the warehouses in Baltimore and Norfolk, wagons were pressed into service, drivers were encouraged by soldiers to perform with a new energy. Even before the weather offered relief to the huddled nakedness of the soldiers, Washington's army began to see meat again, and flour that was untainted by careless handling. In the towns beyond Valley Forge, Greene's men discovered great piles of linen and cotton, the bounty from the French merchant ships, forgotten in seaside warehouses. Making use of the fabric was an overwhelming task for the army's few clothiers, so Greene took the fat rolls of cloth into the towns. In places like Bethlehem and Lancaster, they found women who knew how to sew, who offered their skills as a patriotic service, the one gift they could provide the men of their army. The patriotic pride of a talented seamstress even extended into York, wives of congressmen offering to work as well. What Greene's predecessor had ignored as bothersome cargo, was now cut and fashioned into pants and shirts and stockings, uniforms for men who had for so long gone about their duty in near nakedness. Because of Greene's astounding efforts, Washington realized that so much of the suffering and deprivation his men had endured was due not to a lack of patriotism, nor even a lack of concern in congress. For the most part, it was caused by the astonishing incompetence of the quartermaster department.

HE WAS AT HIS DESK, WAS FORMING THE WORDS, YET ANOTHER PLEA to someone in congress who might settle the nervousness that plagued him still about the rumors from France. He went through the names, thought of Henry Laurens, the president, probably his closest ally in congress. Laurens' son John had become a valuable and efficient member of his staff, and he thought, Perhaps I should have him deliver this letter himself. They might ignore me, but surely Mr. Laurens will not ignore his son. He stared at the blank paper, dipped the pen in the inkstand, held the pen above the paper, but no words came. He stabbed the pen back into the small bottle, said aloud, "I have no patience for this."

He pushed the chair away from the desk, pulled himself up, moved into the hall. There were heavy boot steps on the stairway, and he saw Tilghman step down into the hall, the young man caught by surprise.

"Oh! Sir, may I do something . . . may I be of service?"

"Come with me, Mr. Tilghman. I require some sunshine."

They moved out into the yard, and Washington stepped down into soft mud, saw the grooms responding, the horses led toward them quickly. He climbed up, anchored himself in the saddle, waited as Tilghman did the same. Washington could hear shouts, laughter, said, "That's coming from the river. We should make an inspection. I am in need of good cheer."

He spurred the horse, moved out into the muddy road, down along the bank of the river. The water was swift, no sign of the ice that had lined the banks, and he could hear the laughter again, farther downstream. He pushed the horse through a narrow path in the brush, could see the troops, men barely clothed, jumping into and out of the water, great splashes, thought, Bathing yet again?

"Mr. Tilghman, I thought they had completed this duty. We should not encourage such recreation."

Tilghman was beside him now, said, "I will see to it, sir."

The young man moved forward, and Washington searched the crowd for an officer, someone in command, saw no one he recognized. He felt himself scowling, thought, This is not what I require just now. He jabbed at the horse with his spurs, rode up along a tall bank, could see men now scrambling into the water, then out again. They were not bathing, there was no order, no line. There was motion on the riverbank, small flecks of silver, and he rode closer, eased the horse back down toward the water, could see now, the bank was alive with a slithering mass of fish.

Behind him, more men were shouting, running down from the plateau, joining the commotion, plunging into the river. They carried bits of wood, small pots, blankets, anything that could be used as a scoop. The water was swirling with rippling motion in a section of the river nearly thirty yards long. The shouts brought still more men over the hill behind him. Along the bank, men were tossing their prizes up onto the higher ground, others piling the fish into baskets or larger pots. Tilghman rode back up toward him now, said, "It's a shad run, sir! The river is full of fish!"

"I see that, Mr. Tilghman. Quite a bounty."

He could see the wave of fish passing up to the left, moving away from the gathering of troops. Men were scrambling up the bank, trying to move out in front of the fish, but the swarm was swimming upriver faster than the troops could surround them. Tilghman said, "It seems to be passing, sir. A good catch though. Someone will make a nice feast of this."

Men were pulling themselves out the water, some still carrying their catch, and Washington felt himself opening up to their excitement, said, "I have never seen this before. But they're getting away."

"Yes, sir. It's how it goes. You only catch them when they swim past."

"We shall turn them around then!"

He spurred the horse, moved quickly down to the bank, rode along the edge of the water, caught up to the swirling tide. He looked back, saw men standing in the river, watching him, few moving at all now. He shouted, "Here! I will stop them!"

He pulled hard on the reins, drove the horse straight into the river, the icy water shocking him, soaking his legs. The horse bounced high, reared back, and Washington gripped the reins in one hand, grabbed his hat, waved it low, toward the water. He spun the horse around, and the tide of fish stopped their advance, seemed to back away down the river.

"Now, gentlemen, now! Retrieve them!"

The troops were still watching him with stunned amazement, but finally they understood what he had done. They began to scramble along the bank, some plunging into the water again, into the midst of the fish. The catch began again, the laughter and shouting as men wrestled with fish, gathering them into their arms, tossing them up on the bank. He was still waving the hat, shivering with excitement, soaked through by the cold water. He saw Tilghman on the bank, watching him with a look of panicked concern. He began to laugh along with his men, exhausted soldiers struggling up the bank, some collapsing among the fish. The men were mostly out of the water now, the fish they could not catch slipping past him, out of reach upstream. He eased the horse toward the bank, put the hat on his head, felt the shock of ice water down his neck. The men were cheering him, some holding up fish in both hands, and he climbed the bank, held tightly as the horse shook itself free of the water. Tilghman followed him, and Washington said, "A fine day for a swim, Colonel! A bit chilly yet."

The men were gathering the fish together, hauling them away toward the camp. He sat dripping in the saddle, felt weak with the cold, and the laughter that still rolled out of him.

"A fish dinner, gentlemen! More for salting!"

He waved to the men, heard another round of cheers, said to Tilghman, "I should change my uniform. My wife would have a cross word certainly."

He waved to the men, spurred the horse up the hill, Tilghman close behind. He reached the crest, could see all along the river, the men enjoying their new work, the feast that the entire army would enjoy. He felt the sunshine, stopped the horse.

"I recall our talk in Trenton, Mr. Tilghman."

"Sir?"

"Fishing. I recall that I asked you about fishing."

"Yes, sir. I recall as well."

"This was . . . an adventure. The men enjoyed it, certainly. I don't know how often this sort of . . . shad run occurs."

"It's the springtime, sir. They swim upstream to spawn."

"Ah, of course. The design of the Almighty. This could be more than just an occurrence of nature, Mr. Tilghman. It was a gift, an extraordinary bounty. It is possible that the Almighty is showing us some favor."

"Certainly, sir. This army has endured much."

He felt the sun on his back, a delicious warming. The chill was gone, and he looked upward, closed his eyes, absorbed the heat on his face.

"Indeed, Mr. Tilghman. That we have."

He sat quietly for a long moment, then turned away from the sun. He could see out toward the camp, the commissary officers responding to handle the incredible catch. There was already a sense of order, tables set up for the fish, the process of cleaning them, cloth sacks of salt appearing, barrels of brine. He looked down the long hill to the headquarters, thought of the letter he had tried to write, the annoyance of the day's task. I will not be concerned with that just now. There was another sign here as well, something I should not ignore. There is a spirit to this army, a goodness and a joy in these men that has returned. It is another gift from the Almighty. I will respect that, I will celebrate with them the renewal of our strength, all the good that comes with the new season.

The congress, all his impatience, seemed very far away. He looked back to the river, laughed again, said, "I am fairly certain, Mr. Tilghman, that I have finally experienced a successful day's fishing."

"Yes, sir."

Tilghman didn't sound completely convinced, and Washington looked at the young man, saw a hint of a smile.

"You have something to say, Colonel?"

"Um, no, sir."

"Yes, well, perhaps next time I will attempt to fish from someplace other than the back of a horse."

"Yes, sir."

"You are too serious, sometimes, Mr. Tilghman." He eased the horse forward, saw movement around the headquarters, a rider, and Tilghman said, "It's General Lafayette, sir."

"I see him."

Lafayette rode quickly, pushed the horse up the narrow roadway, and Washington waited for him. The young man was there quickly, his horse bouncing to a sudden stop, and Lafayette said, "General! You should see this, sir!" The young man pulled a newspaper from his coat. "Three days ago, sir! Appears to be a complete text!"

Washington took the paper, saw it was the *Pennsylvania Gazette*, dated May 1. The entire front page was one story, and he fought the sun in his eyes as he read. Lafayette said, "We don't appear to require the confirmation from the congress, sir. Here it is, in full detail."

Washington read further, felt the chill again, but it came not from the water in his clothes, but someplace deep inside of him. He read to the bottom of the page, felt a hard knot in his throat, and Tilghman said, "Sir? What is it?"

He couldn't speak, handed the paper to his aide, looked at Lafayette now, saw tears on the young man's cheek. He nodded, fought his own tears, knew Lafayette was feeling the same emotion, more perhaps. The young man had come to this army as a renegade from his king, and now, in full glorious detail, were the words that Washington had been so desperate to read. King Louis was as committed to their cause as the young marquis. The paper was a full text of the formal alliance between the government of France and the United States of America. No longer would French merchants be forced to perform their business in secret, no longer would the American cause be regarded with hesitation and reluctance. It was the first acknowledgment by a foreign power that America was a nation in its own right and should be free of English control. It was formal recognition, made powerful far beyond the supplying of goods, the extension of credit. France was now preparing to send her own soldiers and warships to American ports, to fight on American soil. France was entering the war.

MAY 6, 1778

It was a grand celebration, a festive display for the entire army. From all over the surrounding countryside, from the towns that had finally risen up to support their troops, the people came, long lines of civilian carriages, entire families, rolling through the outposts of their army to participate in this joyous day. The salutes were boisterous and loud, punctuated by artillery fire, a vast fireworks show for both soldiers and civilians. The parade and festivities would extend throughout the entire day, the army turned out in review, the day concluding with a huge outdoor picnic. It was a marvelous show, and when the civilians finally made their way home, they carried a new appreciation for their army, were surprised by the crisp formations, the precise marching. They had heard all manner of rumor of what was occurring at Valley Forge, the starvation and disease, the army that had virtually ceased to be. But as deep as their surprise, the civilians could not be as profoundly surprised as their commander in chief. Washington had sat tall on the white horse as the men had gone through their drill, had watched in amazement as they performed a stunning feat of musketry, long lines of troops, each man firing his musket in turn, one by one, all along the line, a display of perfect synchronization. It was a show worthy of any professional army in Europe, and Washington had absorbed the spectacle with a brief look to the one man who had brought it into being. Von Steuben had watched the drill with stern-faced pride, the regiments and brigades moving in crisp rhythm, performing the marches with flawless perfection. The Prussian's stiff countenance had broken only once, and he had returned Washington's look with a sly smile, acknowledging his commander's silent salute. He knew, as Washington knew, as every man in formation knew, that this was a different army than what had first come to this place, than the men who had struggled to build their small log city. With the new spring had come a renewed spirit and a new pride. They had, after all, survived the most dire hardships of their lives. And the reward, besides the discipline and camaraderie the Prussian had taught them, was an alliance with France.

For the first time since the war had begun, Washington faced the start of a new campaign with a strange and unexpected eagerness. For the first time, it might not be necessary to wait for the enemy to show his intentions. For the first time, Washington's army was prepared to make a fight on its own terms.

34. GREENE

MAY 19, 1778

HIS VISITS TO THE CAMP WERE MORE FREQUENT NOW. THE QUARTER-master staff in York and in the outposts all through the adjoining states were operating with the same renewed spirit as the army they provided for, and Greene had confidence that they no longer required his heavy hand and his temper to perform their jobs. Though he still held the office, and the responsibility, with the coming of spring came the renewed threat of a campaign by the British, and Washington had made good his promise, that Greene would still hold his command in the field.

He needed very little incentive to return to Valley Forge. When Martha Washington came to headquarters, it had opened the way for other wives as well. Leaving the children in safe hands, Kitty had come down from Rhode Island, she and the infant both now recovered from the difficult ordeal of childbirth. The year before, at Morristown, she had arrived so close to the time the army would return to the field, that their brief time together had been more painful than comforting. But now there was time, and she had made them a home, close to the other commanders' wives. Even if her husband could not always be a part of the dinners and festivities, Kitty Greene had quickly become popular, especially with the foreign officers. She had a moderate skill with French, and opened their quarters to gatherings for those officers whose poor English had often kept them isolated. Her willingness to offer a softer side to conversation was appreciated by the men who had kept so much to themselves, so accustomed only to the companionship of soldiers. She had also become a favorite of Martha Washington, the two women sharing the modest sense of hospitality, both making known their quiet disapproval of card games or excessive drinking. Kitty shared Martha's love for singing, and even if neither woman had a particular talent for the art, together they were formidable partners, could encourage even the most unwilling officer to participate in the after-dinner entertainment.

IT WOULD LIKELY BE A TYPICAL EVENING AT THE HEADQUARTERS, the officers now escorting their wives out of the carriages. He held her arm in his, walked out away from the house, careful to avoid any patches of mud. The roads were hard, broken only by small puddles from a brisk rain shower, a slight chill to the soft morning. But the day had warmed bright and clear, all signs of the dismal winter completely gone. They crossed the road, moved past the blacksmith compound, stepped close to the creek that fed into the Schuylkill. The land was open, gentle hills falling away, another long rise out to the west. There were still flowers on some of the trees, some completely draped in soft white, others flecked with bits of pink and red. But mostly the land beyond was bathed in soft green, the rebirth of woods and open fields. She held tight to his arm, said, "This is a beautiful place. How did you choose it?"

"I had little to do with it. This is close to Anthony Wayne's home. He and General Washington scouted this ground back in December. The French engineer, DuPortail, designed most of the defensive works."

"Oh, yes, of course. Louis."

"*Louis?* You know his name?"

She laughed, said, "You would too if you weren't so formal around those men. Anyone who didn't know the army would walk through here and think every one of you is named *General*."

Greene thought a moment, said, "Do you know General . . . um, Lafayette's name?"

"I believe it is . . . Marie. And General von Steuben is Frederick. His young Mr. Duponceau is . . . Peter."

"Hmph. I never thought of asking."

"Does anyone ever address you as . . . Nat?"

He laughed now.

"Only Daniel Morgan. Calls everyone by their first names, even General Washington. Does break through the stiffness sometimes. Not sure it's good for the army."

They stepped closer to the creek, and he leaned out, looked down into the clear rush of water. He could see a small cluster of minnows, the dark flicker of a tadpole, and he backed away from the edge, knowing she did not enjoy small creatures of any kind.

"We should go to dinner. They're likely being seated now."

He led her back across the road, saw Knox emerging from the mess cabin, the round man coming toward them, quick short steps.

"General! It is confirmed! He will be here tomorrow!"

Greene felt himself sagging, looked past Knox, saw another round form appearing, and Kitty said, "Lucy! Here!"

Lucy Knox moved with the same heavy sway as her husband, joined him, a clasping of thick arms. Greene could not help but share her smile, the one woman who always had something to say, who had added more energy to the camp than anyone had expected. Knox said, "He will arrive tomorrow, General!"

Kitty tugged at him, and Greene knew her question, said, "You are referring to Charles Lee?"

Lucy spoke up.

"Oh, quite! The word is already passing to the entire camp. Quite exciting!"

Knox said, "Yes, indeed! General Washington is organizing a reception, all the senior officers are to ride out on parade, to greet the general when he arrives. It should be an interesting affair, certainly! Well, come along to dinner. General Washington will certainly provide the details."

They moved heavily back toward the dining cabin, and Kitty pulled at him, seemed surprised he did not follow.

"What's wrong, Nat?"

"Wrong? General Charles Lee is coming home. How truly, utterly marvelous."

He did not disguise the sarcasm, and she released him now, faced him.

"Is that not a good thing? I heard they were talking about some sort of an exchange."

"Yes, it was discussed for some time. We released the British general Richard Prescott. He had been captured last summer in Newport. It was considered an equitable trade." He could feel his mood growing darker by the minute. "Damn. I do not understand everyone's enthusiasm. The congress is positively dancing with joy. Most of this army believes his presence is all we require to crush the British."

"You don't? Nat, I have never seen you so . . . agitated."

He looked across to the dining cabin, no one left outside.

"My opinion is of no importance. General Washington requires capable field commanders. It is possibly this army's greatest deficiency. He believes General Lee will make a contribution to our cause. There is nothing more for me to say."

He held out his arm, and she slid beside him. They moved slowly across the road. The wonderful smells were reaching them, and she said something, words that drifted past him. He stared at the ground as they walked, thought only of the scrawny, dirty little man with the yapping dogs. Is it fair of me to hold such a low opinion? He has been away from this army for a long time. Surely he will bring something positive. There is one certainty. The mood of this headquarters is about to change.

MAY 20, 1778

The reception was as Knox described it, officers and guards lining the road in a grand reception line. Greene had watched carefully as Lee approached, looked for some hint of the man's response to this extraordinary show of respect. Washington made the first salute, and Greene saw Lee's curt unsmiling bow to the commander. In his turn, Greene had offered his polite greeting, Lee responding by barely looking at him, moving on quickly to Sullivan, who was next in line. Greene stared straight ahead, the polite show of decorum, could do nothing now but wait for the ceremony to conclude. He was suddenly curious, looked down the line as Lee was introduced to Lafayette. The young Frenchman held out a hand, met Lee with a wide pleasant smile, and Greene winced as Lee ignored the man's hand, responded with silence, a frowning tilt of his head. Lafayette seemed not to notice, discreetly dropped his hand to his side, the smile still in place. Greene felt a hard knot growing in his gut, thought, You cannot even make a show of it? You cannot even offer some small bit of manners?

The introductions and greetings were finally complete, and Greene was relieved when Washington gave the order, the procession falling into line in the road. As they began to move, he took his place in line, saw that he was close behind Lee. He could not avoid looking at the man's uniform, saw that the coat

was somewhat cleaner than he had ever seen it before. Probably
the British, he thought. Dress him up for a fine appearance. They
can't have us think they were mistreating him. I wonder if they
removed the coat before they cleaned it, or just threw him entirely into New York Harbor.

He tried to control the horse, the animal stepping carefully, nervously, as Lee's dogs bounded back and forth in the road. Greene
knew nothing of dogs, saw only barking masses of fur, thought,
Are these the same ones he's always had? How did the British regard *them*? His horse lurched suddenly to one side, and Greene
saw one of the dogs nipping at the horse's leg.

"Be gone! Away!"

The shout broke the quiet solemnity of the parade, and Lee
turned, stared sharply at him. Greene returned the look, then
forced a smile, said, "My apologies, General. My horse is not accustomed to being bitten."

Lee said nothing, turned away, and Greene felt a hard gloom
coming over him. He glanced up ahead, could see the guard
posts flanking the road, Washington leading the officers back
into the camp, the parade coming to a blessed end.

THE DINNER HAD BEEN A SUBDUED AFFAIR, AND WHEN THE PLATES
were cleared Martha had not called them to the hearth for her
usual round of songs. The talk had come mostly from Lee, stories of his captivity, of the fairness and generosity of his hosts,
far too many details of the glorious British dinner tables. Greene
had kept to his manners, inspired by the pleasant smile from
Martha Washington. It was not a time for debate or disagreement, and though Lee's anecdotes were not always in the best
taste, Martha had endured without comment. By the end of the
evening, Greene's patience was a thin taut wire, nearly broken
when Lee summoned his dogs to take their places beside him,
both animals eating their dinner directly from the table, making
short work of the food Lee had provided from his plate. Even
Martha had been bothered by that and, surprisingly, Lee had
noticed, but there was no apology, the man offering only an
abrupt comment about his preference for dogs over human company. It was a concluding note to an uncomfortable gathering,
and Greene had whisked Kitty away to their quarters without ut-
tering a word.

MAY 21, 1778

As he had driven Kitty home, he had seen the rider, had realized it was John Laurens. The young man brought his horse
down the long hill in a hard gallop, surprising for so late an arrival. Greene only knew that Laurens had been in York, had no
idea if the visit was official or familial, but his curiosity had been
resolved soon after. He had not yet gone to bed when the aide
had come from headquarters. It was an invitation from Washington for a meeting the next morning with the senior officers.

Greene had left his quarters well before dawn, could endure
no more of a fitful miserable night. He would not wake Kitty,
slipped out of the house before even Major Hovey was awake.

The only movement was that of the ever-present guards, two
men at each door of the house. They had taken his horse with
quiet efficiency, and he stayed outside, would not disturb anyone's sleep. He passed the time by walking along the creek, then
the river, then retracing his steps. He had not noticed the time,
realized finally that it was nearly full daylight, his thoughts broken by sounds from the door of the house. He watched as Tilghman appeared, followed by Lafayette, the two men stepping down,
moving slowly across the yard, a quiet conversation. They did
not yet see him, and he walked back across the road, caught a
glance from Tilghman, who said, "Oh! Good morning, sir."

"Colonel. Did we enjoy a pleasant night's rest?"

Lafayette said nothing, was staring away, unusual response
from the affable Frenchman. Tilghman seemed nervous, said, "It
was not a good night, General. Forgive me, I should not speak of
it further."

Greene was concerned now, said, "What happened, Colonel?"

Tilghman glanced at Lafayette, who nodded slowly, and Tilghman said, "Sir, I discovered . . . it was most regrettable, sir. General Lee was provided quarters upstairs, near General Washington,
the room that the staff has often used. It was no matter, we have use
of another room. We have been accustomed to close quarters when
a guest was present. It is my duty to wake very early . . ." He
paused, and Greene saw a hard frown on the young man's face.
"General, I must trust . . . you are a man of discretion?"

"Of course, Colonel. What happened?"

"I do not know if General Washington was aware, sir, but

General Lee was not alone last evening. I was in the hall, and was suddenly confronted by a sight . . . I should rather forget. General Lee has imported a . . . mistress . . . a miserable filthy hussy. She shares the general's room even now."

Greene could see that Tilghman was shaken. He fought the urge to laugh, said, "Well, who can be surprised by that?" He looked at Lafayette now, was surprised the young man was as serious as Tilghman.

Tilghman said, "Please, General. I ask you, do not speak of this."

"Have no concern, Colonel. I will not betray your trust. Thank you for confiding in me."

Tilghman began to move away, said, "I should return . . . the general has been awakened. He will require his coffee."

The young man scampered up the short steps, disappeared into the house, and Greene expected Lafayette to share his humor, but the young man was still distracted, glanced back toward the house, said, "General, we should move . . . this way."

Greene followed him, his curiosity growing now, and they reached the edge of the river, Lafayette now staring down into the water.

"General Greene, it was not a comfortable evening in this house."

"No, I cannot say I enjoyed the dinner . . ."

"I do not refer to the dinner. I share Colonel Tilghman's embarrassment for the commanding general, and especially so for Mrs. Washington."

"I understand that. But there is nothing to be done about Charles Lee's personal habits. General Washington believes that he is a valuable commander. We have no choice but to accept his role in this command."

"I am not so certain of that. Before I retired, I engaged in a brief conversation with General Lee. I was attempting to offer my congratulations on his freedom. His response caused me considerable . . . agitation."

"What did he say?"

Lafayette looked at him now, shook his head.

"General Lee has vigorous opinions of the commanders in this camp. I do not repeat gossip, sir. But his words were more than . . . unkind. I have not experienced such a man before."

"His ambitions have been made known to the commanding general before. General Lee feels that what is good for him is good for the country. He places great value in his own abilities and dismisses the abilities of everyone else."

"What *are* his abilities?"

Greene sniffed, thought a moment.

"Apparently, he makes a good prisoner. From all he tells us, the British fell over themselves to make him comfortable. One must wonder what he offered them in return."

"You do not suggest, surely . . ."

"That he's a traitor? I wouldn't go that far. But I must be honest with you, General. I do not believe that man will perform any good service for this army. General Washington would not be pleased to hear me say that. And I am certain General Lee has a good deal to say about me as well."

Lafayette looked down now, said, "I cannot repeat anything, sir. But I cannot believe General Washington would have faith in such a man if he is what you describe."

Greene shrugged.

"General Washington is not blessed with the luxury of opinion or of choice. He must make do with the material he has at hand. I hope to God I am mistaken in my feelings for General Lee. But if I am not, I pray General Washington is not made to suffer some disaster because of it."

THE OFFICE WAS CROWDED, ALL THE SENIOR COMMANDERS PRESent, except for one conspicuous absence. Lee had not yet emerged from his room. Greene could see the annoyance on Washington's face, and Washington said, "We shall begin. Those not present can be advised later. We have been informed of the imminent arrival in Philadelphia of a new delegation from London. They have supposedly been accorded the power to grant concessions toward a cessation of hostilities between our countries. I have been advised that this power excludes one significant concession. They do not come with any offering of independence."

Washington looked around the room, and Greene felt a strange anger brewing in the man.

"I am pleased that the congress is not regarding this commission in a positive light. I am advising you of this so that you do not allow yourselves, and the men in your command, to view this in any way other than as an act of desperation. I believe, and this view is shared by congress, that King George and his ministers have been . . . um . . . the only term I can use is . . . frightened. Word of our alliance with France has certainly burned its way through London. But rather than concede that a wider war, with greater loss of life is so abhorrent that peace should be sought, they have instead responded by an outrageous attempt to divide our country. This is a ruse, diabolical and base. It has one purpose, to distract us from our cause. Any man who might waver from support of this war might now be tempted to see this offer as a ray of hope. The English continue to perplex me with their misunderstanding of the American will. They come to us now, driven by the fear of a new and powerful enemy, and they offer those terms which we sought with such energy three years ago. They ignore that their armies have killed and maimed and distressed so many of us, and offer us a crooked and brittle branch from a poisoned olive tree."

The room was silent, the men glancing at each other. Greene was surprised by the show of rage from Washington, said, "Sir, can we be certain that the congress agrees with your assessment? Can we depend on their firmness?"

"Without question, Mr. Greene. Without question."

"Then, sir, we should not despair the resolve of the American people. If this delegation offers no more than a fantasy of a return to some halcyon days, it is likely that their mission will be brief."

Washington seemed calmer, looked around at the faces.

"I pray to the Almighty you are correct, Mr. Greene. This, however, is not my only purpose for calling you here. My scouts report from Philadelphia that a large quantity of British ships have raised sail and have departed the city. In fact, the suggestion is that a considerable majority of their craft have sailed. I have confirmed this from several good sources."

The room came to life, a hum of comments. Greene looked around, could see the sudden glow of enthusiasm. Greene saw Stirling raise his hand, the man's words hinting of a Scottish burr. "Sir, do we know where they're off to? Might be hightailing it back to New York, eh? Should we be preparing to march, then, sir?"

Washington held up his hands.

"My apologies, gentlemen. Perhaps I was not clear. I meant to say that the British *ships* have left Philadelphia, but not their army. There is no sign that troops are yet going anywhere. The ships are said to have carried sympathetic civilians, and likely, equipment." He paused a moment. "And baggage."

Greene looked at Stirling, said, "If their baggage has sailed away, then a march cannot be far behind."

"Well, then, we had best make preparations for a fight!"

The words came from behind them, and all heads turned toward the doorway. Greene saw Lee, adjusting his dusty uniform, his matted hair standing up stiffly on his bare head. Washington said, "General Lee, thank you for joining us. What do you make of the movement by the ships?"

"Quite clear. They're planning an attack. It will come at us here, or it will come at our cities to the south, Baltimore, Wilmington perhaps. General Howe is certain to strike a hard blow at our weakest point. That would narrow the decision to our position here. We cannot stand up to an attack, not with the command structure we have at present."

There was silence in the room, and Greene felt an explosion building in his chest. Washington pulled himself up out of his chair, said, "I am not clear on just what message the British navy is offering us. I am certain however of the following. Mr. Lee, you have been understandably without communication since your release, due to your necessity of travel. This is an opportune moment for me to inform you, as I intended to inform all of you. We have received word that within the past few days General William Howe has been relieved of command. His successor is Henry Clinton, which should surprise no one."

There were more comments, and Greene saw Washington lowering his head, staring down at the floor, the room growing quiet again.

"I am certain as well that General Clinton would not send his ships *away* from a place where he intended to commence a campaign." He paused, and Greene wanted to cheer, thought, Of course not. There will be no attack here, or anywhere around here. He fought the urge to look back at Lee's smugness, and Washington seemed to avoid Lee as well, said, "I anticipate that we will learn the enemy's intentions soon enough. To that end we shall prepare to leave Valley Forge."

JUNE 1778

Greene rode the horse up on the plateau, moved along past the rows of cabins. He knew Kitty was waiting for him, by now had completed the details of her packing, was preparing to board the carriage that would carry her northward. He had wanted her to come along, just a brief ride through the camp, to hear a final cheer from the men who were making ready to leave themselves, the entire army stirring in a restless awakening. But she had stayed with her bags, and he knew better than to argue. She was fighting the sadness, another good-bye that would likely divide them for many months. He would succumb to it himself, and he knew that this ride was the distraction, delaying the scene that he could not delay much longer. He had experienced it before, knew that the tears would come, her soft crying, her fragile arms holding tightly to him. She would tell him of her prayers, how every night the Almighty would hear her soft voice pleading for his safety, for his return.

He turned the horse, heard his name, a group of men loading rolls of new white canvas into wagons. He acknowledged them with a brief wave, spurred the horse, and moved toward the artillery park. He looked for Knox, didn't see him, wondered if Lucy would be as emotional as Kitty, more so perhaps, a woman who held nothing back. He smiled, could see the two of them together, the Knoxes, a perfect marriage, pure joy in each other, pure joy for life. And Henry Knox, pure joy indeed for the guns in his command.

He rode to the edge of the hill, could see the headquarters, knew that Martha was preparing to leave as well. The women shall be missed, and not just by their husbands, but by the army. When they arrive, it changes the entire camp, and now, when they depart, it will change us again. He turned the horse, stared out toward the southeast, toward the city where so many of the enemy were making their own preparations, some plan he did not yet know. The women may miss us, may even curse us for what we do, but we will not spend *our* nights in tearful loneliness. We have a new companion, coming to life again out beyond those low hills. And before much longer we will receive the reports, and the order will come, and this army will leave behind these cabins, will move down from these heights, this horrible, wonderful place.

35. CORNWALLIS

HE ARRIVED AFTER A JOURNEY OF SEVEN WEEKS, A CROSSING MADE bearable by lengthy card games and grand dinners with the men who were assigned the task of bringing the new peace proposals to America. The ship was the *Trident*, and though passengers were few, the staffs and servants of the peace delegation occupied nearly every available space on a man-o-war that was not constructed for comfort. But the optimism of the peace commissioners set the tone for the voyage, and he was grateful for their lighthearted approach to their mission. To a man, they believed they would reach Philadelphia to find a grand celebration of their certain success. They believed they carried the one means by which this war would draw to a close, two nations blending again into one, ruled by a benevolent king who had made an extraordinary apology for his mistakes. The only man on the ship who had serious doubts about their mission was Charles Cornwallis.

His visit home had been a marvelous rest, a time of peace and comfort. Jemima had welcomed him as he had imagined she would, all the tenderness of tears, the grateful softness of a woman who understands her husband's duty, who holds no resentment or anger for the long absences. But this time there was more than the usual sadness, and as he slipped away from the last touch of her hand he felt an uneasy concern. From the first day of his arrival, he had been surprised at her frailness, Jemima growing thinner in his absence, her laughter and buoyant spirit tempered by a weakness that alarmed him. She had dismissed it, would not admit to any ailment, scolded him for his worries. After too few weeks together, their parting had been as they had always been, more tears and soft kisses. Once at sea he could not think just of Philadelphia and his new duties without wondering if her new fragility was more than just a symptom of his absence.

He was still a member of the House of Lords, though he cared so little for politics. But England was now festering in politics, and so he had obeyed his sense of responsibility and attended the meetings at Parliament. The turmoil was complete, King George's opposition bolstered by the agonizing defeat of Burgoyne and the horrors of the new French alliance with the rebels. The speeches were bold and spectacular, and that one dreaded word had finally made its way into the halls of Parliament, *independence,* sharp calls for the king to conclude the war by a full admission of his government's failings. The prime minister, Lord North, had offered his resignation, but George III knew that a collapse of North's ministry would bring an opposition figure to power. The king would not accept such a shameful defeat within his own government, would not succumb to the will of his hated opposition. North's resignation had been refused. The only alternative was appeasement to the colonies. Cornwallis had endured the debates and haranguing speeches with utter disgust, and a deep embarrassment for his army's failure. The peace delegation believed they carried the only answer acceptable to both King George and the colonies, but Cornwallis had no such optimism.

As the *Trident* made her way across the Atlantic, he had spent many hours gazing at the open water, occupying his mind by searching for some break in the smooth line of the horizon. If there was a French alliance, there was a French fleet, and if the ministry had not responded quickly enough, the waters off the coast of Delaware and New Jersey might already be swarming with warships that would make any peace plan useless. Though none of the others seemed to notice, he had glimpsed the New Jersey coast with relief. As the ship sailed into the mouth of the Delaware River, it was a welcoming hug from strong arms, British warships at anchor all along the wide river. But it was a state of affairs the peace commissioners had not expected, finding this avenue to the British headquarters such a fortified bastion. The commissioners believed the most optimistic predictions of the ministry, expected to find a land where the rebels had been suppressed, their army nearly crushed out of existence, a land where a rebel congress would eagerly welcome a convenient means to ending a hopeless war. Instead, the British warships made it clear that the land beyond the river was untamed and uncontrolled. At any time, at any point, the deck of their ship might suddenly be ripped by musket fire, rebel patrols who regarded the *Trident* as simply one more target.

The wounded optimism of the peace delegation was shattered completely when they reached Philadelphia. While Parliament had consumed long weeks debating the mission of the peace commissioners, word of the French alliance had already reached the congress. The alliance had been ratified, and even celebrated. The terms of the peace treaty offered by King George had been published and circulated to a people who saw it for exactly what it was: desperation, a means of preempting the French alliance, of preventing the colonies from finding the means to a military victory. The proposals were already the object of scorn, in congress and in the streets of American towns. The commissioners were dismayed to learn the very thing that Cornwallis had quietly predicted, that the colonies were too far removed now from British rule ever to go back. If the war was to end, it would have to end on the battlefield.

JUNE 9, 1778

He was not surprised to learn that Howe was already gone. Cornwallis had been told by Germain that Henry Clinton would officially take command in mid-May. He had no doubt that once Clinton arrived in Philadelphia, Howe would make haste to leave. There was embarrassment enough in his resignation and recall, and Cornwallis knew well that neither Howe nor Clinton would feel comfortable in the presence of the other, certainly not in any public setting.

Cornwallis still had to report to his new commander, was making his first ride through the streets of the city, a hot and steamy morning. He moved past the headquarters of so many of the officers, stables of horses, quartermaster depots, small groups of soldiers guarding every warehouse, every official outpost. It had all the signs of a fortified citadel, and none of what had once been a grand and prosperous city. There were few civilians in the streets, and those who still went about their daily routines were sullen, no one saluting him, or even acknowledging him. He rode close to a man carrying a large bundle on his back, the man struggling under the weight. The man glanced up at him, and Cornwallis made a slight bow, said, "Good morning, sir. Do you require assistance?"

The man looked back toward the small cluster of staff officers, said, "If I had my horse, I'd not need anyone's assistance. It was *requisitioned.*"

It was a distinctly military word, the army's ever-present justification, the needs of the soldier taking precedence over the needs of the civilian. Cornwallis had nothing else to say to the man, moved on past, thought, He was paid, certainly, and with the king's currency, not the ridiculous paper the rebels offer. He realized now that there were no horses in the street at all, the few civilians all on foot. Well, of course. It has one meaning. The army is mobilizing. We require all the beasts of burden we can find. There was a sound behind him, the voice of one of his aides, no words, just an odd grunt. Cornwallis turned in the saddle, was suddenly engulfed in a putrid smell, put a hand to his face. He looked down a small side street, a dark alley now a river of black water. There was a flurry of motion, rats, some scurrying through the water itself. He prodded the horse, moved past the scene, looked across the way, another side street, saw two large black birds perched on a large mound, thought, My God, it's a dead horse. He glanced back to his men, saw twisted faces.

"Decorum be damned. Double speed, gentlemen."

The horses' hooves rattled on the stones beneath them, and they were quickly past the grotesque horrors. He held up his hand, slowed them down again, tested the air, the smells still finding him, new sources of filth down each narrow street. He felt impatient anger, thought, Why has no one seen to these conditions? To simply abandon a carcass? Sewage flowing down the streets . . . are we so abusing this place that we ignore common sanitation? No excuse for it. He knew the answer already. From the moment General Howe believed he was replaced, he ceased to concern himself with anything so mundane as sanitation. And, now, Henry Clinton was concerned with nothing but leaving.

He was close to the Penn mansion, the headquarters, could see guards, two dozen or more, lining the narrow drive. He turned the horse, moved between the men who snapped to rigid attention. In the yard, grooms were tending to horses, and he saw one familiar mount, the horse that carried the old Hessian, Knyphausen. He felt relief, had hoped he would see the old man again. He knew there was the chance that Knyphausen might have sailed away with Howe, recalled as well in some kind of show of support from the Hessian king, a gesture to lessen the embarrassment to both Howe and King George. Yet Knyphausen had done nothing to share in Howe's disgrace, and it would make no sense to the army, pulling a good commander away from the troops who needed him. But no one could predict the pride of kings.

He dismounted, handed the reins to a waiting aide. There were other familiar horses as well, tied up in a row along one side of the house, and the relief began to fade. I did not expect a full-scale council. Well, of course, if General Knyphausen is here, they will all be here. He prepared himself for the cascade of friendly greetings, the social banter, saw the wide door pulled open, another squad of unsmiling guards lining the porch. He could already feel the somber mood of the place. The sheer number of guards was Clinton's signature, as though some great cataclysm might suddenly assault the headquarters. It was a distinct contrast to Howe's headquarters, a command that always seemed verged on the brink of a party. As he stepped into the house, more guards manned the hall, stood at each door, the base of the staircase. He could see staff officers in motion, men disappearing into rooms, one man scurrying up the stairs. There was no hint of laughter, no conversation, no sound at all but his own hard boot heels. He stood still for a moment, waited for someone to notice him, could feel Clinton's presence. Well, of course. There is a message here, an aura he must create. This is the center of the entire war.

"General Cornwallis, welcome, sir!"

He was surprised to see John André, the man rushing toward him as though late for an appointment. André stopped just in front of him, somewhat too close. Cornwallis backed up a step, and André said, "By His Majesty's good graces, you have returned to us! I must say, sir, this entire army will receive you with a thousand huzzahs!"

"Thank you, Major. I do not require such a reception." André continued to beam at him, and Cornwallis was suddenly uncomfortable, said, "Major, is General Grey in attendance?"

André understood now, said, "Oh, quite, sir! I am no longer in General Grey's service, well, not directly, of course. I am now General Clinton's adjutant. A most humble honor, sir, most appreciated. I believe that General Clinton required someone who was intimately familiar with the city, and especially the social fabric, as it were. I am hoping that the general will allow me the privilege of arranging another extraordinary exhibition in his honor. I am terribly sorry you missed General Howe's farewell celebration. It was truly marvelous, indeed. A *Meschianza* we called it, Italian, you know. It means medley, and I assure you, sir, a medley of such delightful exhibitions has never been seen on this continent!"

Cornwallis felt himself drowning in the man's enthusiasm.

"A medley?"

"Oh, quite, sir! We could not allow General Howe to retire from his command without a magnificent show, a salute from the army, the entire city. It was . . . truly . . ." He paused, and Cornwallis saw a glint of wetness in the man's eye. André seemed to fight the emotion. "I sincerely wish you had been here, sir. We had jousting knights, fair damsels, a veritable throng of Negro servants in oriental dress. The costumes were my own design, if I may say. The entire army marched past the general, a parade through two magnificent arches, my design as well . . . well, no matter. At the conclusion, a cascade of trumpets, a presentation to General Howe of a laurel wreath, a grand salute by verse, which, I admit, sir, I did compose myself." André stepped back, put his hands together on his chest, recited,

> *Chained to our arms, while Howe the battle led,*
> *Still round these files her wings shall conquest spread*

"There's a good deal more, but I will not trouble you now, sir. Perhaps later I can recite the verse entirely, allow you to capture the moment. I must say, there was hardly a dry eye. The entire evening was a grand ball, dancing until the sun rose to grace the final morning of General Howe's presence among us. I say humbly, sir, no commander in the history of arms has ever departed his army in such a grand fashion."

Cornwallis had no words, could not imagine the scene in his mind.

"Very nice, Major. I'm certain General Howe was grateful for your efforts."

André seemed to swell at the compliment. "Thank you, sir. I would imagine . . . yes. Of course, the general had little time to express such appreciation, but I am certain I shall yet receive some word, once the general settles himself in London. Ah, to be in England, sir! But of course, you were just there . . ."

"Major, may I see General Clinton?"

André seemed to gather himself, said, "Of course, sir! Please follow me!"

He spun around on his heels, and Cornwallis followed him down a wide hall, waited while André opened a door, saw the cluster of uniforms. André said, "General Clinton, forgive the interruption, sir. General Cornwallis has returned!"

All faces turned to him, and he stepped into the room, felt the door closing behind him, André now gone. The silence was a blessed relief, and he met the faces with a smile, Grey, Grant, Erskine, and in their usual place in the corner, the Hessians. Knyphausen was slumped in his chair, his usual posture, the old man seeming to stare away in a haze of thought.

Clinton sat on the far side of a small oval table, was studying a map, pushed it aside, looked up at him with no expression.

"General, welcome. I trust your journey was without incident."

The man's words had no cordiality, and Cornwallis said, "No incident at all, sir."

Clinton returned to the map, his social duties complete, and Cornwallis looked toward the old Hessian.

"General Knyphausen, I hope you are well."

The old man responded to his name, a brief glimpse of recognition. Beside him was an unfamiliar officer, a young Hessian with sharp blue eyes, and the young man leaned over, said something to Knyphausen, who nodded, still stared away. The young man stood straight again.

"The general welcomes your return, sir."

Cornwallis smiled at the unnecessary interpreter, the young man responding with a cordial smile of his own. He suddenly felt the absence of von Donop, the man's rigid formality, so fiercely protective of the old man. He looked at the others now, and Grant said, "A kind welcome to you, sir."

Others joined him. "Indeed."

"Welcome, General."

He could feel the genuineness, the smiles sincere. He looked again at Clinton, said, "Sir, may I offer my congratulations."

"Yes, you may. Thank you. I offer mine to you as well."

Cornwallis watched him carefully, knew the subject might be a tender one. By Clinton's promotion, Cornwallis was now second in command, had received the rank of *full general in America*. It was of little significance to the overall command of the army, but cemented Cornwallis as the successor should Clinton be killed or become too ill to serve. It was the ministry's discreet way of preventing a senior Hessian commander like Knyphausen from assuming command by his seniority of rank.

Clinton had been tormented by Howe's shadow for three years. Now he was casting a shadow of his own, and Cornwallis could already feel the man's discomfort that this time, Cornwallis was in that shadow and might have the same driving ambition for command as Henry Clinton.

"I am honored to serve under your command, sir."

Clinton seemed to weigh his words.

"And serve you shall. You may have observed that the population of this city has been diminished. It is our regrettable duty to accommodate those loyal citizens who wish protection. We have done so by removing three thousand of them to safety in New York, along with their astounding volume of baggage. Doing so has occupied most of the navy's capacity for transport. While some officers have expressed regret that the army has thus been inconvenienced, I believe we would have remained on land in any event. Transporting this army by sea would have caused us unacceptable risk. If a fleet of French warships were to suddenly confront our transports, or should we be scattered by inclement weather, we could suffer a severe disadvantage. For that reason, I believe it is in our best interests to march the army by land."

The questions began to rise in Cornwallis' mind, a sudden wave of doubt. He had seen every sign that the army was preparing to move, that certainly Clinton would begin his command by showing Lord Germain a burst of energy. But why would any new campaign involve the navy at all? Clinton looked up at Cornwallis, said, "Some might suggest that I am exhibiting the same caution as my predecessor. I assure you, I have learned the lessons of our recent past. With respect to General Howe, his command was hesitant to act unless he was assured of certain success. While I admire his devotion to the protection of his troops, the results are well known. Inactivity may prevent casualties, but it accomplishes nothing else. I am not interested in merely achieving the conquest of *land*."

Clinton looked around the room, and Cornwallis saw little response, thought, They have heard this before. He looked to the map, and Clinton said, "General, you have questions? I understand that because of your absence, you would want an explanation. You are entitled to it."

"Sir, I have indeed observed that this army is preparing to march. But I have not been informed as to the overall plan of the new campaign."

Clinton stared down at the map, and Cornwallis felt the familiar rage brewing in the man.

"General Cornwallis, there is no *new campaign*. I would have thought your friends in London . . . well, no matter. This army is preparing to march out of Philadelphia and return to its primary base in New York. Lord Germain has ordered me to detach five thousand troops to our ports in the Caribbean, to defend against an expected assault by French forces there. I am to send another three thousand to our bases in Florida as support. You *were* informed that we are now at war with the French?"

"Certainly, sir."

Clinton turned the map around, slid it toward him. Cornwallis saw crooked lines drawn across New Jersey.

"We have been left with sufficient craft for Admiral Howe to ferry this army across the river. As soon as we are prepared to move, we will do so. We have two possible routes of march. I would prefer to move northward and reach the main road at Brunswick, thence to Amboy. If that route is unavailable, we can proceed . . . here, farther to the south, and, with a rapid march, reach Sandy Hook in short order. In either case we will then be ferried to Staten Island. I expect to receive further orders from Lord Germain upon our arrival in New York."

There was no enthusiasm in Clinton's words, and Cornwallis stared at the map, felt a boiling stream rising in his brain.

"Sir . . . we are to abandon Philadelphia . . ."

"There is no debate on the matter, General. Despite my personal objectives for this army, I cannot find fault with Lord Germain's decision. Philadelphia has proven to be of no value to us. Some would say it has been a veritable prison. This army has suffered moral and physical decay in these quarters."

"No debate, sir. I understand. But sir, *what of the rebels*?"

The words had come out with more volume than he intended, and he expected a hot response from Clinton. There was silence for several seconds, and he could feel his own sharp breathing, said in a low voice, "My apologies, sir."

Clinton stared down at the map, said slowly, "Exercise caution, General."

The words were a low growl, and Cornwallis waited for more, but Clinton sat back now, said, "This meeting is concluded."

The men moved past Cornwallis like children released from school, the door opening to a flow of cool air. He waited as the room emptied, saw Clinton leaning heavily on the table, the man now resting his face in his hands. He wanted to say more, to ask the same question, but Clinton was ignoring him. Knyphausen was rising slowly, helped to his feet by the young officer. He moved slowly past Cornwallis, and he felt a hand on his arm, the old man touching him briefly as he moved to the door. Cornwallis looked at Clinton again, the man frozen, fixed in his pose, staring into his own hands. There was nothing left, no words, and Cornwallis turned away, moved into the hall. He could hear André, out by the main entrance, a fluttering of words to the senior commanders as they made their way outside. He wanted to move the other way, thought, Another entrance perhaps, but then the young Hessian was there, said, "Sir, if it is not a bother, might you accompany General Knyphausen to his headquarters?"

YOU SHOULD REGRET HAVING MISSED SUCH A PARTY, GENERAL."

He could not tell if Knyphausen was serious or not.

"I heard. Major André described it to me."

"Ah, yes, Major André. A man of considerable energy. I admit, General, to some sense of mystery. I am not yet clear why this *Meschianza* was such a positive event."

"It was a tribute, I suppose, to the man, to General Howe. To his tenure as commander."

Knyphausen looked at him now, leaned closer, said, "That could have been accomplished with a toast of brandy at a simple dinner. Forgive my bluntness, General, but Major André's *Meschianza* was a display of decadence and excess, the likes of which no Turkish pasha has ever enjoyed. And, to be honest with you, General, whatever purpose it served was lost on the men in my command. It was, as I heard someone say, 'a marvelous salute to failure.' "

Cornwallis said nothing, felt relief that he had not experienced the show firsthand. They walked out toward the river, the scene much different than his last visit. The river was alive with birds, clusters of white flying low past the few big ships that still lined the wharf, a fleet of ducks gliding slowly along the shoreline in front of the mansion Knyphausen still called his headquarters. He could see the old man had something of a limp, said, "I hope this winter has not caused you any discomfort."

"Every winter causes me discomfort, General. It is the nature of growing old. If you are fortunate, you will learn this for yourself."

Knyphausen moved out in front of him, sat down slowly on a low stone wall, stared at the river, and Cornwallis thought, Fortunate to grow old? Of course. Von Donop. Not all of us will have the privilege of growing old. Knyphausen assumed his familiar drooping posture, gazed down at the ducks slipping by just a few yards below them.

"I should have brought some bread. The birds gather. It is my secret. If I reveal it to my staff, I am certain my young Captain Hausman will use this as the means to put them on our dinner table." Knyphausen laughed now, a slow raspy wheeze. "I knew you would return."

Cornwallis was surprised by the statement, said, "I was always planning to return. Was there doubt?"

"Among some, yes. General Howe, certainly. General Clinton, no. He believes you are here only to take his command."

Cornwallis let out a long slow breath, did not want this conversation.

"I am not here to take anyone's command. It appears, at any rate, that there will be little to take. We are going into a defensive position, retreating to New York. It is not the way I would have thought . . . forgive me, I should not speak further."

"So, you agree we are retreating? General Clinton does not use the word. We are *repositioning*. Your Lord Germain claims it is a new war now. We must take into account the French."

"Damn the French! What of the rebels? Washington has an army twenty miles from here, and we are simply going to march away? For two years we have made every attempt to engage them, to draw them into a fight. Mr. Washington cannot possibly imagine that we are now going to abandon all we have gained."

Knyphausen turned toward him.

"What have we gained, General? This was General Howe's mistake, after all. He believed that by our very presence here we were winning. In fact, Mr. Washington has succeeded in prolonging this war long enough for his rebel government to form an alliance with France. In all the battles we have fought, in all the victories General Howe has proclaimed, with all the cities and rivers and roads we control, nothing is as important to this war as that. You doubt this? The French have not yet shown us a single warship. And yet we are already in retreat. You and I, we might soon find ourselves in Europe, fighting a new Seven Years War, or perhaps we will sail to the islands, and fight in the heat, to protect your king's sugar fields."

Cornwallis put one foot on the stone wall, leaned forward, his arms on his knee.

"Perhaps I *should* have remained in England. My wife . . . I am concerned about her. Now I find that I have no real purpose here. What kind of war can we fight from New York? We will sit in those grand mansions and have our councils, and watch as our officers are corrupted once more by the society women. Mr. Washington will certainly follow us, move his army to the New Jersey coast, strengthen his position on the Hudson. And what then? We abandon New York? That will be the final surrender. His Majesty cannot possibly agree to this. After so much has happened, we just sail away? Pretend this war was never truly important? Are we to consider the men who died in this place to have been merely . . . *players,* another ridiculous pageant from Major André?"

"What would *you* do, General?"

He felt the bait in Knyphausen's words.

"No, I have no plan. It is not my place to instruct or suggest, either to Lord Germain or General Clinton. But I cannot remain here in this situation. I cannot command from inside a fortress. I would rather resign."

Knyphausen raised himself slowly, and Cornwallis watched him, ready to assist. The old man moved away from the wall, then turned, said, "No. You must not do that. And they will not allow it. Your king needs you *here*, in the event of some misfortune to General Clinton." He laughed again. "He cannot have his army commanded by . . . *me*."

The thoughts filled his mind, Germain, the king, Clinton. He knew Knyphausen was right, that Lord Germain would never accept his resignation. No, they will still require me somewhere. Does it matter after all if I lead my men in the colonies or on some battlefield in France? He had a sudden glimmer of pity for Clinton. He has finally received his command, and now, he is but a puppet. His duty might well involve little more than tidying up this theater of the war. He does not deserve such treatment. None of us do.

"General Cornwallis, if you do not mind, I would like to go inside. The heat is tiring me."

He moved closer to Knyphausen, said, "Of course. May I assist you?"

"No, thank you. Captain Hausman will appear, once he sees we are moving to the house. He is observing us now, you can be certain."

The door opened on the wide front porch, and the young Hessian was there, moved out to the top of the steps, waiting for instructions. Knyphausen reached the steps, began to climb, stopped, said, "General, I do not know what the future holds. But I do not agree with you. Wars do not just fade away, armies do not just go home. I do not know what will occur in New York, or what our duty will be. A great many things could still happen which we cannot predict. As you say, Mr. Washington is still out there. And, it is a long march."

JUNE 18, 1778

For nearly a week, Admiral Howe had supervised the transport of the army's supply train, twelve hundred wagons and five thousand horses ferried across the Delaware River. Now, it was time to ferry the troops as well.

The order put the army into motion at 3:00 A.M. The men had been given four days' food rations, but the first leg of the march would take them only five miles. The ships were waiting, and the column moved quickly, men lining up at the makeshift wharves at Gloucester Point. Cornwallis had ridden beside them, had heard a low litany of curses and indiscreet comments from men hidden in darkness. But there would be no punishment. He would say nothing to these men who understood as well as he did that no matter the official tone of the orders, no matter the positive pronouncements from headquarters for a new and glorious campaign, this march was not about anyone's glory. The army was simply abandoning its post.

Before the first light of dawn, his men were marching onto the ships, filling the holds and lower decks. He stayed on the shore, handed the reins of his horse to a groom, watched as the animal was led across a narrow plank to a small flatboat, the ferry for the mounts of the senior command. Across the river the sun was breaking through dull gray dawn, the New Jersey shoreline now visible. He watched the sailors, men climbing up, working the ropes and rigging of the ship, orders called out, and he saw Lord Howe, moving quickly along the wharf. The man cut a narrow figure in the dull light, so unlike the portly mass that was his brother. The admiral saw Cornwallis, moved toward him, said, "Ah, General. Best get aboard. This one's ready to cross."

"Thank you, sir, yes, only a moment."

He looked back along the road, concerned for stragglers. It was an excuse, a reason for delay, for standing just a bit longer on the ground in Pennsylvania. He scolded himself, thought, This is a duty for the provosts. There is nothing left behind, nothing about this place to hold in our memories. We did our duty, made our conquest. Our success will be judged by history, and by King George. I have only one concern, and it is already on board these ships.

He heard hoofbeats, saw a horseman coming quickly through the dull light, the man waving, calling out. Lord Howe was beside him now, watched as he watched. The man rode up close, and Cornwallis could see a bouncing mass of baggage, boxes and sacks tied to the saddle. Now he could see the man. It was John André.

"Ah, Admiral Howe! General! Very good! I pray you hold just a moment! It took me longer than I thought to secure this. May I be allowed to board, sirs?"

Lord Howe moved by Cornwallis, said, "Board immediately. We are departing."

The admiral was gone, no patience for conversation, and André climbed down from the horse, said, "General, you will find this amusing, I'm sure. I was quartered at the home belonging to none other than Benjamin Franklin himself! Jolly rich, that. I took it upon myself to, ah, strike a blow for the king, as it were. Yes. Look here, marvelous."

Cornwallis could see now, the horse was burdened with all manner of personal effects, and André pulled back a cloth, revealing a painting.

"See? It's the good doctor himself. Rather impressive portrait. I thought it quite the appropriate souvenir. Slipped a few volumes from his library too."

Cornwallis felt his disgust growing.

"Major, there are penalties for looting and pilferage. Have you not been informed?"

"Oh, sir, this is hardly pilferage. The man is a confirmed enemy of the king. Before this matter is concluded, Benjamin Franklin will likely face the noose. And if he doesn't, consider, after all, how much longer can the old bird live? It will be a fitting gesture to offer these, um, souvenirs to His Majesty himself! I assure you, sir, I will see to it!"

"General Cornwallis. I must insist!"

The voice came from the rail of the ship, and Cornwallis saw Lord Howe, waved toward him, saw sailors preparing to remove the plank. He had no energy for a discussion with André.

"Board now, Major. If your conscience allows you such things, I am not to dispute it."

He crossed over to the deck of the ship, saw André leading his horse toward the flatboat, the animal weaving beneath André's spoils of war.

As the sun rose high, the breathless air brought the dust up from the sandy roads in a choking haze. Progress was slow, the men encumbered by the line of wagons that was twelve miles long. Cornwallis stayed in the saddle, his uniform wrapping him in a bath of sweat. He moved alongside his column in a slow grinding rhythm, the horse fighting its way through deep sand. The roads led north and east this time, through the heart of southern New Jersey. He did not need the maps, knew that if the rebels did not interfere, they might still go far enough north to reach the good road that led through Brunswick and Amboy, the same road he had already traveled so many times before. But that route was more populous, and there was always the danger of militia, a sudden gathering of farmers to peck and harass their flanks. To avoid the nuisance, the column was prepared to follow Clinton's second route, the open country farther south, that would take them to Sandy Hook. Cornwallis had no interest in passing through Brunswick again, crossing the muddy Raritan again. The memories were still fresh in his mind, the misery of rain and snow, the rebels slipping away from his grasp countless times. No, if we must march across this dismal place, at least we shall see someplace new.

36. WASHINGTON

HE HAD NOT RIDDEN THROUGH PHILADELPHIA, HAD NOT CONSID-ered making some grand show of the British evacuation. The city was now under the command of Benedict Arnold, the man nursing a wound in his leg received during the last great fight with Burgoyne. Arnold commanded a sizable militia, but Washington had no fears for the city, knew that once the British had ferried across the Delaware River, Clinton's intentions were plain. The move had surprised only one man, the one who still insisted that the British would strike southward: Charles Lee. Even as Clinton led his army deeper into New Jersey, Lee challenged every inclination Washington had to attack them, to take advantage of the drawn-out line of march, the slow progress of an army so encumbered by its excess of equipment. Lee held surprising influence over many of the junior officers, and some of the senior staff as well, including Stirling, and even Henry Knox. Washington could not just ignore Lee's suggestions, nor would he simply impose his will on his officers, or on the army. Before any significant move, any major decision, he continued to rely on the councils of war. Washington believed the structure and authority of his command was still fragile, the effects of the intrigue of Conway, Mifflin, and Gates. Lee had already proven he was capable of dissension, but unlike Gates, he was still popular with the troops. If Lee's unusual ideas about strategy exploded into outright disobedience, it could endanger the entire fabric of the army. Washington had no choice but to give Lee his due, to form a strategy that would accommodate the man's ambitious temperament.

Washington's troop strength had grown during the last few weeks of winter quarters, new recruits responding to the spreading word of the health and pride of the army. Von Steuben's drills and lessons had imparted that pride not only to the men who marched under his sharp calls, but to the civilians far beyond the camps at Valley Forge. With their fields planted, a vast number of farmers had enlisted, and some of the unreliable militia were signing up for extended duty, to receive the training that would make them soldiers. By the time the British had made their crossing into New Jersey, Washington was able to mobilize a force of over thirteen thousand men, a number nearly equal to what Clinton had on the march toward New York. Though the British had a head start, their slow progress gave Washington precious time to assemble a march of his own. Despite Lee's insistence that Clinton was simply offering bait to lure Washington into some deadly trap, the pursuit began. Six hundred men marched out under the command of William Maxwell, striking quickly across what Washington believed to be Clinton's intended route of march. Maxwell's troops were to disrupt the roadways, cutting trees, destroying bridges, an effort to slow the British even further. Six hundred skilled marksmen were sent out under Daniel Morgan, a harassing force to torment Clinton's flanks, possibly to force the British to stop marching altogether.

Washington himself crossed the Delaware at Coryell's Ferry, a few short miles from his triumphant assault on Trenton. With the smattering of intelligence that came from the scouts, he began to understand Clinton's dilemma. Washington had marched his men on the more direct route, was now a few miles above Princeton. The alternatives for Clinton were clear: Attack Washington or avoid him. Unless the British intended to provoke a direct engagement, Clinton would have to turn away from the Brunswick–Amboy route, and march out across the sandy farmland to the east.

HOPEWELL, NEW JERSEY, JUNE 24, 1778

Each day had become an agony of delay, the uncertainty that comes from ignorance of the enemy's intentions. The reports from Morgan had stopped completely, the marksmen now making their brief assaults along Clinton's eastern flank, separated from Washington's headquarters by the entire force of the British army. He knew that Maxwell's men had done their work with admirable effectiveness, that the British were making incredibly slow progress. But the plodding march presented problems of its own. Until Clinton made a definite move to either the north or east, Washington could not know where to position his army or what strategy might be best employed. If the British were suddenly to increase their speed, Clinton might move his forces far enough away that Washington could not hope to catch them at all, and the extraordinary opportunity to strike the vulnerable British march would be lost. As he sat in his headquarters, suffering the silence of his scouts, his patience finally gave way. After the evening meal was consumed, he ordered the senior officers to gather in a council of war. There would be no decision made without the involvement of the men who would carry out the plan.

They filled the room, most standing, the few chairs occupied by the men who required them, Greene with his stiff leg, and Lafayette, still recovering from his leg wound at Brandywine. Washington waited for them to find their places, gentle maneuvering, and when the voices grew quiet, he said, "Gentlemen, the primary question before us is whether we should hazard an attack on the enemy. It is my intention not to allow a precious opportunity to escape us. General Clinton has obliged us by providing what could be a target of vast potential. Mr. Maxwell's troops have done admirable work providing obstructions on all roadways in General Clinton's path. It seems as well that the British are greatly encumbered by their train of supply. It is a mystery why General Clinton did not transport such a volume of baggage by sea. However, I am not so concerned with solving mysteries as I am confronting the result."

Lee stepped forward, and Washington had expected it.

"Sir, there is nothing of mystery here. General Clinton is a man of considerable ability. The only possible explanation for his dallying march is the very result we see here tonight. With all respect, sir, you have fallen into his trap."

Lee glanced around the room, seemed to appraise the response to his impertinence. Washington saw nods, many in agreement with Lee's assessment, and Lee looked at him now with a confident smile.

"General Clinton is, at this very moment, sitting in his camp

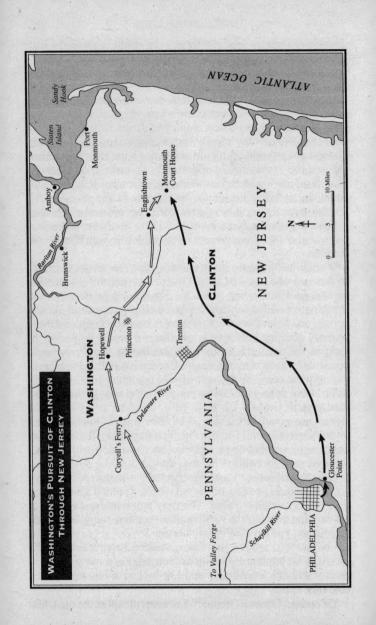

WASHINGTON'S PURSUIT OF CLINTON
THROUGH NEW JERSEY

planning for our demise. He is hopeful that our bravado will carry us straight toward the points of his bayonets."

Washington was becoming annoyed, fought to hide it, said, "May I assume then, Mr. Lee, that you believe the best strategy is to remain passive, allow the British to march unmolested to their destination?"

Lee laughed.

"Of course, sir! Was I not clear? A direct confrontation with the enemy at this time could prove to be a disaster, far worse than any we have previously suffered. To dare to confront such a well-disciplined army with the meager forces we have at hand is not only an invitation to destruction, but the height of arrogance!"

Washington felt a cold weight in his chest, his strength drained by Lee's maddening certainty. He looked at the faces, saw a few frowns, even Lee's supporters uncomfortable with the man's bombast.

"Excuse me! I protest!" The voice was von Steuben's, and Washington could see the man's face reddened by anger. "We are . . . prepared! No one can suggest that this army is not capable!" The Prussian seemed to run out of words, his English failing him, swept away by his temper. Lafayette pulled himself up from his chair, said, "I agree with General von Steuben, sir. It would be a disgraceful display if we allowed the British to march unopposed across New Jersey. If there is danger in a direct confrontation, then we could send a sizable assault against their rear guard. It would be a minor risk, and could provide us with positive results."

Washington could see the room dividing in their opinion, small discussions blossoming, the din now rising. He waited for a long moment, looked now at Greene, who sat silent, a hard scowl on the man's face. The voices were growing quiet again, and Washington said, "There are alternatives before us. We may attack the enemy in strength, we may assault him with caution, or we may allow him to pass. Given the latter, we may assume a defensive posture such that the enemy may be tempted to assault us on ground of our own choosing." He looked at Greene, who stared down to the floor, and Greene said slowly, "Clinton will not attack us. He did not abandon Philadelphia to go on the offensive. With the French now entering the war, he is returning to New York so they can prepare."

"Of course, General Greene!" Lee nearly leapt at the man, his

thin frame leaning close to Greene, who did not look at him.
"The French are the key! Surely *General* Lafayette knows this!
With a French fleet in our service, our victory is assured. There
is no purpose to putting this army in danger. Our triumph will
come to pass in due time! To suggest such a foolish risk is, dare I
say, criminal!"

Washington could see Lafayette stirring in his chair, the
young man absorbing Lee's sarcasm at his rank. It was typical of
Lee to dismiss the abilities of the foreign officers. Since his arrival at Valley Forge, Lee had seemed to make a particular show
of disrespect for Lafayette. Washington believed it was because
of the man's youth, but he had heard the talk, that Lee had made
a target of Lafayette simply because the young man was so close
to Washington. Lafayette put his hand up, said, "Sir, with respect
to General Lee, I propose we do not ignore opportunity when it
is provided. I favor an assault, any assault that might provide us
an advantage. We may never find this opportunity again. A force
of perhaps fifteen hundred men could do considerable damage
to the enemy, without significant risk to themselves."

The voices began again, and Anthony Wayne spoke up, the
fiery Pennsylvanian never one to hold his opinion to himself.

"There is only one option here, sir. The enemy is before us.
We should attack him!"

The opinions came now in a flood, small arguments escalating. Washington could feel the tempers, the room growing hot,
held up his hands.

"Enough! To order!"

He looked at Lee, saw the man's smugness, his thin arms
crossed on his chest, and Lee said, "Should we not vote on this,
sir?"

"Very well. By show of hands, I wish to know your preference. Those who believe we should allow the enemy to pass
unmolested . . ."

Hands went up, and he felt a hard blow to his gut, saw hands
rising from most of the men, was surprised that even Henry
Knox was agreeing with Lee.

"Those who believe we should attack . . ."

Five hands rose, Greene, Lafayette, von Steuben, Wayne, and
the French engineer, DuPortail. He lowered his head for a moment, said, "I will abide by your wishes. However, since I am

still your commander, I would offer a compromise. Mr. Lafayette is correct that there is small risk in moving against the British rear guard. We will do so."

"Really, sir!" Lee was still in the pose, his arms resting across his chest. "Has not the wisdom of your commanders been made clear?"

"General Lee, I do not possess the luxury of perfect wisdom, and I will humbly assume that my officers do not as well. I must answer to a congress and a nation that will question why this army did not strike its enemy."

Lee sniffed.

"*Congress*. A stable of stupid cattle that stumble at every step."

The room was silent, and Lee seemed oblivious to the response to his comment.

"General Lee, your opinion of the congress is your own privilege. However, *this* command answers to its authority." Lee shrugged slightly, said nothing, and Washington said, "There is nothing further to discuss. I shall have Mr. Hamilton prepare a letter for you to sign, documenting your agreement with the decision made here."

Wayne exploded, "I will sign no such letter, sir!"

"That is your privilege, Mr. Wayne. I do not require agreement, just obedience. This council is concluded."

HE DID NOT WANT COMPANY, BUT THE TWO MEN HAD REMAINED BEHIND, and he knew they would not just vanish into the night without a last word. He would not have tolerated anyone else, certainly not the men who had sided with Lee, but he would listen to both Greene and Lafayette, knew they would confront him with the words that were already stirring in his own thoughts.

He was avoiding them for the moment, watched as Hamilton dipped the pen in the inkstand, putting into words the decision of the council, documenting the astounding passivity of his officers, and worse, the dominance of Charles Lee.

In spite of the man's arrogant crudeness, Washington had always liked Lee. He had welcomed his support in the early days, around Boston, when his second in command had been the thoroughly disagreeable and generally incompetent Artemas Ward. When the British evacuated Boston, Ward considered his job complete, would no longer serve under Washington's command. Even before Ward had gone, Lee had proven himself reliable, and a good ally, had done much to give the men in the trenches around Boston a sense that this gathering of farmers and shop-keepers was, after all, an army. And more, Lee had contributed to the essential notion that Virginians could indeed command New Englanders. Washington had tried to believe that Lee could still become the able and supportive commander he had been in Boston, and he had been far more tolerant of Lee's ambition than any of his officers. But since Lee's return from captivity, the man's unfortunate personal habits had been overshadowed by his strident hostility to the officers Washington trusted most, mainly Greene, Lafayette, and von Steuben. If Lee was not yet plotting some intrigue, something to rival the problems that had come from Gates, he was clearly on a mission to elevate himself to a level of influence that even Washington himself would not accept.

He continued to watch Hamilton writing, aware that the two men were seated quietly behind him. He could not erase Lee's smugness from his mind, thought, I overlooked the man's habits, all the blunt arrogance. But am I to overlook this? He has champoned a course that provides no advantage except to our enemy. He looked away from Hamilton's pen, stared at the blank wall of the office. He had heard rumors of Lee's presumed friendship with Howe and Clinton, loose talk of inappropriate cooperation. No, we will not consider such things. I have no reason to believe that Mr. Lee's interests are different from my own. Hamilton raised the pen, said, "This is completed, sir." The young man slid the paper toward him, stabbed the pen into the inkstand, and Washington saw Hamilton shaking his head.

"Is there a problem, Colonel?"

Hamilton looked past him, a glance to the others.

"My apologies, sir. I did not intend to reveal . . . forgive me, sir. It is not my place."

"Reveal what, Mr. Hamilton?"

The young man stood, made a short bow.

"I am ashamed to have written this, sir. It is an embarrassment that so many good officers have been given to a course of such inaction. This document, the decision of the council does honor to no one but a society of midwives."

Behind him, he heard a small laugh from Greene, and he turned, saw the smile removed quickly from the man's face.

"Mr. Hamilton, have this document distributed by the staff. I want signatures by tomorrow morning. You are excused."

"Sir."

Hamilton was gone, and Washington looked at Greene again.

"I do not require anyone to encourage my staff officers to offer such dissent."

"Certainly not, sir. But may your major generals offer a dissenting opinion of their own? Colonel Hamilton is correct, even if somewhat indiscreet."

Washington sat now, leaned out on the small desk.

"Is that all you came to say? I was aware of your disagreement in the council. What of you, Mr. Lafayette?"

"Sir, there is more at stake here than a poor decision. General Lee believes he knows what is best for this army, but he is mistaken, sir. I do not believe he has the best interests of our cause in his heart."

"I will not hear such talk, Mr. Lafayette. No one has yet demonstrated that Charles Lee is anything but a loyal soldier in this army. I am aware he has not regarded you with particular respect. It is simply his nature."

"This is not some cause of my own, sir. He claims that our troops should no longer be put at risk because the French will win the war for us. Do you believe this army should not be called upon to fight, that we sit passively and pray that King Louis provides us with sufficient strength?"

Washington had already made the argument in his mind, said, "I do not agree with Mr. Lee's views. I was dismayed that so many of my senior officers do. But I cannot simply ignore what so many in my command feel is correct strategy."

"Why not?"

The volume surprised him, and he looked at Greene, who repeated the words.

"Why not, sir? When did this command succumb to the practices of a democracy? What army functions by majority decision? Forgive me, sir, but I am dismayed that you would make unwise strategic decisions only to satisfy the greatest number of your subordinates. This is *your* command. This army has never failed to obey your orders, regardless of Charles Lee's formidable presence."

Silence filled the room, and Washington stared at Greene for a moment. Lafayette said, "I wish, sir, that a council of war had never been summoned. It serves no purpose other than to invite men to champion some plan which will give them the greatest personal advantage. I do not understand General Lee's purpose, but I am certain his strategy is wrong. I stake my future in this, sir, that if we attack, we shall find every advantage."

Greene said, "There may never be another opportunity for us. This is *your* command, and *your* decision."

They were both staring at him, and he felt their confidence, was suddenly overwhelmed by affection for both men.

"You honor me with your loyalty and your faith, gentlemen. However, we can make no further decision until we know the enemy's course. I have given my commitment to deploy a limited assault on the enemy's rear guard. For now, I will abide by that commitment. We will see what tomorrow offers us."

JUNE 25, 1778

The report came from von Steuben himself, the Prussian having led a small scouting party that probed the British western flank. Clinton had changed direction, had obviously abandoned his goal of reaching the Brunswick Post Road. There could be no doubt that the British knew of the position of Washington's main force, and Clinton was making it plain that he had no intention of forcing a confrontation. The British were moving to the east, along the one main roadway that would lead them toward their transports at Sandy Hook, the road that led through Monmouth Court House.

The change in direction meant that Clinton was moving directly away from Washington's position, that Lafayette's plan for an assault on the rear guard would result in a small force pursuing a much larger one, with nothing to be accomplished but annoyance. The opportunity was slipping away, and despite the hesitant stance of so many of his officers, Washington changed the plan. He increased the size of the harassing force from fifteen hundred men to a major advance of better than half the army. By marching on a parallel course instead of a pursuit from the rear, Washington's men could make better time, could possibly strike right at the main British line of march.

*   *   *

HE HAD WAITED FOR MORE THAN AN HOUR, MAKING HIMSELF BUSY
with mundane tasks, unwilling to leave his office. He would not
let the staff know that he was bothered by the man's tardiness, or
worse, that Charles Lee might be keeping him waiting on purpose. He checked his watch, nearly nine o'clock, most of the
staff retiring already, the business of the army complete for one
more day. He stood by the open window, stared into starry darkness, low sounds of an army settling into a steamy night's restless sleep. He held tightly to his temper, thought, He has a good
reason, certainly. He is still finding his place here, many new officers. He turned away from the window, sat at the desk, could
feel the stale dampness in his uniform, the window offering no
relief, no breeze to wash away the heat. He listened for movement beyond the door, Tilghman perhaps, some last duty, the
man never retiring without notice, always offering some final bit
of service. But the silence was complete, no boot steps, no voices,
nothing except . . . dogs.

The sound cut through the night air, and he focused, could
hear them louder now, interrupted by the sound of hoofbeats.
The voices came finally, beyond the door, and he could hear the
dogs clattering through the small house, a sudden burst of barking, chaotic excitement. The sounds startled him, ripping through
him, the sounds of a snarling fit, broken by Lee's voice.

"It's all right, Colonel, just having sport!"

The door burst open, and Washington saw Tilghman, the
man's face white with a strange horror, and he said in a hushed
voice, "They near attacked me, sir!"

Lee was there now, did not wait for Tilghman's permission,
the dogs rushing past him, swarming around Washington's desk,
his feet, sniffing and probing. Lee chose his own seat, sat across
from him, laughed.

"Your colonel has no appreciation for the primal needs of the
beast! Never seen a man so frightened. They never come into a
room without knowing all they can of the inhabitants, a lesson I
have learned as well."

The dogs were calmer, circling Lee's chair, finding their own
places to settle down. Washington knew there would be no explanation for Lee's late arrival, said, "Thank you for coming at
such a late hour, Mr. Lee."

"Nonsense, George. Looked forward to it. There was a time

we spoke often, you know. Didn't require such an audience of junior officers to plan the future of these campaigns. Rather miss those days."

He did not share Lee's cheery mood, said, "It was a different time then. Boston was a different circumstance. We have accomplished a great deal."

Lee shrugged.

"I suppose so. Been wondering myself when this war might end. I find it hard to believe what some are saying, that the British are on the run. That's one fine army out there, George. We're fortunate to have survived this far."

Washington let the words flow past, said, "As you know, I have ordered a pursuit of the enemy's march." He reached down into a drawer, retrieved a map, turned it toward Lee. "We will advance along this route . . . here, seeking the enemy's flank at every opportunity."

Lee seemed to ignore the map, sat back in the chair.

"Foolish. Dangerous."

"I cannot ignore our one opportunity, Mr. Lee. And I will not. A force of some five thousand men will advance on that route. I would suggest you become familiar with the map."

"I don't make much use of maps, George. Why this one?"

"This is an important command. As second in seniority, this is a duty that should fall to you. Will you accept?"

"Why your second in command? Why not *you*?"

"I will remain somewhat to the rear of the advance force with nearly equal strength. This will offer us options in the event the enemy changes direction, or some unforeseen danger arises."

Lee thought a moment, shook his head.

"I don't think it's appropriate, George. The men know I don't support this plan. Might make me look a bit foolish to go riding out in front of an attack that I don't expect to succeed. You have a number of good officers, surely you can find one who will accept such a command. Give it to one of your young ones. From what I've seen, some of them require a lesson in strategy. They will learn it from Henry Clinton."

Lee leaned over now, focused on his dogs, and Washington stared at him, the heat rising in his face. He said nothing, watched as Lee made childlike sounds to the animals, and Lee looked up at him, said, "Is there anything else?"

"No, Mr. Lee. You may leave."

Lee stood, the dogs now bounding to life, bursting out through the door, their master close behind. The house was suddenly silent, and Washington felt a dull throb in the base of his neck, massaged it with his hand. His mind was blank, numbed by the shock of Lee's words, his refusal to lead such an important mission. He saw Tilghman, peering around the door.

"Sir? Can I get you anything?"

He looked up at the young man, continued to rub the stiffening pain, said, "Not at the moment, Colonel. You may retire."

"Thank you, sir. With your permission, I will remain a while longer. I have a letter to complete. My brother, in Maryland."

"By all means, Colonel. Offer him my regards."

"Thank you, sir."

Tilghman was gone, and Washington rose slowly, moved to the window, the stifling stillness giving way to a light breeze. His mind boiled with thoughts of Lee, the snide little man so different now than the good subordinate he had once been. He stared into darkness, thought, If Mr. Lee finds this mission so not to his liking, then I shall do as he suggests. I shall offer the mission to one of the *younger ones*, someone who has demonstrated a zeal for the fight, someone who understands that making *use* of this army is the only means we have of success. And I do not believe anyone in my command need learn any lessons from Henry Clinton. He pushed away the image of Lee, thought of the young Frenchman.

"Colonel?"

Tilghman appeared, said, "Sir?"

"Send for Mr. Lafayette. Express my apologies for the late hour, but I require his presence."

"Yes, sir."

Tilghman was gone quickly, and he heard the door of the small house closing, Tilghman's voice breaking the darkness, summoning the groom. He waited for the hoofbeats, moved back to the desk, stood a moment, thought, You have been patient beyond measure, Mr. Lafayette. It is time for your reward. If Mr. Lee does not wish this command, then it shall be yours.

37. LAFAYETTE

THEY HAD MARCHED ALL THROUGH THE NIGHT, AND WERE NOW within five miles of the enemy camp, the crossroads at Monmouth Court House. The night march had been a blessing for the men, most not realizing that it was urgency rather than concern for their well-being. The days had been insufferably hot, the sand and dust of the roads smothering the British soldiers in a blanket of heat many could not escape. Even before Lafayette had begun his march, his men had been allowed to shed their coats and shirts, any baggage that would encumber them in the heat. But the British soldiers had no such luxury. Their uniforms had not changed since the stark days of winter, thick wool, layers of heavy garments that grew heavier on the march. Worse, each red-coated soldier carried arms and equipment that weighed nearly a hundred pounds. The result was an unexpected horror for Washington's scouts, the men who trailed the British column. Instead of stragglers they were finding corpses, men who had simply fallen away from their column, some drifting off the road only to die in the sand and scrub woods. Washington knew that Clinton was driving them relentlessly toward the ships. If the British were not attacked very soon, they would reach the protection of the hill country nearer the coast.

Lafayette had kept his enthusiasm in check, would not reveal to anyone in the headquarters what this command had meant. His first major experience in the field had come during the retreat at Brandywine, where he had received the wound. He had been teased by Nathanael Greene, the Rhode Islander cautioning Washington that this young man was determined to place himself in danger. While the army was making their first preparations to leave Valley Forge, Washington had given him charge of large-scale scouting parties near Philadelphia, one which had resulted in a sharp fight with a regiment of Hessians, another which had nearly cost Lafayette his entire force of three hundred men. It was a daring, and some had said foolish, confrontation with a large body of British regulars under Charles Grey. But the intelligence gained had been crucial, and Lafayette had escaped the danger with a slippery tactic that had left the British baffled. More importantly, the maneuver had demonstrated to Washington that the young man could handle himself well on dangerous ground.

He had his critics still, mainly those French officers who felt some insult at his closeness with Washington. He knew that many of them had come to America for the wrong reason, to return home as heroes, bearing the trophy of grateful appreciation of this new nation. It was all about prestige, a demonstration for King Louis as a sign of their worthiness for a similar role in the French army. Yet most had shown very little in their service to the Americans that would bring any prestige at all, so many of them more concerned with their rank and authority than in doing any kind of good service to a cause. The worst had been Philippe du Coudray, the ridiculous martinet who demanded a lofty position second only to Washington. Du Coudray had then begun his service by suggesting that perhaps Washington should step aside as well. But the problems brought by du Coudray had solved themselves. The man seemed to think himself worthy of a veritable walk on water, the result that he carelessly tumbled himself and his horse into the Schuylkill River. The horse survived. Du Coudray did not.

Lafayette knew that tongues were probably wagging behind him. And as he rode with the lead units of his column, he could not avoid thinking of Louis, what the king might have said when he learned that Washington had given this twenty-year-old such responsibility. He was not sure if Louis was angry at him even now, Lafayette slipping out of France in such blatant disobedience of His Majesty's wishes. But there had been no official summons, no letter of reprimand. He knew that Louis would have his momentary tantrum, spout some heated epithets that would quickly be forgotten. Ultimately, Louis would accept that this young officer would either disappear into this strange American wilderness, a casualty of war perhaps, or would rise as a genuine hero. But as much as he sought a command of his own,

he rarely imagined himself in some kind of heroic role. Lafayette had been driven by a quest that would seem unusually
humble to his king, and to many of the other Frenchmen around
him. Though the most unkind talk assumed the foreign officers
to be of one cloth, the rabid ambitious quest for notoriety, Lafayette had only sought the opportunity that Washington had now
given him.

As the daylight brought another stifling wave of heat over
Englishtown, more troops had appeared, Washington sending
reinforcements to Lafayette's command. He had expected to receive new orders, some update from Washington, word of Clinton's response to this pursuit. But the only word had come from
the scouts, and from von Steuben, who was only two miles from
the British position. Clinton had halted his column around Monmouth, was shifting the marching order of his troops, putting the
more elite units toward the rear, the Hessians more to the front. It
was a logical move with the approach of Lafayette's forces, moving the stronger regiments, the Grenadiers, Queen's Rangers, the
Highlanders, closer to the vast line of British wagons. It was
clear evidence that Clinton believed the wagons would be the
target of such a large force. But Lafayette's orders said nothing
about capturing supplies. He knew that Clinton's halt was simply a mistake, another critical delay that might cost the British a
safe escape.

As the sun climbed higher, the men had rested, and the day
had passed with the army continuing to gather strength, men
now storing up water and preparing food, making ready for the
last march toward the enemy. He watched as another small column appeared from the west, men in white shirts, their faces
shielded from the sun by wide round hats. They moved past him,
and officers appeared, led them into the camp, where the rest of
his men were tending to their muskets. They would gather quietly in the shady places, waiting for the order that would send
them back into the sandy road. The column was past him, and he
still expected to see a rider, some new word from Washington,
was confident that the main army was no more than five or six
miles behind him. He could feel the heat from the horse beneath
him, looked toward a small stand of trees, thought, No need for
you to suffer this. He began to move toward the shade, saw Anthony Wayne, one aide trailing behind him, their horses coated
with a slick wetness.

"General, we are prepared to advance."

"Thank you, Mr. Wayne. We are awaiting final instructions from General Washington. I have sent him the reports of the enemy's position."

"We should not wait too long. I'm certain Clinton won't."

He knew of Wayne's brash impatience, something so very rare in this army. It had led Wayne to some difficulties on the battlefield, and his straightforward tactics had won him both critics and admirers. Wayne's dogged style might not always have been the right strategy, but to many, including Washington, it was a tonic that had often been sorely missed.

Wayne followed him toward the trees, and now both men turned at the fresh sound of hoofbeats in the road. He expected to see Washington's courier, was surprised at the small thin figure leading a pair of hounds. It was Charles Lee.

I MUST ADMIT, GENERAL LAFAYETTE, THAT I DID NOT BELIEVE THIS mission would actually come to pass. Once I was aware that General Washington had increased the number of troops in this command to near six thousand, I felt it was unwise for a junior officer such as yourself to maintain such important authority. This is a position best suited for the second in command of the army. I trust you agree?"

Lafayette read the letter in his hand, Washington's order. It was wisely written, giving Lafayette continued authority if an attack was already in progress. But, with the troops still at Englishtown, Lee could assume overall command with no disruption. He handed the letter to Wayne beside him, said, "Yes, General Lee. You are correct. It is entirely appropriate for this command to be under your authority."

"Ah, yes. Good, then. I shall make my headquarters in this house. You shall report to me here with any information you receive as to the enemy's disposition and activity."

"Yes, sir. Do you have any specific instructions for me, sir? Do you wish to place me in command of any troops?"

Lee seemed surprised by the question, thought a moment, said, "Do whatever you have been doing, General. You're supposed to know your duty. General Wayne, if he's not certain, you may instruct him. Now, good day."

They moved outside, and Wayne stepped out in front of him, passed by the horses, walked out into the dusty roadway. He

spun around, faced him, said, "Instruct you? You are my senior officer. How could you stand before that man and maintain
such . . . calm? He is only here because he suddenly realized he
might miss out on a chance for some glory!"

"The orders from General Washington are clear. General Lee
is in command here. We are not privy to the reasons for his
change of mind."

"It does not require intellect to see that Lee could not just sit
back there while you . . . well, he could hardly allow himself to
sit idly by while a *Frenchman* leads this attack. I mean no offense, sir."

He had held tightly to his disappointment, but did not feel the
kind of anger Wayne was showing toward Lee. The responsibility for a command this size had surprised him. Lafayette
looked to the west, the sun moving lower.

"We are very close to the enemy, a march of two hours. This
night will better be spent in planning the attack. General Lee
must make the dispositions."

"So, dawn, then?"

Lafayette looked at Wayne, saw the deep scowl, the man's disgust clearly evident.

"It is sound strategy, General. There can be no assault now, it
is too late in the day."

Wayne turned in the road again, paced a few steps, turned.

"All right. Dawn. I hope you're correct. If we wait any longer,
Clinton will be gone. I wish I had your faith in General Lee."

Lafayette said nothing, fought through his disappointment still.
It is not about faith. He is in command. We have no alternative.

AS THE SUN WENT DOWN, THE ORDER CAME FROM WASHINGTON. IT
was assumed that by morning Clinton would again begin his
march, would spread his forces in a long vulnerable line. Lee
was instructed to attack wherever opportunity presented itself,
to send his troops in a hard wave against Clinton's flank or rear,
holding the British in place while Washington brought the rest of
the army up to expand the attack into a full-scale engagement.
Late in the evening, Lee had sent out word of a meeting of his senior commanders, and the men expected a detailed briefing on
their places in the line, a map of the tactics they would bring to
the field. As the men gathered at Lee's headquarters, they found
no one waiting for them but an embarrassed aide. There were no

plans prepared, no maps sketched. Lee himself was nowhere to be found, had ridden out into the night, leaving his aide with no instructions at all. The meeting erupted into angry turmoil, Wayne leading the officers back to their camps. They had no choice now but to wait for some further instructions. No one but Lee was authorized to put the brigades and regiments into some order of march, no one but Lee could organize this attack.

Since Lee's arrival at Englishtown, Lafayette had been given no troops to command, no real responsibility at all. As the other commanders stewed furiously in their camps, Lafayette rode out to find General Lee.

THE AIDE COULD ONLY OFFER SOME HINT, THAT IF LEE DID NOT STAY within the boundaries of the small village, he would certainly keep to the road that led north. It was a reasonable guess, the one safe direction.

Lafayette moved the horse in slow steps, then stopped, stared out through total darkness, listened. He had repeated the routine now for several hundred yards, the only sound the low hum and chirp of the insects. He began to move again, but a new sound broke through, and he waited, could hear the slow rhythm of a horse.

"Sir! General Lafayette! We have found him, sir."

The aides had ridden ahead with a trio of guards, Wayne's men, had explored each road and path, knew to find Lafayette here on the main road.

He pulled the match from his pocket, made a short hard stroke against the metal of his short scabbard. The small flame made a soft glow on the road, and Lafayette held the match close to his own face, said, "Thank you, Sergeant. Is he far ahead?"

"No, sir. We came across his aide up the road a ways. The man was scared out of his wits, settin' alone in the dark. Said General Lee's right up the hill there, this open field."

"Very well. I will go alone now. You may remain here. Make yourself heard if there is any sign of trouble."

"Yes, sir."

He followed the man's directions, the trees thinning, the ground rising to a starry sky. He saw Lee now, framed against the horizon. The man seemed aware of the voices in the road, sat upright on his horse. Lafayette moved up the hill, said aloud, "General Lee. It is Lafayette, sir."

The response came from the dogs, a sudden cascade of barking. They were around him now, the horse dancing slightly, avoiding them. Lafayette rode close now, said, "Forgive the intrusion, sir. We were concerned about you."

"Unnecessary. I required solitude. Only way for a man to think properly."

"Yes, sir. You had summoned us . . . the commanders. There is concern about our plan for tomorrow."

"You're damned right there is concern. By morning, the entire British army will be sweeping down on us like a pack of wolves on a chicken coop. I have sent word to General Washington to expect an attack on this front. If we are not vigilant, they may catch us still in our beds!"

Lafayette could hear urgency in the man's voice, tried to see his expression.

"You sent the general . . . you believe we are to be attacked?"

"Those are professionals out there, Mr. Lafayette! The very notion that your outrageous band of amateurs, these farmers, can dare to stand in the same field with the might of King George's finest soldiers! The more I consider the arrogance . . . Washington, Greene, the rest of you! Tell me, *General* Lafayette, what do you know of the British army? What have you come here to do? You dare to hope that these militia will make some brave show? We cannot stand up to them on this ground or any other."

He fought through the shock of Lee's words, felt a hot burn on his face. He stared down through the darkness, said in a low voice, "Sir, we have . . . *you* have General Washington's orders. We are to attack the British in the morning. Do you intend to carry out those orders?"

Lee's voice burst out across the field. "How dare you question me! Certainly! I will follow the instructions I have been given!" He leaned closer, said, "Let me advise you, *General* Lafayette. I will bear no responsibility for the outcome. I have warned Washington, and I am warning you."

NEAR MONMOUTH COURT HOUSE, JUNE 28, 1778

They began the march at three o'clock, none of the commanders having received orders as to their places on the field. By the first light, they could see the ground before them, deep, winding ravines, roadways cutting through on narrow causeways, curving stretches of high ground. Beyond the ravines were high rolling fields, and farther still, the small village, the main road cutting through small houses and the one large courthouse. He could see the vast field was alive with motion, that what had begun as the British march had been abruptly halted, vast formations of red-coated troops forming to receive them. He was surprised to see that the Americans, who had actually marched beyond the British position, were in position to cut off their march completely, turn the lead units back into their main body. He glassed the wide field with a rising excitement, thought, This is truly a . . . marvelous opportunity. With enough of a thrust, they may be driven completely away from this ground, with no escape but the way they have come. He looked to the west, the sky still dull gray. He knew Washington would be on the move already. If there is good fortune on this ground, General, you will arrive in time to confront disarray in the enemy lines. The result could be a perfect rout!

Several of the regiments had crossed over the last of the ravines, and the larger body of men was swarming along the causeways in tight precision, the astounding result of von Steuben's good work. Lee was riding the ridges, and Lafayette moved with him, could only wonder about the man's strange temperament, none of last night's doubts evident in Lee's actions. The brigadiers were sending word in now, aides for Maxwell and Varnum, Grayson, Stewart and Wayne, all seeking orders, some final command that would send the great wave forward against an enemy who was already showing signs of disorder. Lee listened to the requests, sat firmly, silently, raised his field glasses, said, "What are they doing? Is that . . . who is that? Wayne? Varnum? He is too far advanced. Order those men on that rise to countermarch! Where is Grayson?"

The swirl of men around Lee seemed to settle into a strange paralysis, and Lafayette said, "I will find out, sir."

He had no orders, spurred the horse away from the huddled couriers, rode along a narrow strip of high ground. The field beyond was now a mass of troops, a solid line of white and brown. He reached the field, rode hard, the horse skipping through short grass, saw horsemen near the crest of the hill, moved that way.

He would not allow himself anger, not yet, the ground in front of him too near an eruption of chaos. He could see Wayne, shouted as he reined the horse, "What is your situation, General?"

"My situation? See for yourself! The enemy is pulling away! They're giving ground, and we haven't begun the attack! Do you have orders? Are we to attack?"

He could see beyond the lines of Wayne's men, scattered groups of red, some moving behind fences, others slipping into patches of woods. Far up on the main road, a column was advancing, flags and horses, more British troops moving to the field. My God, the time is . . . now! We should reinforce these men! He gripped the reins in frustration, said, "We have no orders, General Wayne! General Lee is concerned you are too far in advance!"

"Too far . . . ? By damn, send me another brigade, and I will sweep the enemy off this ground! What manner of plan is there?"

Lafayette could see the faces of the men, the good troops watching him, hearing the words of their commander.

"I have nothing to tell you, General Wayne, except . . . in the judgment of General Lee, you are in the wrong position."

"Well, then, sir, you may go back to General Lee and advise him I will correct my error."

Wayne spun his horse around, moved out in front of his men, shouted, "Do you see the enemy?"

The line erupted into a loud cheer, and he caught Wayne's eye, a quick nod, the man now turning away, his sword in the air, his troops moving in one sharp line toward the uncertain formations of the British.

Lafayette would not watch, knew that Wayne was right, but it was only one brigade, and the enemy would surely re-form. He pulled the horse back toward the ravine, his heart pounding in his ears, thought, Lee has no plan! There is no plan at all! He is sending orders to men he has never met, to troops he has never seen, in positions he has not scouted. God help us, this day may depend on the brigadiers, after all!

The fight was beginning along Wayne's front, more of the British units coming into line. He drove the horse furiously along the pathway, could see a rising cloud of smoke sweeping across the field, drifting toward the deep ravines.

Far to his right, a new line of British troops was advancing,

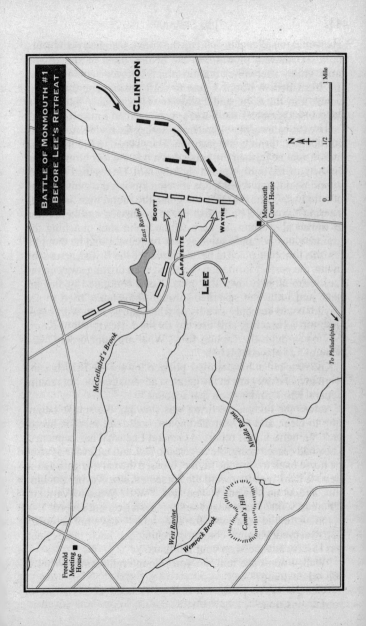

BATTLE OF MONMOUTH #1
BEFORE LEE'S RETREAT

CLINTON

East Ravine

SCOTT

LAFAYETTE

WAYNE

LEE

Monmouth Court House

McGellaird's Brook

West Ravine

Wemrock Brook

Middle Ravine

Comb's Hill

Freehold Meeting House

To Philadelphia

N

1/2   0   1 Mile

bayonets forward, and he held up the horse, searched for Wayne, could see a swath of white in the field, a burst of smoke and flame, volley after volley finding targets Lafayette could not see. The fresh British troops began to shift position, seeking their avenue into the fight, and Lafayette was suddenly jolted by a sharp blast, grabbed the horse's mane, pulled himself around. There were cannon now, guns firing across the ravine, more guns unlimbering, turning into position. They began to fire in regular rhythm, and he pushed the horse down into the low ground, then climbed up, the sulfur smoke choking him. He reached the level ground again, could see Knox moving among the guns, and he rode that way, Knox aiming the guns, the round man animated, cheering his men. The British began to answer, and he felt the air ripped above him, a sharp whine, solid shot punching the ground. Knox began to wave at him frantically, and he thought, Yes, this is not the place to be. He could see the British across the ravine, the perfect formation shattered, men drifting away up the rise, some already over the crest. Knox continued to fire his guns, and Lafayette searched through the smoke, tried to see Wayne, could see only swaths of white shirts, men with bayonets, still advancing, still driving forward. He turned to Knox, shouted through the cannon fire, "What are your orders? Has General Lee placed you here?"

Knox looked at him, smiled, pointed toward the British, said, "I am to place my guns to the greatest advantage. I do not require General Lee's guidance on that account."

Across the ravine, the firing was slowing, the smoke beginning to clear, and he searched again, could see men on horseback, thought, I must report to General Lee what has happened. Knox had ceased firing, the targets too few, and Lafayette spurred the horse back toward the ravine, crossed the narrow path again. He rode hard, moved toward the horsemen, saw Wayne watching him, and as he slowed, Wayne said, "Well? What of Varnum? Where is Scott? I have heard nothing from Lee, not a word!"

Lafayette had no answer for him, said, "I have not as well. I last observed Varnum countermarching . . . back there. Scott was to have advanced on your left flank."

"Well, I don't see him, do you? Countermarching? What in hell is Lee doing?"

"General Wayne, I do not believe General Lee is aware of your disposition."

"Well, you may tell him that my men are very aware! Those were Cornwallis' troops over there! And we ran 'em out of the field! They'll be back before long, and will probably have half of Clinton's army with 'em! You go back to General Lee and tell him we need troops on this ground now! Sir!"

Wayne was shaking in anger, and Lafayette said, "I will go. Try to hold here if you can."

There was musket fire now, more smoke rising farther to the left, along the ravine. Wayne shouted something, moved back toward his men, and Lafayette spurred the horse. The air was cut by a sharp thunder again, and he could see Knox in motion, the guns shifting position.

He drove the horse hard again, one eye on the thick lather that coated the animal's neck, slowed as he moved past Knox, tried to see out to the other flank, the men who should be advancing. But the brush was too dense, and clouds of smoke were still drifting through the ravines. He patted the wetness on the horse, but there was no time for gentleness, and he pushed back across the middle ravine. He expected to see Lee where he had left him, but the ground was empty. He pushed on, could see a narrow trail, thick with fresh troops, thought, Who? Varnum? Dickinson? He turned the horse, moved in behind them, but the men were not holding formation, were milling around. Lafayette saw Charles Scott, the Virginian, sitting high on a horse, staring out toward the sound of Knox's guns, and he moved close, said, "General Scott, are you to advance? General Wayne has made a sharp fight, he requires protection on his flank."

Scott looked at him, and Lafayette saw disgust, the man pointing back toward the main road.

"That man has given me no orders to advance. I have done nothing but march these men back and forth. I was instructed to take command of Varnum's brigade, and someone else would take command here! It's madness! The man's back there spitting out instructions like he's never been on a field of fire! If Wayne commences another fight, I will move these men out there on my own authority!"

Moving away, Scott began to gather his officers, giving his own instructions. Lafayette felt helpless, looked back toward the main road, thought, How can this be happening? I must find him!

He crossed the last ravine, moved toward the road. He could

hear a swelling tide of musket fire behind him, looked out across
the open ground again, his view blocked by distant clouds of
smoke. There was more musket fire far to the left, another confrontation with troops led by someone . . . who? He felt himself
losing control. I must know. Does anyone know? Far down the
road he saw Lee, a cluster of officers, and he spurred the horse,
passed by another regiment still in the road, a formation doing nothing. He reached Lee, saw the man sitting on his horse,
watching calmly as the small eruptions of fire opened beyond
the rugged ground.

"Sir! On the right flank, General Wayne has driven the enemy
back. But they are forming for a counterattack. General Wayne
requests reinforcements."

Lee seemed calm, looked past him, shouted, "Where is General Scott? Did he not receive my order to march to the left?"

The aides were scrambling, men arriving from all directions,
a cascade of questions, and Lee said, "Enough! Gentlemen, there
is no cause for confusion! We must determine where our greatest
strength lies." He seemed to see Lafayette for the first time.

"Did you say Wayne? What in the devil is Wayne doing out
there? Did I not order him to pull back? He is certainly too far in
advance."

"Sir, General Wayne's brigade has driven the enemy! If we
provide reinforcements, he is certain to carry that part of the
field. General Knox has placed his cannon in a most advantageous position. They must be protected!"

The sounds of musket fire were increasing, rolling toward
them, and Lafayette turned toward the fight, could see nothing
for the wave of smoke. The cannon began to punch the air again,
and Lafayette turned to Lee, said, "Sir! We must move closer!
The enemy is sure to counterattack! We must coordinate the
brigades! I would suggest, sir, a general advance, all along the
line! The enemy is not yet formed! The advantage is ours, sir!"

Lee stared past him toward the smoke, seemed to focus for a
moment, raised his field glasses, said, "We cannot stand against
them. We have no choice. We must retreat."

THE UNITS ON THE FAR LEFT HAD RECEIVED THE ORDER FIRST, CON-
fused and furious men withdrawing in good order across the
ravines. Lafayette pushed the horse as hard as he dared, rode
again toward the right flank, the animal stumbling as it moved

past the dense brush. The sounds of fighting were scattered throughout the field, Lee's order pulling men away from a startled enemy. Lafayette knew that Wayne would still be stubborn, that if his men had held their ground, he would not simply back away. He reached the final ravine, could see the wide field littered with bodies, heaps of red, bloody patches of white. The horse seemed to stagger, and he reined up, said, "Not now . . . please. A moment more." There was no one around him now, Knox already in some new position, or withdrawing, as many of the others were doing. Far out along the edges of the ravine he saw horsemen, couriers, and one man was moving toward him, a hard, fast ride. The man slowed the horse as he moved to the causeway, and Lafayette saw the man's face, young, wide-eyed with fear.

"Sir! Sir! I must find General Wayne!"

Lafayette pointed toward the wide hill, said, "Across there."

"Uh, sir, I'm supposed to give General Wayne the message. General Lee has ordered the army to retreat. We're pulling back, sir."

He nodded, said, "Yes, Sergeant, I have been informed." He had thought Lee might yet change his mind, might see that the ground across these deep cuts was there for the taking. But the young man in front of him was the final confirmation, one of many who finally carried some definite instruction to the army Lee was supposed to command. He looked down at the exhausted horse, patted its neck, his own frustrations and weariness giving way to tears. He wiped his eyes, looked up at the man through a thick blur. The courier seemed to sense his anguish, said, "I'm sorry, sir. But can you tell me where General Wayne is?"

He blinked hard, leaned forward, his arms resting across the horse's mane.

"Sergeant, I will give the order to General Wayne. I have a much more important mission for you."

"Whatever you say, sir. I'd just as soon not go out . . . there."

"On my responsibility, you are to go to General Washington. He is advancing on the main road, should not be more than two or three miles back. Tell him, Sergeant, in the most urgent terms, his presence is required on this field."

38. WASHINGTON

THE MARCH HAD BEGUN QUICKLY, SHIRTLESS MEN ENERGIZED BY the enthusiasm of their commander. But as the sun moved overhead, the heat had drained much of the energy away. He had seen men collapsing in the road, helped off by their comrades, knew that others were simply slipping away, seeking some brief comfort in patches of blessed shade. He had tried to gather them in, ordering the provosts to bring the stragglers back to the line. Any delay in the march could mean greater danger for the men already facing the enemy. But the sheer brutality of the heat could not be erased by threats of punishment. The provosts were called off, and he hoped that the men who fell away might regain some strength, might rejoin the army in time to give their support.

As he reached Englishtown, he could hear the steady rumble of cannon, knew that around him, the troops were responding to the sounds as he was. The march became energized again, the men focusing on what lay ahead of them. He wanted to push them harder, fought to hold himself in line with the troops. But the sounds were a message that, finally, the enemy was where Washington needed them to be; that finally, there was a fight erupting in the manner of his plans; that finally, if there was any surprise to be suffered, it was suffered by the British.

And then the sounds began to fade. He spurred the horse, leading the staff forward, moved out toward the advance regiments. The sounds of the horses, of the calls from his men obscured any sounds of a fight, and he crested a small hill, stopped, strained to hear. He felt a twist in his stomach, said in a low voice, "Begin . . . now. Surely. Renew the charge."

He stared ahead, wide fields rolling to the horizon, patches of low trees, deep narrow creeks. And silence.

The column was moving by him still, and he nudged the

horse, could only resume the march. His mind was a swirling torrent of questions, and he looked back, saw the faces of the staff, the expectation of what he would say.

"One of you . . . Mr. Hamilton. Go to General Lee. I must know what is happening. Repeat my order, if necessary, that they press the attack."

Hamilton began to move, slowed his horse again, said, "Sir, there."

A man was stumbling toward them, a ragged mess of a uniform, no weapon, and Washington could see now he was only a boy. The guards were there now, the boy held by two men, and Washington stopped the horse, said, "Who are you, young man? Are you a soldier?"

The boy stared at him with wide ghostly eyes, his red face a smear of sweat and dirt. One of the guards lifted him upright, said, "You will respond to the general."

The boy nodded slowly, tried to speak, and Washington saw the shredded insignia on the man's sleeve, said, "You are a musician? I do not have time for riddles. Who are you, why are you on this road?"

The boy seemed to gather himself, said, "A fifer, sir. I was with General Varnum's brigade. I have lost my fife."

He looked at the wild stare from the boy's eyes, thought, Madness from the heat, certainly. He said to the guards, "See to his care. Send him toward one of the creeks."

The boy seemed not to hear him, said, "Sir, the army is retreating."

The words stabbed at him, and he said, "You will use caution. That kind of talk is dangerous." He looked at the guards now, said, "Hold him under guard. His madness could affect others. We cannot have him spreading such rumors."

He took a last look at the boy, felt annoyance at the weakness of such a child, turned the horse away. He moved back into the road, tried to calm himself, thought, He is a boy, after all. He cannot be blamed for suffering this heat. But if he is correct . . . I must know. He slapped at the horse with the leather straps, began to ride hard out past the front of the column. In front of him, the guards responded, moving quickly. One man stopped, called back to him, pointing, and he saw now, men in the road, a small group coming toward him, dragging muskets behind them. He stopped, waited for the staff, and Tilghman was there now, said, "Sir. Those are soldiers."

"I am aware of the obvious, Colonel. Find out who they are."

Tilghman began to move forward and the guards shouted again, and now the road was coming alive with men, most shuffling slowly, some emerging from the brush. They began to flow by him, most not seeing, some stumbling, one man now falling close to him, the man's musket clattering to the hard ground. Behind them, a larger group of men appeared, were more organized, two columns, a small flag of a regiment. They came on slowly, the men holding themselves in the road with deliberate steps. He saw officers, men on horses, and Tilghman said, "Sir . . . Colonel Shreve."

The faces were familiar, and Washington moved the horse forward again. Shreve moved off the road, let his column move past him, saluted Washington now, said, "Sir. Thank Almighty God."

"What is the meaning of this, Colonel? Why are these men retreating?"

"I do not rightly know, sir. I received the order an hour ago. We had not yet engaged the enemy."

Behind the regiments, more columns appeared, some uneven, men barely able to move, some falling out of line. There were too many for the narrow roads, and the fields out to one side were filling with columns as well. He looked at Shreve, wanted to shout in the man's face, clamped down on the words, said in a growl, "You were ordered to retreat? By whom?"

"I cannot say, sir. The orders came from . . . command."

He stared at the man for a moment, looked now at the column of exhausted troops, said, "Gather these men into a place where they can rest. Refresh them as best you can. This day is not yet concluded."

He moved past the officers, rode between lines of silent troops, thought, This is not a panicked retreat. These men are not beaten by anyone. They have their muskets, they . . . Shreve's words came back to him . . . *had not yet engaged the enemy*. He pushed the horse to a gallop again, threaded his way past the troops. He searched the faces, more officers, some as drained as their men, some moving toward him. He was suddenly at a bridge, a small deep cut across the road, stepped the horse carefully, saw another column in the road ahead, a pair of dogs scampering across the road, saw now, Charles Lee.

He slapped the horse, Lee waiting for him, no expression on the man's face, and Washington pulled up beside him, felt his grip loosening on his temper, the control gone from his voice. He shouted, "What is the meaning of this? Why are these men in retreat? Why is there such confusion?"

Lee stared blankly at him, seemed surprised by his volume, tried to speak, turned slightly in the saddle. Washington's rage was complete, the words a flow of molten rock.

"What have you done, Mr. Lee?"

Lee seemed to stagger under the heat of Washington's glare, a hint of wide-eyed fear. He formed the words, said in a low voice, "There is no confusion here." He tried to gather energy, the smugness beginning to return. "There has been considerable difficulty this morning arising from disobedience of my orders, sir. I have received contradictory intelligence, the enemy has confounded my every move. Officers under this command have failed me in every respect. The ground over which this fight was to be made is wholly unacceptable, a plain so large that no army can make a show for itself. The enemy grenadiers shall surely have destroyed us. As you know, sir, this entire operation was undertaken against my own opinion."

Washington gripped the reins, his fingers curling into hard fists. He glared at the man's smugness, all the perfect excuses, wanted to pull Lee up off his horse, wrap his hands around the man's thin neck. He felt himself choking on the rage, forced his words through a tightly clenched jaw, "You ought not have accepted this plan . . . you ought not have accepted this *command* if you did not intend to carry it through!"

Lee shook his head, said, "Sir, this plan had little chance of success against such a formidable enemy. I tried to caution you . . ."

There was a shout from in front, and Washington saw one of his aides riding hard, the man halting now, "Sir! The enemy is advancing, pursuing our retreat! He is not more than fifteen minutes from our position!"

Washington looked past the man, saw a winding ravine, dense brush, narrow roadways cutting across. Beyond, the ground was a morass of swamps, patches of thick trees, framed by a ridge of high ground.

"As I suspected, sir. We are no match . . ."

Lee's voice sliced through him, a hot sharp blade, and he felt something break inside, the fury and violence now rising, uncontrollable. Lee stopped his words, and Washington saw fear in the man's face, Lee leaning away from him, a small shake of his head, his voice squeezing out one high-pitched word, *"No . . ."*

Washington felt his hands still wrapped around the leather reins, the violence in his mind now a roaring flame. He saw now that men had gathered around them, officers, troops, his staff, all watching him with breathless silence, and he closed his eyes for a brief moment, would not look at Lee. The fury began to slip away just a bit, and he opened his eyes, said, "Mr. Lee, I am relieving you of your responsibility on this field. You will place yourself at the rear of this column."

He did not wait for a response, spun the horse around, saw a new column of troops approaching, more of Lee's retreat, but the men were not staggering, held their muskets on their shoulders, their officers riding stiffly alongside. They moved down through the ravine, then up toward him, and Washington saw their commander, Anthony Wayne, riding alongside the young Frenchman. Wayne raised his hand, and the order went out, and the column came to a crisp halt. Lafayette rode forward still, the young man's face clenched in grim anger.

"General Washington, we received an order to withdraw. General Wayne was compelled to disengage his men from the enemy, and he did so in good order. I wish to report that General Wayne's brigade has performed with the most conspicuous honor."

Wayne moved forward. Seeing red fury on the man's face, Washington said, "Mr. Wayne, we have been informed the enemy is in pursuit of this column. Your troops are in place. Can you maintain a strong defensive position on this ground while we bring the remainder of this army into line?"

"We will not be moved, sir."

"Then proceed."

Wayne's troops began to file out to the side of the road, lining the higher ground, the ravine now to their front, a deadly position for an enemy to cross. He looked at Lafayette, said, "General, we have work to do. I require someone familiar with this ground. It appears to be a good place for a fight."

THE FIRST LINE OF BRITISH TROOPS CAME ON HORSEBACK, A MAGnificent show, cavalry under tall plumed hats guiding their horses in perfect order. Wayne's men were anchored in place, some spread out into the brush along the edge of the ravine, the only movement in their line coming from their commander. He slipped along behind his men, spoke in a hushed voice, caution, patience, unmistakable orders for the men who would only obey them. He knew the British horsemen would make a grand display of their advance, their officers holding them in line to face their enemy as a sign of pride in their power. It was so much tired tradition to Wayne, to so many of the American officers, but it was a tradition that the veteran British regulars carried proudly into every fight, centuries of pomp and magnificence that so often put fear into the hearts of their enemies. But Wayne's men would not run, had seen too much already on this one day, had already pushed hard against the cream of the British infantry. The men on horses were simply more of the same, no matter the finery on their uniforms, or the high-stepping grace of their horses.

The cavalry rode steadily across the swampy ravine, the gait of their horses tied to the sharp rhythm of their drummers. Behind them, along the far side of the ravine, British infantry was moving into position, waiting for the first great thrust from their horsemen to soften up this line of rebels.

Wayne kept up his movement, calming his men, urging them to wait. One of the horsemen pulled aside, and Wayne saw the gold disc on the man's chest, his symbol of rank, the officer who gave the commands. Wayne focused on the man, could see him scanning the lines of troops that blocked his path, and Wayne smiled, knew the order to charge would come from him. He leaned close to the soldiers nearest him. *"Take aim at the king bird."*

The horsemen continued to close and Wayne ignored the nervous glances from the men around him, repeated the words, "Steady. Do not fire."

The horsemen were now within forty yards, the thunder of their drums filling the air, and Wayne watched the British officer raise his arm, point out to one side, the drums changing their beat. The cavalry began shifting their formation, making ready for their final grand assault. Wayne still focused on the officer, was close enough to see the man's expression, the utter contemptuous sneer for these half-dressed men who dared impede the march of the king's own cavalry. Wayne stood up tall, caught the man's eye, raised his hand in a hard fist, then slowly extended one finger, pointed straight into the man's chest, shouted, *"Fire!"*

The rows of muskets exploded in one sharp blast, and for a long moment, there was nothing to see. He shouted again, "Reload! Fire at will!"

As the smoke began to clear, there was a strange hesitation along his line, men staring for a moment at the horrific sight. Horses and their riders were spread along the edge of the ravine, some moving in short fits, blood spreading on both man and beast. The horsemen who could still ride did not remain, were already escaping back across the causeway, and there was no order, no kind of formation. Wayne's men began to fire again, many aiming at horseless soldiers as they tried to pull themselves into some kind of line. But there was no command, no officer to lead them, and before Wayne's men could mount a third volley, what remained of the King's cavalry had limped themselves away.

THE CANNON HAD MOVED INTO NEW POSITIONS ALL THROUGHOUT the afternoon, Knox himself appearing around each battery. The British had responded with waves of their own artillery fire, more than a dozen guns on each side throwing shot and shell at each other, and at the men who fought between them.

Among them was Molly Hays, and she came out to stand with her husband as he worked one of Knox's guns. It was one of the awful fortunes of war that these two armies would wind their way through the New Jersey countryside, to finally collide on this ground, so close to the Hays farm. Molly had come to the deadly fields, as so many of the wives would do. They came to help, of course, but the men would fear more for the women than for themselves, would scold them, command them in fierce language to stay away, to go home, out of the way of the danger. But Hays knew his wife would not endure such a lecture, would certainly never obey one. If she could not stand beside him, then she would offer to perform whatever work was needed. On this awful day, in the killing heat, she found her role, had brought a large clay pitcher, ran from the battery down to a nearby creek, bringing water to the blackened men who worked their guns and themselves with relentless effort.

She had made several trips, the men shouting after her, giving her a playful nickname. She carried it with pride, especially when she saw General Knox himself, the round man sitting high on the horse cheering her as well. The guns had continued to shift position, and she had stayed close, still dragged the water. It was a torturous routine, but she never slowed her efforts. She did not expect to return to the battery to be faced by a silent gathering of men. As they slowly moved aside, she saw him slumped over the axle of the cannon. They pulled him back away from the guns, laid him in the shade of a small tree. But the fight was continuing in front of them, and the men could not wait to give her comfort. As the fire ripped the air, she knelt beside her husband, dipped water from the bucket, washed the blood from his face. She had stayed beside his lifeless body as the fight rolled very close, and Knox had appeared again, shouting warnings, foot soldiers now gathering in line, another officer, musket fire. The cannon stopped firing, the infantry too close in front of them, and the British were responding with muskets, the same muskets that had brought down her husband. But the crisis seemed to pass, and she could see the British troops drifting back through the thickets of brush, the ground in front of the battery a horror of dead and wounded. The foot soldiers were gone, pursuing the enemy, and the cannon began to fire again. She would not stay away now, ran to the gun where he had fallen, stood with the men who had cheered her. She had seen him work the cannon, knew the routine, began by lifting the powder, the heavy shot, swarming around the gun as she had seen him do so many times.

As the day grew late, the battle had shifted away from the battery, the guns growing silent. Knox had come again, had given the order to move once more. She had not escaped his eye, and she watched as the lieutenant spoke to him, saw both men looking her way. She hoped that he was telling General Knox of her husband, her loss. She began to feel afraid that he would scold her, would send her away. Instead, he rode toward her, held out his hand, and as she reached up to take it, he said, "This army shall not forget your service . . . Molly Pitcher."

THE ARMY HAD ADVANCED WITH GOOD PRECISION, AND WASHINGton had placed them along the most advantageous ground. Many of the officers who had retreated under Lee had quickly reorganized their men, bringing them back to the line. Washington had made good use of the men who already knew the contours of the land that lay before them.

He sent Greene to the right flank, Stirling out to the left, both men finding the ground perfect for a strong defense. Wayne had stayed near the center, Lafayette as well, and when the British came forward, their units were separated into uneven lines broken by the rugged terrain. Wave after wave approached the small brushy hills and patches of woods where Washington's men waited. The fights that erupted were brief and decisive. In less than two hours, the British advance was collapsing along every front, brutalized as much by the heat as the men who faced them.

As the British assaults wavered, Washington responded by advancing his men, and gradually the ground around the ravines fell into American hands. The troops maneuvered with a precision that impressed every officer on the field, British and American. One man in particular observed with quiet pride, von Steuben seeing firsthand that his drills and lessons had transformed these men into an army that could stand up to any soldiers King George would send against them.

As the sun settled toward the treetops in the west, the British continued to withdraw from around the swampy ravines, pulling back across the wide fields toward Monmouth Court House. The flower of Clinton's army had had enough.

WASHINGTON LOOKED AT HIS WATCH, AFTER FIVE O'CLOCK, thought, Daylight for two hours, enough time, certainly. He rode along the pathway through the middle ravine, saw cannon moving up across the way, Knox and his officers still maneuvering, still finding the best position to support the steady advance of the foot soldiers.

Across the ravine, the men were spread in thick uneven lines, officers screaming hoarsely, trying to gather the formations. But Washington could see only a few men standing, most simply collapsing in the grassy fields, shirtless, red-faced troops who had exhausted every bit of fire. Even the officers were dropping down, and as Washington rode closer, he saw their faces, men falling to their knees. Few had horses now, so many of the animals falling to the same fate as his own. The grand white steed had died, had simply collapsed beneath him, another victim of the extraordinary heat. He rode a white mare now, a quick replacement found by his staff, its former rider most likely a British dragoon.

He could see up the long rise, scattered bodies of red, gather-

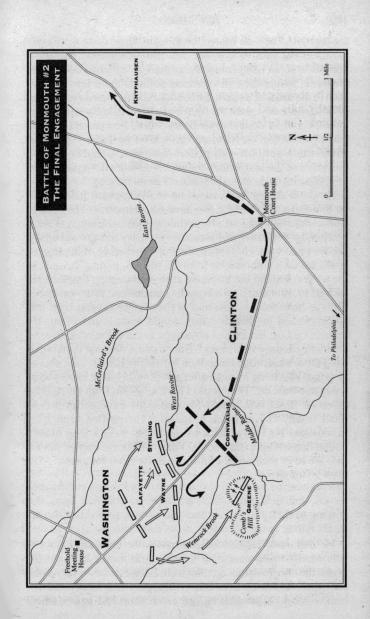

BATTLE OF MONMOUTH #2
THE FINAL ENGAGEMENT

KNYPHAUSEN

East Ravine

Monmouth
Court House

McGellaird's Brook

West Ravine

CLINTON

To Philadelphia

WASHINGTON

LAFAYETTE

STIRLING

WAYNE

CORNWALLIS

Middle Ravine

Wemrock Brook

Comb's
Hill
GREENE

Freehold
Meeting
House

N

0   1/2   1 Mile

ing together. They are beaten, he thought. If we drive them now, they will not survive this day. But the men around him were immobile, some lying flat on the ground. He climbed down from the horse, fought through agonizing stiffness in his legs. He had been in the saddle for nearly fifteen hours, had crossed every piece of this field, every place the fight had gone. He knew so many of his officers had done extraordinary work, Greene and Stirling making the best of the wonderful ground on the flanks. Wayne had continued to perform with perfect discipline, Lafayette holding the center of the line as they fought off assault after assault from men Washington knew to be Clinton's finest infantry.

He stood among them, stared up across the wide field. It will be tomorrow, he thought. We have no alternative. They are in worse condition than we are, certainly. General Clinton is not a butcher, he will not send his men down to try this ground again. So, we must wait. He looked along the gathering of his troops, could see men climbing up from the ravines, joining the men in the field. All along the lines, the army was coming together. He wanted to walk among them, as he had done so many times before, to hear their words, and if they doubted what they had accomplished on this day, they would learn it from him. He thought of Lee, but he had no energy to curse the man, tried to avoid the exercise in his mind. But he could not help thinking of what these men might have done before the British were able to respond. Was it my mistake after all? Should I have known what the man would do? How could I have kept him from his rightful place on this field? Would Mr. Lafayette have performed so much better? The questions rolled up at him, drifted through his exhaustion. He moved back to the horse, took a long breath, pulled himself up to the saddle. There will be no answer, not to-day. We have accomplished all we can for now. Tomorrow . . . it must be tomorrow.

JUNE 29, 1778

He had made his bed under a tree in the open air. Lafayette was nearby, the young man keeping him awake late into the night, the energy to talk coming from Lafayette's own fury at the collapse of Charles Lee. But Washington had finally ordered him to sleep, knew that before much time had passed, there would be repercussions from what Washington had done, that Lee would certainly not go quietly, might even expect to resume some kind of command.

Even in the silence, Washington had begged for sleep, staring up at stars through the leafy branches of a wide tree, and finally the stars were gone, and he had ridden through a great field of cannon and horsemen, all chaos and smoke, realized it was Mount Vernon, the grounds of his beloved home, the shock . . . the house . . . *Martha*.

"Sir!"

The image was gone in the darkness, and the voice came again, a hard whisper, "Sir!"

He raised himself, felt a sharp stab from the stiffness in his back. He heard a match strike, squinted at the glow, saw it was Tilghman.

"Yes, Colonel. I am awake. What is the hour?"

"Four o'clock, sir."

He rolled himself over to his knees, stood up slowly, and Tilghman said, "Should I wake General Lafayette, sir?"

"By all means. I am certain no one will wish to miss a moment of this day."

Now fully awake, he walked out from under the tree, could see the stars again, sharp points of lights covering the entire field. There was movement already, all around him, and he heard the voices, the sound of a tin pot. He felt a thick dryness in his mouth, was desperately thirsty, searched the dark for an aide, someone with a canteen. He moved back toward the tree, more voices in front of him, and Lafayette was there, said, "General. Good morning, sir."

"Mr. Lafayette. I would like you to supervise the formation this morning. You may begin immediately. There can be no delay. At first light, this army will be prepared to advance on my order."

"Sir, right away!"

The young man moved away in the darkness, and Washington could see the faint glow of a fire, the flame hidden deep in the ravine, no target for a British cannon. He thought of coffee, a marvelous luxury. One cup, just one. He looked for Tilghman, heard the young man's voice, the rest of the staff gathering. He stepped that way, thought, One simple luxury cannot do damage. After this day, we may feel like celebrating, indeed!

*   *   *

EVEN BEFORE THE FIRST REAL LIGHT, THE PICKET LINES HAD LED the advance up the long rise, out past the ravines. The men moved with deliberate care, each man waiting for the first flash of light, the British pickets who would be waiting for them. As they spread through the wide field, they discovered a gruesome reality. Bodies of British soldiers were scattered through the grass, the horror deepened by the soft cries from men who were still alive. But there would be no hesitation, and the men of the skirmish line could see the low gray outline of the village. They had expected to find the enemy before now, and the men were flinching at every sound, every crack of a stick. But they kept moving, and behind them, curious officers moved up close, men on horses looking beyond the skirmishers, surprised that Clinton would pull his defensive line back so close to the village. The word began to travel back to the main line, and Washington rode forward, feeling the icy chill in his heart, the low light of the new day revealing what many still could not believe.

The troops continued to advance until they reached the main road itself, the avenue that cut through Monmouth Court House. There were more wounded now, some men on blankets, a few who could pull themselves up, who watched with a new horror as the Americans filled what had been the British camp. But the only other sign of the British army was the enormous amount of equipment they had left behind.

As Washington rode into the small town, his men were pushing beyond the village, the scouts riding hard to the east. He would wait for their reports, but knew already what they would find. It must have begun late in the night, the British gathering those wounded who could walk and putting their men to the march. He sat on his horse in the center of the village and stared east, could see a faint glow, the sun breaking the horizon. The excitement, the anticipation of the morning was gone. Clinton had pulled his army away, had abandoned the field. It was a victory to be sure, a glorious triumph for Washington, for the army who gathered around him. But he could not celebrate, could not feel anything but a numbing emptiness, another grand opportunity to crush the enemy let slip away.

THE BRITISH REACHED SANDY HOOK ON JUNE 30, AND WERE quickly ferried to Staten Island. Despite Washington's distress that he had missed another astounding opportunity, Clinton's command now encompassed nothing more than bases at two American cities, Newport, Rhode Island, and New York. For three years, the British had marched and maneuvered over hundreds of miles of American soil, had assaulted or occupied nearly every major American city. Through a baffling combination of glorious victory and desperate defeat, the king's army now found itself in no better position, with no advantage in either land, morale, or ability, against an army that had demonstrated a maturity and an increasing will to stand tall. Washington had no choice but to assemble his army once more along the Hudson River and wait for the French to make their much-heralded appearance. Clinton established himself once again in the crowded, charred misery of New York, could only begin the effort to convince London that he should at least be given the opportunity to sweep away the legacy of William Howe, some chance to win this war on his own terms.

PART THREE

NATHANAEL GREENE

39. GREENE

WASHINGTON'S LOOKOUTS ON THE JERSEY COAST HAD BEEN GIVEN word to anticipate them, and by the first light of dawn, the topsails were in plain view. They had seen warships before, a constant parade of British frigates and larger ships of the line, the comings and goings of Lord Howe's fleet, or the arrival of new British vessels, merchantmen and transports from across the ocean. As the lookouts watched the sails grow closer, the details of this new fleet began to emerge. It was a stark clear morning, and it was not long before they could count twenty-three ships, many of them much larger than anything the British had in the harbor. By midday the troops in the observation posts were reinforced by a gathering of curious citizens from the farms and villages, a crowd of onlookers massing all along the Jersey shore. To most, the fleet was no different from any they had seen before, but it was the lookouts with the long spyglasses who observed one difference indeed. The flags were French.

They were commanded by Admiral Charles, Count d'Estaing, a man of surly temperament and a long history of service in the French navy. He had received a colonel's commission before he was seventeen, a very young man with what seemed a very bright future. But after thirty years the fire in the young officer had withered, and d'Estaing had become a stodgy and merely competent senior officer. Though he had rarely demonstrated any particular flair for command, his longevity in the service to his monarchs had earned him moderate prestige. From the coasts of India to the English Channel, he had spent his career in combat with one enemy, had built an intense hatred for the British. It was enough reason for King Louis to believe him perfectly

capable of commanding the French expedition to America that
would bring a swift end to such a risky war.

The British warships at anchor in New York Harbor numbered
half the French fleet, and in the city, the British command understood that they were suddenly in a precarious, and possibly fatal
position. But d'Estaing could not simply burst into the harbor
without knowing the waters, would rely on the skill of harbor
pilots supplied by Washington. It was the pilots who turned
American hopes into utter frustration. The French warships were
larger indeed, so much so that they required a depth of twenty-
seven feet. The mouth of New York Harbor was crossed by a
sandbar whose depth at low tide was a good deal more shallow.
If the French ships attempted to enter the harbor, there was a
very good chance they would run aground.

Washington had sent Hamilton and John Laurens to confer
with d'Estaing, but there would be no convincing the French to
pursue such a dangerous course. Alternatives were considered,
and the most obvious choice was made. The French would set
sail for Newport, Rhode Island, to assault the only remaining
British stronghold.

The British force in Newport was close to six thousand men,
commanded by General Robert Pigott. If Pigott's force could be
captured, it would be as serious a blow to the British effort as the
loss of Burgoyne. To d'Estaing, it would be an extraordinary
prize.

While the British had a firm command of Newport, the mainland around them was occupied by barely a thousand continental
troops now commanded by John Sullivan. It was not a force
strong enough to make any threat to the British, and Washington
issued a call to militia in the area, hoping to attract several thousand more. He dispatched Lafayette with another two brigades,
fifteen hundred experienced veterans, and sent them by foot
toward Rhode Island. Though d'Estaing's fleet was a formidable
threat to the British from the sea, Sullivan's command on land
would be strengthened even more by the human cargo the French
ships had brought with them: four thousand French marines. As
the allied forces converged on Newport, there was feverish anticipation in Washington's headquarters. For the first time, a large
British outpost would be confronted by a combined assault from
both land and sea.

* * *

WITH CLINTON'S ARMY NOW CONTAINED IN NEW YORK, AND WASHington securing his outposts all along the Hudson River, it seemed clear that the rest of the summer would pass in a quiet stalemate. Washington's spies were active in New York again, and the reports from Clinton's headquarters showed that as a result of the brutal march from Philadelphia, the British strength had been reduced by nearly two thousand men. Half that number were casualties of either the fight or the heat around Monmouth Court House, but far worse for the British, the Hessians had deserted in astounding numbers, many slipping back toward the various German communities in Pennsylvania. Washington's army was in comparably better condition, and the men welcomed the return to garrison life along the Hudson. With the British now completely off the mainland, the farmers had begun to supply the army again, Greene's quartermaster staff finding a much warmer reception from farmers whose best customers were long gone.

Greene still held the official title of quartermaster, and had no direct command of his former division. The certainty of a quiet summer, and the renewed efficiency of the supply officers meant that Greene could feel comfortable asking Washington for some time with his family. With the march by Lafayette already under way, Greene had offered to serve in Rhode Island in whatever capacity the commanding general thought appropriate. Greene did not hide his desire to make a brief stop at his home along the way, and Washington would not object. Though Greene technically outranked Sullivan, he had readily accepted Sullivan's command for this mission, would serve under Sullivan at the same level of authority as Lafayette. All three men understood that Greene's presence was an asset. The Rhode Islander would certainly add spark to the willingness of his local militia to serve.

COVENTRY, RHODE ISLAND, JULY 30, 1778

Greene sent Major Hovey on his way, to report their arrival to Sullivan, with word that Greene would join him tomorrow. He had arrived at his home knowing that the stay would be brief, one night in his own bed. He had hoped to surprise her, but the sound of horses was unmistakable, and before he could climb down from the saddle, she was standing in the doorway.

She met him with the same teary smile that he had kissed at Valley Forge. He held her for a long moment, could tell from the softness that she had gained weight, the obvious sign of her pregnancy. Her letters had said very little of any difficulties, her attempt to put aside his concerns. But he was skeptical, could not remove the fear for her health until he could see for himself.

He held her out away from him, searching her face, some tell-tale glint in her eye of some ailment she would not disclose. She still smiled, and he felt the fears slipping away, her soft warmth filling the dark places in his mind. She began to pull at him, moving both of them inside the house. He closed the door, and she said, "Come. There is someone you must meet. The general must do his duty."

He could see the humor in her face, and he gently wiped at the tears, said, "The general has remained outside. It is the father who has returned."

He wrapped his arm around her shoulders, and they eased slowly down the narrow hall. She stepped softly, and so he did the same, could not help the nervousness, his heart pounding. She led him to the small bedroom, stood aside.

"Go on in. She's sleeping."

He could not take his eyes from hers, saw the tears coming again, felt his own. He turned slowly into the room, saw a small wooden bed, moved closer, silent steps, sweat on his hands, the pounding in his chest driving an icy chill all through him. He leaned close, could hear the soft rhythm of the child's quiet breathing. He felt suddenly huge, overpowering, a clumsy giant standing so close to such frail perfection. The floor beneath him creaked, and he backed away, would not disturb her, but it was too late. The sound jarred the toddler's sleep, and she turned her head, made a long stretching yawn. She looked at him with wide blue eyes, seemed to study him, curious. Then she raised one hand, pointed at him with tiny fingers.

"Papa."

Kitty was beside him, and he felt her hand slide around his waist, and she said, "That's right, Martha."

He had no words, put his hands out as well, slow, careful, and for the first time, he held his daughter.

TIVERTON, RHODE ISLAND, AUGUST 5, 1778

"We shall be pleased to participate in this plan at your command, General Sullivan. However, we are concerned that your forces here are, forgive me, inadequate to the task."

Greene waited for the explosion, could say nothing. The command was Sullivan's, and no one but Sullivan would respond. Sullivan rose from his chair, and Greene watched the short stout man run a hand through his thinning hair, turn away from the table, pacing slowly. He seemed to be holding tight to his words, and Greene thought, Careful, John. It is time for diplomacy. Sullivan spun around now, hands on his hips, and Greene saw defiance in the man's face, the words slow and precise.

"Admiral d'Estaing, the militia are arriving daily. I had hoped to have more in camp by now, but it cannot be helped. Their commander, General Hancock has assured me that General Washington's plea has reached every village in the area. They *are* coming."

"That would be . . . John Hancock?" D'Estaing seemed impressed now. "We have heard much of this man. He is a great leader. Certainly he will assume command here?"

Sullivan seemed to deflate, and Lafayette said, "Excuse me, General Sullivan, if I may."

Sullivan said nothing, made a quick wave of his hand, and Lafayette said in French, "Admiral, John Hancock commands militia only. He is not an officer in the regular Continental Army. General Sullivan is the commander here."

"Marquis de Lafayette, I have seen nothing here except militia. Even the men you brought here seem unlikely to wage a serious fight."

Lafayette lowered his head for a moment, said, "Admiral, with all respect, the two brigades who accompanied me here are veteran units. They are some of the finest soldiers in General Washington's army." He looked at Sullivan. "My apologies, General. I did not wish to be rude. We should converse only in English."

D'Estaing shrugged his shoulders, said to Sullivan, "The marquis explains to me that this is your command. I am pleased to cooperate. Your plan is sound. Your troops will cross over to the island from here. My ships will approach from the western side. I will land the marines as you make your crossing."

Sullivan stopped his pacing, seemed surprised by the sudden agreement.

"That is fine, Admiral. Thank you. I propose August 10. That will allow us time to complete assembly of the militia."

D'Estaing stood now, his aides behind him rising as well.

"I will return to my ship now."

The men around the table all stood, and d'Estaing made a short bow to Sullivan, marched out of the room. Sullivan waited for them to move outside the house, stepped toward the window, watched as the men were led to carriages, the short ride to the shore boats. He looked back at the men around the table, focused on Lafayette, said, "I trust he will comply with our wishes."

Lafayette nodded.

"General Sullivan, the admiral knows his duty. We should have every confidence in this mission."

Sullivan reached for his hat, moved toward the door.

"I appreciate your hopefulness, General. I assure you, we will complete our part of this." He motioned to the guard beside the door, the door opened for him, and Sullivan said, "I must see to the militia. Hancock promised another thousand by this afternoon. Anyone to accompany me?"

He was out the door now, and the others followed. Greene waited for a moment, then he was alone with Lafayette, said, "It was a fortunate insult."

"In what way, sir?"

"Fortunate that John Sullivan does not speak French."

"Should I not feel the insult as well, sir? Those brigades are my command. I am well aware of their abilities."

Greene sat now.

"I would imagine to a French admiral, we are all militia. We had best become accustomed to it."

Lafayette shook his head.

"It is not necessary for Admiral d'Estaing to insult this army. I fear his attitude may cause some injury."

Greene laughed.

"Not as long as he keeps his insults in French."

AUGUST 9, 1778

The British had responded to the arrival of the French fleet by burning the few ships of their own that lay at anchor around Newport, preventing d'Estaing from making easy capture of the vessels that were so clearly outgunned. Pigott had already abandoned the few outposts beyond the main island where Newport lay, gathering his troops into the strong defenses the British had constructed months before. But even with their forces concentrated on the single island, the British were strung out in a dangerously weak position, and Pigott wisely withdrew his troops southward, concentrating them around the town itself. With the island's northern defenses now empty of troops, Sullivan could not resist taking advantage, ordered a rapid crossing from the mainland, and placed his men in control of that part of the island. The move was concluded with precision, unopposed by any British troops. The only difficulty came from d'Estaing. Sullivan had launched into action a day sooner than the French expected. While the tactics were reasonable, the protocol was not. On the French flagship, senior officers reacted with bristling protest. But the controversy was cut short by a far more serious discovery. Beyond the mouth of Narragansett Bay, a mass of sails began to fill the horizon. The British general Pigott had accomplished much more than the strengthening of his own defenses. His dispatch had gone to New York, and Clinton and Lord Howe had responded. Strengthened by reinforcements from England, Lord Howe had assembled a fleet of his own, more than thirty warships. If d'Estaing did not remove his fleet from the confines of Narragansett Bay, the French could be bottled up and destroyed piecemeal. But more, to a navy man, the British fleet was a target that he could not resist. With Sullivan still expecting the French to land their four thousand marines, d'Estaing suddenly raised his sails, and the entire French force vanished into the Atlantic.

AUGUST 12, 1778

The winds had begun in the middle of the night, and Greene had been shaken from his bed by a screaming gale. With the dawn had come more wind and rain, and through the windows of the small house, he could see that the bay was a frenzy of foaming waves.

For two days, the armies had stared at each other along the large island, both sides eager for some word of what was happening beyond the mouth of the bay. As the storm finally cleared, Greene had a greater concern than the outcome of a naval battle. The camps of his men were a shambles, mud-soaked equipment, tents that had simply blown away. Worse, most of the army's ammunition was ruined. He could only hope that the British camp had suffered as much from the amazing storm.

AUGUST 20, 1778

Sullivan had finally begun the fight, and for five days his troops, backed by John Hancock's militia, pressed the British defenses. Progress was limited, and Greene began to realize that what should have been quick work, the utter destruction of a sizable British force, was instead destined to become a siege. The one element that might yet cause the breakthrough was the addition of the French marines. After so many days at sea, the French fleet began to appear again in Narragansett Bay. As the Americans huddled in their British-made trenches, they cheered the ships. Most had never seen the aftermath of a naval battle, and many stared in shock at the damage. Broken masts hung from rigging, railings were stripped away from decks, planking and gun covers were torn from the sides. When d'Estaing finally made his landing, he did not bring news of any kind of fight with Lord Howe. The two fleets had hardly begun to maneuver around each other before the storm appeared, tossing and scattering the ships, sweeping some far out to sea. Both fleets had suffered equally, neither side capable of any kind of battle. To the relief of the French, Lord Howe had limped his way back to New York.

GREENE BOARDED THE FLAGSHIP, FOLLOWED BY LAFAYETTE. THE *Languedoc* was the largest ship in d'Estaing's fleet, a magnificent fighting fortress holding ninety guns. But her masts were shattered, the rigging still a tangled mess across the decks. Sail-

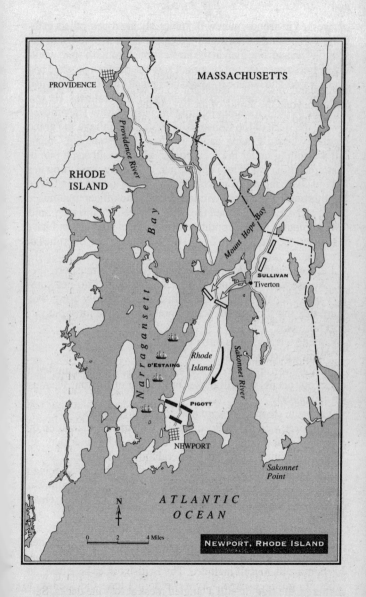

NEWPORT, RHODE ISLAND

ors worked in groups, men with knives, slicing ropes, others gathering what could be salvaged into great fat coils. He heard the
sound of an axe, one man in the bow cutting through a spar, working to free some piece of rigging. From the plank, a passage had
been cleared, and Greene followed the French escort down through
a hatchway, short steep steps that dropped into darkness. He saw
a flicker of light, a candle lighting the passageway. They moved
toward the stern of the ship, and he could see sunlight, the grand
quarters where d'Estaing waited for them. As they entered, Greene
felt a grinding under his feet, broken glass, could see a pile of
shattered china swept into one corner. D'Estaing was sitting in a
tall red chair, facing away from them, staring toward the glow of
light through a shattered window frame. The officer announced
them, and d'Estaing turned the chair, glanced at both men, said,
"My apologies for the condition of my office, gentlemen. I have
instructed the crew to see first to our transport. The amenities of
luxury may wait."

Lafayette said, "I do not understand, Admiral. Transport?"

"We are in a precarious state here, Marquis. I do not know
how many capable vessels the British may suddenly bring. I require that my ships make ready immediately. We must put into
port for repair."

Greene felt a nervous turn in his gut.

"Which port, Admiral?"

"Unless you are aware of some place that is better equipped to
effect our needs, we will make for the port of Boston. We must
set sail quickly."

Lafayette stepped forward now, closer to d'Estaing.

"Admiral, General Sullivan awaits with great anticipation the
arrival of your marines. There is still a fight to be made here, sir.
With the additional strength, General Sullivan believes . . ."

"You may tell General Sullivan that the marines will remain
on board the ships. They will accompany the fleet to Boston. Until I am certain what dangers await these ships, I will not release
them."

Lafayette looked at Greene with a glimmer of panic, and
Greene said, "Admiral, General Lafayette and I have come here
to provide the plan of attack as devised by General Sullivan and
his command, myself included. The British forces here have nowhere to go, no escape. Alone, we do not have the strength to

break their defenses. With your marines, we do. The matter could well be decided in two days. Only two days. That is all we ask."

D'Estaing sniffed.

"General Greene, in two days' time this bay could be a trap for my fleet. Admiral Howe is not a man to sail silently into the night. We do not know what resources he may draw upon in New York. I, however, have no resources at all but what you see here. I have already given the order. The ships in this fleet that are capable of sailing are already doing so. My king was explicit in his instructions, General. Should this fleet meet with any disaster, or should we be confronted by a superior British force, I am to seek safe refuge in Boston. I intend to follow the instructions of my king." He looked at Lafayette. "Do you have any objections to that, Marquis?"

"Of course not, Admiral."

"Well, then, gentlemen, I do not wish to be rude. But I must prepare this ship to sail and concern myself with the care of my fleet. Is that not in your best interest as well?"

Greene thought a moment, could feel Lafayette looking at him, silent caution. Don't worry, young man, I'll not destroy this alliance before it has begun. He said, "Admiral, my concern is for the men in my command, who must now face a formidable enemy without the assistance of our ally. I shall convey your message to General Sullivan. We shall eagerly await your return."

As THE LAST SHIPS SAILED OUT OF NARRAGANSETT BAY, THE REALization that their French allies had abandoned them drained the fight from the militia. Within hours after word had spread, nearly three-fourths of them shouldered their muskets and went home. The sudden weakness in the American lines could not be hidden from Robert Pigott, and the British surged out of their works around Newport and pushed a hard attack into Sullivan's lines. There could be no effective defense, and Sullivan withdrew to the north end of the island, then ordered the remaining troops to be ferried to the mainland. The work was done by Glover's Marblehead fishermen, the same boatmen who had performed such good service so many times before.

Sullivan was furious, and his reports to Washington were hot and undiplomatic, and he unwisely revealed his sentiments to the public. Washington might understand d'Estaing's concerns, but the New England citizenry did not, and a public outcry followed the French fleet to Boston. The civilian newspapers were quick to echo Sullivan's insulting tone, but in the army, there was much more at stake than careless criticism. The alliance was too fresh and too untried to be destroyed by such a swift turn of events, and Sullivan was quickly reined in, his words tempered. Lafayette's temper was boiling as well, as much for his embarrassment at d'Estaing's timidity as for the insults to his country that spilled out in the local communities.

With nothing to be gained by further confrontation at Newport, Washington summoned Greene and Lafayette back to headquarters in New Jersey. There was still hope in the American camp that d'Estaing would yet emerge as the great equalizing force on the sea, that another attempt might be made to assault Clinton's stronghold in New York. But then came word from Boston. The repairs to the French fleet were nearing completion. But instead of sailing back down the coast, d'Estaing would respond to a new urgency, the likely conflict with the British over the islands in the Caribbean. As the final repairs were made, the French fleet raised its sails and disappeared, twenty-three warships and four thousand marines, now on their way to the West Indies.

As Greene rode south, the long hours in the saddle were passed by quiet thought, the sadness and frustration of the mission. There had been failures before, and no one in the army believed that these troops would sweep through every confrontation they would yet have against the British. But Greene knew this failure might have consequences far beyond their inability to recapture a city. All the hopes that had come with the French alliance were suddenly set aside, and Sullivan's anger had spread throughout much of the army as it had spread through New England. No treaty, no alliance was a guarantee that this war would soon be over.

40. CORNWALLIS

THE SHIP SAT HEAVY IN THE WATER, A SOGGY HULK THAT WOULD never see its sails rise again. She was called the *Jersey*, was one of several craft that lay at anchor in the shallows of the bay. Her hull was rotting, her crooked masts bare, and behind the closed covers of the gun ports, her cannon had long been hauled away. The men who served as her crew were not even sailors, were often stationed in this duty as punishment, soldiers or loyalist militia who had shown no talent for facing the fire of the enemy. Some were Hessians, men who had been branded as thieves or worse. Now, they roamed the upper decks of the *Jersey* bearing clubs and whips, while beneath their feet, hundreds of men lay cramped together in a darkened hell. The *Jersey* was now a prison.

One man stared out through an open porthole, the only source of light and air, stared across the East River to the city. He had been captured at the fight for Fort Washington, marched down to the water's edge by angry men in uniforms he had never seen. He had been crowded onto a flatboat with so many others, men from his own company, others strange to him, but all sharing the horror of their defeat. When he first saw the *Jersey*, it had seemed like some glorious blessing. It was a prison ship to be sure, but a place where the men would be safe from the rabble of New York, from the spreading filth of a city too crowded by so many seeking refuge from the war. As he had marched onto the ship, his legs had been chained, and when he was pushed down the hatchway, stumbling in the darkness over men who had gone before him, he began to understand that it was not a blessing after all.

For two years he had survived, had stopped wondering why, his mind stripped clean by the unending horrors. He had one piece of good fortune, his chains were fastened to the bulkhead near one of the high portholes. If he had the strength to pull himself upright, he could see the sunsets, like so many blazing torches settling low over the city, and he had learned to savor every moment, every piece of the fading light. For many months his mind had held away the fear, but time was the enemy, too many nights and too many awful sounds. Now, the darkness brought the madness, the voices and cries holding him frozen, his exhausted mind giving way to the numbing fear, his eyes fighting to see the beasts who made such sounds. At first he had suffered the darkness knowing that the sounds came only from the men whose chains tortured their wounds, or whose sickness had poisoned their sanity. But after two years, his fragile hold on his own sanity had loosened, the voices of the suffering men inseparable from the voices now rising in his own mind.

With each dawn, the demons grew quiet, and the sounds became the voices of the men, so many so close to him, the slow agony of sick minds praying for death. He would not succumb, would pull himself up to the porthole, escape to the peaceful river. On the clear mornings, the river would come alive with the bits of reflection, the sunlight tickling the surface. He had long imagined escape, a dream made real for this one moment, the rising sunlight pulling him out away from the ship like some blessed wave, carrying him over to the city, beyond, his home in New Jersey. But there had been no escape, even for the men who had slipped their chains, bolts ripped from the rotting decks beneath them. Some found the strength to fight, would strike out at the soldiers who brought them food. It was a desperate foolishness that brought bayonets into the hatches, the guards firing randomly into the mass of prisoners. Worse, it took away the food, and for a day or more, nothing would come.

He had learned the skills of the survivor, knew when to reach for the food, knew that many of the men around him were too weak to make the effort. The food would come in scattered heaps, raw, sour pork, hard bread crusted with mold, flour cakes infested with vermin a starving man learned to ignore. For many weeks, he had been charitable, had offered bits of his food to the men nearest him, the men who were too weak to reach for their own. But those men were long gone now, and his generosity was a memory. It was another part of the horror, that each new dawn would find so many more who had not survived the night, who would be dragged up through the hatches by cursing soldiers, corpses to be buried in the soft mud of the riverbank.

It had been the same this morning, the food already eaten, his gut in a hot turmoil, the putrid odors of new sickness rolling through the crowded deck. He had pulled himself up again, stared at the river, the homes along the far shore, had felt the flecks of sunlight opening up the small dark places in his own mind.

He did not know much of Clinton, whether one of the grand mansions was the British headquarters. He knew little of Monmouth or Brandywine, and nothing of Valley Forge. He had heard some rumors of Burgoyne's defeat, loudly denied by the guards. If there was a war at all now, he would know only by the talk of the prisoners, the new men to take the place of so many now buried. For a while, they would have the strength, would speak of their capture, some fight in some place that had no meaning. But soon their voices would grow silent as well, the madness consuming them as it had the rest, what remained of their strength giving energy only to the beasts in the darkness.

He did not know what month it was, but the air cut through the porthole with a sharp chill. He could recall the last time it had been winter, the cries of the beast deadened by the cold. Many men had died then, too many for the guards to notice. It was a strange blessing, food tossed down onto the bodies of those who would not need it, a small feast for those who still survived. The wind ripped at his face, the memories of those months long past, and he felt a hard shiver, wetness in his pants clinging to him. He stared at the rippling sunlight, blessed warmth, saw the reflections in motion, a ship, tall white sails. She was large, a grand man-o-war, moving out through the harbor by the power of the chilling breeze. He watched her until she drifted away, the familiar dream filling him, standing in her bow, the open sky in front of him, the wind carrying him away to some glorious place. He was alone on the ship, no one to cry out, no one to suffer beside him, just the sunlight, washing over him, carrying him home.

The ship disappeared beyond the edge of the bay, and the wind began to bite his face, the tears cutting his cheek. He leaned away from the porthole, his legs giving way, the energy gone, and he sat, settled down into the smells, the cries, and the madness.

* * *

CORNWALLIS HAD BOARDED THE SHIP AT FIRST LIGHT, STOOD ON THE deck in the brisk biting wind. Above him in the East River, he could see the prison ships, a ragged line of useless hulks, motionless, no sign of the grotesque cargo below their decks.

He looked toward Long Island, toward the home he had occupied, a pleasant manor house owned by some Tory aristocrat, the man long gone, imprisoned by the rebels perhaps. Cornwallis would not take up residence in the city, had no need for the astounding debauchery of the place. If he visited the city at all, it was to attend Clinton's headquarters, a grand mansion called the Kennedy House, on the southernmost end of Broadway. Even without the degrading behavior of the officers, the city had become its own nightmare, the ruins from the fire providing shelter for anyone who could not afford to buy themselves into British luxury. The poor, and many not so poor had massed into the ruins to construct a makeshift village of shacks and scraps of tents, which had become known as Canvastown. With the army keeping mainly to itself, Canvastown had become the most dangerous place in the city. Crime and disease were commonplace, and the utter lack of sanitation had created a massive open sewer that far surpassed the horrors they had left behind in Philadelphia.

Cornwallis had attended some of the parties, could hardly decline an invitation from Clinton himself. He had learned quickly why both the officers and their society damsels seemed to bathe themselves in so much perfume. From the depths of Canvastown, and even from the narrow streets that had escaped the fire, the concentration of refugees had created a permanent stench throughout the city that even the elite could not avoid. Since no one had any kind of solution for absorbing the influx of loyalists, they could only try to mask themselves from their presence. Even Cornwallis had to agree that a substantial dousing of perfume was an acceptable alternative to the fog of odor that even the wealthy could not escape.

Though Clinton felt he should remain in the city, that responsibility was not shared by Cornwallis. Long Island had become a place to play. From his new home, Cornwallis had ample opportunity for hunting and fishing, long rides through the hills that two years before had framed bloody battlefields. Many of the senior officers took advantage, and seemed far more enthusiastic about the outdoor distractions than what they left behind in the city. But the carefree life was fragile, and no matter the pageantry of the fox hunts or the pheasant shoots, the stark reality could not be avoided. Long Island itself was far from secure, and every foraging party or social gathering was subject to the presence of guards. Every day, patrols and cavalry units probed and swept across the countryside. Not so far from the shores of the East River, Long Island was a lawless and hostile place, peopled by highwaymen, or worse, common citizens who still felt allegiance to Washington and his rebels. No matter the illusion of holiday, Cornwallis knew that beyond the next hill, past the scenic pasture or meadow might lie a band of musket-toting farmers who would thrill at the opportunity to take aim at a British officer.

Jemima's letters continued to bring despair, hints that she was growing weaker, some frightening affliction that neither of them could name. He knew so little of medicine or disease, had convinced himself that it was his absence that had caused her such misery. All throughout the year, he had thought of her in every quiet moment, and his sanctuary in the Long Island countryside could not erase an aching homesickness. With the army already making plans for winter quarters around the city, Cornwallis knew that, for long months to come, his duty would be painfully dull. He had prepared a lengthy argument, would present Clinton with all the reasons why the army did not require its second in command to endure the New York winter. He had expected protest, had been surprised, thankful when Clinton agreed. The only condition was that Cornwallis make a special effort to visit Clinton's family, to return with some bits of personal greeting from those who inspired a homesickness in Clinton himself.

The ship tacked slightly to the east, and Cornwallis could see the sun finally rising above the horizon, warming him against the sharp wind sweeping the deck. He could smell the salt spray rising from white foam, could feel the ship rolling in slow rhythm to the growing waves. They were clear of Staten Island now, the land falling away. He looked up toward the men above him, sailors doing the good work, tightening and securing the rigging, preparing for a month on the open sea.

SUFFOLK, ENGLAND, DECEMBER 29, 1778

The voyage had been unusually rapid, and a strong westerly breeze swept the ship across the Atlantic in less than four weeks. He had made his official greeting to Lord Germain, but London could not hold him for more time than duty required. Germain had graciously furnished him with a carriage, seeming to sense that Cornwallis had only one priority. Despite the signs of winter, the rolling hills and brown meadows had seemed especially beautiful. He passed by the familiar, hidden places he had explored as a boy, patches of woods, narrow swift streams that flooded him with memories. As he rode up to the house, he was surprised to see no one outside, no gardeners working the beds, only cold silence from the small stable. It was clearly an estate in need of a master.

The home was called Culford, and it was no one's portrait of a grand estate. His father had not been as wealthy as so many who cherished their precious titles, the entire family working their way to maintain the oh-so-important bearing of the aristocrats.

HE HAD BEEN UP EARLY, NEVER ABLE TO ESCAPE THE ROUTINE OF the army. He slipped out of their room with silent steps, leaving her to a fitful sleep that had kept him awake most of the night. The surprise of his arrival had already begun to wear off, and he was dismayed by her strange gloom. For months, the letters from his family had insisted that his presence alone would be the cure she needed, but even the coming of Christmas had done little for her spirit. He had not expected to be home in time for the holiday, the surprise adding to the pure joy in the children. But they were away now, returning to the routine of their schooling. With the house suddenly quiet, he had established a routine of his own, a quiet breakfast alone, while Jemima sought strength from long hours in bed.

Her maid had been in the kitchen before him, would accommodate him by preparing a simple fare, biscuits, a pot of tea on the stove. The maid's name was Ruthie, a short round elderly woman who scurried through the house like some desperate mouse. Ruthie had been with her mistress since Jemima was a baby, and Cornwallis knew to stand aside, that when matters of the house were involved, Ruthie was in absolute command. He had no idea of her age, her plumpness hiding her years. But her loyalty and her love for Jemima were as strong as his own.

It was barely daylight, and he finished his cup of tea, moved up into the main hall, heard no one moving. He peeked into a small parlor, saw a pad of paper, pulled a pencil from his pocket. It was his way of passing the time, his quiet patrolling of the house. The house itself was clumsy in design, dark and dank spaces, a central courtyard that never saw light. He moved through halls that were too narrow, paused at the door to the dining room, shook his head at the thoughtlessness of the design. The room had been placed with the windows facing a setting sun, so that the evening meal was uncomfortably warm. He scanned the room, made notes of the disrepair, rotting timbers. He had seen the dark stains, small leaks beneath the windows that would certainly grow worse. He climbed the stairway, ran his hand over rough plaster, cracks large enough to accommodate a finger. He reached the second level, stopped, the musty smells surrounding him. The bedrooms were small, tight spaces, and he waited for a moment, then eased slowly toward her room, listened for a moment, then slowly opened the door. He peered through the dull light, could hear her breathing, the space in the bed beside her, his space, still vacant. He wanted to move close to her, felt a desperate need to lift her spirits, to give her some part of himself, his own energy, to bring her back to that wonderful time they had once shared. She moved now, soft stirring, a rustle of covers, and he saw her looking at him.

"Is it terribly late?"

He moved close to the bed.

"No. Not at all. Barely daylight. I'm sorry to disturb you."

She lay back again, and he saw the soft smile, the perfect beauty that had captured him so completely.

"I should rise. Ruthie worries so."

He put his hand on her shoulder.

"She worries no more than I do. But if you feel tired, there is no need . . ."

"Charles, will you stay?"

He leaned close, kissed her forehead.

"Certainly. We can spend the entire day in this bed, if that is what you want. Ruthie can bring your breakfast right here."

She took his hand.

"Help me to sit."

He lifted her from behind, and she sat back against the head-board.

"No. Not just today. Will you stay here? Is it so important that you return to that terrible place?"

He felt her gaze, the soft eyes piercing him. He glanced at the nightstand, the pad of paper, his notes, so much to do, so much disrepair. He felt a rush of energy, stood, moved to the small window. He stared out across the bare gardens, the dull brown grass, leafless trees, thought, So much is required, so much that is my responsibility. He thought of Clinton, of New York, the images hard and ugly in his mind. He turned, saw her still watching him, her face framed by the low light from the window.

"There may be no better time. There is so much to do here, and so little to be accomplished over there. I had so hoped it would be concluded by now, that I would be here . . . that I would return to you, to the children."

She seemed surprised by his response.

"What do you mean, Charles? Are you saying . . . you will stay? I did not expect you to agree. Your duty, it is all I hear from the family. Your sister says I should not prey so on your feelings, I should not be such a burden. Your duty is so very important. This awful war."

"I am not certain I even have a duty now. This *war*? I'm not certain that word even applies to what we are enduring in America. Wars are fought by soldiers, men who stand tall on a field and show their courage and their skill by facing their enemy and destroying him. It is the very thing that inspires any man to become a soldier, to test one's own resolve, one's own courage. It is certainly what inspired me." He moved to the doorway, felt himself growing angry, aimed his words out beyond the room. "I am sorry, my love. I do not wish to upset you."

"Nonsense, Charles. You are angry. Please. I have waited so long for you to be here, to tell me all that has happened."

He turned to her again.

"What has happened is that we have created a war only to avoid fighting it! We have made prisoners of our own army! We serve men in London who make war by issuing decrees, who move us about like pieces on a chessboard. We are not even al-lowed to fight. We back away from our enemy and allow him to grow strong. While we delay and debate, we grant him precious time to make powerful alliances. Is there no one in England who desires to *win* this war? Now that I am here, I begin to understand how very far away it is. It is simply not *real*. To the ministry, even to His Majesty, it seems that America is only some place on a map, some piece of the empire that must be preserved because history demands it. But those men know nothing of this war. They could never imagine ten thousand rebel soldiers, they have never seen the king's finest cavalry swept from their mounts by the muskets of farmers. No war can exist without the will of those who must wage it. The rebels *have* that will. I am not certain that we do." He paused, saw her still watching him. "I am so very sorry. I have no right to burden you with this."

"Charles, I am burdened only by your absence. If you are serious about remaining here, I understand what that means. Are you saying you would resign? You would turn away from your command?"

"My command. I serve a man who believes my every moment is spent in conspiracy to replace him. I have come to pity Henry Clinton. He is but another sacrificial lamb. One by one the ministry offers temptation to good men, a place in history, the opportunity to return home to thunderous applause. It has become nothing more than a competition. Who has the greatest ambition? Who can be tempted to believe that going to America might open the way for lasting rewards, the praise of a nation, the favor of our king? Thomas Gage? Johnny Burgoyne? William Howe? The garbage heap of history is a cluttered place." He stopped, realized he was nearly shouting, took a deep breath, lowered his voice. "And yet, they are all good men, they are all good soldiers. Any one of them could have already won this war. Now Henry Clinton has been provided the opportunity to fail. And if the war is still not decided, then who will follow?" He moved to the bed, sat, the anger draining out of him. "Please forgive me, my love. One does not say these things around headquarters. I fear I have held tightly to these thoughts for some time."

She put a hand on his arm, moved closer to him, rested her head against his shoulder. The anger was gone now, and he stared out toward the window. He felt her frailty leaning against him, and she said, "There is much to be done here. The house certainly. The gardens need tending. We could do that together. I should enjoy seeing you get your hands dirty."

HIS FURY HAD PASSED, BUT HIS DETERMINATION TO BE FREE OF THE frustrations of the war had not. His resignation was accepted by the king without debate. He was grateful for George's kindness, the king seeming to understand that the war had become a tedious nightmare for anyone who had the integrity of a good soldier.

He returned to Culford feeling very much the master of the modest estate. The plans for the repairs to the house were more detailed now, and he learned quickly that he had the skills of neither a carpenter nor a mason. He sent word to the village that come spring, services would be required. The winter was bleak and miserable, and there was little for anyone to do beyond the confines of the house. He passed the time with the journals of the estate, a challenge of numbers and accounts. His routine continued, and he actually enjoyed the quiet moments before dawn, had finally relieved Ruthie of the chore of rising so early just to prepare his breakfast.

He stayed close to the house for several days, the excuse always the bleakness of the weather. But Jemima's routine had changed as little as his own, long hours in the darkened room. His resignation from the army had brought her out for several days, and the house had brightened, all the promise of a spring that was still to come. He had been surprised at his own sense of relief, that his retirement had meant more to him than he would ever have believed. He had spent as much time as her energy would allow in talking to her about the repairs, all the projects he was beginning to plan. She had listened politely, pretended to share his enthusiasm, until he finally understood that details of woodworking were boring even to him. Their talk had turned to travel, the chance to visit Ireland perhaps, places he had long taken for granted. Her happiness had opened up a place in him he had never known, so different from a soldier's life. It was as though the war didn't exist, and the very criticism he had voiced of the government had instead become a blessing. It was indeed so very far away, and so very removed from this family, this soldier who was now only a husband and father.

But the winter had dragged on, and the enthusiasm they

shared was weaker now, cut down by the return of her ailment. He still tried to bring her out of the bed, waking her to a new day, hopeful that she would feel the energy. But the humor, the playfulness had faded away. As he slipped quietly from their room, he had grown more afraid that she might never find the strength to share all the joyful plans.

He had fashioned a study out of a side room off the large entrance hall, but could not avoid the uncomfortable dampness that plagued so much of the house. He had been absorbed in his reading, a manual on herbs and flowers, something he had bought for Jemima. He set the small book aside, reached for the tea, cold, had let it sit too long. There were padded footsteps in the hall, and he said, "Yes? Who's there? Ruthie?"

The old woman peered around the door.

"Aye, sir. Would you be needin' a thing from the kitchen, then?"

He glanced at the teacup.

"No, quite all right."

"If you're sure, then."

She did not move away, and he looked at her now.

"Is there something else?"

He could see the concern on her face, and she seemed to hesitate.

"I don't mean to be troublin' you, sir. I'm a mite worried about Miss Jemmi."

He looked down, felt himself sinking into the chair.

"She'll be all right. We must allow her to rest."

The old woman said nothing, backed away, and he said, "What else should we do?"

It was a question he had asked himself every day, and she said, "I don't know, sir. Everyone says that with you coming home, she'll be up and right just anytime. I just don't know . . ."

"It will still be that way, Ruthie. I'm not going anywhere now. Nothing is as important to me as Jemima, and getting her strength back. She has been . . . somewhat better."

"I hope so, sir. It's all she's talked about, you coming home. You two ought to be together."

He stood now, moved past her into the hall. He looked at the stairway.

"You're right. Surely, that's all it will take."

FEBRUARY 14, 1779

The doctor had come, a younger man, had stayed with Jemima for most of the afternoon. But he was gone, no answers to their questions, only reassuring words that convinced no one.

Jemima had not left the room in two days, and Cornwallis had climbed the stairway to look in on her yet again. Ruthie had brought tea, the tray on the floor outside the door, and he opened the door slightly, the small dark room holding tight to the odor of sickness.

"Jemima?"

He waited for her response, small movement in the bed, but the room was silent. He eased inside, put a hand on the blanket, said again, "Jemima? There's tea. Ruthie has prepared . . ."

He saw her face now, the sad frailty replaced by a quiet calm. He moved close, put a hand on her cheek, felt the soft cold stillness. His hand shook, and he backed away, felt a hard icy hole open inside of him. He reached behind him, felt for the open door. He could not look away from her, backed away still, was outside the room now, his eyes fixed on her face. He wanted to speak to her, some words, her name, but there was no voice in him, no sound at all, and with a trembling hand, he closed the door.

HE COULD NOT STAY IN THE HOUSE, WROTE BRIEF DETAILED LETTERS to his family, all the affairs of his life put onto paper. As he rode toward London, there were no thoughts of gardens and estates, or trips and laughter. The countryside was unfamiliar, the carriage carrying him past woods and deep winding creeks whose memories had been swept away. He felt no attachment to the land, the towns, the country. With her death, something had left him, some piece of his own soul taken with hers.

He was on his way to see Germain, had requested an audience as well with the king. There was only one place now where he could feel at home, where no one would speak of wives and illnesses and country estates. If the king would allow it, if the government would only understand that he could still be a good servant, that he still knew something of discipline and honor, then he could still give them what it took to be a soldier. All he wanted was to leave this place. The only comfort left for him now was his life in the army. He would go back to America.

41. WASHINGTON

IT HAD BEEN A STRANGELY MILD WINTER, AND ALL THROUGH THEIR bases along the Hudson, Washington's men had enjoyed a peaceful winter quarters. If there was misery at all, it was due mainly to the boredom.

They had constructed their own cabins, the lessons carried forward from Valley Forge. There had been mistakes made that previous winter, the cabins topped by roofs of mud and grass, which kept the cabins wet and unhealthy. The forests near the Hudson had supplied a greater supply of wood planking, and the new cabins were healthier places. They had flooring as well, another lesson learned, separating the blankets of the men from the ground beneath them.

Despite the depressing turn the French alliance had taken at Newport, the news from across the Atlantic was still positive. The merchant ships had continued to bring their precious cargo, and nearly all of Washington's army received fresh uniforms. There were shoes as well, a better quality and a greater number, and for the first time since the siege of Boston, his men were not forced to perform their drills and marches in bare feet.

As the new year had begun, there had been little sign the British would move at all from their crowded base in New York. There had been raiding parties, foraging expeditions along the New Jersey shore, the occasional bloody confrontation with surprised outposts. But for the most part, Clinton seemed determined to maintain the inflexible British custom of delaying any new campaign until winter had completely passed.

With little activity that required his presence along the Hudson, Washington had gone to Philadelphia, the invitation both social and official. Martha had joined him there, and the city had responded with a series of lavish affairs, grand balls and banquets. He had expected celebrations for the success of his army, the recognition from a grateful nation that their enemy had been driven away. But as the weeks passed, he could see that the festive atmosphere in Philadelphia had little to do with the army at all. It was more a city returning to its routine, a decadent display of excess and wastefulness, as though no one in the city was aware that not so far away, two armies faced each other across a river, waiting to resume their bloody war.

HE COULD NOT AVOID EVERY PARTY, BUT MADE EXCUSES NONETHE-less, finding some refuge in the business of the war. Much of the time had been spent with his friend Robert Morris, the man who had already done so much good work as the nation's unofficial financier. It was Morris who kept the avenues of commerce open to France, who had completed the process begun by Silas Deane. The merchant ships were still under threat from British patrols, but now, with the French fully in the war, the supply ships were protected by French men-o-war, and Lord Howe's warships could no longer make easy prey of the French and American cargo.

Morris had been successful in business long before the war. In the years before the Declaration, many of the colonial merchants had been the strongest voice against any controversy that might endanger their cozy relationships with their British suppliers and customers. Morris had been outspoken from the beginning in his support for independence. But he also possessed the caution of the conservative businessman, and unlike many of the radicals in congress, Morris had thought the Declaration itself was too much too soon. With the keen eye of the economist, he warned that the fledgling nation had no financial foundation to support itself against the might of the British empire. But when the vote had passed the congress, Morris had signed the Declaration after all, and from that moment, had never wavered in his support for Washington's efforts.

THE LUNCH WITH MORRIS HAD BEEN MODEST, AT WASHINGTON'S request. He had suffered several days of an uncomfortable malady, the result of too much feasting at too many lengthy banquets. Morris seemed to understand, and Washington appreciated that his friend had no need to make a display of abundance.

He sat back in the chair, watched as Morris filled a pipe, tamping the tobacco down slowly, carefully. Morris caught his look, said, "My one true pleasure. Virginia's gift to the civilized world." He lit the pipe, extinguished the long match, winked at him. "Well, one gift. She has a talent for supplying good generals."

Washington was surprised by Morris' good spirits, said, "Forgive me, Robert, but I expected you would be in a somewhat sour state. I saw the newspaper this morning."

Morris shrugged.

"Today they assaulted *me*. Last month, those same writers spewed forth so much bilge in *your* direction. I should be flattered at the attention."

"Does it not bother you that some are questioning your honesty? The article today came very near calling you a thief, stealing from the public funds."

"I am neither angered nor threatened by it, George, because I know the source. They are the same voices who have assaulted the integrity of Silas Deane, men of intense ambition and no means to realize it. Jealousy, George. There are men in this nation, men in this congress, for God's sake, who sit on their hands and spout furious criticism at every turn. They speak against me, against you, against your quartermaster, Mr. Greene. They lash out at any policy, any decision that calls for someone to actually *do* something. They are infuriated that the congress is not allowed to exist solely as a social gathering. They bristle at the notion that a congressman should shoulder some actual responsibility. It infuriates them. They find me especially infuriating. I am, after all, in business. I make a profit from what I do. How dastardly of me!"

"There is no shame in business, I would think."

"Naïve, George. Permit me the lack of humility, but I happen to be very good at managing my affairs, and the affairs of my company. I have profited by those affairs, and would have done so whether or not there was a war. That's a simple fact that escapes my critics. It is assumed that anyone who acquires profit in these times must be a thief of one sort or another. Often, that kind of criticism is just. There is immense abuse, George, right here in Philadelphia. You see it everywhere you go. Have you attempted to purchase a saddle for your horse? New boots, perhaps? A bushel of grain? All are necessities of war, you might say. And all are being offered at exorbitant prices by men who have come to see the war as an opportunity to steal from their country. Those people expect only to be considered to be in business as well. Thus it is a simple matter for the newspaper to hang us all with the same noose. My crime? I make a small commission on every shipload of cargo my company receives and delivers. On the other side of the Atlantic, Mr. Deane was guilty of the same offense. Thus we are condemned for feeding at the public trough, as though we should offer our services for free. No matter that I must feed my family by the purchase of meat that is no less plentiful than a year ago, but is ten times the cost."

Washington thought a moment, said, "We are suffering some difficulties at Mount Vernon. I can barely afford the cost of seed, of cloth. All manner of goods have become expensive beyond reason. Yet, all around Philadelphia I see abundance of supply, merchants with full shelves. Is there no sense of patriotism here? Would a man rather have a full storeroom than give help to his country? What kind of man has so little good conscience? You are the expert in such thing, Robert. What is to be done?"

"Bayonets."

Morris continued to draw on the pipe, the smoke drifting into a cloud above him. Washington absorbed the word, saw a slight smile, said, "It is a poor joke, Robert."

"Possibly. But, when the British army was around this city, the talk was survival, not profit. The war has disappeared from Philadelphia, and so, the threat has disappeared as well. One way to change that. Bring in a few more bayonets. Patriotism must sometimes be encouraged. Your Mr. Greene has been a master at stirring that pot. Perhaps he should be given an even freer hand, remind these people that there is more at stake than the value of the paper dollar."

"That would not sit well with the congress, Robert. They protest enough that we have such a presence of troops here now. General Arnold's command . . ." He stopped, saw Morris shake his head.

"General Arnold."

"Is there a problem with Mr. Arnold of which I am not aware?"

Morris pulled at the pipe again, said, "Have you enjoyed all these feasts given in your honor?"

Washington was puzzled, said, "I have thought them to be somewhat excessive for my taste."

"Under General Arnold's command, this city has experienced a revival of excess and decadence that even General Howe would have found distasteful. It seems that Benedict Arnold has been captivated by his newly acquired wife, the former Miss Shippen. Peggy is a very young thing, who has a surprising maturity when it comes to her appreciation of . . . pampering. Forgive my lack of graciousness, George, but she has become somewhat legendary for her, um, *gratefulness* for those who provide her with life's finer adornments. It seems not to matter to her that for a time, those baubles were provided by the British. Now, of course, she is provided for by General Arnold. In my humble estimation, her requirements have provided him with a full occupation."

Washington said, "I have heard very little of this. There are always complaints about any commander who holds a senior post, especially one with the prestige of Philadelphia."

"Just a word of advice, George. This is a place where corruption breeds."

"I will be aware, certainly. If there is a new campaign soon, I will require my best field commanders close by. General Arnold is certainly that."

"You anticipate a campaign soon?"

"I have learned that the British will defy my expectations at every turn. They have shown no sign of movement. It is possible that General Clinton is waiting for the French to show their intentions."

Morris extinguished the pipe, tapped it on the table.

"I am concerned that King Louis considers us a low priority compared to his interests in the Caribbean. If the Newport affair is their best effort . . . God help us."

Washington was surprised at Morris' lack of faith, said, "It was the fault of one man. Admiral d'Estaing was not prepared to subordinate himself to an American commander. I must believe there will be a greater effort to work for a common goal. I have already taken steps to assist that process. Mr. Lafayette is on his way to France now. I have instructed him to use his influence to *clarify* our needs. He has proven himself to be a most worthy ally to my command, and to this nation."

"Are you not concerned about time, George? I have no reason to doubt the young marquis' abilities, but the British could strike out at any moment."

Washington looked down at the table, put his hand flat on the smooth wood.

"The British have accommodated us before. Is it naïve of me to have faith that they will do so again?"

Morris leaned forward, looked at Washington with the seriousness of a man in business.

"You know better than I. But Clinton's inaction may be the best hope we have. Without the French, I do not see how the congress can provide for another campaign. There is no pay for your men, new recruits will be difficult to find."

It was the same story, every new year bringing the same fears. Washington knew that the commissions of nearly four thousand of his regular troops would expire by late spring.

"Then I will continue to hope, Robert. Perhaps General Clinton is content to remain in New York. Perhaps he awaits reinforcements of his own, feels he is too weakened to begin a new campaign. We know from several reliable scouts that he has shipped out a great many men to the southern islands."

"Then you are not naïve after all. You have learned your enemy well, George. It is the mark of a good commander."

AS THE SPRING GAVE WAY TO SUMMER, THE BRITISH EMERGED FROM the city only to continue their small raids on supply depots and farms. Clinton made one serious push up the Hudson, capturing the valuable outpost at Stony Point. It was good strategy, a possible foothold they could use for a much larger campaign upriver toward Washington's main fortification at West Point. But Clinton was careless, and left the newly captured prize undermanned. Washington responded with a quick strike by troops led by Anthony Wayne, and within days, Stony Point was back in Washington's hands. But Stony Point was too weak a position for either army to defend, and Wayne was forced to withdraw, the British occupying the place yet again.

The tit-for-tat confrontations continued in several quarters, from the coast of New England to Virginia, and Washington became more and more confident that Clinton had no intention of mounting a major campaign. He could only assume that the British had as much need of a respite as the Americans. Regardless of what strategy Clinton might be planning for the future, for the present, the British were giving the Americans an enormous gift of time.

While the Hudson was the focus of much of the skirmishing, there was one brief and sharp action farther south, a swampy spit of land called Paulus Hook, which lay along the New Jersey coast opposite southern Manhattan. The British had grown careless again, the outpost manned by five hundred troops who guarded their sandy entrenchments, disregarding any threat from Washington's troops. In the darkness, a handpicked force of three hundred light horsemen burst into the British lines and captured a third of their men, escaping as rapidly as they had come, with a loss of only five American casualties. It was a blow to British pride more than any great strategic victory, but it brought a new officer to Washington's attention. The light cavalry had been commanded by a Virginian, a man whose family Washington knew well. While the young major had shown a talent for horsemanship, the cavalry had yet to prove itself as effective as their British counterparts. But after Paulus Hook, Washington realized that cavalry could be useful indeed, especially if they were led by effective officers, good men like this Virginian, the young major they now called "Light-Horse Harry" Lee.

42. FRANKLIN

Paris, Summer 1779

HE HAD BEGUN THE DAY AS EVERY DAY BEFORE, CONSULTING HIS calendar. The pages were typically a mass of scribbles, and it made no difference if the writing was his or Temple's. The appointments would flow out into the margins of each page, row upon row of names and titles. Each name was accompanied by a time of day, a mild joke now. It was generous of the French to try to appease the American need for punctuality, but Franklin had come to understand that no one would ever arrive at his designated time.

This morning he had followed his usual routine, settled heavily into his soft chair with his cup of coffee, thumbing his way through the calendar to the current day. The result was a glorious discovery. Two pages had been adhered together by some long misplaced morsel of food. The hidden page, now blessedly blank, was for today's appointments. Whether the sloppiness was his or Temple's, he was grateful nonetheless. With pure glee, he had scraped the crusty bit of food from the paper, placed it in a small velvet box on his desk, a memento of an unplanned day of rest.

The house was empty, the maid away at the market. He shuffled through the papers on his desk, glanced at the empty coffee cup. He had made the attempt several times to brew his own coffee, the result never to his liking. There was always someone there to take over, Temple, certainly, or Silas Deane. He sat back in the chair, adjusted the discomfort in his legs. *I am indeed forsaken. Alone and . . . coffeeless.*

Deane had been gone for over a year, recalled by a congress that had been flooded with the tirades of Arthur Lee. Lee had accused every American in France of corruption and thievery, and though Franklin was included in the list, Lee had the good grace to blunt the language of those particular accusations. But Deane had few important friends in Philadelphia, and Franklin had watched him depart under a heavy yoke of defeat. Deane already knew that Lee's accusations would carry great weight in the congress, and Franklin felt sincere pity for this man, who had labored through such arcane difficulties of trade and finance. Now, he would have little help in defending his honor. For a long while, Franklin had believed Arthur Lee was settling into some sort of annoying, harmless insanity. But Deane's recall was serious, the man never likely to receive his due, an otherwise decent man who might now be made the scapegoat for any impropriety Lee wished to raise. Deane's departure was an affront as well to the French, who trusted the man and had relied on him to help engineer the delicate negotiations of trade.

The congress had put its best foot forward and replaced Deane with John Adams. Adams had arrived in Paris a man clearly out of his element, and everyone in the French court was quickly aware of it. He spoke no French, and seemed unable, or perhaps unwilling to learn, and Franklin had found himself in the strange role of interpreter. Franklin knew he had Adams' respect, but he also knew that Adams was a man accustomed to carving his own path. With Franklin so firmly entrenched as the primary negotiator with the French, Adams had bristled at accepting a role he had not been expecting, that of Franklin's subordinate. Franklin had seen immediately that the Massachusetts lawyer truly had no idea what his job was supposed to be. In a short while, Adams had learned to grumble less and support Franklin by adding his flair for neatness to the somewhat sloppy office management of Franklin and his grandson. But Adams had never warmed to Paris, and after several months he was gone as well, returning to Massachusetts to tend to the affairs of his home state.

Franklin thought of rising from the chair, working the misery from his legs, but the soft leather had captured him completely. He reached over to the inkstand, picked up his pen, looked at the tip, a blob of ink hanging precariously. He studied it for a moment, then realized he was wearing white pants. He eased the pen back to the well, thought, That would never do. Placing an indiscreet smear of ink on myself would probably result in a sudden visit from the king. Or worse: Madame Brillon.

He grunted, pulled himself up from the chair, one hand on the desk, supporting himself. The gout gave him both good days and bad, and today seemed to be neither. He picked up the coffee cup, shuffled slowly toward the kitchen, thought, I should not allow Temple such freedom. This is when I require him most, not just when the visitors parade through here. I can endure the people. It's the coffee that gives me such difficulty.

His grandson had been whisked away to Paris, the guest of some society belle in the village. He was gone often now, and Franklin had come to realize that if he did not give the young man specific instructions, Temple would interpret that to mean his presence was not required. Franklin moved into the kitchen, thought, He should decide if he intends to be a boy or a man. A man has responsibilities, after all. He is my secretary. A man does not allow himself to be pursued by women to such an extent that he loses his senses. Only a boy would seek such comforts. Well, no, a boy will not have the same interests. It is the man . . .

He set the cup down on the marble counter, smiled. Your logic is deteriorating as quickly as the rest of you, old man. I should find fault with him because he obeys the same instincts that have so pleased his grandfather? He listens more than I give him credit. Franklin recalled the lecture he had endured from some local busybody, who had scolded Franklin for the numerous visits from the ever-energetic Madame Brillon. He recalled the man's finger, poking menacingly into Franklin's face, the shrill tone of his voice. He laughed now, thought, That fellow could only regard women as objects to be feared, was positively certain that men are of so much more value. No doubt, his own home is void of anything feminine. Franklin had responded with his own view of man, a violent and mischievous creature responsible for a lengthy list of ills. He tried to recall the man's name, Guy . . . something, the man clearly unreachable, and thus, not worth remembering at all. He is simply jealous that a woman with the charms of Madame Brillon should ride past his home on her way to mine.

He moved out of the kitchen now, having given up on the idea of coffee. Ah, Temple. Go forth, young man. Surrender yourself to the captivity of the softer gender. For one day you may be as old as your grandfather, and given to such daydreams.

He returned to the parlor, stood at the window, stared out to the empty road. This is not at all how my day should be progressing. Being alone in the house is an astounding accomplishment. And I am bored. Surely, at least one French visitor will mistake this day for tomorrow, and seek his appointment. It is so much their way. He moved toward the desk, reached for the calendar. He thought of Benny now, the empty silence of the house reminding him of the cascade of noise from his younger grandson. Benny was away at school in Geneva, a choice Franklin had made out of concern that Benny was becoming too . . . French. I find them a most amiable people to live with, he thought. They are not as cruel as the Spanish, or as avaricious as the Dutch. They are certainly not as stupidly proud as the English. They seem to possess no real vices at all, other than some harmless frivolities. But I would prefer my grandson to be a Presbyterian and a republican. It will make his path much less challenging in America. At the very least, he would be more punctual.

He heard a carriage, stared out with a surge of hopefulness. It passed by the house, disappeared beyond, and he grunted, said, "You should at least stop and pay your respects."

He returned to his calendar, peered through his glasses, and now a carriage was suddenly close, moving in the drive. He closed the book with a small flourish, said, "Well, there you have it."

He thought of sitting in the chair, not appearing too anxious for company, thought, No, then you have to pull yourself up again. Far too much work. He moved to the door, his pride gone, pulled it open, watched as a French army officer emerged from the carriage. The man was unfamiliar, very young, removed his hat to reveal a high forehead, topped by thinning red hair. The young man tucked his hat under his arm, turned toward the house, noticed Franklin. He swept the hat low to the ground in a deep bow, said in nearly perfect English, "Please forgive the intrusion, Dr. Franklin. I am the Marquis de Lafayette."

HE CARRIED A LETTER OF RECOMMENDATION FROM WASHINGTON, and Franklin felt amused that the marquis seemed to think he required some formal introduction. Franklin returned to his chair, and Lafayette continued to stand, seemed to pulse with movement, a broad grin on the young man's face.

"Truly, Doctor, I had thought we had established our meeting for this date. I can return tomorrow. It is a grievous error on my part."

Franklin ignored the calendar, pointed to a chair, said, "Please, sit down. If you continue to stand, you will exhaust me."

Lafayette moved quickly, seemed suddenly concerned, sat in the chair, rigid, his back stiffly upright.

"And, by all means, relax. Is this the result of your service to George Washington? Does he whip you into submission, or are you just naturally afraid of comfort?"

Lafayette seemed to ponder the words, and Franklin could tell he was trying to decide if the old man was serious.

"Sir, it is my honor to place myself in your company. I shall sit in whatever manner is pleasing to you. I do not wish to be a bother. Is your health good, sir?"

"That would depend on whom you ask. I am told frequently that I am maintaining good form for a man of my years. I believe that is meant as a compliment. I am not sure what *form* is appropriate for a man of sixty-seven." He waited a moment, saw a puzzled look on the young man's face. "Ah, see? You have heard otherwise. Some continue to insist I am seventy-three. However, I made a decision some time ago, that once I attained the age of seventy, I would begin to compute my years in the opposite direction. Three years hence, I am now sixty-seven. No one has yet shown me that there are rules that forbid this practice. Once a man reaches seventy, he should be entitled after all to establish his own rules."

Lafayette stared at him, his mouth slightly open.

"My new rule is maddening of course to those who believe I have grown too old to exist in their world. In the case of Mr. Arthur Lee, I am constantly in violation of staying around too long. However, as long as the women do not object to my company . . ." He stopped, saw the smile returning to Lafayette's face. "You're too young to have such notoriety. You should be parading about the parks of Paris with my grandson."

"I am indeed married, sir."

"Yes, of course. My apologies. I heard that your reception at the royal court was an embarrassment to the king."

Lafayette frowned now, said, "I certainly hope not, sir."

"Don't be concerned. King Louis requires a bit of sobriety occasionally. From what I was told, the audiences cheered you more loudly than anything His Majesty has heard in a while. Your accomplishments and the respect you have earned in America are gratefully appreciated here. Perhaps that will influence both the king and Count Vergennes the next time they choose a man to command French troops in America."

He was testing Lafayette's reaction, and the young man seemed to choose his words carefully.

"Doctor, I regret the difficulties which arose in the affair at Newport. Count d'Estaing is a most capable man."

"More than capable. I have heard that his forces are faring well in the West Indies. The British are in something of a lather, loud voices in Parliament calling on King George to focus more of his attention to the islands than to his, um, colonies. I am privy to such things."

"That would be a fortunate decision for America, Doctor."

"As fortunate as the Marquis de Lafayette assuming command of the next French force to cross the ocean?"

The young man's guard seemed to slip away, and Lafayette showed the enthusiasm again.

"Thank you for that kindness, Doctor. I only hope to give assistance to General Washington in the manner he will find useful. I admit to having some ambition to command such a force. There would be no difficulties such as we had at Newport."

"I agree. However, my influence is limited, General. Is it acceptable to refer to you as general?"

"I accept whatever title you wish, sir. In the French army, I am but a captain."

"Hmm. I prefer *general*. It is likely that before much time has passed, your king may agree."

"Thank you, Doctor."

"I have recently been called upon to assume the office of Superintendent of Naval Affairs for America. Marvelous title, yes? The congress has added that one to my ever-increasing list. I'm not yet sure what it entails, except that French naval officers are now adding their appointments to my calendar. There is some discussion of a plan to mount an invasion force to threaten England directly. Are you aware of this?"

"More than aware, sir. The plan was, in principle, my own. I had hoped to command such a force. It is the primary reason I asked to meet with you, Doctor."

"Thank you for your candor, General. Now, I must be candid as well. Your government is not comfortable with your plan. There is concern that the effort required in the West Indies could leave the French navy in a precarious position should a serious fight erupt in the English Channel. I cannot speak of what your role should be, and I dare not insert my views in places where they do not belong. Your notoriety and your value to General Washington will ultimately determine where your duty is best performed. As for causing injury to the British from the sea, I have my own view. It has come as a surprise to many here that America has in fact produced something of a navy. Thus far, there has been one extremely useful benefit of this. American ships have begun to appear in foreign ports of call, patrolling European waterways, protecting American shipping interests. It both amuses and distresses me that until our ships appeared in their waters, some European governments considered America as some strange mythical place. It is a peculiar notion that my country was little more than a rumor until our flag appeared from the masts of warships."

"Doctor, from what I have heard in America, there were some in your country who knew nothing of King George until his warships destroyed your towns. People often believe what is convenient."

"Quite so. Your king and some of his generals may not believe it is *convenient* to have you off commanding an army somewhere. I can understand your disappointment. But that does not mean we will not cause our own havoc."

Lafayette could not hide his mood, but Franklin saw curiosity as well.

"General, a French warship has been refitted and offered to an American captain, to use as he will in the waters around the English coast. With the additional support already promised him from several French vessels, I believe he can cause considerable discomfort in British ports. I have advised him only to avoid barbarism, not to exact revenge on British civilians for the brutality their navy has inflicted in America. His family is Scottish, and he's a Virginian now. Perhaps you know him? His name is John Paul Jones."

THE SHIP WAS NOW CALLED THE *BONHOMME RICHARD*, A TRIBUTE to Franklin himself, his *Poor Richard's Almanack* now extremely popular throughout France. Captain Jones had become popular himself, had already given birth to a reputation in France as a keen naval officer who preyed effectively on British merchantmen. But he had yet to face a challenge from a British warship, and when his small fleet sailed for British waters, the French officers he commanded were not yet convinced this American could even survive a serious naval battle, much less command one.

The British ship was the *Serapis*, a forty-gun frigate that was newer, larger, and far more maneuverable than the *Bonhomme Richard*. The fight began at dusk, the two ships swirling about each other in a storm of fire and smoke. When Jones could not outflank the *Serapis*, he rammed her, his crew casting hooks over her rails. With the two ships locked together, their gunners poured a continuous hell of grapeshot and canister into the faces of the enemy. On the *Bonhomme Richard*, Jones sent marksmen up into the rigging, musket fire now adding to the carnage below. On the deck of the *Serapis*, no man could survive, and finally, with both ships taking on water at a dangerous rate, an American shell was lobbed into the main hatchway of the British ship. The explosion ripped the *Serapis* apart from within, and with both crews exhausted and bloodied, Jones himself aimed a single gun at the main mast of the *Serapis* and fired. As the mast toppled into the sea, the British lowered their flag.

The extraordinary victory had been achieved within sight of a stunned audience on the British shore, and though the destruction of both ships could not be measured as any sizable loss to either side, the prestige gained by the fledgling American navy sent a shock through all of Europe.

The *Bonhomme Richard* did not survive another day, the damage too great, the leaking hull finally giving way. But her captain would fight again, and no matter his future, his place in history had been secured. It was the first American naval victory against a foreign man-o-war. Those who survived the fight would remember the two ships locked together, both captains fighting with sword and pistol. For a long while, the victory had seemed to favor the *Serapis*, her captain facing his foe with a haughty demand that the *Bonhomme Richard* accept certain defeat and lower her flag. It was the reply of her captain that would be remembered, the voice echoing out through the smoke and fire, heard by the men on both sides:

"I have not yet begun to fight."

43. CORNWALLIS

SEPTEMBER 1779

HE HAD RETURNED TO NEW YORK IN JULY TO A COMMAND THAT had absorbed the despair of the city around it. Clinton had put on a good show of welcoming him back, and if nothing else, his arrival was a distraction from the mundane duties of a paralyzed army. But the glad tidings had been swept away in a matter of days. Every officer in New York knew that Clinton saw Cornwallis as the primary threat to his authority, and the acrimony only worsened the mood in the headquarters. Cornwallis was not surprised by Clinton's hostility, but he would not engage in the gossip and disparaging that seemed to provide an entertaining distraction to bored officers. He had returned to America because there were, after all, some personal connections for him in the army. He had rarely allowed himself to dwell on friendships with fellow officers, the nature of the army so mobile and transient. As he began the search for familiar faces, he learned that James Grant was gone, had been chosen by Clinton to lead the force that sailed to the West Indies. But others, Leslie, even Knyphausen, had welcomed him as the friend he had become. He was surprised they knew of Jemima's death, the personal so often separate from the official. Their warmth had surprised him, as well as their kindness for the obvious pain he carried.

He felt no trace of homesickness for England, could not even picture his children in his mind, a tormenting guilt that forced him awake in the late hours of sleepless nights. Their anguish was no less than his, but he was still consumed by grief, her death draining him of compassion so that he felt he had nothing to offer even his own family. He tried to forgive himself, reminded himself that his sister and brother had children of their own. They had always accepted his son and daughter in a spirit of family, and accepted them now. But the guilt would drive him to quiet tears, and he could not escape that they were so much a part of her, so much a part of what had been torn away from him. If it meant he was a failure as a father, that was a chain he would wear another day.

He spent most of his time in the house on Long Island, and it was no less a garrison now than it had been before. On every road, past every peaceful farm and field, cavalry was stationed, and the simple joy of a ride in the countryside was made ugly by the necessary presence of guards. But his love for the outdoors had not returned, and long days were made longer as he stayed close to his office. As much dread as he felt for any meeting with Clinton, the couriers who brought the orders had at least provided him some distraction. Though the summer heat had magnified the stench of the city, the discomfort of his own boredom took him to headquarters hoping that perhaps this time, some new plan had been approved. Despite Cornwallis' personal despair, he had to have faith that Lord Germain and Henry Clinton would stumble far enough through their ongoing war of words to agree on a strategy, some plan to take this army again into the field.

CLINTON SAT HUNCHED OVER BEHIND HIS DESK, THE ROOM SILENT, poised for another round of explosions. His face was red, a permanent state now, and Cornwallis waited with the others for the tirade to resume.

"Do they find some sport in this? I only imagine this to be some sort of perverse game. Lord Germain, Lord North, prancing around the drawing rooms of their grand estates in a brandy-soaked quest for some new means to torment me. It is a game they have mastered. This one, however, I must assuredly credit to Lord Sandwich. As first lord of the Admiralty, this would be his doing."

The conversation was one-sided, and Cornwallis knew the rest of the officers would simply endure.

He was not surprised that Admiral Lord Howe was gone, had already returned to England. The two brothers Howe were in many ways a team, and though each man had responsibility for his own branch of the service, no one truly expected Richard Lord Howe to remain in America while William Howe was skewered by Parliament.

Before he had sailed from England, Cornwallis had been summoned to the official hearings, but would not provide ammunition for William Howe's detractors. It was always so simple for the king's opponents to make a target of one man, to hold him up as a symbol of so many failures of policy. Cornwallis knew both the successes and the failings of William Howe, knew that it was the failings that would plague Howe for the rest of his life. It was not up to Parliament to make it worse.

Admiral Howe's replacements thus far had been a strange merry-go-round of inept commanders, and Cornwallis had observed the appointments from England with bewilderment. It was as though Lord Sandwich was toying with American naval operations as a means to provide his aging commanders their one final hurrah. As each man was shuffled into place, his incompetence would be revealed usually as an unwillingness to perform any real duty at all. For several months, the result had been a powerful navy willed into inaction by men who cared more for the peaceful glory of retirement than for actually confronting the French.

Clinton's fury was directed at yet another man who had been dredged from the halls of the Admiralty, Marriot Arbuthnot, perhaps the most abrasive, unpleasant, and bombastic officer in the navy. Arbuthnot had been commander of the naval force in Halifax. Now, growing feeble in his late sixties, he was the latest selection by Lord Sandwich to rescue the war from the army and in the process, torment Henry Clinton.

"We will be graced presently by another of the highly exalted *Old Ladies* of the Admiralty. Certainly most of you have some acquaintance with Admiral Arbuthnot."

There were small groans, and Clinton seemed pleased at the response.

"Yes, well, we shall come to know him in much more detail. If there is one benefit to his arrival, it is that he will not remain here long. There is some urgency in London that this command provide assistance to the governor of Jamaica. Apparently, the French fleet in the West Indies is preparing an invasion of that island, for what reason I have no possible idea. However, such a threat to the king's interests must be answered, and this command has been ordered to supply troops. It is of no concern to Lord Germain that this post has already been depleted to the extreme. However, orders will be obeyed. Admiral Arbuthnot is to sail to Jamaica, transporting a force numbering some four thousand men. Someone in this room will command that force. Despite my better judgment, I would ask for your involvement."

Cornwallis felt a ray of light cutting through him, said, "If it is acceptable, sir, I will go."

The room fell quiet, and Cornwallis could see the surprise on Clinton's face, twisting slowly into a smile.

"I am greatly pleased by your suggestion, General. I had thought a junior man, but, no, this matter requires our most serious consideration. You are a most appropriate choice. So it will be!"

LATE SEPTEMBER 1779

The mission was organized with astounding speed, and Cornwallis had no doubt that Clinton's sudden efficiency had much more to do with his glee over his departure than with any concerns for Jamaica.

He had thought little of the conditions he would find in the tropics, or the heat and misery he might endure. No matter what challenges Cornwallis would confront, the mission would carry him far from the challenge of maintaining his sanity in New York. The bonus lay in the mission itself. Once in Jamaica, for the first time in his career, Cornwallis would have a truly independent command.

They sailed into a rising sun, the transports and escorting warships turning southward, sliding briskly along the New Jersey coast. They had been at sea three days, enough time for the troops to rid themselves of seasickness, the open air cleansing the depths of the largest transports. On the long voyages, Cornwallis had once passed the time by writing letters, most of them to Jemima. But now, he stayed on deck nearly all day, a slow methodical pacing, focusing first on the low dark strip of land to the west, then the amazing contrast, the open sea, the great yawning abyss to the east. When the call came from the lookouts, he had paid little mind, heard something from the officers of a signal from a small courier vessel. But when the ship lowered her sails, he forced himself to accompany the grotesque Arbuthnot to receive the smaller boat sliding alongside, the courier with the message. The ship had come up from the West Indies, and the news was not what anyone was expecting. Admiral d'Estaing had sailed north out of the Caribbean, not west. If there was a danger from the French fleet, it was now toward New York, or perhaps a second campaign to Rhode Island. Cornwallis was bewildered by Arbuthnot, the old man insisting the French must certainly invade Halifax. Regardless of the French intentions, it was clear that the threat to Jamaica was gone.

As the fleet turned about, Cornwallis went to his cabin and passed another three days in quiet despair. They would return the troops to New York, and once again, he would plant himself beside Henry Clinton, while the ministry tried to figure out what to do next.

OF ALL THE THIRTEEN COLONIES, THE LEAST SETTLED AND THUS, the least political was Georgia. For the past year, the British had pushed up from their bases in Florida, had outmanned what resistance the colonial troops could offer. The spoils were Savannah and Augusta. While the loss of those two cities was not likely to change the outcome of the war, it was a clear sign that, with adequate leadership and sufficient force, the British could easily gain the upper hand. Though Georgia could be described as liberated from rebel control, much of the citizenry there had no great loyalty to either side. Subsistence and survival against hostile terrain and hostile Indians drew far more attention than whose flag might fly in the fortified cities. But the British had established a base from which they could look elsewhere, another incursion perhaps, another colony that might be reclaimed for the king.

As Cornwallis endured another long month in New York, the mystery of d'Estaing's intentions became known. The French fleet had arrived at Savannah, obviously intending to recapture the port from British hands. It was a doomed effort, too reminiscent of the debacle at Newport. In an astounding reminder of d'Estaing's first failure, a violent storm scattered and damaged much of the French fleet, effectively ending the mission. The colonial forces in the south now had shared the same frustrating experience as Greene and Sullivan at Newport. D'Estaing responded by dividing his fleet, returning half his ships to the West Indies, while d'Estaing himself led the remainder back to France. Though Savannah was still British, d'Estaing had accomplished one unintended success. Clinton continued to sit quietly in New York.

The population, as far as we can determine, is evenly divided. Where we have failed in the past, General, was in believing that New Jersey and Pennsylvania would provide this army with overwhelming support. Time and again, General Howe's expectations were not met."

It was an accurate statement, and Cornwallis nodded slowly, still not certain why Clinton was telling him this.

"South Carolina holds opportunity. While I am not quick to leap to the same conclusions of my predecessor, nonetheless, it is a favorable climate for us. Am I wrong to anticipate considerable support for us there? I do not believe so."

Clinton had answered his own question, and Cornwallis knew when his opinion was not required.

It was unusual for Clinton to summon him alone, and he was

still not comfortable, felt as though the private meeting was meant to mask something, protect Clinton from some later blame for a plan that might emerge right now. Clinton had still not revealed any reason for the meeting, continued to talk.

"It has always been difficult to secure the approval of Lord Germain for some plan of which he is not the author. But I have prevailed. From London, the war must seem like one grand theater, from Boston to the islands, one place indistinguishable from the other. The king places enormous value on the West Indies, and thus, we move troops to the West Indies. If he feared for Pensacola, we would no doubt be called upon to send troops to Pensacola. I have protested that weakening New York to such a degree has placed this army in grave peril. Those concerns have been ignored, until now. Perhaps it is perseverance on my part, perhaps the ministry has suddenly remembered that we are still fighting to preserve *all* of the empire, not just the land of sugar cane. In any event, Lord Germain now agrees with me that we cannot make war with the French and simply ignore the colonies. We have afforded Mr. Washington too many advantages as it is."

Cornwallis would not allow Clinton to bait him into some criticism of William Howe.

"I am relieved, sir, by Lord Germain's change of heart. I had feared the rebels would be allowed to remain unmolested. It can only add to their strength, and their arrogance."

"The arrogance, General Cornwallis, is ours! From the beginning of this war, we have done exactly what the rebels would ask of us. We have assaulted them at their strongest point! From the horror we inflicted on ourselves at Breed's Hill, to John Burgoyne's stubborn invasion, we have pointed our spear in one direction, and allowed the rebels to slap it aside. Would you have us repeat that absurd strategy?"

Cornwallis took a deep breath.

"Sir, does not the defeat of Mr. Washington end this war? Should that not be our goal?"

"How often have we defeated him thus far, General? We drove him out of New York, we drove him out of New Jersey, we drove him out of Philadelphia. What has it achieved? Look at us! For nearly a year, this command has been hampered by London's indecision. We weaken ourselves further, send troops to all corners of the earth, while across the Hudson River, our enemy

stands tall and taunts us. Now, I am criticized in London for having done so little. How dare those mindless politicians insult me
so! For nearly a year, they have granted me a free hand to make
raids along the coast. Admirable work, that! Throw terror into
farmers and fishermen! Well, General, now there is a new plan!
My plan! We have learned a valuable lesson from our success in
Georgia, and that success will be repeated in South Carolina. We
are no longer going to strike the enemy at his strongest point. We
are going to consume him in pieces, one powerful thrust at a
time. Once the Carolinas are in our control, we will launch a major assault into Virginia, conquering both that colony and the
Chesapeake Bay. What will become of this war if the colonies
lose half their territory?"

"I suppose . . . the rebel congress could be compelled to end
the war."

"Yes, General. Then we are in agreement. I will summon the
senior staff. General Knyphausen will remain in command in
New York, with sufficient force to keep the rebels at bay. I am
withdrawing General Pigott and his command from Newport, to
add to our defenses here. With the change in the direction of our
campaign it is no longer necessary to extend our forces so far to
the north. You and I will lead the rest of the army to an assault on
Charleston!"

The word punched him, and Cornwallis could see the fierce
gleam in Clinton's eye. Of course. Charleston. The overall plan
could work, the Carolinas peopled by enough loyalist support
that the rebels would have no means to hold the place. But first
would come the landing, the necessary capture of the one place
that was a dark stain on Clinton's record. It had been an embarrassment for Cornwallis as well, his first confrontation of the
war, a clumsy and arrogant attack against an invulnerable position, manned by rebels who were commanded by Charles Lee.
That was an embarrassment as well, even though the rebel prisoners themselves had no respect for Lee, claimed only to serve
William Moultrie. Moultrie had constructed the fortification
that Clinton and Admiral Peter Parker had tried to destroy, and
the result was catastrophic for the British navy. Both the strategy
and the planning had been disastrous, the first experience Cornwallis had with arrogant assumptions of rebel weakness. Whether
Clinton had learned those lessons from nearly four years before re-

mained to be seen. But Cornwallis knew that if Charleston was the first objective, those memories would be hard in Clinton's mind.

DECEMBER 1779

"Do you believe he is correct?"

Cornwallis studied the old man for a long moment, said, "Does it matter?"

Knyphausen shouted the words, "Of course it matters! No matter if General Clinton is right or wrong, it will matter! This war cannot last for so many more years. I receive news from my king. He is concerned that already this war is bankrupting your empire. Now we fight the French as well? You cannot sail to South Carolina and pretend you are simply doing the bidding of your commanding officer! You have a part in this! You owe that to your king!"

Cornwallis accepted Knyphausen's scolding, felt weak, a dull sense of shame.

"I will perform what duty I am required to perform. I do not believe General Clinton will allow me much authority. He still believes I am his enemy."

"He believes every officer in this command is his enemy." Knyphausen laughed, surprising Cornwallis. "I have never seen anyone like him, General. He is truly skilled at strategy, far more than General Howe. But I wonder if he has the ability to take a plan from the paper to the field. That must be your duty. You are the skilled hand at tactics. Together, the two of you are an ideal command. Ah, but to General Clinton, there is no . . . *together.*"

"How will you fare here?"

The old man shrugged.

"There will be no trouble here, unless the French navy comes. Even then . . . I am not too concerned. Both of you, your navy, theirs. Is it so difficult to find an admiral who does not sail his ships like a blind man stepping through rocks? It is fortunate for both you and the French that you build good ships. You do not build good sailors."

Cornwallis would not argue the point, said, "They are still good men. They are used poorly. Someone will emerge, when there is need."

Knyphausen raised a finger, smiled.

"Ah, but on which side?"

Cornwallis stood.

"I should return. The men are boarding the flatboats. The loading is to commence."

Knyphausen rose slowly, and Cornwallis saw a sadness on the old man's face. Knyphausen moved toward him, stood close, touched his arm.

"When next I see you, it is possible the war will be over. You may be the hero. I wish that for you."

Cornwallis felt a hard knot in his throat, lowered his head. He felt angry at himself, embarrassed. Since his return, it had been difficult for him to control his emotions. The soft wound inside him was opened up too easily, and he wiped at his eyes, took the old man's hand.

"My apologies, sir. I shall miss your counsel. It is quite possible that you may be the hero as well."

Knyphausen shook his head.

"No. General Clinton has chosen the right man to stay behind. You must make certain he has chosen the right man to lead his attack."

DECEMBER 26, 1779

It took more than two weeks to move the army to the big ships. The weather had turned quickly, erasing any hope that this winter would be as mild as the one before. December had brought dark days of deep cold, and the harbor was alive with floes of ice. The fleet finally set sail in a hard gale, snow driving across the decks of a hundred ships. From the first day at sea, there were destructive problems from the weather, some transports blown uncontrollably to founder in the shallows, one disappearing altogether, far beyond the horizon to the east. As the fleet worked its way southward, the storms were relentless, and the pitching waves shattered bulkheads and cracked masts. Though the conditions were so very different from Howe's disastrous journey to Pennsylvania, the results were eerily similar. Horses could not endure the tumbling chaos of the holds, and many died, carcasses cast overboard. The men fared poorly as well, sickness magnified by the sharp cold and icy rains.

The journey required more than a month to complete, and the fleet was so badly damaged, any thoughts of an immediate assault on Charleston were set aside. By early February, the army was put ashore near Savannah, and within a few weeks, they finally began the mission by a march over land toward Charleston.

The rebel forces in the city were commanded by Benjamin Lincoln, a Massachusetts man who had distinguished himself from the first days of the siege of Boston to the defeat of Burgoyne. Lincoln had nearly four thousand men in his defenses, and continued to call in every militia unit and other strength he could gather into the fortified city. It was a disastrous mistake.

Clinton did not repeat his errors of four years before. Despite a stubborn unwillingness to cooperate with Clinton's detailed plans, Arbuthnot wisely did not attempt to engage the impregnable position at Fort Moultrie, instead slipped his warships quickly past the rebel artillery. Within days, Clinton was preparing the first of three major siege lines, and Lincoln's strong defensive position became irrelevant. The maneuver required weeks to perform, and inspired uncomfortable memories of the slowness of William Howe. But even Cornwallis understood that a siege requires time. The final piece of the trap was laid when Cornwallis moved inland and severed Lincoln's escape route. With the British lines moving ever closer to the city itself, the rebel command had no alternative. Benjamin Lincoln was forced to surrender the city, along with the entire army under his command. The collapse rivaled the rebel disaster at Fort Washington as their worst defeat of the war.

MAY 1780

With Charleston secure, Clinton had sent Cornwallis inland, establishing outposts at key crossroads and larger towns. Despite Clinton's optimism, Cornwallis still expected resistance, but the occupation progressed with almost no confrontations. With Lincoln's surrender, any organized command of rebel forces had disappeared.

Clinton had issued a proclamation, requiring the citizenry either to pledge an oath of allegiance to King George, or sign a parole, pledging not to take up arms against the British for the remainder of the war. Cornwallis had unpleasant memories of William Howe's decrees, which seemed always to prompt more protest and hostility than any benefit the British received. But South Carolina was a different place from New Jersey, and Cornwallis was surprised to see the outpouring of signatures on the official ledgers. To Clinton, it was confirmation that South Carolina had never truly been an enemy of the crown. But Cornwallis saw past the signatures to the people themselves. In each small town they would come out and receive the British troops with quiet curiosity. Their names on a piece of paper meant little more than a means of easing their fears. Most never read the document, signed because men with bayonets stood close by. If the papers were signed, the bayonets went away. It made little difference what uniform the soldiers wore.

Cornwallis spent much of his time in the town of Camden, extending British control like the spokes of a wheel. With Clinton in Charleston, Cornwallis' duty was relatively calm, and the entire command beneath him seemed to go about their duty as grateful as he was to be away from New York.

CHARLESTON, JUNE 3, 1780

He traveled to the city with the Irishman, Francis Rawdon, a young colonel who had recently arrived with his regiment of Irish volunteers. Rawdon had sailed from New York just in time to witness the fall of Charleston. He was in his mid-twenties, but carried himself with the bearing of an older man, the result of strict aristocratic breeding. As he rode beside Cornwallis, the two men were a marked contrast, the general's wide girth settling heavily in the saddle, while Rawdon sat tall, a dark lean man who easily conveyed a sense of command and authority. Rawdon had formerly served directly under Clinton, but had resigned his post, chose instead to lead his Irish troops in the field. Cornwallis knew that to be the official version. The truth was that Rawdon despised Clinton, had gone so far as to author an inappropriately scathing letter to the commanding general as a prelude to his resignation. Clinton had no difficulty releasing Rawdon to other duties. Cornwallis liked the young man immediately.

In Camden, the troops were still organizing their bases of operation and defense, but no one had any reason to make haste.

The countryside had been swept virtually clean of any rebels by the swift and utter brutality of another young man, Banastre Tarleton. Colonel Tarleton had been with the army for some time, and commanded the light cavalry known as the British Legion. But he had performed no service worth any serious mention, until now. It was the same with so many of the young officers, that once they were clear of the oppressive influence of New York, they seemed to blossom into their roles. Tarleton had engaged in attacks on several groups of militia, some who had attempted to aid the rebels in Charleston, others simply escaping from South Carolina altogether. The results had been consistent. Tarleton had quickly established a reputation in both armies as a master of savage brutality. His horsemen pursued their foe without pause, and fought them without mercy. To the rebels, and to the civilians, Tarleton was a beast. To Cornwallis, he was a godsend.

In Camden, he had left behind Colonel Nisbet Balfour, a man with a few more years and a few more distinctions on his record than the two younger colonels. Balfour had served as far back as Boston, had been wounded at Breed's Hill. He was another man who appealed to Cornwallis as dependable, one who would manage his own post without the necessity of Cornwallis keeping him on some leash.

It was the nature of the army that the familiar names would fade away, and new ones rise to the surface. Along with James Grant, Charles Grey was gone as well, had returned to England to pursue a more fulfilling service than he had found in America. Cornwallis had thought he would miss the familiar faces, that the army would suffer from such changes in command. But there was energy in youth, and the young subordinates had already proven that they were prepared to command in this new theater of the war. Whether or not Clinton approved, or even recognized their service, Cornwallis had already begun to shape them to suit his own style of command.

He had wondered if Clinton would remain in Charleston, or like William Howe, if Clinton would feel the appalling need to ride beside his troops in their daily routines. The morale of his command was rising daily, and Cornwallis had fretted that Clinton's arrival in Camden could sweep all of that away. But the fretting had been short-lived. Word had come of a new French fleet mobilizing across the Atlantic. There was no hint of its intentions, but Clinton had to believe New York was now under threat. It was a logical decision, and with Charleston, and presumably all of South Carolina in solid British control, Clinton had no need and no desire to remain. He was going back to New York.

The thought of returning northward, of remaining planted beneath the insufferable weight of Clinton's authority had driven Cornwallis nearly to sickness. But there was a pleasant surprise in the dispatches he received from Charleston. The decision whether or not to accompany Clinton was given blessedly to Cornwallis himself. Neither man had any desire to remain close to the other, and the opportunity handed him by Clinton was a generous gift. It was the easiest decision of Cornwallis' career. Clinton would maintain overall control of the army from New York. But the command in the Carolinas would now belong to Cornwallis.

He had not yet spoken to Clinton face-to-face, and the ride to Charleston had begun as a formal departure ceremony, that certainly both men could offer a civil, perhaps even friendly farewell.

CORNWALLIS READ CLINTON'S DECREE WITH A COLD HARD KNOT IN his stomach.

"What's that you have there, General? My letter of authority? Should be quite pleasing to you. I believe we have addressed every issue."

Clinton had been generous with his authority, allowing Cornwallis broad discretion, a crucial necessity, given the distance and the time it would require to receive orders and instructions from New York. But the paper in his hand was different, and Cornwallis read a moment, then showed it to Clinton, said, "No, sir. This is your latest decree."

"Ah, yes. What do you think? Consider this my parting gift to your command. This should solidify the entire colony to your service. You may, of course, use this as a model for North Carolina, when the time arrives. There is another document . . . ah yes, the troop dispositions. I feel justified in returning to New York with a significant portion of the troops here. Whether or not the French arrive, I am certain Mr. Washington is expecting us to mount a considerable campaign against his army. We shall not disappoint him."

Cornwallis felt his mouth hanging open, measured his words.

"Sir. You are *reducing* our troop strength here?" He looked at the paper, counted the regiments, examined the different commands. "You will leave me with approximately . . ."

"Five thousand men. Sizable force. Should be quite sufficient for your needs. I expect you to make considerable use of the loyalist militia. Once this new decree is spread across the colony, you will receive a considerable number of new recruits, mark my words."

Cornwallis backed away from Clinton's desk, turned to one side, could not look at the man. Rawdon was behind him, said, "General, may I get you something?"

He shook his head, tried to pull himself upright, felt no strength, his legs softening rubber. He said, "Excuse me, sir. I require some air. The long ride, no doubt."

Clinton seemed unconcerned, said, "Out you go, then. Perk up a bit, then I will discuss with you my plan for the conquest of Virginia. Magnificent, I must say. Two-pronged attack. We may force George Washington to sign his surrender papers on the front porch of his estate!"

Cornwallis did not respond, moved out into the hall, Rawdon close beside him.

"Sir, are you certain you are all right?"

"Outside, Colonel."

He moved toward the door, a guard pulling it open, and the sunlight blinded him. He eased his way toward the short steps, saw chairs along the porch, guards down in the yard, Negroes tending the horses. He stopped, moved along the wide porch, close to one chair. He put his hand on the woven cane of the arm, sat slowly. The sun was still in his face, the heat filling him, and he waited for Rawdon to sit, then said, "What is it about command? When a man is promoted, is afforded such responsibility, such authority . . . is it so necessary that his mind stop functioning?"

"Forgive me, sir. I don't know what you mean."

"I have endured much in this army, Colonel. But no matter the training, no matter the experience, nothing has ever prepared me for an assault of such astounding stupidity."

Rawdon smiled, and Cornwallis glared at him, the smile vanishing.

"He will leave us with five thousand men. He believes the loyalists will flock to our banner. He will return to New York to commence a new campaign aimed at the strength of Washington's army, the precise strategy he once believed would utterly fail. And, if all of that is not sufficient . . . his decree."

"I'm sorry, sir. I did not yet read it."

"We have subdued this colony, Colonel. The civilians have returned to their lives, comfortable that this war has finally passed them by. We have asked no more of them than to pledge their allegiance to the crown. It was no threat to the peace, it gave no cause for controversy or protest. But now General Clinton has taken one very large step in the wrong direction. His new decree demands that every citizen of South Carolina sign a new oath of allegiance proclaiming their willingness to participate in the establishment of a royal government."

"Why is that a problem, sir?"

"Colonel, despite General Clinton's assumption that the citizens of South Carolina are merely waiting for their opportunity to take up our muskets, my experience has been that most of these people wish only to tend to their farms and manage their shops. General Clinton is compelling them to state their allegiance to our cause, with the warning that a refusal to do so implies treasonous behavior. We are forcing these people to choose sides, when in fact, the war for them should be over."

Rawdon shook his head.

"I'm sorry, sir. I do not understand the problem. Should we not expect loyalty?"

Cornwallis felt the energy slipping away.

"Colonel, the army is not in the business of ensuring loyalty. Our purpose here is to win victories. With victories, loyalty will follow. An essentially peaceful citizenry is now being informed that they will lend us vocal and active support, or they will be treated as our enemy. It is the seed that sprouts resentment, Colonel. Admiral Howe attempted this in New Jersey, and his brother in Pennsylvania. Ask yourself, Colonel. Did either of them succeed?"

JUNE 8, 1780

In a final blow to Cornwallis' command, Clinton decided to transport the experienced units of British regular cavalry back to New York. There was no explanation required from Clinton, and no explaining the decision in the camps. Cornwallis had met the news with grim acceptance, sent word to Colonel Tarleton that his Legion would now be more than just a mobile force to strike at the enemy, but would in fact be the army's only eyes and ears.

As Clinton's ship sailed out through the harbor, Cornwallis rode back to Camden. His troop strength had been stripped, his expectations of a quick victory swept away. He had no confidence that loyalists in any number would emerge to assist his army, that once he manned the outposts with enough strength to hold the colony safely in British hands, what would remain to march into North Carolina would be a pitiful force. But he had confidence in his officers, and the morale of his diminished force was high. Despite every suffering torment he felt from Henry Clinton, nothing could overshadow that finally, for the first time in his career, Charles Cornwallis was truly in charge.

44. WASHINGTON

PREAKNESS, NEW JERSEY, JUNE 1780

NEWS OF THE CATASTROPHE AT CHARLESTON REACHED HEAD-quarters on the last day of May. He had held out hope that there would be another magnificent victory there, the city defended with the same courage and tactical brilliance of four years ago. But his optimism had been tempered. He knew that the first time Clinton had made enormous mistakes, mistakes he was not likely to repeat. He was not, after all, William Howe.

But Washington had believed the colonial troops there were prepared as well. The army was better equipped and better trained, and was led by a man Washington was convinced could stand up to any British threat. The collapse of Benjamin Lincoln's defense was a baffling mystery, and the cost of the failure far exceeded the cost of the city itself. Lincoln had assembled most of the trained militia available in South Carolina, and all of the regular continental troops. Now, the vast majority of that effective fighting force was held captive by the British. Those who had escaped the sabers of Banastre Tarleton had scattered piecemeal, disappearing into the hills to the west, or stumbling slowly northward to find refuge in the colonial outposts in North Carolina.

It was devastating enough for Washington to consider the sudden wave of problems in the Carolinas. Now he had to confront a new problem closer to home. The morale of the army along the Hudson River had suffered from their inactivity, and many of those with expiring enlistments had gone home. There had been almost no new recruits, the states around New York lapsing into a bored complacency that was shared by the congress. With word of the disaster in South Carolina, morale had plunged even lower, a new tide of hopelessness that drove bored men to desert. The British and Hessians in New York numbered better than ten thousand soldiers, yet Washington's defenses along the river could muster barely three thousand men fit for duty.

The congress had evaded the responsibility for raising troops by throwing the job back to each individual state. Washington launched a new wave of pleas to Philadelphia, as he had done so many times before, begging the congressmen themselves to return to their home states to exercise their influence directly on the state assemblies, imploring them to send whatever volunteers they could muster. Almost no one complied.

Washington watched New York carefully, fearful that Knyphausen would discover the weakness of his enemy just across the river. The colonial troops made a show of parading along the palisades on the Hudson in regular drills, large clusters of campfires lit in patches of open ground all down the coast. It was a feeble effort at deception, to convince Knyphausen that Washington could still defend the coast with great numbers of troops, an army that could well pose a serious threat to the city itself if Knyphausen was careless. But the effect was the opposite of what Washington intended. Instead of staying put, Knyphausen answered the threat by launching an assault from Staten Island. Washington was not certain of Knyphausen's ultimate plan, but knew he had no force to put in Knyphausen's path. With no fight to be had, the Hessians had occupied themselves with pillaging the farms, yet another plague on the civilians who remained in the area. Washington could only watch from the highlands around Morristown, had no idea if Knyphausen had some larger goal in mind. The answer came quickly, and Washington was surprised and relieved to see the Hessians suddenly pulling away, crossing back over to Staten Island. Then he heard from his scouts. Clinton had returned, and Knyphausen had been ordered back to the city. Once again the enemy would settle into their base in New York, while Washington could only wait for some new plan to reveal itself from the mind of Henry Clinton.

IT BEGAN AS SO MANY RUMORS BEGAN, FROM FEAR AND SPECULA-
tion. With the collapse of Lincoln's army at Charleston, many of the continental troops along the Hudson began to hear talk that Washington would soon be marching to the Carolinas with those troops who could be spared, or whose homes were closer to the new threat. But the defenses along the Hudson were far too weak to drain them of any more strength. Washington had already called for the troops in Philadelphia to march northward, an agreeable strategy suggested by Benedict Arnold. Arnold had been insistent on leaving the city, on returning to the field where he might perform a more valuable service. Washington had to agree, Arnold having already proven himself in every campaign he had participated in. Arnold was even quite specific on the duty he wished to receive, and Washington had complied. Arnold was now in command of West Point, the crucial outpost upriver that prevented the British from opening a clear route into Canada. More importantly, West Point was the strongest fortification for many miles, the first major obstacle to the British should they once again attempt to divide the nation in two.

Washington rode along the palisades with Greene, had to address a new wave of verbal assaults on his quartermaster. Most still came from the Board of War, and even Greene knew that his outbursts of anger had grown tiresome and ineffective. The congress had evaded that responsibility as well, calling on each state assembly to supply goods and equipment for the men in Washington's command. It was an inefficient system, the states concerned first for their own defenses, supplying first the militia who remained inside their own borders. Now, Greene was making his demands to a congress with even less power than before. Greene's enemies found a convenient excuse to ignore him, while those who understood the urgency would request, or even beg the states to comply. Despite Greene's outspoken disgust, most of them did not.

Washington knew that Greene's role as quartermaster had gone on for longer than either man had expected. But all he could offer Greene was a sounding board, and do what he could to deflect the high-volume complaints aimed at the man who was simply trying to do his job.

They passed by a battery, four twelve-pound cannon anchored deeply into the rocks. Washington halted the horse, looked for the officer in charge. He could see dark openings in the hillside itself, the mouths of small caves, convenient shelter from the oppressive heat. The gun crews emerged, men saluting him, one man raising his hat. He saw an officer, a surprised lieutenant, and the man scrambled up the rocks toward him, said breathlessly, "Good day, sir! And General Greene! My apologies. We were not expecting you."

The man seemed more annoyed than apologetic, and Washington said, "Don't be concerned, Lieutenant. Just passing by. Your guns appear to be in good order. Fine work."

"Thank you, sir! We would be honored if you would call upon us to join with General Lee's command."

Washington was baffled, glanced at Greene, who shared the look.

"Of what do you speak, Lieutenant?"

"The Carolinas, sir. I have relations in southern Virginia. I am honored to defend their homes, sir. General Lee will give the British no quarter, that's for certain!"

Greene leaned forward in the saddle, said, "*Charles* Lee?"

"Yes, sir. The word is, he's been ordered to command again, to march to North Carolina."

Washington shook his head.

"The word indeed. Lieutenant, your enthusiasm is appreciated. However, Charles Lee is no longer a part of this army. Unless I am mistaken, he has returned to his home in Virginia."

"But, sir . . . the word is . . ."

"The word is *wrong*, Lieutenant."

Greene's short temper was betraying him, and Washington put a hand out, a silent restraint.

"General Greene is quite correct, Lieutenant. It would do a service to your men, and to this entire command if these rumors were stopped."

The man seemed crestfallen.

"As you wish, sir."

Washington could not just ride away, felt an odd sense of affection for a man who was still so eager to serve.

"What is your name, Lieutenant?"

"Johnson, sir. Irvine Johnson."

"Mr. Johnson, there will no doubt be further rumors on our plans for the Carolinas. By now, there should be no need for secrecy." He looked at Greene. "I was going to tell you on this ride, General. Now is as good a time. The congress has indeed made their selection for that command. This is not a rumor, Mr. Johnson, and you may tell anyone that you heard this from me. General Gates will soon be in North Carolina, and he will be organizing an army to confront the enemy."

He could feel Greene's silent amazement, thought, We should move away. He will certainly have something indiscreet to say. Johnson was smiling now, said, "Thank you for your confidence, sir. That is good news indeed. The hero of Saratoga himself! Thank you, sir!"

"Good day, Mr. Johnson. Man your guns well."

The man stiffened, saluted.

"Sir! God bless you, sir. God bless General Gates!"

Washington turned the horse, saw Greene staring at him with an open mouth.

"Let's ride, Mr. Greene."

They rode in thick silence, and Washington was relieved that Greene held his words, waited until they were clear of any troops. He heard a long exhale, and Greene said, "I had some suspicions Gates would go there. Too many in the congress still believe he is our *Zeus*. How could you have allowed that?"

"I was not consulted as to my opinion on Mr. Gates' suitability for command."

Greene sat upright. "Not consulted? How can that be? They cannot simply appoint commanders as they see fit!"

"Calm yourself, Mr. Greene. They can do precisely that. It has been clear to me for some time that my command of this army does not extend south of Virginia. It has never been a necessary source of discussion until now. Many in congress feel that the entire thirteen states is too large an area for one man to cast his authority. I cannot find fault with that. Communications and intelligence cannot reach this headquarters in time to answer a crisis."

"But . . . Gates?"

"He has the respect of the people, Mr. Greene. Consider Mr. Johnson, there. Gates still commands the respect of the men throughout this command. That respect is essential to assembling an army. The people of North Carolina will receive him well, and will respond to his call for troops."

"How will he be supplied?"

It was a question from the quartermaster now, and Washington smiled, thought, You accepted this better than I would have thought.

"The farms in North Carolina should offer sufficient bounty. Once Mr. Gates has established his presence in South Carolina, young Mr. Laurens will travel there to seek assistance from the state assembly. I have discussed this with his father. The congress will offer their usual request for assistance, but there is no better means of expressing the urgency than from the voices of their own. The Laurens family has considerable influence in that theater."

They rode silently for a moment, and Greene said, "Does Gates truly have your confidence?"

"It matters not, Mr. Greene. Our first priority is here, right across this river. The Southern Department is now his priority. It is his command."

He knew Greene would have the final word, waited for it.

"God help us."

THEY RETURNED TO THE HEADQUARTERS TO A STRANGE JUBILATION. As the sound of their horses reached the house, the staff emerged, assembled into line. Now Lafayette came out, and Washington could see that this maneuver had been carefully rehearsed, the young man stepping crisply to the front, a paper in his hand. Washington remained on the horse, looked at the wide grin on Lafayette's face.

"What is it, Mr. Lafayette?"

"We have received news, sir."

The entire staff was sharing in Lafayette's game, and Washington put aside his weariness from the ride, would play along.

"From what quarter?"

"From Newport, sir."

"Newport?"

"Newport, sir. I am pleased to inform the commanding general that the French fleet has made port. By now, the French troops are on American soil."

Greene was not as playful, said, "How many?"

Lafayette smiled at Greene as well.

"Ten warships, sir. Six thousand troops."

Greene looked at Washington now with wide-eyed surprise.

Washington began to feel the jubilation of his staff.

"You see, Mr. Greene? The Almighty has a way of providing. For now, we shall not concern ourselves with Mr. Gates. I would rather occupy myself by fashioning an appropriate greeting to our new allies."

LAFAYETTE HAD RETURNED TO THE ARMY LATE THAT SPRING. WASHington had met him with unconcealed joy, but the young man brought more than his own presence to Washington's camp. He brought the promise from King Louis himself, a fleet of ships and a new spirit of cooperation, the French monarch clearly intending to correct the mistakes both sides had learned from the failures of d'Estaing.

The young man had brought news both official and personal. His wife had given birth again, a boy this time, and Lafayette had made the announcement to the entire headquarters: the boy was named *Georges Washington Lafayette*. It was an honor that Washington had received with quiet emotion, but there was emotion as well for the young man's more official news. The French navy had assembled a new fleet, and though the number of ships was not sufficient to engage the British in a major sea battle, they would provide considerable protection for the troops they carried.

Their commander was Jean Baptiste, Count Rochambeau, a thirty-year veteran of French combat on bloody fields from Minorca to Prussia. Washington knew little of Rochambeau, but knew that protocol and diplomacy were as important now as ever before. Someone would have to go to Newport, to greet Rochambeau's command, to welcome their arrival. The only logical choice was Lafayette.

THE BRITISH HAD RESPONDED TO THE ARRIVAL OF THE FRENCH BY detaching a sizable force of warships to Newport. Though Clinton might have little confidence in Arbuthnot's abilities, the plan was simple and straightforward. No great naval battle was required. To the French and to Washington, it was clear the British were content to blockade Narragansett Bay, to bottle up the small French fleet, keeping them harmlessly out of the way. Washington's scouts began to send word from the city that Clinton was preparing to move, British and Hessian troops already loading the transports. The strategy was obvious, Clinton feeling pressure to confront the French soldiers. But Washington did not want a major engagement to develop so far north, in a theater of the war he could not support himself. He did not have the troop strength to send anyone to Newport, and if the French infantry were crushed by a sudden British assault, it could be a disaster worse than Charleston. The entire alliance might collapse.

THE LETTERS WERE SENT OUT BY COURIER, WRAPPED IN A LEATHER pouch, the messenger riding hard and quick, darting through darkness on the road that led to the King's Bridge, the northernmost access point to Manhattan Island. Even in darkness there was danger, British patrols always moving, guarding against any sudden assault that Washington might send at them from above.

The courier moved slowly, as quietly as the horse would allow, could see lanternlights at the bridge itself, the British guards not yet aware he was there. As he turned the horse in the road, the pouch of letters was dropped, the leather strap loosened enough so that papers would peek out, catching the eye of the first British patrol who passed that way.

Within a day, the letters had found their way to Henry Clinton. The headquarters congratulated themselves on the vigilance of their cavalry, the horsemen finding what had been so carelessly misplaced by the rebels. The letters were in Washington's own hand, and the hand of his secretary, orders to his subordinates, the details of a plan to push a hard assault into New York. It was a logical and intelligent strategy, the British defense there weakened by the loss of the troops who would sail to Newport. But the rebel plan had been discovered in time, and all around New York, Washington's scouts were surprised to see the flatboats returning from the transports fully loaded, the British and Hessian troops marched again to their barracks. From the camps near the city, a column of several regiments had marched quickly up to Harlem Heights.

As Washington sat high on the palisades and glassed across

the Hudson, the reports began to come in from his spies. Clinton had canceled the mission to Newport, had instead ordered his army to stand on alert, to prepare to receive Washington's massed attack.

Washington could only smile.

HARTFORD, CONNECTICUT, SEPTEMBER 1780

I have arrived here with all the submission, all the zeal, and all the veneration I have for your person and for the distinguished talents which you reveal in sustaining this war forever memorable.

The tone of Rochambeau's letter was certainly designed to erase any doubts Washington might have about French willingness to cooperate, but Lafayette brought another message as well, more direct, that Rochambeau now insisted on a meeting with Washington himself. With the British naval blockade still outside Newport, and Clinton's massed army in New York, neither Rochambeau nor Washington was comfortable making a journey far from his own command. It was logical that the meeting would take place halfway between them, at Hartford.

Lafayette had given Washington his own version of the meetings with Rochambeau, cordial certainly, Lafayette relaying Washington's desire for a campaign as soon as the French were ready to march. Rochambeau had resisted, and Lafayette had returned to New Jersey in a strangely sullen mood. Washington had immediately agreed to the meeting, was still waiting for Lafayette to reveal more about the man, some personal information that might help Washington know how best to proceed. But the young man seemed unable to give any more details than the gist of the unproductive meetings.

Washington was accompanied by an escort of forty guards, rode with Lafayette and Hamilton. As they crossed the Hudson, Washington was losing patience with Lafayette's unusual sulking silence. He had resisted pressing the young man, but Hartford was close now, and sulk or not, Washington needed more than Lafayette had given him.

The road was well traveled, and the guards obeyed Washington's orders, were polite to the carriages and horsemen they passed. He moved past an open hay wagon, a farmer slapping the team, moving them aside. The man looked at the guards, seemed annoyed at the inconvenience. He noticed Washington now, glanced at his uniform with no recognition.

"You best be gettin' this war done, now! People in these parts is runnin' out of patience!"

The words punched him, and he wanted to stop, talk to this man, felt a surge of annoyance that this farmer would presume to understand so much. Hamilton was close beside him now, said, "He's just a farmer, sir. There's four little ones riding in there behind him. Has to be difficult for these people to make do."

Washington was surprised that his reaction to the man had been so obvious.

"Thank you for your counsel, Mr. Hamilton."

He was annoyed more at himself now, thought, You do not have the luxury of anger. He is one man, one farmer who worries for his children. He has the right to show concern, to question why these soldiers cannot prevail against an enemy that the man has probably never seen. I have yet to convince the congress. Why should I believe I can convince anyone else?

He looked ahead, the road widening a bit, thought, The town is close, certainly. Time is short, I know what to expect.

"Mr. Lafayette."

Lafayette had stayed back behind him, rode forward now. "Sir?"

"Remain beside me. Mr. Hamilton, you may fall back a bit, if you don't mind."

Hamilton understood, slowed his horse. Washington kept his voice low, said, "Mr. Lafayette, you have provided me with the substance of your meeting with General Rochambeau. You will now provide me with something more. Your behavior has convinced me that there is more purpose to this meeting in Hartford than convenience."

There was a silent moment, and Lafayette said, "You are correct, sir. My conversations with General Rochambeau were somewhat difficult."

"Why? Do the French not wish to cooperate with us? Is this man no different than d'Estaing?" His voice was rising, and he closed his eyes, held tight to the frustration. "I am weary of riddles, Mr. Lafayette. What challenges do we face in Hartford?"

"General Rochambeau is a superior commander, sir. The fault is mine. I was perhaps too outspoken in my meeting with the general. You should know, sir, that General Rochambeau is a veteran of many wars, of much good service to the king. I did not understand that he would receive my authority with such resistance. It gave me some offense. It was not the proper stage for our discussion."

"Why should General Rochambeau find you objectionable?"

"In France . . . General Rochambeau is aware that I made great effort to place myself in command of his forces now in Newport. He is aware that I am welcomed frequently at the royal court. It is a privilege that some find to be . . . superfluous. Some in the army, the men of experience, do not believe I should be here in such capacity as I enjoy."

A fog seemed to lift in Washington's mind. Of course, Rochambeau is an old professional. Lafayette is a young, ambitious man who has gained a position of some influence here. Energy and zeal from the young is not always appreciated by aged men who feel they have labored long to earn their own position.

"So General Rochambeau wishes to meet with me because he prefers not to grant you such a place of importance in this command."

"That is a fair statement, sir. The general believes I was too zealous in seeking the command more suited to his experience."

"He may be correct, Mr. Lafayette. Do not take offense. You have a place in this army, and my absolute confidence. In General Rochambeau's army, you are still a captain. You must respect that. Did you leave your meeting on good terms?"

"Yes, sir, I assure you. I offered the general my apology, and he responded by assuring me that he bears no ill will. He considers that we are much like father and son."

Washington hid a smile.

"I rather understand that, Mr. Lafayette."

ROCHAMBEAU WAS A SHORT, THICK MAN, A DARK MOTTLED COMplexion on a round face. He met Washington with a wide grasping hug, and Washington had accepted the gesture with some discomfort, was not accustomed to such a physical display from either his officers or anyone else. But Rochambeau filled the awkward silence with a generous flow of compliments, much like the effusive deference in his letter. Lafayette interpreted, and Washington observed both men carefully for any sign of hostility that might cloud the meeting. But Rochambeau seemed unaware of any difficulty with the young man, and after more cordiality, led them to a long oval table, wineglasses already filled. They sat, Rochambeau not taking his eye from Washington. He knew he was being appraised, accepted a toast in French from one of Rochambeau's officers, followed Lafayette's lead with the wineglass. Around the table, the talk grew quiet, and Rochambeau said, "I am pleased to tell you, General, that I am in your service. You should know that my orders are to subordinate myself and my soldiers to your superior rank."

It was the answer to the first looming question, and Washington smiled.

"Cooperation between us can only ensure success, General. Thank you."

"You should also know, sir, that my king has been very specific that I not endanger my men by removing them from the support of the navy."

Washington waited for the words to filter through Lafayette, who finished the thought with a slight frown. Washington absorbed the meaning, said, "I had hoped to begin a campaign to remove the British from New York."

"Ah, yes, sir, and is it appropriate for me to ask if you have the strength in your command to accomplish this?"

"No, General, I do not."

Rochambeau showed a mask of concern.

"You desire my forces to support yours, yes? It is a reasonable request. However, we are in some difficulty here. By my orders, I cannot abandon the fleet to the dangers from the British blockade. And, if we were to break the blockade, the fleet is not of sufficient number to defeat the British navy at New York."

"I had hoped, General, that a larger fleet would soon arrive here."

Rochambeau put his hands in front of him, turned his palms up, a slight shrug.

"I am very sorry, General. That is not so likely to happen. Our efforts in the West Indies, and along our own shores have exhausted our resources."

Washington felt the air leaving the room. So, there are six thousand French troops who will not leave Newport, and ten warships that are too few to make any attack on the British. Rochambeau drank from his wineglass, said, "Forgive me, General, but I must ask you a question that is commonly heard in my country. Why have you been unable to raise such strength as you require? A nation this large would suggest an army that could not be contained from one British base in New York. I apologize if this is offensive to you, General Washington, but we do not understand why America has not already won this war."

It was not offensive, but Washington felt the familiar frustrations, the same questions and pleas he had made to the congress. He waited for a long moment, and Lafayette was staring at him, seemed ready to burst. Washington put a hand out toward the young man, shook his head, a silent command, *quiet*.

"General Rochambeau, you ask a fair question. I do not have the most satisfying answer. We are a nation who knows little of building armies. We do not have great feudal estates peopled by workers who lay down their shovels and axes and take up the swords of their lord because he requires it. It is not our way. The American people are concerned that one tyrant will replace another. If we defeat the British, what will follow? Will there be another oppression, from the hand of our own soldiers perhaps? We created this nation from a collection of ideas, words on a piece of paper. There is no ruling order, no class of warriors to call on. From the beginning, we relied on militia, to take to the field when there is need. We have learned that it is a system that does not serve well in the face of a strong enemy, or in the face of a wider war. A man in Connecticut can be expected to defend his home, but it is not so simple to convince that man to fight for Virginia. Under my urging, the congress has granted this command the power to raise a Continental Army, and we have been somewhat successful. But those troops serve for a period of time, and when that time expires, they are free to go home. My men have given so much to this cause, and many of them ask the same question as you. Why does not the great mass of citizens turn out in support? Perhaps, General, they must be given guidance. Perhaps there are many people who do not yet understand that this cause is worthy of sacrifice. Perhaps they have not been offered a leader who inspires them. I . . . simply do not know."

Lafayette completed the translation, then said, "It is not true, General."

Washington motioned him to silence again, then looked at Rochambeau, saw puzzlement, thought, He does not understand. How can I expect that, when I do not understand myself?

He put his hands flat on the table, leaned forward, said, "General Rochambeau, what must we do to gain your cooperation?"

"I am here only to obey, General. But we have been inconvenienced by our enemy. It is the nature of war. We must allow ourselves patience."

Patience. The word bit him. He thought of Greene, imagined him at this table, that word so likely to inspire an explosion. Rochambeau seemed to read him, said, "General, the British are not going to leave their base in New York very soon. We must seek opportunity. You spoke of faith. Perhaps this is the example. I have already made a study of this war, of your adversaries. General Clinton is a man of lofty planning and poor execution. Allow him the time to open the door. My troops will remain a formidable presence in Newport. We will not abandon you, General."

The meeting was concluded, and Washington was saluted again with the inflated tokens of affection.

He began the journey back to his headquarters in a somber silence. He scolded himself for having such high expectations, for believing that Rochambeau could be a savior. He felt drained of hope, absorbed the rhythm of the horse, staring blankly ahead. His thoughts settled into dull blackness, and he fought and grappled with his own despair. The struggle was too familiar, and he knew that tomorrow would cleanse much of it away. Once he was back at his headquarters, the business of the army would occupy him, consume him, push the despair into some dark hole in his mind.

He rode now through a cascade of falling leaves, a warm breeze that pulled them from the tall trees. He looked up, the roadway darkened above him by soft blankets of red and gold. It would not be so long before the trees were stripped bare yet again, another winter for his army to suffer. He focused ahead, thought of West Point. He had sent word of his arrival, had thought a pleasant night there might ease his mood. It had been a long while since he had enjoyed a comfortable meal with a couple as pleasantly sociable as Benedict Arnold and his charming young wife.

45. ARNOLD

He waited in the back room of the house, stared out to thick woods. He focused on the shadows, longer now, nearly gone, the sunlight high on the trees. He had eaten nothing, his stomach a hard cold knot, the smell of the food reaching him through the closed door, sickening him. He heard the sharp clink of the utensils, the spoon stirring something in a pot, each bit of noise burrowing into his brain. Their voices were unavoidable, loud and crude, and he was filled with the disgust, could imagine food slopped on plates, the men eating with their hands. They were laughing now, some obscene joke no doubt, and he shivered, strange, uncontrollable, tried to focus his mind only on the fading light beyond the window.

The three men did not share Arnold's nervousness. Two of them were merely laborers, ordered by his authority to row a boat out into the Hudson, to make their way to a British warship, the *Vulture*, anchored downstream. If they were nervous at all, it was for the darkness, a river watched by guns of both sides. But Arnold had assured them by providing documents, allowing passage through any official blockade, permission to carry the third man, Joshua Smith, to an important meeting on board the British ship.

The house belonged to Smith's brother, William, a Tory who was now a refugee in New York. But Joshua Smith was a patriot, offering the use of his brother's house as a wayfaring stop on the road from New Jersey to Arnold's headquarters opposite West Point. Smith had accepted Arnold's invitation with nervous glee, the opportunity to perform some important task for the Continental Army, a rare opportunity to throw a slap in the direction of his brother. Smith's mission was to carry a letter from Arnold to the *Vulture*, a letter to confirm Smith's identity as Arnold's trust-worthy agent. If all went according to Arnold's plan, a passenger would accompany Smith back across the river. Smith knew that the man was very important to General Arnold, had been told only that the man's name was John Anderson. Smith would have his men row his passenger back to a quiet place near Smith's house, where Arnold would join Anderson for a private meeting.

Arnold had given Smith the broadest hints, had planted the notion of great secrecy, a meeting of certain value to the army. Arnold had told him that the man called Anderson could be of great help to Arnold, could in fact open a passageway into New York for all manner of valuable intelligence. Smith had learned his part of the mission with complete enthusiasm, accepted his responsibility as a patriot. All they needed was darkness.

AS FAR BACK AS 1775, ARNOLD'S SERVICE IN THE FIELD HAD BEEN extraordinary, the capture of Fort Ticonderoga, then the first mission to Canada. During the futile assault on Quebec, he had been wounded, but maintained control of an impossible night-mare, men trapped by a hard winter in a hostile land, their mission a complete disaster. The fault had been in the plan itself, not in those who carried it out, and Arnold had brought back the sur-vivors to an army that was suffering far greater disasters from its defeats in New York. Neither the congress nor the commanding general had time to give Benedict Arnold his due.

As the war seemed to expand beyond his reach, Arnold had sought opportunities to serve, flashes of duty in quick fights, but never the key role, never the position that would bring the atten-tion he deserved. Washington had finally recognized him, the commanding general including Arnold in the promotion lists. But many in congress believed that Connecticut had given the army too many generals, and he was passed over. It was a hard slap at his ambition, and to Arnold, the congress seemed far too impressed by men who were prominent in defeat.

When the army had gathered to confront Burgoyne, Arnold had seen another opportunity, only to be swept aside by the abysmal Horatio Gates. Gates had done nothing to secure the victory at Saratoga, and every officer on the field knew that with-out Arnold, and men like Morgan and Lincoln, Gates would likely have ended up in a British prison. Instead he was the savior, the great hero, and made an obscene parade of himself to the congress, while Arnold nursed a leg wound so serious he could not walk for several months.

Arnold finally received his promotion to major general only because Washington sliced through the blather in congress, convincing them to reward the man who had earned the rank. When the British abandoned Philadelphia, a crippled Arnold was assigned to command the city. But for long months, Arnold's bitterness toward the congress festered, a growing hatred of the generals who seemed to have such talent for putting their names into the public eye. His passion for the cause began to fade, and Philadelphia became an opportunity of a different type. It was a place where the enterprising and the ingenious could profit, and Arnold took advantage. The grand social scene there had brought him alive again, and despite the hostility and the accusations of corruption, Arnold had found a comfortable home. But the congress was too close, and he began to feel the wrath of jealous men, men who envied the stature of the senior commander. He was charged with serious offenses of corruption, and congress ordered him to stand for court-martial. But the evidence was scant, the man too skilled at covering his tracks. In the end, he could only be convicted on charges so minor that a relieved Washington could eliminate the issue with a mild reprimand.

Despite his notoriety, Arnold still attended the grand ballrooms, and he was astounded to attract the eye of the most sought-after beauty in Philadelphia. Peggy Shippen seemed to adhere herself to him, and the gossip that swirled around him only increased. She was half his age, but he fell in love, and when they were married, the gossip turned more toward her than her husband. He was completely dazzled by her, jealous of the attention that even her marriage had not discouraged. He knew she was spoiled, and he enjoyed it, allowed her every indulgence he could provide. When his own resources did not satisfy, he was amazed at her own resourcefulness, her ongoing relationships with those now in New York, the Tory civilians who had gone with the British, as well as the British officers themselves. Her needs continued to grow, and he continued to accommodate her. Their private hours were the most passionate he had ever known, and he would have done anything to keep her close to him. When she began to show sadness for the loss of British elegance, whispering to him in those soft moments, yearning for the grandeur she missed, he began to see a new path, a new means to take her out of the despair of this never-ending war. The more they spoke of it, the more bitterness he had for the cause of her unhappiness. There could be no peace in Philadelphia, no peace serving in an army that abused and punished its best commanders, while elevating men like Horatio Gates to such a lofty perch. His time in Philadelphia had given him a feel for business, a flair for delicate finance. As he began to explore a new world for her, new possibilities, he was grateful that she agreed, and within a short time, it was her discreet contacts, her means of reaching her acquaintances in New York that opened the door.

He did not wrestle with a moral dilemma, did not hesitate to offer himself as currency. Peggy swept away any last doubts by observing that there could be no treason to a country that never truly existed. He anticipated that Henry Clinton would find him to be a valuable asset, worthy of significant reward by his service alone. But Clinton had disappointed him, seemed more interested in what Arnold could bring with him as a prize. It was suggested that Arnold lead a body of troops in some unwise mission, allowing himself to be cut off, forced to surrender. But there were no troops for him to lead, no looming fight that would offer him either the command or the opportunity. Instead, there would have to be a place, an outpost, a garrison, someplace Arnold could weaken with such discretion that his officers would not detect it. He could supply the plans, the details of weakness, of troop placement, all the tools the British could use for an easy conquest, a prize that Clinton would receive with grateful rewards. When Clinton agreed to his terms, it was a night of grand private celebration. Not only would she have the luxuries of New York, or perhaps even London, but he would have the means to pay for it all. As his wounds healed, and his plans hardened in his mind, he needed only to secure command of the most appropriate garrison. Washington had obliged him. All that was left was to furnish the British the advantages they would need to capture West Point.

THE THREE MEN HAD DISAPPEARED INTO THE DARKNESS, HAD BEEN gone for better than three hours. He paced outside the house, tried to see his watch, had gone through the same routine every few minutes. The agony of time had finally passed, and he caught the reflection from the house, the low light of a lantern. It was nearly midnight. It was time.

He climbed the horse, moved into the road. There was no moon, the black sky pierced with stars. He pushed the horse slowly, the hoofbeats drumming in his ears, muffled only by the thunder from his own heart.

He rode for several minutes, could see the gap in the trees, the designated spot. He stopped the horse, listened for a long moment. The woods around him were a cascade of noise, the roar of so many small creatures filling his ears. His breathing came in hard short gasps, and he put a hand on the icy stone in his chest. He moved the horse carefully, the trees opening into a narrow patch of grass, and ahead, the wide patch of stars broken by the tall points of fir trees. He continued on, stopped, heard different sounds, a voice perhaps. He waited, heard it again, thought, Yes! A voice, surely. Now he heard a horse, muffled sound, coming toward him, and he waited, heard a low, hard whisper.

"General?"

"Here. Right here."

He could not see Smith's face, the man only a dark shape, moving up close beside him, and Smith said in a low voice, "Done as you said, sir. He's right back there, the edge of the tall firs. My men and me will wait out on the road. You come get us when you're ready for him to go back."

Arnold was shivering, the sweat in his clothes chilling him. He nodded, tried to make a sound, his voice choked away by the nervousness, whispered, "Yes . . . yes, good."

Smith began to move away, and Arnold searched the darkness in front of him, the tops of the trees. Behind him, Smith said, "I hope he can give us some help. This country could use some good fortune."

Arnold stared ahead, said, "Indeed."

He walked the horse to the edge of the trees, stopped, dismounted. He waited a moment, took a step, said in a low voice, "Mr. Anderson?"

He heard the steps, the man moving toward him. He saw the dark shape, a small man, shrouded in a long coat. The man moved close to him, said in a low voice, "I don't believe we are detected, General. Hardly the time for disguises, eh? Allow me to offer my introduction, sir. I am Major John André."

*   *   *

THEY TALKED FOR FOUR HOURS, NEGOTIATIONS AND TERMS, DETAILS and tactics. When the talking stopped, Smith was summoned, but now there was a problem. It was after 4:00 A.M., and there was not sufficient time for the darkness to shroud André's journey back to the *Vulture*. They rode instead to Smith's house, to wait through a long day for the darkness to return. Arnold had gone out close to the river, could see the British ship in the distance, the safe haven for André. As the sun rose high, the air was suddenly streaked by bits of fire. The *Vulture* was a tempting target, and he realized that along the edge of that part of the river, there was at least one battery that could find the range. As he stared in desperate agony, the *Vulture* began to take damage. In barely an hour, the ship had moved to safety, disappearing far down the river, beyond the range of the guns that Arnold himself commanded. Now there was a new urgency. With the darkness would come a different task for the accommodating Mr. Smith. The man that Smith knew only as Anderson would have to reach the protection of British patrols overland, crossing a dangerous no-man's-land patrolled only by bandits, men Arnold knew as *irregulars*. André accepted his fate, rode out with Smith carrying a pass Arnold had provided him. He also carried documents from Arnold that were meant for the eyes of Henry Clinton. As Arnold rode back to his own headquarters, he fought through his fear, eased his mind by thoughts of Peggy, pictured her waiting for him at his headquarters. André would certainly make the journey, and he swept his fears away with a marvelous daydream. Yes, very soon, she will be on my arm, strolling through the galleries of the city. They will stand aside as we parade past them, admiring the beautiful Mrs. Arnold, holding proudly to the uniform of her husband, the celebrated British general . . .

46. WASHINGTON

HE HAD NOT REACHED ARNOLD'S HEADQUARTERS IN TIME FOR THE evening meal, had sent his sincere regrets, advising Arnold instead that he would arrive for breakfast. Along the way, Knox had joined him, the artillery commander on his own mission to inspect the batteries that spread along the Hudson. The fortifications had not been tended to in a long while, and Washington had considered the pleasant social evening at West Point to be a lower priority than accompanying Knox to examine his guns.

The headquarters house was across the river from the fort itself and slightly downstream. It had been the home of Beverley Robinson, a prominent Tory who had escaped the wrath of his neighbors by fleeing to New York. Washington had not questioned the location, knew the house was well guarded by thick woods and tall, close hills. The house was a suitable mansion for such an important command, could accommodate a large staff as well as room for visitors.

As he rode into Arnold's yard, he knew they were late yet again, Lafayette and Hamilton chiding him gently to speed up the inspections. The young men were clearly looking forward to the breakfast as much as he was. Washington was surprised by the lack of activity, the yard empty. He had expected a grand reception from the man who had been so very grateful for this influential command. But there was no concern, his mind occupied by the view of the wide river, the long sweeping vista that reminded him so much of Mount Vernon.

Hamilton had dismounted, and Washington still expected Arnold to emerge from the house. As Hamilton moved toward the entrance, Washington saw an officer appear, a small thin man, his hat in his hand. Hamilton spoke to the man, then both men moved across the yard toward him.

"Sir, this is Major David Franks, aide to General Arnold. The general was called away. Some business across the river."

Franks moved closer now, seemed embarrassed.

"My apologies, General. General Arnold received a note, and left immediately. He said he would be at the fort, and requested you be rowed across. I am truly sorry, sir."

Washington glanced toward the river, said, "No matter, Major. I should enjoy inspecting West Point as well."

He left the officers behind, sat in the stern of the wide boat. The fort was a looming hulk of stone, gripping the stark rocky face like some huge claw. He examined the gray walls, the gun ports that lined the rocks, felt a pride, the sense of power. They will never strike here, he thought. Not even Clinton would be so arrogant to think he can sweep through this place.

The boat was pulled ashore, and Washington was surprised that no one was waiting for him. He saw the same surprise on the face of the sergeant, the man who commanded the oarsman.

"My apologies, sir. They don't seem to have been expecting you. I'll fetch a guard."

The sergeant scrambled up the hill, and Washington heard shouts, a flurry of activity above him. He stepped out of the boat, climbed up over small round rocks, could see the guards, surprised men sliding quickly down the trail. He saw an officer now, recognized the man, John Lamb.

"Sir! My deepest apologies, sir! We were not informed of your arrival."

He was growing weary of that word.

"*Apology* not necessary. Colonel Lamb, did not General Arnold inform you I would be joining him here?"

Lamb seemed confused by the question.

"Um, no sir. I have not yet seen General Arnold, sir."

"He is not here?"

"No, sir. I assure you, sir, I would be aware."

Now Washington was confused. He looked back across the quiet river, said, "Well, Colonel, since I am here, perhaps you will allow me to inspect your command."

"By all means, sir. I would be honored."

"Perhaps, in time, we will find what has become of General Arnold."

*   *   *

HE HAD RETURNED TO THE MANSION TO FIND ARNOLD STILL ABSENT, his aide reporting only that the general's boat had not returned. He expected nonetheless to pass the time by the pleasant company of the young Mrs. Arnold, but she had yet to emerge from her bedroom. Arnold's aides could only offer the familiar apologies.

He was shown to a small bedroom, a polite accommodation offered by Major Franks. As the aide escorted him into the room, Washington could not help a glance above him, seeking some telltale sign that Peggy Arnold was stirring in the upstairs bedroom. Franks caught the look, said, "General, my deepest regrets. Mrs. Arnold was not well this morning. I had hoped she would make her appearance by now, but I have learned that it is best not to disturb a woman in such a state."

"Quite so, Major. Think nothing of it. Once General Arnold returns, I'm sure we shall have a fine gathering."

Franks moved away, and Washington closed the door. He removed his coat, brushed his hand over his shirt, wiping at the dust of the long ride, the grime from the construction of the still-unfinished fort. He sat on the small bed, glanced around the small room. It was typical of so fine a home, a soft narrow bed, one tall window, a spray of sunlight that fell across a small chest of drawers. He noticed a fat china vase, bursting with flowers. It was a touch that Martha would have approved, and he said a silent thank-you for the attention to the small pleasant detail. He looked down at his dusty boots, thought of removing them, heard a small sound above him, a slight squeak from a bed. He listened for footsteps, but there was only silence, and he frowned, disappointed by whatever ailment had kept her upstairs.

He had known Peggy's family for many years, knew the girl as a young teen. He had always suspected she would marry well. Even as a youngster her charms were magnified by her lack of shyness. When he learned that Arnold had won her, he was surprised. He attributed her affections to the strange effects of war. He would never mention this, of course, assumed Arnold had endured enough discomforting talk at the hands of the society belles of Philadelphia.

Peggy had seemed to be comfortable in any setting, especially in those social gatherings where the elite were certain to take notice. Washington found her behavior refreshing, this young confident girl who refused to play the expected role of the shy

coquette. He had anticipated visiting with her as much as with
Arnold himself, knew the young officers who accompanied him
felt the same way. He cast his eyes toward the ceiling again,
smiled, thought, Yes, it was always so. The young men are all in
love with Peggy.

There was a sharp knock on the door, and Washington said,
"Do come in."

Hamilton was there, and Washington saw a bundle in his hand.

"Sir, these just arrived. The courier has a message from a
Lieutenant Colonel Jameson, sir."

"Yes, I know Colonel Jameson. He is in command of the outposts along the British frontier down the river."

"It seems the colonel was most insistent that these be delivered only to your hand, sir."

Washington took the letters, spread them on the bed. He saw a
sketch, a crude drawing, held it up, could see now, it was the lay-
out of West Point. He felt a stirring in his brain, looked at the
other papers in turn, saw a letter from Jameson himself. He read
for a moment, and his hands shook, a burst of cold spreading
through him.

"A man has been apprehended, name of Anderson, bearing
these documents on his person. And, bearing this as well, a pass
signed by General Arnold. Mr. Hamilton, summon Mr. Lafayette and Mr. Knox. *Now.*"

Washington scanned the papers, could see details of troop
numbers and placements. There was one other note, written in a
different hand, a flourish of lines and swirls, the hand of a man
with a talent for writing. It was a lengthy request for leniency, a
strange explanation of deeds not detailed. Washington scanned
down, more of the same, wordy explanations why the man should
not be considered a spy. And then, one line caught his eye:

*The person in your possession is Major John André, Adjutant
General of the British Army.*

The hall was filled with motion now, and Washington saw
Lafayette buttoning his shirt, looking curiously at the papers on
the bed.

"I was preparing for dinner, sir . . ."

"Is there still no sign of General Arnold?"

"No, sir."

"Then it seems we have been betrayed." He shouted, "Mr.
Hamilton!"

"Sir!"

"Ride quickly down the river, go to the King's Ferry outpost. Determine if they have observed the passing of General Arnold's boat. If not, make every effort to apprehend it."

"Apprehend . . . General Arnold, sir?"

"*Now,* Mr. Hamilton!"

His hands were shaking, and he scanned the papers again, saw a page with familiar words, realized they were his own, notes from a meeting with Arnold a few weeks before. He felt a swirling fever of anger, a hard black fist coiling up in his brain. He looked up at Lafayette, said in a low growl, "We must make every determination of the damage this has caused. But first, I should like to see Mrs. Arnold."

HE KNOCKED, HEARD NOTHING, HAD NO TIME FOR MANNERS. HE pushed the door open, saw her curled up on the bed, holding tightly to her infant child. He had not expected to see the baby, had forgotten entirely that she had given birth. She looked at him with hard, wild eyes, and he said, "Mrs. Arnold . . . Peggy. Do you know where your husband has gone?"

"He cannot protect me! He is gone!"

She began to cry, heavy sobs, holding the baby close to her chest, the baby now crying as well. Washington felt suddenly helpless, and behind him, Arnold's aide was there, said in a soft voice, "Mrs. Arnold, it is General Washington. He will protect you."

"No! It is not General Washington! *He is here to kill my baby!*" she screamed, sat up in the bed, backed away from him, staring wild-eyed, the picture of utter madness. The baby was in her lap now, and he could see she was wearing only a dressing gown, the thin material now pulled askew. He turned his head, embarrassed at her immodesty, and she stopped crying, said, "Yes! *You are the one!* My husband cannot protect me from you! He suffers so! They have put hot irons on his head!"

She crawled toward him across the bed, her gown falling open completely, and he backed away, felt the door behind him, said, "Mrs. Arnold, I am not here to kill your baby. Please."

She began to cry again, and Washington backed out of the room, stood in the hall, saw Lafayette staring past him, wide-eyed, and Lafayette said, "My God. Poor suffering child."

Arnold's aide moved again into the room, the soothing words again. Washington felt a hot twisting in his stomach, moved down the narrow stairs. He saw Franks, said, "Major, what transpired this morning?"

"Sir?"

"You said General Arnold received a note from Colonel Lamb?"

"Um, well, yes, sir. We assumed it was Colonel Lamb. The general did not reveal the contents. He received the note, then returned to his room. He spoke to his wife, then . . . called for his boat."

He heard hoofbeats, and Franks opened the front door, said, "Major Hamilton has returned, sir."

Washington pushed through the door, saw Hamilton halting his horse, the young man jumping down. Hamilton ran toward him, said, "Sir! We encountered a courier from King's Ferry! General Arnold was observed down the river, but he has gone, sir. The lookouts report that he was seen boarding a British ship . . . the *Vulture*, sir."

Washington stared out to the river, said, "At least he had the decency to say good-bye to his wife."

OCTOBER 2, 1780

Word had traveled quickly, and Washington began to receive entreaties through the British lines. The most insistent came from Clinton himself, that André be released, some absurd excuse that the man was under a flag of truce. André himself had attempted long-winded explanations of his capture, each contradicting the one before. Despite all the pleas, Washington would only agree to one term for André's release: a simple exchange, John André for Benedict Arnold. Clinton refused.

He could not find reason to arrest Peggy Arnold, and once she was allowed to leave, and provided transportation to Philadelphia, her condition seemed to improve dramatically. Washington granted her a favor. If she desired to be joined with her husband, he would not object.

Among his own staff there was disagreement on how Major André should be regarded, whether the man's favored position in the British command required special circumstances. But Washington would hear no pleas for leniency, for treating André as anything other than a spy. The trial was brief and the verdict definite. No argument could be offered to prevent André's execution. Despite André's own request that a man of his lofty status be allowed to choose the manner of his own death, Washington made the decision himself. On October 2, John André was hanged.

47. GREENE

HORATIO GATES HAD ARRIVED IN NORTH CAROLINA TO ASSUME command of a ragged and exhausted army. Several regiments of continental regulars had been marched southward, adding to the few survivors from Charleston. They were accompanied by cavalry, a necessity in this part of the country, where so much flat open land invited rapid assault. The newly arrived troops had made a torturous march through inhospitable land, and when Gates arrived, many were still suffering the effects of their ordeal. The horses of the cavalry were in poor condition as well, many not surviving the long ride south. Gates was met with urgent requests from the officers that the entire army required time to refit and replenish their strength. But Gates would not wait. If the cavalry was not prepared to ride, they would be left behind. The men would fare as best as the land would provide. Gates started them on another grueling march, his eye focused squarely on the British outpost at Camden. It was a ripe target, unsuspecting and vulnerable, and as Gates gathered militia units from North Carolina and Virginia, he had begun to see his army as invincible. Camden would be his first prize.

If Gates believed his attack would be a surprise, the British commander, Francis Rawdon, disappointed him. At first, Gates seemed to have the upper hand, and presented his forces in such a way that the British wisely pulled back. Gates interpreted the move as an all-out retreat, but Rawdon was merely buying time, reorganizing and reinforcing his lines. By the time Gates met the British again, they were stronger and better prepared, and now, were commanded by Cornwallis himself.

Gates pursued the attack with perfect vigor, but he had positioned the raw Virginia militia along a key position of his line. Confronting Cornwallis' regular infantry, they fired one volley, then turned and ran, completely abandoning the field. Their collapse endangered Gates' entire position, and inspired a massive panicked retreat. The only units that held their ground were the veteran regiments from Maryland and Delaware, William Smallwood's regulars, who had shown their astounding bravery as far back as Long Island. With most of Gates' army dissolving in front of him, Cornwallis turned his entire force on Smallwood, a power the veterans could not resist. With no alternative except annihilation, Smallwood retreated as well.

While the fight had been a crushing defeat, it was Gates himself who placed the final punctuation mark on a perfectly disastrous ordeal. As his army fled piecemeal through woods and swamps, Gates himself rode hard and fast, as he made his own retreat as well. When he finally brought himself under control, he had ridden for better than three days, to Hillsboro, North Carolina, a distance of one hundred eighty miles. Though his report to congress insisted he was seeking a point from which to best reorganize his command, his beaten army had a different view. As his junior officers rallied the scattered troops toward Gates' new sanctuary, the men themselves understood that Horatio Gates, the hero of Saratoga, the savior of their cause, had in fact led them to utter disaster, and then, abandoned them on the field.

PREAKNESS, NEW JERSEY, OCTOBER 22, 1780

"Mr. Greene, we are faced with a crisis of some urgency."

He looked at Washington with a strange urge to laugh, the words so completely familiar.

"Yes, sir."

"You are aware by now of the difficulties which Mr. Gates has suffered. This army has survived an astounding volume of catastrophe, and I am confident we will survive this one as well. It has become something of a lesson for me, that positive change is often born of disaster."

"Would it not be better if we could avoid disaster altogether?"

Washington looked at him, cocked his head to one side.

"Who, in this army, is capable of such a feat?"

Greene knew the question applied to him as well, his own failure at Fort Washington still a scar.

"Mr. Greene, the congress has placed in my hands the authority to select a successor to General Gates. In times of crisis, their confidence in my ability shows considerable increase." Washington paused. "No, that is not appropriate. There are many still in that body to whom this nation is indebted."

"And a good many to whom we are not, sir."

Washington said nothing.

"My apologies, sir. I did not mean to suggest the congress is opposed to our cause."

"Mr. Greene, there is no one who has endured the arrows of that body more than you. But you have friends as well."

"I may have friends, sir. The quartermaster general does not."

"That's why I sent for you. Your duties in that department have, for the most part, been terminated. Once your accounts have been settled, you are free to assume a new post."

Greene had already heard the talk. As word of Gates' defeat flew through the army, it inspired all manner of speculation, some aimed directly at him. The summons to Washington's headquarters had put the rumors in a new light, Greene allowing himself to believe that the talk was not so far-fetched after all.

"Most of my accounts are settled now, sir. There is some dispute as you know, some members of the congress who will not accept anything I submit without assuming some dastardly scheme on my part."

"Those voices have grown quiet in recent days, Mr. Greene. One more benefit of a sudden crisis. I am recommending to the congress that you be granted the appointment as commander in chief of the Southern Department."

He had expected it, but the words seemed unreal. He looked at Washington, saw no change of expression, the message matter-of-fact. Greene didn't know what to say.

"May I assume this meets with your approval, Mr. Greene?"

He could not hide his smile.

"Quite so, sir."

"I have not been informed of either the strength of the enemy's forces, or our own. I can give you no particular instructions. I must leave you to govern your actions entirely according to your own judgment, and the circumstances of that command. You may realize nothing more than embarrassment, Mr. Greene. But I can rely on no other officer in this army with a responsibility so grave."

"Thank you, sir. Will the congress agree?"

Washington smiled, the first break in his sober mood.

"Consider, Mr. Greene, your most vocal opponents. Whether or not they appreciate the gravity of this duty, or the depth of my confidence in you, some of them will certainly delight in seeing you gone."

NOVEMBER 1780

The appointment required Greene to appear before the congress, and he was surprised to see that Washington was entirely correct. Even those who had spoken of him with such bile made a show of gratefulness toward his good service, so many offering their unguarded assurances that command in the Southern Department would now be in the most qualified hands. Whether his former enemies shared Washington's faith in his abilities or simply wished him to disappear southward, his appointment received the full support of congress.

He had been accompanied by von Steuben and Harry Lee, both men essential to the strategy of his new command. Washington and Greene agreed completely that Gates' failure had much to do with the lack of training in his army, and von Steuben had already proven himself the master of that particular problem. Lee would command his legion of cavalry, would correct the enormous error made by Gates in ignoring the value of the light horse.

As they moved south, Greene had insisted on visiting Mount Vernon, a favor to a grateful Washington. It was purely social, and Martha offered as much generous hospitality as Mount Vernon could provide. But Greene would not linger, could see the house in disarray, Martha already preparing for another journey north, yet another Christmas with her husband in the bustling confines of a new headquarters. Though the visit was brief, polite small talk of Kitty and his children, he did as much as he could to send her on her own journey with words of encouragement, a playful challenge that she would now have new generals and a new army to charm. This time they would be French.

Greene knew that the key to success, and possibly survival in the Carolinas, would be the availability of supplies that would originate in Virginia. But that state was a chaos of military disorganization, a product of the philosophy of its governor, Thomas Jefferson. Like John Adams, and so many of those who had fashioned the very existence of the country, Jefferson believed a permanent army was a potential threat to liberty. Even the periodic raids from British warships could not alter his perception that local militia responding to a crisis was a far better solution for Virginia than a regular military force. Though congress had authorized Greene to raise continental regiments there, the resistance in Virginia was fierce. To confront that challenge, von Steuben was left in Richmond, to put his considerable energies into convincing Jefferson and the rest of Virginia that there was truly a greater need beyond their own borders.

What remained of Gates' forces had gathered around Charlotte, and as Greene rode southward through North Carolina, he began to dread the meeting, the first confrontation Greene would have with the man he had come to replace.

CHARLOTTE, NORTH CAROLINA, DECEMBER 2, 1780

The town was small, barely two dozen homes, and beyond its streets lay the camps of the army. Greene was followed by his staff, Majors Burnet and Forsythe. Burnet was businesslike and studious. Forsythe was more outgoing, and Greene used him more as the liaison with the subordinate officers. Major Hovey was gone, had returned to his home near Boston, and though Greene felt his absence, he could not have denied the young man's resignation. It was a common problem for the senior officers, finding energetic young men who accepted the grueling responsibilities of managing a command. It was unusual for a staff officer to survive the crushing work, and Hovey had kept to the

job longer than most. Too many of the others came to the headquarters with dreams of their own command. Some sought the
self-importance they gained from such closeness to authority.
Greene thought of Hovey often, knew the young man had every
ability to perform the job, had shown the same tenacity as Tench
Tilghman. But Hovey had his own dreams, some notion of going
into business, a bookseller perhaps, his quest receiving an enthusiastic endorsement from another former bookseller, Henry
Knox.

Greene rode at the head of a small column of men who had
once been North Carolina militia, two companies now signed on
for a full enlistment. As he had journeyed southward from Virginia, he was surprised to find militia officers waiting for him,
assembling their men in their village squares. It was more than a
cordial welcome, many of the men now joining the ranks of the
Continental Army. There was considerable shame in their ranks,
the embarrassment for the collapse of the Virginians at Camden.
In the small towns, Greene heard more details of that fight than
he had received from Washington, certainly more than Gates
would include in his official reports. The militia units themselves understood that their performance was poor, that if
Greene was going to succeed, these men would have to become
better soldiers.

He halted the column, and the officers took over, moving the
men out of line, marching them toward the clusters of dingy
white tents. Ahead, he saw a small tavern, and beyond, some sort
of boardinghouse. Officers began emerging from the house, and
he pulled the horse to the side of the wide road, studied them as
they studied him. One last man came out, short and round, thick
glasses perched low on a hawklike nose. It was Horatio Gates.

Greene dismounted, took his time adjusting his coat, annoyed
with himself for his nervousness about confronting Gates. He
fiddled with his saddle for a moment, saw a groom waiting patiently for the reins to the horse. Greene took a deep breath,
handed the leather straps to the groom, who led the horse away.
The meeting was unavoidable. Gates was right in front of him.

"General Greene! Welcome to Charlotte! A dusty ride, certainly. Come, we have some refreshment inside."

The man's politeness disarmed him, and Greene said, "Yes,
certainly. Thank you."

Gates led the way, the others standing aside, not following, clearly obeying some previous instruction from Gates. Greene moved inside, trailed Gates to a dimly lit dining room, a fat wooden table perched in the center. There was a lantern on the table, and Gates adjusted the light, the room now opening up in a dull yellow glow. Greene saw a bottle, something dark, and Gates retrieved two glasses from a small cabinet, said, "This potion is not what one would expect in New England, but it is passable. Some kind of grape, or perhaps not. A gift from General Sumter. Ah, but you have not met him. You will. Please." Gates pointed to another chair, and Greene moved slowly, feeling wary, one animal circling another. He still expected some hostile burst from Gates, sat slowly. Gates held up a glass.

"To your success, General, the success of our cause."

Greene raised his glass, tasted the liquid, something like wine, very sweet. Gates set his glass down, waited for a moment, said, "Is there something you need to tell me, General?"

"Yes, sir. I suppose I should make this official. General Gates, by order of the Congress of the United States, you are relieved of command of the Southern Department of the Continental Army. I am your replacement."

"I acknowledge your command. Congratulations, General Greene. May your fortunes be blessed to a greater degree than my own."

It was not the reception he expected.

"Thank you, sir."

"Please, Nathanael, formalities are not required."

"You still outrank me, sir."

"Not any longer. With your arrival, my service to this army is concluded. I shall return to my home in Virginia. I have learned that there is no place in this army for a man who trusts too deeply in the abilities of his soldiers."

Greene was not yet prepared to regard Gates as a civilian, said, "I'm not certain I understand, sir."

"Unlike so many in General Washington's command, I have been a champion of militia. I have always believed that a man will fight more fiercely and more dependably if he is close to his own home. Without the support of militia, I do not believe I could have defeated General Burgoyne. However, the Almighty has played a tragic game in this theater. I had every reason to believe these men would show the courage of their brothers at

Saratoga. A foolish mistake. They have done me in, Nathanael. They have put an end to my career, erased my laurels. Your journey here took you through Philadelphia, certainly. Tell me what you heard."

"I'm not certain I can comply, sir."

"Then I'll tell you. 'He ran away. The gallant Gates abandoned his army.' They weren't here, Nathanael. It was shameful in the extreme. No man should be expected to lead such a rabble of cowards and misfits. I believed in them, and they rewarded me with disgrace. I take my leave of this place with no apology. If these men did not do their duty, Nathanael, it is no fault of mine."

Greene was grimacing at the sound of his own name, thought, Does he believe he is my friend? Why is he even trying? Gates took another drink from the glass, and Greene saw the familiar smirk, the arrogance of a man with full confidence in everything he does. There was nothing Greene could say, no argument about strategy or mistakes that Gates would hear. There was nothing left for Gates to do but leave.

"Sir, if I may inquire, what is the troop strength here now?"

Gates laughed, poured his glass full again.

"Troops? Oh, you have some men scattered hereabouts. By my count, perhaps two thousand. Of those, not more than half fit for duty."

Greene absorbed the numbers, far fewer than he had expected.

"Are there still units to be assembled here?"

Gates laughed again.

"You mean, men from my . . . *former* command? Not likely, General. If you intend to build an army, you will do it from fresh recruits. I am certain that this colony will offer you little support at all. They seem rather to prefer the British."

Gates' word stuck in his mind: colony. Greene felt more uncomfortable now, could not avoid thinking of Charles Lee. Gates and Lee were both Englishmen by birth, with deep connections to the British army. Neither man had been particularly missed by their former commands, and now Greene realized that Gates was perhaps more inspired by revenge against those British officers who had forgotten him than by a devout allegiance to America.

Gates finished his second glass, said, "I am told you brought some fresh militia. Virginians?"

"North Carolina. I am pleased by their willingness to sign full enlistment papers." He stopped, thought, Tell him nothing. He claims, after all, to be a civilian now. He need know nothing of my plans.

Gates seemed oblivious to Greene's sudden caution.

"Did the militia cheer you, Nathanael? Did they welcome you with glad tidings, vast expressions of loyalty? Do not be fooled. If you trust them, they will carry you to your doom."

Gates seemed unsteady, the effects of the odd brew. He poured himself another glass, and Greene slid the chair away from the table, said, "Excuse me, sir. I should see to my men. There is much to be done."

He stood, and Gates seemed not to notice, the man absorbed in his own gloom. Greene turned away, stepped to the front door, moved out into a bracing chill, the air washing away the staleness of the house and its occupant. The officers had gathered, seemed to be waiting for him. He saw a few familiar faces, acknowledged them with a nod.

"Gentlemen, the transfer of command is complete. Mr. Gates is, by his own admission, no longer a part of this army. I am aware that we have considerable labor before us if we are to engage the British on favorable terms. I would advise you that you do not discuss our strategy, nor seek the counsel of General Gates. While I will extend every courtesy to him, as I would to any prominent visitor to this camp, let there be no confusion. This department is commanded under the full authority of the congress and General Washington. From this moment forward, we shall have but one purpose. We shall make every effort to organize, train, and equip the men of this command to confront and defeat our enemy. There is no other reason for anyone to be here."

HE WAS DISTRESSED TO FIND THAT GATES HAD BEEN ACCURATE WITH his numbers. As Greene inspected the camps, he discovered better than half the men present unfit for duty, either from sickness, wounds, or injuries from their retreat at Camden. The morale was worse than their physical condition.

Washington had ordered him to prepare his own report on the conduct of Gates, something that would stretch beyond the certain bias of Gates' own version. To gain as much information as he could, Greene listened to anyone who would offer their own story, details of what had happened at Camden. It was clear that Gates had relied far too much on the raw militia, and by striving to meet the British on favorable ground, he had driven his men mercilessly in long night marches, neglecting their need for food and rest. The more Greene learned, the more he realized that with the tactics Gates had used, he was fortunate to have kept two thousand men.

The flow of supplies began to increase from Virginia, von Steuben's efforts showing results. Greene had sent William Smallwood home to Maryland, considered that his skills at recruiting were of even more value to the army than what Smallwood brought to the field. The new recruits began to arrive, some already influenced by von Steuben's zeal, entire companies marching with good order. Others simply wandered in, stragglers who had escaped Charleston or Camden, who had no better place to be. There were others as well, farmers who left their land for the winter months, to offer what help they could. Greene welcomed them all. As the training began in earnest, Greene used the lessons he had learned at Valley Forge, and though the numbers grew slowly, the men in his command were indeed becoming an army.

JANUARY 1781

It was a show Greene had seen before, the huge Virginian announcing himself with a grand parade. Back in the summer, Daniel Morgan had been ordered to accompany Gates to the Carolinas, but had resigned from the army instead. Morgan claimed sickness, but many in Washington's camp believed that Morgan simply refused to serve under Gates. Greene was among them. With the collapse at Camden, Gates had sent an urgent request for Morgan to reconsider, and surprisingly, Morgan had complied. Gates had assigned him to command a unit which, for Morgan's own reasons, was rarely in the same camp with Gates. Now, with Gates gone, Morgan had decided that joining Greene was more to his liking.

Greene had watched as Morgan passed the headquarters, the last bit of his grand entrance, leading his familiar riflemen, those men only a small part of his command now. He had inspired his usual audience, the troops coming out of their tents, gathering along the road, most of them cheering. Morgan was no stranger to this army, and even the men who had never seen him had heard tales. Greene knew that some of the stories were accurate, though, of course, many more were not. Greene had caught Morgan's attention, a short nod from the big Virginian toward the window where Greene watched him. A summons was not necessary. Morgan knew his duty, would make his appearance at the appropriate moment.

Greene was still writing his report on Gates, struggled with the words. Morgan's arrival had been a welcome distraction, but Greene had returned to the work, driven by thoughts of Washington, the request to sort out the truth.

His thoughts were jarred by the cascade of sounds outside. The door opened, and Burnet said, "Sir. General Morgan is here."

"He knows I'm here, Major!" Morgan burst past the startled young man, seemed to fill the room, leaned across the desk, put a huge hand in front of Greene. Greene took the hand, felt the man's strength, a hearty shake, and Morgan sat heavily, said, "Thank God Almighty, Nat! That's what every one of 'em is saying! Thank God Almighty! Now we have a commander!"

"Welcome to headquarters, Daniel."

"It's a different army already! All over the countryside, all the way to the mountains. Those boys over there, rowdy bunch. Had nothing good to say about Gates, but they like you, Nat! The word is, old Cornwallis is done for. He just don't know it yet!"

Greene felt engulfed by the man's joy.

"That's all very kind, Daniel. But we require more than good wishes, or strong morale. We require good officers, men who can both lead and train their men. You know as well as I do that General Washington has never had great confidence in militia. Yet militia is nearly all we have to work with."

Morgan laughed.

"That suited Gates just fine, you know. He loved to ride through their camps, just to hear the salutes. You know, Nat, the real reason he kept so many green troops around is that they'd never take him anywhere so he'd come under fire. It used to be a joke, Nat. After Camden, not so funny anymore."

"My fear, Daniel, is that Cornwallis will not allow us the time we require to train them. Where do we get the officers? Sending untrained militia into battle against a professional army is suicide."

"No, Nat. Worse. It's murder." He looked at the papers on Greene's desk. "You writing up a report for Washington?"

"Yes. Trying to be fair . . ."

"Fair? God Almighty, Nat. The man should be hanged! No, first he should be whipped by every orphan he created. Damnably stupid man!"

There was fury in Morgan's words, and Greene put a finger on the papers in front of him, said, "Shall I include your opinion to the commanding general?"

"Damned right. But be clear on one thing, Nat. Gates failed because he wore out his men, then stuck a bunch of scared Virginia farmers in line against Cornwallis' best infantry. But you can't just fault the militia. This is a different place than up north. These boys down here live in some pretty rugged country. Some of them spend their whole lives trekkin' through the mountains, keeping Indians away from their families. They can fight. Look at what happened at Kings Mountain."

Greene had been amazed by details of a stunning victory just below the South Carolina border. The men were militia, scattered units from the Carolinas and Virginia, an assembly of rough troops who had never shared any field. They had been commanded by their own officers, names unfamiliar to anyone in Washington's camp, Shelby and Campbell, McDowell, Williams and Cleveland. But they led a perfect assault against the ultimate display of British arrogance. Colonel Patrick Ferguson marched his troops blithely through the region, claiming to sweep the last semblance of rebel influence out of South Carolina. When Ferguson learned of the rebel force pursuing him, he chose not to seek the safety of the British outposts, instead invited an assault by perching his men up on a rocky, narrow hill. The militia surrounded him, and methodically worked their way up through the rocks, and the result was a near massacre. The militia swarmed completely over the British position, killing Ferguson along with most of his men. It was an amazing accomplishment that erased much of the stain and despair of Camden. Yet, farther north, almost no one had yet heard of Kings Mountain. Since Gates himself had not been involved, he made scarce mention of it in his own reports. There was, after all, no credit he could claim.

Greene had realized that a good many of the troops who were adding to his ranks were there because of the heroic performance of their own militia. Morgan was right. It was a different place.

"So, Nat, you got any spirits around here?"

Greene pointed to a small cabinet, the same one Gates had used.

"Look in there. Some interesting potions."

Morgan poked through an assortment of bottles, retrieved one, studied it.

"Ahh, do you suppose?" He pulled a cork, took a short sniff, twisted his face. "Yessiree! Marion's brew. He calls it *Swamp Elixir*." He looked at Greene, raised the bottle toward his mouth, said, "You mind, Nat? Just a shot."

Greene waved his hand, and Morgan took a short sip, waited a brief moment, then took another. He squinted hard, said, "Woo! Yep. Those boys over there work some kind of magic. You had any dealings yet with those fellows? Marion? Sumter? The *Swamp Fox* and the *Gamecock*. Quite a pair."

"I haven't had the pleasure. Will they fight with us, Daniel?"

"They'll fight, that's for sure. They been a plague to the British from the start of the war, well before anyone up north thought this place was important enough to fight for. Can't say they'll line up beside you and march. Not their way. They pop out of the swamps and hit hard, then disappear. They don't have enough men to do much more than that. Francis Marion's not usually got more than fifty or a hundred men under him. But, I bet you Cornwallis don't know that. They fight like half a division."

"Will they follow orders?"

"If the orders make sense. After Camden, they wouldn't even talk to Gates. He ignored them, thought they were a bunch of bandits. Big mistake."

"I shall not ignore anyone who can assist us."

"It's like that all over this place, Nat. Partisans and militia. But the word is out there. They're hearing that finally, the whole country is joining their fight. Washington has done sent his best man. You draw up a plan, they'll carry it out. That goes for me, as well."

Greene pushed the papers aside, could see a smile on Morgan's broad face, the telltale gap of missing teeth.

"Well, then, Daniel, as soon as the men here are fit, I think it's time we take this fight back into South Carolina." He pointed at the bottle cradled in Morgan's hand. "If you don't mind . . . if I'm going to fight with these fellows . . ."

Morgan seemed to hesitate, then handed the bottle across the desk. Greene pulled the cork, the aroma ripping into his nose. He held the bottle away, looked at the strange clear liquid.

"If they have the courage to drink this . . . no wonder they can fight."

48. CORNWALLIS

WINNSBORO, SOUTH CAROLINA, JANUARY 1781

HE HAD CHOSEN A HEADQUARTERS THAT WOULD PLACE HIS REGU-lar troops close enough to give support to as many of the out-posts as possible. They were many and spread far apart, from Augusta and Charleston to Camden, Ninety-Six and Rock Hill. It was essential to offer the citizens of the colony a visible pres-ence, a reminder that this place was ultimately under the control of King George. But the display alone would never be effective without the power of the army. Every examination of the maps, every plan for a new campaign brought out his wrath for what Henry Clinton had done to his army.

Each of the outposts had come under some assault, some sharp probe from at least one of the partisan rebel commanders who ran rampant through the rugged countryside. The result was that a substantial part of his meager army had to remain in place, guarding the crossroads that united the army in this loose-knit web of supply lines. If he was to make any move northward, any invasion of North Carolina that would have good effect, he des-perately needed more men.

He had summoned Alexander Leslie from Virginia, with a major portion of the troops Clinton had sent to the mouth of the

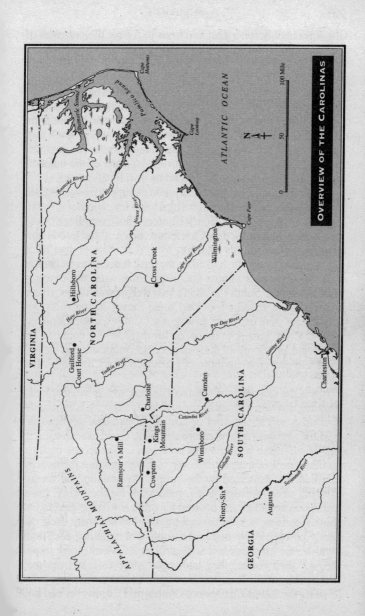

OVERVIEW OF THE CAROLINAS

Chesapeake. Clinton's plan had been to follow the conquest of the Carolinas with a massed assault on Virginia. The troops there were included in Cornwallis' command, and despite Clinton's blanket optimism, Cornwallis knew that his diminished army would need considerable help in South Carolina before any further campaign could begin. Leslie had brought another twenty-three hundred troops, easing the strain on the outposts. But there were other problems besides vulnerability to attack. Each outpost had to be fed and supplied, and though South Carolina was ripe with fertile and productive farmland, none of the outposts could safely draw forage far beyond its own fortifications.

Cornwallis had established a system of supply that originated in Charleston, but the transport ships were few, another infuriating lack of support from Henry Clinton. Those supplies that did arrive were warehoused in Charleston, much of the goods now in useless piles. On his return to New York, Clinton had taken not only the cavalry, he had taken the draft horses and wagons as well. So there was almost no means of moving the essential goods overland. South Carolina's vast web of waterways, rivers, and navigable streams provided some means of transport, but small boats were as scarce as wagons. Clinton's assumption had been that the vast population of loyalists would come to the army's aid, providing all the transportation required. But the loyalists had proven to be more of a headache for Cornwallis than a help.

It was the sad result of Clinton's decree, which had inspired a stunning display of brutality throughout the colony. Anyone who coveted a neighbor's land or had some personal grudge, any creditor who wished to pressure his client, could exact his toll by simply claiming his target to be a rebel. Old scores between feuding families were settled now with outrageous violence, the criminal acts protected by the simple explanation that the aggressors were loyalists, doing good work for their king. Cornwallis was appalled, and ordered his officers to intervene, to find some means to stop the absurd abuses, but the army itself was nearly powerless. No matter the outrage or injustice, even those loyal to the king knew that regardless of which army moved through their towns, they had much more to fear from their neighbors.

After the fall of Charleston, Clinton and Cornwallis had both assumed that South Carolina could easily be controlled by the army's establishment of a civil authority. In fact, Cornwallis now understood, the British had no control at all. Far from sweeping away the last dying groans of a rebellion, the British army had stumbled into a colony that was engulfed in its own civil war.

Since Clinton had left him with barely enough troops to maintain civil order in the larger towns, it was essential to bring as many Tories under arms as he could. But any enthusiasm the loyalists had for carrying British muskets had been swept away at Kings Mountain. The only true British soldier there had been Patrick Ferguson, and both Ferguson and his loyalist militia had been annihilated. Worse was the butchery that followed, and never were the signs of civil war so apparent. Many of the loyalist prisoners had been massacred by the rebel militia, retribution for so many of the atrocities committed by the loyalists. Nowhere in the entire theater of the war had the violence been so brutal between American civilians, with almost complete disregard on both sides for the authority of their army.

Clinton had sailed away filled with confidence that the colony was indeed wiped clean of rebel influence. In the months that had followed, that confidence had been strongly reinforced by Cornwallis' spectacular success against Gates. That would certainly satisfy Clinton, and Cornwallis had even trumpeted his optimism to London. It had seemed certain that in a few short months, North Carolina would come under control as well. But then had come a dozen minor battles, the amazing show of strength and fighting ability of the rebel partisans. Every supply line, every depot, every unguarded troop position was subject at any moment to a sudden torrent of musket fire. Cornwallis had responded by sending Banastre Tarleton and his brutally efficient horsemen stampeding after the elusive rebels. But Tarleton's success was most pronounced against small units often in retreat, refugees or stragglers the Legion pounced upon with a terrifying lack of mercy. But Tarleton was not always successful. In one sharp fight against Thomas Sumter, at a place called Blackstock's Plantation, Tarleton had been severely embarrassed, losing twenty percent of his strength. Though Cornwallis continued to have faith in the Legion as his most valuable weapon, his frustration grew. If anything was to be accomplished in the Carolinas, he could not merely sit and wait for rebel militia to make a mistake. There was still a war, and there was still a rebel army to pursue. In their one confrontation, Cornwallis had nearly destroyed Horatio Gates and his entire force. He could do the same to Nathanael Greene.

HE WAS UNCOMFORTABLE WITH THE REPORTS HE HEARD ABOUT Tarleton's Legion, claims of brutality from rebel prisoners, other protests coming even from loyalists. But Cornwallis would not press the man for details, would not lecture his most effective fighter on the proper rules of war. The militia on both sides had shown complete disregard for mercy and civilized conduct in the field. Cornwallis would not condone such brutality, but he could not deny it had become a very real ingredient of the war in South Carolina. If Tarleton strayed beyond the bounds of decency, Cornwallis did not have the luxury of shifting troublesome officers from one post to the other. Tarleton seemed immune to the protests, and if the young man was not impaired by the outcry that followed him, Cornwallis could readily accept that. Tarleton was simply too important to his plans.

He waited for the young man in his office, glanced at his watch. He was becoming accustomed to Tarleton's habit of arriving late, but he was annoyed, had lost his tolerance for affectations, especially from a subordinate officer. His capacity for patience had been crushed by a serious illness, the same fever that had stricken many of his men. Though Cornwallis had pronounced himself free of the disease, the weakness and its effects on his mood were not entirely gone. He called out, "Lieutenant?"

A young man appeared at the door.

"Send word to Colonel Tarleton. I am not amused by pacing around my office."

"Right away, sir."

He moved to his desk, thought of the aide, said in a low voice, "Must they always be so young?"

He had spent so many days of misery, first the sickness, then the complete boredom of keeping himself in his headquarters, essential to maintaining the web of outposts. He had tried to encourage the friendship of the junior officers, something unusual in the British command. It was certainly unusual for him. But despite the responsibilities and the tormenting details of command in such a hostile place, and though he certainly did not miss Henry Clinton, he found himself missing the meetings, the councils. He shared so much experience with men like Grey and Grant and even Howe, but now, with the army spread in such a wide array of outposts, he rarely saw his own senior staff. Balfour commanded in Charleston, Rawdon in Camden, Leslie still down in Ninety-Six. It was a strange surprise to him that he felt the need for company, for someone who could engage him in some kind of intelligent conversation. The only other possibility was Tarleton, a man young enough to be his son.

"Sir, he's here."

Cornwallis moved around behind the desk, waited for the usual show. Tarleton never entered a room without appraising it first, halting at the door, careful to note who his audience might be. He was there now, removed the plumed hat with a slow flourish, no smile, a brief look of impatience.

"Do come in, Colonel. I trust you are not ill? Horse managing all right?"

It was an attempt at sarcasm. Tarleton was oblivious.

"Quite, sir. Ready for a go, I'd say. The Legion is rested and fit."

"Sit if you like. I wish to know details of your intelligence reports."

Tarleton did not sit, stood stiffly just inside the door. It was another affectation, some strange habit of making himself the first one in any meeting to leave the room.

"Information is difficult to gather, sir."

He saw Tarleton staring out past him, and he thought, Not if gathering it is your job.

"That may be, Colonel. However, anything you can provide is far superior to what I have here." Cornwallis picked up a piece of paper, read, "I walked as far as the fishing creek, and there I saw Willy McBride's wife, who told me she saw Tom Ridgely who saw Sam Wiley's wife who said she saw some men walking on the Sibley road last Tuesday." He put the paper down, saw an amused smirk from Tarleton. Cornwallis was not smiling. "This is not intelligence, Colonel. But it's all I have. The rebels have cut off every avenue of information. The civilians are too frightened to offer anything useful. We cannot pass dispatches between here and Ninety-Six without losing a courier to an ambush. Now, I will repeat my request. I wish to know of your intelligence reports."

Tarleton seemed to deflate, and Cornwallis waited.

"We do know, sir, that General Greene has divided his army. The reports of my scouts show General Morgan has been detached, and is advancing on a route from the northwest, moving possibly toward Ninety-Six. General Greene's movements are not certain."

Cornwallis stared at him, said, "Did you not consider that sufficiently important to mention it without my asking?"

Tarleton seemed bruised, said, "I had intended to inform you, sir. I thought I should prepare as well a plan of attack. I have assembled the Legion, and suggest an accompaniment of infantry." He pulled a paper from his coat, handed it to Cornwallis. "By my figures, sir, a thousand men should be sufficient."

"What is Morgan's strength?"

"We're not certain, sir. He has possibly been joined by some of the partisans. I am not concerned on that account."

"All right, Colonel. The mission is yours. You will seek out General Morgan's force and prevent him from completing his mission, whatever that might be. Since you have approximate knowledge of his direction of march, I would advise you to make haste. There is no reason to allow the rebels time to amend their plans. I cannot assume their intelligence is as ridiculous as mine. As for Greene, I have ordered General Leslie to rendezvous with what small force I have here. Combined, General Leslie and I will field some three thousand men. If you can eliminate Morgan as an effective force, Greene should offer us a very satisfying target."

The meeting concluded, and Tarleton swept out of the office with his usual dramatic flare, a wave of the hat, a sharp spin on his heels. Cornwallis could not sit at the desk, began to pace again. He felt an odd clarity, imagined Greene in his mind, a man he had never seen. This is not, after all, about militias and partisans and outposts in some bloody miserable frontier. It is about armies and generals, and what kind of fight we will drive into their hearts. I have allowed myself to dwell on absurd distraction. Loyalist atrocities and rebel butchery will matter very little if Greene is swept away. I have to trust Colonel Tarleton's information, and so, I must believe that Greene has divided his army. It is a significant mistake. Now, we shall show him why.

49. MORGAN

HIS MEN HAD BEEN STRUNG OUT ON A MARCH THAT WAS TAKING FAR longer than he had hoped. It was typical of Morgan to get bored riding with the main column, fighting the temptation to ride out ahead, to do the work of the skirmishers. Usually it was simple impatience, but this time he was anxious, uncertain, and now, he might be in serious trouble.

The scouts had come to him with regular reports, and too many of them had brought the same information. He was being pursued, and very soon the pursuit would become an engagement. If his men continued to march in such a ragged formation, spread out along the roads, Banastre Tarleton would cut them to pieces.

He knew of Tarleton only by reputation, a fiery young man who loved the saber. Morgan was amused by the nightmarish descriptions of the British Legion, the hushed talk around campfires of beastly men who showed no hesitation in butchering prisoners, who, in the aftermath of battle, would walk among the wounded with sabers flashing, to finish their gruesome job. But the danger was now very real, and it had less to do with some monstrous quality to Tarleton's men than the vulnerability of Morgan's position. Once Tarleton's pursuit was confirmed, Morgan spread the word to every unit. There was no reason to keep it secret. If the men knew it was Tarleton in their rear, it would most certainly quicken their march.

The cavalry unit Greene had given him was commanded by William Washington, a relative of the commanding general. Morgan had sent Washington's horsemen to the rear of the column, keeping a sharp eye on the enemy who pursued them. Out to the front, Morgan had sent scouts, militiamen familiar with the land, their mission to find good ground, a safe place to make camp and, possibly, the place where they would make their stand.

Morgan's original mission was to march all the way to Georgia, to inspire a wave of new recruits to join Greene's army. But it was clear now that the plan was far too dangerous. Cornwallis had made the correct response, and Morgan realized that he could not have free rein to march around the main British position without attracting the kind of attention he was getting from Banastre Tarleton.

Morgan had believed much of what he had told Greene about the spirit of the partisan militia, but nearly a third of this column were raw recruits, men from North Carolina and Virginia. The remainder were veterans, tough partisan militia plus continental regulars, the regiments of Marylanders, the men from Delaware, who had stood tall through nearly every major battle of the war.

The guides were commanded by Andrew Pickens, a tall lean Scotsman. Pickens was another of the partisan commanders, whose harassment of the British had been centered mainly near his home at Ninety-Six. Morgan had been surprised by Pickens' stern demeanor, a prim, devoutly religious man not given to the fits of drunken vulgarity that seemed so common in some of the camps of the partisans. Pickens had not begun the war with quite the coldhearted hatred toward the British that inspired men like Marion and Sumter. When Ninety-Six fell under British control, Pickens had offered his parole, had gone home expecting only to tend to his large farm. But he could not escape the violence that rolled across his state, and eventually his home had been destroyed by the mindless plunder of loyalist troops. It proved to be a costly mistake for the British. The fire had been lit, and Pickens tore up his parole and returned to the fight. He now led a command of more than a hundred riflemen, men whose pride in their marksmanship rivaled that of Morgan's Virginia marksmen.

FOR TWO DAYS, THE ROADS HAD BEEN GUMMED BY THE SOAKING misery of a winter rain. The misery had extended into Morgan as well. He suffered from rheumatism and other ailments, waves of pain that would tear through his back and hips. The muddy roads and the thick mist in the air had increased his suffering, souring his mood and his patience. He had tried to walk, hoping to relieve the torment from the horse's uneven gait. But walking through thickening mud was even harder on his back, and he had climbed onto the horse again.

He looked up through the bare trees, could see the dull gray clouds finally thinning out, bringing an end to the rain. Daylight was beginning to fade, and Morgan's temper was scraped raw by the jolts of pain and the lack of information from Pickens' scouts. He was waiting for confirmation of a place they had told him about, where a vast meadow spread north toward the Broad River. For many years it had been used by cattle farmers, a natural clearing that offered forage to large herds. It was called Hannah's Cowpens.

He finally succumbed to the urge, looked back to the officers behind him, said, "Stay here. I'm going ahead. Dammit."

The air was finally dry, the horse finding its way with a steady gait, giving blessed relief to the throbbing in his hip. He knew his men would not allow him to just ride out alone, and he waited for someone to appear beside him. He expected a junior officer, some young man willing to endure his profanity. It was a more acceptable duty than bearing a message to General Greene that they had lost Daniel Morgan in the woods.

He heard hoofbeats, was surprised to see William Washington beside him now.

"Well, hello, Will, you tired of following our tracks?"

"I was coming up to see you, saw you riding ahead. I assumed you decided to take a look for yourself."

"We can move fast or slow, Will, but we're going to end up in that Cowpens place sooner or later. I have to know if it's sooner. How far back is old Benny?"

"Sir? You mean . . . Tarleton? Five miles, not a bit more. It was ten yesterday."

"So he's wearing out his men."

"Definitely. He clearly intends to catch us no matter the cost. They haven't stopped for more than a few minutes since last evening."

The woods began to thin, and men began to appear along the road, emerging from dim trails that cut out through the tall trees. He saw confused expressions, recognized several of Pickens' scouts.

"Fall in with us, boys! We're not done looking yet."

He cleared a large patch of tall hardwoods, the ground rising in front of him, and he stopped, said, "Can someone tell me if this is the place?" There was silence, and he turned in the saddle, a sharp burn cutting across his back. *"Where the hell are we?"*

He heard a young voice, a nervous quiver in the man's words.

"This is the Cowpens, sir. Straight ahead, about five miles, is the Broad River."

Morgan straightened his hips in the saddle, the pain easing slightly.

"I thought as much. Let's have a look."

He led them out into the clearing, moved up the long rise, saw a ridge stretching across the field, beyond, higher ground still, another ridge. Along the edge of the fields were small patches of tall trees, and he pushed forward, stared out.

"The Broad River?"

"North and northeast of our position, sir. Five miles, or less. Should we bring the column up quickly, sir? Not much daylight."

He turned the horse, looked for the voice. He saw a young man, a burst of red hair over a mass of freckles.

"How old are you?"

The young man glanced at the others, and Morgan heard small laughs.

"I'm old enough to fight, sir."

"I'm not looking to send you home, boy. I just wanted to know how old you were."

"Seventeen, sir."

"Well, Mr. Seventeen, let me explain how an older man sees this ground. You're thinking we should make for the Broad River. You think old Benny Tarleton might be too much for us to handle. You live around here?"

The young man was beginning to wilt under the attention, and Morgan could still hear the low laughs, smart comments from the others.

"Yes, sir. Up . . . thataway, sir. Across the river. My family's got a farm . . ."

"Yes, I'm sure it's a right lovely place. You itching to go home, then? It's all right, boy, we're all itching for something. Let me tell you what would happen to you if we crossed that river. You'd be thinking about that damned farm, your soft feather bed. Your mama probably cook up a big meal for you, your sweetheart would come cryin' to you, all lathered up cause you're home at last."

"Sir, I wouldn't run away . . ."

"Hell yes, you would, boy. A good many of your friends too. The rest of you, with your smart mouths. Militia, the lot of you. Some of you would stay with me, but the rest of you, you'd be like Mr. Seventeen here. Smell your mama's cooking. Off you go. That's why we're going to stay down here, this side of the river."

He looked out across the field.

"There's another reason we're going to stay here. You doubt I know something about the British?" He turned the horse, his back to the men, peeled off his coat. He pulled his shirt up, fought the stiffness in his back, the shirt now up to his shoulders, his bare back to the men. He heard the quiet gasps, smiled, said, "A long time ago, had some British boy about your age, Mr. Seventeen, thought he was an officer. Tried to tell me left was right, and when I argued the point, he slapped me with his sword. Ought not to have done that. I knocked him out of his boots." He pulled the shirt down, turned, saw what he had always seen, wide-eyed stares, even from Washington. "They claimed they gave me five hundred lashes, but the British don't count too well. There's only four hundred ninety-nine. I told 'em they weren't done, but they insisted. They still owe me one." He let the story sink in for a minute. "If I know something about the British, it's their arrogance. Benny Tarleton's no different, maybe the worst of the lot. He'll keep chasing us 'til he catches us. The only way to take care of him is pick the place. Let him find us where we *want* him to find us." He looked at Washington, saw the man gazing out across the rolling grassy fields.

"You agree, Will?"

Washington nodded.

"We probably wouldn't make the river anyway. Tarleton's pushing his infantry hard. My cavalry's not strong enough to hold him off for long."

"Didn't think so. Well, then, Mr. Seventeen, tell you what we're going to do. You're looking here at a very nice place to make a fight. I want you to go back and find Colonel Pickens, and tell him I need the militia up here as quick as they want to eat their supper. Take one of these smart mouths with you. We'll camp out there, beyond that far hill. Get moving, boys!"

The young men seemed grateful to leave, pulled their horses around, and were gone. Morgan looked at Washington again.

"Bring the cavalry up here too. Plenty of hay in these fields. The horses will need their rest. If I'm right, Tarleton will be here in the morning. His men will have marched all night, and probably not eaten anything but the mud off 'n their shoes. He'll look to make quick work of us. He'll prance out here, stand right on this spot, and he'll probably laugh, see us spread out up there in that grass, and think he's got us. He'll make some joke to his officers, that we've made a jolly well bloody mistake." He leaned forward on the horse's neck, looked at the sun settling behind the tall trees. He patted the horse, said, "This could be more fun than a barn dance at Fat Lucy's."

HANNAH'S COWPENS, JANUARY 17, 1781

"You gentlemen claim you can shoot."

The line of men seemed to stiffen, one man holding up his rifle, and the man said, "I'll put Lilly here up against any of your Virginia boys, sir!"

There were laughs now, and Morgan smiled.

"Is it custom for you Carolina boys to carry your sweethearts into battle? I'd be concerned about being distracted, especially when you go to loadin' 'em."

There were more laughs, and Morgan glanced up, could see the stars fading in the gray light.

"You think you're better marksmen than my Virginia boys, so I want you to prove it. You'll line up across the face of this ridge, spread out near three hundred yards. The enemy will come out of those trees, show themselves way before you'll have a shot. Keep a sharp eye, but don't get nervous. No wasted shots. They'll see you, and commence to marching straight at you. Every damned one of you is going to have a clean shot. I want you to take two. Any man here ever thought about putting his fist into an officer's teeth?"

Hands went up, more laughter, and Morgan said, "Now's your chance. Look for the fancy uniforms, but if he's not right in front of you, pick out a sergeant. I want to see their whole command taken down. You'll throw so much fright into those boys, they may up and run. But don't depend on that. Take your second shot at the man with the bayonet. If he's still coming, it means he's as brave as you. Then I want you to pull back quick. Don't stand there and try to fistfight 'em. They'll be too many of 'em. Behind you, there'll be a solid line of militia, watchin' you with big scared eyes. Show 'em how to be soldiers. Pull back into their line in good order, and keep shooting. The militia will get the same orders as you. I'm headin' there now. They'll fire two shots, then run like hell."

THE MARKSMEN HAD SPREAD OUT IN THE FIELD, AND THERE WAS just enough daylight that he could see the faces of the militiamen.

"As you boys form your line here, there's one thing I want you to remember. In General Washington's army, we have learned one lesson. The best way to use militia in a fight is to put 'em square in the center of the line. And then, when the first man runs, we shoot him."

He waited for the effect, heard low voices.

"Which is why you're gonna like this particular plan. All I need you to do is stand tall for a little while. You'll see the marksmen out there in front of you, and they're gonna put on a show for you. Every one of 'em thinks he can shoot the head off a bird at three hundred yards. But I already told 'em. The first man who tries that today . . . I'll shoot *him*. I need them to let the enemy march right up in front of 'em. They'll do their job with their rifles, and fall back toward you. They are not running away! That is, after all, your job."

He was enjoying this, could hear nervous laughter all down the line.

"Most of you have never seen the enemy in a battle line. Scary damned thing. All fancy and proud, sticking those bayonets out toward you so's you think about that before they get to you. We're gonna give 'em exactly what they're looking for. When those Carolina marksmen fall back to your line, all I ask you to do is wait, and watch the enemy parade. When they get close enough, your officers here will give the order, and you'll take your shot. Don't forget to aim. The British never aim. You know that? Damnedest stupid way to fight a war I ever seen. Those fool generals put so much work into making their uniforms all parade-ground perfect, and then they forget to teach their soldiers how to shoot a musket. They shoot from the chest, and so, every volley goes high. Right over your heads. Watch them. You'll see for yourselves. But I don't want you to watch too long.

I want you to do what Benny Tarleton expects you to do. I want you to turn and run like scared rabbits. Shoot twice, if you can, then pull back to the left flank. There's a line of continentals behind you to give you cover. Nobody's gonna catch you. The British don't run worth a damn. Once you're back out of harm's way, don't start building no campfires and thinking about cooking dinner. Just stay put. We may need you again."

HE COULD HEAR THE DRUMS FIRST, A LOW ECHO ROLLING UP FROM the mist of the trees. He rode slowly forward, kept his field glasses focused out beyond the line of marksmen. He saw flickers of motion now, a small group of horsemen. They came up through the mist, and he could see details, green coats, tall hats of thick black plumes. They stopped in the same place he had stopped the day before, and he could see one man pointing, the others spreading out slowly, examining the ground. He smiled, said, "Good morning, Benny."

Then just as quickly, they were gone.

He looked behind him toward the second rise, could see the continentals in a tight line. Just in front of him the militia had spread into a thinner line, Pickens sitting up high on a horse beside them. He nodded to Pickens, who stared ahead with a hard frown, and Morgan thought, Nothing I can say to him now. He knows the plan. Every man has his own thoughts before a fight. Pickens is probably deep into some prayer, talking to the Almighty. A good many of those boys doing the same thing. He thought of his orders to the militia, and it nagged at him. He had heard enough low protest to understand that he had given offense to some of them, inexperienced men who believed they could stand up to anything. He had seen it before, big talk, hard words from men who marched out to face the enemy, then collapsed into tears. I don't want anyone trying to prove me wrong. The orders were plain enough. If this plan is going to work, they must shoot, then run away. No heroes today.

He could still hear the sound of drums, raised the field glasses again, saw only the mist. Won't matter, he thought. When this line starts to go, they'll all go. Some of 'em might even keep going. He looked out to the side, toward the thin trees beyond the field. No swamps. That's a blessing. Anytime there's a swamp, it's the first place they head to. He put the glasses down again, felt his hand shake. He realized he was nervous, felt a sharp chill.

The pain in his hip was nagging him slightly, but not serious, and he said his own prayer. Punish me tomorrow if You have to. But give me today. Not too much to ask, dammit. If this doesn't work, there won't be much of a tomorrow anyway.

He saw motion, raised the glasses again. Horsemen rode out of the trees, and he tried to count, guessed four dozen. They spread out into a single line, and he saw red coats, thought, Not Benny's boys. The dragoons instead. He'll save his Legion for later, for the last glorious charge. He sniffed now, felt a wave of disgust. That way, Benny, you can claim the prize, your boys alone clearing away the last of the rebels. All right then, I'm depending on you. Before this is over I want to see those green coats of yours. Show me why you're so damned tough.

He could see behind the British dragoons now, a thick line of infantry, marching up out of the trees. The drums were louder, a hint of a rhythm, the sounds still deadened by the mist. The lines advanced in a steady march, the precise movement of white pants and black boots beneath the solid lines of red. The scouts had told him that Tarleton had brought only British regulars, no Tory militia, and he could see it for himself, thought, So, Benny, you don't care much for militia either.

He focused again on the horsemen, caught a glint of metal, their sabers drawn. He felt his heart racing, thought, All right, redcoats. Do your job. Push those skirmishers back. The dragoons began to move more quickly, now, and he fought the urge to ride ahead, to see the charge from up close. It was always the most glorious show, men who carried the pride of their own history, who faced their foe and by the sheer gallantry of their ride, drove so many enemies into panic.

"Come on, my boys. Come on!"

He had trouble holding the glasses still, his own nervousness affecting the horse.

"Easy, easy. Just a bit closer . . ."

The marksmen were mostly down in the grass, and he saw puffs of smoke, rising in a thin line above the ground. Now the sound reached him, a hundred clapping hands, and he could see the line of dragoons suddenly lurching about, riderless horses turning in all directions. He lowered the glasses again, saw heaps of red down in the grass, the dragoons pulling together, backing away. He strained to see, thought, A third of them went down.

And no horses, no one shot at a damned horse. Nice shooting, boys. I'm impressed so far.

The dragoons vanished behind the massive line of infantry, and now the rhythm of the drums was clear, the foot soldiers advancing up the gentle rise. For a long minute there was only the sound of the drums, the thick red line sliding forward through the brown grass. The marksmen fired a second volley, then Morgan could see the British line punched by small gaps, officers swept from their horses. He raised a fist, a silent cheer, watched as the gaps healed, the line solid again, the good work of their sergeants. The marksmen were up now, pulling back toward the line of militia, and he was surprised that some of them were firing still, reloading on the move. Well done, boys. You can stand beside my Virginians for certain now.

He turned the horse, spurred hard, moved farther behind the line of Pickens' militia, pulled the horse around high on the second ridge. The marksmen had completed their withdrawal, were blending into Pickens' line. Morgan saw riders, a company of dragoons emerging on each flank of the British advance. He heard a sudden sharp thud, saw smoke from both flanks, British field cannon beginning their work. He watched the militia, shouted, "Stand there, dammit! Not yet! Wait!"

He could see Pickens moving quickly along the line behind his men, could hear the shouts of the officers, of the men themselves. He repeated the words in his mind, *not yet,* tried to gauge the space between the militia and the red line. Seventy yards . . . sixty-five. *Not yet.* Sixty. Wait, dammit! He heard a new sound, could see the British line erupt in cheering, the troops breaking their discipline, men holding their muskets high. Yes, you bloody devils, sing for it! Cheer for your grand attack! Cheer for your damned history, and the power of your damned army, and sing for that damned butcher who leads you. Now, I'll show you what a butcher can do!

He saw Pickens raise his arm, and the line erupted into fire and smoke. The field below him was obliterated by the gray fog, and Morgan rode forward, had to see himself, could hear scattered pops. Now he saw the British formation, their advance falling into pieces, more riderless horses, a vast gaping wound in the center of their line. Their officers were moving quickly, trying to mend the break, and Pickens fired again, another surge of smoke covering the sight. He heard more cheers, but it was not

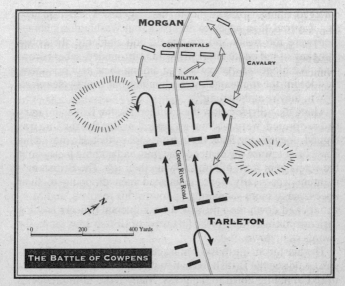

MORGAN

CONTINENTALS

CAVALRY

MILITIA

Green River Road

0   200   400 Yards

TARLETON

THE BATTLE OF COWPENS

the British. Pickens emerged from the smoke, his sword high overhead, and the militia line began to pull back, a perfectly chaotic retreat. They were coming close to Morgan, a steady stream to the left, and he shouted to them, "Run like hell!"

He looked down toward the British line, could see the dragoons coming forward on the left, in pursuit of the fleeing militia. He spun the horse, moved with Pickens' men, then turned again, rode straight up the hill, the last crest, toward the line of continental troops, shouted, "It's your time, boys!"

He moved through their line, spun the horse around, could see the dragoons closing on the retreating militia. There was genuine panic, the inexperienced troops racing to stay ahead of the steady pursuit from the British horsemen. The surging retreat was moving past the left flank of the continentals, and Morgan watched the dragoons, thought, Stay your course. Don't turn this way. Chase them, dammit! The dragoons were moving into the retreat itself, sabers doing their vicious work on Pickens' men. He punched a fist into his hand, said quietly, "It's time, Mr. Washington!"

From behind the left flank came the thunder of a mass of horses, and around the crest of the hill, Washington's cavalry emerged, riding hard, straight into the dragoons. The British cavalry wavered, then began to pull back, but Washington's horsemen were too many and too quick, and suddenly, the entire company of red-coated horsemen was surrounded, sabers dropping, Washington's men swarming among their new prisoners. Beside him, the continentals were shouting, one man's voice clear.

"Sir, they're still coming!"

Along the hillside below the continentals, the British infantry had re-formed, were pushing up the hill again. But the line was ragged, uneven, one flank far in front of the other. He moved his horse back toward the center of the line, had nothing to say now, the veterans in front of him knowing their job. The British momentum was nearly gone, exhausted men dropping to their knees, many more staggering up toward his regulars, and Morgan looked down the line, saw the continental officers holding their swords in the air. As the first wave of British drew close, the swords went down.

The blast from the mass of muskets jolted his horse, and Morgan could see the British formation through the gray haze, a sea of red tumbling down in the grass. Many more of the redcoats had simply stopped, some facing his men with muskets dragging, hands rising in the air. The continentals advanced around the British troops, taking prisoners of their own. He spurred the horse, moved toward the right flank, could see the British dragoons on that side of the line still in tight formation, the foot soldiers there still pushing up toward the continental line. The British advance had extended to the right beyond the end of his own line, and he moved out that way, saw John Howard, the Marylander, shouting orders to his men, the flank pulling back at a right angle to the main line. Morgan watched as the British moved close, heard a strange screaming sound, realized now it was bagpipes, the Highlanders, coming hard toward Howard's outnumbered flank. Morgan felt the familiar chill again, the excitement now mixed with a stab of fear, Howard's line too weak to hold away the assault. He drew his own sword, and Howard saw him, the man's face a deadly glare. Howard pointed to the apex of the angle his men had created, shouted something, his voice drowned out by a sudden eruption of sound. Morgan looked out past the flank, could hear cheers, a loud squalling cry, tried to see the source, could see the Highlanders suddenly halt, some firing their muskets in a scattered volley. Now the voices had form, and Morgan was surprised to see Pickens leading a wave of militia toward the stunned British assault. The Highlanders made a fight, but the militia were on them quickly, a violent collision of bayonets, fists, and clubbed muskets. He watched in stunned amazement, looked back to the rear, realized that the retreating militia had gone completely around behind the main hill, circled right back into the fight. Now the Highlanders were dropping their muskets, men backing into groups, arms rising, the bagpipes silent.

Morgan pulled the horse around, the fear turning to laughter, shouted, "Pickens, you wonderful son of a bitch!"

He spurred hard, his sword still in his hand, rode down across the field where his men were gathering prisoners, some already tending to the British wounded. The sounds of the fight had passed, no music, the rhythm of the drums now silent. He reined the horse up, looked down toward the trees. Washington's cavalry had continued down, more prisoners gathered up, and he could see Washington himself in a sharp fight with a small group of British horsemen. But it was not dragoons, the coats were not red. They were green. Morgan retrieved the field glasses, focused on the final clash, the last bit of action on the field. The fight was brief, and Washington seemed to let them go, and Morgan thought, Yes, wise, no need to pursue them farther. Keep the army together. He saw the green-coated horsemen riding hard down toward the trees, slowing their retreat, not pursued by Washington's men. They had nearly disappeared, and Morgan saw one man stop, staring up toward him, field glasses of his own. Morgan felt the sword in his hand, waved it in a slow arc, said aloud, "Go on home, Benny. We'll take good care of your boys!"

50. CORNWALLIS

JANUARY 18, 1781

THE REPORT CAME IN BY THE HAND OF A GREEN-COATED HORSE-
man, but the shame on the man's face showed him more of what
had happened than Tarleton's words on paper. Nearly eleven
hundred of Cornwallis' finest soldiers had engaged Morgan's
rebels, and less than three hundred had come away. He didn't
know the exact casualty count, but Tarleton's report made clear
that most of the British troops engaged at Cowpens were now
Morgan's prisoners.

As word of the disaster raced through the camps, Cornwallis
began to hear the hot words against Tarleton. It came mainly
from the veteran officers, outraged that this *boy* should have had
such a command, should have been allowed the opportunity for
such a spectacular failure. Cornwallis expected the criticism,
knew it was just one more part of any defeat. If Tarleton had
crushed Morgan's army, the same critical old men would have
climbed over each other to be his champion.

He had not yet written his official report to Clinton or Germain. That would come later. He would wait for Tarleton himself
to arrive, to offer more details and, perhaps, some acceptable explanation how such a disaster could have occurred. But he knew
Tarleton well enough, knew that the young man possessed that
one ugly trait so common to men of ambition. His priority would
be the high-sounding excuse, that no matter the judgment Cornwallis would hold, Tarleton would be more focused on the response of King George, on how his exploits would read in the
London papers. Such men always dream of titles, medals, procla-
mations in Parliament. Rarely did such men seem to understand
that, first, they had to win a war.

Cornwallis only had seven hundred troops around his headquarters, was desperate for Leslie to arrive from Ninety-Six with

the reinforcements. The added strength would give Cornwallis enough of a force to make a serious pursuit of Morgan's rebels. It was the only reasonable strategy, the strategy Clinton would insist upon. No enemy who had inflicted such a deadly strike should simply be allowed to wander off. It mattered little if Morgan intended to pursue some further assault, or if he was content to retreat and rejoin his army to Greene's. The only possible disruption to Cornwallis' plan could come from Greene himself, if the rebels showed some sign of launching a two-pronged attack on the British outposts. But Cornwallis had heard nothing of an advance by Greene. Thus Morgan was the target. Whether it was sound strategy mattered less than pride. The army would expect it, Clinton would expect it. It didn't even have to make sense. It was simply the rules.

OUR ASSAULT WAS PLANNED WITH COOLNESS, AND EXECUTED WITHout embarrassment. I had thought, sir, that the main body of the army would have come to our support."

Cornwallis stared at Tarleton with no expression, thought, So that's the best you can do? Of course, I cannot be surprised. I did not launch an all-out assault to assist you. Never mind that my total command here was two-thirds the size of yours.

Tarleton stared past him, his usual pose, seemed not to care if Cornwallis responded or not.

"Will there be anything else, sir?"

"General Leslie's men have arrived here only this morning. We will pursue the rebels as soon as those men have rested. I will require your eyes on the march, therefore I am hopeful we will succeed in gathering the remnants of your Legion." He paused, said, "How many men will that be, Colonel?"

Tarleton showed no reaction to the question, said, "I would estimate two hundred or more. There will be sufficient strength, sir."

The young man's arrogance was grating on him, and Cornwallis said, "You are dismissed, Colonel. See to your men."

Tarleton was gone without another word, and Cornwallis stared at the open doorway, felt drained by the young man's arrogance. There would be no lectures, no public shame for Tarleton. Cornwallis had never agreed with that kind of bombast, public embarrassment so often heard from Henry Clinton. The facts of the engagement alone would stain Tarleton's reputation to the entire army. The young man had returned to camp with fewer than seventy of his Legion, and many of them were already talking, relaying the last bit of the story that Tarleton himself would never repeat. When the battle had been clearly decided, Tarleton had called for a final assault by his Legion, a hard charge that might yet have turned the fight. The green-coated horsemen were fresh, rested, had not yet been a part of the battle. But on his command, most of the Legion, over two hundred fifty men, had responded to his order by simply riding away. In a battle that had claimed eight hundred of their comrades, Tarleton's Legion never faced the enemy. They had already begun to straggle into camp, but the shame of their performance would infect Tarleton more than his men. It was a punishment far more severe than anything Cornwallis could say. He still stared out through the open door, thought, No, young man, this is not how *legends* are created.

RAMSOUR'S MILL, NORTH CAROLINA, JANUARY 25, 1781

His intelligence from the civilians was worthless, no real information about Morgan's line of march. With the defeat at Cowpens, the loyalists had simply disappeared, no one having any faith that the British army could be counted on to provide them any protection. The loyalist militia was nearly nonexistent as well, other than those units still manning the important outposts at Camden and Ninety-Six, men who were close enough to their homes to risk fighting for their own land. His scouts had finally picked up Morgan's trail, and the best guess was that the rebels were marching northeastward, possibly to move along the Catawba River, deeper into North Carolina. Cornwallis had received word from farther east that Greene's main body of troops had pulled out of Charlotte and was marching north as well.

He allowed the army to gather and rest around Ramsour's Mill, a small cluster of homes perched on the Little Catawba River. They were close to Morgan's march, but not close enough. Those citizens of Ramsour's who had remained had been certain in their claims that Morgan had crossed the river two days earlier.

Cornwallis had ordered his staff and his own baggage placed in a tent. He did not intend to remain long enough to annoy some local farmer by moving into his home. As the last of the troops had marched into Ramsour's, he had stood out by the main road, examining the men as they moved by him. They had found a vast pile of leather, the good work of some industrious tanner, and as his men marched past him, Cornwallis had seen the ragged condition of their boots. The order had already been given, each man to resole his own shoes. He did not know how far they would have to march, but for a while, at least, they would not go barefoot.

Cornwallis watched as the rear guard escorted the wagons, the painfully slow progress, a variety of farm wagons and carriages piled high with all the baggage of the army. As they moved past him, they turned into a wide field, and Cornwallis had seen enough, thought of returning to his tent. But an officer caught his eye, a high screeching voice, arms flailing madly, oblivious to Cornwallis, the man clearly in command of his private world. Cornwallis was curious now, could see the officer was one of the quartermasters. He was guiding the wagons into line, silent stares from crusty wagon masters, weary horses hauling their teetering loads. Another officer appeared, more high-pitched shouts, the two men directing their wrath at each other. The argument turned quiet, some crucial decision reached, and the first man shouted to the wagoneers, pointing out to one side. Whips began to crack, and the wagons jerked into motion again, shifting their position. It was a dark comedy, but Cornwallis was not smiling, could see wagons extending down the road beyond his sight. He turned away, stared toward the river, thick woods on the far side, tall timber on rolling hills, thought, We are *two days* behind them. Tomorrow it will be three.

The infantry that pursued Morgan to Cowpens had not begun their march until they had been stripped of every nonessential piece of equipment and baggage. The result was a division of British light troops who could cover far more ground in far less time than usual for such a large number of men. But the light troops were gone, most of those who survived Cowpens now marching under Morgan's guards, to some destination Cornwallis did not yet know.

He began to walk back toward his tent, the words still pricking his brain. He is *two days* ahead of us, and we cannot even park our wagons without a decision by committee.

*   *   *

I WANT IT ALL BURNED. EVERY PIECE OF CUMBERSOME EQUIPMENT,
every wagonload of extra uniforms, every officer's finest ballroom garb."

They stared at him with open mouths, and after a long, silent
moment, Leslie said, "The officers . . . ?"

"Especially the officers, General. What is the purpose of this
pursuit? Is it not to catch our enemy? At our present rate of
progress, if I may use that word, we will lose more ground every
day. We do not even know the country, must still seek out the
fords of the rivers. Many of Morgan's men *reside* here."

The two men absorbed his words, staring into the campfire.
Each was perched on a short stool, both men balancing a china
teacup on one knee. Cornwallis looked out into the utter blackness, heard the night sounds, waves of insects, strange croaks
and cries from the river. Leslie spoke now, said, "But, sir, the
men will not respond well to such a sacrifice."

"What is the greater sacrifice, General? Leaving behind your
brandy and extra store of molasses, or marching this army to exhaustion while our enemy continues to thrive in the field? If we
eliminate the encumbrance of our wagons, we will greatly enhance our pursuit. We will maintain the bare necessities of medical supplies, salt, other essentials. The men can carry what they
require on their backs."

The officers looked at each other, and he saw resignation in
their faces, nods of approval.

"This is all I require of you, gentlemen. You must see past old
habits. Look at this camp. We march with so few men that one
significant engagement can decide our fate. The enemy has shown
he can draw men from these colonies in great numbers, can replace his wounded, even his deserters. We can do nothing of the
sort. General Clinton, when he chooses to write, never concludes
a letter without expressing his utmost confidence that we will yet
receive an outpouring of loyalist troops, waves of new recruits at
every outpost, every village on our march. What choice do I
have but to play out the farce? In every town I perform the same
ritual, post the notice, issue a call to loyalists to join us on the
march. This afternoon, I witnessed a gathering of six men, and
when the provost attempted to lead them to the recruitment station, they claimed only to be curious, had never seen a British
soldier before. Loyalist sympathy? Allegiance to His Majesty's

cause? No, gentlemen, they wanted to know what we *looked* like." He saw his own mood reflected on their faces, and he realized it was something he had not seen since New York. He was too accustomed to the arrogance of Tarleton, the other younger men who seemed to have no understanding of the difficulties they were facing. He was grateful for the presence of Leslie, and the other man, Charles O'Hara, one of Leslie's brigadiers. Both men were closer in age and experience to Cornwallis, both men seeming to understand that this could possibly be their last good opportunity to destroy Greene's rebel army. O'Hara was a dark, handsome Irishman, had risen in rank through the Coldstream Guards, one of the most prestigious units in the army. He stared into the fire, said, "General, how far do we pursue? How do we force an engagement with the rebels?"

"General O'Hara, if we do not engage the rebels, we have no purpose in being here. General Clinton believes that by simply maintaining our outposts in South Carolina, we have claimed a victory, that the rebellion in that colony has ended. I would suggest that Colonel Tarleton has experienced otherwise. It is entirely within my authority to withdraw our forces to those outposts and simply remain there. We might as well sail for England. The decision must be made. If we remain immobile, we will face certain ruin. If we advance, and pursue the rebel army, we face infinite danger. General Clinton has his view. Mine is somewhat different." He paused, shook his head. "I admit to being puzzled, gentlemen. Why do the rebels retreat? Morgan won a significant victory, and yet, instead of becoming emboldened by his success, he chooses to withdraw."

Leslie said, "Morgan cannot assume we will make another such mistake."

He knew it was a veiled reference to Tarleton, would not allow Leslie the opening.

"Whether or not it was our mistake or their good fortune is not my concern. By their retreat, the rebels have chosen the path of this war. If we are to claim victory, we must engage them. To engage them we must catch them. Once we have shed our baggage, I intend to pursue General Greene to the ends of the earth!"

IT WAS ALREADY A MASSIVE BONFIRE, AND CORNWALLIS STEPPED through the gloomy throng of soldiers, carried a fat heavy trunk. They backed away, and he turned, saw them all watching him.

He turned to the fire, the flames growing higher, far taller than he was. He felt the heat on his face, the weight of the trunk in his arms. There was a voice, "Sir! May I assist you?"

He did not respond, stepped close to the fire, squinting against the heat, and with one heavy grunt, launched his trunk into the blaze. He looked at them again, saw officers coming forward, more baggage, the men following his example. Before the night was over, the fire was fueled by the excess baggage of the entire command, excess grain, rolls of cloth, wool and cotton, and all but a handful of wagons. By morning, the shock had settled on every man along the march, that behind the long column, no wagons followed, nothing to slow them down, to keep them from pushing their pursuit of the enemy.

FEBRUARY 1781

They continued northward, led by the word from Tarleton's scouts, who pushed out ahead of the column, probing the roads for the direction of the enemy. They captured the usual rebel stragglers, who brought news Cornwallis had not expected. Greene himself had apparently left the main body of his army, had ridden across country to join Morgan's retreat. It was curious news to his officers, but Cornwallis understood. Greene appreciated the gravity of Morgan's position. If Cornwallis himself was in pursuit, Greene would take charge of the men being pursued.

At each river crossing Cornwallis was forced to halt the army in a maddening routine, stopping the march while scouts sought out a shallow crossing. Every few days the rains would come, and the men had no choice but to huddle in soaking misery as they waited for the clouds to clear, and then for the river levels to drop. It was more frustrating because Greene was not so disadvantaged, and Cornwallis was beginning to appreciate the man's tactic. Along many of the roads, he had seen the tracks of the rebels punctuated by narrow ruts in the mud. He assumed it was cannon. But soon the scouts brought him the word: The rebels were actually transporting their own boats, rolled along on makeshift axles. To add to the rebel advantage, Greene had sent men ahead to secure more boats, small fleets of craft that ferried their men safely and quickly across each river. Cornwallis had no such luxury, could only march his men along the water's edge until a crossing was found. Some were hazardous still, men pushing chest deep through swift currents, while on the far side, militia would wait in the trees, along the banks, to harass and pick at the helpless men with deadly musket fire.

After each crossing he expected Greene to make a stand, that finally the rebels would have had their fill of the unending retreat. But Greene pushed on, and when the rebels reached Guilford Court House, the two wings of Greene's army united. But even then, Greene did not stop, drove his men northward, and Cornwallis knew now that the rebels intended to march all the way to Virginia. Cornwallis could only continue the pursuit because he had no good alternative. He pushed the column toward the last barrier out of North Carolina, the Dan River, thought, Surely, now we will find him. But Greene had planned well, and the Dan was no different than the rivers before. There were boats as well, and merely twelve hours before Cornwallis reached the Dan, the last of Greene's army was landed on the northern banks, safely across the river.

As Cornwallis stood on the banks of the Dan staring into Virginia, it was a miserable reminder of Trenton, the enemy escaping him beyond the Delaware River. He was as exhausted as his men, took no comfort from the thought that Greene would be worn-out as well.

It was called a victory for the British and would cause celebration in London, would garner congratulations from Clinton and Germain. For the first time since the start of the war, not one continental soldier stood on Carolina soil. But Cornwallis did not celebrate. For now he truly understood Greene's plan. Cornwallis' army was barely two thousand strong, the men brutally punished by the extraordinary march. Their grand parade uniforms were as ragged as the clothes of the rebels, their newly soled shoes worn away again, their horses emaciated and sick. And, worse, the soldiers were starving. Greene had surrendered the Carolinas, and in the process had nearly destroyed Cornwallis' army.

51. GREENE

HE HAD NOT INTENDED TO RETREAT AS FAR AS VIRGINIA. ALL ALONG
the extraordinary march, he had sent letters to von Steuben, requesting that the Prussian send down the new recruits he had
raised in northern Virginia. But von Steuben had a crisis of his
own, a considerable surprise in the person of General Benedict
Arnold, now a brigadier in service to King George. Arnold commanded a force of twelve hundred men who had landed at Yorktown. Soon they had pushed hard up the Virginia peninsula,
causing panic in Richmond. The influence of Thomas Jefferson
had forced von Steuben to keep his recruits close at hand. Even
if von Steuben had more men than he might require, the Virginia
recruits had little interest in marching south to join a distant fight
in the Carolinas when the danger to their own homes was so
immediate.

With his men safely on the north banks of the Dan River,
Greene began to deal with the miserable condition of his troops.
Clothing was scarce, the men marching in rags, much as Greene
had seen throughout the campaigns in New Jersey. Shoes were
scarcer still, and most of the continental regulars were once
again barefoot.

For all the difficulties he faced, the one most personal to
Greene was the failing health of the man who was the most capable subordinate in his command.

I CANNOT REPLACE YOU, DANIEL."

"That's probably so, Nat. But beggin' won't help. I can't do
this, not anymore. It near kills me just to climb on my horse."

Greene sat slumped in his small camp chair, could see Morgan twisted slightly, the man's broad shoulders curled forward.
Even hunched over, Morgan seemed to fill the tent. Greene saw

the man's face clamped tight, no sign of the mischievous smile, could see sweat on the man's brow.

"You're hurting. You have some spirits?"

Morgan shook his head.

"Won't matter. Can't climb my horse drunk or sober. And it's a long ride. Probably better I can see straight. Don't need to be falling off my saddle." He paused. "I'm sorry, Nat. I'm going home."

There was already talk in the camp, an unkind slap at Morgan from officers who felt his antics and oversize reputation had pushed some of the more deserving of them out of their rightful place in the sun. All of his reasons for refusing to serve Gates were magnified now, as though the big man was some sort of whining brat, who either got his way or went home crying. The new rumors were that Morgan didn't care for Greene's tactics, would have preferred to stand and fight Cornwallis at any point during the retreat. As a result, Morgan was now going to sulk his way back to the Shenandoah Valley.

Morgan had ignored the talk, seemed to appreciate that Greene did as well.

"Nat, what you proposin' to do? You need more people."

"Pickens should return soon. I still expect militia from up north. General Smallwood sent word, he's sending some new recruits to add to the Maryland line."

"That's not the people I'm talking about, Nat. You need veterans. Cornwallis may be beat to hell over there, but he's still got the flower of his army. The more time you give him to rest up, the stronger he gets."

"I don't intend to give him time, Daniel. I'm sending the cavalry down, Washington's men, Harry Lee's Legion. They'll keep an eye on him, keep Tarleton from running roughshod along the river. Cornwallis has pulled back to Hillsboro, waiting to see what we're going to do. We won't keep him waiting much longer."

Morgan tried to sit up straight, grimaced, leaned to one side.

"I wish I could stay with you, Nat. I'm no good to this army now. This has been comin' on for a while. It was just a damned nuisance, but now . . . well, hell, I'm not going to cry to you. You ain't my mama. If I could ride, I'd ride. If I could fight, I'd fight."

"Go, rest up. Maybe you'll be back yet."

"Don't think so, Nat. I'm crippled up. This ain't something that's just gonna go away."

There was a silent pause, and Morgan said, "You think you can beat him?"

"Cornwallis? I don't think we have to, Daniel. All we have to do is hurt him once or twice. He's too far from Charleston, and he has the same problem we have: He can't get ammunition. That's why I need people, Daniel. I need to hold him as long as I can. He's a very long way from his outposts in South Carolina. He can't refit, and he has no close base of supply. The one thing I cannot do is risk destroying this army. Another reason I need the reinforcements. The only way Cornwallis succeeds is if he annihilates us. I don't intend to let that happen."

"Pick your ground, Nat. Make use of the militia. But don't depend on them." Morgan paused, shook his head. "You don't need my pea-brained counsel. You've had the best teacher a soldier can have. If I see George before you do, I'll let him know how his student turned out. Not bad for a book-learned Rhode Islander."

Morgan stood slowly, and Greene could see hard pain on the man's face. Morgan raised one arm, a slow stretch, put his hand against the canvas above him.

"When I get home, I'll see what I can do to round up some cloth. Half this army's runnin' around naked."

Greene smiled.

"I've given that some thought. Could be to our advantage. Imagine an attack led by a line of naked men. Would strike certain fear in the hearts of the enemy."

Morgan managed a small laugh.

"I don't think the commanding general would approve. Unless, of course, it worked." Morgan turned away now, moved to the opening in the tent, stopped.

"I ain't much for sentiment, Nat. You got some good men here. Hope you make the best use of 'em. God help me, if I could fight with you, I would."

GUILFORD COURT HOUSE, NORTH CAROLINA, MARCH 15, 1781

Toward the end of February, Greene ordered his army to re-cross the Dan River and advance carefully along the roads where

Cornwallis had withdrawn. The British did not wait quietly, Cornwallis throwing Tarleton forward in strike after strike, to find some way to maneuver Greene into the fight the British wanted. Though Greene knew he had to prevent the British troops from recovering from the damaging march, he was not yet prepared to offer a fight of his own. He felt his army was still too small. He could only hope to keep the British on the move by teasing them with the threat of an engagement. Cornwallis responded in the only way he could, seeking a confrontation with as much energy as Greene used to prevent one. After nearly three weeks, Greene's careful dance around the guns of the British accomplished what he'd hoped it would. The reinforcements finally began to arrive.

Greene expected to hear a great deal of Banastre Tarleton, the one man Cornwallis would rely on to seek the vulnerability in Greene's position. But Tarleton's effectiveness had been countered by the good work of William Washington and Harry Lee, sharp duels and crisp clashes, a violent chess game by the horsemen that allowed Greene the necessary time to gather his army. He had time as well to find the one piece of ground that would offer the best advantage for a good fight.

So much of the land close to the Virginia line was dense woods, no place for either army to make a stand. But on the long retreat, Greene had passed through Guilford Court House, where a patchwork of farms and open fields divided the forests. As his cavalry continued to clash swords with Tarleton, Greene moved his army back to Guilford. Finally, he was prepared for a fight. He summoned the horsemen to Guilford, placed them as Morgan had done at Cowpens, behind the flanks of his army.

Greene had his numbers, over four thousand men now spread in lines west of the small town. He had his good ground, the wide ridges, open fields surrounded by stands of trees. He could only wait for his invitation to be answered, for the enemy to understand that if they wanted a fight, they would have to march to Guilford. Cornwallis did not disappoint him.

MORGAN'S TROOPS WERE NOW COMMANDED BY COLONEL OTHO Williams, a brilliant young Marylander. Williams had been with the Maryland regiments since Boston, had been seriously wounded and captured at Fort Washington. Later exchanged for a British prisoner, Williams was one of the few bright spots in

Horatio Gates' disaster at Camden. Greene believed he was capable of taking the reins from Daniel Morgan. Greene's other senior commander was a brigadier, Isaac Huger, who had once commanded the militia in Georgia and South Carolina. Huger's family was prominent in South Carolina, but Greene had come to rely on the man for more than his recruitment value. After Cowpens, when Greene had left the main body of the army to travel northward with Morgan, Huger had been left behind to command the retreat. He had executed his assignment with the same dexterity and skill as Greene would have done himself. Once the two wings of the army had reunited, Greene knew that Huger was more than some aristocratic product of plantation wealth. He was a capable leader of troops.

THE STARS HAD BEEN SWEPT AWAY BY A CLEAR ICY DAWN, THE grassy fields touched by a soft white blanket of frost. Greene had ridden forward, down along the edge of a wide deep valley, thick with tall trees. The road out of Guilford continued westward and Greene moved out into the center, stopped, held up his hand, his staff halting as well. They kept silent, listened for the sounds of some kind of fight, some sign that Cornwallis was close. He stared down the road into the dull light of the silent forest, said, "Difficult to hear anything here. The trees will mask the sounds." He looked to his staff, said, "Major, send a rider. He should find Colonel Lee on this road. If the enemy is advancing, it is likely that Colonel Lee will be engaged. I must know his disposition."

The order went out, and a horseman was past him now, dropping off down the steep hill, the man's hoofbeats quickly muffled by the terrain. Greene glanced at his pocketwatch, *eight-thirty,* stabbed the watch back into his coat. He turned the horse, looked back up the long rise. He had hoped to see the courthouse itself, the small buildings of the town. But the view was blocked by a thick mass of trees. That will make it difficult, he thought. The officers will have to manage their own part of the fight.

The road climbed up through a long open field, black earth flecked with the remains of cornstalks. Out in the center of the field, a ragged fence intersected the road, and behind the fence, the first line of militia stood ready.

He had taken Morgan's experience to heart, the extraordinary strategy that had worked so well at the Cowpens. The first line would be the men from North Carolina, nearly a thousand nervous militia, most of whom had never seen their enemy. The fence would give them blessed protection, split rails stacked in a snaking line. It was Morgan's lesson, to put the least reliable men in a place where they had little to do but make a show. Greene stood now where the enemy should first appear, and he guessed, four hundred yards to the fence, perhaps more. The open ground in front of them would offer ample opportunity for several clean volleys, and once the British had moved close, the militia knew to withdraw. The militia were protected on their right flank by William Washington's cavalry, and companies of veteran marksmen, most of the men hidden in the woods that lined the cornfield. Once Harry Lee returned, his horsemen would take up position on the left flank, more protection, and a perfect position to enfilade the British advance.

Behind the North Carolinians, the woods engulfed the road, and here Greene had placed the Virginia militia, another thousand men, huddled now in the protection of the trees. Behind them, another open field led to the town itself, where Greene had placed his most seasoned troops, two regiments of Virginia Regulars under Huger, and two regiments of Marylanders under Otho Williams. If the British advance reached the third line, they would confront the finest soldiers Greene had on the field.

He pointed up the rise, said, "We will take up our position behind the regulars. Until we hear from Colonel Lee, we have no alternative but to wait."

He heard hoofbeats, looked back down the draw, saw riders rounding a distant curve. They climbed the hill, were clear of the tree-sheltered road. He could see now, it was Harry Lee.

Lee reined up, saluted him, his horse blowing clouds of hot breath, still jostling the young man about. Lee pulled hard on the reins, said, "Whoa, easy there! Sir, I'm surprised to see you here! You intend to start this fight yourself?"

Lee's joviality was always infectious, but Greene was not in the mood for pleasantries. He looked past Lee, stared down the road, could see the rest of the horsemen in column, moving quickly up the hill.

"You have a report, Colonel?"

"Indeed, sir. Right down thataway is a whole flock of redcoats. A few greencoats too. We had a little confrontation with Tarleton's boys. Did like you said, held them up a bit, made sure they knew what direction we wanted them to go. As I said, sir,

unless you plan to take your place on the skirmish line, I'd be
moving on back. Should I send my men out to the left flank, sir?
I see the militia boys are set."

Greene stared down into the woods, moved his horse a few
steps forward, listened. Lee's horsemen were moving past him
now, and Greene said, "Yes, proceed to the left flank, Colonel.
Dismount your men, put your best marksmen in front."

Lee gave the order, his officers now leading the way. Lee
moved up beside Greene, and, after a long moment, the woods
seemed to pulse with a low sound. Gradually the sounds grew
louder, and Lee said, "Their drummers are in fine form today,
sir." Lee pointed down into the woods, and around the far curve
riders appeared, men with green coats, a flag, the drums rattling
a sharp rhythm up the hill.

"As I reported, sir. You were hoping for a fight. I think you
have one."

IT WAS MIDDAY BEFORE THE BRITISH EMERGED IN FORCE ON THE
low road. They spread into a heavy line, began as they always began, stepping in unison through the field, pushed on by the
sounds of the drums. Yet it was not quite like Cowpens. Guilford
Court House was a much more vast area, the heavy stands of
trees blocking Greene's view of his deployment. There was another difference as well. The British strength was double what
Tarleton had led to Cowpens, and were not commanded by
an impetuous young cavalryman. They were led by Cornwallis
himself.

From his vantage point near the courthouse, Greene could
only know when the British appeared by the first hard thump of
his cannon, two six-pounders placed in the road that divided the
fence line. The British field guns responded, smaller pops of the
light three-pounders. He knew it was more for demonstration
than for any real effect, that the British would cease their fire
when their troops marched out into the field. After a duel of several agonizing minutes, the British guns finally fell silent. It was
the first genuine sign that the battle had begun.

THE BRITISH MOVED OUT TOWARD THE FENCE LINE, FACED THE MILI-
tia, but the discipline was not in those men, and many of the
North Carolinians fired their first round when the British were
barely in range. The redcoats absorbed the uneven volley and

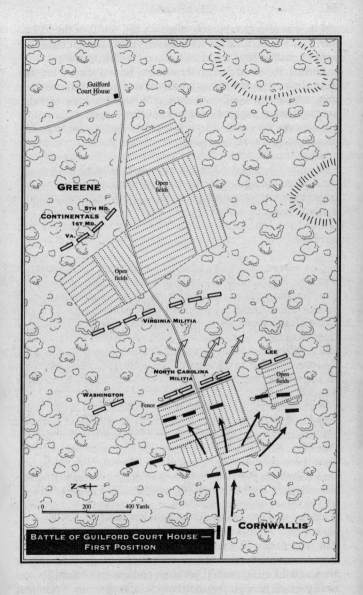

BATTLE OF GUILFORD COURT HOUSE —
FIRST POSITION

kept their near-perfect march to within fifty yards of the fence. Then they stopped, the drums suddenly quiet, and, for one long moment, the two lines faced each other. The British pointed their bayonets to the front, every man in their line focusing on the terrified faces of the men along the fence. Behind the frozen stares of the North Carolinians, an officer moved his horse slowly, raised his sword, shouted a single word, the command that would decimate the arrogance of the British formation, would sweep away the enemy in front of them.

"Fire!"

But the men along the fence did not answer the command, were consumed instead by the fear of the bayonets, and in one sudden massive wave, they pulled away, threw down their loaded muskets, and ran.

AS THE BRITISH CONTINUED THEIR ADVANCE, THE CAVALRY AND riflemen in the woods on either flank took careful aim, and small gaps began to appear in the British line. But it was not enough to hold them back, and the British saw there was safety in the trees. In the dense woods, the Virginia militia held their positions, and when the British marched into the edge of the trees, the thick underbrush erupted into sharp volleys that rolled back the first British line.

Greene could see only the woods, a long thick cloud of white smoke rising through the treetops. He paced the horse, raised field glasses, but there was nothing else to see. He rammed the field glasses into their pouch, felt angry frustration at his blindness. He thought of riding forward, moving up close behind the woods, but he could do no real good there. Ultimately, the most important part of the day could come right where he was. He had expected to see the Virginia militia retreating back out of the woods by now, and the frustration gave way to curiosity, and then, outright surprise. The Virginians weren't pulling back at all. They were making a fight of it.

He had seen remnants of the chaotic retreat of the North Carolinians, men without muskets, shedding coats and blankets, canteens and packs, furious officers riding among them, swatting them down with the flats of their swords. But the panic was complete, and the militia would not be stopped, many of them far beyond the field now. He began to realize, of course, the Virginians had seen that as well. They would not bear the same disgrace. They had, after all, the protection of the dense woods.

The fight in the trees was a solid roar of sound, and he stared in amazement, thought, The longer they hold, the greater the chance the British will back away! If so, the continentals should advance, give support. He began to move forward, rode out in front of the regular troops, heard cheers now, all along the line, but it was not for him. He looked down to the trees, could see a wave of men emerging from the right, some of the Virginians finally pulling away from the fight. He raised the field glasses, could see officers, some sign of order, a ragged line as they retreated up the hill. There was still musket fire in the woods, but not as steady now, most of the sounds coming from the left, from the men who were still holding their position. He scanned the officers on the right, too far away to see faces, thought of the commanders, Stevens and Lawson, men he barely knew, men he never expected to hold their ground against the full might of a British advance. The smoke began to drift away, and more of the Virginians emerged from the right, some pulling the wounded back with them. The quiet spread all down through the trees, the left now starting to give way as well. The retreat was uneven, the right already falling back behind the flank of the continentals. On the left, the Virginians were just now emerging from the trees, just beginning their climb. As the musket fire in the woods grew quiet, Greene was surprised to hear another hard fight, far out to the left, well beyond the woods, thought, Lee! He is still engaged on the flank! He scanned the continentals on both sides of him, thought, There is nothing we can do to assist him. Lee is too far forward. They must have assaulted him directly. He saw horsemen now, Washington's cavalry, following the retreat of the Virginians, protecting their withdrawal on the right. I cannot send them to Lee. We must still protect the right flank. He felt suddenly helpless, the great strength of his army beside him, no way to send any help to Lee's fight. Couriers were close behind him, and he pointed that way, said, "Send a message . . . Colonel Lee cannot allow himself to be cut off! If the enemy continues to advance, we will require his horsemen on our left flank! Unless a withdrawal will place him in jeopardy, he must retreat to our main position, and assume the flank! Go!"

The courier was quickly gone, and Greene stared down at the trees, the last wave of Virginians now coming up from the left, many turning to fight the enemy still hidden by the woods. Yes, by God! You have done your job!

He could see movement along the timberline to the right, bits of red, felt his heart jump. Very well! We shall see what you have left!

The British emerged in a ragged wave, and a cheer went up around him, and he thought, A salute to the Virginians, or perhaps . . . their enemy. Greene rode down to the left, out in front of the Marylanders, who could finally see the British troops. He turned toward them, raised his hat, and more cheers went up, the men seeing him, all of them knowing their part of this fight would now begin.

He faced the enemy again, could see British officers strengthening their line, evening the formation. He saw one man, clearly in command, a small staff following the man as he rode behind his troops. I should like to know you, sir. What do you see at this very moment? You have been battered and bloodied by men you must certainly have believed could not fight. Now, you must face the finest soldiers in America! Are you even aware of that? Let us see what you will do!

The British line began to move, but they were compact, not spread across the field, their officers pulling them tighter, a heavy fist, moving up the rise, shifting toward the left half of the continental line. Greene jerked the horse, moved farther that way, saw Otho Williams, sitting tall in the saddle, watching the advance draw up directly toward him. Greene moved close, said, "It will be your fight, Colonel! It seems Cornwallis has chosen to make his assault on Maryland!"

Williams was nervous, stared at the vast red wave moving closer.

"Then we shall show him his mistake, sir!"

The Marylanders held their fire, the perfect discipline of veterans. The British were close now, less than a hundred yards, and Greene felt the tightness in his throat, searched for the flag, their commander, found him now, could see the man's scarlet coat glistening in the sharp clear sunlight, points of gold light from his polished brass buttons. Greene felt a surge of raw fury, glanced beside him, thought, A musket, just this one time. Or better, the lines should part, and we should ride out, meet close enough so that I may strike you down myself. He drew his sword, held it high, brought the point down slowly, focused on the

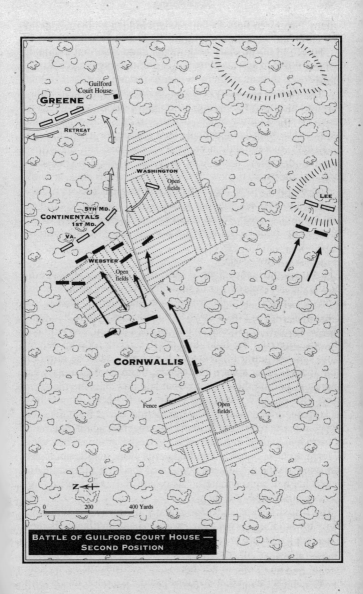

GREENE

Guilford
Court House

RETREAT

WASHINGTON

Open
fields

LEE

5TH MD.
CONTINENTALS
1ST MD.

VA.

WEBSTER

Open
fields

CORNWALLIS

Fence

Open
fields

Z

0   200   400 Yards

**BATTLE OF GUILFORD COURT HOUSE —
SECOND POSITION**

man's chest, studied every part of him, the white dusty wig, the calm stare on the man's face. The British line halted now, thirty yards in front of the Maryland troops. Their front line suddenly dropped down to one knee, two rows of muskets pointed straight at the troops in front of them. Williams did not wait, and Greene heard his shout. The Maryland line fired first in a massive volley. Greene felt himself shouting, a hot angry cheer, saw Williams rush forward, shouting orders, driving his horse close up behind his men. The Marylanders made their charge, swarmed through the British line, the fight now with the bayonet. But the British held their discipline, some firing as well, the Maryland line staggered by the sudden blow. Williams drew them back, a withdrawal in good order, the British stumbling back as well, then drawing up, coming together again. There was musket fire on both sides now, and Greene could hear the sharp whistle of the ball past his head, felt a hand on his arm, saw Burnet, pulling him back.

"Sir! Withdraw! Sir!"

He turned the horse, glanced back, tried to see the British officer, but the field was a mass of smoke and writhing bodies, heaps of bloody horror, the fight growing into a deafening chatter. He spurred the horse, moved down to the other Maryland line, men not yet engaged. These were Williams' men as well, but Williams was still directing the fight on his left. Greene rode up behind them, saw the junior officers watching him, could see relief on their faces. Down toward the woods, more British units were emerging, finding their way to what had now become the main fight. In front of Williams, he could see British troops falling back again, driven away by the thunderous blows from the First Maryland. The retreating British came together again, but many of them had shifted into line with the fresher troops. They were re-forming now, barely a hundred yards away, and he could see that many of them had seen enough of the First Maryland. He waved his hat high, shouted, "Maryland will stand tall today! Show them, boys! Show them!"

The British began to advance again, and Greene saw Williams, riding toward him, his hat gone, sword in hand. Williams shouted to his men, "Prepare to receive them! Wait for the order to fire!"

Greene backed his horse away, could see down to the woods, the last British troops to emerge. They were advancing well up the rise, and he looked at Williams, said, "Colonel, this is your command. I must see to General Huger. If the Virginia Regulars will make such a fight, this day is ours!"

He heard the first roar of Williams' new fight, turned, expected to see a vast wave of smoke, more devastation along the British advance. This part of the Maryland line was the Fifth Regiment, and they were not the veterans that had come through so much of the war. They were Smallwood's fresh recruits, men who had not yet seen a fight, who did not yet know what it was to stand tall in the field. The thunderous volley had not come from their ranks, was all on the side of the British. Greene stared, was stunned to see the entire line suddenly pulling back, men running without firing a single round. The British seemed as surprised as he was, began to advance again, but the fresh Marylanders did not have the steel of their brothers, and before the British could even make use of the bayonet, that part of Greene's main line was simply gone.

THE FIGHT CONSUMED TWO HOURS, AND FACED WITH A CONTINUING pressure from Cornwallis' disciplined army, Greene finally had no alternative but to order a retreat. By nightfall, his exhausted army found their way nearly seven miles, to an easily defensible position in a place called, ironically, Troublesome Creek. Though Tarleton's men eventually attempted a pursuit, the wooded countryside after dark was no place for cavalry. Greene was able to gather in many of his stragglers and lead the orderly march himself. He rode beside the proud and infuriated veterans, the men who had so nearly prevailed but were denied the victory by the curse so common to this army now, the failure of the inexperienced soldiers.

CORNWALLIS HAD REMAINED IN THE OPEN FIELDS AROUND GUIL-ford Court House, but it was not some symbolic claim of the victor. It was bloody necessity. For two days, the wounded on both sides were gathered and treated, every home, barn, and shed now a hospital. Cornwallis had sent letters to Greene, imploring the Americans to provide for their own, and Greene responded with wagons of medical supplies, surgeons, any means he could provide to ease the suffering of the wounded.

He had expected Cornwallis to pursue him, and he put his men into as good a defensive position as the land would allow. But the enemy did not come. Very soon he understood why. It was the surgeons who sent word, along with their urgent requests for more help. Cornwallis had lost a quarter of his strength, nearly six hundred casualties. The British were in no condition to pursue anyone.

Greene had tried to make some estimate of his own casualties, and none of the officers believed they had lost more than four hundred men, out of four thousand engaged. But there was a far greater problem. The North Carolina militia had not only deserted the field, they had deserted the army. Over a thousand men had simply disappeared.

The day after the battle, the rains had come, adding to the utter misery of those unsheltered wounded. Greene was concerned as well for the morale of his entire army, especially the hard veterans, whose victory had been thrown away. As the rain turned the river's edge to deep mud, Greene stayed close to his own tent, receiving the reports, putting together the final numbers he would have to send northward.

He had kept Harry Lee's Legion in the field, scouting for any sign of movement by the British. He still expected to hear some word of a British advance. Though Cornwallis had been badly mauled, he was still very far from his base of supply. Greene had to be prepared that Cornwallis would have no choice but to continue the attack.

TROUBLESOME CREEK, NORTH CAROLINA, MARCH 18, 1781

The rain was relentless, the tent leaking in a dozen places. He had placed the small camp desk in the one dry corner, stared at blank paper, his first attempt at preparing the report for the commanding general.

"Is this the sanctuary?"

He looked up, saw a dripping Lee, the young man smiling as he wiped the rain from his eyes.

"You may enter, Colonel. Sorry to say, it's not much drier in here."

"Oh, I would disagree with you, there, sir. My horse would like to come in as well, if that's all right."

It was Lee's usual mood, and Greene did not share his smile.

"No? Well, I suppose not. If I may sit, sir?"

Greene nodded, pointed to the low camp stool.

"Thank you, sir."

Lee shed his heavy coat, tossed it in a heap outside the tent. He sat now, his knees up in front of him, and Greene stared at the blank paper.

"I assume, Colonel, that the enemy is enduring the same misery we are?"

"More so, sir. They don't have tents. We picked up a couple deserters who said Tarleton was wounded. They lost a barnful of officers."

Greene thought of the one man, leading the assault on the First Maryland. I should have killed him myself.

"Names?"

"Not yet. We'll find out, sir."

Greene still studied the paper, and Lee said, "Excuse me asking, sir, but you writing a letter? I can come back."

"It's all right, Colonel. It's my report to General Washington. Or, it will be. Not sure how to begin."

"Well, sir, I'd start by telling the commanding general that this army has bested the finest army in the world."

Greene looked at him, saw the same smile.

"I'd prefer to tell him the truth, Colonel. You object to that?"

Greene was not in the mood for conversation, saw Lee's smile slip away, and Lee said, "You think, sir . . . because the British are sitting in those fields, that we lost that fight?"

"Don't you? Colonel, I was given the responsibility to command this department for one reason. General Washington believes I have the ability to achieve success. I have not done so. It is my duty to inform him of that fact."

Lee was wide-eyed, said, "General, I'd appreciate it if you would set that paper aside for now. You need to see the facts in the daylight, sir. This rain's soaked right into your brain . . . pardon me for saying."

Lee let out a breath now, and Greene was surprised at the man's frankness. He pushed the paper away, said, "Is there anything else, Colonel?"

Lee started to stand, thought better of the effort, settled back down on the stool.

"Sir, we whipped the British good back there. The only thing they won was that piece of ground. Excuse me, sir, but I'd sell them another piece of ground at the same price."

"We paid a price as well, Colonel."

"You mean the North Carolina boys? We didn't lose anything by it. They weren't soldiers, and they didn't do anything for this army. We have a bigger problem with the Virginia boys. I hear they're going home."

It was one more ingredient in Greene's despair.

"They only agreed to six-week enlistments, Colonel. I imagine in a week or so, they'll all be gone. Twelve hundred men. And, unlike the men from North Carolina, the Virginians *did* fight. When they go, we'll have barely sixteen hundred continentals left in this camp. How much success will that ensure us? We have an enemy not more than a day's march away, who knows he must either fight us or go home. I don't know how much more I can ask of these men."

Lee looked down between his knees, thought for a moment.

"Sir, you asked me if there was anything else. My apologies, sir, but when General Washington hears what you did down here, well, sir, he's going to agree more with me than with you. It's not just the battle. Don't you see that, sir? Once this rain stops, two things can happen. The enemy will come after us, or they won't. If they attack us, these boys will fight again. But if they don't, if Cornwallis marches away from here, it means . . . by God, sir, it means you've won . . . the campaign."

52. CORNWALLIS

MARCH 18, 1781

HIS MEN HAD EATEN NOTHING FOR NEARLY A FULL DAY BEFORE THE battle. For a day after, they suffered the utter misery of the torrential rains. But finally the rains stopped, and the quartermasters had conjured up barrels of rancid flour, enough to provide some kind of ration for the march.

He had already sent forward as many of the wounded as could travel, over four hundred men, who filled a column of confiscated wagons. The army would follow, knowing that behind them, a

hundred more had been left in the town, too severely injured,
cared for by those few surgeons he could spare. Any man who
survived the horror of the makeshift hospitals would certainly
become Greene's prisoner.

The march was strangely quiet, even the musicians subdued.
There were far fewer drummers and fifers now, some killed at
Cowpens, many more killed or captured at Guilford. For a while
Cornwallis could hear one drum, far in front of him, one man
who still had the spirit, who would still offer a proud rhythm to
the march. But the steady beat had suddenly grown quiet, and
soon Cornwallis understood. He had ridden past the drum itself,
tossed aside, punched and ripped by the angry stab of a bayonet.
It was not a surprise that Cornwallis' own sour mood would be
reflected by the men.

He had issued yet another proclamation, a call for loyalists to
celebrate their victory at Guilford by flocking once more to the
king's flag, and for any rebels who surrendered themselves to be
pardoned for all crimes. As soon as the notices were posted, he
regretted the decision, scolded himself for such a mindless show
of optimism. It was more than a sad joke this time, it was cruel
and deadly to anyone naïve enough to respond. Once he realized
he had to abandon Guilford, he knew that anyone who actually
tried to comply would find no protection at all, would certainly
be set upon by the rebels.

The reports would be written soon, and he knew that Guilford
Court House would be described as a glorious victory, another in
a long series of crushing blows to the rebellion. By the time the
reports reached London, they would be received according to
the political bent of the reader. The king's men would trumpet
the success as one more sign the war was going their way. The
opposition would have a different view, and he imagined the
speeches in Parliament, the king's enemies growing more bold
with each bit of news. No matter how much Germain and Lord
North colored the facts, the opposition would know what Cornwallis knew himself. Throughout most of the war, the British
had proven superior on the field, the rebels reduced to fighting
from positions of weakness, resorting to tactics that would make
bandits proud. On every field where Cornwallis had led the assault, his regulars had driven the rebels away. But now, as he
marched his army away from their tragic victory at Guilford, he

understood that the rebels could only succeed in a war fought exactly as they had fought it. And now, six years after it had begun, the rebels were clearly winning.

He had begun to see their commanders in a different light, appreciated now that their talents exceeded what a trained officer typically brought to the field. He had never thought of Washington as a military mind, had viewed Fort Washington and Brandywine as stupidly executed disasters. But the rebels were a different kind of army, and so, their commanders were different as well. Both Howe and Clinton had allowed too much time to slip by, too many opportunities for the rebel commanders to learn from their mistakes. The rebels had grown into their roles, men like Greene and Morgan and Lafayette learning how to shape their tactics around the abilities of their men. Greene's retreat from Guilford was perfectly timed. As Cornwallis moved his men into position for a final grand assault, the rebels were exactly where Cornwallis needed them to be. Then, Greene had pulled them away, and Cornwallis knew now that Greene had saved the rebel army from utter destruction. And so, one more disaster had become instead one more valuable lesson, and today, Greene would be a better commander.

Ah, he thought, but Greene gave us the field. That is what will matter to Henry Clinton and George Germain. I will be congratulated, no matter that I now have barely fifteen hundred hungry, shoeless soldiers. And if we do not find supplies soon, we may simply collapse into no army at all.

He had sent word down to the outposts both at Wilmington and Camden, an urgent order for forage and food to be sent to Cross Creek. The town was a vibrant Scottish settlement sprawling along the headwaters of the Cape Fear River. It was believed to be a solidly loyalist area, the Scots fiercely proud of their allegiance to the king. The quartermasters had already marched ahead, leaving behind encouraging words for the troops, that once they reached Cross Creek, the army could rely on a fresh outpouring of loyalist sentiment in the form of both supplies and recruits. It was optimism Cornwallis had heard before.

He was not surprised to learn that Greene's army was pursuing him, though the only confrontations had come from the cavalry, Tarleton's men holding away the light horse of Lee. But Greene would stay close, and even if the rebels were too badly bruised to make a fight, he knew Greene would trail him to Cross

Creek, seeking some opportunity to strike. It was all the incentive Cornwallis needed to push his army in a desperate march.
Though he had to believe his troops would still have the spirit for
a fight, they were lacking one essential ingredient. Since they
had burned their wagons at Ramsour's Mill, there had been no
means to resupply their cartridge boxes. Though food was an urgent necessity, a lack of ammunition meant they could not force
a general engagement. Even if they relied on the bayonet, they
could not survive another *victory* like Guilford.

CROSS CREEK, NORTH CAROLINA, MARCH 29, 1781

The Scotsmen had met Cornwallis' call for support the same
way most of the Carolinas had responded. The British were ignored. As the army marched into Cross Creek, they were delivered only four days of forage for the desperately weak horses,
the quartermasters admitting sheepishly that the countryside
was devoid of the essential needs for the men. They would again
survive on hard biscuits and miniscule rations of dried beef.

The wagons of the wounded had stopped at Cross Creek as
well, the horrified citizens reluctantly opening their homes as
hospitals. One house had been reserved for the officers, and
Cornwallis stepped up on the porch, could already smell that familiar, awful odor, dropped his head for a moment, then stepped
through the door. He saw women, a mother and two girls, a heap
of clothing already torn into brightly colored bandages. The
women ignored him, and he moved past them, followed the
smells to a parlor, peered inside. O'Hara was on a small narrow
bed, looked up at him, said, "Ah, General, you here to part me
from my miseries? I had feared seeing the Almighty before I saw
you, sir."

He was surprised at O'Hara's spirits, said, "I thought I should
see how you're faring." He looked at the thick bandage on
O'Hara's leg, and O'Hara said, "That's the one that hurts, I admit." He put a hand on his chest, patted gently. "I have been assuming, of course, that this one would be the final blow. The
surgeon tells me I barely escaped the reaper. Not so . . . some
of us."

O'Hara's buoyant mood had no energy behind it, the smile
quickly gone. Cornwallis was ashamed, had forgotten that the

man's son did not survive the battle. Lieutenant O'Hara was an artillery officer, had been buried where he was struck down.

"I regret the loss of your son, General."

"He died the best way a man can, sir. His mother will not understand, of course. Women don't appreciate those things a soldier accepts. He was a good lad, sir. They are all . . . good lads."

There was a silent moment, and Cornwallis saw O'Hara fighting himself to hide the emotion.

"I'm hoping, General, that we will have you back in action quite soon." He paused, said, "How's General Webster? Any word?"

O'Hara seemed to welcome the change of subject, said, "Webby hasn't been awake for a while, I'm told. Poor chap. Did the best work of any of us. Took his people straight into that Maryland bunch. Hardest fight of the day. He's in the rear bedroom. He'd appreciate you looking in on him, sir."

Cornwallis nodded, knew that O'Hara's appraisal was right. Webster had driven his men straight up to the heart of Greene's third line, had been struck down in a horrific confrontation. O'Hara said, "I hear young Tarleton lost a finger."

"Two, actually. He was fortunate."

"We are all fortunate, General, those of us who can tell about these exploits. If you don't mind, sir, can you tell me what our plan is now? I hear the rebels are on our tail."

"We must continue the march. I had hoped the citizens here would provide more than their parlors."

O'Hara tried to sit up.

"It is a singular outrage, sir! These people have benefited from His Majesty's every favor. All the reports of their loyalty, their generosity. They have proven false in every particular. We should not remain another day in the company of such ungrateful people. Scotsmen, indeed!" He dropped back, and Cornwallis saw a twist of pain on the man's face.

"Easy, General. It is not necessary for you to exert yourself."

O'Hara was breathing deeply.

"Quite right, sir. It won't happen again. So, if I may, sir, when do we march?"

"Tomorrow. I have decided to make for Wilmington."

O'Hara looked at him for a long moment.

"I would have thought . . . Camden."

It was Cornwallis' private debate, the agony of a decision only he could make.

"If we continue toward the coast, the rebels will likely follow. That will prevent any danger to Camden, or the other outposts. Wilmington will afford us the protection of the navy, and a reliable source of supply. This colony is a spiderweb of infernal rivers, and I must consider that the rebels will seek opportunity to strike us at vulnerable points. The route to Wilmington is not so inconvenient."

O'Hara looked away for a moment, and Cornwallis thought, He knows as well as I. If we march to Camden, it is a declaration of defeat, the termination of this campaign.

Cornwallis backed away.

"I will look in on General Webster. You will be put on a wagon in the morning."

"Thank you, sir. I trust you will order the engineers to smooth out the rough ride."

Cornwallis managed a smile, turned, moved out into the main room. The women were gone, and he heard low voices, the rear of the house. He lowered his head, took a long hard breath, fought again through the smell.

HE HAD BEEN SURPRISED THAT GREENE DID NOT FOLLOW HIM PAST Cross Creek. Every report suggested that the rebels were moving southward, returning to South Carolina. The information caused a new debate, a decision whether to make some effort to reinforce Rawdon. But Greene had the head start, and if the rebels intended to strike hard in South Carolina, Cornwallis was simply too far away to prevent it.

Though Greene's army was gone, the march out of Cross Creek was an ordeal nonetheless. He had expected that the Cape Fear River would provide a comfortable avenue for moving his men, but the waterway was not as navigable as he had hoped. Nearly all the men were barefoot, and the rigors of the march shredded the remnants of their uniforms. As the country flattened into the sandy plains of the coast, they were met by astonishing swarms of insects, every night a torturous misery of mosquitoes and other unseen tormentors. During the day, rebel partisans seemed to spring out of every patch of woods, peppering the army's misery with musket fire. He would make no effort to confront them, knowing that these people were at home in their swamps, that any troops who pursued them would gain no advantage, would only slow their progress. For seven agonizing days, the soldiers pressed forward, their numbers shrinking as the sick and weak fell away. He had endured the march as well as the strongest of his men, but then came one hard jolt, the news sent back from the wagons to the front. James Webster had died. Cornwallis had tried to shield himself from what he could not deny, that Webster's wounds had indeed been mortal. It was yet another cruel reminder of the price of their glorious victories.

WILMINGTON, NORTH CAROLINA, APRIL 1781

In just a few days the army had become healthier. O'Hara was up off his bed, was slowly making his way back to duty. Cornwallis sent a steady stream of messages to Charleston, orders for Balfour to relay any news from Rawdon's post at Camden, any sign of a confrontation with the rebels that might endanger the other outposts as well. But each transport that arrived in the harbor brought little news that would cause Cornwallis to sail his troops for Charleston. It was a blessed relief.

He had moved the headquarters staff into an extraordinary mansion that had been abandoned by its loyalist owner early in the war. The headquarters there had been established by Major James Craig, who had come to the Carolinas with Alexander Leslie. While Cornwallis felt enormously rested by the languid atmosphere of Wilmington, it was an uncomfortable reminder of Philadelphia, the grandeur of stately homes, memories of dress uniforms and ballrooms. But there was one stark difference. In Wilmington there was no Howe or Clinton. It was his command, and his headquarters. There was one other difference as well. With the approach of summer, the Carolina coast became a nest of suffering, the men assaulted by a far more dangerous enemy than the rebels. It was fever season. He had seen the consequences of it in Charleston, heard the stories from Savannah, had even suffered the effects himself the year before. Whatever the source of this particular plague, he knew it could devastate his army. They could not remain in Wilmington.

He had been stunned to learn of Benedict Arnold's sudden rise to command, especially in a place as crucial as Virginia. Technically, Virginia was under Cornwallis' command, but Arnold had been sent there by Clinton without ever seeking Cornwallis' approval. Cornwallis had never corresponded with Arnold, and had no wish to do so now. A traitor is a traitor no matter his uniform, and Cornwallis could not think of Arnold without considering the fate of John André. André had always seemed a pitiable excuse for a British officer, but by circumstances Cornwallis did not yet understand, André had become trapped in a ridiculous and worthless web of intrigue, his execution strange and grotesque. If André's execution was justified, there should be some kind of justice for the man who had put him in that position. If it was not to be Henry Clinton, it must surely be Benedict Arnold. As much as Cornwallis had disagreed with the strategies of Henry Clinton before, he could not stomach the thought of treating Arnold as some sort of trusted subordinate. Now he would not have to. Though the flow of letters from Clinton had been blessedly scarce, one letter had given Cornwallis enormous relief. Clinton had sent William Phillips to Virginia to take the command away from Arnold. Even better, Clinton had provided Phillips with better than two thousand reinforcements. Phillips was a capable, if not brilliant officer, a fat, affable man that Cornwallis had known well for twenty years. Phillips would serve well as Cornwallis' junior, and if Arnold was to remain in Virginia at all, he could be Phillips' problem and not his own.

The heat began to settle on Wilmington, lengthening days, steamy nights. He had heard almost nothing from Rawdon, and little from the scouts he sent into the countryside. The British intelligence system was nonexistent, and he could only assume Greene was still moving southward. The feeling was familiar to him, warmer weather fueling growing impatience, frustration that once again, a very good army was sitting idle, while its commander consumed his time pacing through someone's luxurious home.

The plan began to form in his mind, the idea tempered by concerns for events that could still occur in South Carolina. He would ponder it in the dark hours, would wake in the middle of the night to sweating bedclothes, a warm breeze that filled the curtains like great winds billowing the sails of the stout ships. With the sleep erased he would stare up in darkness, his mind working over the maps, counting the regiments, imaginary discussions with the officers who were far away. In the daylight, he would go to his office, put pen to paper, the maps again, and then, letters, to Phillips first, seeking his agreement. The letters went as well to Clinton and Germain, but he expected no answer. By the time they could respond, it would make no difference anyway. Their letters would not find him quickly enough. There would be ample time for him to exercise the discretion Clinton had given him, to put into motion the one plan that he believed might still work. Clinton sat idly in New York with a great mass of power, while in the Carolinas and Georgia, the British held tightly to the important towns and crossroads. It was a plan Clinton would have to approve, even if Cornwallis did not need him to. The most important colony in America had become Virginia, the great yawning abyss that lay between north and south. The Chesapeake was always crucial, but never more so than now.

The more he tinkered with the plan, the more his old enthusiasm returned. He had erased all thoughts of South Carolina from his mind, had to trust that his commanders there could hold away any assault Greene would offer. Phillips would await him with the fire they had shared as young officers, two men who could depend on each other to stand tall against their enemy. It was nearly too simple a concept, and as he organized another long march, he tried to imagine the reception he would yet receive from the king, from Germain, even from Clinton. The campaign would be brilliant by its very simplicity, a weakly defended colony that held the key to the entire war. If Virginia fell, America must follow.

On April 25, Cornwallis led what remained of his army, fewer than fifteen hundred men, on a march through the lowlands of coastal North Carolina. As they forded the rivers, the Tar and the Neuse, his men marched again through relentlessly hostile country. But then they crossed the Roanoke, and the misery of all they had endured in the Carolinas was behind them. By early May, Cornwallis was in Virginia.

53. WASHINGTON

JUNE 1781

THE INVASION OF VIRGINIA BY BENEDICT ARNOLD HAD INSPIRED Washington to counter the move by sending Lafayette southward with as many troops as could be spared. Von Steuben's efforts at raising militia were encouraging, and with the young Frenchman's arrival there, Arnold's threat could be minimized. Washington had given Lafayette one more order as well. If at all possible, Arnold was to be captured.

For several weeks, Lafayette had prevented any effective British campaign, and Arnold's men had done little more than pillage the countryside, terrorizing civilians whose farms and villages had already been stripped bare by the needs of their own army. Virginia seemed to have settled into the same kind of stalemate Washington had endured in New York. And then, he learned that Clinton had sent reinforcements and that, surprisingly, their commander was no longer Arnold, but Cornwallis himself.

The news was agonizing for Washington, for reasons both military and personal. If Cornwallis secured the conquest of Virginia, Mount Vernon and, indeed, Martha herself might fall into British hands. Though he could not take his eyes off Clinton and the continuing threat of a British surge out of New York, he could no longer assume Virginia had the troop strength to defend itself. Weakening his army once more, Washington reluctantly sent Anthony Wayne southward, with another thousand troops. If Cornwallis did indeed force an engagement with Lafayette, at least the young Frenchman would have the power to mount an effective defense.

Though Greene was technically in command of the Southern Department, he still deferred to Washington's authority. The difficulties lay with communication. Letters took a month or more to travel from the Carolinas to Washington's base along the Hudson. But Greene had done nothing to shake Washington's confidence, and the news of Cornwallis' departure from Wilmington had to be accepted as stunning evidence of Greene's success. With Cornwallis gone, Greene would confront an enemy in South Carolina who seemed resigned to its fate. Though the British would certainly fight to maintain their outposts, their positions were isolated and unlikely to be reinforced. While Greene still had a great deal of work to do, his return to South Carolina would bring the partisans to his side, and, certainly, the people themselves.

FOR LONG AGONIZING MONTHS WASHINGTON HAD PLANNED AND plotted for some means of assaulting New York. But the reality was pure frustration, Clinton's strength actually increasing with a sudden arrival of reinforcements. Washington's spies confirmed that New York was now bristling with nearly fifteen thousand British and Hessian troops. If there was to be any assault at all against Manhattan Island, Washington could do nothing without the support of the French.

Washington had gone north again for another conference with Rochambeau. The French were maddeningly gracious, politely receptive to his maps and strategies, Rochambeau quick to repeat his assurances that he was there only to serve Washington's needs. Washington endured the grand dinners and lavish parades, all the European pageantry that was designed to impress on him their respect for his command. But through each formal ceremony, and each toast to his name and his health, Washington was acutely aware that the French troops were still idle, the inadequate force of warships in the harbor at Newport were continuing to lie at anchor, while in New York, the British grew stronger still. The question burned inside of him, shielded by his smiling politeness to Rochambeau. Why were the French on American soil if they did not intend to fight?

As Washington fumed about his headquarters, he was still convinced that the ridiculous stalemate could be broken. He had formed a plan for a quick strike into New York from the north, directed toward the King's Bridge. But the plan required the added power of the French infantry. Rochambeau had finally agreed, and on July 4, while Washington endured more long weeks of French preparation and delay, the first French infantry forces finally arrived at Peekskill. But the intended assault was not to be. The plans were too complex, and the British outposts and sentries were simply too alert. By the time an assault could be launched Clinton was fully prepared. For Washington, it was one more piece of churning disappointment. The entire operation was called off.

ROCHAMBEAU'S INTERPRETER NOW WAS MAJOR GENERAL FRANÇOIS-Jean de Beauvoir, Chevalier de Chastellux. He was also one of Rochambeau's senior commanders, and the most educated and literate man Washington had ever met. While Chastellux was perfectly pleased to be interpreter, it was clear he was taking advantage of his position to gather information for a revealing book about life in America. It was a source of intense curiosity to Washington, if not somewhat intimidating. Washington realized that Chastellux might well record on paper every word Washington spoke.

Rochambeau had made himself at home at Dobbs Ferry, a pleasant village perched in the Hudson highlands. The graciousness had continued, dinners in Washington's honor, invitations to inspect the French troops. He had become accustomed to the arrival of parcels of all size, gifts from Rochambeau and the senior officers in his command, an amazing array of trinkets and artifacts that Washington accepted with polite appreciation.

He accepted yet another invitation to visit Rochambeau, to witness some display of drill and small arms that the Frenchman seemed especially proud to demonstrate. But Washington had seen enough of the perfect white uniforms, had come to know by heart the particular regiments, signified by the color of their finely stitched trim. The display had been predictable, more about show than combat, the perfect precision of men on parade. Washington smiled with his host, applauded at what seemed to be the appropriate moments. It was not so different than what von Steuben had brought to Valley Forge, but to Rochambeau, and his entire command, it seemed a particular point of pride.

The event had concluded, and Washington was already tired, was nagged by a dull pain in his jaw. His teeth had been giving him considerable difficulty, adding to his sour mood. But his hosts were all smiles, and Washington forced his own politeness. As the senior staff retired into Rochambeau's lavish quarters,

Chastellux moved close to him, said, "General, if you are so disposed, General Rochambeau wishes to speak with you privately."

"Certainly." It was somewhat unusual, Rochambeau not often particular about the number of staff or officers who attended their meetings. Chastellux led him into Rochambeau's office, stood to one side, and Rochambeau was there now, pulled the door closed behind him. Rochambeau did not sit, looked at Chastellux, who began to translate, "I must inform you, General, of a somewhat troublesome situation."

Washington felt the throb in his jaw, a hard burning pain. *What now?*

"If we are to commence a new campaign against the British, the fleet at Newport is inadequate to serve our needs, as you are aware. Admiral Barras has been most insistent that since the infantry has removed itself from his protection, Newport is a dangerous place for him to stay. I admit to you, General, with some embarrassment, that this is a disagreement that is annoying to me. The admiral wishes to remove his fleet to Boston, and has even suggested he begin a naval operation with the intent of assaulting British interests at Newfoundland."

Washington could not hold back.

"Newfoundland?"

Rochambeau smiled. "It is not of concern, General."

Washington moved to a chair, his weariness betraying him, sat down, said, "General Rochambeau, it is entirely my concern. If Admiral Barras does not intend to provide his warships for our assistance, we cannot accomplish a great deal anywhere in this theater of the war."

Rochambeau glanced at Chastellux, said, "General, I am in sympathy with you. Let us consider another possibility. Another theater, perhaps. If it was suggested that another fleet of warships was to arrive on this coast, a much larger fleet, would you agree that this could be put to valuable service?"

Washington saw a puzzled look on Chastellux's face, Rochambeau's words obviously unexpected.

"Certainly, General. Valuable indeed."

"If I was to tell you that a powerful fleet, commanded by Admiral de Grasse, might arrive, perhaps, at the Chesapeake Bay, would you consider that to be of value?"

Washington said nothing, looked again at Chastellux, who seemed visibly uncomfortable. Washington was beginning to understand now, thought, there is nothing *perhaps* about this. Washington knew of de Grasse, a reputation as one of the French navy's finest commanders. De Grasse had been sent from France to the West Indies with a sizable armada, was one of the primary reasons the French were faring so well against the British navy in their confrontations there.

"General Rochambeau, is Admiral de Grasse en route to the Chesapeake Bay?"

Rochambeau shrugged.

"Perhaps. If he was, how would you respond to that news, General?"

Washington's mind raced, all the talk, all the planning and the meetings, Rochambeau's stubbornness against assaulting New York. For all the man's claims of subservience, he thought, they have their own plans, their own strategy for fighting this war. They will allow me to know those plans when I solve their riddle. He was angry now, the toothache putting him close to an explosion. Chastellux said, in English, "I am sorry, General. I knew nothing of this."

Rochambeau waited patiently for Chastellux to finish his words, seemed to know what his subordinate had said.

"General Washington, we all fight for the same cause here. You must understand that my king must keep his eyes on all the world, not just America. You are not experienced in the consequences of war. I respect you because you have endured against a much more powerful enemy. But I must support my government's caution. A direct assault against a powerful foe in New York could have disastrous consequence. Indeed, your war could end at the very moment our forces were defeated. It would prove an embarrassment to my king."

Washington felt the heat in his brain slipping away from his careful grasp.

"General Rochambeau, if our forces are defeated, I have lost my home, my country, and my life. I have never championed any strategy that proved to be unwise. I am not certain that New York should be our priority, only that General Clinton's defeat there would hasten the end of this war."

"Thank you for your honesty, General. I will be honest with you as well. Admiral de Grasse has agreed to sail from the West Indies to the mouth of the Chesapeake because he believes there is an opportunity to destroy a British fleet that is forming there.

From all we can gather, General Clinton is establishing a formidable naval base at Portsmouth, on the Virginia coast. If the British fortify that position, it could put our naval operations in America in some jeopardy. The British would have a base more central to operations either north or south."

Washington's anger was easing, and he said, "It is a sound plan. Might I suggest that if Admiral de Grasse is successful, he could *then* weigh the consequences of an assault on New York?"

"That is possible, General. I must mention, however, that Admiral de Grasse believes our forces should unite. His fleet and . . . your troops."

Washington absorbed the words, realized that Rochambeau was offering him the decision, a symbolic show of Washington's seniority.

He had received Lafayette's estimates, that Cornwallis had nearly eight thousand regular British troops on the Virginia peninsula. Even if de Grasse confronted the British fleet for dominance of the Chesapeake, Cornwallis would hold tightly to the state itself. If the British supply lines over water were cut, Cornwallis would simply extend them inland, another campaign of plunder and destruction that Lafayette was not powerful enough to stop. If the British were to be defeated in Virginia, it would have to come by both land and sea.

"General Rochambeau, should Admiral de Grasse choose to appear at Virginia, he could be of immeasurable service to our cause. I would suggest that we prepare to join him there."

AUGUST 1781

The danger was enormous, Clinton perched in New York with a force large enough to crush both Washington and Rochambeau, if they allowed themselves to be caught on a vulnerable march. Washington's plan was to offer a perfect deceit. The columns paraded close to the Hudson clearly visible to Clinton's lookouts. Clinton's spies could not help but observe rebel militia along the Jersey shore assembling vast fleets of small boats. Rochambeau ordered his troops to build huge ovens, in clear sight of the harbor. It was a convincing show that the armies would form their camps and their main supply base not far from what Clinton would believe to be their primary target:

Staten Island. For days, the drums sounded, and troops filed into place near Newark and Amboy, the troops themselves believing that they were preparing to invade New York. Throughout the entire operation, Washington and Rochambeau were the only two men who knew the true plan. The lookouts kept him advised, but Washington would see for himself, would climb the observation posts to study the British warships at anchor in the harbor. There was no change, no flatboats, no troops in motion. Clinton was sitting tight, convinced, as was every man along the Jersey shore, that a massive engagement was imminent, that very soon, New York could be under siege.

When the orders came to march yet again, Washington's troops still believed they were preparing to cross the narrow waterway. But their march took them through Brunswick, and then Princeton, and by the time they reached the Delaware River, the troops realized it was a different mission altogether.

The march would take them through Philadelphia, to the delight of a citizenry who cheered their disheveled army, shoeless men in ragged shirts. But then the real show began, and the crowds stared in utter amazement at this new army who followed them, the perfect, beautiful uniforms and fat healthy horses. The combined force totaled six thousand men, and few but their commander understood the extraordinary risk. Washington had left behind barely five thousand men, an uncertain combination of regulars and militia, manning the outposts along the Hudson. They shared the desperate hope, with their commander, that Clinton had truly been deceived, that the enormous British force would remain in New York. Once past Philadelphia, Washington could not look back, could only think of the vast ocean to the south, whether or not the French admiral de Grasse was good to his word, whether the French navy would actually appear. But for his soldiers, there could only be one goal now, completing a journey of four hundred miles to the shores of the Chesapeake Bay.

54. CORNWALLIS

THERE HAD BEEN NO JOVIAL AND SENTIMENTAL REUNION WITH HIS friend William Phillips. As Cornwallis had brought his army close to their Virginia base, he had received word that Phillips had been stricken by a fever, and only three days before Cornwallis arrived, Phillips had died. It was not the welcome into Virginia he had expected.

There was one blessing to be found. Benedict Arnold was gone, summoned by Clinton to take part in some vaguely detailed campaign to the north, possibly another assault against Newport. The news had lightened Cornwallis' spirits considerably.

Throughout the summer, the Virginia campaign had been an ordeal of marches in all directions. Cornwallis was determined to engage Lafayette's forces, but the young Frenchman seemed to know his own weaknesses. As Cornwallis would push his army up the Virginia peninsula, Lafayette would back away, maintaining a safe distance. Cornwallis suffered the same disadvantage of every British commander, an army that moved too slowly, encumbered by its own girth. Cornwallis realized that the young man had no desire to stand up to a general engagement with British regulars who were a far superior fighting force than the mix of continentals and inexperienced Virginia militia.

If Cornwallis could not compel Lafayette to a general engagement, it did not mean the rebels could be ignored. Lafayette had learned from the triumphs of Washington, that the most effective fight he could make against Cornwallis was the quick burst, targeting the mistake, or tormenting the rear guard. While Cornwallis still believed Virginia lay open to occupation, with Lafayette dogging him at every turn, it would not be a simple conquest. Since the British infantry was vulnerable to the rebel annoyances, Cornwallis had one good alternative. He sent his horsemen after the rebels, Tarleton's Legion, and the Queen's Rangers, under John Simcoe. Simcoe was only slightly older than Tarleton, and nearly as cocky. The two units operated separately, and Cornwallis encouraged the rivalry with discreet prodding for each young horseman to outdo the other. But the results were unspectacular. Simcoe managed one minor clash that embarrassed von Steuben and his Virginia militia, while Tarleton nearly captured Governor Thomas Jefferson right out of Jefferson's own home at Monticello. Their raids made for boisterous conversation and would certainly go far to enhance each man's opinion of himself, but Cornwallis recognized their accomplishments for what they were: lost opportunities. Cornwallis had seen this all before, an ineffective campaign against rebels who were adept at biding their time, stretching out the campaign while the British exhausted their enthusiasm for the fight.

He still believed in the soundness of his strategy, that a large-scale offensive in Virginia could succeed at bringing the colony firmly under British control. Besides separating the Carolinas from contact with the northern colonies, Virginia was obviously an important source of food for rebel troops still gathering under Nathanael Greene. Cornwallis could not just sit quietly and allow a sound strategy to go wasting. In a forcefully worded letter, he suggested to Clinton that New York be abandoned, that Clinton move the main army to the Chesapeake. Against such a force, neither Lafayette nor Washington could save Virginia. The rebellion could be brought quite effectively to a close. Cornwallis believed resolutely in his plan. Henry Clinton had other ideas.

THE LETTERS HAD AWAITED HIM FROM HIS FIRST DAYS ON THE PENinsula, arriving in small clusters. It was the disadvantage of distance, Clinton penning the letters days apart, Cornwallis received them in one mass all at the same time. He laid them out on the table, cocked his head toward O'Hara, said, "Would you suggest I read these in the order they were written, or would it be more prudent to relay them to you in the order of their insanity?"

He had lost his fear of speaking indiscreetly about his superior, emboldened by distance, of course, but more, by what seemed to be a collapse of Clinton's ability to command. O'Hara was not as comfortable with Cornwallis' whimsical attitude, said, "The most recent would be the most important, I would think. It would be a product of the latest information, would contain the orders that we would be expected to follow."

Cornwallis ignored the minor admonition from O'Hara.

"All right then, General, but I should warn you. You will not appreciate the level of comedy under which I must function if all you hear is the latest order. No matter, here it is. June 28. We are to . . . embark that portion of the army which is available, and proceed with appropriate artillery and wagons, for the purpose of assaulting the rebel positions around Philadelphia. Once any resistance has been suitably dispatched and the rebel supply stores have been destroyed, the force will continue to New York, to reinforce the main body of the army."

"Philadelphia?"

"Ah, see? I told you. As entertaining as we may find that order to be, it pales in comparison when taken out of its context. You see, here, June 8: 'Dispatch with all speed those troops not required for your immediate defense, and hasten them to New York.' And, here, June 14: 'Recall any troops you may have embarked to New York, and make all effort to securing a secure naval base at Portsmouth or Old Point Comfort.' "

O'Hara seemed even more uncomfortable now.

"The most recent one, June 28 . . . must be obeyed, sir."

"Oh, quite! And obey it we shall! That is, only until we receive the next one."

His good humor was a mask for the complete fury that had boiled up inside him. He looked at the papers spread on his desk, closed his eyes for a brief moment, then said, "I have ordered General Leslie to make ready for boarding the transports now at anchor at Portsmouth. The commanding general has ordered us to sail for Philadelphia, and sail for Philadelphia is what we shall do. I have considered it a Divine blessing to have been in command so far from the reach of that man. Never was that so clear than right now. For better than a year I have engaged the enemy at every bloody opportunity. I have given my king everything a soldier must give. My reward is to endure haranguing buffoonery from my superior who sits in idleness in his mansion in New York and wrestles with demons of his own creation. The rebels are planning to attack New York. Or perhaps not. The French navy is a threat to us, so we must build a secure port. Or perhaps not. When I arrived here, I received word that General Clinton was displeased that I had sailed away from the Carolinas. I am wondering if I should return there, transport this command back to Charleston. Not only would General Clinton find that pleasing, but it might be the only means I have of escaping him."

"Sir, surely there is good work for us to do here."

"Where? Virginia? New York? Philadelphia? I am to maneuver this army by whim. We are without strategy, without the guiding hand of a commander who sees beyond his own convenience."

O'Hara shifted in his chair again.

"Sir, we must still obey our orders."

"Without fail, General. Without fail."

SIMCOE'S RANGERS HAD ALREADY BOARDED ONE TRANSPORT SHIP, while onshore, Leslie was supervising the loading of the horses. Along the crude wharf, men were moving into line, troops who stared at the ships with utter despair. It had not been so long ago that they endured the journey southward, had marched and fought and marched again, and now, would embark on the misery of yet another sea voyage. Rumors had already infected them, talk of a massive French armada, somewhere *out there*, poised to swarm over this small fleet. They knew little of the French, just the stories told by their fathers, who described them as a savage enemy, uncivilized men who would throw a murderous broadside into a transport ship and dance in the rigging while the helpless soldiers screamed for mercy.

Leslie had already heard the ugly rumble of panic, had quietly armed the marines, spreading them around the perimeter of the wharf. Leslie had chosen Simcoe's men to board first with good purpose. The horsemen would be certain to show their bravado, adventurers setting the fearless example for the foot soldiers who watched them. The first infantry regiments were lining up now close to the boarding plank, and Leslie heard his name, turned to see a rider coming hard, a dispatch in the man's hand. He read it with openmouthed amazement, then motioned to his aide, said, "Stop them. Have the Rangers disembark, return to the wharf. Orders of General Cornwallis. It seems General Clinton has changed his mind."

THE NEW ORDERS WERE SPECIFIC, AND CARRIED THE ENDORSEMENT of the navy. Cornwallis' troops would remain in Virginia after all, would focus on the construction of the seaport. The naval commander was, once again, Thomas Graves, replacing Marriot Arbuthnot, who had returned to England in some dispute over rank. Clinton's orders to Cornwallis bore the signature of Admiral Graves, the man familiar with that part of the coast of Virginia. Though the particular location of the base was suggested as Old Point Comfort, centered on the eastern end of the Virginia peninsula, the final decision would be left to Cornwallis and his engineers.

SIR, WITH ALL RESPECT TO YOUR ORDERS, I MUST REPORT THAT IT will not be suitable."

The man was nervous, and Cornwallis said, "Lieutenant Sutherland, you may stand at ease. I will not strike you." Sutherland seemed to jump at his words, was more stiff now than before. "My word, Lieutenant, do I inspire this much fear in all my officers?"

"I don't know, sir. I mean . . . by no means, sir. My apologies. I was concerned that the general would find my report most distressing."

"I find a great many things distressing, Lieutenant. Engineering reports are not among them. If Old Point Comfort is unsuitable, then you will find another location. My orders are to locate a suitable port, and construct a deepwater base."

"Yes, sir, I understand. That place is not Old Point Comfort. There is no suitable material available for fill, and there is no protection for shipping from the shelter of a natural harbor. I have made some notes, if I may, sir."

"By all means, Lieutenant."

Sutherland scanned his paper.

"There is no existing port in this part of Virginia which offers every advantage. I have considered the sites available to us, sir, and examined the ground. There are details on this map . . . here, sir, with your permission."

Sutherland placed the paper on Cornwallis' desk, turned it toward him, and Cornwallis saw the precise lines, the writing of a trained engineer, numbers and formulas.

"What am I looking at, Lieutenant?"

"The location I believe is best suited, sir. With your permission, we can begin work immediately." The young man leaned forward, put his finger on the paper, said, "Here, sir. Yorktown."

AUGUST 30, 1781

Clinton's orders continued to arrive, but there was less contradiction, and more of a tone of caution to Cornwallis that soon,
any part of the British command might be under threat of attack.
Clinton and Admiral Graves seemed to accept the choice of
Yorktown as a base of naval operation, and Cornwallis ordered
the construction of wharves, fortifications, and shore batteries.

Clinton's orders were specific in another way as well, that
Cornwallis was not to commence any new offensive in Virginia.
Though Lafayette's rebels sat astride the peninsula just beyond
his reach, Cornwallis was under direct orders to place his army
into a defensive posture. As the engineers focused their labors
on constructing the seaport, Cornwallis had no choice but to fortify the town against land assault as well. While Sutherland
worked the waterfront, O'Hara supervised the digging of fortifications in a wide perimeter around the town. Cornwallis could
find only one ray of optimism through the gloom of his assignment. If Lafayette made any attempt to assault him there, the
rebels would meet with disaster.

By the third week of August, the laborers and soldiers were
toiling in a scorching sun, molding Yorktown into a formidable
British port. As he paced the waterfront, he appreciated the engineer's eye, could see the aspects of Yorktown that might be a disadvantage for a seaport. The York River was wide, could be
passed easily by ships under sail. But across from Yorktown the
river was squeezed like an hourglass by the intrusion of a point
of land, Gloucester Point. The only way effectively to block the
river to ship traffic was by placing an outpost on the other side,
separating them from the protection of the main army. It was
dangerous, and those troops would have to be strong enough to
withstand an assault on their own. Cornwallis felt he had no
choice. He ordered batteries to be placed at Gloucester Point as
well. Once that work was completed no one could pass up the
York River without taking serious damage from British cannon.

He waited each day for some new bit of torment from Clinton.
He fully expected that the work around Yorktown would suddenly be stopped, some outrageous orders suddenly calling for
another mad scramble to New York. There was still fear of the
French warships, intelligence received from the West Indies that
a large fleet under de Grasse had been making ready to sail

northward. The British command in the islands discounted the
reports, could not fathom that de Grasse would weaken the
French forces so severely. But Clinton and Graves accepted the
strong possibility that the intelligence was accurate, both men
certain that New York was the intended target. Graves had finally
ordered the British ships into action, and from the West Indies,
Samuel Hood had sailed northward with a fleet of fourteen warships. Cornwallis had seen Hood's flagship, a cluster of sails
suddenly appearing out beyond the mouth of the wide river. But
the British fleet was fast on their way to New York, and Hood did
not stop at Yorktown. His visit was only a quick inspection, making sure there was no immediate threat to Cornwallis' port.

Cornwallis walked the waterfront, ignoring the work of the
engineers, felt the chains from Clinton's orders wrapped tightly
around him. Already he was suffering from boredom, chafing at
the quiet atmosphere of a new headquarters, another fine mansion made ready just for him.

He had been forced to send Leslie back to the Carolinas, a
sudden need to replace Francis Rawdon. Rawdon had endured a
miserably hot summer facing the ongoing threat of assault by
Greene's rebels, and the brutal climate had finally destroyed the
man's health. Cornwallis had no choice but to approve Rawdon's
return to England. He moved O'Hara into Leslie's position, confident that O'Hara was the one officer in his command who
would not require Cornwallis to peer over his shoulder. He was
also the one man Cornwallis felt comfortable with pouring out
his vitriol against Henry Clinton.

"Sir, the wharf is nearly complete. Fine work, those chaps."

O'Hara's words slipped past him, and Cornwallis said, "What's
that? What chaps?"

"Sir, the wharf. The engineers have done a fine job, I'd say."

"Fine job."

They continued their walk, and Cornwallis could feel O'Hara
glancing at him, stopped now, said, "Am I causing you some discomfort again, General?"

O'Hara seemed to flinch, said, "Oh, my, no. I'm sorry, sir. I
am concerned, that's all. Perhaps my accompanying you was a
bad idea. You would prefer to be alone, it seems."

Cornwallis stared out toward the open water, said, "*We* are
alone, General. We are firmly and completely in a prison of our
own making. Not even Admiral Hood would risk landing here,

to suffer the monotony of this swamp. General Clinton might as well order us into winter quarters. It would hardly matter that in this damnable place, winter is defined by a brief lack of mosquitoes." He continued to walk. "I have never been one to ignore my enemies, General. Now, I have been ordered to do precisely that. That . . . *boy* is out there with his band of rebels, wondering why I do not pursue him. I'm quite certain *General* Lafayette felt it was bloody good sport. Now, we can do nothing until General Clinton and the navy sort out their fears and find some reliable piece of information about our enemies. In the meantime, we must endure a holiday in Yorktown."

He realized O'Hara was not beside him, and he turned, saw the man staring out toward the open water, the mouth of the river.

"Sir. It seems we are not so alone after all. It appears Admiral Hood has returned."

O'Hara retrieved a small pair of field glasses from his coat, raised them, said, "Yes, his entire fleet, I would say. I can see a number of sails. He must have decided to make port here, after all, inspect our good work, as it were."

He handed the glasses to Cornwallis, who focused, stared out, could see small clusters of white clouds spread along the horizon. Behind him, he heard excited shouts from the lookout posts, men watching as he watched, the fat white sails growing closer, driven by a hard stiff breeze. O'Hara continued to talk, a babble of enthusiasm for the sudden security of the naval force, livening the town, the certain competition between soldier and sailor, games, perhaps, to relieve the boredom. Cornwallis continued to stare for a long moment, O'Hara's words flowing past him.

"Is that not a capital idea, sir? I'm certain Admiral Hood would agree. Athletics, perhaps, pass the time with the fine art of competition. Army versus navy. Could give the men quite a boost, sir."

Cornwallis lowered the glasses now, saw a young sergeant approaching, the man pointing out toward the fleet.

"Sir, beggin' your pardon. The lookouts report, sir. The ships . . ."

"I know, Sergeant." He raised the glasses again, could see bits of color now, stared for a long quiet moment. He felt a cold mass growing in his stomach, and his hand shook, clouding his vision. He lowered the glasses again, said, "General O'Hara, we should postpone your festivities for the moment. That fleet . . . is French."

55. LAFAYETTE

THEY HAD SPENT MOST OF THE SUMMER IN A RAPID SCRAMBLE FOR survival. Instead of cursing Lafayette for their constant state of motion, the men seemed to understand that the young Frenchman was in fact showing exceptional skill at maneuvering his army. The British had spent long weeks on marches that accomplished nothing, and with little to show for their exhaustive efforts, Cornwallis finally conceded the futility of his mission and withdrew his army down the peninsula toward Williamsburg. Lafayette had followed, fully expecting some sudden turnabout, Cornwallis trying to catch him unaware. It was clear that the British had the strength, and if Cornwallis wanted to drive his troops all the way to Maryland, there was little Lafayette could do to stop him. But as they backed away from him, Lafayette knew to press forward, and when the opportunity had presented itself, he turned aggressor. He had kept as close to Cornwallis as he dared, and if the sight of enemy campfires made his men especially prone to panic, it also offered Lafayette the opportunity to strike quickly. With Anthony Wayne now in his camp, Lafayette knew that the Pennsylvanian the men now called Mad Anthony could be the perfect officer for a rapid assault.

The place was called Green Spring, a swampy lowland near Williamsburg, along the north side of the James River. The scouts had brought word that Cornwallis was pulling away from his base at Williamsburg, had gathered boats for a crossing of the James. Lafayette assumed that the British were intending to gather and resupply at their base at Portsmouth. Wayne was given the command of a force of five hundred men, who would slip rapidly toward the crossing, and with good fortune might time their assault to catch Cornwallis vulnerable, with the British spread across both sides of the river. Wayne had advanced with his usual speed, and seemed ready to make a decisive blow at what seemed to be the British rear guard. But Cornwallis had learned of his approach, had hidden the main body of the British army behind Wayne's intended target. The result was a trap, a hot fight that Wayne barely escaped. Though he was nearly engulfed by the entire British army, Wayne continued to press his attack, surprising his own men as well as the British who faced him. Lafayette quickly pushed forward reinforcements, and arrived on the field barely in time to pull Wayne back from a lopsided engagement that could have wiped out a sizable portion of Lafayette's command. It was a valuable lesson. Though Wayne was possibly the most capable field commander he had, "Mad Anthony" had not gotten his nickname by accident.

For Cornwallis, Green Spring had been an opportunity lost. The British had simply run out of daylight, and by the next morning, Lafayette had pulled his army together into a strong defensive position. The British resumed their crossing of the James, and made no further attempts to engage Lafayette again. Though Green Spring had been a seriously close call, Lafayette had been suspicious of Cornwallis' retreat, had not believed the British would simply pull away from him without attempting another major assault. As Cornwallis continued to shift his strength across the peninsula, Lafayette assumed he was still gathering his forces, forming some new plan to sweep the continentals out of their path. Instead, there had been another surprise. The British had begun to dig themselves into Yorktown. Lafayette had eased his army forward, closer still to his suddenly immobile enemy. And then, the French fleet arrived.

HE HAD BEEN INVITED TO JOIN DE GRASSE ON HIS FLAGSHIP, SURprised that a senior admiral would even acknowledge his authority. The memories of Rochambeau were still sore in his mind. Rochambeau had made it plain that the senior French commanders had little respect for Lafayette's rank in the American army, as though he was still some pretender, seeking adventure and a lofty reputation. It was little satisfaction to Lafayette that most of the strutting martinets who had done so much to dazzle the congress were gone. Some had returned quietly to France, some had vanished westward, to find some savage adventure on the Indian frontier.

The French fleet had blocked the capes at the mouth of the

Chesapeake, and effectively sealed the York River from any traffic. But de Grasse had not sought any engagement with the British onshore, and the few British frigates anchored at Yorktown wisely made no attempt to engage a fleet that was vastly superior.

Lafayette did not know de Grasse beyond the man's extraordinary reputation for naval command, and his legendary temper. De Grasse had sent his flatboat north of the British outpost at Gloucester, a dangerous landing given the proximity of the British lookouts. But the British had made no efforts to expand beyond their shore batteries, and Lafayette had already placed a body of militia on that side of the York River, to keep close watch on the British fortification. As de Grasse's boat rowed him close to the magnificent flagship, Lafayette began to feel his youth, a very nervous young man about to stand before a mighty father. He had not met the man, and already, he was intimidated by him.

He was helped up the ladder, stood on the deck of the massive warship, the *Ville de Paris*. The crew had come to full attention, and officers were falling into line. He saw an officer bound up from the main hatchway, stand stiffly aside, and now another man emerged, older, moving slowly, a regal rhythm to his steps. The older man stepped up onto the deck, and Lafayette stared wide-eyed, the man towering over him, taller even than Washington. He was near sixty, looked at Lafayette with deep-set, heavy eyes, seemed to examine him with a quick appraisal. Lafayette waited, felt even more of a child now than before, his dread in full blossom. De Grasse said, "Welcome, General Lafayette. I am Admiral François, Count de Grasse. I am at your service."

THE GOBLETS WERE SILVER, THE WINE A DEEP RED, FAR SUPERIOR than anything Lafayette had enjoyed in his own camp. He examined the artifacts that adorned the office, an extraordinary collection of prizes and decorations. De Grasse allowed him a moment to be suitably impressed, then said, "I have sent word to General Washington and General Rochambeau that I can remain here but a short time, not more than a few weeks. I have a pressing need to return to the islands. Do you anticipate we may complete our campaign here in good time?"

"Sir, that is a question best put to the commanding general. I cannot say precisely what our campaign should involve."

"I assume, General, that you intend to destroy the army of General Cornwallis."

It was a concept Lafayette had never truly considered.

"Yes, sir, that would be an exceptionally fine plan. My mission has thus far been to obstruct the enemy's movements and seek some opportunity to annoy him."

De Grasse seemed amused, a slight smile, said, "General Lafayette, I have sailed here with a force of thirty-four of His Majesty's finest warships. The ship on which you now sit carries one hundred guns, and is the most powerful warship on this earth. I don't wish to dispute your orders, but I imagine General Washington intends that this fleet do more than . . . *annoy* the enemy. Perhaps your situation would be improved by the addition of my particular cargo."

Lafayette had barely touched the silver goblet, watched as de Grasse sipped his wine. The reception from de Grasse was still overwhelming him, and he glanced at the attendant, a junior officer standing stiffly to one side, a man older than he was. The man caught the look, said in a whisper, "Yes, General? Anything you wish?"

Lafayette shook his head. "Oh . . . no, thank you."

He looked at de Grasse, the man's words settling into his mind.

"Sir? Cargo?"

"General, I have transported something over three thousand infantry, who, I am quite certain, would prefer making camp on land than spending one more day in the comfort of my ships. Might you have some good use for them?"

"Three thousand troops? You would offer them to . . . my command?"

"I am told that General Washington places his highest confidence in you. Is there any reason why I should not do the same?"

"Thank you, sir. I am honored by your respect, by all you have offered me. Yes, Admiral, your troops can be put to considerable effect."

SEPTEMBER 5, 1781

The French troops came ashore on the island of Jamestown, led by the Marquis de Saint-Simon. Saint-Simon was another of the capable French commanders who, like Lafayette, had received some attention in the military on the strength of his aristocratic family. Surprisingly, he showed Lafayette the same courtesies as de Grasse, conceded immediately that this was, after all, Lafayette's command.

Lafayette understood that he had the troops now to do what he had feared before, place a barrier close to Yorktown that had enough strength actually to discourage the British from sweeping him aside. As Saint-Simon completed his landing, Lafayette united his ragged army with the fresh French troops. They pushed forward, Lafayette anticipating that Cornwallis would strike at any time. But the British remained behind their fortifications. Within two days, the combined French-American force had established a new line of defense at Williamsburg, a day's march from Yorktown.

With the lines secure, de Grasse continued to consult Lafayette. Though no significant move could be made without orders from Washington, Lafayette received a message that the commanding general was on the march, somewhere in the area of Philadelphia. But there would be no peaceful wait. De Grasse sent word: He was raising his anchors and moving out to sea. The British had finally responded to de Grasse's presence, and a fleet had sailed out of New York under Graves and Hood. The sails had been sighted, and de Grasse would have to move out far from shore to allow his ships maneuvering room for what could certainly be a critical battle.

Lafayette waited with his entire command, focused on the vague thunder that rolled in a steady rumble from the open sea. He knew Cornwallis was waiting as well, listening as he was, both men aware that the great naval battle would not only decide who would control the Virginia peninsula, but who would control the Chesapeake as well. Lafayette was surprised that the fight seemed only to last a few short hours, and as the sun dropped behind him, he caught a glimpse of a sail, then more, ships moving close to the mouth of the York River, one fast packet moving up the James. The ship reached Williamsburg the next morning with a message from de Grasse. The fight had been indecisive, no great advantage for either side. But the British had absorbed the brunt of the damage, and Graves had withdrawn his fleet, seemed to be withdrawing to his base in New York. The

French fleet would resume their former position inside the Chesapeake Bay. Cornwallis was bottled up again.

SEPTEMBER 14, 1781

Lafayette stared through field glasses at a dozen horsemen, the familiar coats of the British cavalry. They had come every morning, close enough to scout his lines, not so close as to draw fire from the pickets. In just a few days it had become a routine, Lafayette and Wayne riding out, waiting for the British horsemen to appear. Wayne was beside him, glassed the men who glassed him back.

"They keep this up, we should lay an ambush. If this is a game, it has become tiresome."

Lafayette saw the British horsemen turn away, disappear into a row of trees, as they had done each day.

"I'm concerned it is not a game. The enemy has one avenue left to him. We are standing upon it."

Wayne lowered his glasses.

"You think he'll try it? It would be foolish. We'd cut him up bad."

"Perhaps. If he came in one tight formation, drove into one flank or the other, I'm not sure we could stop him. Not completely."

"Then let him come, sir. We're ready, that's for certain. Your French boys over there would probably like a shot at those lobsterbacks too."

Lafayette turned his horse.

"I should see General Saint-Simon. Caution him to guard his flanks. The British might even attempt some movement by night. Surprise us."

Wayne moved beside him.

"Why? General, I don't understand your concern. It would be a slaughter for the British to try to bust through here."

Lafayette could not escape the nagging discomfort inside him. He had not enjoyed a meal for several days, his own body protesting every bite. He was suffering his breakfast, some strange pudding of cornmeal, sweetened with molasses, now a brick in his gut. He looked at Wayne, saw a strange smile, and

Wayne said, "Sir, all they can do is exactly what we want them to do. We're ready for them."

"General, if they move against us here, it is because they have no other alternative. Cornwallis certainly knows he is trapped. Any move he makes now is likely born of desperation. That makes him very dangerous. If the British are faced with the choice of surrender or fight, I am not so certain that they will choose surrender. Our strength is nearly equal, yet we still employ a large number of militia. He has only his regulars, and they will fight like animals to escape."

"No animal can stand up to a musket, sir. With all respects. Are you telling me you're afraid of a confrontation? What do you think we should do, pull back?"

"Certainly not, General. I am only concerned that we not allow ourselves to feel . . . relaxed. We are in a stalemate here. Until General Washington arrives, we are not strong enough to change that."

HE HAD SPENT THE REST OF THE DAY LEADING HIS SMALL STAFF ON a nervous ride from outpost to outpost, from picket lines to the main fortifications. He knew Wayne thought him overly cautious, the outspoken Pennsylvanian probably joking about him behind his back. The French troops were as nonchalant as Wayne, Saint-Simon holding them at their posts with mild impatience, wondering if their young commander truly had the backbone for a fight. It added to his nervousness that the officers he now commanded didn't seem to understand that they had a beast in a cage, and that the cage could be weaker than they believed. He yearned for spies, the kind of men Washington had in New York. He had marveled at their astounding courage and ingenuity, men who could learn the most secret of orders, could impart such amazing misinformation that had fooled the British command, possibly saving Washington's army. No, I must only sit here and watch their cavalry scouts. And if I am fortunate, Cornwallis does not have *his* spies. For if he does, then he will know my fears, he will find our weakness. Surely he must try to escape us, must break out of this cage. There is only one route, and it must pass through here. If he breaks past us, even part of his army, he can march into North Carolina again. And I will have failed General Washington.

It was nearly dark, Williamsburg a distant scattering of candle-light. He could smell the smoke of the campfires, the empty rumble in his stomach warning him of the inevitability of an-other miserable meal. He turned the horse, climbed a hill, moved into a wide road. The sun was low in the far treetops, the ground a soft gray haze. The two aides were close behind him, the squad of guards behind them. There had been no protest from his men, who seemed not to care if he led them over every inch of his lines. He glanced back, said, "Time to eat, gentlemen. You would certainly be hungry."

There were low mumbles of approval, and he nudged the horse, saw a flicker of light coming toward him from the town. The guards were already responding, and they moved up past him, intercepted the hard ride of a horseman, a man with a lantern. The man halted his horse, his light reflecting on the faces of the guards, who surrounded him. It was a civilian, and the man said, "General Lafayette! You should come quickly! By all means!" The man turned, and the guards let him pass. He moved quickly, his horse galloping back toward the town. Lafa-yette felt annoyed, said, "I suppose it is important. I do not so much enjoy mysteries. If you gentlemen do not mind, we will wait a moment for supper."

He spurred the horse, could still see the man out in front of him, the horse carrying the man around a corner, disappearing past a small house. Lafayette followed him into the town, moved his horse into the wide hard street, saw more lanterns, a crowd of people surrounding a cluster of men on horseback. He pushed the horse forward, curious now, and the faces began to turn toward him, more people emerging from the houses, lining the street. He could see the horsemen clearly now, the uniforms, saw the big man now moving out in front, walking the horse toward him. Lafayette reined the horse, felt a hard lump in his throat.

"Good evening, Mr. Lafayette."

The fear, all the nervous uncertainty was gone now. Washing-ton had arrived.

56. WASHINGTON

THE ARMY HAD MARCHED TWO HUNDRED MILES IN FIFTEEN DAYS.
After their brief parade through Philadelphia, Washington had
led them to the Head of Elk, the uppermost reaches of the Chesapeake Bay, where French transports had boarded the men and
ferried them the rest of the way to the James River.

The route of his surprise march had angered many of his
troops, New Yorkers in particular, who had no desire either to
see Virginia or to fight there. But Robert Morris had come to his
rescue, had negotiated an agreement with Rochambeau. The
French provided hard specie so that Washington's entire army
could receive back pay. As they marched out of Philadelphia
with silver in their pockets, the mood of the men was signifi-
cantly improved. The morale was heightened further by rumors
that their mission to Virginia was aimed specifically at the capture of Cornwallis himself.

Washington led them out of Williamsburg through a soft
green countryside that he had known as a child. But the beauty
of the land, low rolling hills, patches of deep woods, had been
changed by the war, farms abandoned, fields unattended. This
time of year, the harvest would be near, and the land would be
ripe with the bounty that made Virginia such a marvelous place
for a young boy. But now, the wide road carried them through
desolation and destruction, some of the houses reduced to burnt
timbers. It was the result of the raids, the same horror he had
seen in New Jersey. There it was the brutality of the Hessians
but this had been done by Englishmen, Tarleton probably, and
the sights sickened him. There was always sadness for the families, the innocent who must suffer this devastation, but he was
sickened as well by the thought of the soldiers with their axes

and pikes and torches, asking himself what kind of civilized men could do this.

The horse carried him past a house that had been battered and broken, no glass in the windows, the doors ripped away, walls punched through. Every piece of furniture was smashed and scattered, every piece of clothing ripped, every mirror shattered. It was all the pieces of one family's life cast about the yard with calculated design. He stopped the horse, stared for a long moment, the house familiar, some place he had visited a long time ago. The army continued its march behind him, men calling out to him, reading his emotions.

"We'll make them pay, sir!"

"We'll take it to them, sir!"

He stared at the destruction for a long moment, felt Tilghman beside him, said, "There is nothing of war in this, nothing of strategy and tactics. This is no more than barbarism, inflicting permanent scars on the innocent. It is the dying gasp of an oppressor, brutality handed out by an army who knows its own defeat hangs above. There is no other reason for it, no reason to torment people who you claim to embrace."

Tilghman said nothing, and Washington jerked the reins, moved back up into the road. He had not often felt this kind of rage, the pure hatred for the British soldiers. This kind of savagery does not come merely by the order of a commander. This was done by a mob, hateful men who have lost their honor. Whether it was Tarleton or Simcoe, or nothing more than a band of stragglers, these men do not have the right to wage such a war. It is time to bring this to an end.

He marched beside the column of continentals, the French following behind. His command now included better than sixteen thousand men fit for duty, with two thousand more in support. It was the largest body of men he had led in any march, the greatest strength ever placed into his hands. As they drew closer to Yorktown, that strength filled him, energized his mind and his heart, his anger focusing on the one simple mission that lay before them.

HE HAD EXPECTED SOME OBSTACLES TO THE ADVANCE, SOME ATtempt by Cornwallis to slow the march by harassing the flanks, dragoons perhaps, some quick strike. But the British had stayed entirely inside their own defenses. His column was within two miles of Yorktown, and he could see the great spread of defenses, a hard line dug into the sandy ground, a wide arc that enclosed the town. The landscape in front of the British lines had been wiped clean of trees and underbrush, would surely be covered by a mass of artillery. He had expected this would be a serious fight, a bloody awful confrontation. From all he could see now, Cornwallis was well prepared to give him one.

He arranged the army in a wide line to conform to the British defenses. The French were placed to the left, the Americans on the right. The ground closer to the town was cut by streams, a shallow ravine, swampy land that gave the British natural barriers for their defense. The British flanks seemed to end at the York River, and beyond, their frigates stood ready, guarding the waterfront with rows of heavy cannon that could enfilade any assault. Behind the British works, he could see the town, a few larger homes, smaller buildings, perched close to the river. As he glassed the entire scene, it was strangely peaceful, a light salty breeze drifting through wisps of grass and thin brush, leaves in the trees above him whispering with the soft voice of autumn.

For so long, he had depended on the rapid march, the desperation of the quick escape, an army who consumed so much of its energy fighting just to survive. But now the enemy was right in front of him, outnumbered and outgunned, and all the desperation was finally on the other side. From the first days in command at Boston he had never studied his enemy from such a superior position, had never felt this astounding sense of calm. He tried to imagine the mind of Cornwallis, was certain the man understood the crisis in front of him. The British had only two alternatives, escape by water, up the York River perhaps, moving deeper into Virginia, or a direct assault straight at Washington's army. Washington knew his own mission was clear. He must prevent either from happening.

He knew they were looking to him, that Rochambeau had made quite clear to his own officers who was in command. In his own line, the principal divisions were commanded by Lafayette, von Steuben, and Ben Lincoln, who had been exchanged for British prisoners captured at Saratoga. The division commanders were served by veteran brigadiers, Wayne and Gist, Dayton and Muhlenberg and Hazen. The militia were commanded by Thomas Nelson, the new governor of Virginia, who had only recently replaced Thomas Jefferson.

The first duty would be the construction of their own entrenchments. As the tools were issued, and the engineers went about their work, Washington began to think of the days ahead. He began to focus less on Cornwallis' puzzle and more on his own. He had arrived at Yorktown expecting to launch an assault, confront the British the same way they had tried so often to confront him. But with the British so well prepared, the results could be as disastrous for his army as it had been for Gage at Breed's Hill, or for Cornwallis himself at Guilford. Washington realized now he had another alternative, a siege, to strangle the enemy in a slowly tightening noose. The decision was difficult. He did not want to risk the slaughter of his men, and would not order Rochambeau to charge such a strongly fortified position without the man's complete agreement that it was the best course. A siege required time, and had to be executed with precise care. That strategy had one distinct disadvantage for him. Washington had no idea how to mount a siege.

IT IS A MATHEMATICAL CALCULATION, GENERAL. YOU MEASURE your own strength against that of the enemy. You measure your ability to supply your troops against his ability *not* to. How long can he survive? If he cannot feed his men, he must capitulate."

Washington felt foolish enduring the lecture from Rochambeau, but it was not the Frenchman's fault. He had admitted to the French command that the only man in his army who had any experience in siege warfare was von Steuben. The Prussian's skills had already been put to use, supervising the disposition of Washington's lines, and the construction of the first entrenchments. If pressure was to be applied to the British position, it was essential that the artillery be moved close enough to provide a steady barrage that would both overpower and terrorize the enemy defenses. Washington was delighted to learn that Rochambeau and many of his officers had engaged in numerous sieges. The French seemed delighted that Washington requested their advice.

"Parallel trenches, General. The ability to move your troops safely forward, to a position of advantage. If executed properly, the talent of your remarkable riflemen could be put to considerable use."

Washington glanced at von Steuben, who nodded to him slowly.

"Yes, General. I agree completely."

Washington looked at Rochambeau, said, "General, what of time? Admiral de Grasse has insisted he must sail by the middle of October. Can we accomplish our goals by that time?"

Rochambeau laughed.

"General, I will speak to Admiral de Grasse. With your permission, of course. I believe he can be persuaded to remain in place a while longer. The admiral appreciates that the success of this operation will be of benefit to *him* as well as to his king. I have discovered that naval officers must often be reminded that there is a world beyond the sea. As long as the British fleet does not arrive in sufficient force to compel the admiral to leave, we will have his support. General Cornwallis will not escape us by water."

"I am concerned, still, about the river."

It was something of a sore point to Washington, his repeated requests for de Grasse to storm past the British batteries at Yorktown and place enough power upstream to prevent the British from using that escape route. But de Grasse could not be persuaded, believed the batteries too dangerous to risk losing one or more of his ships. Rochambeau seemed to know of Washington's concerns, said, "General, we will press forward with all speed. Once our artillery has advanced within range of the town, the enemy will be unable to load any kind of transports at their wharves without great hazard." He looked at von Steuben. "If your troops will make good use of the shovel, the enemy's fate is sealed."

SEPTEMBER 30, 1781

They spent the long hours of the night in rapid construction of their entrenchments, men working in shifts, battling the insects and the sudden thunderstorms as they cut their way through the sandy ground. As the men worked, the artillery from the British lines peppered the night air with scattered blasts. There was little damage and almost no casualties, the gunners throwing out their shells toward targets hidden by the darkness and the earth they piled in front of them. When the sun came up, Washington had expected more firing from the British, had made it a priority to protect his workmen by ordering von Steuben to plan a careful routine to their movements. As the dawn spilled slowly onto the barren ground in front of them, they faced only silence, no activity in the British works. Gradually, curious men began to peer up, scanning the earthworks across from them for the telltale signs of movement, the usual glimpse of red, the flash and smoke of the cannon. As the sun rose higher Washington's men could see clearly that something had changed. They began to slip out from the entrenchments, moving carefully forward. Washington moved to his observation point, glassed them as they slipped out into the open ground. Their officers were as nervous as he was, and close in front of him, riflemen stood poised to cover his men should they need a rapid retreat. The men moved up close to the British works, and Washington watched them with a hard pounding in his chest as they climbed through the cut trees and pointed sticks, up and over, disappearing into the silent trenches. Then he saw their celebration, hands up high, hats tossed in the air. It was a stunning surprise. The British had completely abandoned their outer works. Cornwallis had pulled his men back to their defensive entrenchments closer to the town, a much more compact line.

The tactic of a full hard assault against the British lines was still in his mind, the temptation to capture this magnificent victory in one powerful thrust. But a frontal assault now would have to concentrate in a narrow area, into a much greater mass of power. A slaughter would be a certainty. If Washington had any doubts about conducting a siege, he understood now that Cornwallis had made his decision for him.

OCTOBER 6, 1781

For several days, the engineers had given instructions, and a thousand men had spread out behind the lines into the woods, cutting and gathering great masses of sticks and cut limbs, bundling the timber into stout bales. It was the same kind of work Washington had seen at Boston, the bundles used to assemble a wall of fortifications. At Dorchester Heights, the work had been done in one night, and when the British woke, Boston was suddenly under the guns of Washington's army. The enemy then had been William Howe, and Howe had responded by abandoning the city. Now, the enemy was a different kind of commander, a man who was pinned into a desperate hole and would certainly seek some vulnerability, some means to strike out at his enemy. If the parallel trench was to be dug and fortified, it would have to be accomplished with the same efficiency that Washington had seen at Dorchester Heights. They would have to complete the task in absolute quiet, in only one night.

Nearly four thousand men took part in the work, half serving only as guards to protect the laborers in the event the British launched an assault. They were blessed by a light rain, which blanketed them from moonlight and muffled any sounds. The engineers worked the men for eight hours, long shifts of the fittest men armed only with shovels. As each new section of trench was dug, the bundles of sticks were carried forward, placed up in front of the workmen. All through the night, British cannon barked out across the open ground, but with no good aim, no sign that the British had any notion of the work that progressed well within the range of their guns. When the sun rose, it was exactly as Washington remembered on Dorchester Heights, stunned British lookouts staring in amazement at the fortified works so close to their defenses. The work could continue by day now, the trenches protected from British fire by the high mounds of sand and sticks. For three days they labored still, the trenches widening into strong fortified lines, gun pits constructed, the cannon brought forward in complete cover. They pushed on, used the nights to move closer yet, and each morning the lines had been dug farther forward, forming a second parallel. When the sun rose, Washington heard the enthusiasm of the marksmen, already moving into place, carving out niches for their long rifles. He stood beside them, marveled at the work of the laborers, shovels flying around him still, more cannon rolling forward. He glassed the British as the marksmen studied the range, knew what they knew. A good marksman could now find his targets. The British defenses were only three hundred yards away.

OCTOBER 9, 1781

The invitation had come from Knox, the rotund man's cannons nearly all in position. Washington never gave thought to this sort of ceremony, but Knox had insisted. He stood now with the gun crew, the men still tending to their gun, one man wiping the barrel with a dirty cloth. Knox said, "Prepare to fire!"

The gun was rolled back, the barrel swabbed by a man with a ramrod, another man stepping forward, stuffing a thick cloth sack into the barrel. The ramrod went in again, pushing the sack deep, and now Knox said, "Sir, should you wish to select the particular ball?"

"Mr. Knox, you are far more expert in this sort of thing. I would leave that to you."

"Very well, sir." Knox leaned forward, ran his hand over the mound of black iron, a dramatic pause. He pointed now. "This one."

The cannoneer lifted the ball, carried it to the front of the gun, placed it in the muzzle, the ramrod going in again. Now the gun was rolled forward, and Knox made a show of sighting down the barrel.

"We have chosen that house, there, the white roof."

He took a small fire stick from his gunner, handed it to Washington, said, "We are prepared if you are, sir. I would only suggest you stand . . . in this manner. The gun will recoil somewhat."

Washington had tried to keep a calm demeanor, allowing Knox to have his game. He had told himself it was good for the men, had not thought the moment would affect him so, his heart pounding, a slight quiver in his hand. He held the stick, followed Knox's instructions, blew on the glowing tip, a small flame now engulfing the stick. He glanced at Knox, could not help sharing the man's smile, braced himself for the sound, touched the stick to the fire hole. The cannon erupted in a massive roar, jolted back toward him, Washington jumping as well. The sound deadened his ears, and he stared out past the muzzle of the gun, tried to see, a vast cloud of smoke blinding him. To one side he heard a cheer, an officer, glassing out, the man shouting, "Hee! A hit! Knocked a hole in the house! Busted it all to bits!"

Washington could still not see the target, backed away from the gun, deafened, the crew doing their work again. Knox moved away with him, and the men were cheering him, a crowd of troops lining the trench. But their voices were drowned out by the sound of cannon erupting all down through the trench. He tried to hide the excitement, felt it still in his shaking hands, realized he still held the fire stick, handed it sheepishly to Knox, who said, "There you have it, sir! I'm honored you would consent."

The smoke began to fill the trench, hot choking sulfur, and Washington moved back farther, found clear air, took a long breath. He looked toward the front, the field out beyond the trench a vast sea of smoke, the guns firing in a steady pounding rhythm.

"The honor is mine, Mr. Knox."

He moved away, while behind him, a mass of artillery launched their deadly charges, a gathering of power like nothing he had ever experienced. The orders were clear, the guns would maintain their fire as long as they had targets in front of them, as long as the enemy continued to hold to their positions.

He returned to his headquarters, the tents back in the trees, close to Rochambeau. But along the way, something still rose in him, something very young, a boy's pure excitement. The siege of Yorktown had begun in earnest, and it was a moment he would never forget. He had fired the first shot.

57. CORNWALLIS

OCTOBER 10, 1781

THE FRENCH BATTERIES HAD FOUND THE RANGE, AND THE AIR above the town was streaked with smoke. The targets were the few ships, anchored close to the Yorktown wharf. The shells were burning as they flew, and when they punched through the hull of the closest warship, the decks exploded in flame. In minutes, the *Charon*, a forty-four-gun frigate, was fully ablaze. Those of her crew who could still save themselves had jumped overboard, some swimming to the shore, others swept under by the cascade of debris that rained upon the water.

He watched from the shore, from the opening in his tent. The sun had set, the fire still high, the *Charon* finally beginning to collapse upon herself. Along the bank of the river, men had gathered, staring silently, as he was, watching His Majesty's fine strong warship begin its slow disappearance to the waterline. The flames danced on the water, as though the river itself was burning, the hands of hell rising from below. He glanced behind him, up toward the town, could see the flames reflected on the houses, eerie skeletons of grand homes now smashed and broken by the steady barrage of shot and shell.

He could only stare as the flames did their last bit of work. The fire began to die, a large piece of the ship's bulkhead falling away, a muffled splash that spread a low wave toward the wharf. For a long moment, the flames settled down to a hard red glow, the last bit of the hull just above the surface. Soon the embers gave way to a rush of steam, the hull pierced by her own decay, the final glow extinguished by the water. And just as quickly, the darkness of the river was unbroken.

He glanced up toward the town again, was suddenly aware of the silence, a pause in the artillery barrage. But the moment passed quickly, the air ripped again by the sharp whines, a hard splash close to the wharf, more sounds now, the sky reddened by sharp bursts. He backed into the tent, stumbled to find a chair, sat slowly, thought, So, the rebels enjoyed their spectacle. Their gunners stopped long enough to watch the ship burn. It must have been . . . a bloody delight.

HE HAD MOVED OUT OF THE TOWN ITSELF, AWAY FROM THE LARGE mansion that had been his headquarters. It was too close to his defenses, too obvious a target, had already absorbed a horrific assault, walls punched and broken. He had ordered a tent pitched right on the edge of the river itself, protected by a high embankment. The bank was dug out by the flow of the river, years of erosion carving out caves and pits in the soft earth. It provided shelter for the civilians, who had once thought themselves safe in the town, who could never have foreseen such terrifying destruction. His army had no such luxury, the men out on the main defensive line digging themselves down into whatever shelter they could manage. There was no safe place, no protection, and the rebel gunners, now so well reinforced by their French counterparts, had thrown a relentless and unceasing barrage into every part of the British defenses.

The carnage continued into the night, the darkness no obstacle to the rebels. The British gunners could only respond periodically, the sheer number of rebel shells so overwhelming. And worse, Cornwallis knew, his gunners were running out of ammunition.

OCTOBER 14, 1781

He heard the musket fire begin, was already moving forward before the aide could reach him. In the darkness there was no fear, and he stood tall, climbed up to the top of the mound of packed dirt. Barely two hundred yards away, he could see the flashes, could hear the shouts, screams, both of his redoubts engulfed by a nearly invisible assault. The pops of the muskets stirred in his chest, and a new sound reached him, metallic, a strange chattering of . . . bayonets. He closed his eyes, lowered his head. They are inside. He looked again, nothing to see but darkness. We were strong, he thought. But if they would come at all, they would come in strength. He saw another burst of fire, a short row of muskets from high on the wall, then a brief quiet moment, broken by the sharp voices of men. He knew the sound, the hard shouts of the victors, the harsh gathering of prisoners.

Beside him, men were staring out still, unaware he was there, some filling the silence with a hopeless cheer for their own.

"Push 'em back, lads!"

"Bayonets! Use the bayonets!"

He stepped down off the dirt wall, unable to see anything in the darkness, stood still for a moment, the cheers around him growing quiet. Out in the redoubts, a new cheer went up, and along the dirt wall close to him, the men began to talk, low voices, the murmur of shock. He refused to hear it, felt his way slowly back, moved into the streets, back to his tent by the river.

ON THE MAPS, THEY WERE LABELED REDOUBTS #9 AND #10, TWO large circular fortifications. They were strong, heavily protected by a wide dry ditch, each filled with cut trees and sharpened sticks. The redoubts were the hard anchor for the left flank of Cornwallis' defense, were the only barriers preventing the rebels from completing their parallel trench all the way to the river. The assaults on the redoubts had been a masterwork of coordination and surprise, two groups of assailants, one rebel, and one French. No matter the troop strength he had placed in each, a well-trained and well-equipped body of regulars, the enemy had used all its advantages. Now the redoubts would be absorbed into the rebel lines, the last link in the chain that held Cornwallis tightly entrapped.

From the first withdrawal into Yorktown, he had believed it

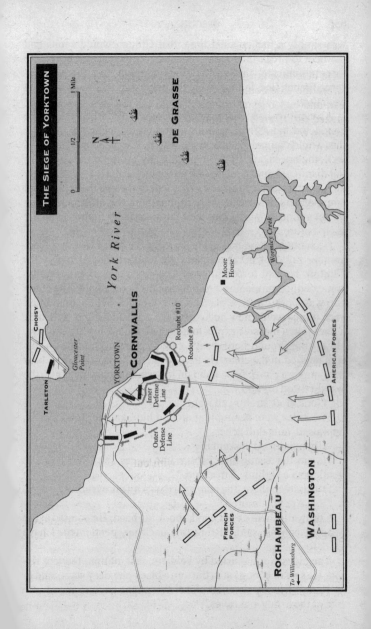

THE SIEGE OF YORKTOWN

0   1/2   1 Mile

N

DE GRASSE

York River

CHOISY

TARLETON

Gloucester Point

YORKTOWN

CORNWALLIS

Redoubt #10

Redoubt #9

Inner Defense Line

Outer Defense Line

Moore House

Wormley Creek

AMERICAN FORCES

FRENCH FORCES

ROCHAMBEAU

WASHINGTON

To Williamsburg

was simply a race against time, that Clinton would soon send the fleet to break the French blockade. They had still been able to communicate, fast packet ships slipping past the cumbersome French line, letters taking the better part of a week to travel each way.

Around his headquarters tent there was little business to be conducted, no formal meetings, nothing of tactics or strategy that would compel his officers to gather. It was too dangerous as well, the unceasing artillery making any group of men a potential disaster should a rebel shell strike too near. He stayed mostly along the water's edge, took to his tent to receive the regimental commanders. It was the daily routine now, the officers arriving one at a time, bringing him their latest casualty figures from the night before.

He sat in his tent, had made his tally, the horrible losses from another night of bombardment, yet another dismal report for Clinton. He had forced himself to enjoy a cup of tea, a rarity, some civilian producing a gift to ease his fierce mood. The china cup was empty, and he glanced at it, thought, Who would think such things would now be luxury? He was suddenly punched by a hard jolt, a massive explosion, the tent collapsing around him. He hit the ground hard, heavy canvas pressing him down, his legs tangled in the chair. He tried to shout, no words, could hear men moving close, felt a hand on his arm now, saw daylight, the weight lifted off him.

"Good God, sir! You all right?"

The aides were scrambling around him, and he stood slowly, appraised, only dull aches.

"I'm unharmed, it seems."

He saw the teacup then, broken into pieces, said, "We owe that gentleman a shilling, I'm afraid."

O'Hara was there, the man's face torn by pure panic.

"Sir! Are you injured?"

Cornwallis held up his hand, shook his head. He pointed at the heap of canvas, said, "Bring this back up, gentlemen. I have work to do."

The aides were assisted by soldiers, fast motion, the tent rising. He saw one long rip in the top, a black powdery stain, said to O'Hara, "Bloody damned close. We might have to move into one of those dug-out caves."

O'Hara was still staring at him with wide-eyed horror.

"Sir! You were nearly killed!"

The tent was secure now and he said, "What would you have me do, General?"

He moved into the tent, O'Hara close behind him.

The aides had pulled his desk upright, the papers stuffed into the small drawers. He pulled out a handful, scanned them, now held one up.

"This is the last letter I have received from General Clinton. He confirms that he is sending a sizable fleet, and a sizable body of infantry, and that they should set sail by October 5. A week ago."

"Well, yes, sir. If that is the latest . . . I have seen that previously. Then we can expect relief at any moment!"

Cornwallis shifted his chair, sat, the chair rocking on the uneven ground.

"You are a man of optimism, General. That is to be admired. I find I cannot avoid General Clinton's particular mention:

It is supposed the necessary repairs of the fleet will detain us here to the fifth of October and . . . you must be sensible that unforeseen accidents may lengthen it out a day or two longer; I therefore entreat you to lose no time in letting me know your real situation.

He put the paper down, saw the same glimmer of hope on O'Hara's face, said, "I have given the commanding general every account of our *real* situation. As I asked you before, General, what would you have me do? According to General Clinton we are to wait for rescue, by a great and powerful fleet that may or may not have sailed October 5. I have received no word of any movement by the French fleet, thus I cannot assume Admiral Graves has made his presence known."

Outside, another hard blast buffeted the sides of the tent, more shouts, one man screaming. O'Hara seemed to flinch, and Cornwallis held himself tightly down on the chair, expected the tent to collapse again. O'Hara was scanning the canvas above him, and Cornwallis felt something give way inside of him, shouted, *"What would you have me do?"*

O'Hara seemed to cower at his volume, looked at him with

stunned horror. Cornwallis felt his hands shaking, curled his fingers into hard fists. They sat in silence for a long moment, and he said, "My apologies, General."

"Not necessary, sir. What possibilities do we face? Surely, sir, you know better than I."

"We can attack, we can flee, or we can await our deliverance at the hands of Henry Clinton."

"I must assume, sir, that you would choose to attack."

OCTOBER 16, 1781

They slipped out past the British lines shortly after four in the morning, a handpicked assault force of three hundred fifty men. There could be no general advance by the army, the rebel numbers far too superior, so the target would be specific, to open a chink in the rebel armor by eliminating the effectiveness of several key artillery positions. The British soldiers were to move quickly, silently, a rapid surge into the closest French batteries. His men would be less concerned with the troops they confronted than the destruction of the French guns, one squad of men given the task of driving spikes into the fire holes, rendering the cannon useless.

The first wave accomplished its mission and immediately pushed on to the second battery. The guns were spiked again, but now, the response came, a wave of French troops that met the British advance with more force than the British had expected. The fights were brief and sharp, both sides suffering casualties. Before the sun had come up, the mission was over. By midday, the French had repaired their cannon, the big guns again hurling a steady rain of iron and fire into the British lines.

He had stayed in the tent, had long given up hope of sleep. As the brief skirmish had echoed in the darkness, there was no cause to venture out, no need to place himself in any more risk than he was in now. He would wait instead for the message to be sent back from the mission commander. But there was no courier, no dispatch, the word was brought to him by the mission commander himself, Robert Abercrombie, one of Cornwallis' finest officers. Abercrombie had lost more than a dozen men, only inflicting minimal damage to the cannon and the troops he had encountered. To Abercrombie, it was an embarrassment. To Corn wallis, it was the outcome he had to expect. Despite every instinct that told him to push hard into the enemy in front of him, he had come to accept that his army was simply too outnumbered.

The shelling continued, the town ripped by fire, the list of casualties growing by the hour. He pulled himself up from the small chair, moved out to the opening in the tent, stared across the river. Gloucester Point was a mile away, fortified by the same good work of the engineers who had done their best around Yorktown. But Gloucester had not yet come under the siege guns, seemed for the moment to be in no real danger. He had placed Tarleton in command there, the most logical course, removing the horses from Yorktown. There was no forage in the town, no means to feed the animals, and the horses would be impossible to protect, would be too easily slaughtered by the artillery bombardment. He knew that Tarleton was hemmed in by a strong French force, but with reinforcements from this side of the river, Tarleton might create the one opening the army could use.

THE BOAT HAD BROUGHT TARLETON QUICKLY ACROSS THE RIVER, the artillery seeming to ignore it as an unworthy target. The young man stood before him now, still held to his glow of self-importance. Cornwallis said, "I regret I do not have an additional chair, Colonel. Undamaged furniture is something of a rarity. I require you to send over those boats in your service. How many can you provide?"

Tarleton hesitated, said, "Do you intend to bring the army across to Gloucester Point, sir?"

"What I *intend* is for you to send your boats, Colonel."

He had no patience for answering questions, felt the ground shake beneath him from the impact of a shell, a shower of dirt raining on the tent. Tarleton seemed to be unaware, looked past him, the habit Cornwallis found more annoying now than ever.

"Sir, I merely wish to know if we are finally going to advance the army into the countryside. You will certainly require the services of my Legion. With all respects, sir, I should know your plans."

Cornwallis held tight to his words, said in a low hiss, "I would prefer it, Colonel, if you would *look* at me when you address me."

The bravado began to slip away from the young man, Tarleton's eyes slowly finding him.

"Much better, Colonel. My plan is to evacuate this position this evening and place the army in a position to break out of your works across the river. Am I correct that the forces to your front would be easily removed?"

Tarleton was looking at him now, said quietly, "Yes, sir. They number no more than a thousand, perhaps fewer."

"Once we are on the march, it will be difficult for Washington to pursue us. His numbers are too many, his supply train no doubt too cumbersome. The advantage of mobility, for once, will be ours."

Tarleton seemed to light up, a small glimmer of excitement.

"Quite, sir! There will be nothing to stand in our path. We can make straightaway for Carolina!"

He felt none of Tarleton's excitement, thought a moment.

"Colonel, does it not bother you that we would be marching away from what is presumed to be our salvation?"

"I'm not sure what you mean, sir. Are you referring to General Clinton? The fleet? If I may be so frank, sir, I have not had much faith in such promises of salvation."

"You may *not* be so frank, Colonel. Return to Gloucester Point immediately. Send me those boats."

The young man was gone quickly, and Cornwallis walked outside the tent, could smell a hard odor of sulfur, the smoke from the town drifting out past him. He would not watch Tarleton's boat, could not endure any part of the young man's arrogance for a second more. He tried to think ahead, the march, his battered army moving again into the Virginia countryside. They would leave behind every piece of baggage, every conveyance for supply, would abandon the few ships still at anchor, and possibly the sailors who manned them. Any wounded would be left behind as well, the army keeping to its feet with all the energy the men could muster. The word stuck in his brain: *Carolinas*. It was an extraordinary distance for an army with no food supply and few if any friends along the way. The horses would be the first casualties, forage no doubt impossible to find. In the end, it might come down to the sacrifice of those noble animals. He had already harbored the awful thought, slaughtering the horses for meat, possibly the last desperate means to feeding his army.

A shell whistled close overhead, solid iron smashing against the wharf, shattering timbers, then bounding in a high arc and landing with a hard splash in the water. He did not move, felt a cold numbness in his legs, spreading through his whole body. He looked overhead, thick gray clouds rolling down the river. Perhaps there will be no moon tonight. Perhaps there will be a Divine hand in our escape from this place. He looked out across the river, could see the small craft carrying Tarleton to the far shore. He looked out toward the capes, the mouth of the river, could see small clusters of sails, the French fleet. No word, no sign. For all his smirking and arrogance, Colonel Tarleton is correct. There is no Clinton, no Graves, no bloody marvelous rescue. There is just . . . one more night.

THE CLOUDS CONTINUED TO DARKEN THE SKY, AND BY DUSK, THE rains began. Tarleton had sent sixteen boats, and they had begun to load at dark, each filled with as many men as could safely be rowed across. The rain had grown heavier, but the boats had made their first crossing, were beginning to return now, lining up along the wharf to receive the next wave of troops. He stood out on the wharf, defied the rain, but the storm was growing worse, the wind beginning to howl, the few remaining trees along the water's edge bent and whipped by a sharp gale. The troops were filing into the boats, and he tried to see their progress, but there could be no lights, nothing to guide the enemy's cannon. The storm brought light of its own, the soft glow of lightning, the slow rumble of thunder. The boats began to push away, but already the water was rough, hard waves splashing high over the wharf, the spray driven by the wind. He heard shouts, men trying to control the boats, a flash of lightning illuminating the chaos along the wharf. A man was close to him, the voice of O'Hara.

"Sir! We must halt the crossing! The boats cannot maneuver! We should wait, allow the storm to pass!"

He nodded, leaned close, put a hand on O'Hara's arm.

"Order the crossing to cease. Wait for my order to resume."

Cornwallis turned away, looked for the dull white of the tent. He stepped away from the wharf, felt his feet deep in mud, trudged his way toward the bank. He ducked inside the tent, the ground still muddy beneath him. Water dripped through every part of the tent, and he shivered from the chill of his uniform. He looked out, shielding his eyes, the rain hard and steady, the wind buffeting the tent, driving the rain into his face. He backed away, felt for the chair, the seat a pool of water. He sat, stared down into nothing, every part of him feeling the pure misery of another disaster.

OCTOBER 17, 1781

The rain did not stop until well after midnight. By then there was not enough time for the numerous crossings it would require to ferry the army to safety. As the river once again grew calm, he sent the boats across empty, with one order to Tarleton. Return the men who had made the first crossing. With the dawn approaching, he would need every man in Yorktown.

With the passing of the storm had come a different storm, the rebel artillery again showering the town with fire. The wounded now filled every house, and no home was free from the sudden burst of a shell. He walked through the darkness into the main street, moved carefully, the street gouged by craters, covered with the debris of houses and trees. He knew to wait for the next shell, nearly a rhythm to it now, the sharp streak, the hard burst of fire lighting the street, showing him the obstacles. He turned down a side street, moved toward the front lines, where so many of his men still huddled, sleepless and frightened. He eased his steps forward, water masking the depth of every hole.

The clouds were still clearing, and he could actually see now, a low gray light, and with the first bit of dawn came a new wave of shelling. He heard a whistle high above, the ball bursting in a shower of sparks back close to the river. He moved quicker, could see his way through the debris. He was not sure yet where he was going, had told his aides only that he would see the hospitals, that it was unnecessary for anyone to follow him. It was unwise, of course, that should something happen to him, it might be a while before anyone knew.

His own guns had nearly quit firing altogether. Their location was too familiar to the rebel gunners, and so many of his guns had been destroyed. The gunners knew as well as he did, there was no good purpose to returning fire, the rebel works far too protected. There might still come the infantry assault, a vast wave of men suddenly emerging out of the rebel lines. Those few shells his gunners had would be desperately needed.

He was nearly clear of the town, the ground around him sandy, mostly covered by storm water. He navigated around a wide puddle, stopped, was suddenly engulfed in a hard grotesque smell. It was something he had smelled before, and he backed away instinctively. He could see now, the puddles were littered by heaps of broken men, pieces of bodies. He looked down, saw a man's arm close to his own feet, felt the sickness coming. He stepped back, then stopped, scolded himself, You are not some recruit!

He looked out toward the defensive line, uneven mounds of dirt, shattered trees, could see movement, men rising as they saw him. They began to pull away from their cover, moving closer to him, recognition now. "Sir! It is dangerous here! You should get back, sir!"

He stepped past them, moved closer to the mounds of dirt. There was a new smell, sulfur, the odor rising from the ground, replacing the smells of death. He stared out above the mounds, the men calling to him, hard whispers, "Sir! Lower yourself, sir!"

He ignored them, tried to see some movement, some sign of the rebels, something beyond the low haze of smoke. He thought of Trenton, his fury at the empty trenches, Washington slipping away in the middle of the night. It has happened to both of us, he thought. At Monmouth it was Clinton, leaving *you* behind, a pleasant little surprise for *you* to discover. And I would have done it here. Or will it be you, Mr. Washington? Could it be that you will oblige us once more and just . . . march away? Perhaps you believe you have done all the damage you can do, that we can endure no more.

It was a ridiculous fantasy, and he focused on the batteries across the open ground, thought, No, they are present indeed. And I have no further possibilities. My king may condemn me . . . but we cannot all die here for no good reason.

He saw the flash, and the men shouted at him, "*Down,* sir!"

The shell whistled past, burst into a house back behind him, the house that had once been his headquarters. All down the enemy lines more flashes came, a new wave of firing, shot and shell now echoing all down through the town.

"Sir! Please! You best be lowerin' yourself!"

He backed away from the mound, said aloud, "I require an officer."

"Yes, sir! May I assist you, sir?"

The man scrambled low toward him, and he recognized the face, a young lieutenant, the name swept away in the clutter around him.

"You have a drummer here?"

"Quite, sir!" The man turned shouted, "Mr. Brown! Attend!"

Cornwallis saw the boy's face, filthy and scared, the drum bouncing against his knee. Cornwallis said, "Do you know the cadence for a parley, young man?"

The boy seemed terrified, glanced at the lieutenant, then at Cornwallis.

"Yes, sir. That would be . . . three hard . . ."

"Climb the parapet there. You will commence to call for a parley."

The boy seemed ready to cry, and the lieutenant motioned. "Go on! Do as your general commands you!"

The drummer climbed the mound of dirt, began to rap on his drum, the beat echoing down the line. The lieutenant was close to him now, said, "General, with all respect, it can't do any good. With the shelling, he can't be heard."

Cornwallis waited a moment, the young man still drumming, and now the beat seemed louder, the steady rhythm cutting through the rumble of the guns. The lieutenant looked out toward the rebel lines, said, "The shelling . . . they're ceasing their fire."

Cornwallis still looked at the drummer, said, "They may not hear him. But they can *see* him. Lieutenant, do you have a handkerchief?"

"Yes . . . yes, sir."

"Place it on the tip of your sword. You will advance out beyond your drummer. Do you understand?"

The young man retrieved a white cloth from his pocket, and Cornwallis' words seem to reach him now.

"Sir . . ."

Cornwallis saw tears in the man's eyes, fought to hold his own. He touched his pockets, felt for a pencil, his fingers finding the short stub.

"I require paper."

He realized now that more men had gathered, emerging from their shelters. He saw officers, his own aides now approaching. He said again, "I require paper."

It was there now, and he moved to a flat piece of wood, a shattered box, dropped down to one knee.

"Lieutenant, when you advance you will hold your sword high, and you will carry this in your coat. You will present it to whoever makes himself available. Someone, I am certain, will make himself available."

He moved the pencil in his fingers, stared at the blank page for a long moment. His mind was a fog, no words, the sleeplessness weighing him down. The men watched him silently, and there were no protests, no angry calls, no one disputing what he was about to do. His mind was filled with the sound of the drummer, and he glanced up, saw the faces all staring at him. They knew as well as he did. They had come to the end.

> *Sir,*
>
> *I propose a cessation of hostilities for twenty-four hours, and that two officers may be appointed by each side, to meet at Mr. Moore's house, to settle terms for the surrender of the posts of York and Gloucester . . .*

---

58. WASHINGTON

THE BRITISH OFFICER HAD BEEN BLINDFOLDED, LED TO THE REAR OF the American lines. Washington had not been comfortable with Cornwallis' suggestion of a twenty-four-hour truce, knew that time might yet favor the British. He still expected a British fleet to reappear, assumed Cornwallis might feel the same way.

Washington had received letters that originated from his spies in New York that Clinton was putting his army into motion, the fleet there bolstered by reinforcements from England. Despite the willingness of Cornwallis to capitulate, should Clinton and Graves suddenly appear on the horizon, de Grasse would again be forced to meet them at sea. The trap around Cornwallis might suddenly spring open, and any talk of surrender could suddenly be terminated.

The terms were sent back to the British lines, and after more exchanges of notes, some minor quibbling, Cornwallis agreed to a meeting the following morning. For the first time, Washington had a sense of the despair in the British camp. For all the haggling over issues of pride, there was no argument, no disputing that Cornwallis was conceding the surrender of his entire position.

OCTOBER 19, 1781

The meeting at the Moore House consumed an entire day, and extended into the following morning. Washington had named two representatives, the young South Carolinian, John Laurens, and a French counterpart, the Viscount de Noailles. After much rancorous debate about issues Washington considered more symbolic than strategic, the documents were prepared for signatures. By late morning, word had come to his headquarters. Cornwallis had signed the papers, and within the hour, the British would march out of Yorktown.

FOR SEVERAL DAYS WASHINGTON HAD GLASSED THE DESTRUCTION of the British defenses, the stout earthworks proving too weak to stand up to the heavy French guns. The artillery barrage had virtually destroyed the town, and occasionally he could see glimpses of panicked civilians scrambling to salvage some personal belonging, then disappearing down toward the edge of the river. It was a horror he had not expected, the terrible cost to the innocent, the mysterious hand of the Almighty selecting these people, this tranquil place to be the focus of such catastrophe. It was a strange and disturbing notion to him that the nation had so often failed to support his army because they were so far removed from the war. It was difficult to convince citizens who never saw a British soldier that they should send their food and their money and their men to some remote horror in some far removed place. It was a challenge even for the congress, who seemed to believe this war should not be allowed to inconve nience the civilians. It was certainly a mystery to the French, who had a far better understanding of the ways of war. Any king would have absolute access to his nation's treasury, and could always compel his army to comply with his strategies. It was the very system from which the Americans were trying to free themselves, and yet Washington knew now that if this war had been lost, it was possibly because the American people didn't understand their responsibility. With their town in ruins, the people of Yorktown *would* understand, as did the people of Boston and New York and Charleston. Once the war has touched your home, disrupted your life, once you share the sacrifice of those nameless soldiers, it is your war as well.

He sat on the horse, backed by his generals. His army extended out in front of him, spread along the right side of the road that led straight into the British works. On the left, Rochambeau and his commanders sat, their army facing his across the road. The contrast was obvious and astonishing, the French in their perfect white uniforms, the decorative and colorful trim, the officers each adorned with some display of medals or pendants. His men faced them with as much regal bearing as they could muster, most in torn and filthy hunting shirts that had once been white or light brown. Behind the regular troops, the militia had formed, and their dress was rougher still, every man in the clothes he happened to bring from home, most with no shoes.

He could see that the continentals were standing more formally than usual, a show for the Frenchmen who faced them, who might still hold some notion of the barbarism of this uncivilized rabble. But there would be none of that today, the men on each side of the road now gazing quietly at the other, measuring, silent respect, motionless salutes.

The bands had been playing for a long while, the French and Americans alternating, a joyful competition for musical dominance. Washington had smiled at the attempts by his men, but it was clear even to the continental musicians, the French were professionals. Music had come as well from the British, the distant playing of bagpipes, fifers trying to send their tunes down this long road, as though asking to be included in the game. But now the music stopped, quiet orders from the officers. There was a more serious game to be played.

He was consumed by nervousness, could not help staring out

beyond the town to the open water. He knew that de Grasse was scanning the horizon, searching for any sign of sails, sharing Washington's concern that suddenly there would be a new chapter to this fight.

He steadied his hands by holding tightly to the reins, felt the unexpected chill of the cool clear day. He stared down the open road for a long silent moment, and the horse raised its head, a sniff of protest. Washington realized he had drawn the reins up tightly against his chest and straightened his arm now, loosening the tension on the horse. He leaned forward, patted the horse gently on the neck, a silent apology. He straightened again, glanced at Rochambeau, who sat rigidly in his saddle. The Frenchman did not look at him. No, this is not the time for words. It cannot be long now.

Far out in front of him he heard the sound of a single drum, a slow cadence, steady rhythm. Behind him came a sharp breath, someone reacting to the sound, and he smiled, his officers as nervous as he was. He could see the horsemen now, no sign of a flag, one of the conditions Laurens had insisted upon, thought so harsh by the British. But the horsemen were complying, and behind them he could see the column of red, following their commanders out of their works.

He was sweating in the cool air, watched them coming closer, could see the man in the lead, smaller than he had expected, and as the man drew closer, Washington saw his face, a dark ruddy complexion, thought, Can that truly be General Cornwallis?

The officer stopped a few yards in front of him, dismounted, looked toward the French, purposeful, direct, drew his sword, and stepped toward Rochambeau.

"Sir, I am Brigadier General Charles O'Hara. I regret that General Cornwallis has taken ill this morning. In his place, I hereby surrender to you the general's sword."

Rochambeau looked at O'Hara with a hard silent glare, then gave a quick look to his aide, a brief low command, and the aide said, "Our commanding general is there . . . across the road."

O'Hara looked at Washington, and his face was a mask of despair. He moved across the sandy roadway, held the sword up, said, "General Washington, allow me to surrender . . ."

"General O'Hara, since your commanding officer has not consented to deliver his sword in person, it is not proper for me to accept it. You will offer your surrender to one of my senior officers." He looked behind him, said, "General Lincoln, please advance."

Lincoln rode forward, and O'Hara lowered his head.

"Certainly. I understand, sir."

He held the sword up to Lincoln, who took it, held it in both hands for a brief moment, then leaned down, returned it to O'Hara's hand. Washington looked at Lincoln, the man who had endured the shame of the defeat at Charleston, who had been denied the honor of marching out of Charleston with his flags flying. Now the same condition had been exacted from the British, the perfect justice for their arrogance, their scorn for this ragged army. Washington saw tears on Lincoln's face, said, "General Lincoln, you may give the order. Commence the surrender."

Lincoln nodded, wiped his face with a hard hand, said, "General O'Hara, you will order your men to lay down their arms."

NEARLY EIGHT THOUSAND MEN FILED SLOWLY INTO THE OPEN FIELD, surrounded by French guards. The muskets and cartridge boxes were tossed in a great heap, some men reacting with outbursts of violence, throwing their weapons down in a fury, others sobbing openly.

He sent Lincoln to the open field to supervise the surrender, an exercise in control, preventing some possible outbreak of violence on either side. Washington stayed out on the road with Rochambeau, the two men saying very little. As the column passed slowly through the field, a British band was playing, the music plain now, some tune he had not heard in a very long time. The notes were unsteady, the emotion of the men who played them, but the tune was clear to him now, the title coming into his mind. It was an old British song, called "The World Turned Upside Down."

He felt a powerful disappointment toward Cornwallis, wondered now if it was a weakness in the man's courage. He could not accept that, thought, Perhaps it is something very different, some part of being British, the importance of pride, the horrible disgrace the man would take home to his king. The sting of defeat must be unbearable to a monarch who so believes in his perfect superiority, that he can suppress every part of his empire by the tip of a sword. "The World Turned Upside Down" . . . indeed.

OCTOBER 27, 1781

The people had returned to Yorktown, weeping civilians who sifted through the destruction, farmers from around the area who came to offer help. The French and American armies were still in place, Washington doing as much as he could to replenish his supplies, tending the wounded and sick. The militia had mostly gone, some escorting the vast sea of British prisoners to the Shenandoah Valley, to the prison camps that had been assembled around Frederick, Maryland, and Winchester, Virginia. The senior British officers had made their reports, many boarding the one frigate Washington allowed to sail for the safety of New York.

Out beyond the French fleet, toward the wide ocean where de Grasse still focused his spyglass, the sails of the single British frigate were suddenly met by many more. Clinton had been true to his word, had responded to Cornwallis' pleas for help. The British had assembled thirty-five warships, a fleet powerful enough to cause considerable problems for de Grasse's blockade. They carried seven thousand rested and fit British and Hessians troops, a force strong enough to have changed the entire balance of the siege, a force that could not only have rescued Cornwallis, but once again, could have turned the tide of the war. As the anxious de Grasse scanned the busy horizon, the British flagship was receiving the report, Clinton himself reading the accounts of the devastating defeat at Yorktown. Within a few short hours, the fleet had turned itself around, and sailed back to New York.

59. WASHINGTON

To the congress, and most of the people north of Virginia, Yorktown was the victory that had ended the war. But Washington could not enjoy their celebration, cautioned against assuming the British would simply vanish with barely a whimper.

The command in the Southern Department was still Nathanael Greene's, and the news of Yorktown had not slowed Greene from the enormous task that still confronted him. The names meant little to people in the north, Hobkirk's Hill and Ninety-Six and Eutaw Springs, but each was a fight worthy of anyone's comparison to Brandywine, Princeton, or Monmouth. Though Greene claimed none of these extraordinary fights as victories, the British were so bloodied that their commanders were forced to abandon their inland outposts and withdraw the entire British command to the safety of Charleston.

After Yorktown, Anthony Wayne had gone south to reinforce Greene, and by the following spring, Wayne's ragged army had cleared the British completely out of Georgia. By the summer after Yorktown, the entire British presence in America was reduced to the city of Charleston and the main headquarters at New York.

Though Washington was still hesitant to claim victory, in England, the government there was doing it for him. Henry Clinton had been recalled, replaced as overall commander by Governor Guy Carleton of Canada, the fourth man to hold the command. By all rights, that position should have fallen to Clinton's second in command, but Cornwallis knew that Yorktown was a catastrophe that no one could overlook. Even worse for King George, the news of Yorktown, and all its implications had reduced Lord North's cabinet to a shambles. King George had no choice but to accept a new government, run now by the principal voices of his hated opposition.

Throughout the entire war, the most significant and impactful pieces of news that had reached England had been the defeats of their army, from Boston to Saratoga, and now Yorktown. Even the king conceded that his army could no longer hope to prevent American independence. By early 1782, a new peace commission was established, with none of the pretense or arrogance of their predecessors. They would not sail to America with lofty demands, would not pose and preen before the congress. They would go instead to Paris, and they would negotiate the final and humiliating terms of a peace treaty. The man to lead the negotiations for the Americans would, of course, be Ben Franklin.

As with every communication, the distance between Philadelphia and Paris and London would make any process a slow one. Though the negotiations dragged on for more than a year, the outcome was rarely in doubt. Every condition the Americans insisted upon was agreed to. On September 3, 1783, the treaty was signed by delegations from both sides. The following January, it was ratified by the United States Congress. What most Americans had known since the fall of Yorktown was now made official to the entire world. The United States of America had earned its rightful place as an independent nation.

New York, November 1783

Washington had waited for the last of the British command to set sail before he would ride into the city. There would be no purpose for meetings or even social gatherings. He had admitted to himself that his hesitation was symbolic as well, something he rarely focused on. He simply didn't want to be in the city with *those* people, didn't want to hear sorrowful congratulations for his efforts, no empty platitudes about a war justly won. His deeply sown hatred for the British was muted now, no one in the British camp he could single out with particular prejudice. But the city itself had been the victim, and it was one more symbol of the horror, the despair, so much tragedy that the British had inflicted. He didn't want to discuss it with anyone. He simply wanted them gone.

As he rode down into the city itself, the crowds had emerged, but they were not a grand and boisterous mob. It was so much like he had seen in Boston, seven years before, the faces of a people scarred by the brutality of their experiences. A fourth of the city was still in black skeletal ruins, naked chimneys rising above cavelike dwellings. Though the crowd was sparse, their suffering was an overpowering sign of what the city had become, a festering sore for those people who were too poor or too crippled to escape, Americans loyal to their cause who had no means, and no other place to go.

There had been a great many more suffering souls, the mass of humanity that had once packed into the city, the Tories who had scampered to the safety of the British guns. He cared little for the suffering of the loyalists, so many refugees with the means and the wealth to escape the wrath of their neighbors. After Yorktown, the loyalists were the only real source of bloodshed in the north, bands of marauding Tories who still sought revenge on the citizenry who had swept them from power. Their violence had infuriated Washington. They were not soldiers at all, were no better than bandits, exacting retribution on the poor and powerless. When Washington responded with violence of his own, they had scurried back to New York, shoving the desperate residents deeper into their holes.

But nearly all the loyalists and Tories were gone, most seeking escape by sailing to England, some going to Canada. The people they had left behind were the people Washington saw.

As he rode farther into the city he looked out across the East River, toward the place where his own horror began, the awful fight on Long Island, the shameful wounds to the confidence of his army. He cared little for the accolades that would have met some grand triumph. He thought instead of all those who had looked to him for leadership, had followed him to that first devastating fight. In every battle, he had borne that weight, the responsibility to the men who followed him, from the officers to the barefoot militiamen, so many who had believed he would lead them to victory over that polished and efficient professional army. For so many, it was never to be, so many of those faithful men still out there, buried somewhere in the fields around Brooklyn. But the river was a harsh reminder of a worse horror, so many thousands stuffed into shallow graves in the mud of the riverbank, those tragic souls who had not survived the rotting hell of the prison ships.

That so many had followed him through it all was a mystery to him. The small victories could not erase the stain of hopelessness he had so often carried, the despair he hid so well. And yet, despite the marches and the starvation and the nakedness, so many still stood tall and faced the awful challenge. Their courage and sacrifice had cleansed him of the disdain for those Americans who had done so little to help their cause. He held no grudge, no thoughts of vengeance against those whose concerns were so petty, whose selfishness threatened to destroy any chance that this nation would survive. Many in the army did not share his generosity, and he had confronted the ugly talk, officers and their men succumbing to the basest emotion of revenge. They had threatened to march upon the congress, to exact punishment on those whose thievery and ambition had done so much to damage the cause, those who did not deserve to be called Americans. But Washington had confronted them, had eased the anger as he had eased their frustrations in the past. He was still no orator, could only offer the soft word, the emotional plea that they return home. No paper, no treaty, no congress could carry their nation into permanence without their hands, the strong, the dedicated, the men who knew so much of sacrifice. It was not his words that calmed them, it was his presence, the large man now bent with exhaustion, beaten down by his own sacrifice, standing before them with little to offer but his own dignity. They had obeyed.

NEW YORK, DECEMBER 4, 1783

The gathering had been planned at a tavern close to the waterfront, attended by those few officers still near the city who could join him for some sort of celebration of his final day in New York. It would be a lavishly prepared banquet, white tablecloths and silver, the extraordinary effort of their host, Samuel Fraunces.

They were not many, less than a dozen men, but he would show no disappointment. So many had gone home, so many others were still involved in the business of the army, spread out all through the nation. As he sat at the head of the table, he realize the small number of men was something of a blessing, that h could speak to each of them, try to offer some kind of personal appreciation. As the food was set before him, and the wine goblets filled, he knew it was not to be. There was no appetite, and no conversation. Every man in the room looked down to his plate with emotion too deep for anyone to speak. After a long moment of silence, he said, "I am sorry . . . I had hoped this would be a time of elation. I am fortunate to be allowed to return to my home."

He saw nods, most of the faces still turned away. He reached for the wine goblet, his hand shaking, and he steadied it on the table, said, "We should have a toast." He raised the goblet. "With a heart full of love and gratitude, I now take leave of you. I most devoutly wish that your latter days may be as prosperous and happy as your former ones have been glorious and honorable."

He let out a breath, raised the goblet, took a sip of the wine. The men around the table followed, the goblets now back in place. He had hoped someone would speak, ease the hard emotion he could not escape. He looked around the table, Knox, von Steuben, no response. He looked to the far end, Tench Tilghman sitting beside Benjamin Tallmadge, the man who had organized Washington's spy network in New York. No one spoke still, and he nodded to Tilghman, the wonderfully reliable young man, thought, Perhaps you can assist me . . . one more time. But Tilghman returned the look with red eyes and a quiver in his lips, and Washington felt the man's loyalty now in some deep place he tried to hide. It was affection now unembarrassed and pure, and he realized that he loved them all, the men in this one room, and those so far away. Lafayette was already sailing for France, Greene was still in the Carolinas. It is good they are not here. As it is . . . I have no words to give these men. He reached for the goblet, stopped, took a long breath, felt the tightness in his throat.

"I cannot come to each of you, but shall feel obliged if each of you will come and take me by the hand."

Knox was first, stood, steadied his wide frame against the table, stepped close to him, stood as straight as he could, held out his hand. The gesture was simple and honest and removed the last hard barrier to Washington's emotions. Knox was already crying. Washington put his hands on the man's shoulders, and they came together for a brief, silent embrace. Washington was blinded by his own tears as the men moved close to him in a single line, each one repeating the gesture. The last was Tilghman, and the young man stood frozen for a long moment, tried to speak, and Washington shook his head, no, it is all right. He embraced him as well, could not hold his emotions, felt Tilghman's sobs matching his own. There were still no words, nothing he could say to any of them. He moved to the door, turned to face them, and von Steuben suddenly snapped hard to attention, the Prussian holding a firm salute for a long moment. Without a word, Washington turned, moved out into the street.

HE WAS COMPELLED TO VISIT THE CONGRESS, THAT IF HE INTENDED to resign his command, there would be a formal ceremony, and most certainly a litany of speeches. He had not expected the congress to respond to him with as much emotion as he had received from his officers. But he could not speak to them without emotion of his own, that after so many years, the controversies, the hostility, he could not ignore that this one body of men was still the genesis of everything he had fought for. For nearly nine years he had been in their service, had suffered and endured and triumphed. The faces were many and different, but the body and all it commanded was still intact.

There had been talk of receptions and balls in his honor, but he would not be detained, that once his resignation had been accepted as official, he had one priority, one destination in his mind.

The horse responded to his every command, carried him in a steady trot through the lush green hills, across the quiet streams and bare wintry trees. He fought the urge to push the animal harder, to make the journey quicker, and the horse seemed to know, brought him along in a steady hard gait on the roads so familiar now. With a hard leap in his chest, he turned the horse up the long drive toward Mount Vernon, studied the grounds through teary eyes, the gardens, the fields, all the precious lands that had missed his caring hand. It would be his again, the very soil beneath him would feel his touch, the house itself would know his strength. He rode up close to the rear entryway, glanced out past the house to the stunning vista of the Potomac, more beautiful now than he had ever remembered. He stopped the horse, sat for a long moment. His mind was already racing forward, all the tasks, the wonderful joy of the work, but his thoughts were halted by the slow motion of the door. He saw her now, th small woman dwarfed by the tall entryway, and she made a small cry, put a hand to her mouth, stepped out onto the porch. He climbed down from the horse, and in one quick sweep was up the short steps, had her firmly in his arms. He could feel her strength again, felt her energy filling him. He had wanted to say so much, tell her of all his plans for the house, the land, so much they would share now, all the sacrifice behind them. She held him tightly still, small soft sounds, and he felt his energy slip away, a broad smile opening up inside of him. Of course, it can wait. There will be time, after all. And, it is Christmas Eve.

AFTERWORD

CHARLES, EARL CORNWALLIS

It may be doubted whether so small a number of men ever employed so short a space of time with greater and more lasting effects upon the history of the world.
—BRITISH HISTORIAN GEORGE TREVELYAN,
 ON WASHINGTON'S VICTORY AT TRENTON

I shall never rest my head on my pillow in peace and quiet as long as I remember the loss of my American colonies.
—KING GEORGE III

BENJAMIN FRANKLIN

He freed men by enlightening them.
—COMTESSE D'HOUDETOT, 1781

He becomes the central figure in the tedious and diplomatically sensitive negotiations with the British for the peace treaty that will officially end the war. Suffering from weakening vision, he confronts the challenges of his new task by fashioning a combination of reading glasses and an aid to distant vision, thus, he invents bifocals.

Suffering from the continuing effects of the gout that has plagued him for so long, and weakening from both age and the strain of the work he must perform, he requests that congress release him from his official responsibilities. He leaves France in July 1785. During his work with the peace treaty, he is stricken by the first symptoms of a bladder stone, the misery of which ends most of his social appearances. Thus the rumors of his lechery and sexual conquests of young French maids is made even more ridiculous. Observing that his critics, including John Adams, seem to assume the worst because of the attention he draws from Frenchwomen, he writes:

> *This is the civilest nation on earth. . . . Somebody, it seems, gave it out that I loved ladies; and then everybody presented me their ladies (or the ladies presented themselves) to be embraced; that is, have their necks kissed. For as to the kissing of lips or cheeks it is not the mode here; the first is reckoned rude, and the other may rub off the paint. The French ladies have, however, a thousand other ways of rendering themselves agreeable: by their various attentions and civilities and their sensible conversation.*

In late 1783, Franklin witnesses a phenomenon that has all of France in an uproar: the launching of a lighter-than-air balloon, and later, the first such launch that bears human passengers. In response to skepticism that a balloon has no usefulness, he says, "What use is a newborn infant?"

His farewell to France inspires universal sorrow in that country, and he returns to America as the most celebrated and famed private citizen in the world. Arriving in Philadelphia, he is received with all the respect and acclaim appropriate to his long years of extraordinary service and accomplishments. His return is marked by an artillery salute and a continuous ringing of church bells. But his public service is far from concluded. Elected to the Pennsylvania State Assembly, he is voted by that body to be "President of Pennsylvania." As the new nation begins to feel the pains of creating its first true government, in 1787, at age eighty-one, Franklin is selected as a delegate to the Constitutional Convention. As he suffers the increasing strains of age and the stone that torments him, his presence becomes as much ceremonial as practical. Though he proposes several suggestions as the foundation for the new government, including a single house of legislature, none are adopted. He accepts the diminished stature of his role with grace, regards his presence as a post of honor, and behaves accordingly. Though becoming too frail for the grueling debates required to shape the document, for those who seek him out, he is never without humor, counsel, and wisdom.

Increasingly inactive, he only occasionally attends the convention, and as the particulars of the document continue to be disputed, he offers one final bit of counsel: *"I cannot help expressing a wish that every member of this Convention who may still have objections to it would, with me, on this occasion doubt a little of his infallibility, and, to make manifest our unanimity, put his name to this instrument."*

He is among the first to sign it, and is a key force behind the ratification of the document by the state of Pennsylvania.

He continues to be sharp of mind, but his body's failures increasingly confine him to his home. He receives friends and noted visitors, and finds enormous pleasure in the company of his grandchildren. To the amused annoyance of his friends in Philadelphia, he disputes the adoption of the bald eagle as the symbol of the new nation, prefers instead the turkey, "a much more respectable bird."

Despite the tormenting misery he suffers from the bladder stone, he will not consent to an operation. His daughter Sally remains constantly by his side, and when she seeks to comfort him with the wish that his life will yet be long, he replies, "I hope not." He is stricken with an infection in his lung and lapses into a coma, from which he never awakes. In the presence of his two grandsons, he dies on April 17, 1790. He is eighty-four.

Franklin's writings are preserved primarily by the efforts of his grandson, Temple, who serves as editor of a definitive six-volume collection of Franklin's essays, experiments, and witticisms, published in 1818.

Historian Carl Van Doren writes: "Franklin was not one of those men who owe their greatness merely to the opportunities of their times. In any age, in any place, Franklin would have been great. He moved through the world in a humorous mastery of it. Whoever learns about his deeds remembers longest the man who did them. And sometimes, with his marvelous range . . . he seems to have been more than any single man: a harmonious human multitude."

The portrait of Franklin stolen from the Franklin home by British Major John André remains in possession of the descendants of General Charles Grey until 1906, when Albert, Earl Grey, Governor of Canada, offers its return. The painting hangs today in the White House in Washington, D.C.

*All the days of my life I shall remember that a great man, a
sage, wished to be my friend.*
—MADAME ANNE-LOUISE BRILLON

NATHANAEL GREENE

During 1782, he continues to maintain his post in the Carolinas, and when the British evacuate Charleston, Greene occupies
the city as his headquarters. He spends long months assisting the
state of South Carolina to rebuild its government. He is thus rewarded with enormous gifts of both land and money from the
three states in his department, the Carolinas and Georgia. In August 1783, he travels home to a hero's welcome in Rhode Island,
but returns to the south with prospects for settling into the life of
a gentleman farmer.

His personal reputation is severely damaged by a scandal involving the finances he had worked to secure for the feeding of
his army, a problem that Washington had eliminated through the
support of Robert Morris in Pennsylvania. But the Southern Departments are too far removed from the concerns of congress,
and Greene learns that those he trusted to secure the debts necessary to provide for his men have squandered the funds. Despite
his reception in the southern states as an heroic savior, he is
nonetheless held accountable for the financial pledges, and thus,
most of the gifts he has been rewarded are reclaimed by the
states as payment.

In the summer of 1785, he moves Kitty and his now four children to the one remaining property he holds in Georgia, called
Mulberry Grove. His years of frustration in dealing with the
congress, both as Washington's subordinate and as quartermaster general, give him considerable insight into politics, and he
writes often about the critical need for a central government. His
principles and suggestions mirror many of those eventually
written into the Constitution. Though he is considered a likely
candidate for several political offices, he refuses any offers, has
had enough of life so far removed from his family. He settles
well into the pleasant life on his farm, surprises himself that he
shares Washington's enthusiasm for the soil. He is surprised
even more when he learns his passion is shared by a new neighbor, "Mad Anthony" Wayne.

But Greene's New England upbringing has given him a weakness he cannot predict, and despite so many campaigns and so much physical distress in war, it is the summer sun that strikes him down. Accompanied by Kitty, he journeys to Savannah in an unsheltered carriage, and the oppressive heat gives him a fever from which he never recovers. On June 19, 1785, attended by Kitty and Anthony Wayne, Greene dies. He is forty-four.

He is one of only two general officers who serve in the army continuously from the first siege of Boston through the surrender. The other is Washington, who, after the British surrender, salutes Greene with what is now an ironic note: "I congratulate you on the glorious end you have put to hostilities in the Southern States. The honor and advantage of it I hope you will live long to enjoy."

Strangely, Greene is often overlooked by early historians, and his greatest notoriety emerges first from the pens of the British. Sir John Fortescue writes: "Greene's reputation stands firmly on his campaign in the Carolinas. His keen insight into the heart of the blunders of Cornwallis and his skillful use of his troops are the most notable features of his work. He is a general of profound common sense."

Greene's friend and subordinate, Henry "Light-Horse Harry" Lee, proposes to congress a resolution that a monument to Nathanael Greene be constructed in the nation's capital. The motion passes with no controversy, but the matter is strangely forgotten. In 1875, the issue is reopened by Rhode Island's two senators, and ninety years late, the monument is finally constructed in Washington, D.C.

As long as the enterprises of Trenton and Princeton shall be regarded as the dawning of that bright day which afterward broke forth with such resplendent luster, so long ought the name of Greene to be revered by a grateful country.
—ALEXANDER HAMILTON, 1789

MARIE DU MOTIER, THE MARQUIS DE LAFAYETTE

Upon his return to France in early 1782, he finally begins to receive the respect due him from the "veterans" of the French service. His close acquaintance with King Louis XVI ensures a prominent position in French foreign affairs, and when Thomas Jefferson is sent to Paris as United States minister to France, Lafayette becomes his invaluable liaison in the often dark halls of French government.

In 1789, he is named commander of the National Guard, the elite troops close to King Louis. He continues to serve his king during the early months of the French Revolution, and single-handedly rescues Louis and Marie Antoinette from one notable explosion of mob violence.

He is promoted to lieutenant general in the French army in 1791, is prominent as commander of the French forces when war with Austria erupts in 1792. Swept out of power by the outcome of the French Revolution, he flees the country, only to be captured and imprisoned by the Austrians. Freed by Napoleon in 1797, he returns to France to find a very different land, under the control of a dictator whom Lafayette respects but will not serve. Napoleon continues to offer him positions in his government, including the prestigious post as representative to the United States. But Lafayette refuses, chooses instead to pursue a peaceful life as a civilian. He settles into the farm country outside Paris until 1818, then succumbs to pressure to return to politics. He serves in the French Chamber of Deputies for six years, but resigns to accept an invitation from President James Monroe to tour the United States as an honored guest of a grateful nation.

In 1824–25, his yearlong parade through America is met by an extraordinary show of affection and admiration from a people to which he had been so dedicated. He returns to France every bit the hero who has captured the love of the American people.

He writes his memoirs, describing himself in the third person and making no attempt at modesty. But few can deny that the accounts are among the most accurate of those set into writing by one who was so centrally involved in the struggle for American independence.

Nearly bankrupted by the French Revolution, he never seeks reimbursement of his considerable expenses during the war in America. Congress awards him a small fraction of what he is due, but provides him a sizable grant of land, mostly in the new territory that is Louisiana.

He returns to politics, but never enjoys the prestige and power of his early years. He lives out his life as a beloved man of modest means and dies from a flulike ailment in May 1834. He is seventy-seven.

HENRY KNOX

The modest, obese bookseller who becomes the self-taught master of Washington's artillery is appointed to succeed George Washington as the second commander in chief of the American army. In that post for only a year, he becomes secretary of war in 1785, though that office is not yet given official status by the constitution. He remains in that position under President George Washington until 1794.

He falls into the trap that ensnares so many continental officers, and involves himself in land speculation in what becomes the state of Maine. He is nearly bankrupted, though he and Lucy continue to own a sizable piece of farmland near Thomaston, Maine. After resigning his position under Washington, he moves his family to their home there, called Montpelier, which is one of the finest mansions in that part of the country.

Lucy gives him twelve children, of whom only three reach adulthood. Throughout Knox's life, he and Lucy continue to inspire the admiration of their friends for their childlike affection toward each other. They become the center of society in their small world, and Knox's lust for food and high living is well known. On one occasion he writes, "On July Fourth, we had a small company of upwards of five hundred people."

He dies in September 1806, at age fifty-six. Lucy lives until 1824, her widowhood described by friends as a "joyless endurance."

CHARLES LEE

After being removed from the field by Washington at the Battle of Monmouth, Lee never again serves the country in any public capacity. He is outraged at the humiliation handed him by the commanding general, and requests a formal court-martial to clear his name of the *"cruel injustice"* Washington has inflicted upon him. Instead of clearing his name, he is convicted of all

charges. His continued criticism of the rank amateurism in
Washington's army inspires Frederick von Steuben, Anthony
Wayne, and John Laurens to challenge him to duels. The only
actual confrontation is with Laurens, who gives Lee a minor
wound.

In July 1779, he returns to his home in Virginia, and in January 1780, the congress officially dismisses him from the army.
He dies in Philadelphia in 1782, at age fifty-one.

DANIEL MORGAN

After retiring to his home in the Shenandoah Valley, he returns briefly to service under Lafayette to assist in the defense
against Tarleton's Virginia raids, but his health continues to
plague him, and by mid-1781, his days of active service in the
Revolution are at an end.

In 1794, he accepts Washington's request to serve during the
Whiskey Rebellion in western Pennsylvania, returns home to
Virginia, where he is elected to Congress in 1797. He takes his
four hundred ninety-nine scars to his grave in Winchester, Virginia, in 1802, at age sixty-six.

Morgan is one of only eight men to be awarded congressional
gold medals for his service during the war.

HORATIO GATES

After his humiliation at the Battle of Camden, Gates returns
to his home in Virginia. Incensed at the widespread and vocal
disregard for his abilities, he demands an official inquiry into his
performance. In 1782, a congress that is focused on the much
more important task of forging a peace clears him of miscon-
duct, though no one will speak publicly on his behalf. Returning
briefly to the army, Gates is the power behind much of the fiery
talk aimed at inciting the army to lay siege to the congress,
which Washington defuses.

After the peace treaty, Gates returns to Virginia, suffers the
death of his wife, and soon proceeds to offer his hand in marriage to several prominent women, including the widow of the

heroic General Richard Montgomery, who was killed at Quebec. His quest finally lands him a marriage to a wealthy New Yorker. He dies in 1806, at age seventy-eight.

ANTHONY WAYNE

Promoted to major general in 1783, "Mad Anthony" retires to the plantation given him as a reward for his service to the state of Georgia. But he discovers that farming is not always profitable, and after several financial setbacks, he returns to his home in Pennsylvania, where he serves in the assembly, and then, in 1791, is elected to Congress.

He serves the army again in an attempt to deal with Indian violence in western Pennsylvania, and in 1794, routs a large force of Indians, bringing an effective end to the conflict. On the journey home, he is stricken by illness, and dies at Erie, Pennsylvania, in December 1796. He is fifty-one.

FREDERICK VON STEUBEN

He leaves the army in March 1784, and is granted full citizenship by his adopted country. He moves to New York City, and establishes himself as a lion of society. Always an honored guest at parties, he obliges with his martial bearing and boisterous manner. Though popular with the New York society ladies, he never marries. Granted a pension by Congress, and a significant land grant in New York state, he retires to his new home in the Mohawk Valley. He is stricken by a sudden, unexplained illness, and dies, November 1794, at age sixty-four. Leaving no heirs, his estate is bequeathed to the two adjutants who had served him throughout his experience in the American war, Majors Walker and North.

In 1910, in recognition of his extraordinary contribution to American independence, Congress erects a statue of him in Washington, D.C. A duplicate of this statue is erected the following year in Potsdam, Prussia.

TENCH TILGHMAN

Washington's most trusted and loyal aide resigns from the army in December 1783. He returns to Maryland, settles, and marries, in Baltimore. With an eye toward learning the relatively new business of banking, he is assisted by Robert Morris in establishing a small financial company. But he dies suddenly in 1786, at age forty-two.

HENRY "LIGHT-HORSE HARRY" LEE

Lee remains with Nathanael Greene for the concluding chapters of the war and distinguishes himself and his Legion in every major fight Greene undertakes.

In February 1782, he resigns from the army, claims ill health. He returns home to Virginia, marries his cousin, Matilda Lee, who dies in 1790. He then marries Anne Carter in 1793. He is asked by Washington to command the troops organized to put down the Whiskey Rebellion, and succeeds in restoring the peace without the loss of a single man. He serves in the United States Congress for five years, until 1788, as governor of Virginia until 1795, and returns to Congress in 1799.

Lee engages in several unwise business dealings, shows such an astounding lack of business sense that he becomes completely destitute. His creditors show no mercy to the former hero, and in 1808, he is confined for two years in a debtor's prison. Upon his release, he travels to the West Indies, presumably to heal old war wounds, but more likely to escape his creditors. In 1818, returning to Virginia, he dies en route, and is buried at Cumberland Island, Georgia. He is sixty-two. In 1913 his remains are moved to the Lee family vault at the Lee Chapel at Washington and Lee University in Lexington, Virginia. He rests there alongside his son, Robert E. Lee.

Henry Lee's memoirs, published in 1812, are widely considered one of the finest firsthand accounts produced during this era of American history.

SILAS DEANE

Attacked relentlessly by Arthur Lee's influential friends in congress, Deane retires from public life a broken and humiliated man. He returns to France in 1781, and sinks into a personal despair that inspires him to write extremely unwise letters that pass through the hand of his secretary, Edward Bancroft, who is in fact a British spy. The letters are an exercise in bitterness, with Deane claiming that America should not continue its quest for independence. Bancroft reveals the letters so that they are made public in both England and America, and Deane has now sealed his fate. Accused not only of financial misdealings, but treason as well, he endures his remaining years in exile. He dies en route to Canada in 1789, at age fifty-two.

The man so responsible for engineering crucial French financial support does not receive his due until 1842, when Congress recognizes that Arthur Lee's conspiracy against Deane was without basis, and that in fact Deane's ledgers are accurate and his accounts entirely honest.

ROBERT MORRIS

The man so responsible for sorting out the financial quagmire of the Revolution rarely receives credit for repeatedly saving Washington's army. Those in congress who possess none of Morris' worldly understanding of commerce regard him instead as a man never to be trusted. Caught up in the controversy that surrounds Silas Deane, Morris' services to congress draw to a close. Despite vicious criticism of his business practices from such notable writers as Thomas Paine, Morris still carries the enthusiastic support of George Washington, and Washington's friends in congress, including John Adams. Morris is appointed superintendent of finances in 1781, a precursor to what will become the post of Secretary of the Treasury. With considerable financial assistance from the French, he founds the Bank of North America in 1782, and does much to prevent the utter collapse of the fledgling American economy. Receiving little support from either the congress or the states, he resigns in 1784. Exhausted and embittered, he declines Washington's offer to serve as first

Secretary of the Treasury, instead represents Pennsylvania in the United States Senate until 1795.

He continues to play a high-stakes game of business speculation, at one time owns the parcel of land that will eventually become the District of Columbia. He is dealt a serious financial blow by the aftermath of the French Revolution, and despite his considerable land holdings, finds himself with no liquid assets. Unable to pay his creditors, he is jailed for three years in a debtor's prison, released under a clause in the new federal bankruptcy law. He dies in Philadelphia in 1806, at age seventy-three. To this day, Morris receives little credit for winning the financial battles that allowed the creation and sustenance of the Continental Army.

JOHN SULLIVAN

Having served with Washington from the siege of Boston, Sullivan never rises to the level of achievement of Washington's other subordinates, notably Greene and Lafayette. His lackluster performance during most of the early years of the war is redeemed in 1779, when he is chosen by Washington to lead a large-scale assault into the Wyoming and Cherry Valleys of northern Pennsylvania. Sullivan leads a force of nearly four thousand men against a combined force of Indian nations, who, inspired by their alliance with the British in Canada, have pursued a campaign of brutal terror against the civilian population. Sullivan's campaign is a complete success, is effective in removing hostile Indians from the region, and shocks the British in Canada.

He returns feeling the ill effects of the extraordinary physical ordeal, and resigns from the army in November 1779. He becomes active in New Hampshire politics, serves as attorney general, governor, and finally, as a judge. He dies in 1795, at age fifty-five.

ALEXANDER HAMILTON

Washington's aide yearns for service in the field, and after some acrimony develops between the two men, Hamilton is a lowed to leave his headquarters post. Serving under Lafayette at Yorktown, Hamilton commands one of the two assaults against the final remaining British redoubts, and leads his men in a successful conquest of Redoubt #10.

He resigns from the army in December 1783, and moves to New York, where he opens a law practice. He founds a newspaper, the *New York Evening Post*, which becomes a mouthpiece for his strong views about the necessity of a strong central government. Appointed in 1787 to the Constitutional Convention, he becomes the leading advocate and most vocal supporter for what is now called the Federalist movement. He is appointed by Washington as first Secretary of the Treasury in 1789, and does much to salvage the young nation from the disastrous financial crisis in which it finds itself. He serves until 1795.

In his philosophy of Federalism, he becomes the polar opposite of Thomas Jefferson, and the two men become the leading spokesmen for their opposing causes. This serves to divide the government into distinct political parties, which survive in various forms throughout American history.

In 1795, he returns to his law practice, which becomes enormously successful. He returns to the army in 1798, to respond to a potential conflict with France, and is awarded the rank of major general.

Always vocal about his politics, Hamilton campaigns vigorously against John Adams for president. He then wages a hostile campaign against Aaron Burr for the privilege of running against Thomas Jefferson. Hamilton is widely quoted as calling Burr a "dangerous man," and Burr responds by challenging him to a duel. In July 1804, they meet and Burr prevails. Hamilton dies the next day, and is buried at Trinity Church in New York City. He is forty-seven.

AND ACROSS THE ATLANTIC . . .

CHARLES, EARL CORNWALLIS

On November 4, 1781, he leaves Yorktown and sails for New York, where he endures a final meeting with Henry Clinton. He returns to England the following spring, but receives surprisingly little condemnation for his part in the disasters of strategy that have plagued the English high command. In 1786, he is appointed to a much-sought-after position as governor-general of India, where he erases any stains from his American experience by his complete efficiency, both militarily and as the civil administrator of that part of the Empire. For his services, King George awards him the title of First Marquess Cornwallis, in 1793.

He returns to England, and in 1797, accepts the lucrative posts of commander in chief and governor-general of Ireland, and serves as Plenipotentiary to France. The honors are more symbolic than enjoyable, and he yearns to return to India, for which he has developed a deep affection. He arrives in 1805, but contracts an illness and dies soon after. He is sixty-seven.

Ironically, it is in America that his name carries the stigma of the man who "lost" the Revolution. In England, he does not receive any of the public censure that is given to Howe, Burgoyne, or Clinton. His one grave mistake was marching his army to Virginia without the consent of his superior, but fault must be placed far more at the feet of Henry Clinton for failing to recognize Cornwallis' crisis at Yorktown.

King George shares the sentiments of the English people that during this most unfortunate war, Charles Cornwallis was the one capable officer, who, if he had served under a capable commander, would likely have destroyed Washington's army.

JEAN-BAPTISTE, COUNT ROCHAMBEAU

While not entitled to full credit for engineering the strategy that resulted in the astounding victory at Yorktown, he is nonetheless the man who convinced Washington to look beyond New York as a means of ending the war.

He remains close to Yorktown until January 1783, then returns to France. King Louis grants him considerable favors, and for his heroic role in the American Revolution, Rochambeau receives the highest regard of the French people, second only to Lafayette. He serves King Louis in various government posts and in 1789 is named military commander of the Alsace Region which borders the incendiary Germanic states.

During the Reign of Terror in the French Revolution, he is imprisoned, but returns to the army to serve Napoleon, who pro motes him to marshal of the French army in 1803. He dies in 1807, at age eighty-two.

Though so many of the French senior command viewed their American allies as no more than a rabble, Rochambeau is credited with both patience and tolerance of the continentals and their commanding general. His obedience to Washington, against the sentiments of so many of his subordinate officers, provides the most important link in the chain that connects the alliance, and thus secures the American victory.

FRANÇOIS, COUNT DE GRASSE

The French admiral sails away from his triumph at Yorktown in November 1781, and returns to action in the West Indies. In one of the largest naval battles to that time, he is soundly defeated by the British, captured, and imprisoned in London. Released in August 1782, he returns to France and serves as the go-between for the crucial peace negotiations between France and England that will end their part of the war.

Loudly blamed for the naval catastrophe, de Grasse seeks to exonerate himself by laying blame on a lengthy list of subordinates, which instead lowers him further in the eyes of both the French people and King Louis. He dies near Paris in 1788, at age sixty-six. His descendents escape the Reign of Terror by sailing to America and settling in the Carolinas.

CHARLES GRAVIER, COUNT DE VERGENNES

The French minister most credited with helping to finance the Revolution continues his active role in American affairs by participating in the negotiations of the final peace with England. Though King Louis is seen by most Americans as their financial savior during the war, it is the persuasiveness of Vergennes that influences Louis' policies. His closeness to Louis creates enemies, and his generosity to the Americans is blamed for the financial chaos that grips France in the mid-1780s, which many believe contributes to the French Revolution. While he certainly would have been a primary target of the Reign of Terror, he escapes by dying in 1787, at age seventy.

WILLIAM HOWE

On his return to England, he begins a lengthy campaign to exonerate himself for his failings in America. But no conclusions are drawn by either Parliament or King George, and Howe is allowed to languish in relative inactivity. He is promoted to full general in 1793, and named to a key position to defend England from Napoleon, though the British Isles are never directly threatened. Upon his brother Richard's death in 1799, he becomes the fifth viscount Howe. In 1803, his health begins to fail, and he resigns from the army, becomes governor of Plymouth, England. He lingers for a decade as a sickly invalid, and dies in 1814, at age eighty-five.

His legacy is often more satirical than military, and thus in many ways he is a tragic figure. Several poems are written to his dishonor, including some that mention his noted relationship with his mistress:

Sir William he, snug as a flea,
Lay all the time a snoring,
Nor dreamed of harm as he lay warm
In bed with Mrs. Loring.
—FRANCIS HOPKINSON

In amazing contrast, Charles Lee writes:

He is all fire and activity, brave and cool as Julius Caesar . . .

BENEDICT ARNOLD

After leaving Virginia, he commands a mission to assault the town of New London, Connecticut, which accomplishes nothing militarily except the wanton destruction of much of the town. He convinces Henry Clinton to allow him to raise a special legion in his name, assumes that loyalists will flock to a man of such lofty stature. Barely two hundred enlist, and the project is abandoned.

With little to do, he and Peggy sail to England in December 1781. Though he makes every attempt to place himself in friendship with prominent Tories, including King George, he is for the most part ignored.

In 1785, frustrated by the army's unwillingness to grant him any further command, he sails to Canada and embarks on a business career, which fares no better. He returns to England in 1791, spends his final years as a bitter, dejected man, whose dreams of fortune and fame die with him in 1801. He is sixty.

Peggy Shippen Arnold survives him by only three years and dies in 1804. In America, those who participated in the affair of Arnold's treason, including George Washington, continue to believe that Peggy had nothing to do with Arnold's decision to betray his country. It is only after the deaths of nearly all concerned that an account by Aaron Burr surfaces, revealing Peggy's frank admission of the extraordinary acting performance she had exhibited for the sake of Washington and his men. Though Burr's reliability is discounted by many historians, irrefutable documentation is unearthed in British military archives in 1920, which contains damning evidence that there were *two* traitors at West Point.

HENRY CLINTON

After the disaster at Yorktown, he returns to England to find his name has become synonymous with defeat. The British government is sufficiently satisfied by those conclusions that it refuses Clinton a Parliamentary hearing, unlike what had been performed for William Howe. He publishes his memoirs, which contain scathing criticisms of everyone but himself, and which inspire a hostile exchange with Charles Cornwallis that continues for the rest of his life. He serves in Parliament, and though he is given no significant military duties, King George promotes him to full general in 1793. He becomes governor of Gibraltar in 1794, and serves only until his death in 1795, at age sixty-five.

WILHELM, BARON VON KNYPHAUSEN

He endures the final months of the war with Clinton in New York, but in 1782, his failing health causes him to resign. He returns to his home in Hesse-Cassel, where he is appointed military governor. The quiet life of the respected old soldier rejuvenates him, and he spends a lengthy retirement in the company of his family, survives until 1800, until age eighty-four.

BANASTRE TARLETON

After Yorktown, he returns to England, immediately begins work on his memoirs. Published in 1787, they are a one-sided assault on anyone who ever disagreed with him, most notably Charles Cornwallis. He dismisses his former commander as an utter incompetent, though his analysis is rife with errors of fact, and thus, his work is rarely taken seriously. Tarleton tries his hand at politics, and after several attempts, he gains a seat in Parliament in 1790, serves until 1806. He continues to serve in various army posts, from Portugal to Ireland, is promoted eventually to full general. For his sheer longevity of service, he is knighted in 1820 by King George IV, and survives until 1833.

In a fitting irony, Tarleton's name virtually disappears into English military history. He is remembered primarily in America, not for his skills as a capable cavalryman, but as a petty, cold-hearted and vindictive brute, his name a symbol of the worst kind of ruthlessness.

CHARLES O'HARA

Cornwallis' most capable field commander returns to England early in 1782. On the strength of Cornwallis' energetic recommendation, he is promoted to major general. In 1792, he is appointed lieutenant governor of Gibraltar. In 1793, he is captured by the French and imprisoned in Luxembourg. Released in 1795, he returns to Gibraltar as governor, and dies there in 1802, at age sixty-two.

AND,

GEORGE WASHINGTON

I am become a private citizen on the banks of the Potomac, and under the shadow of my own vine and my own fig tree.

Free from the bustle of a camp and the busy scenes of public life . . . I am retiring within myself, and shall be able to view the solitary walk and tread the paths of private life with heartfelt satisfaction. I will move gently down the stream of life until I sleep with my fathers.
—GEORGE WASHINGTON TO LAFAYETTE, 1784

In 1787, the gentleman farmer accepts a call from Virginia to participate as a delegate to the Constitutional Convention, and upon his arrival in Philadelphia, he succumbs to considerable pressure to become president of that body.

As the Constitution is ratified by the states, it is apparent to Washington that no other person is considered a suitable candidate for the office of the first president of the United States. Though he has spent precious few years at his beloved Mount Vernon, he accepts the inevitable, and in 1788, moves Martha into the presidential mansion in what is now the nation's capital, New York.

He governs from the strength of his neutrality, preventing unwise American involvement in the various violent conflicts in Europe, realizes more than many in his own cabinet that the United States must meet its own challenges before pursuing alliances that could lead to further war that America cannot afford. Naïve in the ways of politics, he steadfastly holds the government together despite the enormous strain of the two factions led by the bitterly opposed Hamilton and Jefferson. As his term nears expiration, there is little enthusiasm for any other candidate to succeed him, including his vice president John Adams. From every part of the nation he receives entreaties to remain in office for a second term, and despite personal exhaustion, and the furious disappointment of Martha, he accepts election to a second term.

In 1797, he adamantly refuses to consider a third term, despite a wave of pressure to do so, and finally retires to Mount Vernon. He lives out the brief remainder of his life in the soft comforts of his wife, who has endured long years of sacrifice both by the absence of her husband and the death of all four of her children. In December 1799, while tending to the chores of his farm, he is stricken by a severe throat infection, and two days later, on December 14, 1799, with Martha beside him, he dies. He is sixty-seven.

For three days, he lies in state in the dining room at Mount Vernon, then Martha orders his body placed briefly on the porch of the mansion, for his last magnificent view of the Potomac River.

To measure his impact on history, one must consider the world as it might have been without him. Of those who had serious designs on his position as commander in chief, from John Hancock to Artemas Ward to Charles Lee to Horatio Gates, it is impossible to envision anyone maintaining such a dedicated grasp on the tormenting necessities of the army, the congress, and the people.

Not even his dearest friends and most ardent supporters claim perfection in the man. He possessed none of the oratorical skills of Patrick Henry, none of the scientific inventiveness of Ben Franklin, none of the instinct for political science of John Adams. Few claim he was the most expert military tactician, or the most efficient politician. But without Washington, there would have been no Trenton, no Monmouth, and no French alliance. Without Washington, there would have been no General Lafayette, General Greene, or General von Steuben.

Throughout the entire ordeal of the American Revolution, and throughout the exhaustive historical studies of this time, no other name has risen, no other name has ever been placed into the same historical arena as George Washington. By his patience, dignity, perseverance, and his unwavering devotion to his cause, he is entitled to claim absolute responsibility for those triumphs that ensured the existence of the United States of America. He is indeed, the Father of His Country.